WHITE HAVEN WITCHES

BOOKS ONE - THREE

TJ GREEN

White Haven Witches Books 1-3
Mountolive Publishing
Copyright © 2019 TJ Green
All rights reserved
ISBN 978-0-9951163-6-8

Editing by Missed Period Editing
Cover Design by Fiona Jayde Media

To My Mother - Thank You

Other Titles by TJ Green

Tom's Arthurian Legacy
Tom's Inheritance
Twice Born
Galatine's Curse
Tom's Arthurian Legacy Box Set

White Haven Witches
Buried Magic
Magic Unbound
Magic Unleashed

Invite from the author -

You can get two free short stories, Excalibur Rises and Jack's Encounter, by subscribing to my newsletter. You will also receive free character sheets of all the main Whitehaven Witches.

By staying on my mailing list you'll receive free excerpts of my new books, as well as short stories, news of giveaways, and a chance to join my launch team. I'll also be sharing information about other books in this genre you might enjoy.

Details can be found at the end of *White Haven Witches*.

Cast of Characters

Avery Hamilton - owns Happenstance Books
Alex Bonneville - owns The Wayward Son pub
Reuben Jackson - owns Greenlane Nursery
Elspeth Robinson - owns The Silver Bough
Briar Ashworth - owns Charming Balms Apothecary
Mathias Newton - DI with Cornwall Police
Caspian Faversham - CEO Kernow Shipping

BURIED

WHITE HAVEN WITCHES (BOOK 1)

MAGIC

TJ GREEN

Prologue

We are witches, born from generations of witches, and our magic has been passed down through the centuries. But it seems we have more power than we ever thought possible.

When things that were hidden come to light, an enemy is awakened. Our ancient grimoires were hidden for a reason; now we are in a race to find them first.

1

Avery always liked to read the tarot cards on a full moon, outside if the weather allowed, and today it did. It was mid-June and hot. The earth smelled rich, and the scent of lavender drifted towards her.

She sat at her garden table. The brick-paved patio area was flooded with silvery light and the garden beyond was full of plants, lost in the shadows despite the full moon. The only things visible were the white roses that nodded from the depths of the borders, and the gravel paths that snaked around them.

Earlier that day she had sensed a shift in the normal path of her life; a premonition that required further investigation. Out of long practice she sat calmly, shuffling the cards and then placing them out in the cross before her, turning them one by one. She shuddered. Change was coming, and with it, danger. The cards revealed it and she could feel it. And it would happen soon.

Avery leaned back, perplexed, and then jumped slightly as she heard the click of the gate. Alex, another witch. She recognised his scent and sound. Her worry over the reading was replaced by curiosity.

He stepped into view, his expression invisible with the moon behind him, casting her in shadow. He was tall, with broad shoulders and a lean, muscular build. It was like a wall had stepped between her and the moon.

"What do you want, Alex?"

"What a lovely greeting, Avery," he said, his voice smooth. He pulled a chair out and sat opposite her, looking down at the cards. "So you sense it, too."

"Sense what?"

"You know what." He sounded impatient. "That something is coming. Don't you think we should work together?"

"No."

He leaned back, shifting slightly so that the moon lit his face, showing his day-old stubble and his long dark hair that fell just below his shoulders. His brown eyes looked black in the light. "This is ridiculous. You have no reason to distrust me."

She refused to be drawn. "I have no reason to trust you, either. You disappeared for years, and now you're back. I have no idea who you even are anymore."

"I'm the same witch I always was. People travel, you know. That's life!"

Even now Alex could make her blood boil with his infuriating superiority. She wanted to throw something at him, like a lightning bolt. "Why are you here?"

They stared at each other across the table, Avery only able to see a glint of moonlight in his eyes, until he said with forced patience, "There are five witches now in White Haven, five of us who wield the old magic. We should meet. Pool our resources. I can't believe you haven't already."

"We've had no need to form a coven, and I like working alone." She inwardly chastised herself. Why did she have to sound so defensive? It was okay to work alone.

"I've been talking to Elspeth. She'd like to form one."

Avery rolled her eyes. "Of course she would."

"There's nothing wrong with that! We can share ideas, share our strengths."

"We're all witches! What do we need to share?"

"Oh, let me see," he said with a sigh. "El can work metal, brilliantly, metal and gems, in fact. Far better than any of us can. Have you seen what she's been producing lately?"

"No."

"You should. And of particular use for us, she can weave magic into an Athame, and other useful objects we use in our rituals."

"I can do that, too," she said impatiently, "we all can. We're witches."

"Not as good as she can," he persisted. "And Briar is excellent at using herbs and healing. Better than all of us," he said, cutting her off before she could protest. "Gil is particularly good at using water magic. And then there's you." He stopped and just looked at her, his expression unfathomable. He was making her uncomfortable.

"What about me?" She was annoyed with him for being so very logical, and she felt the wind stirring around her as her annoyance increased.

He laughed, the white of his teeth bright against his shadowed face. He looked around and the breeze made strands of his hair float around his face. "Am I making you cross? I'm sure you're causing that wind."

She frowned and cut it off, the wind dying instantly.

"Air. You manipulate it so easily. And new spells, your intuitiveness—those are your strengths."

She was so unnerved at his knowledge of her that she responded with sarcasm. "And what about you, Alex? What can you bring?"

"My ability to scry, to prophesise, my astral abilities. And fire." He glanced at the candle that sat on the side of the table, unlit, and it suddenly flared to life, the flame shooting a foot into the air before it settled down to a small, orange flame. The light illuminated his grin. "I burn hot, Avery. Nice on cold nights."

"How lovely," she said, trying to dispel the images that rushed into her head. She put the flame out as quickly as he had lit it, the smoke eddying between them.

He leaned forward. "I'm calling a meeting. The others should know that we've sensed something. We need to be on our guard. My place, tonight at ten." He stood, once again blocking the moon briefly before he headed to the gate, his gait long. "By the way, your defences on the house need strengthening. See you later, Avery."

Alex was 29, a year older than her, and they'd been to the same schools and shared the same powers, and yet he infuriated her. She watched him go, then looked up at the moon and wanted to scream, but the moon counselled silence, so she swept the cards up, shuffled, and dealt again.

2

Avery woke at dawn after a restless sleep, the barely-there light filtering through the blinds in the bedroom. She had been thinking more about Alex than the ominous reading, and that annoyed her more than anything. She hated the way he just slid into her mind and stayed there.

By the time she got to work she felt irritable. Work was a bookshop called Happenstance Books, which she'd inherited from her grandmother, along with the building it was in. They stocked new and old books, fiction, non-fiction, and the esoteric—witchcraft, divination, angels, devils, and all things in between, as well as tarot cards, incense, greeting cards, postcards, and other occult-related objects. The shop was well placed, halfway up a small side street that wound up from the sea, and wedged between a coffee shop and a gift store selling local trinkets to tourists. It was stacked with high shelves that wound around the walls, as well as through the middle, making the interior a section of narrow passages. A selection of comfy chairs and a small sofa were placed in strategic locations to encourage reading and lingering, and it smelt pleasantly of old paper, coffee, and incense.

Sally, her friend and the store manager, was already in their stock room at the rear of the shop, unpacking a box of old books Avery had brought a week ago in a house sale. She knew Avery was a witch, although she never called her one. It was inevitable she should know after their years of friendship, although Avery made out it was something far more wishy-washy than it really was and Sally indulged her accordingly.

Sally looked up and smiled. "You're early! Someone kick you out of bed?"

"Funny! Bad night's sleep. What about you?"

"You know me, always an early bird. Coffee's on if you want some."

"I don't want some, I need some!" she said, heading to the small galley kitchen, inhaling the coffee fumes gratefully. She hesitated a moment and then called out, "Alex came to see me last night."

There was a moment of silence as the rustling of books stopped, and Sally came to the door, leaning against the frame. "I thought you didn't get on?"

"We don't, sort of. But he sensed the same thing as me." She looked at her, trying to decide what to say. In the end she just said it all. "I was reading the cards last night and I thought I saw something. Something dark. I have no idea what, but Alex saw it, too. He came to talk. At two in the morning!"

"So he knew you'd be up," Sally said, raising her eyebrows quizzically. "Have you two got some psychic link?"

Avery shook her head, leaned back against the counter, and sipped her coffee. Sweet and strong, just as she liked it. She might just start to feel human soon. "No! At least I hope not. It's very disconcerting."

Sally shuffled against the doorframe. "I like him, I don't really get why you don't. He's honest, and runs a great pub! He's got a fab chef at the moment. Have you been?"

"No, not since he arrived."

"Are you sure nothing's happened between you two?"

Avery rolled her eyes. "No. Anyway, he wants to talk at his pub tonight. He's calling a meeting with the others." Sally would know exactly whom she meant by the others.

"It's probably a good idea," Sally nodded. "There's strength in numbers."

"Oh, don't you start."

Sally grinned, raking her hand through her blonde hair. "I wouldn't hesitate if Alex invited me over. He's very good-looking."

"And he knows it. And besides, you're married with two kids!"

Sally married her childhood sweetheart when she was 20 years old, and within a couple of years they had their first child, swiftly followed by a second. Avery had no idea how she managed the shop and her home life so efficiently.

"I meant, if I was single!" Sally changed tack, looking slightly worried. "So, is this serious, what you and Alex saw? You've never mentioned anything like this before."

Avery immediately regretted saying anything, and shook her head. "No, probably not. I've probably got a rival with a new bookstore opening. I'm sure it will be fine. It was just sort of spooky, Alex turning up when he did, and I've probably read more into it than I should have. Anyway, anything good in that box?"

Sally headed back to the store room, Avery trailing after her, and pulled a book out of the box she'd been unpacking. "Old editions of the classics, but nothing riveting. Not yet, anyway. I've got to do another house visit later. Unless you want to? One of us has to update our inventory." She had a smirk on her face, knowing Avery hated doing the inventory.

Avery smiled sweetly, "I'd love to pick up those boxes! Thanks Sally. Where am I going?"

"Do you remember that little old lady who used to come in here sometimes? Anne? She was a bit of a local historian."

"Yeah, I think so." Avery kept it light, but she did remember her. People poking about in the town's history always made her worried. She didn't want them to turn up anything she'd rather keep hidden. She'd been polite to Anne, but had otherwise tried to keep her distance.

"Well, she died the other week, and she's left us some books."

"Oh," Avery suddenly felt bad and also slightly relieved. "I'm sorry to hear that. Sure, I'll go. Who arranged it?"

"Her son, Paul. I haven't met him, he just phoned. I arranged to pick up mid-morning, at her house. Are you all right, Avery? You look a bit odd."

The feeling of unease had rushed back like an incoming tide and Avery felt dizzy. "No, I'm fine, bad night's sleep, remember? Need more coffee." She headed back to the kitchen, trying to subdue her worry.

***

Avery pulled up outside a large, old house that sat on a rise overlooking the sea on the edge of the town. The second she saw it she felt a shudder pass through her. Something had alerted her witchy senses, something magical. It was only a trace, but it was there.

She looked at the house thoughtfully. Anne hadn't presented any inkling of magic, so why could she sense something here? And what of her son, Paul? They certainly weren't related to the other four witches in the town, and she was pretty sure there weren't any others. Was this a trap? But surely if he'd been a witch he'd have tried to disguise the wisps of magic she could sense.

The house was built from the mellow, creamy stone that many houses in the area were built from, and that also made up the old boundaries snaking across fields and along roadsides. It sat down a drive that was overgrown with bushes and trees. The paving was cracked, the paint on the door and window frames was peeling off, and the whole place looked like it needed a complete overhaul. At one point, this house would have been one of the most coveted houses in White Haven, and probably would be again after a ton of money had been thrown at it. She looked down the lane. All of the other houses here were in much better condition. She bet the neighbours were looking forward to the renovation. But was something hiding behind that cracked facade?

She sat for a few minutes, watching the house and trying to detect if there was a threat, but other than the whiff of magic, she sensed nothing.

Avery looked in the rear view mirror and checked her appearance. Her long, red hair was loose and relatively neat, and her pale green eyes had lost the tiredness from earlier in the day. Coffee was awesome. She touched up her makeup, grabbed her phone and checked there weren't any messages, then exited her old green Bedford van, something else she'd inherited from her gran, locking it behind her. She smoothed her long, dark blue maxi dress, keen to make a good impression.

As she walked up the drive, she scanned around the garden, but noted nothing unusual until she came to the front door where a vigorous pot of thyme and one of sage was placed either side of the door. Common plants, but they also offered protection. And on the corner of the doorframe she saw a small mark. Another symbol of protection. This was getting weirder. She rang the doorbell and waited for a few seconds, flexing her fingers in case she needed to defend herself, before finally hearing footsteps approaching. The door swung open to reveal a harried-looking man who appeared to be in his sixties. He looked at her, confused.

"Can I help you?"

"I'm Avery, from Happenstance Books. You must be Paul? You asked me to collect your mother's books—Anne Somersby? Is this a good time?" She smiled encouragingly.

"Oh, yes, sorry, of course. I'm a little distracted—I'm sorting through some paperwork. Come in, please." He leaned forward and shook her hand. "Just follow me and I'll show you the library." He laughed, "Well, it's not really a library, but it does have a lot of books."

Avery relaxed slightly. She didn't detect anything magical or threatening from him. He walked ahead of her, leading her down the long hallway to a room at the back of the house, looking out onto extensive gardens.

She paused at the window, "Wow, what a beautiful garden."

He laughed, "It was a beautiful garden. Now it's a mess."

She laughed, too. "Well, you know what I mean. It will be again." She looked around the room she was in, "And this is amazing, too!"

"You're a book lover. I just see more stuff I have to move. But yes. It is."

The ceilings were high, and the room was lined with heavy oak shelves filled with books. The small amount of exposed bare wall was panelled with the same dark oak. And the magical something was here—Avery could sense it more strongly now. She tried to contain her excitement, schooling her face carefully. "Did Anne leave me all of these?"

He gestured around the room, "Everything, although of course, you don't have to take them all." He looked puzzled. "Did you know her well?"

Avery shuffled awkwardly. "If I'm honest, not really. She came into the shop, chatted sometimes, bought books." She shrugged. "I'm guessing that's why she left them to me—to bring them back home. I'm sorry to hear she died."

Paul smiled sadly. "Thank you, but she'd had a rich life." He gestured at the shelves. "There were some old town histories she'd put together herself that she particularly wanted you to have. Insisted, in fact, before she died. Made me promise I wouldn't forget. Are you a history fan, too?"

Avery tried to cover her surprise with a small lie. "Very much so. You can't live in White Haven without loving history. We sell a lot of history books in my shop."

Paul laughed, "Quite a murky history, in places! What with witches, caves, smuggling, and wrecks at sea—the place is riddled with strange deeds!"

Avery's heart had skipped at beat at the mention of witches, and she laughed along with him, feeling the hair rise on the back of her neck. "True, but no more so than many old villages along the coast, I guess."

Paul nodded. "Anyway, I better get on. I'll be in the study going through more papers." He sighed. "She accumulated everything, you know. Would you like coffee?"

"Yes please, sounds great. Black, two sugars."

He disappeared, and for a second Avery stood still, thinking, while her heart pounded uncomfortably. She sensed magic, and Anne had requested

18

she come here. Had she known what she was? She couldn't think about that now. She turned back to the books. It took all her self-control not to run over and start pulling them from the shelves.

Something was definitely here; her witchy senses were tingling all over. She quickly scanned the shelves. They were crammed with old, worn paperbacks, hardbacks, and books with old leather covers—a mixture of classics, romances, thrillers, and reference books. She focused on where she could feel the pull of magic, and looked up.

There, in the far corner, on a top shelf, was a row of old leather-bound books. Just as she was about to pull a chair out to use as a step, the door opened and Paul came in with her coffee.

"See anything you like?" he asked, as he put the coffee on a side table.

"Lots of thrillers and classics that would sell well, and some of the reference books, too." She tried to keep the excitement out of her voice. "Where else did your mother get her books from, do you know?"

"No idea! And I imagine she got them years ago. She didn't go out much as she got older." He looked at the dust and general dilapidation of the room with its dated decoration. "I don't think she did much of anything, except look at family trees. You probably know that she was a bit of a local historian. She would go to the library and look at the archives, and then she got a computer and would do what she could on there." He brightened at the thought and smiled. "I was quite impressed when she got a computer. She didn't let age stop her learning!" He pointed at the shelves. "The files she particularly wanted you to have are in that section. She was especially interested in old families of the area. You'll probably find them amongst that lot."

Researching old families? That gave her another prick of unease. Her family, Alex's, and Gil's would have been amongst the oldest. All magical. All with secrets. "I'll look out for them."

"Sorry, you'll have to contend with a lot of dust."

"It's fine. I'm used to it. I clear quite a few books from old houses."

He nodded, "Okay, I'll leave you to it."

As soon as he'd gone, she pulled the chair out and stood on it, reaching up to the row of books. As she pulled a few volumes out, dust billowed around her and she coughed and blinked. Grabbing a handful of them, she carried them to the table under the window. The names gave nothing away: A Reference Book of Wildflowers, The Cave Systems of the West Country, Herbs and their Properties, English Folklore, Legends of the South. Not what she was expecting, but interesting. She picked up a few and flicked through them. Nothing interesting. Then she picked up the book on cave systems and shook it, and a black and white photo fell to the floor, releasing the scent of magic.

She picked it up and held it under the light, and almost dropped it with shock. The photo was of a house, slightly unfocused, the gardens manicured, and a big bank of trees behind it. In front of the house were a woman and two small children staring at the camera, unsmiling and grim. But it was unmistakable. She knew that house—it belonged to Gil. Was that his mother? No, she corrected herself. The photo was too old. It must be his grandmother, maybe even great-grandmother? And the children must be either his mother or father, and an aunt or uncle. She could never remember whom he inherited his magic from.

After the shock, her initial reaction was one of disappointment. Gil was a witch—maybe the photo had come from his house? Was that why she could sense magic? She turned the photo over to reveal a scrawl of writing that looked like it had been written in a hurry. "The real Jacksons."

Her hands shook and she looked around the room as if she was being spied on. She had known Gil all her life. She liked him, a lot. He seemed so trustworthy, and now she had doubts running through her mind. This suggested that Gil was not a real Jackson. And if that was the case, who was he?

3

Avery lived in White Haven, a small seaside town on the Cornish coast. It was an old and charming place, with its old stone buildings with mullioned windows, tiny lanes, cobbled streets, quayside views, and boutique shops and restaurants, all swirling down to the sea, where fishing boats bobbed in the harbour. Outside the shops and pubs were hanging baskets and potted plants, and the whole place was picturesque. Beyond the town were rolling downs heading up and away from the sea.

This was the place she called home, a place that was filled with magic. It had a special quality to it, like a few of the ancient towns and villages that carried their old magic through the years. Many sensed it, and it attracted new agers, wiccans, mediums, pagans, and spiritualists, although she doubted that any knew that real witches actually lived among them.

It was now nearly 10:00 PM, her tea of beans on toast was hours ago, and she was starving again. Part of her wished she'd gone to the pub with Sally for their usual post-work drinks with friends, but she had really wanted to read Anne's notes before meeting the other witches.

The traffic was always nightmarish in town, so she walked from her shop down to the pub, thinking about Alex and trying to dispel the annoying feelings he always provoked.

She'd always felt he thought he was better than her, and she'd resented him for it. A few years ago he'd left White Haven, and she had no idea why or where he'd been. He'd returned a few months ago, taking over the old pub on the quayside that belonged to his uncle, and it had been a shock to see him back. She'd seen little of him since his return, other than when he came into her shop to say he was back. It surprised her that he thought to tell her. He was as good-looking as always, more so now that he was older. He'd looked around her shop, waiting for her to be free, and then he sauntered over to the counter, grinning. "Long time, no see, Avery. Thought I'd let you know I'm back, in case you ever need anything."

"Thanks, Alex. Very generous of you. But I think I'll be okay."

"Same old Avery. When you change your mind, you know where to find me." And then he strolled out the door.

Since then she'd bumped into him at a few parties, and in a few bars with mutual friends where they'd chatted a few times, but that was all. And yet last night he'd come to see her, had known she would have seen something coming.

The Wayward Son, Alex's pub, was on one of the quayside roads, looking over the small harbour with its collection of fishing boats. She could smell the brine. It always made her tingle.

As she walked in, the sound of chatter and music swelled around her; the pub was packed. She headed to the bar and saw Alex make his way towards her from the far end, leaving his two bartenders to attend to the other customers. His dark hair was tied back, but he still hadn't shaved; dark stubble coated his chin and cheeks. He wore a black t-shirt and old jeans, and he looked way too good. "Evening," he said, a lazy grin on his face. "What's your poison?"

"A very large glass of red, please. And a packet of cheese and onion crisps."

He reached behind him and grabbed a bottle of merlot. "I predict the lady likes a full red with a hint of spice. Sound good?"

"Perfect, thank you," she said, feeling churlishness wouldn't be a good idea in his pub.

"Drink's on the house, and don't worry about the crisps, there's food upstairs."

"Is there?" she asked, all animosity towards him temporarily forgotten.

"Of course, I like to feed my guests." He gestured towards the stairs at the back of the pub. "Head up, I'll be with you soon. You'll have to unlock the door, but you know how," and he promptly turned to another customer.

She grabbed her glass and headed through the crowded main room to the back, as instructed. A set of stairs was tucked to the rear of the small room that looked out onto the beer garden. Outside a breeze bustled around the courtyard garden, jostling the strings of fairy lights that lit up the drinkers still sitting outside. The back room was much quieter and darker than the main part of the pub, lit only by more fairy lights, candles on tables, and discreet up-lighting in the corners. It seemed that only locals were in here, and she nodded in greeting to a few she recognised.

She headed up the stairs and onto a broad landing, shrouded in shadows, and found a locked door. She whispered a spell to unlock it, and hearing the lock click, she turned the handle and went in.

Avery knew Alex had the whole of the first floor to himself. He didn't rent any of the rooms out, saying it was too much work, but she had never seen it before and she was surprised at how good it looked. He had knocked through as many walls as safety allowed, and consequently his flat was large and roomy, with an open plan kitchen and living area, exposed brick walls, and a massive fireplace. A tan leather sofa, enormous and squashy, dominated the living area, and a large rug covered the polished floorboards. She was impressed. Alex had style. Taking advantage of being the first there, she had a quick peek around and found there was a single bedroom leading off and a bathroom, and that was it.

Drawn by the thought of food, she headed to the kitchen, and found a few covered dishes of crackers, olives, and pickles. She nibbled a few olives and sipped her wine, wondering where the others were, but within seconds the door opened and Briar arrived, halting with surprise when she saw Avery in the kitchen.

Briar was about the same age as Avery, late-twenties, with hazel eyes and chestnut brown hair that fell in waves past her shoulders. She was petite, barely past five feet, and slim. She wore lace and lots of white and pastel shades, and of all of the witches was not only the best with herbs and potions, but also at healing. Briar sold creams and lotions, herbal medicines, and old remedies in her shop, Charming Balms Apothecary. She had deliberately made it old-fashioned and everyone loved it, especially because her stuff worked. Skin did look better, eyes were brighter, nails were stronger, old ailments were eased. The magic was subtle, but it was there.

There was something very soft and gentle about Briar, usually. Avery detected a slight prickle to her at the moment, however. She shut the door behind her and said, "So you came! I really didn't expect you would."

Avery felt a bit shocked. *Was she that unsociable?* She gave a half-smile. "I wasn't sure I would either, but here I am." She wondered if Briar was put out. "How are you? It's been a while."

"I'm fine, Avery. Just busy. The shop is very popular at the moment. Can't complain, it's summer season. It will slow down soon enough."

"I know what you mean," Avery nodded. "I've been busy, too."

Briar didn't waste time. She leaned against the counter from the living room side, sipping her white wine. "So what's this meeting about? It must be important, you don't normally come here."

The word 'normally' gave Avery a jolt. "No, I don't," she answered. "But Alex insisted."

Briar laughed. "And when has that ever made a difference?"

Before she could answer, Gil, Elspeth, and Alex arrived together, bringing in a jumble of laughter and chatter.

Alex looked surprised. "Great, you're here too, Briar! I didn't see you arrive."

"You were busy," she said, hugging him. "Simon served me."

Avery was already feeling like the outsider; they all looked pretty comfortable together. She wondered if it showed when Elspeth came round the counter into the kitchen and hugged her.

It had been a while since Avery had seen her, and she'd forgotten how gorgeous she was. Elspeth was tall and graceful, with long blonde, almost white hair that cascaded down her back. She always wore red lipstick that looked even brighter against her pale skin, but she also wore lots of jewellery. Rings, a nose piercing, necklaces, and lots of bangles, and she nearly always wore skinny black jeans, biker boots, and rock t-shirts. Elspeth owned a jewellery shop, and sold her own designs as well as things she brought in. All of her jewellery had a little magic woven through it. She sold charms and amulets that really worked, as well as pendants, rings, earrings, hair clips, pins, and brooches. She had spelled positive energies into them, and used gemstones as well. She must be making more things lately, from what Alex had said.

"Avery! It's great you're here. Alex said you were coming, but I didn't believe him."

"Elspeth, hi," she managed to murmur through the hug.

"El, please, not Elspeth! I love your hair, Avery, it's such a beautiful colour."

"Thank you," she said, suddenly conscious of her long, dark red hair.

In contrast, Gil stood next to El looking quite homely. He was shorter than Alex, his short dark brown hair was neat, and he wore a plain t-shirt and dark blue jeans. Gil ran a plant nursery called Greenlane Nursery out of the extensive grounds of his house, and it was very popular. He employed half a dozen locals, supplying hanging baskets to shops and businesses, and helped White Haven to compete in an annual garden competition, Britain in Bloom.

He sold the usual annuals, perennials, and shrubs, but he specialised in herbs. Gil's family were rich and he had inherited the house and grounds, most of which were private, apart from the nursery and show garden.

Gil grabbed her in a bear hug. "Lovely to see you, Avery."

Avery felt flustered, and tried to laugh it off. "Well, it's nice to be wanted. I think." She took a large sip of wine, and a few deep breaths while the new arrivals grabbed drinks from the fridge, and Alex pulled out cheese and pate.

He loaded up a tray and handed it to Avery. "Would you mind?"

"No," she stuttered. "Where do you want it?"

"The coffee table," he directed, and picked up another tray and headed to the living room.

The group trailed after them, Gil and Elspeth sitting on the couch, while the others sat on huge floor cushions. Avery felt a whisper of magic and the lights around the room dimmed, as the fire flared in the fireplace.

"That's better," El said. "I was starting to feel chilly." Her long limbs were crossed beneath her on the couch, and she took a large slug of bottled beer.

Avery realised it really had been a long time since she'd seen them, and she felt suddenly guilty, although she couldn't work out why. She thought of the photo of Gil and again wondered what to do. As if he read her mind, Gil caught her eye and smiled.

"Come on, then," Briar said. "What's going on?"

"Does anything have to be going on?" Alex said. "Can't five witches get together for Friday drinks?"

"Four witches sometimes get together—Avery does not. Therefore, something must have happened."

Alex glanced at Avery. "We've both had a premonition. Enough to merit bringing it to everyone's attention."

"What kind of premonition?" Gil asked, concerned.

"Ladies first," Alex said, winking at her.

Avery tried not to glare at him. "I read the cards and saw that something is coming. Something dark. Something that will threaten us. I read the cards several times and saw the same things—the Tower, Death, the Fool, the Moon, and many sword cards. And then Alex came to see me." She turned to him and found him watching her, his eyes narrowed as he listened. "What about you, Alex? You never said what you saw."

"I was sitting here—well, at the counter, actually," he said, nodding to the long counter that separated the kitchen from the living room. "I was just looking into my coffee thinking about what I had to do that day when I experienced a rush of darkness, almost a blackout, and I saw a man coming. He was dark-haired but faceless, and he brought danger. I could see blood and steel, maybe a blade. And a burning anger and desire. It was so strong, I knocked my cup over and almost scalded myself."

Gil leaned forward, "Did you recognise him? Anything that was familiar?"

"Nothing." Alex was a joker, a tease, but there was nothing light about his mood tonight. "It felt personal, though."

"But what could he want?" El asked. "We have nothing that anyone who knows magic could desire. Nothing unusual, nothing powerful." She looked around the group, perplexed and questioning, "Well, I haven't, anyway."

Avery shook her head slowly. "Me, neither." The others agreed, although Gil looked down at the floor, lost in thought. Avery looked over at Alex. "But how did you know that I would have seen it, too? It was bit odd that you simply arrived at two in the morning."

He hesitated for a moment, and then said, "You, more than any of us—well, other than me—have the gift of sight. As soon as I had my vision, I knew you had sensed something, too. I waited all day to see if the feeling would go, and it didn't. It woke me up and I had to see you, straight away." He shrugged, looking at her with an unusual intimacy, "I can't explain it other than that."

Avery made a decision, and she looked around at the others. "I did find something interesting today, although I don't know if it's anything to do with our premonitions. I was gifted some books by a lady who recently died, and I visited her house today to pick everything up from her son. She had compiled files and family trees on lots of old White Haven families, as well as histories on shops, buildings, and an interesting collection of old town maps. My family tree was in there, as was Alex's. I haven't had chance to go through it all properly yet. " She omitted the part about the photo. "It was a bit spooky, actually, like I was being spied on."

The atmosphere changed, and they all lowered their drinks and leaned forward.

"Who was it?" Alex asked immediately.

"Anne Somersby, she lived on Waverley Road. She was an old lady who was a bit of a local historian. Every now and again she'd come into the shop and look to see what books we had on the area."

"What do you mean, our family histories?" El asked.

"All of us. I haven't gone through everything yet, though."

"What kind of family histories?" Gil asked, his beer on the table forgotten. "I mean, was there anything in mine?"

Was that more than natural concern she heard in his voice? "I haven't had a chance to have a good look, Gil, they look like family trees with a brief bio on some family members. Although, she's done the same to lots of old families in the area. Not just those with the craft."

"Was there any mention of magic?"

"No! None." She again omitted the scent of magic she had discovered.

"What have you done with all the records you've found?" Alex asked.

"They're in my flat, which is sealed and warded, so they're safe."

He nodded, satisfied, but then he surprised her by asking, "The son, is he staying there? At her house?"

She looked at him, confused, "No idea. Why?"

"I think we should check the house out. See if there's more there."

"Are you mad? That's breaking and entering!"

"We won't do any harm! We're just looking."

She couldn't believe she was hearing this, but no one else seemed to putting up a fight. "No way! What if he's there?"

"Take a look at those papers tomorrow, and then see if you can find where he's staying. I think we should look, but not tonight. We'll wait until you find out more."

El had been watching them both. "Do you think this has to do with your premonition then?"

Avery shrugged. "Maybe. Or it could be some weird, random coincidence."

Gil shook his head. "We know better than that. There's no such thing as coincidence. It all means something. Maybe she'd found something."

The room fell silent because they knew he was right. The fates moved in odd, unimaginable ways, and just because they couldn't see the cause of something, or see where it led, didn't mean there weren't connections. It was like a web all around them; you just

had to know where to look.

4

The next day the shop was busy and Avery was tired, especially as she hadn't arrived home until late the previous night.

At just after five when the last customer disappeared, she locked up, said goodbye to Sally, and passed through the internal door at the rear that was normally kept locked for privacy, and up the stairs into her flat.

The building that housed her shop and flat was 18th Century, and had originally been three buildings, until years ago when her family had bought them all and converted them into one. The bookshop was on the ground floor, and the next floor contained an open living room, dining room and kitchen, a bathroom, and a spare bedroom. The top floor was in the attic and housed her bedroom and an en suite bathroom, while the rest of the space made up her spell room and workspace.

The spell room was her favourite room in the whole house. The floor was made of polished wooden floorboards, slightly scuffed now, and covered in a variety of colourful old rugs. Two worn leather sofas and an old armchair sat facing each other in the centre of the room, a small table between them. At the far side of the long room were an old oak cupboard, drawers, and a wooden table. Against the walls were shelves packed with books, many old, their pages worn, and all of her magic equipment, including her herbs, tinctures, syrups, and potions. And it was messy, like most of her house. She accumulated books, objects, pictures, and art, and they spread everywhere in random and haphazard collections.

She walked through the living room and threw open the balcony doors, letting a warm breeze flow through the house. She headed to the kitchen and lit a bundle of herbs to clear her head, and then grabbed a glass of wine.

The boxes she'd inherited from Anne were still spread over the living room floor, so she opened them up to check what was in each, and then started to categorise them, deciding to put all the notes on families and the family trees together, reference books in another pile, and the fiction in another.

The logical place to start would be with the notes on Gil's family. She felt she was prying but it was clearly important, and he hadn't said no. Within the box file was a large family tree that went back generations; the writing was small and immaculate, and must have taken her a long time to create. There were copies of birth certificates, marriages and deaths, and a history of the house, all the way back to the 1500s. She didn't have to go far to find what she was looking for.

Gil was definitely on the family tree, which was at first a relief, until she realised he could still be an imposter. But how would he have fooled his whole family, unless there was the whole 'switched at birth' thing happening? And that would have included his family in the collusion. It was only when she looked closely at the dates of birth of his grandfather and his great-uncle that she realised what Anne's scribbled statement meant. Gil's great-uncle was actually the oldest son, and his children were the true heirs of the Jackson estate. Gil was actually not in the direct line of inheritance.

Avery leaned against the old sofa behind her and the papers dropped onto her lap. Was the family in the photo Gil's great-uncle's family? Were any descendants still alive, and did they know about their thwarted inheritance? She pulled the photo out and looked at it again. It must be them; the photo was of that era, although there was no date or any other identifying notes on it.

She stared at the man in the photo, and a cold chill swept over her. His eyes were dark and compelling, but up close there seemed to be an unflinching gaze staring back at her, offering a challenge. He was younger than she had first assumed, and the children at his feet were toddlers. She checked the family tree again. Gil's great-uncle's name was Addison—a popular name for the oldest male. What was even odder was that there was no date of death recorded next to his name.

Another chill ran through her. He must be dead; he'd be over a hundred by now. Perhaps Anne couldn't find any death certificates. His wife Philippa's date of death wasn't there, either. His children were named, but there was no further history on them at all. No dates of death, or recorded marriages or children. It was as if the whole family had disappeared.

There were several questions that now needed answering. Did Gil know? How had Anne found the photo? And where was the family now? And for no discernible reason, the words black magic kept pushing to the front of her mind.

Suddenly, the lamps inexplicably switched off, the doors slammed shut, and a wild wind carried around the room, lifting all the papers up and dropping them again. A presence seemed to fill the space, and Avery suppressed the urge to scream. She jumped to her feet and summoning her powers, sent a blast of light outwards from her hands and lit every single light, electric and candles, until the room dazzled with brightness.

The bulb overhead exploded, but the lamps remained on and the candles blazed.

Avery looked around, unnerved, her heart pounding. What had caused that? But the darkness had fled and she went to one of the windows overlooking the street to see if she could see anything unusual. It was after seven now, but it was midsummer and still light, and people strolled about heading to pubs and restaurants. Everything looked perfectly normal. Although she hated to admit it, she was seriously disturbed. She needed to have people around her, and despite her reservations, the best person to speak to was Alex.

The premonition was right. Something was coming, and she thought it might be connected to Gil.

*** *** ***

Avery entered The Wayward Son and made her way to the bar, catching Alex's eye. His eyes widened quickly with surprise and he headed over, a look of concern on his face. "What's happened? You're as white as a sheet."

Avery lowered her voice and leaned in, although with the noise in the pub she doubted anyone could hear. "I don't know, if I'm honest. A weird, supernatural wind flew around my flat when I was looking at Gil's family tree, and I felt something there. A presence. I think I've found something." So close to Alex, she could smell the faint scent of his aftershave and resisted the urge to inhale deeply.

He fell silent for a second and then pulled a menu from the side of the bar. "Are you hungry?"

"Starving, actually." She realised she hadn't eaten since lunch.

"Grab a seat in the back room, and I'll come and take your order. I should be able to join you." He added, "It's on the house."

She frowned. "Don't be ridiculous, I'm happy to pay."

He pushed a glass of wine into her hands. "Just sit and look at the menu! I'll be with you soon."

Avery snaked through the crowded pub to the room at the back she had passed through the previous night. It was quieter here, and a few tables were free. She wondered if Alex had cast a spell to keep it that way. She sat at a small table under the window looking out on the courtyard garden and wearily sipped her wine, trying to shake her mood.

The menu was in front of her, but she gazed outside, thinking about what the incident in the flat could have meant. She ran through various scenarios but kept coming back to black magic, and wondered if someone knew what she had found. Or rather, what Anne had found.

A few minutes later, Alex sat opposite her and plonked a pint of beer on the table. "What you having?" He nodded at the menu.

She picked it up. "I haven't looked. What do you recommend?"

He didn't hesitate. "The steak."

"Sounds good." She pushed her chair back, "I'll go and order."

"No!" He waved her down. "I'll get one, too. Medium rare okay?"

"Fine." She was too tired to argue, and decided that letting him order would be the easiest thing to do. If she was honest, she wasn't sure she should be here telling him anything. She wasn't sure she trusted him.

When he came back, he said, "Go on then. What happened?"

She wasn't sure where to begin. "How well do you know Gil?"

He just looked at her for a few seconds, confused. "As well as you do, I suppose. Why?"

"Do you know anything about his family?"

"Not really, other than they're super rich and he's got a huge house. And a rich magical legacy, obviously." He leaned closer and dropped his voice. "What's this about?"

"Do you trust him?"

"As much as I trust anyone."

"I found a photo in Anne's collection of notes. It was a photo of Gil's home, very old, black and white, and scrawled on the back was a line saying, 'the real Jacksons.' It freaked me out, so I went through Anne's family tree on Gil, and I found that he's not the real heir. He's descended from the second son. His great-uncle Addison's family should have inherited everything."

"Okay, that's slightly weird, but maybe Addison was bad news, or he argued with his parents and was disinherited." Alex looked slightly disappointed. "Is that all?"

Avery persisted. "But there's no death date for either him, his wife, or his kids. That is weird. And it was right after I read that, that this hideous wind rolled around my flat and it went really dark. Something was in there with me."

"It didn't hurt you?"

"No, I summoned light and blasted the flat with it, but it made me jump. That's not normal."

He shrugged. "We're not normal. But yes, it's weird. And no dates of death?"

Avery shook her head.

"Also weird, but maybe Anne had trouble finding their records." He leaned back in his chair watching her for a few seconds, and then he gazed out of the window, thinking.

"And another thing," Avery added. "There were signs of protection around Anne's house when I went yesterday. Well, at the front door, anyway."

"Is there anything else you've neglected to tell me so far?" Alex asked, a dangerous edge to his voice.

"No!" she shot back. "I don't think so, anyway."

"I may not have been around for a while, but I am quite trustworthy, you know!" Alex frowned. "While you're in the mood to share, would you like to tell me exactly why I piss you off so much?"

"You're very sensitive. You don't piss me off." That wasn't strictly true, but she was buggered if she was going to explain.

"Liar," he smirked.

"If the rest of the evening is going to be spent like this, I'll go!" Avery went to push her chair back and felt it locked in position. She glared at him and said in a low, threatening voice, "Release my chair right now!"

"No. Food's coming, and I don't want to eat alone."

One of the bar staff headed over, grinning. "Here you go, two steaks. Bon appetite, boss!" He nodded at Alex and left them to it.

At the smell and sight of the food, Avery thought she might die soon if she didn't eat and picked up her knife and fork. "Do you pin all your dates to the chair like this?"

"I didn't think this was a date," he grinned.

"Oh, sod off and let me eat." She cut a large wedge of steak and took a bite.

They fell silent for a few seconds while they ate, and Alex looked deep in thought. "Why don't I help you look tomorrow? We'd work quicker together, and there's safety in numbers."

Before she could answer, her phone rang and she pulled it out of her bag. She frowned at the unknown number. "Sorry, I better get this. Hi, Avery from Happenstance Books. Can I help?"

"Hi Avery, great. It's Paul, Anne's son. I've found something else Anne wanted you to have."

Avery looked up at Alex, and almost stumbled over her words. "Oh, that's great. Is it more books?"

Alex watched her carefully as he continued, and she mouthed at him, It's Paul.

"Well, no actually," Paul answered. "I don't think so, anyway. I've found a big box in the attic with your name on it. It's all taped up, so I haven't disturbed it. Do you want to come and get it? Maybe tomorrow?"

"Yes, perfect. What about ten in the morning?" she said, thinking she could do with a small lie in.

"Excellent. See you then." He rang off before she could ask anything else.

"Well?" Alex asked.

"This is getting really weird. Anne's left me something else. A box in her attic with my name on it!"

"Well, I'm coming with you, so you'd better pick me up." He looked at her and grimaced. "Don't argue. It could be a trap. You have no idea who this Paul guy is, or if he knows something."

"If he was going to attack me, he could have done that yesterday. But," she added, seeing his mutinous expression, "I'll pick you up anyway."

"Unless you stay here tonight. It's probably safer."

She shook her head, thinking that staying with Alex would be far too intimate. "No, I'll be fine. The cats will keep me company."

As if he'd read her mind, he said, "I'll be on the couch."

"Yes, you would be!" she said haughtily, "But honestly, I'm okay. Thank you."

He grinned, "Another time, then. In the meantime, have another glass of wine and tell me about this Paul guy and everything you haven't told me so far."

5

If Paul was shocked or disappointed to see two of them at his door the next morning, he didn't show it. "Come in! Two of you. Great idea. That box is big and heavy—I couldn't get it down the attic stairs. I've found a few other things, too."

Alex shook his hand. "Nice to meet you, Paul. Lead the way."

Paul led them upstairs and along dusty corridors. The decorating, like downstairs, was old fashioned and floral, and through open doors they could see dusty bedrooms and an outdated bathroom. Both of them were on their guard, but Avery was aware of Alex's solid presence behind her, which was very comforting.

At the end of one corridor was a small door almost hidden in the panelling surrounding it. "They liked to disguise their attic doors years ago," he said by way of explanation. It creaked as he opened it, and they followed him up the bare, wooden steps.

As soon as they reached the attic door, Avery felt the gentle pull of a spell and she glanced around uneasily. The attic was dim and shadowy, lit only by very small windows that at the moment were on the wrong side of the house to catch the morning sun. Paul flicked on the light switch and a single, bare bulb in the middle of the room lit up the space. It was filled with lots of old crap from what Avery could see. Old chairs, broken furniture, and boxes and boxes of stuff. He led them to a box in the far corner.

"Here you go. It wasn't until you'd left on Friday that I read Anne's note again. She'd left me a list of who's to get what in the will,'" he explained, looking harassed. "I have quite a few things to give to others—you know, jewellery and stuff. She said there were a couple of boxes, as well as the books for you, and I had to come searching for them. I wasn't planning to come up here for a while, so it's lucky I read her instructions again."

Avery was barely listening, looking instead at the box, mystified. She had expected an old cardboard box, but this was a big wooden crate, completely sealed. A note was on top of it, with her name on it. She glanced at Alex and then at Paul. "Wow, Paul, that's pretty big. I wasn't expecting that. Are you sure you're happy for me to have it? I mean, you don't know what's in it. It could be valuable."

She could feel Alex glaring at her, but she ignored him. They had to do this right. She didn't want any repercussions. Paul shook his head. "No, it looks battered and decrepit. I'm a little embarrassed to be giving it to you, if I'm honest."

"No problem, I'm happy to take it off your hands. You have enough to clear," she said, smiling. "Did you say you found a few other things?"

"Just this, really," he said, reaching for a small box on the floor. "It has a big chunky key in it. Not sure what that's for, but there you are."

Thanking him, she put the box into her bag, and said to Alex, "Shall we lift together?"

Paul waved her off. "Let the men do it."

"Too right, you follow us down," Alex agreed, but when Paul's back was turned he mouthed at her, Look around! He pointed to the herbs hanging above them. It was a hex bag. Desperate to have more time in the attic, Avery whispered a small spell and a loud knock emanated from downstairs.

Paul looked annoyed. "Sorry, I better go and get that, I've got someone else coming to pick up some old furniture. Are you okay to wait?"

"Of course, don't rush," she reassured him. "I'm sure I can help manoeuvre it to the door, at least."

"I'll be back in a minute," he said, and almost ran across the attic and down the stairs.

Alex grinned. "Well improvised!"

"My pleasure," she said, grinning back for a second before becoming serious. "What the hell is in this box, and what's with the herb bundles?"

"If she didn't know magic, she knew someone who did." Alex looked at the box at their feet. "I'm really worried what we're going to find in there." He reached up to the herb bundle and pulled it gently from the ceiling. "Protection again. Quick, let's check out the rest of the room while we have a chance."

They both darted around, searching corners and rafters. Alex called softly from the window. "Another sign of protection."

"I wonder," Avery said, heading to the attic door. She checked the frame inside and out and pulled up some peeling wallpaper along the edge. Beneath it was another rune scratched into the wall above the centre of the frame. "Alex," she hissed. "There's another sign here."

He joined her at the door. "This is too odd. The sooner we look in that box, the better."

"I'm not so sure. I have the horrible feeling we're going to wish Anne had never left me anything."

***

An hour later they were back at Avery's flat, the box in the centre of the living room. It wasn't as heavy as it looked, but it was bulky and Avery had struggled to lift it, Alex taking more than his share of the weight. After frequent stops they had finally wrestled it up the stairs and they now stood looking at it with worried expressions.

Alex had brought a big crow bar with him from the back of the garage, and he tried to prise under what looked like the lid, but he couldn't get it to move. "There's no edge. It's completely sealed."

Understanding began to dawn. "The spells of protection in the attic have been hiding this box. Could we be seeing something that's been disguised? I mean, it's probably not a crate." Avery ran to the spiral stairs that led up to the attic. "I'll grab my grimoire. I have a few spells that might work."

When she returned, Avery put her spell book on the coffee table, faced the box, and started to recite the most likely spell. Nothing happened, and she flicked through the pages, Alex peering over her shoulder. "I'll try another," she murmured. It was an old spell, a counter-spell, in fact, to dispel veils of illusion. As she uttered the words, strange things began to happen to the box. A mist seemed to rise from it, and Avery's vision blurred and she blinked quickly. The box continued to shimmer until the image of the wooden crate completely disappeared, and instead they saw a sturdy, dark wooden box, carved on all sides with strange symbols. A thick iron band was wrapped around it, and in it was a keyhole.

"Holy crap. That looks sinister," Alex said. "Where the hell did Anne find that, and how did she know to give it to you?"

He was right. The symbols, old runes by the look of them, seemed to impart a warning.

"I'm not sure I even want to open it," Avery said, trying to stop her mouth from gaping open.

"Where's your sense of adventure?" Alex said, dropping to his knees. He ran his fingers over the box, feeling the carvings. "How old do you think this is?"

She shrugged. "I have no idea. Hundreds of years old, probably. I don't do furniture, I do books."

"Gil might know. He likes antiques."

"This might be about Gil's family. Stuff they wouldn't want us to know. And at the moment, I don't know what to think about Gil. I want to trust him, but I don't think we can involve him yet."

"I agree," Alex said. "We keep it between us. We don't even tell Briar or El yet. Come on; let's protect this space before we open it."

She sat on the rug opposite him and he reached his hands out. "I'll lead. There's a spell I think will work well here. Will you let me?"

She nodded and put her hands in his. They were strong and warm and he gripped hers tightly.

"Can you feel anything here?" she asked.

"From yesterday? No, can you?"

"No. Whatever it was has gone."

"You chased it off," he said, squeezing her fingers reassuringly. "Anyway, let me start."

She fell silent as he started to chant. The language was old English, an ancient spell that she was familiar with but had never used. He spoke it well, and power whipped around her quickly, giving her a glowing sureness of protection as it spread across the room. She felt his presence reach across to hers with an unexpected intimacy, and as they connected, the power surged stronger until the room resonated with it like a clear bell. The candles placed about the room sparked into life, chasing shadows from dark corners, and she felt herself relax like she hadn't in days.

"Good. Done." He released her hands and turned to the box. "You should open it. It's gifted to you, after all."

She nodded and pulled the box with the key in it from her leather bag that lay next to her on the floor. Nervous, she fumbled and then slotted the key in the lock. It took several attempts to turn it, until finally the old mechanism clicked and the lock released. She flipped back the heavy bar and lifted the lid, gently resting it back against the coffee table.

A musty, old smell escaped, and glancing at each other nervously they both peered inside. The box was full of magical objects. There was an ancient Athame—a witch's knife used for spells—an old bowl or cauldron, several objects that had been wrapped in paper discoloured with age, and some folded paper. A decayed bundle of herbs in a cotton bag were wedged into a corner.

A tremor of excitement rippled through Avery, and she reached into the box. "This stuff is old. Really old. And it's proper magical stuff."

She pulled out the paper and unfolded it gently, and Alex moved next to her, his arm pressing against hers, so he could look, too. Trying to ignore the tingle it sent through her body, she attempted to read the first few lines.

"It's a letter, or a note."

"From when?" he asked.

She tried to read the writing on the first page. The ink had bled in places, but it was just about legible. "October 1589. The Witchfinder General is coming to White Haven."

She felt her breath catch and her fingers trembled, and she looked at Alex in shock. "The witch hunter? Holy crap, Alex. Where has this stuff come from?"

They both knew what had happened when the Witchfinder arrived. Helena Marchmont, Avery's long distant relative, had been burnt at the stake.

"We'll read it later," he nudged her softly. "I have a feeling it will take a while to decipher that writing. I'm wondering if the rest of this stuff is from the same date." He pulled one of the paper-wrapped objects out and as he peeled off the paper it cracked as if in protest. It was a glass jar. "An alembic jar—for potions."

Avery unwrapped another package and found a second jar, this one conical, the glass old with small bubbles in it. "Someone liked potions."

They pulled the other packages out until a range of old glass jars were placed in front of them.

Alex shrugged. "It looks like alchemy to me. Maybe someone was trying to find the secret of immortality."

Avery laughed, "Or was trying to turn lead into gold."

"Both are possible, and anything else. The time fits." Alex shuffled his position slightly, crossing his legs, his weight pushing against her, making her acutely aware of his heat and strength. "We should examine the box. Didn't Anne leave you a note?"

"Yes! Good thinking." Avery realised she'd been so caught up with what was inside the box that she'd forgotten to look at the note. Glad of the excuse to pull away, she knelt forward and pulled the envelope with her name on it from the lid. Inside was a sheet of paper. She read it aloud.

"Dear Avery, I appreciate this will be a shock to you, but I've been aware of your—special skills, shall we call it—since you were little. Don't worry, your secret was safe with me.

"White Haven is a magical place, and for years I've been guarding and researching its rich heritage. I was once friends with Gil's grandmother, Lottie, and it was she who revealed the secrets of the old families to me. She knew I would treasure their memory and protect it. And I've protected it well. It was Lottie who taught me simple spells of protection, and Lottie who inscribed the signs around my house. I'm not one of you. She revealed these secrets to me, and asked me to be Guardian, because she knew no one would suspect me, and if anyone came looking for these things, and the other things that are still hidden, there would be no greater protection.

"However, I'm dying. I need to return these things to you and the other families. There's no one I can speak of this to. My son does not know, by the way. He is merely the messenger.

"I'm not a fool, Avery. These things have been hidden for a reason. Witchcraft is both light and dark. Lottie's own uncle was banished from the house for his persistence in black magic, his name stricken from the family records. I'm not sure Gil knows of this. But Lottie always feared he would be back. He or his descendants. He was searching for the old grimoires. The originals. You must find them first. Lottie says the spells they contain are powerful. When the witch hunter arrived, they were hidden for everyone's sake. When Helena Marchmont was burnt at the stake, the others fled, fearing if she wasn't safe, then no one was. It was only years later that the families returned here, and as you know, some never stay long.

"I have done what I can to help you in my small way, but Lottie didn't know, and I certainly haven't discovered, where those grimoires are. I've researched the

town and the family histories—yours, Alex's, Gil's, Elspeth's, and Briar's—but I couldn't find what happened to Gil's great-uncle Addison. It was as if he simply vanished.

"I wish you luck my dear. I think you'll need it.

Yours, Anne Somersby."

A chill rushed through Avery's body and she felt everything shift, as if her life had suddenly changed in ways she couldn't yet comprehend. She looked at Alex. "Did you know about any of this? The missing grimoires, the banished brother?"

He rolled his eyes. "Are you mad? How could I possibly know! That's what a secret is, you muppet." He grabbed the letter and skimmed it again.

"I'm not a muppet!" she said, outraged.

"So then don't ask stupid questions."

Despite Avery's annoyance with Alex about all sorts of things, mainly for just being Alex, she realised she was incredibly grateful that he was here with her now. She ran her hands through her hair. "Sorry. I'm feeling nervous."

"I know." He grinned, "That's why you have me here. To protect you. It's my pleasure."

"You are so annoying."

"So are you," he said, and rose to his feet, stretching.

She ignored him. "We're going to have to let the others know. I guess this leaves Gil in the clear."

Alex nodded. "I think so. We need to find out about these other grimoires. If I'm honest, I'm not surprised." He stood at the window, looking out onto the street and then looked back at her. "The date on our family grimoire is from 1790. What about yours?"

She shuffled over to look at the front of her grimoire, and saw the date scribbled at the top, the long list of witches' names beneath it, Avery's being the latest. "1795."

"Well over two centuries after the witch trials swept the country." He looked at the boxes strewn about the room. "If Anne's done a good job, there'll be lots in there to help us."

Avery nodded, resoluteness now pouring through her. "So, someone's coming. For us and the grimoires—wherever they are. We need to prepare. You better get your magic on, Alex."

6

After contacting the others to come around later, Alex spent the afternoon helping Avery carry everything she picked up from Anne's house into the attic so they'd have more room to spread out. It would also mean other casual visitors to the flat would have no idea what they'd found.

He'd looked at her living room, perplexed and amused. "Do you normally have so much stuff around?"

Avery looked at the stacks of books, magazines, and the clothing strewn around the room and wondered what he was talking about. She liked ethnic everything, and there were candles, wall hangings, and throws strewn across the couch, as well as large, bright kilim rugs on the wooden floor. Her books and magazines were strategically placed next to favourite spots, and houseplants were everywhere. Yes, it was slightly chaotic, but she loved it. It was warm and comfortable—her nest. "Er, yes. I like it lived in."

"Congratulations. It certainly looks it." He smiled at her, one eyebrow raised, and Avery felt a flush of colour on her cheeks. Was he insulting her house?

"What's wrong with it?" she retorted.

"Nothing! It's not a criticism," he said, still grinning at her in his infuriating manner. He gestured at her, an all-encompassing sweep of his hand that travelled from her head to her toes, and she looked down at her long dress and back at him. He continued, "It's an observation. It's very you. I like it."

She narrowed her eyes at him, wondering quite how to take his last comment, and decided it was better left ignored.

When they'd finished moving everything, they collapsed on the attic floor, both of them hot and sweaty. Alex lay sprawled on the rug in a patch of late afternoon sunshine, like a cat basking in the heat, while Avery leaned against the sofa looking at the carved wooden box as if it would explode.

"What are you thinking?" Alex asked, still prone and eyes closed. "I can hear your mind whirring away from here."

"I'm wondering what that note says."

He rolled to his side and propped himself up on his elbow, fixing her with his dark brown eyes. "Well, we've got a couple of hours before the others get here. Why don't we read it? Or rather, you read it, and I'll listen."

"Do you think we should wait for the others?"

"No, it'll probably take ages to decipher that spidery writing."

"Good. I was hoping you'd say that." She leaned across him to reach into the box, trying not to touch him while all the while remembering the flash of well-toned abs she'd seen when he'd carried the boxes up the stairs.

She was aware of him watching her and she tried to ignore him as she swiftly grabbed the papers and leaned back against the sofa. He grinned at her and leaned back again, closing his eyes. "Have at it!" he said dramatically.

Unseen, Avery rolled her eyes. There were only a handful of pages, and she turned them over gently, scared she'd damage them, as the paper crackled beneath her fingers. "I'm really nervous. What if we find out something terrible?"

"It's a million years ago, Ave," he said, shortening her name in an unexpected intimacy. She quite liked it and watched him speculatively, feeling like a peeping tom because he couldn't see her. His long limbs were muscular and strong, and his jeans hugged his thighs in all the right ways. One hand was under his head, the other rested on his very flat stomach. She dragged her eyes away and back to the diary.

"But whoever's written this letter could be one of our ancestors."

"Yes they could, probably Gil's, but it's not going to read itself!"

"All right!" Slowly and hesitantly she started to read. She said the first line again and felt her stomach lurch.

"October 1589. The Witchfinder General is coming to White Haven.

"We have been lucky here in White Haven. We are far from the cities and have remained quiet and insular, those of us who practice the craft able to keep our magic a secret. But a sickness is sweeping the country. The rumours swirl and thicken and we hear that the Witchfinder General is coming—only days away. He has stopped in small

towns along the way and we hear of interrogations and public shaming, drowning, and even a burning at the stake. But they are not real witches, not as we are.

"We cannot run and start again elsewhere, it is too obvious. And besides, there are other things to consider, things that will have long term implications. We have decided we must hide our books and practices, bury them deep before he arrives, before he burns us all. Our magic is not as powerful as it once was - for reasons I cannot explain here, but to use it in front of everyone will endanger not only our children, but the whole town. All our grimoires will be hidden about White Haven and our properties. We must decide where, swiftly.

"I choose to hide these tools beneath his very eyes, and he will not see them. These items are covered with wards and seals. The others think I am mad, but I am confident of my own magic. He will not find these objects, although the book I will put elsewhere.

"I am hopeful that he will leave town without finding anything, and then in a few months I can reclaim what is mine, and my family's heritage. But if not... I cannot shake this fear that something will go wrong and that we will all die before any of them can be found. We prepare for the future, however. Our magic will not die. It will course through the veins of our children — it is our legacy. But it is this fear that causes me to write this note — just in case. I see things others don't, and I see the long, dark shadow of the Witchfinder General and I see blood and fire. I tell myself it is my imagination, but that is to deny my power.

"If someone else finds this note then I am dead, but I hope it will not be too late to find the book. I believe I have hidden it wisely. Our book has old spells from the dark times, and our power of spirit and fire. Whoever you are, when you choose to look for it, think of what we do. It will be there. And then guard it well.

Imogen Bonneville."

Alex shot upright, looking at Avery in shock. "Did you say, 'Bonneville?'"

She swallowed, "Yes."

"But that's my surname."

"I know. I did warn you it might be one of our ancestors!"

His dark eyes were troubled, and he stretched his hand out and took the note. "I know, but thinking it and knowing it are two very different things."

Avery leaned back, watching him and thinking. "At least one of your ancestors wasn't burnt at the stake." She shuddered. "I know it happened a long time ago, but it suddenly feels like it happened only last year. It's one of those things I push to the back of my mind. I still can't believe Helena didn't use her powers to escape."

"It would put everyone at risk, the letter said as much. Can you imagine if that happened now?"

"There must have been more to it than that. She said, 'Our magic is not as powerful as it once was.' And I don't want to think about that happening again. We may have to use our magic more openly if we get threatened, and then what?"

"I'm not sure we can afford to do that now, any more than they could then." Alex looked at the note. "Imogen mentions a prophecy, and a legacy of fire, so they are clearly skills that run in my family. But how did this box end up at Gil's house?"

"Another mystery to add to the many," Avery observed, thinking that life was about to get far more complicated, and probably dangerous.

***

Briar, El, and Gil looked at them both in amazement. The box sat in the middle of the attic floor in pride of place, the rest of the files and books surrounding it, spread on the floor in all directions. They perched on floor cushions, rugs, and the sagging sofas. Candles filled the room, and the scent of incense drifted around.

"So, you found this box in Anne's attic?" Gil asked, again.

"Yes. I know it's weird, but she's been hiding it for years," Avery explained for what seemed the hundredth time. "And she got it from your great-aunt."

"But it actually belongs to me," Alex added.

Gil closed his eyes and leaned back on the sofa. "I need time to think."

"But Gil," Briar said insistently, "you really had no idea about your crazy, black magic-seeking uncle?"

"Great-great-uncle," he murmured without opening his eyes. "No! I did not."

"And what about your brother?" she asked, referring to Reuben, Gil's younger brother who generally avoided all magic.

"I doubt he knows, either." He remained prone on the sofa, hands over his eyes.

Alex interrupted, "Briar, can we give Gil a moment without the twenty questions?"

Briar looked at him wide-eyed. "They're important questions, Alex. Some crazy person from his family is after some old hidden grimoires, and we are at risk!"

"Yes, thank you, Briar, I know that. But this is not the time for blame. It's not Gil's fault. And actually, we don't know what we sense yet. It could be Gil's family, or it could be someone completely different."

Avery suppressed a smile, enjoying the fact that Briar was at the receiving end of Alex's sarcasm and not her. If she was honest, Briar was a little brittle tonight. As soon as she'd arrived at Avery's flat, she looked around suspiciously, and narrowed her eyes when she saw Alex already there, leaning against the kitchen counter with a beer in hand. *Did she fancy Alex?* Avery wouldn't be surprised. He was very good looking, she had to admit. He had that rugged self-assuredness that was infuriating but mesmerising all at the same time. She found his closeness surprisingly unsettling.

Avery tucked a strand of her dark red hair behind her ear and coughed slightly. "So, to get back to our plan. We need to go through all of this paperwork and see if we can work out where the old grimoires are."

El spoke for the first time in ages, "And see what else our old histories may show us."

"Exactly," Avery looked at El gratefully. "We also need to look at the old town plans, records, and anything else. And we need to work quickly, before someone else works it out before us."

"How come none of us knew about the old grimoires?" Briar asked. "Surely family members would have passed them down."

"Oh, I can tell you why." Gil sat up and rubbed his hair so that it spiked upwards. "Fear. After Helena died, I would imagine they were only too happy to let them disappear completely."

"But the grimoires are our strength," Avery reasoned. "Surely when the risk was over, at least one family would have gone back for theirs."

El shrugged. "Another mystery. And what about the box? Have you examined it?"

"Every inch," Alex said. "I recognise some symbols, but not all. Runes are not really my speciality. It's a bit weird that it may have been carved by or for my family."

El shuffled forward and sat next to the box, her silver bangles jangling as she ran her hands across the surface. "It must be several centuries old, right?" She looked up at them, "And we think these objects are from the 1500s?"

"We think so, yes," Alex confirmed. "If we use the letter to date it."

"I'm familiar with runes, and these ones offer protection. They ward off evil, and hide it from prying eyes."

"If they could do this, why didn't they do it with the grimoires?" Briar asked.

"Still too big a risk, I would imagine," Avery said. "Anyway, I've started looking through the history of the town. Do you know where your old family houses would have been?"

"Well, you know where mine is," Gil said. "We haven't moved in years. I would imagine our grimoire is hidden within the grounds, but maybe I'm being simplistic."

"Well, it sounds like your great-great uncle Addison had been looking for it, and he must have looked everywhere," Alex reasoned. He looked at Gil, puzzled. "Did you really have no idea about him and your disappeared line?"

"No, none." Gil looked at them, still raking his hand through his hair. "I'm in shock, actually. I'll have to speak to Reu about it, but I'm sure he knows nothing, either. As you know, he prefers to ignore our magic."

Avery didn't really know Reuben, but he was closer to her age, and very different to Gil. "Are you sure he doesn't like magic, Gil? I would have thought he would have moved from White Haven if he wanted to ignore his history. Like my sister did." Sometimes magic didn't run strongly in all family members, and sometimes they just preferred to ignore it and bury their talent. Her sister, Bryony, had buried it for years and moved away, unlike Avery who had honed and practised her magic, becoming stronger every day. The thought of finding the old family grimoire filled her with excitement.

"I don't know what he thinks, Avery, we just don't talk about it anymore."

"How does it work with your wife, Gil?" Briar asked. She sat cross-legged on a cushion, watchful, and it seemed to Avery, still annoyed about something. "Does she know about your magic? I mean, I presume she does, but…"

"I hide it," he said. "All of it."

Avery felt a jolt of disbelief, and looked at him, shocked. Gil was the only one of them who was married, or in fact in a relationship of any kind. It wasn't that any of them hadn't been in relationships, but they didn't last that long. She presumed for his marriage to have lasted, his wife, Alicia, must have known.

"Really?" Alex also seemed surprised. "How is that even possible? You live with her every day. Aren't you hiding part of yourself? Your real self?"

Gil thought for a moment. "I've broached the subject, you know, of the history of this place, and what would she think if there really were witches, but she looked at me like I was mad." He looked at the others, a rueful smile on his face. "I left it, and kept promising myself I'd bring it up later, but chickened out." He looked at them all and laughed. "You should see your faces! I know it's mad, but I've made it work." He became serious, dropping his gaze to the floor for a second, before looking up sheepishly. "I was lonely, and I needed her. I *need* her now. I don't know how you do it. We're so different from everyone else, I just needed a connection."

El, Avery, Alex, and Briar looked at each other, a flash of understanding passing between them.

"It's all right, mate," Alex said awkwardly. "You don't need to explain yourself to us."

El smiled sadly, and leaned against the wooden box. "I envy you, Gil. It is hard, that's why I came back here. It's why I like hanging out with your brother. He might not practice magic, but at least he understands it. And me."

Avery tried to hide her surprise. Elspeth, like Briar, had moved back to White Haven a few years ago. Their families had moved away when they were children, and both had felt White Haven's magical pull, returning in their early twenties. She had no idea El spent time with Reuben, and realised there were so many connections she didn't know about.

Gil obviously knew, because he just nodded. "I know. I'm hoping you'll change his mind."

El shook her head. "I think it would take something big to do that."

"Well," Briar said, looking regretful, "My last boyfriend loved that I could make all these cool potions and creams, except when he suspected they might really work. He just couldn't get his head around it, no matter how much I tried to play it down. It was the midnight herb gathering that really freaked him out. The whole relationship thing exhausts me. Unless I meet someone who understands me, I've sworn off it for the future." She glanced at Alex and then stared into distance, lost in thought.

"And what about you, Avery?" Alex asked.

His stare was so direct; it felt intimate, even with everyone else there, and Avery stumbled over her words. "I guess I've had the same experience as everyone else. Old boyfriends have thought I was odd, with endearing hobbies—you know, my tarot reading and book obsessions—and I really played them down. I thought my last boyfriend was okay with it, but it turns out, he wasn't. But lucky me, we remain good friends!" She shrugged, feeling embarrassed, even though there was no need to. "And what about you, Alex?" she asked, returning the question. "No secret girlfriends hidden away?"

He laughed. "Several, all at arm's length."

"No surprises there, then," Avery said, rolling her eyes as everyone laughed.

"Liar," El said, unexpectedly, watching Alex with her head tucked speculatively on one side. "You don't fool me, Alex Bonneville. That ladies man thing is just an act."

Alex's response was just as unexpected. He threw his head back and laughed. "No comment. I reserve the right to privacy. As do my women. And there's always room for more." He winked at El, Briar, and Avery.

"You're revolting!" Briar shrieked in mock horror, and threw a cushion at Alex, who laughed again.

Gil tried to bring them back to order. "If we can move on from Alex's harem, what's the plan with these grimoires?"

Avery answered, trying to shake off the memory of the glint in Alex's eye. He was way too dangerously sexy. And unobtainable. Instead she voiced something she didn't really believe, but thought she'd say anyway. "Maybe we should leave these grimoires alone. To find them could change everything. We've managed all these years without them."

"It's too late for that, "Alex said. "I think that the moment Anne Somersby died, something was set in motion. And we both know something else is coming," he said, looking pointedly at Avery. "We have no choice, we have to find the grimoires first, and whatever else is hidden from our past. And we have to stick together."

"I can't take any of this home yet," Gil said. "Do you mind if I leave it here?"

"No, of course not," Avery said, shrugging. "Where do you hide your grimoire at home, though?"

He grinned. "There's a hidden room in the attic. But I rarely go up there. The spells I need for my garden I know by heart. Alicia just thinks I have eccentric gardening habits. She doesn't like gardening, anyway, and her job keeps her busy."

"Well, I don't want to move this box, not in the daylight, anyway," Alex said. "If that's okay, Avery? I'll take the files, though. Exciting bedtime reading!"

"Sure, whatever you want."

El agreed. "I'll take my family papers, too, but all the general stuff on the town and that, maybe we should leave here?"

"I agree," Briar added. "Let's meet again, soon. Share what we have."

Avery nodded, "All right, Wednesday night?"

"What are we all doing for the Solstice?" Alex asked. "That's only a week away. We should celebrate it together."

Avery had never celebrated it with anyone else before, but before she could protest, a chorus of agreement rang out. Alex grinned, a triumphant smile as he glanced at Avery. "Good, I'll start planning."

7

When she wasn't working at the shop, Avery spent every spare moment in the attic looking at her family tree and piecing the history of her family together, while also reading up on White Haven's history. Anne had really done her research, and Avery's head swam with details.

She had a meticulous family tree, going back to the 1500s. Whether Anne couldn't find anything before then, or had given up at that point, it wasn't clear. She'd also glanced at Gil's, and that went back to the 1500s, too. It must have taken Anne years. It was odd, to spend so much time on someone else's history. Some of the names on her family tree coincided with names written in the front of her grimoire. She remembered adding her own when she was sixteen, her mother encouraging her in the family traditions. The only time she had, actually. Shortly after that her mother left White Haven, and she hadn't revealed anything about a previous spell book, lost or otherwise. Maybe she didn't know about it.

Amongst Anne's papers was a map of White Haven and the surrounding area, marked with numbers and letters, and Avery pinned it to the wall, removing a few prints to make room. She marked Gil's house on there. It was the only one that they knew had belonged to the family through the years. But where had everyone else's family once lived? She was pretty sure that the bookshop and the house it was in only belonged to the family in the late 1800s.

It was a couple of evenings after their discovery, and Avery lifted her head from her research and looked around at the attic, wondering about the other witches who had stood there working their spells. It was cluttered with papers and books from Anne, her own spell book, and books on herbs, metals, and gems. Her tarot cards were on the table, folded in silk and placed in their own special box. The carved wooden box still sat on the floor, although she had pushed it to the side, under the window. It drew her eye all the time, no matter where in the room she sat.

As the light faded and the shadows lengthened across the floor, Avery felt unsettled and restless. She grabbed a bundle of sage from the shelf and lit the end with a flash from her fingers. The sage sizzled and smoked, and she marched to a corner of the room, chanting a cleansing spell as she worked around the room, clearing the air.

With another click of her fingers, she lit the candles, and the dark corners pooled with a warm yellow light, immediately comforting her. She sat and pulled out her tarot cards, shuffling them thoroughly and focusing on what she wanted to ask them. Alex's image came to her mind, but she pushed it away. She wanted to know if something was still coming. A stranger, a threat, or what?

The pack warmed beneath her hands and she slowed her breathing as she started to place out the cards. As she turned each one, she saw representations of herself, Alex, and a card that could be Gil, and then the major arcana cards came, chilling her blood. The Devil, the Tower, and the Moon, and too many sword cards, ending with the King of Swords.

She swept the cards up in a hurry, jumping when she heard a knock on the door. Attackers didn't usually knock, she reassured herself, as she ran down the two flights of stairs to her front door. She could see Alex's silhouette through the glass and she felt relieved, if puzzled. She opened the door and he stepped in, grinning and waving a bottle of wine. He looked good tonight, his long hair loose and freshly washed; he smelt of something musky.

"I come bearing gifts!" He hesitated as he looked at her. "Are you all right?"

"I'm fine, I've just read the cards again and they look awful. You made me jump, that's all."

"Well, good job I'm here then. Do you mind if I look at that box again?"

"Of course not, it's yours."

He looked at her expectantly. "Glasses?"

She grinned. "Carry on up, I'll grab them."

By the time she returned to the attic, Alex had dragged the box to the centre of the room again, and now sat cross-legged in front of it, examining it closely. He had pulled a book from his canvas pack and it lay open next to him, revealing pages illustrated with drawings and descriptions of runes.

Avery sat next to him and picked up the book. "Where did you get this from?"

"El. She's had it for years and has marked a couple she thought looked familiar." He pointed to one on the side of the box. "This one is for protection and repels demons." He looked at her with a raised eyebrow.

"Demons? As in, red-eyed, evil smoke and brimstone demons?"

"I guess so." He pointed to the opposite side, where another strange mark was carved into the wood. "And this one repels spirits." He pulled the book from her hands and flicked through a few pages. "See, here."

Avery compared the two, and felt a flutter of excitement start to override her fear. "And the one on the top?"

"Incomprehension, blindness—a deflection, almost, of vision. The one that stopped us from seeing the box." He leaned closer, looking at the details. "See, there are lots of tiny little runes, too, all around the rim of the lid of the box."

The lid was deep and solid, with more runes on the inside. "And what do these mean?" she asked, pointing at them.

"Another spell." Alex's voice rose slightly with anticipation. "They combine to make a sentence." He looked back and forth between the runes and the box, flicking pages impatiently, muttering under his breath.

While he looked, Avery ran her fingers over the runes, feeling their smooth contours. She had the feeling they hadn't been carved by hand, but had been magicked in, burnt by fire. *Should they even be trying to open it?* She sat back on her heels, thinking. It was deep enough to hold a grimoire. Maybe Imogen Bonneville had been lying in her letter. She felt a thrill race through her. If this did contain the grimoire, they were ahead of whatever was coming.

"Alex, I think the grimoire is in the lid."

"What?" he said absently, still pre-occupied.

"Your family grimoire. The original."

He looked up at her in shock. "But the note…"

"Meant to confuse—I think so, anyway."

He looked back to the pages in front of him. "Okay. This makes sense. I think I know what the runes say. It requires a blood sacrifice."

"What!" Avery jolted back. "We don't do those." They never did such things. That was darker, older magic, now forbidden.

"Hold on—it's not what you think. It needs my blood." He may have said the words calmly, but he looked worried.

53

"Go on." She took a slug of wine, trying to ease her racing thoughts, and Alex reached for his glass, too.

"It needs something of me, something to prove who I am, and that I am worthy of it."

The room felt very dark suddenly, and Avery shivered. "Your ancestor surely wouldn't want to cause you harm?"

"I think it's also an act of faith."

"There's a lot of *thinks* here." As much as Alex annoyed her, she didn't want him dead or maimed. And she didn't relish the thought of black magic unleashed in her home.

"Will you help me?" She hesitated, and he carried on. "I had another vision. More blood, more destruction. I see death, Avery."

"What if it's this?"

"It's not this. This will help us."

"The cards I saw earlier predicted it, too. Destruction, I mean. Change." Her well-ordered life, weird as it may be to some people, was also safe, and now it felt threatened. She sighed. "We can't walk away from this now, can we?"

He shook his head, his long dark hair falling round his face, and in the candlelight she became aware of just how attracted to him she was. He had an animal magnetism, a sheer masculine force that she couldn't ignore, but really had to. She was pretty sure he wasn't interested in her at all, and if he was, she was only one among many. And, she reminded herself, he was a superior bastard at times.

"It's a simple spell; it just requires some herbs and my blood. I don't actually need you to do anything, just be here in case something crap happens." He grinned and winked.

"That's not funny. I'm not the witch cavalry. Should we call the others?" With the night closing in around them, her attic felt threatened and vulnerable. More witches were a good idea.

"No, it would take too long. Let's get on with it," he said decisively, rising quickly to his feet. He headed to her extensive collection of dried herbs and selected some jars, declaring, "I need this, this, and this."

While he was preparing the herbs by crushing them in the pestle and mortar, she flicked through the rune book, looking at the designs and comparing them to the box. "Are you sure you know what you're doing? I'm familiar with a couple of these, but…" Her voice trailed off as she tried to work out the meaning.

"My grandmother was good with runes," he said from where he stood at the long wooden table. "She taught me some, a long time ago. I remember a few of them now—vaguely. I must have her books somewhere, or maybe she took them with her."

"Where's your grandmother now?"

"Not here," he said with a sigh. Before she could ask anything else, he bought the herb mix over. "Now, I just have to mix my blood in it."

"We need a black candle," Avery said. "It will enhance the spell, discover the truth of it, and banish negative energies." She headed to the shelf to where a number of baskets sat, and after rummaging in one of them, she pulled out a brand new candle, while Alex marked out a circle on the floor with salt.

"Salt?" She looked at him, confused.

"I'm taking precautions. Just in case something unhealthy appears." He shrugged. "I'm sure it won't."

She resisted the urge to glare. "In that case, we need purple candles, too."

Alex placed the box in the centre of the circle, and then Avery lit the candles on either side.

He looked at her, serious all of a sudden. "Ready?"

"As I'll ever be."

"Step away, just in case."

He waited until she was across the room, standing by the table, and then he stepped into the circle and sat cross-legged in front of the box, withdrew a penknife, and slashed it along the centre of his palm. Avery winced as she watched him. He clenched his hand and let the blood drip into the bowl, all the while chanting under his breath. He mixed the blood and herbs with his uninjured hand and started to smear the mixture over the runes in the lid and the tiny ones all the way around the edge. All the while his blood dripped into the bowl, and he seemed to smear a lot of it over the box.

As Alex chanted, the pressure dropped, and Avery realised she was having difficulty breathing. She started gasping for breath, and noticed Alex was doing the same, but she daren't speak. Something, good or ill, was happening. With a weird sucking sound the pressure dropped again, and Avery felt dizzy as every single candle in the room went out, and then the lamps, until only the two candles in the circle remained lit.

Avery concentrated on Alex and the box. Long, wavering shadows made him look demonic, and it looked as if the runes on the box were moving.

Just as the pain in her ears was becoming unbearable, there was a loud bang like a gunshot, and the wooden lid of the box cracked down the middle. Thick, black smoke began to pour from it. The candle flames on either side of the box shrank to tiny sparks, and Alex chanted louder, lifting his head to stare at the smoke.

Avery stepped forward, raising her hands, ready to send a blast of energy at whatever it was, but the thick smoke stopped within the circle's protective walls. She remembered Alex's words. *He said it was a test, but was it?* The signs on the box provided protection from spirits and demons. Maybe something was locked in.

She stood transfixed. Alex's voice was strained and he was enveloped in the blackness, almost shouting his chant. She stepped forward again, wondering what else she could do, when suddenly the blackness crackled like it contained lightning and disappeared, leaving Alex slumped on the floor. The candle flames on either side shot high before shrinking again, and the pressure in the room returned to normal.

Whatever it was, had gone.

Avery used her pent up energy to relight every single candle and ran to Alex, pulling him out of the circle, until she fell over backwards on the rug, with him sprawled on her lap.

She eyed the box warily, but nothing else happened, and she quickly felt Alex's neck for a pulse. She sighed with relief. It was there, strong and steady, but he was a dead weight and completely unconscious.

She leaned over him awkwardly, and shook his shoulders. "Alex, Alex, can you hear me?"

Nothing.

She shouted louder, "Alex. Wake up!"

She had a sudden, horrific thought that he might be possessed, and then chastised herself. *This wasn't Supernatural. But could it happen?* She and the others used the elements, did spells of protection, but they never messed with blood magic. Well, never until now. *What the hell had they got themselves into?*

She looked at his inert form. He was really heavy. And solid. His arms were sinewy with muscle, his shoulders broad, and his shirt had rolled up as she dragged him over, revealing a smooth flat stomach. Her gaze travelled down his legs, and she swallowed guiltily. Tearing her eyes away she focused on his face and shouted again, "Alex, wake up!"

Still nothing.

She glanced at the box and decided she needed to complete the salt circle again. She felt vulnerable and open to attack, having no idea what had been in the black smoke. Sliding out from under Alex, she rested his head gently on a cushion and scooted over to the box, all her senses alert, as she peered into the crack in the wooden lid. She could see a hint of silver. *Something* was in there, but she'd leave it for Alex to look. She grabbed the salt and completed the circle once more.

Avery was tempted to wake him using a spell, but decided against it. He must have used up a lot of energy, and only rest would restore that. His hand was still bleeding from the cut he'd made across his palm, so she fetched a bandage from the bathroom and dressed the wound. Then she angled a pillow under his head, and threw a blanket over him, trying to make him as comfortable as possible.

The room felt chilly now, even though it was summer. There was a small fireplace in the wall between her bedroom and the attached en suite bathroom, and the rest of the attic space, as the main chimney breast rose between what had once been two separate houses. She lit a small fire, the bright orange of the flames making her feel warmer already.

She wondered how the others were getting on with their research. The past had always felt close to her, and now it felt even closer. She had the feeling that old secrets were ready to be uncovered, whether she wanted them to be or not. Shivering, she pulled a blanket around her shoulders and lay on the sofa, a cushion under her head. It wasn't long before she slept, too.

8

When Avery woke the next morning, she found Alex gone and his blanket draped over her. He'd left a note on the table.

I didn't want to disturb you, so I'll see you tonight. The others will be coming, too. Don't touch the box until we arrive. Thanks for your help. I'm all right.

> *- Alex*

Of course, it was Wednesday. She looked around the room, expecting to see the room disturbed in some way after the events of the previous night, but in the pale dawn light, everything looked fine, apart from the broken lid of the wooden box. She felt sorry Alex had left; she would have loved to know what he'd experienced, but that would have to wait.

After showering and applying makeup, she pulled on a long cotton skirt in dark blue and a short-sleeved cotton top before she headed downstairs to the shop. The day was overcast and promised rain, and that was usually good for visitors. On Wednesdays, only she and Sally were in the shop, which kept them busy. On other days, a post-grad student named Dan would come in for a few hours, which relieved Avery from needing to be in the shop all day. She didn't like leaving Sally on her own.

Sally grinned at her when she arrived. "What have you been up to? You look like you had a late night."

"Nothing that exciting," Avery lied. She'd already decided on how she would explain seeing more of the others. It would be unusual enough for Sally to comment. "You know when Anne Somersby left us some books?"

"Yes," Sally said, leaning her hip against the shop counter.

"She left me some papers on some old family histories and the history of the town. They include Alex's, Gil's, and a few others—you know Elspeth from the jewellery shop, and Briar with the lotion store?"

"Yes." Sally drew the word out quizzically, a slight frown behind her eyes.

"Well, I let them know, and we've decided to finish her investigations," she said lightly, while making herself busy tidying shelves. "Alex came over last night and it ended up being a late night, that's all. They're back this evening."

Sally's voice went up an octave. "What do you mean, 'came over?' Are you two—?"

Avery leapt in before she could finish the sentence, whipping round to face Sally. "No! It was just a chat."

"A late night chat." Sally smiled smugly. "Call it what you want to, I'll make a cuppa," and she disappeared into the back room.

Avery sighed and rested her head against the bookshelf. This would now go on and on. She hoped customers would keep them busy all day.

***

By the time they closed the shop, Avery was knackered. They had been busy all day, so she hadn't had time to worry about other things. She locked up and headed upstairs to her flat.

El arrived first, looking excited. "Hey Avery, that stuff you gave me from Anne is great." She rested a big, slouchy leather bag on the floor, bulging with papers. Her white-blonde hair was scraped up in a messy bun on her head, and she wore faded jeans and a t-shirt, revealing a glimpse of the tattoos on her upper arms. "I've found out so much more about my old family history than my family ever told me."

"Who gave you your grimoire then, El?" Avery asked, curious.

"My great aunt. And she was sneaky about it, too. Made me promise not to tell my parents, or anyone else in the family. Magic was a big no-no to them."

Avery was in the open kitchen area, preparing tea and coffee. "So how did she know that you would be okay with it?"

"She noticed things that the rest of my family either couldn't see, or didn't want to. I was always clever with making things, and she noticed that I made things slightly differently. She made a point of visiting as I was growing up, and then one day she asked me if I wanted to spend the weekend at her house. It was a creaky old place, but over the course of that weekend she told me about our family, as much as she knew anyway, and she started to teach me magic. After that, it was our little secret." Elspeth smiled and shrugged. "She was amazing. It if wasn't for her, I may not even be here."

Avery passed her a mug of coffee. "I guess I've been lucky. At least it wasn't something to be hidden in our family. Not from each other, anyway. Although not all family members have embraced it."

"Strange, isn't it, how some people are scared of this stuff?" Elspeth laughed, "And then a whole load of other people wish they had what we have."

"I don't know if they'd want what we have now. Things got weird last night."

Before she could elaborate, the others arrived. Alex looked tired.

"Are you okay?" Avery asked. "You really worried me last night."

"What's going on?" Briar asked, a look of concern crossing her face as she looked between the two of them.

"It's all right, I'm fine," Alex said. "Sorry I didn't stay," he said to Avery. "I woke at about three in the morning and didn't want to wake you, so I left. Are YOU all right?"

"I wasn't the one smothered in weird black smoke. I'm fine, thanks. Weirded out, but fine."

By now the others were looking bewildered, and Alex quickly said, "The runes on the box, it was a test, for me. Come and see."

They followed him up the stairs to the attic, which looked peaceful, if messy, suggesting nothing of the events that happened the night before. The wooden box rested in a patch of sunlight, highlighting the crack on the inside of the lid. The line of salt still surrounded it.

"What the hell happened?" Gil asked. "Is that *blood*?" He stood close to the box, examining the smear of herb paste that ran over the runes, and the bowl the paste had been mixed in. Alex's knife was still on the floor, too, and he looked at Alex's bandaged hand. He straightened up, suddenly serious. "What did you do?"

"The box needed my blood to prove who I was. Or rather, my ancestor did. It was a rune spell, and I deciphered it."

"And then decided to cast it! Blood magic?" Gil looked at Alex incredulously, and then at Avery. "And you let him do it?"

Avery had never seen Gil like this before. She knew Gil as the laidback witch from across the town who came from one of the old families. But then again, they'd never performed magic together, either.

She stood next to Alex, in solidarity. "I actually didn't want him to, but we knew something was in the lid. It's still in the lid. We think it's the grimoire." The tension in the room was palpable. "Look, I know it was dangerous, but we were careful, you can see that. And I trusted Alex." She felt Alex give her a quick glance, but she kept looking at Gil.

Gil's shoulders dropped and he sighed. "I wish you'd have called us first. Anything could have happened."

Alex explained, "There wasn't time, and besides, I didn't think we needed you. And I'm fine."

"And the black smoke?" El asked, hands on hips, not wanting to let them off that easily.

He grinned sheepishly, "Well, that *was* odd."

"It wasn't smoke though, was it?" Briar said, standing next to the circle. "It was a spirit form."

Avery's mouth gaped. "It was a *what?*"

"She's right," Alex said. "It spoke to me. Well, sort of. I could feel it in my head, probing, checking me out." He shook his head, as if to shake out the intrusion. "I felt I had to fight to prove who I am. It was exhausting."

"You passed out. It must have been," Avery said, frowning at Alex. "I didn't know whether to try and intervene, but then I thought if you're right, and it was a test …" She trailed off, and looked at Briar. "It was crazy. Anything could have happened, but we had to try. How do you know it was a spirit?"

Briar gently probed around the crack on the box's lid, and then brushed her fingers across the symbol on the side. "This sign. It seems logical now."

"Well, hindsight's a great thing. You could have been killed. Both of you," Gil said, still annoyed. He sat on the edge of the sofa, looking at the box warily.

Alex strode forward to join Briar. "Well, we weren't, and it's about time we looked at what's in here."

He inserted his fingers into the long crack in the lid and pulled, the fractured wood splintering to reveal a large, thick grimoire covered with scuffed black leather. Alex lifted it out gently and as the light hit it, a faded

61

silver image glinted on the cover that Avery struggled to recognise. Alex carried it to the oak table that Avery used to prepare her spells, and they crowded around him as he opened the cover. A list of names was written on the front page in different scripts, and the date at the top said 1309.

"This was 300 years old when it was hidden!" he said, shocked. He turned the pages, and it seemed everyone held their breath. The pages were covered in dense, tiny writing, all spells starting on a new page, the same as in their existing grimoires, the language old, and the script hard to decipher. There were simple illustrations too.

"What kind of spells are they?" El asked, craning to see.

"Some of them seem the usual types," Alex said thoughtfully. "Charms of protection, healing spells, some curses, and …" He paused, looking at them, "Spells to control spirits and demons."

"Demons?" Briar asked, her eyes wide.

He nodded. "Many more than I've got in my existing book."

Avery felt another flutter of worry pass through her. She had been taught as a child that to manipulate spirits and demons was something that could be done only occasionally - it was too dangerous. "Does this mean they summoned demons more than we do now?"

"I guess so." Alex continued to turn pages, mesmerised. "These spells are sophisticated, complex. And potentially more powerful than I've used before."

It took a few seconds for this to sink in. Older, more powerful spells. A hidden legacy of magic they could now learn. Avery shivered, not sure if it was with excitement or trepidation. "Do you think the other grimoires will be like this?"

"They must be," Gil reasoned. "Is there anything in there about immortality? Or anything that looks particularly dark?"

"Other than *demons*? No idea at this stage." Alex looked up. "I really need to spend time looking through this properly. The writing's hard to decipher in places."

"Why are you asking that?" El asked Gil.

"Just wondered if it's something my missing relatives might have been interested in."

Briar interrupted, looking horrified. "Has anybody actually summoned a demon?"

"Never," El said. "And I have no intention of doing so either."

"I wonder," Avery said, "If it was Anne's death that triggered something coming in the first place. I mean that her death released knowledge of the box she'd hidden away for so long. After all, it was just after she died that Alex had his premonition and the cards foretold an event."

"Alex," El mused thoughtfully, "what are the MAIN types of spells in your book?"

"I'm not sure, it's difficult to define. Astral projection, out of body walking, spirit talking." He was sitting now, head on his hand, leafing through the book, his attention completely caught in it. "I've never seen stuff like this before."

"So it's a symbol for Spirit!" she exclaimed. "The image on the front of the book, I mean."

Avery was annoyed with herself for not realising sooner. "Of course! And it *is* Alex's strength."

"So does that mean the other grimoires focus on the other elements?" Gil asked.

"Fire, Air, Water, Earth. The strengths of our family lines?" Briar observed.

Avery grinned. "We could grow our magic! Learn new things. Tap into a magic that's been hidden to us for centuries!"

Gil brought her back to Earth. "If the spells are as powerful as we think—as Alex thinks his are—then the books could be trouble. A whole shit ton of trouble. If someone else knows these exist, it's no wonder they're coming for them."

9

The following morning, Avery was up and out early. The streets and lanes of White Haven were quiet, and wisps of early morning mist started to clear as the sun rose into a pale blue sky.

Avery walked up the hill away from her flat and Happenstance Books, and at the top looked back over the town and the sea beyond. She never tired of this beautiful view. She loved the old cobbled streets and tiny lanes that snaked into each other as they rose and fell with the land, finally leading down to the sea. Fishing boats were heading out, but the sailboats remained in the harbour, their bright sails furled. Beyond the town, the houses were spaced out along the hills and fields. It was such a pretty place, and she wanted it to remain that way. She didn't want a witch war breaking out in White Haven in the search for old grimoires.

Last night, once the other witches had gone, she'd made herself a chamomile tea and shut the door between her bedroom and the attic. She sat in bed with the lights low and the window open, and spread Anne's papers across the duvet. Her cats, Circe and Medea, had curled up on the end of the bed, keeping her company, ears pricked, eyes closed, while she'd scrutinised old maps of the town. And that's when she saw Anne's mark on the page, a small green-inked squiggle that looked like an 'H.' *Could that be for Helena?*

That spot was where she was heading this morning.

Avery turned from the view and headed along the lanes until she found the one she needed. Besom Lane. It wasn't somewhere you would pass by chance. It was tucked out of the way, and lined with tiny cottages. She meandered along it, admiring the hanging baskets and pots, the neat curtains and whitewashed walls, and carefully noted the numbers. The lane was long and winding, and she eventually arrived at the cottage she was looking for.

This tiny place could have been where Helena and her family lived all those years ago. There was a window downstairs next to the front door, and two small windows upstairs, the cottage identical to the others on either side. It was strange to think she had lived so close to this place and had never known to whom it had once belonged.

Avery leaned back against the wall of the house opposite and gazed at it, her thoughts jumbled. *Was Helena dragged from here to the stake, or was she already imprisoned somewhere in the village?* She looked again at the map. It was fuzzy and unclear compared to modern maps, and although Anne had noted a number, for all Avery knew, the numbers might have changed over the years. The map showed small square gardens at the back, and this row was almost buried in the slope of the hill behind it. But whereas the lanes were isolated back then, now they were surrounded by streets lined with more recent buildings—well, 18th century as opposed to 16th century.

What now? Would the old grimoire be hidden here? Avery wracked her brain trying to think about what Anne's note had said. The cottage must have withstood many changes and renovations; it would be a miracle if they found it here. She sighed. It was time for coffee and breakfast. She'd go and see who else might be awake.

***

Avery pushed open the door to Briar's shop, the door chimes ringing pleasantly as she entered. She carried two hot lattes in a cardboard tray, and a bag of croissants was wedged into the top of her shoulder bag.

As soon she entered the shop the scents of lavender, rose, and geranium wrapped around her. She inhaled deeply and looked around with pleasure. Briar's shop looked like an old fashioned apothecary. Shelves lined the walls, filled with different ranges of skin lotions, hair products, soaps, creams for ailments, and all sorts of dried herbs, books on herbs, scented candles, and other products used around the home. All of them were made with natural ingredients, either by Briar or other small companies. You could tell which were Briar's products, because they were all in unusually shaped bottles with pale pastel colours. It was a comforting shop, and Avery immediately relaxed.

Briar looked up from behind the long wooden counter at the back of the shop and smiled, puzzled. "Hi, Avery! Is everything all right? I don't normally see you in here." She'd been filling some jars with a creamy lotion that looked like moisturiser, and she finished her work, putting the jug on the counter.

"Don't let me stop you! Yes, I'm fine—sort of. I've bought coffee and croissants so I can pick your brain." She plonked her bag and the rest of her load on the counter. "Your shop looks great!"

Briar smiled. "Thanks. I've been doing well, so I expanded my range." She grinned and leaned forward, grabbing a coffee. "People often comment on the unexpected benefits of using my stuff."

Avery laughed. "I bet! If they only knew."

"Probably best they don't." Briar sipped her coffee. "This is good, thank you." She dipped the croissant in and took a bite. "Even better!" She watched Avery as she chewed. "So, what are you picking my brain about?"

Avery looked around to make sure the shop was still empty. "Old grimoires, of course. I'm worried we'll never find the others."

"Well, if we don't, maybe someone else can't find them, either. It might be a good thing, from what we saw in Alex's book."

"Do you really think that? It's our heritage!"

Briar licked her fingers. "It's been five hundred years since we've seen those books, and our magic has survived. It's brought us a good life." She gestured to the room around her. "We've never needed them before, and we don't need them now." Briar looked calm and composed, and very resolute.

"Does this mean you're not going to look for your book? Or where you used to live?" Avery felt herself floundering. "Or anything?"

"I don't know. We have a lot to lose."

"We have a lot to gain, as well. And someone's coming."

Briar sighed and rolled her eyes. "But who? I mean, really? This is just too weird. Anne dies, you and Alex are seeing the same stuff. All of this hidden information is suddenly revealed. It feels like a set-up. I'm not sure this stuff should be found."

"But Alex already has his. The box. The grimoire. The message from Imogen, his ancestor. From Gil's." Avery appealed to Briar, feeling she needed to make her see sense. "I thought you were excited about the news?"

"I was, and now I'm not so sure." Briar started to fill her jars again, the smell of geranium wafting between them. "I have a bad feeling about this. I don't like dark magic, and I won't do it."

"I don't, either. And we don't know if this IS dark magic. It could be about harnessing untapped potential."

Briar shook her head, the long dark curls framing her pretty face. "I'll see how the rest of you get on. Until then my papers about my family tree and my place in White Haven remain locked away."

Avery was suddenly disappointed, and then curious. "How did you end up here, Briar? El was telling me that her great-aunt told her—it was their secret."

Briar nodded. "I know, she told me that, too. For me it was different. I found out through letters."

"Letters?" That certainly wasn't the answer Avery was expecting.

"Yes. Sent by my parents to each other, debating back and forth as to whether they should tell me or not." Avery must have looked baffled, because she smiled. "My father travelled a lot for his work, and he and my mother wrote to each other all the time. There was an incident at school—I had a rush of magic and did something that freaked a few in the class out. I can't even remember what now, nothing major. My mother told me I was special and hinted at powers, and then she said nothing else. A few years later my dad died in an accident, and a few years after that, so did she. That's when I found the letters. The conversations were veiled, but I understood enough to know what they were referring to. They wanted to shield me. So I came here, to the place they used to call home."

"How did you learn to use your magic, then? It would have been hard if no one taught you."

"I taught myself. Although they had given up the life of magic, they couldn't bear to part with everything. Or, my mother couldn't. I found lots of books and the family grimoire. And then I came here and met all of you, and Elspeth has taught me lots. So has Gil."

Avery's mouth fell open in shock. She had no idea that Briar had been such a novice when she arrived, or that the others had helped so much. And then she felt incredibly guilty. "I didn't realise. I'm so sorry; I should have helped you, too."

Briar shrugged. "It's okay, Avery, you've always done your own thing. You like it, I don't. I need the others."

Lately Avery had started to wonder how true that was, but she turned the conversation back to Briar. "But you've learnt so much. You're brilliant. A natural!"

Briar smiled ruefully. "I don't know about that."

Avery shook her head, feeling a rush of annoyance. "Briar, I'm confused. You could learn so much about your past now. And yet, you're turning your back on it!"

"It's complicated. I feel I'm only just getting to grips with things, and now this happens. I move at a different pace than you."

Avery felt bereft all of a sudden, and frustrated. She was only just starting to understand Briar. "Will you still come to the Solstice celebration?"

Briar smiled. "Of course. I'm still a witch."

10

Avery's next stop was El's jewellery shop. She wanted to reassure herself that El wasn't having second thoughts, either. As much as she was trying very hard to respect Briar's annoyingly sensible decision, she was annoyed with her for being so, well, *annoyingly sensible*. Really, was this the time to have second thoughts, when old magic and new powers were so close?

The closer she got to El's place, the crosser she became.

El's shop was close to the seafront, down one of the lanes that ran off from the quayside. The strong smell of brine oozed around her as she arrived outside. The shop front was a big window made up of small square bevelled panes that made the interior hard to see, especially because a display was set up under the window, showing necklaces and earrings in unusual designs, as well as a collection of decorated knives.

Once inside, Avery found that El's shop was much darker than Briar's, and smaller. The walls were lined with dark-patterned wallpaper, and the display cases were lined with black velvet. The lighting was low, and fairy lights were placed around the displays. High above the counter at the back of the shop was a selection of knives and swords. They looked wickedly sharp, as well as ornamental. On the far side of the shop was a collection of metal bowls and objects used in witchcraft. El had clearly decided to market herself as Wiccan, and a strong smell of sandalwood incense swirled around the shop.

She had to push through a group of girls who were admiring the jewellery, holding earrings against their ears in front of a mirror. A young woman stood behind the glass-topped counter that was used to display more jewellery.

Avery introduced herself. "Hi, I'm a friend of El's. Do you know where she is?"

The young woman had black hair cut into a blunt bob, the ends died purple, and she wore a tight black dress that showed every curve. Her face was pale but expertly made up, her lips painted a blood red. In comparison, Avery felt underdressed. As usual, her long red hair was loose and she wore one of her ankle-length flowing dresses with flip-flops. She felt like a wild woman in front of this groomed creature, and she had a sudden longing to send a wind whipping through the shop to ruffle her immaculate hair.

The woman gave Avery a quick appraising glance and called back over her shoulder through a partially open door behind the counter. "El! You have a visitor. Some red-haired chick."

Avery grinned. Chick! She hadn't been called that in while.

She heard El shout back, "Is that you, Avery?"

"Yes!"

"Come on in."

Without saying a word, the woman gave Avery another long look, and then lifted up the hatch at the end of the counter, allowing Avery to walk through. A practitioner of magic, Avery could tell. She had a quality of knowing. It was unmistakable.

Not bothering to speak either, Avery went into the back room, which was painted a dark red instead of black, and almost stopped in shock. El wasn't alone. Reuben was there, lounging in a chair next to glass doors that opened out into a tiny courtyard. And great Goddess, he was seriously hot.

El grinned. "How are you, Ave? You've met Reuben, haven't you?"

"I'm not sure I have, actually. I've seen you around, of course. I know your brother better." Was she gabbling? She felt heat starting on her cheeks, and she hoped she wasn't blushing.

Reuben nodded, "I know. And no, we've never met." He jumped to his feet and extended his hand, and she was surprised by his height. She'd never been so close to him before. He was tall, with an athletic muscular build, very tanned, with tousled blonde hair that had been bleached by the sun. He wore a sleeveless top that had seen better days, and it showed his strong muscular arms, which were covered with a half-sleeve of tattoos. He was wearing board shorts and he had the smell of salt and sea about him. It looked like he'd been surfing. She shook his hand; it was warm and firm and he grinned a gleaming smile. She hoped she wasn't going to giggle like a schoolgirl.

"Want some coffee?" El offered, interrupting her train of thought and providing a welcome distraction as Reuben dropped back into the chair, his long legs stretched out in front of him. El was standing next to a wooden counter than ran under a window overlooking the courtyard. Her hair was piled on the top of her head, and she wore pale blue jeans and a skinny grey tee. Next to her, a collection of jewellery and gems were laid out, and it looked as if she had been working.

"Why not? Tachycardia never hurt anyone."

"What?" El said, confused.

"I've had a lot of coffee today."

El looked at her watch. "Already? It's only ten!"

"Long story." She looked at Reuben, wondering how much to share.

"It's okay," El reassured her as she poured a cup of coffee from a percolator on the bench and passed it over. "He knows everything."

"Oh." For a few seconds, Avery wasn't sure what to say. As far she knew, Reuben wanted nothing to do with witchcraft.

"Your secrets are safe with me," he said, looking amused.

"It's not that," Avery explained, leaning against a cupboard at the back of the room. "I just thought you weren't interested."

"Interested, just not a practitioner."

"I wanted to know what he thought of the whole, weird thing," El explained.

"And?" Avery asked him.

"It sounds dangerous. But intriguing." He shrugged, non-committal, his bright blue eyes assessing her.

"Well, Briar thinks it sounds too weird. She's not doing anything for now," Avery said, trying to keep the annoyance out of her voice and failing. "I wondered if you'd had second thoughts, too, El?"

"No way. Reuben's gonna help me hunt for my grimoire. I think I know where to look." She frowned. "Seriously, Briar's not looking?"

She rolled her eyes. "Not yet. And wait a minute—you know where to look already?" Avery had a rush of relief that El was still in, and then a rush of panic as she realised she didn't have a clue where to look for her own.

"It's just a theory," El continued. "According to Anne's paperwork, my family lived up on the hills above the town. The old crofter cottage—Hawk House."

Avery knew the one she meant immediately. "That was yours? But it's a wreck now."

El grinned. "Exactly. We can check it out without interruptions."

"When?"

"Tonight. No time like the present. You look like a small kid, Avery. Do you want to come?"

"Yes, please! I presume you mean tonight, in the dark?" She faltered for a second, wondering just how creepy that might be.

Reuben smiled a slow sarky grin. "Scared, Avery?"

She narrowed her eyes at him, hating to be called out. "No! I'm coming. Just tell me when."

***

Avery's final visit of the day was to Alex. If she'd had time she'd have visited Gil, but his house was on the edge of town, and she really should get back to the shop. Sally would think she'd been kidnapped. In fact, she should call her. She pulled her phone from the depths of her bag and saw she'd missed half a dozen calls. *Crap.* She'd left her phone on silent. She guiltily called her, bracing herself.

Sally's voice rang out in her ear. "Are you okay?" She sounded grumpy.

"Of course—I'm fine. I've been catching up with a few things, and honestly didn't think I'd be this long."

"Bloody hell, I wish you'd have left a note. I've been calling you all bloody morning."

"I know. I'm sorry."

"The shop is really freaking busy."

"Sorry, really sorry. I'll be back by lunch." She checked her watch. *Hopefully.* She was right next to The Wayward Son now.

She heard Sally exhale loudly. "Dan's here early, so you can take your time. It's a good thing someone answers their phone."

Avery bit down a reply. She employed Sally; she should chill the hell out. But Sally was her friend and a fantastic manager. Without her, the shop would be a disaster. She adopted her most conciliatory tone. "I'm really sorry. I'll see you soon. Thank Dan for me."

She headed into the pub, deciding she had to buy cake before she headed back. Something to appease her staff. The smells of the kitchen hit her as soon as she entered, and the place already looked busy. The lunchtime rush had started early. She saw Simon, one of the bar staff she remembered from the other night, and she leaned on the bar as he came over, wondering if it was too early to get a pint. It was a quick decision. "Pint of Doom, please."

"Sure." He grabbed a glass and started pouring her drink.

"Alex not working today?"

Simon nodded his head, up towards the ceiling. "Up there. Said he's doing some stuff."

She took her pint and paid. "Cheers."

Avery headed to the back room and went up the stairs, hoping Alex wouldn't mind her dropping in. She knocked and shouted, "Alex, it's me! Avery."

She heard the thump of footsteps and then the door flew open. Alex looked half asleep, his long hair tangled, his stubble darker and thicker than usual. He leaned on the frame, yawning, and then he grinned. "Avery!" He stepped back. "Come in. You'll have to excuse the mess. I was up half the night."

"Bloody hell, Alex. This place *is* a mess. It's worse than mine!"

The room was gloomy, the blinds still down and semi-closed. Papers were strewn across the rug in front of the fireplace almost covering it completely. Half-drunk coffee cups were placed randomly around the room, and a selection of empty beer bottles sat on the kitchen counter. A large corkboard was propped on the floor, leaning against the kitchen workbench, scraps of paper pinned to it.

He pushed his hair back, and then opened the blinds in the kitchen, allowing sunshine to stream in. He squinted for a second, letting his eyes adjust. Even looking half awake, he was still very hot. She had a sudden vision of waking up next to him and wondered what he'd look like naked. Reuben was good looking, but Alex had a smouldering sexiness that she just couldn't ignore. What was the matter with her this morning? She hoped his psychic abilities meant he didn't read minds.

He put the kettle on and called over, "Do you want a coffee?"

She looked guiltily at her pint. "Er, I'm drinking."

He looked at her pint and then at his cup. "That's a way better idea." He pulled a beer from the fridge and popped it open. "Cheers." He took a long slug.

"So, I guess you were researching all night?" Avery looked around the room. "Where's your grimoire?"

"Under that pile of papers." He nodded towards the rug in front of the sofa. He grinned again, dispelling the tiredness. "You should see what's in there, Avery. Hold on, let me get it."

He padded barefoot over to the grimoire, and unearthing it from beneath the papers, he carried it to the kitchen workbench that separated the two rooms.

Seeing it again gave Avery a shock. She had forgotten how much older it was than their existing grimoires. It oozed age and arcane knowledge, the cover guarding long forgotten spells and secrets. She turned the pages, admiring the old script and the drawings in the margins. She was itching to find her own. She looked up to find Alex watching her.

He smiled. "It's beautiful, isn't it?"

She nodded. "Now that you've had a good look at it, what spells have you found?"

He excitedly turned pages, trying to be gentle. "I don't know how this has kept so well, but it's in really good condition. I presume it was the spell on the wooden box. I doubt they knew how long it would have to be hidden for."

Avery frowned. "I doubt the intention was more than a few years. Or even months. Helena's death must have had far-reaching consequences."

"The families fled. Her death would have been catastrophic. Unbelievable, even." He sighed. "It depresses me to think about it. Can you imagine that happening here? Now—to us? Anyway. Spells. Let me show you this." He found the page he was looking for. At the top was an image of linked bodies. Beneath, written in tiny script, was a list of ingredients and a spell.

"What's this?" Avery asked.

"Spirit walking."

"What?"

Alex laughed. "Another word for astral projection. But with someone. What do you think?"

Avery was confused. "Well, I thought that's something you could do, so why do you need a spell?"

"Because I've never done it this way. Or with someone. Shall we?"

Avery looked at his dark eyes, all traces of sleep in them gone. Her heart was beating incredibly fast; he was so close. She had an overwhelming urge to kiss him, but instead said, "Are you insane? You want to spirit walk with me?"

"If you've never done it before then it will be a safe way for you to do it. I'll help you, protect you." He winked, his gaze falling on her lips before he met her eyes again. "I can't think of anyone else I'd rather spirit walk with."

Avery's stomach lurched. *Was Alex flirting with her?* It would be so easy to be seduced by him, and she wasn't completely sure that would be a good thing. "Really? I'm not entirely sure I trust you that much. I thought spirit walking was dangerous."

"Only if you don't know what you're doing. And I do." He was still smirking at her in his insufferable way. "Go on. You know you want to."

As much as she had the feeling she should run in the opposite direction, she really wanted to see what spirit walking was like. "All right. What do I have to do?"

He grinned. "You have to come back here later tonight, when you're already tired. I'll prep the spell and we go from there."

"But I've promised to help El and Reuben search for El's grimoire tonight." She wasn't sure if she was relieved or not.

"Great! El has a plan. And help from Reuben—interesting. How come?"

"I've no idea. He was there at her shop. Looked pretty comfortable, too. Said something about being interested in magic, but not practising it," Avery explained, but thought she'd keep the fact that he looked very hot to herself.

Alex nodded. "Where are they looking?"

"The old Hawk House, up on the downs above the town. It seems it once belonged to her family."

Alex thought for a brief moment, and then decided, "They don't need your help. Not the physical kind, anyway. I'll text her that we'll help in other ways."

"What other ways?"

"Astral ways," he said, grinning.

11

The rest of Avery's day passed in a blur, and all too soon she was back in Alex's flat, her heart pounding uncomfortably, her mouth dry. She leaned against his door before opening it, wondering briefly if she'd gone mad, and why she thought to touch up her makeup before arriving. She wished she were heading to the downs instead.

Before she even knocked, the door flew open, and Alex ushered her in, saying, "Your nervous energy preceded you. I could sense you a mile off."

"Exaggerator," she said, pushing past him.

He locked the door behind her. "We really don't want to get interrupted."

His flat was completely transformed. All traces of the mess from earlier had gone. Despite the warm night, the fire was on low, and the room glittered with candles. In front of the fire was a soft warm blanket, big enough for two. There was no other lighting in the room, and the rich smell of incense drifted around. Avery could feel her mouth dropping open in surprise, and Alex laughed.

"It's easy to get cold when you're lying still, so we need the fire, and we need to be comfortable. The lights help induce a relaxed state."

Right now, Avery thought she would never relax. "I bet that's what you say to all the girls," she shot back, thinking her heartbeat must be audible.

Alex just laughed again, and led her to the rug. The grimoire was on the coffee table behind them, a selection of coloured candles next to it, as well as Alex's Athame and a silver goblet filled with a dark, murky liquid.

"We need to create the protective circle, then take that drink—it will help us enter the right state and help us link, and then we say the spell."

"What's in the drink?" Avery asked, eyeing the concoction warily.

"Valerian, clary sage, vervain, amber, gold leaf, lavender, and bay. And a couple more."

"All right, if you're sure you're not going to poison us."

"Trust me, Ave, I'm a pro."

She resisted the urge to comment, and instead joined him as he used the Athame to create the protective circle by drawing in the air and on the floor. She followed him, lighting the candles and placing them on the four points of the compass. He sat in the middle of the rug, and she sat opposite him, legs crossed, knee to knee. The soft yellow candlelight gave everything a warm glow, and despite herself, she relaxed.

"Do you feel okay?" Alex asked.

"Surprisingly, I do."

"Good."

He took her hands in his, closed his eyes, and took a few deep breaths. Avery did the same, willing her heart to slow as she dropped her shoulders. After a few seconds, he squeezed and released her hands and she opened her eyes to see him holding the small, engraved silver goblet with the liquid inside. He took a few sips and grimaced, and then handed it to her. Avery took a few sips, too and shuddered. It was horrible. Bitter, with a slightly burnt taste to it. She handed it back to Alex and he placed it on the edge of the circle, and then he lay down on his back facing east, and she lay next to him. He took her hand in his and squeezed it again. "Ready?"

"Ready."

Alex started to recite the spell and she closed her eyes again, feeling the energy in the circle change, and her awareness heighten. As he chanted, her breaths deepened and her body relaxed, her limbs becoming heavy. Within seconds she heard Alex's voice in her head, but instead of jolting her awake, it intensified her experience and she embraced his voice. It was like a soft blanket wrapping around her and she wanted to hug it close. As if he could sense it, his presence encompassed her and she responded again, the intimacy almost overwhelming. And then she could see him, his entire form lying a few feet above her. But it wasn't his physical form. He was a pale, silvery blue and he smiled down at her.

"Come on Avery. Join me."

He took her hands and pulled gently and with a *whoosh*, she felt herself sliding up and out of her body until she floated next to him. For a second, a wave of panic washed over her, and then Alex's presence wrapped around her again, calming and reassuring her.

"I'm okay," she said. She saw her physical form lying beneath her, and a long, thin silver cord connecting her spirit to her body, and the same with

Alex next to her. "This is so weird," she thought, forgetting Alex could hear her.

"But great, isn't it?" His eyes glowed with a pale light, and as if sensing her discomfort, he said, "Let's just move around the room so you can get used to the feeling. Just move slowly."

He floated away from his body and pulled her with him. The room was dim and shadowy, its colours drained, the candles bright points in the darkness. A powerful purple aura emanated from the grimoire. "Look," she pointed.

Alex nodded. "Magical energy. Very strong, too."

As she followed him, she felt stronger and safer. This was actually fun.

"If you feel worried at any point," he said, "just envision yourself lying here, and follow the cord back to your body."

She nodded as her eyes followed the cord spooling across the room. "Can we go outside?"

"If you feel ready."

"Yes!" She grinned. "This is awesome."

Avery again felt Alex's essence squeeze her own gently, and she responded as he laughed. "This is so cool—way better than doing it on your own. For now I'm going to keep hold of your hand, is that okay?"

"Yes, I'd prefer that."

"Great. This is going to be odd, but don't panic."

He turned and pulled her towards the wall and then through it. She was aware of the strange sensation of brick and stone and then she was free and the stars floated above her. She gasped. "Look!"

Avery rolled onto her back as if she was swimming, and watched the stars glowing in swirls of incandescent light. They looked bigger than she was used to, and the rest of the town below her was pale in comparison. She could see waves of energy flowing around everything. Beyond the pub, she could see the sea, and the immense force of the waves as they rolled in and out further along the beach. The raw power on display was amazing—it was so tangible.

"This is what you draw on, Avery. Do you see it?" Alex asked, his hand the one warm constant in this sea of change around her.

"I do. I feel as if I could touch it." She gasped again as people spilled out from the pub below them. "Look, I can see their auras." The people were dim, but their auras glowed white, or purple, or orange.

"It's easy to see auras here," Alex said. "You'll find it becomes easier when you return to your physical form, too. How're your energy levels?"

"I feel fine. Great, even!"

"Good, let's head up to the downs."

"Can we go that far?" Avery asked, worried.

"Your cord will travel a long way, as long as your energy is good," Alex explained with another squeeze of reassurance. "Come on."

Alex pulled Avery up higher and away across the town to where it became dark, the lights and the people disappearing behind them. In the distance she could see dark purple clouds washing up from where the surf pounded at the cliffs heading out of town. And then she saw the ruined house on the moors, tucked into a curve of hillside, and the pale blue auras of two figures poking around amongst the ruins. Elspeth and Rueben. There was flare of light along the foundation; it seemed El was using magic.

"She must be using some kind of locator spell," Alex said. "Can you see the lines beneath the earth?"

For a second, Avery couldn't understand what he meant, and then she saw the silvery lines growing stronger by the second, marking the foundation of the old house, some stretching further back up the hill. "Did El do that?"

"She must have. Can they see it, though? Look," Alex gestured further up the hill. A slab of silvered earth glowed for a few seconds, and as they drifted over it, it disappeared.

Avery felt of rush of excitement. "Is that where the book is?"

But before he answered, she felt another wave of energy hit her, but different this time. It felt dark, angry. She tensed and looked up at the same time as Alex. A dark red glow was heading towards them, and Alex quickly pulled her to his side as a figure became clear ahead of them.

"What the hell is that?" Avery asked, panic racing through her.

"Another spirit walker," Alex said, "and he doesn't mean well."

The figure raced towards them and a wall of power pulsed outwards. Almost simultaneously, Avery sensed Alex push something like a force field towards the approaching figure. The two met with a clash, and although Avery couldn't hear anything, she felt an almost tidal surge of electricity rush around them.

Now was not the time to panic, and Avery stayed close to Alex, doing as he did and summoning her own powers. She was a witch—if she could do this in her physical body, she could do it now.

Alex was totally focussed on their attacker, but she felt him anchoring her, and she joined her force to his, strengthening the shield he had created. Their attacker's form was blurry, non-human, and it was impossible to make out what he or she was. One thing was certain. It was trying to hurt them. The figure pushed closer, trying to crack the protective shield that glowed a pale blue ahead of them. Avery didn't ask what would happen if it broke.

"We need to withdraw, Alex. I don't know what I can do to help."

"To withdraw we have to push it back, to give us time. We do not want it following us back."

"Will it hurt Reuben and El?"

"No, it can only watch. I hope. Listen, we must push together. Let it think it's overpowering us, and then push. Hopefully it will be enough to throw it off balance. And I have a trick up my sleeve."

Avery was vaguely aware of the scene below. The two witches were continuing to work the spell, following the lines beneath the earth, but Alex pulled her attention back.

"We need to protect them, too, give them privacy." He grinned at her, his teeth glowing with a silvery light, his eyes sparkling. "Follow my lead."

The dark mass ahead was pushing against them. Its anger was palpable. Avery felt Alex's energy pull back, and she matched him, allowing their attacker to come closer. She saw two red eyes glowering malevolently, and she felt its premature wave of pleasure at their perceived weakness. They allowed it to creep closer and closer, until Avery was worried it may be too close to repel. Red waves flared like fire around the shield, licking like flames trying to crack their defences.

Alex whispered, "Nearly time. Wait. Wait. *Now!*"

He pushed suddenly, striking out in one massive hit, and Avery joined it, amazed at the strength they created together. Into the middle of it Alex projected a strike like lightning—a silvery bolt that crackled with searing heat. It punctured out through their shield and into their attacker's, sending it shooting backwards.

They barely had time to enjoy their victory when Alex pulled her away, and she did as he told her earlier. She thought of her physical body next to the fire and followed her cord back, racing along it in a blur, Alex next to her. Their attacker was a long way behind them.

Avery returned to her physical body with a *thump*. Her limbs felt heavy, but her mind was alert in an instant and she tried to sit up. A searing pain exploded in her head and she cried out, falling back.

She heard Alex. "It's okay, take your time. You've used a lot of power."

She turned to him, blinking, and the room focussed. The warm orange light was soothing, and the fire still crackled, bathing them in heat. Alex was lying on his side, head propped on one hand, watching her. She took a few deep breaths and felt the pain recede quickly.

"Better?" His voice was a balm to her senses. It almost replaced losing his warm presence that had wrapped around her earlier.

"I think so." She shivered, despite the warmth. "Shouldn't we be doing something? Like joining El and Reuben?"

His close proximity made her nervous, but her gaze wandered from his dark eyes, across his delicious stubble, down to his full lips.

"In a minute," he said softly. And then he leaned forward and kissed her, gently at first.

A flare of desire raced through Avery and she leaned into his kiss. Within seconds his hand was on her back, pulling her close, until she felt his whole body pressed against hers. Her hand snaked around his waist, feeling his muscular build and his warmth. His kisses deepened, and she felt herself falling away, losing herself completely in him.

He eventually pulled away, gazing at her. "I suppose we should go and check on El and Reuben now." But he didn't move, waiting for her response, his gaze still travelling from her eyes to her lips and back again. His hair fell around his face, grazing her cheeks, and his scent enveloped her.

She felt breathless and giddy and wanted nothing more than to stay right there. "I suppose we should."

He grinned, and she melted a little more. "In another minute." And he kissed her again, all playfulness gone as she arched into him, drawing him closer. When they broke apart again, both were breathless.

Avery pushed him away, her hand against his chest. It took every ounce of her willpower. "You're a very bad influence, Alex Bonneville. Our friends could be in trouble."

He reluctantly pulled away. "Come on, then. I'll drive." He pulled her to her feet, and while he grabbed his keys, she extinguished the candles with a word.

12

The narrow lanes were as black as pitch; only the car's headlamps lit the way ahead, giving Alex and Avery brief flashes of hedges, gates, and fields.

"I didn't think a spirit walker could physically attack someone," Avery said. She peered through the windscreen, trying to see if she could see anything in the sky overhead.

"They can't, normally." Alex drove quickly, his eyes on the road. His car was a classic Alfa Romeo Spider, Boat Tail, and it whipped through the country lanes. "I expect El and Reuben will be fine, but I don't know what attacked us. I'm not even sure it was human."

Avery felt a heaviness settle into her body as she thought of demons, ghosts, and other creatures of the night. "What could it be?"

"Either someone wielding dark magic, or a demon."

There. The word was out now.

"But they don't exist." Her voice sounded tinny and weak. She looked at Alex's profile as he concentrated on the road, willing him to agree with her.

"We both know they do." He flicked her a glance. "We just haven't encountered one before."

"Necromancy was very popular hundreds of years ago. Do you think our ancestors summoned demons?" It was a horrible thought.

"They must have done, or why have I got so many spells about them in my grimoire? From what I've seen so far, they certainly engaged in darker magic than we have. And you must have some demon related spells in yours."

She had to grudgingly admit she did. "I thought it was more theoretical than practical."

"Everything's theoretical until you decide to act on it."

A thought struck her. "How did you learn to do the whole lightning bolt-thing?"

"The grimoire, of course. And there's a whole lot more in there, too. No wonder someone else wants them."

They crested a rise and the hedges fell away, the headlights spilling onto the downs. Alex turned down a rutted lane and the car bounced as they raced along. Avery braced herself against the sides, hoping she wouldn't be brained on the car roof. The Alfa didn't like the uneven surface.

They could see the bleached outline of the building ahead of them, but there was no sign of El or Reuben. Alex screeched to a halt next to El's battered 4x4 Landover. They bounded out, the slamming of the car doors loud in the silence.

By unspoken agreement they looked around carefully, and the silence of the night fell around them. Nothing moved. Even the normal night sounds had fled. From here they could see White Haven, its lights twinkling, and out at sea the lights of the boats. Close by, however, there was only darkness, the downs invisible, with only a sense of the openness of the unseen landscape. Avery directed her energy so it formed a ball in her hands, ready to fling at any unwanted visitors, and then focussed her senses outwards, looking for something, anything, but there was nothing else there. Only Alex.

She looked up, but the sky above was clear, the stars unflinching, with no sign of whatever had happened earlier. Was she imagining it, or could she detect a strange smell? It was like an unnatural rot.

Satisfied there was nothing waiting to attack them, Avery walked to Alex's side, and together they headed into the remnants of the house. They passed through the shell of rooms, with their broken walls and a trace of foundation showing like bones. There was still no sign of El and Reuben.

Alex whispered, "The lines ran up the hill, remember?"

He led the way, watchful and silent. They both muffled their presence with a spell, cloaking their bodies so they appeared like shadows. The locators of El's spell were still visible, pale lines marking long vanished foundations of maybe an earlier dwelling. Within a few minutes they came to a black hole in the ground, its opening several feet below the surface. Piles of earth and stone stood either side, and a huge stone square like a flagstone lay upended to the side. The smell of rot was stronger now, coming from the hole.

"What now?" Avery asked. "If we go down there they could attack us by accident, or what if something's down there with them?" She trailed off, her meaning apparent.

"I'll look." Alex dropped to his knees and put his head in. He summoned light, and projected a pale light from his hand downwards. Avery stood close by, hoping nothing would emerge from the surrounding blackness.

After a few seconds Alex said, "It's an old cellar. Follow me."

He gripped either side of the opening and dropped from sight. As soon as he was in she took a last look around and followed him. She felt him grip her waist and hold her, gently lowering her to the ground.

A passageway snaked away from them, a pale light ahead. They had only taken a few steps when a scream rang out, and then a shout of rage. Alex ran and Avery followed, her heart pounding. She again summoned energy into a white-hot ball in her hands, and as Alex rounded a corner, he came to a stop. A few passages opened up, but only one was lit, and he again raced down it, following its turns. Another scream echoed around them; Alex stopped and she thudded into the back of him. He stepped aside quickly and for a brief second, Avery took in the room.

It was long and low, lined with rough brick and rotten timbers. The smell of rot and damp was strong. A lamp hung from the ceiling and the faint yellow light showed a wooden box on the floor against the far wall. Reuben was standing in the centre of the room facing a shadowy beast in the corner that crackled with heat. His arms and legs were wrapped in coils of flames that seemed to be trying to pull him towards the beast—or pull him apart. Reuben was straining to pull back, roaring with pain. As they entered the room, the flames disappeared, and Reuben fell to the floor.

The beast swelled in size, and red eyes glowed within its centre. Avery could just make out misshapen limbs; it exuded malevolence. It was a demon, and El struggled and writhed in its grip, screaming as flames crackled around her.

Alex ran to Reuben and dragged him back towards the entrance.

If they attacked the demon, they attacked El, but the box was intact, and it looked similar to Alex's. It must be the other grimoire. Avery directed her ball of glowing witch light at the box and shouted, "Release her, or I destroy the box."

For a second the demon waited, its flames slowed and the crackle subsided.

Avery felt rather than saw Alex move next to her. She shouted again. "I'll do it! El means more to me than the grimoire." The ball of light swelled in her hands and she stepped closer to the box. The demon needed to know she meant business. She sent the blast towards the box, engulfing it, and the demon roared with an unearthly howl.

Avery waited, the ball of light cradled within her hand again. "Release her now!"

From deep within the depths of the demon a column of fire rushed towards her and she rolled, flattening herself against the far wall as Alex threw up a shield in front of both of them. "Blast it again, Avery!"

She threw another blast at the wooden box and the demon howled again, this time flinging El to the floor as it charged across the room towards them. Avery redirected her aim to the demon and Alex joined her, battering the demon with their combined powers. Avery saw El staggering to her feet and she joined them with another blast of energy. The demon was surrounded, but it grew in size, filling the centre of the room.

The room now sizzled with heat and magic, and the white-hot blast surrounding the demon was almost blinding. Was it feeding off them? Avery was dimly aware of the dampness in the walls and the earth surrounding them, and she changed her focus, drawing on water instead. A jet of water shot from her hands and this time steam billowed around them as the demon howled with an unearthly cry that covered her skin in goose bumps. With a final flash of power the demon streamed upwards and out of the cellar, and suddenly the room was empty.

El fell to her knees and Alex rushed over to her. "Are you all right?"

"I'll be okay, I've just used a lot of energy, and that thing sucked some from me. Is Reuben all right?"

Avery felt dazed and exhausted, but she turned and checked Reuben and found him groggy and weak. "I don't know, but he's alive. We need to get out of here before that thing comes back."

"We're not going anywhere without that box," El said, standing on slightly shaky legs.

"Oh, we're definitely taking that box," Alex agreed. He looked at Avery, "Are you okay?"

She nodded. "I'm fine. I think. Better than Reuben, anyway." She turned and pulled Reuben's arm, trying to avoid the blistering already coiling around his forearms. "Hey Reuben, you need to get up. We have to get out of here."

He looked up at her, his skin ashen, his tattoos even more vivid against his pallor. Avery could see blistering around his calves, as well. He extended his hand and she pulled him to his feet.

"I feel like crap," he said with a grimace.

"We need to get Briar. She's better at healing than any of us," El said, looking worried.

"Go," Alex said. "I'll bring the box. We need to get out of here, before that thing comes back with friends."

* * *

They met at Elspeth's flat. Unlike Alex and Avery, Elspeth didn't live above her shop. She lived on the top floor of an old, converted warehouse overlooking the harbour. The walls were a mixture of warm brick and ornate dark wallpaper like her shop; the floor was made of solid oak, and the windows were long and metal framed. And it was small. "I love it, but it costs me a fortune," El had once complained. Lamplight pooled in the corners and incense filled the air—a protection spell.

They had squashed into the rickety lift and mostly fell into her flat, all of them exhausted. The wooden box was on the floor, looking ominous. Avery gazed out of the window at the harbour below, illuminated by the streetlights, and watched the gentle rise and fall of the waves and the boats bobbing gently on the swell. She could feel the box behind her. Half of her wanted to see what was in it, half of her wanted to be at home, tucked up in bed, asleep. Or maybe with Alex. She was aware of his presence everywhere, like a tickling of her senses, and she longed to touch him again.

A loud knock at the door disturbed her reverie and Briar came in, followed by Gil.

"I wasn't sure you'd be able to come," Alex told him.

Gil frowned. "Reuben's hurt. Of course I'm here." He rushed to Reuben's side. "How you doing, Reu?"

"I've been better," he said. He sat on the sofa, sipping a strong coffee. "The burns are the worst. That thing lashed me with these weird flame ropes."

"It was a demon," Alex said seriously. He stood leaning against the kitchen counter. "We have to call it what it is."

Gil and Briar looked shocked; the others were used to the term now.

"When you said it over the phone, I thought it was a joke," Briar said. She sat on the floor next to Reuben, unpacking her bottles and salves. She was pale without makeup, her hair bundled on top of her head.

"It's no joke," El murmured from where she sat in front of the fireplace, black candles burning there instead of a fire, to ward off the spirits. "That thing wrapped me up in its demon fire. I'm lucky I wasn't burnt either. I presume it needed me - maybe to open the box."

"I have some salves for burns, and a spell for spirit fire. Let's hope that helps," Briar said, choosing a pot.

"Tell us everything," Gil urged.

Alex started, telling them about the spirit walking, and then El told them about their investigations which had led to the house. She turned to Alex and Avery. "So you saw something during your spirit walk? Was it the same thing?"

"I don't know." Alex shrugged. "But we were above you and it rushed at us. It was a dark mass. It looked like the demon in the room, but it could have been someone with dark energy disguising themselves."

Avery leaned back against the window frame, its cold steel digging into her shoulder. "If the demon was controlled by necromancy, then it could be that whatever—or whoever—was spirit walking sent the demon."

Gil had been watching Briar expertly tend to Reuben's wounds, but now he looked at Avery. "You're saying somebody controlled that thing. The demon."

"Why would a demon need a spell book, Gil?" she asked. "They don't. Witches need spell books. Witches control demons. Or at least, some do. It was very popular in medieval times. And someone clearly is willing to do anything to get those grimoires."

It was a horrible thing to acknowledge, but they had to. She watched Gil and Reuben. They were both so different. Reuben the handsome surfer who had supposedly turned his back on magic, and Gil, his older, quieter brother. Gil's hair was darker and shorter, and he was slightly thicker set, but now that they sat next to each other, Avery could see the family resemblance around their eyes, and the set of their mouth.

"So instead of healing and nurturing magic, we're now dealing with dark magic?" Gil looked at Avery accusingly. "You've caused this, by finding that box and those papers."

Avery felt like she'd been punched. "Sod off, Gil! I didn't cause this! And I didn't find those papers, or even look for them. They were left to me. If you want to blame anyone, blame Anne!" She was angry now, and she could feel her magic ready to sizzle again. "In fact, blame your relative. She's the one who dragged Anne into all this."

The tension in the room was palpable as Gil stood. "We only have Anne's word for that. It could be a lie, or a double cross. Something to draw us into looking, all for someone else's purposes. Anne went to a lot of trouble to point us in the right direction. When she was dead. Very convenient."

Avery stepped towards Gil. "You had no idea about your history. Stop trying to blame someone else. It's probably your mad uncle Addison who tried to kill us tonight."

"Stop it. Both of you." Alex stepped between them and then looked at Gil. "You have to accept this, Gil, like it or not. I suggest you start looking for your own grimoire. You too, Briar. The gods only know what's in there." He turned to Avery, a ghost of a smile in his eyes. "I'll help you find yours." He then announced to all of them, "And we need to stick together. I don't know about you, but I have no idea how to summon a demon, control one, or destroy one. That thing we encountered tonight is only banished. It will be back. And we need to be ready for it."

13

Avery woke late and stretched in her bed luxuriously. And then she winced. She felt as heavy as lead and she had a dull headache. Last night's activities had depleted her energy levels, and she needed to replenish them.

The sunlight filtered through her blinds and in the warm light she wondered if last night had been a nightmare. So many things had happened. The spirit walk had been magical—well, most of it. And Alex. What had happened there? The feel of his kiss still lingered on her lips, and she hoped it would happen again. And then, of course, the demon had changed everything.

She looked around at the room for reassurance; at her pictures, the shelves with her favourite objects displayed, her soft bed linen, and her old drawers and wardrobe. Here she felt safe. As she moved her feet down the bed she pushed against something heavy and heard a meow. She looked down and found Circe and Medea blinking at her. Time for breakfast.

After she'd showered, she headed down to the shop. It was only Friday, one week since she had been given the box and the letter from Anne, but it felt like a lifetime had passed.

The shop was open, and a few customers were already browsing. The mellow sounds of John Coltrane played in the background. Sally looked up as she entered. She was straightening cards and tidying shelves, but she took one look at her and said, "Let's talk."

Avery caught Dan's eyes from where he stood at the counter, and he grinned. Dan was tall, dark, and skinny, and he was far more tolerant of her erratic behaviour over the last few days than Sally.

Avery headed to the coffee pot in the back room and poured herself a large mug. She looked at Sally. "Would you like one?"

Sally leaned against the doorframe, arms folded across her chest. "Don't try to distract me, Avery. What's going on with you?" Her lips were pursed into a thin line, and she looked genuinely worried.

"Nothing's going on; I've just had a few busy days and late nights." Avery sipped her coffee and felt the warm rush of caffeine thaw her sluggish brain.

"I have never known you not come into work before—or forget to call me! And you look like shit today."

Wow, Sally wasn't pulling any punches. "Thanks, Sally. You're so sweet to notice!"

Sally sighed. "I'm saying this because I'm your friend and I'm worried about you! Your behaviour is weird."

She needed to reassure her—quickly. "The stuff I had from Anne has thrown up some questions about my family, that's all. I've just been doing some investigating. And that's meant some late nights." Sally knew her family was a touchy subject. Hopefully she wouldn't ask anything further.

"You know a woman was killed last night? I hope you haven't been wandering the streets on your own. It's not safe."

Avery almost spilled her coffee in shock. "Who was killed? Where?"

"A car was found crashed on the road over the moors. There was blood everywhere, apparently. The police aren't saying much at the moment, but there's no other cars involved, and it's really suspicious."

Avery felt dizzy and she groped for a stool. "On the moors? What— miles away?"

"No! Just outside the town." She lowered her voice. "I saw Joe this morning as I was opening up. He said he's never seen anything like it. It was like she'd been attacked by an animal."

Joe was one of the local policemen. He'd been to school with Sally and knew her well. And besides, in a small town, news travelled fast.

Avery's brain didn't seem to want to process anything. "But I thought you said it was a car accident? That can cause a lot of blood."

"Joe wouldn't say, but I think there was something else."

"So they think a crazy person did this? That there's some sort of killer in the area?"

Sally clammed up. "I don't know. But it's weird. You should be careful."

"Well, so should you, then," she retaliated. Avery desperately needed to speak to the others. Was this a human attack, or had the demon attacked some poor woman? As horrible as the thought was that there was a murderer on the loose, it was far preferable to a demon. "Look," she said in an effort to appease Sally, "I haven't done anything to endanger myself. Don't worry. And I'm sure this accident is just that. Okay?"

"You're heading out the door again, aren't you?"

"Just for a while. I won't be long."

Before Avery left, she went back up to her flat and covered it in every ward and protection spell she could think of, and then she protected the shop, too. She would take every precaution she could.

***

Avery's feet seemed to know where she was going before she did. They led her straight to the pub. Part of her wondered if it was wise to see Alex again so soon. She was confused about the kiss. *Was it something that could happen again, or was it a spur of the moment flirt that meant nothing?* Well, to him. It meant more than it should to her. As much as she might try to deny it, she was attracted to him. Maybe she should try to put up some barriers. Self-protection was a good thing.

The streets were getting busy. Shoppers meandered along the streets, enjoying the bunting that had appeared over the last few days, and shop owners were decorating their window displays for the summer Solstice. As White Haven was a town that embraced its witchy history, witch-hanging included, it also embraced the natural rhythms of the seasons, and the Solstice was one of them. Tomorrow night there'd be fires and parties on the beach, and the pubs would be offering specials. Unfortunately, at this moment, The Wayward Son was closed.

As much as she was itching to wake Alex, she figured she should let him sleep. Instead, she headed for El's shop to see how Reuben was. The door swung silently in, and she found the same woman from the other day behind the counter. Instead of letting her through, she said, "She's still at home. And I know nothing." She held her hand up to ward off further questions and Avery turned round and headed to the quay, convinced she knew more than she was letting on.

The entrance to El's flat had a big lobby with bare brick walls and a call system at the bottom. She pressed the buzzer and without needing to speak, El said, "Come on up, Avery."

Presuming the Dread Guardian of the Shop—as Avery had started to call her—had phoned ahead, Avery headed through the doors that El had released and into the lift. Within seconds she was in El's flat.

Sunlight and a light breeze streamed in through the big windows, and she saw the harbour sparkling in the sunshine, the boats bobbing on the sea. She had a moment of pleasure as she looked at the beautiful place she lived, before her eye was drawn to the box in the centre of the lounge. It was open.

El sat on the floor in front of it, objects strewn around her. She looked up at Avery. "It's similar to Alex's. A goblet, an Athame, a ritual bowl, a small chopping knife, and some jewellery—a beautiful old pendant." She held it up the light and Avery took it from her, turning it. The silver chain was long, and the pendant was a blood red stone. She must have looked puzzled because El said, "Carnelian. To protect and confer endurance and courage. If I'm honest, it's what I need right now."

Avery dropped onto the rug next to her. "Have you heard what happened on the moor last night? After we left?"

"No. What?"

"A woman had a car accident. Except it's probably just meant to look like an accident."

El was already pale, but if it was possible, she turned paler and her hand flew to her mouth. "No!"

"Yes. I'm wondering if it was the demon."

El closed her eyes briefly. "What have we got into, Avery? This isn't what I love about magic. Demons, blood, unbridled power. I want to protect people, make them happy, tap into nature, live at one with our surroundings."

Avery snorted. "We haven't got unbridled power, and I doubt we will. Besides, we choose what we do with our magic."

"But we can't control a demon. And I'm not sure I want to."

"Good. Neither do I. But we're going to have to, because it will come for us again." Avery looked around the room and could hardly believe what she was saying on such a bright, beautiful day.

"Do we know who the woman was?"

Avery shook her head. "No. Not yet."

"Do the others know?"

Avery shrugged. "I don't know, haven't spoken to them yet." She looked around the room. "Where's Reuben?"

"Gil took him home; he wanted to keep an eye on him." El's pretty face fell into a sullen frown. "I don't think he trusted me."

"He's his younger brother—he's just worried."

"The thing is, Reuben didn't even argue. I think he's mad at me. He barely looked at me as he left."

Avery wasn't sure before, but she was sure now. El and Reuben definitely had something between them. El looked like she might cry. Avery patted her shoulder. "He had a horrible shock. He knows you, and he knows what you are. Hell, he's a witch, too! He'll come round. He might even accept his gifts." Avery nodded towards the box. "What about the grimoire? The box is virtually identical to Alex's. Different markings, but that's all. The grimoire must be in the lid."

El seemed pleased to focus on something else. "They're runes again. One to protect against spirits and demons, but the ones around the lid are different. I'm not opening it here, though. Not alone. I was thinking of bringing it to our Solstice celebration tomorrow. I want to open it while we're all together."

"Okay," Avery nodded. "Seems sensible." Although under the potency of a waning gibbous moon, and in the open, they might attract more than they were ready for. However, she kept her thoughts to herself. "We're celebrating in my small garden. It's already warded and protected, and I'll add to that today."

They both jumped as the intercom rang loudly. El headed over and pushed the button. "Hi, Elspeth here."

"This is Detective Inspector Newton. We'd like to ask you a few questions, please."

El looked at Avery in shock, and mouthed SHIT! She turned quickly to the intercom. "Certainly, can I ask what about?"

"We'll explain when we see you." He sounded stern, and Avery felt her stomach flip. "Are you going to let us in?"

"Of course, come on up." She pressed the release button and turned to Avery, stricken. "Bollocks, and triple bollocks!" And then her gaze fell on the box, which even in the bright sunlight looked distinctly magical.

"We'll cover it with a spell," Avery said quickly. "Help me drag it to the corner."

El ran over and between them they wrestled it under a table as Avery quickly murmured a spell that made the box invisible.

"What can they want, Avery?"

"Maybe they saw your car on a camera. Stay calm. You were going for a drive in the moonlight and saw nothing. That's allowed, you know."

They were interrupted by a knock at the door, and after a final look around the room, El went to the door, while Avery stood in the kitchen making tea and trying to calm her nerves.

El opened the door and without waiting for an invitation, a tall man with dark hair swept into the room, followed by a younger man with reddish hair. They both looked around, stopping briefly when they saw Avery, and then finally looked at El. She now looked very composed and shaking their hands said, "Hi, I'm Elspeth. Please come in." She gestured further into the room.

The dark haired man spoke first. "Detective Inspector Newton, and this is Officer Moore."

Moore nodded and followed the DI into the room. They seemed to fill the space of El's small flat. Avery thought Newton looked as if he was in his mid-thirties, and he was handsome, the clean lines of his face exuding both confidence and suspicion. He wore a single-breasted grey suit and a crisp white shirt, and it looked good on him. Moore's suit, in comparison, looked a little rumpled.

Avery came out from behind the open-plan kitchen counter and shook their hands as well, trying very hard to make a good impression. "Hi, I'm Avery, El's friend."

Newton nodded, looking her up and down. "I know your face. You run the occult store."

"The bookstore," she corrected him, a stone in her stomach. All storeowners had regular interactions with the police as part of community policing and safety, however she had never met Newton before. "Can I get you some tea? I'm making some anyway."

"No thanks." His face was grim, and he turned to El. "There was a death last night on the road across the moors. We've been combing the footage of the cameras leading out of town along that road, and your car was seen leaving at 11:07 PM and coming back into town around 1:15 AM. Where had you been?"

"Just out for a drive. I like to sit on the cliff top and look over the sea. I also found out recently that my old family home used to be the old Hawk House, up on the moor. I wanted to see it."

"At night?" he asked, watching El closely, every now and again flicking a glance at Avery, while Moore scribbled away.

Avery risked a glance under the far table, and satisfied that the box couldn't be seen, busied herself with tea.

"I was with Reuben. It seemed romantic, you know, gazing at the stars."
She smiled and winked, but Newton ignored her.

"Who's Reuben?"

"Reuben Jackson. He's a local. Works at Greenlane Nursery."

"One of the Jacksons from Greenlane Manor?" he asked, his eyes narrowing.

El nodded, "Yes."

He glanced at Moore, who again scribbled furiously, and then asked, "Did you see anything on the moors?"

"Nothing, except a few passing cars. Why?"

"You didn't hear anything?"

El folded her arms across her chest. "No. Why are you asking me questions if there was a car accident? I mean, I'm sorry that someone is dead, but I didn't see anything. I would have stopped, obviously. And I certainly didn't hit anyone, you can check my car."

Newton hesitated a moment and glanced again at Moore, who gave the faintest of nods. He looked at El and then beyond her to where Avery stood, now sipping tea and desperately trying to calm her rapidly beating heart. "We're not worried about another car. We're worried about something far darker."

He watched them and the silence in the room seemed to solidify, anchoring Avery to the spot. "What do you mean, 'darker?'" El asked.

He changed tack. "You two, and a few others in White Haven, have a certain reputation."

"We do?" Elspeth said, looking confused.

He smiled, unpleasantly. "Yes. And while some people may think it's interesting, even exciting, I think it's dangerous."

"Detective Inspector, you're going to have to be a bit clearer with that. I really don't know what you mean," El said, remaining very composed. Maybe there was a flicker of glamour there, too. Avery silently applauded her.

"Magic, is what I mean," he said looking her straight in the eye. "Magic that uses the laws of nature for her own ends."

Avery's eyebrows shot up, but El continued smoothly. "Magic respects nature, it does not abuse it, and neither do I. While I may have a certain reputation, it's all for the good. I sell simple trinkets, necklaces, bracelets, and rings that have the natural properties of the gemstones I use. That's not magic."

"So why do people whisper that if they need certain charms or protections, they should visit your shop?"

"I merely capitalise on the glamour of magic, but I'm just a silversmith."

He looked across the room to where Avery stood silently watching and feeling quite annoyed. "And you. You sell books on the occult, mysticism, divination, tarot cards."

"I also sell books of romance, action, thrillers, and fantasy. It's not illegal," she said, her anger building. "This is not the dark ages. This town has a rich history, built on the witch-hunts and the burning. If you haven't noticed, the whole town is full of soothsayers, fortune tellers, herbalists, and angel believers. That's why tourists come here. I sell what people are interested in." She could feel a breeze whipping up around her again, and she saw Newtown narrow his eyes as a strand of hair lifted in front of her face. She quickly tucked it behind her ear.

His grey eyes darkened like a storm. "The woman on the road had had her throat ripped out. Car accidents don't do that."

El's hand flew to her chest and Avery gasped and said, "I'm sorry to hear that, truly sorry, but we had nothing to do with it." She hesitated a second, and then thought she should come clean—after all, he'd have seen Alex's car. "I was with Alex Bonneville last night; I know you'll have seen his car, too. We met El at Hawk House, but that's all. We didn't see anything, either."

Newton's face was like granite. "So you all met at the Hawk House site, a couple of days before the Solstice, and a young woman died violently."

"I can assure you, those events are not connected," Avery said, her voice icy as she glared back at Newton.

"We'll need to speak to Alex Bonneville and Reuben Jackson." Newton gave them both a long, searching look, and then he looked around the room carefully, as if something would suddenly reveal itself. "That's all for now. Do *not* repeat what we told you about the way the woman died. If you think of anything, come and see me. And don't go anywhere."

He pulled his card out and laid it on the coffee table, while Moore pocketed his notebook. He had said nothing throughout the entire interview, and he followed Newton silently out the door.

As soon as they had left, Avery snorted. "Don't go anywhere! Where the hell does he think we'd go? I live here!"

"Holy shit, Avery. We're persons of interest in a murder investigation and a woman is dead!" El collapsed on the sofa and Avery walked over and sat next to her, cradling her now lukewarm tea and bringing one for El. They were silent for a few moments, and Avery leaned back, closing her eyes, trying to rationally think through the events of the night.

El interrupted her thoughts. "What do we know about demons, Avery?"

"Not much. Dark entities that need blood or souls to feed on—powerful, unruly, vengeful, and they don't belong in our world. They can be summoned and controlled with necromancy. If you're insane." She opened her eyes to find El staring at her. "Well, that's what I know. What about you?"

"The same. To be honest, I never thought they were real. I thought they were a magical figment that belonged in the dark ages. Manifestations of people's fear."

"Well, it wasn't a manifestation last night. It killed someone and attacked Reuben."

"If it's here, it will kill again. We have to stop it."

"So now we have three problems," Avery said. "We have a premonition, a suspicious detective, and whoever's attacking us and their pet demon to sort out. I better let Alex know he's going to get visitors, and you need to tell Reuben." And then she pulled her phone from her bag.

***

Avery decided she wanted the rest of her day to be normal, without any more drama. She stopped at the bakery and brought a selection of cakes, pastries, and three double-shot lattes with a sprinkling of cinnamon. When she arrived at the shop at just after eleven, she found Dan sitting on a stool behind the counter, reading a book. The music had changed, and Led Zeppelin's "Kashmir" was now playing.

"Hi," she grinned, trying to put her nerves behind her. "I've bought snacks."

There were only a couple of customers in the shop, browsing in the thriller section, so she plonked the goods down on the shop counter and took a long drink of coffee. Sometimes she felt caffeine was the only thing getting her through the day.

"So the wanderer returns!" Dan said with a wry smile, and he put his book down and reached for a latte. "This is great. Cheers."

"Quiet morning?" Avery asked.

"A bit of a rush earlier, but it's quietened down now. What have you been up to? You've made Sally a very grumpy woman."

Avery decided to come clean. "I've been questioned by the police, actually. All because me and Alex took a late night drive out to the moors."

Dan's face fell. "That poor woman. But they questioned you? I thought it was an accident?"

"A suspicious accident," Avery explained, not wanting to say more. "Anyway, I think he was happy-ish with our explanation. Obviously, we know nothing." Which wasn't strictly true, but she wasn't about to go talking about demons. Dan would think she was mad. In fact, she might be. "Where is Sally?" she asked, looking around.

"Out the back. Sally!" he yelled. "Coffee's here." He reached for a pastry. "Wow, these are awesome."

"Oh, you're back!" Sally said, coming from the back room, a mixture of relief and annoyance on her face. She looked at the coffee and cakes. "A peace offering?"

"Sort of. Sorry, Sally. It's been a hell of a week."

Dan spoke through a mouthful of pastry, "And she's been interviewed by the police."

"But I'm fine," Avery rushed to calm Sally. "It's just a misunderstanding."

Sally leaned closer, glancing at the customers to make sure they were out of hearing range, and said quietly, "Things have changed since you picked up Anne's stuff. Why?"

"It's nothing," Avery said, also leaning forward. "She just gave me some family histories, that's all."

"We both know about your—" she hesitated for a second, "practices. And it's the Solstice. Do you need our help?"

Avery was so shocked that she almost spit her coffee out. "What do you mean—'practices?'"

Dan smiled. "This is a witchy town, but we all know there's more witch in some of us than others. And that includes you, Avery. And don't panic."

"I make no secret of my interests," she started, defensively.

"Oh bollocks, Avery. We're not talking interests. We're talking practices," Dan said, brushing pastry flakes from his shirt. "We respect your abilities, but they're not a secret, not to us, anyway."

Avery felt the hairs stand up on the back of her neck. She had tried so hard to hide her powers, and she hoped they didn't know the scope of them.

She must have looked shocked because Sally added, "Don't worry; only a few people really know. Locals. We respect your privacy. But if something weird is going on, they will start to ask questions. We know you're safe, but magic is magic, Avery."

They both fell silent as Avery sipped her coffee and tried to think of something to say. Today was going to be one of those days, and with the impending Solstice, it could be weirder than most. "All right," she said, making her mind up and glancing once more over her shoulder. "I have certain abilities. It's hereditary. I am safe with my abilities, as in, I do not intend harm, but there are others who do. Things may not be so safe around here at the moment, so I want you both to be careful. I'll prepare something for you to carry, and I want you to promise me to carry it always. At least for a while."

Dan and Sally's slightly jokey tone now disappeared. "So something IS going on?" Sally asked.

"Yes. But that's all I'm saying. Now, if you don't mind, I'm going to head upstairs and prepare a little something for you." She looked at their shocked faces and allowed herself a small laugh. "Well, you did ask."

✳✳✳

Avery headed up to her flat and first checked her main living area to ensure nothing remotely magical lay around, just in case DI Newton wanted to visit, and then she did the same in the attic. She shoved the wooden box into the working area, where her shelves were filled with her supplies, and performed a spell to dissuade visitors from looking too hard in that particular area.

Satisfied with her work, she crossed the small back alley to the walled garden and entered it through the ornately decorated gate that was imbued with spells. She always kept it locked, but it also had protection added to it to ward off prying eyes. Once inside, she looked around with pleasure and sighed in relief. Her garden always calmed her.

It was surrounded with four high walls covered with climbers and espaliered fruit trees. It seemed bigger than it really was, because it was impossible to see it all from one spot. Pergolas and gazebos added height and structure, and everywhere you looked the plants were growing with a giddy profusion. There were roses, irises, dahlias, verbenas, geraniums, lavender, hollyhocks, delphiniums, lupins, shrubs and small trees, and much more. Gravel paths wound through everything, and everywhere she walked, she brushed by plants so that their perfume filled the air.

She bypassed the garden table and chairs where she had seen Alex the other night, and pressed on to where the herbs grew. She stopped and filled a basket with a variety of cuttings, and decided she'd come back later as the light fell to collect some roots. They were best gathered at dusk.

They would welcome the Solstice here tomorrow, and they would be undisturbed. In the centre of the garden was a grassed area, as smooth as velvet and perfect for rituals. Although the garden was surrounded by other buildings, only her own flat was high and close enough to see into it.

Avery saw Dan and Sally once more before the end of the day to give them their hex bags. She called them into the back room, and left the door part way open to watch for customers. "Here you go," she said.

Dan looked bemused at the small muslin bag that was filled with herbs and tied at the neck with cord. "What do I do with it?"

"Wear it." She pulled the cord free of the bag. "See, you can hang it around your neck, tucked under your shirt, or put it in your pocket. Whatever you choose. Just wear it."

Sally looked at her wide-eyed. "It just looks like the herbs I put in my underwear drawer. Does it do anything?"

"It does plenty. Just take it and use it," Avery said.

Sally leaned forward and touched it gingerly, and then lifted it over her head like a necklace so it rested under her shirt, as Avery had suggested, while Dan put his in his jeans' pocket.

Avery felt as if a huge weight had been lifted off her shoulders, and although she was sure that feeling wouldn't last long, she decided to enjoy it while it lasted. It was nice to be able to be even a little bit honest with two people who weren't witches. "Excellent, now, be careful."

"What are you doing for the rest of the day?" Dan asked. "We're going to The Mermaid for a pint if you want to come?"

Avery shook her head. "No, I'm having a quiet night, thanks. Just me, the cats, and the TV."

"You sure?" Sally said, looking worried.

"Absolutely. See you in the morning."

Once they'd gone and the shop was locked up, Avery enjoyed the laziest night she could, not even wanting to look at Anne's research. The previous night's events had exhausted her, and the woman's death had depressed her.

Magic was the last thing she wanted to do. And besides, the Solstice would be a busy day.

14

Saturdays were always busy, customers streaming in and out of the shop, and all the talk was about the celebrations on the beach later. Avery, like many others, had decorated her shop window. The day passed in a whirl of chat and sales, and she barely had time to think about their own celebrations that night.

Neither Dan nor Sally made any mention of their conversation from the previous day, and Avery was relieved. On his way out the door, Dan asked, "Are you going to any of the celebrations on the beach later?"

"No. I'll be celebrating privately tonight. Are you?"

He grinned. "Sure, who doesn't enjoy a good bonfire, a bit of chanting by our local pagan druid, and a few beers?"

She laughed. One of the town councillors liked to officiate at the Solstice and Equinox celebrations, proclaiming himself the local druid. Visitors and locals loved it, although there was no real magic involved at all. The crowds should be enough to keep the demon and whoever was controlling it away. "Good. Stay with the crowds. And enjoy!"

The pale blue sky seemed like a lid on the town, trapping the heat of the day within the lanes and buildings. One of the pleasures of mid-summer, Avery thought, was the light that lasted late into the night. She headed into the garden, spending the next few hours preparing for the other witches' arrival, and trying to ignore her growing hunger pangs. Some magic needed an empty stomach so Avery hadn't eaten since breakfast.

They had decided to celebrate the Solstice with a very non-witchy BBQ after their celebration. Avery's brick-built BBQ hadn't been used since the previous summer, so she scrubbed it clean. She prepared salads for later, and made sure there were plenty of candles to supplement the low electric lighting that illuminated the garden paths, plants, and the table; the whole place would look pretty and magical.

Alex arrived first, letting himself through the gate. Avery heard the crunch of the gravel as he headed down the path. She sat at the table sipping water and smiled as he came into view. Last week, she had wanted to strangle him, but now her heart raced a little quicker as she remembered that long, lingering kiss.

He sank into the chair opposite hers. "How you doing?"

"I've been better."

He placed his proffered beer in the cooler and took a swig of water. "Thanks for the heads-up yesterday. DI Newton arrived with his silent witness in tow. What a creepy pair they are."

"They *do* have a murder to investigate."

"I know. I'm trying to make light of a bad situation. I'm not normally suspected of murder." He looked around. "I can feel you've increased your protection."

"Yep. And I gave Dan and Sally an amulet bag, too."

He raised his eyebrows.

"Apparently, a few locals know I'm a witch—and you too, probably. They mentioned *others* and I didn't ask. I'm really not sure how much they know of what we actually can do, but we're trusted to do the right thing, apparently. So I did. Has anyone ever said anything to you?"

"About magic? Never. But I work in a pub, not an occult bookstore. And I think people associate women far more with witches than men. Doesn't sound like they'll be hounding you out of town, anyway," Alex said with a grin. "Did you ask El what happened at Hawk House—you know, how the demon arrived?"

"No, Newton arrived before I'd had a chance to find out. We'll ask later."

His eyes darkened and his gaze fell to her lips, and it seemed he was going to say something when the gate opened again, and she heard El and Briar arrive. Avery wasn't sure if she was relieved or disappointed.

Briar was looking her most ethereal. Her dark hair was loose and she wore white everything—a long skirt and a lace-trimmed cotton shirt. El was wearing her usual black, and her white-blonde hair glowed in the evening light. She was carrying a large object wrapped in a blanket.

"No Gil yet?" El asked.

"No. Any news from Reuben?" Avery asked.

"No," El answered, with a slight grimace.

Briar looked at all of them. "I feel I'm missing something."

"We'll hang on for Gil and then we'll fill you in," Avery said. "What are you carrying, El?"

"I've brought a sword, bound with ceremonial magic. I thought it would be great to draw our circle." She unwrapped it and Avery's jaw dropped in amazement.

"Wow! That's so cool!"

The sword had a simple hilt, a mix of silver and what looked like copper. The blade had a fine engraving running down the centre. Alex leapt to his feet. "May I?"

El grinned. "Of course."

Alex lifted it and then swished it around. "I like this."

"Better not let Newton see you with it, or he'll be accusing you all over again," Avery said.

Briar was silent, but she watched Alex admiringly, and for a second Avery felt a flash of guilt as she remembered their kiss from last night. She was sure Briar fancied him, but it seemed Alex was oblivious. His muscles flexed as he moved, and Avery felt desire stir within her.

El laughed. "Seriously, Alex, you're holding it all wrong." She stepped in to adjust his grip when Gil arrived, surprising everyone when Reuben appeared behind him.

For a second El didn't move, she just looked at Reuben with wide, questioning eyes, and the place fell silent for a brief second as Alex strode towards them. "Gil, good to see you. Reu, how are you? We've been worried sick."

Despite the attack a couple of nights before, Reuben looked as handsome and rugged as ever, and he broke into a grin. "It'll take more than a demon to finish me off." He looked serious for a moment. "Thanks for your help the other night. Without you two," he glanced at Avery, "things would have been very different." He looked at El. "How are you?"

Relief washed over her face. She had been so worried he wouldn't forgive her. "Feeling guilty. I could have killed you."

"No, the demon could have. It wasn't your fault. You could have died, too."

"What about the burns?"

Reuben showed the angry red welts at his wrists, arms, and legs. "They're still there, but they're healing—thanks to Briar's poultice."

Avery relaxed, relieved that El and Reuben seemed to be okay.

Gil sat at the table. "Well, I'm pissed at all of you. This is still insanity to me."

Alex put the sword on the table. "You'd better get used to it, because it's not going away."

Gil looked up at him. "I don't appreciate the police coming to visit, either."

"Neither do I!"

"Or me!" El added, annoyed.

Briar intervened. "The police? What's happened since I last saw you?"

"Didn't you hear?" Avery asked, having a feeling she was about to ruin Briar's night. "A woman died on the moors that night."

She nodded. "A car accident. What's that got to do with us?"

"It wasn't a car accident. It was the demon."

Briar looked horrified as the reality of their situation sank in. "The one that attacked you?"

"Well, there better not be another," Alex said dryly. He turned to El. "How did it attack you? You never said."

"We were already underground," she said, thinking. "The spell showed us the foundation and led us to the underground cellar's entrance. Up to that point we were alone. Obviously it was dark, but I didn't sense anything, and there wasn't a sound, except for the occasional car on the road beyond. It arrived once we were in the cellar room with the box. I don't know where it came from—it was just there. I didn't sense a thing." She exhaled heavily. "I feel pretty stupid. It grabbed me and it was like being held by a cord of electricity. It was horrible. I could sense this darkness and hunger for power. And I couldn't get free—that was really scary."

Reuben stirred. "It's true. It was just there. As it grabbed El, it struck me."

"But the box was there," Avery said, puzzled. "Why didn't it take it?"

"The wards," Briar said. "They would have repelled it."

Alex nodded. "Good point. Maybe the demon was to keep you there until whoever was controlling it could get there to get the box. We're lucky we were closer."

Gil stood up. "If I'm honest, I'm not feeling that celebratory. However, we are here to celebrate the Solstice, so let's get on with it."

"Well, I'm going to celebrate my first encounter with a demon and surviving," Reuben said with a grin.

"Good point!" Alex agreed. "So, you're joining us?"

"After last night, I've decided I can't ignore my magic any longer. Especially if I want to survive. So yes, I am."

"Before we start, I need a hand to get the box in," El said. "You're all going to help me get my grimoire."

***

They stood on the grassed area in the centre of the garden. El held the sword with the point turned down, touching the earth, and starting in the East, she walked around in a full circle, large enough to hold all of them. The other five followed, all murmuring the ritual words to create the circle.

They stepped into it, and as the circle was sealed behind them, Avery felt the outside world falling away as the sacred space enveloped her. All other evening sounds disappeared: cars, the murmur of people talking that carried from the road, and even the sound of the breeze rustling through the trees.

They had decided their celebrations should encompass giving thanks to the gods and the elements for their magic and an appeal to give strength for the coming year. They spoke in unison, their voices weaving together as they repeated the well-known lines, rising and falling with changing cadence. They moved around the sacred space in a steady dance, exchanging candles between them, and Avery acutely felt the cold grass beneath her feet, dry and brittle.

As the light diminished and the first stars appeared in the sky, Avery felt the turn in the season, the acknowledgement that they were moving towards winter already, the longest day almost over. With the silence came power, and she felt it soaking into her skin and bones, renewing her for the challenges she knew were to come. Within the circle, the candlelight at the four points of the compass burned steadily, throwing a flickering light over their ritual, but outside it was black, and it seemed to press in on them.

Avery had no idea how long the ritual lasted. Time within the circle seemed to slow, but her gaze fell on the box in the centre, and she wondered if opening it would be as challenging to El as Alex's was to him.

Gil broke the silence that had fallen at the end of the ritual. "When do you want to open your box, El?"

"Now's as good a time as any." She walked over to the box, opening the lid, which like Alex's was deep with small runes carved around the edge.

"Are all the grimoires hidden in boxes?" Briar asked, watching El carefully.

"Maybe," Avery said. Briar looked worried, and Avery still wasn't sure if she wanted to find hers at all.

Reuben spoke from opposite Avery, his face in the shadows. "It's interesting, isn't it? If we find another one like this, we have to presume they were all hidden together."

"It makes sense though, doesn't it?" Gil said. "The Witchfinder was on his way, and they all needed to hide their grimoires. Perhaps they'd had the boxes prepared for some time."

"How do you want to play this, El?" Alex asked. He stood next to Avery, and his strong presence resonated beside her. As if he sensed her looking, he glanced at her and winked, and she felt her stomach flip. Now was not the time to think about their kiss, and she looked back to El.

El sighed. "I have no idea. I'll say the runes as you did, Alex, and hope for the best. I've written them all down. Are you ready for whatever may emerge?"

"As ready as I'll ever be." Gil looked at Reuben. "Are you sure you want to be in the circle?"

"I'll be fine, brother."

"Is blood needed again?" Gil asked, disapproval in his voice.

"No." El sat cross-legged in front of the box, took a deep breath, and started the incantation.

Much as when Alex had started reading his runes, Avery felt the air pressure change, becoming heavy, as if it was smothering her. El's voice filled the air, and for several seconds, nothing happened. The pressure continued to build and then shapes began to manifest around them. Avery blinked, thinking she was seeing things, before they became clear. Large, black crows screeched and flapped their wings, buffeting the air. In seconds, there seemed to be hundreds of them. She shouted and pushed a crow away as it flew at her face, scratching and clawing, and then more flew at her, tangling in her hair. She could barely see; the circle was full of them and they had nowhere to go. She was dimly aware of Alex and Gil on either side, also struggling against the onslaught.

They had to open the circle.

As Avery struggled to the East to open the doorway, she fell to her knees and grabbed the sword. She uttered spells of banishment, but nothing worked. If anything, the crows were multiplying. She could hear shrieks and swearing, and she tried to protect her eyes as she rose once more to her feet. El remained seated in a private bubble of protected space, the crows unable to touch her. An enormous *crack* resounded, and she glimpsed the lid flying open, split in half.

In three swift movements Avery drew the sides of the door and opened the circle, breaking the wall of protection. The air pressure dropped like a stone, and the crows streamed past her. She fell to her knees once more and covered her head with her arms until she felt the rush of beating wings subside. Then she heard the *boom* of her protective spells breaking, and looking up, saw the arrival of large, dark shadows in the garden beyond their circle.

Demons.

Alex yelled, "Avery!" He pulled her behind him and taking the sword, quickly closed the circle again before the demons could step inside.

All six witches quickly faced outwards, bracing themselves for attack. El was seemingly unharmed after the spell.

Two demons prowled around them. Like at Hawk House, their forms were hulking black shadows with misshapen limbs, but their red eyes glowed.

Briar's voice shook. "I know you told me what happened the other night, but I didn't really picture it. I still can't believe it."

"My injuries not enough for you, Briar?" Reuben said snarkily.

"Hey, look on the bright side," Alex said. "Whoever it is, sent two. We must be a bigger threat than they thought."

Gil sounded as shocked as Briar. "What are we going to do now?"

The demons moved closer to the protective wall around them, as if testing it for weak spots. As they touched the wall, a bright blue flash crackled like electricity. The demon roared and released a stream of flame at the wall and it lit up again, shielding them. Avery knew that no matter how good their protection was, it would give way eventually.

"El, maybe you should check that book to see if there is anything on demon banishment," Alex suggested. "Reuben, you okay?"

"I'd like some revenge." Reuben clenched his hands into fists.

"I'm not sure punching them will work. Will your magic be strong enough?"

"Combined with everyone else's, yes."

"How did you banish them last time?" Gil asked, his eyes never leaving the prowling demons.

"Fire seemed to strengthen it, but it didn't like water. I pulled the water from the walls, combined it with energy, and blasted it. It just disappeared," Avery said, thinking about the chaotic fight.

"Well, there's six of us, and two of them, so I figure we have good odds," Alex said. "But, we need a plan. Renewing the protective spell will only trap us here all night. Have you got a pond in your garden, Avery?"

"Not really—it's a tiny, ornamental thing," she said thinking of the small pond by her herb garden.

While they talked, the demons prowled, pulsing with power, their shadowy mass growing and shrinking as if they were breathing. They had split up and were attacking them from opposite sides, enveloping them in flames. The walls around them again crackled with a blue, protective light.

"We're going to have to break the protection spell to attack," Gil said.

"Not until we have a plan!" Alex said, his voice curt.

While Gil and Alex argued about what to use to banish the demons, El crouched on the floor, flicking through the grimoire, desperate for something they could use. She looked at Avery. "I can barely read a word of this," she said, frustrated. "Especially in this light."

Briar interrupted. "There's water in the earth, Avery, lots of it. We just need to draw it out."

"And add wind, lots of wind," Reuben suggested. "This is not their environment. If we add enough elements, it will surely overwhelm them."

"It's worth a shot," Alex said. "Gil—you, Briar, and Reuben draw on water and earth together, and we'll support Avery with wind."

"I have another suggestion," El said. "Use the sword to channel the elements. Either air or water. It will act as a conduit."

"Brilliant idea," Alex said. "I think air will work better, though, if that's okay with you, Briar?"

"No problem."

They all nodded in agreement, and Avery saw El put the grimoire back in the box and cover it as best she could. Alex gave Avery the sword. "Let's dissolve the circle together."

They stood back-to-back, hands held, saying the words that ended their protection. Within seconds the demons rushed at them, shooting long, forked tongues of flames that flickered like whips around them. Avery felt the white-hot lash of one as it whipped across her bare arms and she suppressed the urge to scream. She focussed only on air and the cold metal of the sword. Fortunately, her anger was enough to draw it quickly—it was the element that leapt quickest to her aid, as if it was always waiting to be called on. Instinctively, Alex and El had broken off from the others and now all three stood together, surrounded by a whipping vortex of wind. As one, they directed it at the demons, while the other three sent a deluge of water at the same time.

A tornado of wind, rain, and damp earth surrounded them all, blinding in its intensity, and Avery heard a shriek. She couldn't be sure if it came from the demons or one of them. The demons continued to lash out with tongues of fire, but struggled against the onslaught of elements.

Avery gathered their combined power and focussed it into one massive blast. The sword felt like an extension of her being, and her power seemed to magnify down it and beyond, directing it like a laser. She wielded it quickly, slashing back and forth as the air howled and her hair whipped around her. The group's combined attack was too strong, and soon the demons disappeared.

As Avery lowered her energy, the wind dropped. She thought she'd feel exhausted, but adrenalin soared through her. Her fingers tingled and her awareness was razor sharp.

She looked around at the others standing in a ragged line. Although the wind, rain, and earth had just raged around them, they all stood untouched. She grinned. "We did it!" Every single one of them looked at her in shock. "What's the matter?"

Alex pointed at the ground. "Feel anything different, Avery?"

She looked down and found she was hovering about a foot above the earth. Avery wasn't sure if she felt panic-stricken or excited. No, she was definitely excited. She looked up at them again. "How am I doing this? Oh, wow! This is so cool!"

"Can you stop it?" El asked, bemused. She paced around Avery, as if she was looking for strings.

She giggled. "I'm not sure I want to!"

"It might cause a problem with the locals, though," Alex observed, also trying not to laugh.

Avery heard a cry from Briar and saw her look at her feet. Although less obvious than Avery's response to the wind element, Briar's feet were now buried up to her ankles in soil. "You too, Briar," she said.

"It must be as if the elements recognise us," Briar said, as she pulled her feet out with a grimace. And then a smile flashed across her face. "You know, I was so busy with that demon that I didn't think, but it was an incredibly grounding and powerful experience. For a few seconds, I felt I could do that all night."

Gil didn't look amused at all. "Fun though this is, those demons might come back, and I'm not sure I have enough juice to do that again. I'm not sure that your garden will survive, either. It's a bit worrying that your protection spells didn't last, Avery." He lit the candles again with a turn of his wrist and all the garden lighting flickered on, too, illuminating the darkness beyond.

Avery saw chaos beyond their circle. Plants had been lifted and flung out of position, and her lawn was churned up, as if a herd of elephants had trampled across it. As reality hit her, her energy levelled out and she slowly floated back to the grass, her feet gently touching the ground.

"El, your book!" she cried with alarm, suddenly remembering the grimoire.

El turned and headed to the box, lifting the lid carefully, but she sighed with relief. "It's fine. It was protected enough, especially in the middle of all of us."

Briar was kneeling down, her hand on the earth. "I can help put your garden back together, Avery. You just need to leave me to it."

"Well, I'm starved," Alex said, running his hand through his hair and scratching his head. "I'll get the BBQ going while someone helps Avery renew our protection. Nothing ruins a good BBQ like demons."

***

By the time Avery returned to the BBQ area with Gil, the smells of sausages, burgers, chicken, and onions was wafting around them. She was starving. Battling demons was a good way to work up an appetite.

Strings of fairy lights were draped in the trees and they twinkled like fire flies, and candles illuminated the table. The smell of incense and sage mixed with the smell of grilled food. Someone had performed a cleansing ritual, purging the space of any negativity left by the demons.

Alex was wearing an apron and sipping beer while turning sausages on the grill. He threw her a grin as she joined them. Reuben was sitting next to El, beer in hand, looking through the grimoire. Whatever had driven him away from magic seemed to have gone, and he appeared to be as interested in the book as all of them.

Avery pulled a few beers from the chilly bin of water, and giving Gil one, chinked his and took a long drink as she sat down at the table.

Reuben looked up. "Where's Briar?"

"Still healing my garden," Avery said. "Oh no, here she is."

Briar walked into the light like a garden spirit, except the bottom of her white dress and her feet were muddy. "I think I need a shower," she said, and she tried to brush the dirt from her hands. "The good news is, your garden will survive, but I suggest you turn the hose on it tomorrow."

"Thanks, Briar," Avery grinned. She handed her a beer. "Grab a seat."

"So, what delights are in that book?" Gil asked, with a weary tone. He dropped into the seat next to Reuben.

Reuben looked baffled. "Weird stuff. Diagrams, spells, and what looks like alchemy."

"It's definitely alchemy," Elspeth said. She leaned back in her chair. "I have simpler versions in my usual grimoire, but these spells have much more detail. There are spells here to trap powers into metal, and protection spells that are sealed in rings or lockets. There's also a spell that traps a person's essence into a sealed jar."

"Essence! What's a person's essence?" Avery asked, alarmed.

"Their soul."

Silence fell, broken only by Alex dropping his metal spatula. "Is that a joke?" he asked, leaving the grill and coming over to the table.

El looked very serious. "No. And don't even ask me to read the spell out. It's hideous. And no, I won't ever try it."

Avery felt sick imagining murder, torture, and worse. "Do you think anyone has tried it?"

"Well, it's in there, isn't it?" Gil pointed out. He stood up, his chair scraping back loudly against the gravel. He paced around the table. "I told you I didn't like this. We don't do this kind of magic."

"And we're not going to," Alex said, looking in annoyed amazement at Gil. "We're not bloody animals. I've got a knife, but I'm not about to start stabbing someone!"

Avery laughed. "He's right, Gil. There are thousands of things we could do every day, but we don't. We still exercise our judgement."

"I suppose so," Gil said. "I guess I'm worried what I'll find in my book. It makes me think our ancestors were crazy."

"I don't think they were," Reuben said. "They were people, like us—just a bit closer to their magical roots."

"Well, considering what's happened over the past few days, I've decided I will look for mine," Briar said. She had a streak of dirt across her cheek, and as she brushed her hair back from her face, she added another one. "We can't run away from our past, especially since it seems to be insistently knocking on our door."

"Do you know where to look?" Gil asked, finally sitting again.

"Not yet. Do you?"

"Well, it seems our mad great-uncle hunted everywhere for it, so I'm wondering if it's on our grounds at all. What about you, Avery?"

"I know where my old ancestor used to live. It doesn't mean it's still there, though. And besides, someone else is living there now."

El had returned to looking at her grimoire, but now she stirred. "You know where Helena lived?"

"Yes. Well, I think so. I presume it's where she lived."

"Have you ever been to the witch museum?"

"Er, no. Well, not since I was a child," Avery said, wondering where El was going with this. "I feel self-conscious there. Why?"

El looked thoughtful. "There's something about Helena there—I visited the place when I first moved here. We should go tomorrow."

"Yes, I'm sure there'll be instructions for the hidden grimoire on display," Gil said with a note of impatience.

"Actually, it has a detailed history of the Witchfinder's visit. There may be more there than we realise, now that we're looking at it with fresh eyes."

"Awesome. I've got plenty of staff on tomorrow so I can get out for a few hours." Alex said, interrupting them. "Food's up. And while we eat, we can discuss our witches' day out." He grinned at Avery and she felt her stomach flip again. He really was too damn sexy for his own good.

15

In the end only El, Briar, Alex and Avery met at the museum. Reuben had persuaded Gil that it was time to search their grounds for the grimoire, and reluctantly, Gil had agreed.

The museum was a solidly constructed stone-walled, low-roofed, sixteenth century building that looked like a pub. It was close to the quay and had a small car park next to it. They had agreed to get there early so it would be quiet, but had a shock at the entrance to find a police car and yellow tape across the front door.

"Oh no, what now?" Briar said, worry creasing her face.

Avery felt fear pricking its way up her spine. "It could just be a break in?"

"Let's hope so. I think we should get out of here," Alex said, and he started to walk away, pulling Avery and El with him.

Unfortunately, before they could go anywhere, a dark sedan pulled up and DI Newton stepped out, the silent Moore exiting the other door.

"What a surprise to see you here," Newton said, his tone accusatory. Despite the early hour he looked freshly showered and shaved, and very sharp in his well-cut suit. "Revisiting the scene of your crimes?"

"Not funny," Avery said, bristling. She pulled free of Alex and stepped up to Newton, sick of his bullying tone. She wanted to slap him. "We haven't committed a crime."

"Here for a visit, were you?" he said, his eyes narrowing suspiciously as he eyed them all in turn. His gaze lingered on Briar. "I haven't met you yet, but I think you own the potion shop."

"It is not a potion shop!" Briar said, almost spitting. *Wow, Newton had a real knack for getting under their skin.*

"Let me introduce DI Newton and Officer Moore," Avery said, gesturing with a flourish.

"Newton?" Briar repeated, puzzled. She looked as if she was about to say more, when Newton interrupted.

"Now that you're here, I'd like your opinion on what happened in the museum."

"Why?" Alex asked immediately. He had also stepped closer to Newton, as if challenging him.

"Calm down, Bonneville. I just want your opinion. And I'll get your alibis later. Wait here," he said, as he stalked off into the museum, Moore close behind him.

"Alibis!" Avery huffed, feeling like she wanted to rip Newton's head off. "Why should we need to provide an alibi? He clearly wants to blame us for anything and everything! That supercilious bastard."

"But what if the demons have attacked again?" El asked, worried. "What if someone else is dead because of us?"

Alex shook his head and sat on the stone wall that edged the car park. "Not because of us. We didn't cause this. We didn't summon demons."

Avery was too annoyed to sit, so she paced restlessly. "Who is out there, doing this? We need to find them!"

"We need to do lots of things," El said wearily.

Briar was sitting quietly on the wall next to Alex, but she finally broke her silence. "Is the name Newton familiar to you?"

"Er, the DI?" Alex asked, looking at Briar as if she'd gone mad.

"No! I mean, other than him. I've read the name somewhere."

Avery now felt her annoyance turning to Briar. "Haven't we got other things to be worried about?"

Briar looked at her, ignoring her tone. "It's an old name in this town, isn't it?"

"It's not an uncommon name anywhere," Alex said. "Besides, lots of people have lived here for years."

Briar looked perplexed. "I think I know the name from some of that info we got from Anne. I think he's from one of the *old* families."

Avery glanced at the other two, and was relieved to find they looked as confused as she felt. "Briar, please explain. It's too early, and my brain's full of other crap."

Briar remained unruffled by Avery's sarcasm. "I mean the old families with *magic.*"

El laughed. "What! Newton and magic?"

"He might not have magical abilities, but I'm sure his ancestors have."

"It might explain why he's anti-witch, and has an unhealthy interest in our habits," Alex said.

Their conversation was broken by a shout. They looked around to see Newton beckoning them from the open door.

"Yes, sir," Avery muttered under her breath as they walked over.

"I'm breaking protocol by letting you in, so don't touch anything!" he ordered. Without another word he headed inside, and they followed him in.

The inside of the museum was lit by the unnatural glare of overhead lights. The windows were small and let in only a small amount of daylight. Small, yellow spotlights lit up the displays, and Avery presumed that would normally be the only light source when visitors were here.

For a few seconds Avery gazed around the museum, taking in the numerous displays in glass cabinets, both against the walls and in the middle of the floor. They were filled with old maps, manuscripts, and lots of other objects, but her attention was swiftly drawn by a display that had been smashed, and on the wall was a large, complex Sigel written in what looked like dried blood. Avery felt her skin prickle as she recognised it and all her annoyance at Newton drained out of her.

She could sense the power from the sign, and all four them had stopped in the middle of the room.

Newton stood next to the sign, looking at them curiously. "So, what is it?" he asked.

Alex spoke first, and he walked closer to the display. "It's an ancient ward, essentially a warning to stay away."

That was an understatement, Avery thought. She swallowed her fear and joined him, with El and Briar close behind.

Newton looked sceptical. "Really? Because you have all gone very pale. Now is not a good time to be holding something back."

Alex glanced at her, a questioning look on his face, and she felt something shift within her. This wasn't a time to be keeping secrets, and Alex knew it, too.

Avery looked at Newton, trying to gauge his reaction. "It marks a doorway, and within it is a warning to stay away. It essentially says this place is claimed."

To give him credit, Newton wasn't at all fazed by that statement. Instead, he narrowed his eyes and folded his arms across his broad chest. "A doorway to what? And claimed by who?"

"A doorway to another dimension. One in which unnatural, non-human forms live. And it is claimed by whoever made the sign."

"How does the doorway work?"

"I can't speak for the others, but I don't know HOW it works. I just know what it is. But it's powerful, I can sense that."

Newton looked at them one by one, as if trying to read their minds. "I'll rephrase the question. It's a doorway, you say. Will it open? Or is it just some gimmicky sign that someone with a weird sense of humour has put up."

"In theory," Avery said, "if you say the right words, it will open."

"And then what?"

"It will allow things—*beings*—to pass through to our dimension. And back again. But no human would ever survive there."

"So it's more for something to come through?"

"Yes. But someone may be taken through as a type of... sacrifice." Avery could scarcely believe she'd said that.

Newton's tone changed, and he ran his hand through his hair, looking worried. "The cleaner's missing. There's blood in the kitchen, and blood in that sign. Could something have taken the cleaner through there?"

Avery felt sick. "Maybe, yes. But Newton, you have to understand—we don't do this. I know you don't like us for our interest in the esoteric and natural magic, but this—" she gestured towards the sign. "I really don't know how this works, only the theory."

Alex was looking at the destroyed display, the glass smashed and the objects beneath it scattered. "How do you know the cleaner is missing? He could have had an accident and gone to the hospital."

"There's far too much blood there for anyone to have survived. Haven't you noticed the blood?" He pointed at the floor, and for the first time, Avery saw the smear of blood that ran from the door at the back to under the sign, and beneath the musty smell, she could detect the sharp, metallic odour of blood. "There's more in the kitchen."

"But who called you?" Alex asked.

"The lady who manages the place on Sundays. She's out the back with Moore. She's in shock and we need to get her out of here, but I wanted your opinion first."

"What was in the display?" El asked.

"You'd better come and ask her. I'll take you around the long way—I don't want you walking in anything." Newton headed back across the museum and they trailed after him as he led them around the back of the building to the kitchen and storage area.

Moore was sitting in a small stock room with a uniformed police officer and an older lady who sat on a stool, looking tearful and clutching a cup of tea in a paper cup that someone must have gone to fetch her. A doorway showed a glimpse of the kitchen, and Avery saw a lot of blood on the floor and splashed up the walls. She shuddered.

Newton put his hand on the lady's shoulder. "I'm sorry Mrs Gray," he said, gently, in a tone Avery had never heard him use before. "I need to ask you another question. I have some people here who I've asked to help." He nodded towards them. "What was in the display that was destroyed?"

She looked at them, clearly bewildered by the turn her day was taking. "It was a display about the Witchfinder and his visit to White Haven back in the 16th century. There are also some things relating to Helena, the witch who was hanged here years before." She looked at Avery sadly. "Sorry, my dear, I know she was your ancestor."

Avery experienced a moment of shock. She hadn't realised anyone outside of their circle had connected her to Helena. She was amazed this woman could show any compassion, considering what she'd witnessed in the kitchen. She thought she'd be accusing her, not sympathising.

"Was there anything new in the display, Mrs Gray?" Briar asked, surprising them all. She was normally so quiet.

The old woman shook her head. "No. That display has been like that for years."

Newton interrupted. "Any other questions? I'd like to take Mrs Gray to the station now, for her statement."

"No, thank you." Alex answered for all of them.

"I need a few more words with Mrs Gray. Can you wait outside for a minute?"

It wasn't really a request, and they filed out, blinking in the warm sunshine. Avery felt as if she'd been in a cave and had forgotten it was a beautiful summer morning. She headed to the stone wall that looked over the harbour and sat down, vaguely aware of the others next to her.

The harbour was filled with boats grounded on the sand. The tide was edging out, and pools of water gathered in the sand beneath the harbour wall. The sound of gulls mixed with the passing of cars and the occasional barking dog. Everything seemed so normal.

"Do you think the cleaner has really gone?" Briar asked. She sat next to Avery, her hands clasped in her lap.

"Yes," Alex answered. "I don't think they'll ever find a body."

"We need to seal that doorway," El said. She was pacing backwards and forwards. "If we leave it open, it can keep coming back. It's right in the middle of the town!"

"How do we seal it?" Alex asked, annoyed. "I haven't even seen one before, except in illustrations."

Avery thought about the books she had in the store and in her attic. "I have some old books about necromancy. I'll look as soon as we get back. What about you two? You have the oldest grimoires. Is there anything in them?"

El shook her head, bewildered. "I don't know. I've barely begun to look at it. I'll check it as soon as I get in."

"Well, you know there are demon and spirit related spells in mine, but I'm inexperienced when it comes to that type of magic, and if I'm honest, I've avoided studying them," Alex said. He looked across the car park to the museum. "They'll surely close the museum. I guess we won't see inside there again."

"I can't believe Newton let us in at all!" Avery said.

The sound of a door slamming made them turn. The uniformed officer and Moore were escorting Mrs Gray to a police car, and Newton was heading their way.

He stood in front of them, looking far calmer than Avery felt. Maybe he was just better at holding it together than them. He smoothed his tie down, patted his pocket, and brought out a packet of cigarettes. He swiftly took one out and lit it, inhaling deeply.

"So," he said, watching them carefully, "What are we going to do about that doorway?"

Avery looked at Newton with new appreciation. He said 'we' and he didn't argue with the notion of the other dimensions or beings. "You're not going to arrest us, then?"

"Not unless I find your fingerprints everywhere. SOCO's on the way now," he said, referring to scene of crime investigators. "And if it reassures you to hear me say it, I don't think you're murderers, anyway."

Briar still sat next to Avery, watching the exchange. "You're one of *those* Newtons, aren't you?"

Newton took another long drag on his cigarette and exhaled slowly. "What do you mean by *those* Newtons?"

"There are several old families in this town, Detective. We know some of them have a more diverse history than others. I'm pretty sure you do, too. And your family is one of them."

"I'm aware of my personal history, Briar," he said softly. "I stay away from it. But yes, I know all about it, and about you, too. It's my business to know. And I know it wasn't an animal that attacked that woman the other night, either. What's going on?" He watched her intently, his eyes sweeping across her face.

Avery had the distinct impression that this was a test of honesty. Of trust. He was gauging how much he could trust them, and they were wondering the same about him.

"Honestly," Briar said, "we really don't know. But we know someone wants something badly enough to call on any type of help they can."

"You're lying—all of you. You know more than that. But that's okay. You'll tell me eventually. I just hope it's before there are more deaths, because whatever's happening here, you're probably the only ones who can stop it." He took one final drag from his cigarette and threw it on the pavement. "You have my number. Call me when you decide to help."

16

Avery sat in a cafe around the corner from the museum with a large coffee and a plate of bacon, eggs, and toast in front of her. She sipped at her coffee appreciatively, wishing there was brandy in it.

"My day is not turning out the way I'd planned," Avery said, in between mouthfuls of food.

"That cleaner's isn't, either," Alex replied. He'd ordered a full breakfast, and Avery was amazed at the speed with which he was putting it away.

"Cheers, Alex. I was trying not to think about that."

"That's all I can think about," Briar spoke up. She was picking at her toast. "I keep smelling that blood."

El had ordered a large slice of chocolate cake with her coffee. "As soon as I've finished this, I'm off to look at my new grimoire." She lowered her voice conspiratorially. "We have to at least find a spell that will prevent whatever comes out of that doorway from going any further."

"I've been thinking about that," Avery said. "We could use a protective circle like we cast last night."

"It needs to be stronger," El said, dipping some cake in her coffee. "That wouldn't have lasted long. And we're not going to be there when it comes back. I hope."

"We have to find out who's causing this," Briar said. "I wonder how Gil and Reuben are getting on?"

Alex pushed his plate away. "Better than we are, I hope! Anyway, I'd better go. I'm on the lunchtime shift. I'll call you later," he said to Avery as he pushed his chair back, and then he disappeared out the door.

Avery watched him go, wondering what his final comment meant. Was there something more to, "I'll call you?" When she turned back to the table, El and Briar were looking at her speculatively.

El broke the silence. "He'll call you?" She grinned. "Is there something going on we should know about?"

"No! I presume he just wants to know if we've made progress later." Avery sounded evasive and lame. She picked up her coffee in the hope that someone would change the subject.

Briar shook her head, a sad smile on her face. "No, I don't think so, Avery. That's a different 'I'll call you.' He said it with meaning."

"Oh, yeah. There was definitely meaning there," El agreed, smirking.

Avery gave her a hard stare and then looked at Briar. "Er, Briar, you can tell me to butt out, but do you like Alex, or something like that?" Wow. How sad was that? She sounded like a schoolgirl.

"Something like that," Briar admitted, still picking at her now very cold toast. "But it's not going to happen. I think he's way more interested in you." She shrugged. "Win some, lose some."

Now Avery felt like crap. She didn't know Briar very well, and hadn't spent much time with her until this week, but she liked her, and for some inexplicable reason now felt really guilty. "Well, nothing has really happened. He's just a flirt, and he likes to keep his options open."

El shook her head. "I disagree. He acts the flirt, but I don't think he is, not really."

Avery grunted and decided it was time to change the subject. "Whatever. What do you think of Newton?"

"He looks good in his suit," El said, grinning.

"But he smokes!" Briar grimaced into her toast.

"No, he's smoking!" El countered. "Anyway. I also need to go. Avery, you need to come up with a better protection spell. I hear you're good at that sort of thing. What about you, Briar?"

"I need to prepare some stock for the shop, and then more research." She looked back at Avery. "If you can, get that spell prepared for tonight—we need to secure that doorway."

"You mean, break in to the museum?" Avery asked, shocked.

"Or, we could call DI Newton," Briar said, grinning. "He wants to help."

***

Avery opened the door of her flat and took a deep breath of relief at being home. She was lucky she had Sally as her manager and Dan to help out, or she wouldn't have as much freedom to pursue hunts for hidden grimoires. The last few days had been a whirlwind of action, revelation and danger. She did, however, need time on her own, and on Sundays the bookshop remained closed.

In one week her entire life seemed to have changed. While she had always enjoyed her magical skills, her magic was always benign. This was how it should be. She tended her garden, harvested ingredients, read books on the subject, and tested her abilities. She had hundreds of dried herbs prepared, access to fresh ones, and she liked to try new spells. She didn't know how Alex had known, but he was right. She got that from her grandmother. And yes, there was Alex. The other night their kiss had been unexpected, but not unwelcome. If she was honest, she really wasn't sure what she thought about it. And she had no idea what he thought; he hadn't said anything, other than the enigmatic—I'll call you.

She decided that before she did anything else, she would clean the flat. The mundane occupation would help her process things. For the next hour, she vacuumed, tidied, and polished. The cats either scooted out of her way or watched inquisitively.

When she'd finished, she headed through the gate and into her garden. The energies of the previous night had settled, but she still sensed the disturbance that the demons had brought. She followed the winding gravel paths until she reached the grassed area at the centre. Briar had done well. The grass was back in place and as smooth as a bowling green. In fact, it looked better than it had before. The plants from the surrounding beds were tucked back into the soil, and apart from a few damaged stems, looked none the worse for their ordeal. It was hard to recall the horror of the previous night, standing here in the bright warm sunshine. She suddenly recalled Briar's advice about water, so she pulled the hose from the shed and then turned it on the borders.

The events of last night were so confusing; she couldn't say where the demons had come from. It seemed that they had arrived as soon as she had opened the door of their protective circle and the ravens had flown free. Ravens. That was an interesting bird to have manifested from the box. They were bringers of news, dark omens, and wisdom. What a mix.

She could only presume that the demons had been waiting somewhere in another dimension for a manifestation, or some sign of magical activity, and had attacked as soon as the birds were released. It would have taken a huge amount of power to control them.

Avery finished watering the plants, turned off the hose, and then lay on the grass and closed her eyes, thinking again of last night. Could anything else have been there? She couldn't sense anything at the time. Maybe the witch who was hunting them had been above them, spirit walking. Or had at least had been above the town, waiting and watching for a magical disturbance. Alex hadn't been sure what had attacked them before, but maybe the witch controlled demons both in the spirit dimension and the material. Whoever they were was one step ahead of them. She laughed to herself. No, they were several steps ahead. They needed to do a lot of catching up.

The doorway to the other dimension in the museum was an unexpected development. She wondered if this was an easier way to control the demons. Manifesting out of the air must take a lot of control. Creating a doorway would require less energy. Well, once the initial sacrifice had been made. Two people were dead. Two too many. The sunlight played across her face, and it was tempting to sleep, but there was too much to do. She opened her eyes, gazing at the sky above. It was a deep, endless blue, with just a few clouds scudding by. Someone, somewhere would be mourning a loved one.

They had to seal that doorway. Did their adversary presume they were so weak that they couldn't defend the town? That they didn't care? She was determined to prove them wrong. She leapt to her feet, her energy renewed. It was time to prepare.

Avery sat at her worktable in the attic and pulled out several old books she had on necromancy, spreading them in front of her. They were filled with diagrams of circles of protection, summonings, invocations, and lists of the type of demons that could be summoned and what they could be used for. The diagrams were complex and she felt her heart growing heavy at the mere thought of doing them. She saw an image that looked familiar and reached for her own spell book.

Her grimoire was filled with spells, all written by different hands through the years. The first spells were written in ink, and there were blots and splashes in places, while others had been written meticulously. Some spells were illustrated, with pictures of herbs, roots, and images of the moon. There were spells she knew by heart because she used them regularly, but there were others that she hardly used or ever looked at. The more modern spells were written in ballpoint pen, and she had annotated several spells that she had tested and found needed improving. These she had rewritten, and there were many pages filled with her own handwriting of reworked spells and new ones.

But there were spells at the back that she hardly ever looked at. These spells came with a warning. Magic should never be used to harm, but many of the spells in the back of the grimoire were for exactly that purpose. There were warped love spells, spells to bind, to silence, to dull the wits, to confuse, to bring bad fortune, to cause infertility, and many others. And there were spells to control and summon spirits. While this didn't really include demons, she assumed the principles would be the same.

Avery turned the pages slowly, making notes, and ran through several scenarios in her head, testing out protection spells until she had something she thought would work. She grabbed her cutting knife and headed to her borders. She needed roots and fresh leaves—catnip, peppermint, chamomile, geranium, Solomon's seal, garlic. And she needed fresh seaweed; she would have to go to the beach. Some plants would need harvesting at dusk, but she could begin some preparations now. Of her dried plants, she would need mandrake, foxglove, and rose hips. She needed to make two potions.

While she worked, she wondered if it would be worth phoning her grandmother. She was in a home now, her mind a shadow of its former self. But of all her family members still living, she had the best knowledge of witchcraft. Her mother had walked away from it and White Haven, and her sister had quickly followed, leaving her alone. Her father had long gone, unnerved by the family legacy. But Avery couldn't deny her blood and had remained, working her magic alone. She shook her head. No, she couldn't disturb her grandmother. She had to do this on her own, but maybe, after tonight, she would visit her, and ask her what she remembered about the Jacksons.

Once she had what she needed, she headed back to her workroom and started to prepare her ingredients. She lost herself in the work as she meticulously chopped and ground the herbs, saying the necessary words. Circe and Medea watched her all afternoon until she had finished. Avery petted them and then headed down to the kitchen to feed them. She heard the thundering of their paws as they jumped off the table and followed her to the kitchen.

Once she'd fed them she grabbed an oilskin bag and headed to the beach. It was time to get the seaweed and make the potion.

***

Avery eased her van to a stop on the car park overlooking the deserted beach. The cove was virtually empty, as she'd expected. It was about fifteen minutes outside White Haven, and access to the cove was down a long, winding path from the cliff top.

She had chosen to come here because there wouldn't be too many people to see her small rituals as she picked up seaweed. As much as she loved White Haven, on a bright day like this, the harbour and surrounding beaches would be full of families and children.

A cool wind blew in from the sea, and she wrapped her cardigan around her as her long skirt buffeted around her ankles. When she arrived on the beach, she kicked off her flip-flops and put them in her bag, feeling the damp sand underfoot as she made her way to the shore. In the far distance she could see a man walking his dog, but otherwise the beach was deserted.

Avery headed to the rock pools, looking for seaweed still attached to the rocks. She trod carefully, and finding what she needed, brought her cutting knife out, its silver blade flashing in the light, and whispered the necessary invocation as she cut the seaweed free and put it in her bag. She wandered to the far edge of the beach where the cliff stretched into the sea, enjoying the silence, and watched the man head up the rickety wooden steps, the dog prancing around his ankles, and then he was gone and she was alone.

In a sheltered spot, out of the breeze, Avery piled up some driftwood and uttered a simple spell to create fire. She brought out her small, blackened cauldron and placed it among the flames, adding saltwater and chopping the seaweed into it. For a few minutes she watched, and when it was time, she added some of the other herbs she had brought with her. Passing her hands over the mixture she said the spell that would bind them together.

There. It was done. Wrapping a cloth around her hands, she took the small bowl out of the flames and put it on the sand to cool, and then stopped for moment. She had heard a noise. A soft sound, like a call on the breeze.

Avery stood and looked across the beach and up at the cliffs, but no one was in sight. And then she heard her name floating on the wind. She jumped, and a shiver passed through her. Who was that?

The voice grew louder and stronger, like a seagull crying on the wind. It came closer and closer, but there was still no one in sight. She grounded herself, preparing for whatever may come next.

126

Without warning, a man appeared on the sand a short distance away. He was tall and dressed in black, his dark hair short, and he strode quickly towards her. Her heart started thudding and she raised her hands. If demons appeared now, she was toast. She looked around, but there was nowhere to run. The crags of the coast were at her back, and rock pools lay between her and the sea.

She turned back to him, keeping her energy raised and ready to strike.

He stopped when he was a few feet away, allowing her to see his features clearly. He was older than her. Early forties, maybe. His dark hair was streaked with grey, and his pale blue eyes fixed on her intensely as he took in her every detail.

She found her voice. "Who are you?"

He laughed. "I'm one of you, Avery."

"What does that mean?" she asked, already annoyed.

"From one of the old families."

"Well, most people I know don't manifest out of thin air, so that doesn't surprise me. But which family?"

He laughed, showing even white teeth against his tanned skin. "I like your spirit, Avery, but then again all of the women in your family have a certain boldness."

She glared at him, not liking to be on the back foot. He was an arrogant prick on a monumental scale. "Excellent, so glad I meet your approval. I presume all of the men in your family have a similar streak of dickishness." She was being deliberately prevocational in order to wipe the arrogant smile off his face. It didn't work.

"My, my. How polite you are."

"Oh, cut the crap. I presume you're the one responsible for the demons?"

He smiled, but it didn't reach his eyes. "Maybe. I'm here to offer you a warning, before anyone gets hurt."

"Too late. Two people are already dead."

He shrugged. "Not our people."

"They were still people!" She was incensed and wanted nothing better than to strike him, but she knew that would be pointless. She had no idea how he'd appeared out of thin air, which meant he was clearly more powerful than her.

"Forget them, Avery. You need to think about you, Alex, Briar, Gil, Elspeth, and Reuben. You are in possession of things we need. We don't want to hurt you to get them, but we will, if we have to."

Her blood ran cold. He knew them all. "Can we skip the cryptic messages? What do you want?"

"The grimoires, of course."

"But they're not yours. They belong to us."

"To be blunt, you don't deserve them. You've let your powers grow weak." He looked at her in disappointment.

"Well, maybe now we have a chance to grow stronger again." She was making empty threats and he knew it, but she wasn't going to be walked over. And the more she stood there, the more she knew she wanted her grimoire. Now that she knew they existed, it had tripped a desire that she couldn't switch off.

"And maybe we have a chance to grow stronger." He tipped his head to the side, watching her reaction.

"No. Absolutely not. They're ours."

He sighed. "I'm not sure you should answer on behalf of everyone else. Ask them. They may disagree. I can take possession of Elspeth's and Alex's as soon as they are ready."

She thought for a moment. She was pretty sure Alex and El would tell him to get lost, but Gil or Briar? And then another thought struck her. If he was more powerful than them, why couldn't he just take them? Breaching their protection spells could be easy for him. Maybe there was a reason he couldn't?

"I'll ask them. But don't get excited. May I tell them who called today?" she asked with an exaggerated politeness through gritted teeth.

"Caspian Faversham. I'm not sure Anne will have heard of me," he said with a smirk.

And then he disappeared in a swirl of air and sea spray, and Avery was left alone on the beach.

17

As soon as Avery was back in White Haven, her mobile phone rang. It was Briar, and she sounded excited.

"Avery, I got hold of Newton, and he agreed."

"Agreed to what?" she asked, trying to pull into the side of the road while she spoke. She still felt flustered by her encounter on the beach.

"To let us into the museum."

Avery was silent for a moment, dumbfounded. She hadn't really thought Briar would call him, and she certainly didn't expect him to agree. "Are you kidding? I mean, you actually asked him?"

"I said I would. I told him we would try to close the doorway, and he agreed."

"Wow. I did not expect that." She gazed out of her window at the traffic which snaked its way through the narrow streets in the centre of the town. Sundays did not make the place any less busy. "What time?"

"Late. After midnight. But can we do it?" Briar sounded worried. "I mean, have you got a spell ready?"

"I have something that may work, but I'd like to see if El or Alex have had any luck."

"Alex is working, remember?"

Avery exhaled slowly. "I forgot. Look, Briar, I met someone on the beach, and he threatened us."

"Are you all right? What happened? Who was it?" she asked in a breathless race.

"I'm fine. He materialised out of thin air, and he's called Caspian Faversham. It's a stupid name." She snorted, glad she could ridicule him in some way.

"Who the hell is that?"

"I have no idea. Look, I can't talk now, I'm parked precariously. Come around to mine later, and I'll explain everything. And we can talk through the spell I've tweaked."

Briar was silent for a moment. "I'm not sure I can cope with demons again."

"I'm not sure I can either, so we better seal that doorway."

***

Avery returned to her worktable in the attic, and this time spread Anne's research around her. The need to find her own old grimoire was now more urgent than ever. There was no way that she would let Faversham get it.

Anne had been rigorous in her documentation. Her family tree was exhaustive and fascinating. It was strange to see her family line travelling back so many generations. Her finger ran across the paper as she focussed on old names, all of them unfamiliar except for the most recent and Helena; her name was a beacon for all the wrong reasons. She could kick herself for not going to the museum sooner.

And what if Briar was right? What if Newton was from another old family who had abandoned their witchcraft and their place in the town history? What did this mean about the DI? It seemed he knew more than he wanted to say. Any normal person would have scoffed at supposed doorways to another dimension, but he didn't blink. And moreover, who was Caspian Faversham? And were there others they had no idea about? What did these old grimoires really hide? She sighed. So many questions. Avery thought she knew the history of White Haven, and her place in it, but now she sensed there was a lot that had been hidden.

She soon abandoned Anne's histories, and instead pulled a couple of books towards her that described the history of White Haven. They were small imprints, written by local authors. One was only a few years old, and the other had been written decades ago.

She looked at the most recent. The cover had a black and white photo of White Haven on it. She skimmed the contents. It seemed the book described the history of the town from the Doomsday records, but a lot of the content was on the witch trials, and then progressed on to the smuggling in the later centuries—the Cornish coast was renowned for it—before it reached the present. She flicked to the back cover and found a picture of the author, an older man named Samuel Kingston, and wondered if he still lived locally. She'd check later.

She glanced at her watch. She'd text Alex and El about meeting later; she was sure they'd be around to help. But for now, everything she needed for the spell was prepared. She could finally relax and read.

***

Avery roused later from a light sleep, stretched out on the old sofa, her book on the floor. Shadows were creeping across the room, the temperature had dropped, and her stomach was uncomfortably empty.

She headed down to the kitchen to heat some soup and thought about what she'd learned from the history book. It seemed the Witchfinder General had come searching for several locals who were renowned as cunning folk— the term used for those who helped their local communities through pagan beliefs and healing. Although they were generally respected, when hysteria started to sweep the villages, fear superseded rational thought and a few were accused of witchcraft. Kingston mentioned the names of several women and men who had been interrogated, but she only recognised a couple. Helena's, and the surname Jackson, which she presumed must be Gil's ancestor. According to the records, two locals had been drowned through the testing of their witch abilities—if you survived the attempted drowning you were condemned as a witch anyway, and Helena was burned at the stake.

Avery was embarrassed by how little she knew about the actual facts of the investigations. All she'd really known about was Helena. She had no idea about the drowning tests. And disappointingly, there was no name of Faversham in the records, or Newton, for that matter. Kingston must have had access to all the records of the trials, and she wondered if she could access them, too. Maybe there was more he hadn't published; more names that could explain what had happened. Avery still couldn't believe that Helena wouldn't have used her powers to escape, despite what Alex said about saving the others. Something just didn't add up.

She sighed, frustrated, and took her soup and toast to the sofa and switched on the TV. She needed a distraction, something normal. Unfortunately, she found the news. There was a local report about the break-in at the museum and the cleaner's disappearance. At least there was no mention of sorcery and doorways to other dimensions. The trouble was, would it stay hidden?

There was a knock at the door, disturbing her musing, and she found El outside, looking determined.

"Are you okay?" Avery asked, as she welcomed her in.

El slung her heavy backpack onto the sofa. "That grimoire is baffling, amazing, and frustrating. I've already found out so much that I could use in my metal work, but there's stuff I need time to get my head around. And," she paused, looking at Avery as if wondering how to phrase what she was going to say next.

"Go on," Avery said. "I have a feeling things are going to get a lot weirder around here."

"Well, I now have spells to summon demons and spirits, specifically to help work with metals and fire. I'm pretty freaked out." She looked around the room. "Have you got beer?"

"Sure," Avery said, her heart sinking a little as she headed to the fridge and pulled out two bottles. She popped the caps off and handed one to El. "If I'm honest, I was expecting this. It seems there was a lot of magic our ancestors used that we're not comfortable with now. Necromancy was common in the medieval period. And it was all in Latin. The church condemned it, and yet the priests controlled it."

"But I really didn't expect to find this in our family grimoires." El took a swig of beer and leaned on the counter, her long hair falling forward and framing her face.

"I think we all have to expect it." And then Avery had a thought. "Hey, this is actually really good timing, El. I've been working on a spell to seal the doorway. Those spells in your grimoire could help—although I think I have one that will work. Have you brought it with you?"

"Sure, it's in there," she said, nodding towards her pack. "Briar told me what we're doing later. Have a look."

Avery put her beer down and gently pulled the grimoire out, putting it on the counter between them. She couldn't help but grin. "Wow, El, this is so cool! I mean, look at it!"

The leather cover was dark brown, and a triangle, the sign for the fire element, was burnt into the centre of the cover. Avery ran her hand over the leather, marvelling at how soft it felt, worn over the years by thousands of hands. She looked at El. "I'm jealous. I want to find mine."

El smiled encouragingly. "You will. I'll help."

Avery turned the pages made of old, thick paper, the handwriting changing as the owners had over the years. The language of the early spells was difficult to decipher, and some were in Latin. She found the spells about summoning demons early in the book, written by the witches from the medieval times. The drawings were complex, but made carefully and precisely. There were pictures of pentagrams, circles, double circles, inverse pentagrams, and invocations, all with instructions beneath them.

Avery took a deep breath and exhaled slowly, looking at El. "Wow. Again. Let's go upstairs, compare it to what I have, and see what you think of my spell. Although, I'm not planning to mess with the doorway. I just want to seal it into a protection circle."

"Sure," El said, gathering up the book. "I'm going to call Gil and Reuben about tonight, if that's okay. Strength in numbers."

Avery nodded. "With luck, we'll seal the doorway and won't see any demons at all."

***

The museum stood dark and forbidding that night, and the group sheltered in the shadows of the back wall. Police tape sealed the front and rear entrances, and the only sound around them was the crashing of the waves against the sea wall.

They had parked up the road, out of sight, and walked down, immediately heading to the back of the building where they couldn't be seen by the casual pedestrian.

Alex looked at them and grinned. "Is this ninja witch night?"

Briar shivered, despite the warm night air. "I don't feel like a ninja."

"I don't either, but I'll do my best," Reuben said, from where he stood next to El, his silhouette lean and tall.

Avery looked at them, and despite her nerves, had to laugh. They were all dressed in black—black tops, black jeans, and boots, and everyone with long hair had tied it back. Reuben and El had even pulled black hats over their bright, light hair. She looked at Alex. "Well, we do need to be discrete."

"Even with a police escort? Where is he, anyway?" he asked, referring to Newton.

"He'll be here soon," Briar assured them.

"I'm not sure I even like the guy," Gil said. "He could arrest us after this." Gil had been reluctant to come, thinking the whole thing felt like a trap.

"I'm not sure there are laws about prosecuting witches anymore," Alex reasoned. "Anyway, here he comes."

They looked across the car park and saw the tall figure of Newton approaching. When he reached them, they could see he had come dressed in similar clothing to them—the suit had gone. He looked more approachable in his casual clothes, and his short hair was ruffled.

He glanced at them at all, but spoke to Briar. "Thanks for the call. You did the right thing."

"We're not murderers, Newton, despite what you think of our beliefs," she said, a hint of annoyance in her voice.

Gil stepped forward, his face grim. He was shorter than Newton, but he looked up at him, meeting his stare. "Forgive my disbelief, but the police don't normally encourage magic on the site of a murder. In fact, the police, like the general public, usually refuse to believe in magic at all."

Newton's face was implacable, especially in the dark. All Avery could see were the firm lines of his cheeks and chin, and a dark glimmer in his eyes. "Well, I'm not most police, and I certainly don't want any more deaths in White Haven. Are we going to get on with it?"

Gil remained silent, trying to assess Newton, but Alex answered. "Yes, let's get it over with."

"Have you got what you need?"

"Yes," Avery answered. "It's all in my pack, and Briar's."

Newton nodded and led them to the back door, pulling away the police tape and taking a key from his pocket. Avery watched him as he turned the key, opened the door and listened for a moment, then stepped inside and gestured to them to wait.

Avery swallowed nervously, her heart pounding, hoping he'd return and that something wasn't already lurking. The wait seemed to last forever, but then he was back, calling them inside, and they shuffled in after him, the last one in shutting the door behind them.

The inside of the museum was pitch black, other than the broad beams of their torches, and Newton led the way into the main room. "Watch the floor. The blood's still here, but it's dried now. And don't go in the kitchen."

Avery glanced in there as she passed and saw there was a large pool of congealed blood still on the floor. The smell was stronger than ever, and she stepped quickly past the opening, focusing only on what she needed to do.

Once in the main room, she looked around, assessing the space and where best to position themselves. She looked at the archaic symbols drawn on the wall with renewed interested now that she had been studying others like it all afternoon. There were similarities, but also strong differences. It looked even more menacing than she remembered.

"So, what's the plan?" Newton asked.

"We have no idea how to close the doorway," Avery said, "so we can't prevent anything from coming through. But, we do know how to make a powerful protective circle around it, and we can make a devil's trap within it."

"A what? I thought this thing let demons and spirits in?" Newton asked, his eyes narrowing.

"It's called a devil's trap, but essentially it will trap any spirit, ghost, or demon form that comes through there. In theory."

"So, it might not work?"

Alex rolled his eyes. "Well, it's not something we do every day, Newton, so no, we're not sure."

"But you *are* witches?" he confirmed, his arms crossed as he looked at them.

Avery felt the knot in her stomach intensify. This was a subject they'd been dancing around with Newton.

"Yes," El finally said, looking him squarely in the eye. "Good ones. And by that I mean good in intent. But we're not as powerful as whoever made that."

"What were you doing up at Hawk House the other night?" he asked.

"None of your business," El snapped.

"I'm just going to get on with preparing everything," Avery said jumping in, and placed her bag on the floor, well away from the blood and the area they were going to seal.

Alex and Briar bent down next to her while the argument and interrogation about the other night continued. She pulled out a selection of candles, incense, her chalice, cauldron, the chosen herbs, and the potion she had made earlier.

Briar fetched a huge bag of salt from her bag and Avery's grimoire. "Here you go, Avery. I'll mark out the circle." She walked off and left her with Alex.

"So, how are you feeling?" Alex asked, watching her. He sat on the floor, his presence unexpectedly calming.

"I'm okay. Getting used to dealing with demons, I guess." She looked up at him, and he held her gaze.

"You should come over to my place later. There's safety in numbers."

Avery's heart immediately started racing, but instead she said, "Er, yes, maybe."

He looked slightly nonplussed. "Maybe?"

"You're distracting me, and I need to concentrate," she said, looking away and feeling flushed. *Was she suddenly fourteen again?*

"I make a great breakfast," he said, still watching her with a speculative look on his face and the hint of a grin. "But I'm serious. There's safety in numbers, and there's a lot of crap happening."

She smiled, but it faltered as she thought of her encounter on the beach. "I know. And there's something I need to share with all of you later. Something that happened earlier."

"What?" he asked, his grin disappearing.

"Later. We need to get this done."

He sighed. "All right. Now, tell me what we need to do again."

Avery had already outlined the spell she'd planned, but she went over it again before pulling another old book on necromancy from her bag. She flicked through it until she found a picture of a pentagram surrounded by a double circle, filled with images and runes. "This is the devil's trap. We need to draw it on the floor under the doorway."

"What with? Please don't say blood."

She grinned. "A mixture of my own design." She pulled a dark bottle out of her bag that was stoppered with a cork and cupped it gently, a warm glow suffusing out of her hands and into the potion in the bottle. She said a few words quietly under her breath, and the light increased, even as she passed it Alex. "There you go. I'll be with you in a minute—don't start it yet!"

He leapt to his feet, taking the bottle and the necromancy book with him. Avery called over to El, Gil, and Reuben, who were still arguing with Newton. "Hey, guys. We need to prepare the room. Here are some candles, and we need them placed at certain points."

The arguing stopped immediately and they placed the candles as instructed, while Briar placed some just outside the large salt semi-circle she had made that touched the walls on either side of the dimensional doorway.

While they were getting the room ready, Avery prepared the altar on the floor within the semi-circle, and she saw Newton watching. "Are you sure you don't want to leave?"

"No. I need to see this."

"But nothing will happen, hopefully. At least nothing will come out of that doorway."

"You don't know that."

She sighed. "No, I don't. Something may come out of it right now, and then we'll all be in trouble. But you know more about this than you're letting on."

He remained silent.

"Now who's being stubborn?" She looked around at the others. "Are we ready?"

They nodded and she turned back to Newton. "Stay back—whatever happens."

Alex stood ready to begin marking out the trap, the dimensional doorway looming over him. The rest lined up along the inner edge of the salt circle, the altar in front of them. Avery recited the spell line by line, the others repeating it. She felt the energy in the room start to rise as Alex daubed the floor with the mixture she'd given him, copying the trap carefully and precisely.

It took some time to complete, and as they continued to chant the spell, the air crackled with power and the complex design of the trap glowed in the muted light.

As soon as Alex had completed the final outer circle, he stepped back to meet the others, their hands linking as he joined them in the spell, and their voices rose on the air as if they had developed a life of their own.

There was one final step Avery needed to complete, and she reached for the bowl containing the other herb spell mixture she had brought, looking up at the complex shapes and runes of the doorway. It pulsed with a dark power that emanated from whatever was beyond; she could feel it far more acutely now. She sensed its malevolence and an age-old evil that was unlike anything else she'd experienced. When she started this spell, a large part of her was worried, fearful even. It was so different from anything she had done before, but now as the power of the others flooded through her, she felt excited at what they could do together. They were far more powerful than Faversham realised.

While the others continued to chant, Avery daubed the mixture on the cardinal points of the devil's trap, the salt circle, and on the wall. She then stepped back to the altar and invoked the Horned God and the Goddess, calling on them to strengthen the spell.

Once again Avery floated off the ground, pulled upwards by an invisible force as energy raced through her like a lightning bolt. There was a crack in the air like thunder, and for a brief moment, the devil's trap and the protective semi-circle flashed with a dazzling bright white light, throwing them all out of the circle. They landed with a collective *thump* on the floor, and the candles went out, leaving them in complete darkness.

For a few seconds, there was only silence.

Avery was bone tired. The floor felt cold, hard, and dusty, and the energy that had raced through her body had gone, leaving her spent and exhausted.

Gil called out, "Is everyone okay?"

There was a general rumble of consent, and someone lit the candles, their warm glow once again illuminating the museum.

"I don't think I've ever channelled that much energy before," Briar said.

"I think I need to sleep for a week," Reuben added. He lay motionless, looking up at the ceiling. "I'm not used to that."

"You did well," El said, reaching over to pat his arm. "You're just out of practice."

"But it worked," Alex replied. She could hear the excitement in his voice. "That was amazing."

Avery rolled onto her side and looked over at him, grinning. "I know."

She heard footsteps and looked up to see Newton emerge from the shadows, his face grim in the half-light. She sat up. "Newton. I'd almost forgotten you were there. Are you okay?"

He stood looking over them. "I don't think I fully appreciated what you were before." His voice sounded flat and hard. "I didn't like it then, and I certainly don't like it now."

Disappointment coursed through Avery, but what did she expect? He wasn't a witch, whatever his background may be.

"Like it or not," Alex said, "we have protected that doorway. Now it doesn't matter what comes through. It won't get any further."

Newton glared down at them, his arms folded across his chest. "I will be keeping an eye on all of you, and for now, I'll be checking in EVERY SINGLE DAY. And I expect one of you to come and check on this place *every single day*. Do you understand?"

Gil rose to his feet, belligerent. "Yes, we understand. But we're not the enemy, Newton."

"Well, until I know who the enemy is, you will remain firmly under my observation—unless, of course, you want to tell me exactly what is going on here?"

They remained silent, and he sneered. "No. I didn't think so. Well, I have a new job for you. You need to work out exactly how to get rid of that demon doorway so it's gone for good."

***

The group met at Alex's flat. By then it was nearly three in the morning and Avery was tired. The flat was warm and inviting after the chill of the museum, and they lounged around on the sofa or the floor, sipping beer or coffee. Avery had just told everyone about her encounter on the beach.

"So, who is this Faversham guy?" Alex asked. He lay on his side on the rug in front of the fireplace. "I already want to punch him."

Avery shrugged. "That's the trouble. I have no idea. He's not local—well, to White Haven anyway, and he's not in the written histories we have so far."

"Well, he seems to know a lot about us," Gil said, annoyed. "And Newton's pissed me off, too. We're not his bloody lackeys for him to be giving us stuff to do."

"Well, no," Reuben reasoned. He sat on the sofa, his legs stretched out in front of him. "But we want to get rid of the demon doorway, anyway."

"But how dare he tell us what to do! Like he controls us or something," Gil continued to complain.

"He was pretty mad," Briar agreed. "I'm not sure I'm comfortable with him knowing that much about us, but we don't have much choice."

"Wrong, Briar," Gil said, turning on her. "We could easily have broken into that place and done it without him."

"But we'd have risked being more implicated in the whole thing," El said. She was curled up in the corner of the sofa, sipping coffee. "I'm glad he was there. At least he knows we're trying to help, even if he was being a miserable git."

"What are going to do about Faversham?" Alex asked. "At least in our homes and at work, he shouldn't be able to materialise out of thin air and attack us. But we're vulnerable anywhere else. We need to know more about him so we can defend ourselves."

"I'm going to go and visit that local author, if I can," Avery said. "He may have information he didn't share in his book."

"That's a good idea," Briar agreed, nodding. "I'd come with you, but I have to open up the shop all week."

"Me, too," El said, and most of the others agreed with her.

"That's okay. I'm happy to go alone."

"I'll come, if you can visit on Thursday. It's my day off," Alex explained. "I think from now on, we should probably work together."

Gil had been silent for a few minutes, but now he spoke. "This guy, Faversham, isn't a ghost. He's real. Have you looked him up?"

Avery suddenly felt incredibly stupid. "Er, no, actually. I was busy preparing spells. I didn't think."

Gil pulled his phone out of his back pocket. "Let's look now." It only took him a few minutes. "Thank the gods for Google. Caspian Faversham, head of finance at Kernow Industries in Harecombe." Harecombe was the next town down along the coast. He turned the phone around and showed Avery a photo. "This him?"

She reached for the phone and had a closer look. His smug, handsome face was looking back at her, all smiles in his sharp suit. "That's him!" She passed the phone around so the others got a look at him.

Gil grinned. "Well, at least we know who he is now. Our enemy number one."

"I've heard of that company," Briar said.

"Everyone's heard of them, surely," Alex said, handing the phone back to Gil. "They're huge."

"And," Gil added, after looking after at his phone again, "his father is the head of the company. Mr Sebastian Faversham. And what a silver-haired fox he is," he said snarkily, showing them his photo, too.

"So," El said, "he doesn't mind us knowing who he is, or he'd have never told you his name. He'd have known you'd look him up."

"Eventually," Gil said, teasing Avery.

"Oh, sod off, Gil. I was busy," Avery said, fearing she'd never live this down. "So he's a powerful witch—or sorcerer. Do you think silver fox Faversham is a witch, too?"

"Probably," El said. "Feels like a declaration of war to me. Sort of—this is who we are, and there's nothing you can do about it. They have money and power. And he must be the one who placed the doorway on the wall."

"So he's a murderer, too," Reuben said.

"But we have what they want," Alex put in, grinning from his spot on the rug.

Avery nodded. "I presume then that you two," she said, looking at El and Alex, "are not prepared to give up your grimoires?"

"No!" they both replied.

"Good. Not sure how he'll take that news, though."

18

Avery spent the week working hard, both in the shop and reading Anne's work. Faversham hadn't reappeared, and there were no further deaths. Although their trap hadn't captured any demons, at least none had been unleashed on the unsuspecting community, either.

She had managed to contact Samuel Kingston, the local author, and had arranged to meet him with Alex. It was Thursday morning, and outside it was cloudy and threatened rain. They sat in Avery's battered van in front of an unassuming cottage on the edge of White Haven.

"Well, it looks safe enough," Alex decided, peering at it.

"He's a historian; what did you expect?"

He shrugged and turned back to her. "Maybe I'm paranoid, but I'm expecting a lot of weird things at the moment."

She looked at him properly for the first time after picking him up on the corner outside the pub. "You look tired. What have you been up to?"

"Oh, cheers." He flipped down the passenger sunscreen and looked at his reflection in the mirror. "I do a bit, don't I?" He ran his hands through his hair and gave her a rakish grin. "I've been experimenting with my grimoire. It was four in the morning before I got to sleep today."

"I hope you're not doing anything too dangerous," she said, starting to feel a bit worried.

"Just stretching my powers a bit."

"Like what?"

"Honing my psychic skills, spirit-walking, practising banishing spells." He paused, looking at her with raised eyebrows.

"All right, I'll bite. Banishing spells?"

"For getting rid of unwanted spirits and demons and other creatures that may cross dimensions they shouldn't." He leaned back, looking pleased with himself.

Avery had to admit she was impressed. And infuriatingly, his dishevelled, smug face looked just as handsome as he normally did—not that she wanted him to know that. "Great! So hopefully you'll be of some use now!" she said cheekily, and hopped out of the car before he could respond.

He leapt out of the passenger side. "You're not that funny, you know that?"

She grinned and headed up to the house. "Come on. Kingston will wonder what we're doing out here."

The cottage, like many in the area, was old with a thatched roof. The windows were small, and there was a pretty garden running riot with summer plants on either side of the garden path.

They knocked, and a middle-aged woman opened the door. She was dressed in a smart blue skirt and blouse, and she smiled at them immediately. "You must be Samuel's guests?"

Avery smiled back at her. "Yes, I'm Avery, and this is Alex."

She stepped aside. "Come on in. I'm his daughter, Alice. I'll take you through. He's so excited to have visitors and to be able to talk about his book. I hope you're ready—he may just talk you to death." She shut the door and led them down the long hall to the back of the house. "I'm heading out to work, so I'll leave you to it."

She led them past old photos and watercolours of the local area. The cottage had been modernised. The floors were stripped back to beautiful wood that shone with a high gloss varnish, and the walls were painted muted pastels. She led them into a conservatory at the back of the house, filled with greenery and looking over the back garden that was as packed with plants as the front.

"Dad," she called, "they're here."

She turned to them. "You may have to speak up. His hearing's not as good as it used to be."

An elderly man turned to them from a large cane chair that sat in front of a long window. His shoulders were bowed, his hair shot through with grey, and he had glasses perched on the end of his nose. He squinted up at them, and Avery smiled. As he saw his guests, he tried to rise to his feet with a beaming smile.

"Hi, Mr Kingston. I'm Avery—I spoke to you on the phone about your book. I've brought my friend along, Alex, if that's okay?"

"Of course, of course," he said, reaching forward and shaking their outstretched hands. Avery immediately liked him. He seemed so sweet and was so pleased to see them. He looked beyond them to his daughter. "Can you bring us a pot of tea, dear, before you go?"

She nodded. "Give me two minutes."

Samuel ushered them into seats; a small table sat between them, filled with papers and a plate of biscuits.

He smiled at them again. "I don't often have visitors wanting to talk about my book. This is a real treat."

"It's treat for us too, Mr Kingston," Avery said. "I was so impressed with your research."

"Call me Sam," he insisted. "It took me years, my dear, but I love White Haven. I've lived here all my life. It's my tribute to the place."

Alex leaned forward. "I confess I haven't read it yet, Sam, but I will."

He waved his hand as if brushing something away. "That's fine. You're young, you have time."

Before Alex could answer, Samuel's daughter came in with a tray containing a pot of tea, cups, sugar, and milk, and placed it on the table. "Right, I'm off," she said to him. "Got everything you need?"

"I'm fine. Stop worrying," he said to her.

She smiled at Alex and Avery over his head. "Have fun, then." And she left them to it.

After a few minutes of small talk, and settling them all in with tea and biscuits, Samuel started to tell them how he came to write the book. He asked, "Is there anything in particular you were interested in? I cover a lot of history."

"I'm interested in the witch trials," Avery said, placing her cup on the table and taking a biscuit. "I was wondering where you got some of the information from, and if there was anything you left out?"

He looked at her speculatively, his mind lively despite his physical frailty. "Left out? Why do you ask that?"

She glanced at Alex. "I'm aware there are certain old families that have lived in White Haven for generations, and you mention several of them in your book. Obviously there's Helena Marchmont who was burned as a result of the witch trials, and some others who were drowned. You mention the names of those who were investigated, such as the Bonnevilles and Jacksons, but I wonder if there are some you didn't mention? Some families that may still be around today."

He nodded slowly and sighed. "The witch trials were dark times, very dark. A time of madness, it seems to me. Neighbours turned on neighbours, you know. Old friends betrayed each other, while others tried to protect each other." He paused for a moment, thinking. "I wanted to say more, but my publishers wanted me to stick to the facts. They said I would be speculating, and we might upset any descendants who still lived in the area. They didn't want to risk being sued. I can see their point, but I knew I was right."

"Right about what?"

"I think Helena was betrayed."

Avery couldn't have been more shocked if he had reached across the table and slapped her. A quick glance at Alex showed he was as surprised as she was.

"What do you mean, *betrayed*?" Her biscuit lay forgotten in her lap.

Samuel took a deep breath in and looked out at the garden, his eyes narrowed in thought. Avery's heart was beating fast, and she tried to calm herself down. The old man might be getting excited over nothing.

He eventually spoke. "In the archives, you can see the old names, the ones who had money and stature in the village, mentioned time and time again. You've mentioned some, the Bonnevilles and Jacksons, but there were also the Ashworths and Kershaws." Avery recognised Elspeth's and Briar's family names. Samuel continued, "These families would have known each other, were probably friends. It's hard to say, of course," he hedged, spreading his hands and shrugging. "But they were of equal standing in the community, so it makes sense. But there were other families mentioned who were equally well known. One family were ship owners, wealthy, who lived outside of White Haven, but had a big presence in it. They employed people in their shipping industry. I mention them because they testified against Helena Marchmont, and I believe, because of their standing in the town, heavily influenced the trial against her—despite protestations of innocence from the other families I've mentioned."

"Who were they?" Avery asked, fearing she already knew the answer.

"The Favershams. Because of them, I had to leave their name out of the book."

Avery felt a cold shudder run through her, and she looked at Alex, trying to gather her wits.

"I'm confused. How did they know you were going to put them in your book in the first place?" Alex asked. He leaned forward, his elbows on his knees, looking at Samuel intently.

Samuel shrugged. "I interviewed them. It's part of the process. They're well known, and when I saw their name I thought it would be good to get a present day perspective on the whole thing, thinking it would be a bit light-hearted. I had no idea they would take against the idea so strongly." He thought for a moment. "It got very ugly, very quickly. Before I'd even got home they'd phoned my publisher, and that was that. I was going to look at other local interviews, but that got quashed, too."

"Did they give a reason?"

"No, not really. Other than that it would damage their reputation." He gave a short bark of a laugh. "It's over 500 years ago! Who cares, really?" Samuel looked at them, perplexed. "It was their reaction that actually made me more suspicious. Do you know that since then those archives have been locked?"

"Locked!" Avery finally found her voice again.

He nodded. "Most of the records are kept at the Courtney Library in Truro. That's where I got a lot of my information. Now, that particular archive is locked." He smiled sadly. "Money can buy you a lot."

Avery took a deep breath. "Wow. That's fascinating. Thank you, Samuel. You didn't have to share that."

"My dear, I'm getting older, and who else can I share it with? No one else can see those records now, and I doubt anyone cares to." He leaned forward, a twinkle in his eye. "Why are you asking?"

The last thing she wanted to do was endanger the old man, but he'd been honest, so she felt she should be too. "I'm related to Helena Marchmont, and I've become interested recently in what really happened back then."

His eyes widened with surprise. "Ah! I should have realised." He tapped his head. "I'm slower than I used to be. Of course, you're from Happenstance Books."

She nodded. "And Alex is a Bonneville."

He looked at Alex, who shrugged. "I guess we've both got the history bug lately."

"Well," Samuel said, "I wish you luck on your research, but I'm not sure you'll get very far."

"Have you got any copies of the old archives?"

Samuel shook his head. "No, unfortunately not. It was all in my old notes, and I regret to say I haven't got them anymore. I just didn't have the room when I moved here. I burnt the lot of them." He fell silent for a moment, and then said, "I never used to believe in witchcraft, despite the fact that I've lived here for years. It's a magical place, and the town thrives on the history, but I always thought it was all a bit of fun. But after meeting the

Favershams, I became a believer. Be careful around them. They're dangerous."

19

Avery was sitting at a table in a beer garden overlooking the sea and Alex sat opposite, each with a pint of the local lager called Doom in front of them. It was another hot day, just before the lunchtime rush, and they had secured a table under a broad umbrella that gave them some welcome shade.

"I think we need to go to the Courtney Library," Alex said, looking out at the sea thoughtfully.

"Now?" Avery asked, surprised. "What's the point? We can't see anything."

He turned to her and grinned. "We can see what it looks like, where the archives are, and check that the restrictions haven't changed. And then, if we need to, we can break in at night."

She nearly choked on her pint. "Are you insane? What do you mean, 'break in?'"

"We want to see those archives, right?"

"I'm not sure we need to. We already know who the Favershams are and that they testified against Helena. I'm not sure any more details will help." She took a sip of her beer. "What we need to do is work out how to protect ourselves against Faversham."

"But the more we know," Alex argued, "the better prepared we'd be. There might be a useful nugget of information about the trials that could unlock everything for us."

"And we might get arrested and learn nothing."

"We're witches, Ave. Stop thinking so laterally. We can spell ourselves into shadows, disarm alarm systems, and sneak in." He tapped his head. "Think!"

"Alex! I don't do magic to get sneaky stuff done."

"We don't normally fight demons and make devil's traps, either. Times change."

They were interrupted by the arrival of the waitress with their lunch. Avery had opted for seafood chowder, and Alex had steak and chips. Once she'd gone, Alex continued.

"We have to be the aggressor here, or we'll be trampled on. We need to up our game. I don't like being on the back foot." He took a large mouthful of steak.

Avery's stomach grumbled and she took a sip of the chowder as she thought about Alex's proposition. "I guess it won't hurt to look. And I suppose that also explains why there's no mention of Faversham in Anne's stuff."

Alex nodded and pointed with his fork. "Correct. And there may be more old families Samuel didn't think to mention, including the Newtons. I'd rather look myself and know for certain."

"I wonder if our Newton knew about this?"

"Maybe not. If we know so very little of our own history, why would he?"

As Avery looked up, she saw a man approaching them from across the beer garden and her throat tightened. "Alex. Caspian Faversham is here, and he's heading this way."

"What?"

Alex spun around on his seat, simultaneously pushing his plate away. They both stood as Caspian made his way through the tables and arrived next to them. He looked at Alex, assessing him. They were matched in height, but Alex was broader in build. Caspian was dressed in a shirt and smart jeans and looked like he was about to visit a country club; Alex was dressed in an old t-shirt and faded jeans, and his long hair was loose. They were like chalk and cheese.

Caspian gave a thin-lipped smile and acknowledged Avery with a dismissive glance. "Mr Bonneville. Why don't we sit?" he said in his irritating, condescending tone.

"Because I don't want to," Alex said. "Who the hell do you think you are?"

"Now, now," Caspian began, looking around as heads turned towards them. "Let's not cause a scene."

He sat on the bench next to Avery so he could face Alex, and Avery edged to the far end of the bench to get some distance between them.

Alex grimaced, but finally sat down. "I know what you want, and the answer is no," he said, cutting through the niceties.

"I see. Have you thought through the consequences?" Caspian watched him, his hands resting together on the table.

"Whatever the consequences are, it's still no."

"So, you don't care that your friends, or you, may die when I come to take your grimoire?"

"What makes you think you're stronger than us?" Alex asked, his eyes hard.

"I know I am. I have been practising my magic for years. You have simply played with yours."

Alex smiled. "Sticks and stones, Caspian. Those grimoires are ours, left to us by our families. You have no right to them. Besides, if your magic is so superior, what do you need our grimoires for?"

"Let's just say we are owed them, but were cheated out of them many years ago."

"Bullshit," Alex said. He paused, watching Caspian's face. "You know what? I think all this talk about the Witchfinder General is a cover for why the grimoires were really hidden. Our ancestors were hiding them from your family, and you've been waiting and watching. Well, you can keep on waiting. We're on to you, Faversham. Now piss off, and go tell your daddy there's no deal."

Caspian jerked back as if he'd been slapped. "Your family has always been stupid." He turned to Avery, "As has yours. You have no idea what you're messing with."

Avery once again felt the wind whip around her. "Maybe not, Caspian, but we'll find out. And when we do, we'll come looking for you."

Caspian stood up and looked at them both with disdain, but also with something else. Was there a flash of fear in his expression? "Another time, then," he said, before he turned his back and left them.

Avery took a deep breath and exhaled slowly. "I'd love to know how he keeps finding us."

"Probably a simple finding spell," Alex guessed. He grinned. "I think we successfully pissed him off. Although, he has interrupted a perfectly good lunch."

"What made you say that the Witchfinder General is a cover?" Avery asked, remembering what he'd said to Caspian. "We've never discussed that before."

"Just a feeling I have. It popped into my mind while I was looking at his smug, arrogant face. I'm right, though—I'd put money on it."

An idea started to form in Avery's mind, but before she could say anything else, Alex's phone rang, and he pulled it out of his pocket.

"It's Gil," he said, and quickly answered it, leaving Avery worried something else may have happened while they'd been away. "Hey Gil," he said, "what's up?" Avery watched him as he nodded, and grunted, "Yes, no, really?" He looked at Avery, eyebrows raised. "Yep, we'll head back now." He put his phone down and said, "Eat up. They think they know where his grimoire may be. They want our help. And we need to change clothing."

Avery paused, a chunk of bread halfway to her mouth. "Are you kidding?"

"Nope." He winked. "We'll put off our visit to the archives for another time."

***

Avery and Alex turned off the road and onto a long drive that wound through tall trees and dense bushes, until the drive ended in a broad sweep in front of a sprawling manor house. It had originally been built in the 14th century, but had been added to over the years so it featured a variety of styles. Avery loved it. It was old and welcoming, made of mellow stone with mullioned windows.

The grounds were extensive; a mixture of lawns, gardens, and woodland, and the garden directly behind the house descended in a series of terraces down to the sea, where they ended at a steep cliff. A large section of grounds at the front of the house were accessed by a different driveway, and housed Gil's plant nurseries that were open to the public.

Avery parked at the side of the drive and they headed around the back of the house and down to the glasshouse where Gil and Reuben were waiting for them. El was there as well, but there was no sign of Briar. All three of them were dressed in boots, jeans, and hooded tops. They carried backpacks, lanterns, and torches.

The glasshouse behind them was huge. It had a brick base with high, arched windows and a glass roof housed in cast iron above it. It was beautiful.

"What's going on?" Avery asked.

"We're heading into the tunnel beneath the glasshouse, that's what's going on," Gil said, running his hand though his hair.

"There's a tunnel beneath the greenhouse?" Alex asked, squinting at it.

"Glasshouse," Gil corrected. "And yes, a smuggling tunnel. Our family has a dubious history, and access to the beach."

"You'd always known about the tunnel?" Alex asked.

Reuben answered, "We knew about the cellars and the tunnel that ran to the ice house, and we think there's a tunnel that runs to Old Haven Church, but we didn't know about *this* tunnel!"

Avery started to feel excited. "Why? Where does it go?"

"Over there," Gil said, pointing to the small island that sat off the coast.

"Are you serious?" Images of dark, dank passages filled her brain. And of course there was the risk of drowning, which at this point overshadowed the fear of attack by demons.

"And how did you find it?" Alex asked, equally amazed by the look on his face.

"It's a long story involving family archives, Anne's notes, and our existing grimoire. And luck. We found the entrance just before we phoned you, but thought the more the merrier."

"Probably a good idea," Alex said, and he described their latest encounter with Caspian. "We need to look into something that can protect us from his unexpected visits—something that will block us from his search spells."

"I've been thinking about that," Reuben said. "I have an idea, if you're open to having a tattoo."

Alex shrugged. "I like ink. But why?"

"I'm working on a design for a tattoo that will protect us from prying eyes—including demons. I think we should try it."

"Well, I've never had a tattoo, but I'll try anything to keep Faversham away," Avery said, thinking that it was great that Reuben was getting more involved. "So, what's going on with you and magic, Reuben? Are you in, or out?"

He shrugged. "It complicates my life, and I don't like complicated. I like ink, the wind, and the surf. But I also don't like being attacked. So, for now, I'm in."

Avery nodded. "Fair enough."

"What's the plan this afternoon?" Alex asked.

"We've found the entrance, we're pretty sure we know where it goes, so we're going to check it out. And that's the plan," Gil explained.

"Simple. I like it. It's vague on the finer points, but hell, we were planning to break into some archives before you phoned."

El looked at them both. "Okay, sounds like you have more to catch us up on. In the meantime, let's head to the tunnels. Briar can't make it, and I've bunked off work. Let's go."

They followed Gil into the glasshouse. Long benches ran along both sides and down the centre. Tender plants jostled with seedlings and tomato plants, and the smell was rich and pungent. Gil led them down to the far end where there was a hatch in the ground, and he headed down into the darkness, his torch flickering to life.

"Why is there a tunnel under here?" Avery asked, feeling more and more baffled. She pulled her torch free as she spoke, preparing to follow the others.

El jumped in to explain. "It seems there's a heating system for the glasshouse, from way back. Pipes, a furnace, water. Very sophisticated. There would have been an outside entrance at some point, but it was bricked up and the chimney removed. And there's a hidden doorway. Well—not hidden anymore!"

At the bottom of the steps there was a room stretching the length of the glasshouse. It had a brick-lined floor and a low ceiling, the cast iron pipes clearly visible above them.

Gil spoke from the shadows. "This glasshouse fell into disrepair before World War I. The structure completely collapsed, and it was overgrown. It wasn't until the Second World War that it was repaired—you know, to support the war effort. I think that's why my crazy uncle never found it. We came down here as a last resort, really. "

"I'd almost forgotten about him," Avery said. "How does he tie in with the Favershams?"

"No idea. He may not be linked at all."

Gil turned and led the way to the wall where an old furnace sat. To its left was a long row of shelves, now deconstructed and stacked on the floor. Wooden panels lined the wall behind the shelves with numerous hooks attached, but within the panels a door-shaped black space loomed.

"Voila!" Gil exclaimed, looking pleased.

Alex laughed. "Wow. How did you find that?"

"By a systematic poking and prodding of panels and pulling of hooks."

"Yeah, right," Reuben said, his voice dripping with sarcasm. "It was *so* random."

"Cheers, Reu," Gil murmured. "And now, onward we go."

Gil set off with an enthusiastic march, and the others followed him into the passage beyond. Avery shivered. It was cold, damp, and musty, and she wrapped her hoodie more firmly around her as they headed further along the passage.

Their torches illuminated the brick floor and walls, which curved in an arch overhead, but as they went deeper the tunnel changed into bare earth and rock, the surfaces rough and unfinished. Water dripped from overhead, and the air smelt stale.

"It must have been years since anyone walked down here," Avery mused, carefully watching her step.

"Probably close to a hundred at least," Reuben called back.

The ground sloped downwards, following the gradient of the hill towards the shore, and then it quickly got steeper, with rudimentary steps carved out of the earth. Every now and again they passed brackets for torches on the walls, but the torches were long gone. Eventually they emerged into a larger space, where the remnants of broken and rotting crates were on the ground.

"Are we all okay to carry on?" Gil asked.

"May as well," Alex said. He looked around with interest. "Is this a smuggling cave?"

"Maybe. This could be where they stored some stuff."

Alex laughed. "Well, I wouldn't have taken your family for smugglers, Gil, but I guess you had to get your money from somewhere!"

"Sod off!" Gil said, annoyed. "We were doing people a favour."

"I'm kidding!" Alex said, rolling his eyes. "You know, you were probably stealing from the Favershams, and anything that upsets them is fine with me. I don't know them and I hate them."

"Why the Favershams?" Gil called back.

"Because they were a trading company."

"Good, I hope we really annoyed them," Reuben put in.

They pressed on, and the passage became wider and higher. Every so often a small clump of earth appeared on the ground as if there'd been a slip, but in general the passage looked in good condition.

"How long does this go on for?" El asked.

"Until we get to the island, I guess," Reuben said. "It's half a mile off shore."

They were now a long way from the entrance, and deep underground. Water streamed down the wall in places and it was muddy underfoot. The passageway started to rise again, and then opened out, and they stumbled into a large cave.

The group let out a collective sigh of wonder. The cave was full of wooden crates.

"Excellent! This could be it!" Gil said, as he headed to the nearest crate and lit his lantern.

"It's going to take ages," Reuben grumbled. He flashed his torch around and up, revealing a high, rocky ceiling. "I think we must be under the island now, so there has to be an exit here somewhere. In fact," he stood and listened for a moment, "I can hear the sea."

He was right. Avery could also hear the soft shush of the waves, and the occasional louder crash as waves hit rocks. "I'll help you find the entrance, Reu, while the others search the crates."

"Sure," he nodded, and they headed off to the far side of the cave, leaving the others to discuss spells to help reveal the crate.

"What if it's not here?" Avery asked Reuben, as she played her torch along the cave wall.

He shrugged. "We keep on searching."

Avery caught sight of sand on the ground and headed towards it. "Reuben, it must be over here." She saw an exit behind a jutting wall of rock leading into another passageway, a light trail of sand snaking down the centre. Avery grinned. "Shall we?"

"After you," he said.

The further they travelled, the thicker the sand became, and the louder the sound of the surf. And then they came to a dead end.

"It must be a hidden door," Reuben said. "After all, you don't want everyone finding a smuggler's cave."

"I guess not. Do you think it's sealed with magic?"

"I doubt it. Not all smugglers would have been witches."

They started to feel around the wall and the floor, looking for a hidden catch or mechanism, until Reuben shouted, "Got it."

He had reached his hand into a natural crack in the rock about halfway down the wall. Avery heard a *click*, and the wall in front of them opened a fraction down the right side. She pushed it open cautiously, but it was stiff from lack of use, and she pushed against it with her shoulders until it creaked open.

Beyond the door was a pale light and Avery stepped onto soft sand, Reuben close behind her. They were in another cave. This one was long with a low roof and the ground was covered with soft white sand; up ahead was a slight break in the rock where a pale light filtered in.

They made their way cautiously to the gap and peered through into another cave that opened up to the sea. It was empty, and there was no one in sight. The entrance to the cave was covered in brambles, bushes, and stunted trees, but beyond the greenery they could see the blue-grey sparkle of water.

"We're on the far side of Gull Island," Reuben said. "If I remember correctly, there's a huge hill of rock above us. It would hide any ships docked out there."

They peered through the branches onto the shore beyond. It was a mix of rock and sand, and sharper rocks broke through the surface of the sea. "They'd have to bring a small boat through those. It would be tricky to navigate," Reuben observed.

Avery turned towards the back of the cave. From where she stood, the narrow entrance to the cave beyond was completely hidden by the curve of the rock wall. She nodded. "Very cool. I wonder if anyone else knows about this place?"

"Not anymore, I'd imagine," Reuben mused, shaking his head. "From the sea, you wouldn't be able to see this cave." He slipped through the tangle of branches until he could stand on the shore, and he looked up. "It's so steep above us, no one could clamber down. Not unless they had climbing equipment."

Avery joined him, trying to not get scratched, and looking up realised he was right. "They chose this place well. I wonder how they ever discovered it?"

"I guess we'll never know." Reuben looked at the sea and the small cove. "I bet this place would be pretty inaccessible on stormy nights."

For a few seconds, Avery tried to imagine what it would have been like centuries before, with ships anchoring off the coast and trying to bring their goods ashore under the cover of darkness. She shivered. A lot of people died smuggling, and she doubted it would have been any different here.

"It must be weird, knowing your ancestors were smugglers."

"It's even weirder knowing they're witches," he said, laughing.

They sat on the shore, enjoying the warmth of the sun on their faces, and Avery turned to look at Reuben's strong profile. "You wish you were surfing, don't you?" she said, smiling.

"Not there I don't," he countered, looking at the rocks.

It wasn't often that Avery was alone with Reuben, so while she had the chance she asked, "Why don't you use your magic?"

He dropped his gaze to the ground and then looked at her, his expression honest. "It feels like cheating, I suppose. When I'm surfing, it feels like it's just me and the sea, and if I used my magic it would make it too easy. I stopped using it in my teens, and haven't really used it since. Until now, of course. The spell the other night to cast the devil's trap was harder than I thought. I've been knackered for days."

"Have you been practising?"

"Yeah, just learning how to control it, really. I forgot how natural it felt. It's coming back, though, quicker than I thought. I've been practising on the grounds and in the attic when Alicia's not around."

"Do you think she knows? I mean, about you two? It seems mad to me that you could be with someone that long and not know," Avery said, finally expressing her doubts about Alicia's ignorance of their magic.

Reuben looked thoughtful for a few seconds. "I don't think she does, but sometimes I wonder."

"Why?" Avery pressed, unsure as to why it should even matter.

"It's like she wilfully turns away if Gil even starts to talk about things that aren't everyday-normal, like she doesn't want to encourage the discussion."

"Maybe she's uncomfortable with it, and would rather pretend it doesn't exist," Avery reasoned. She could understand that. She'd like to do the same with demons.

Reuben added, "But he's been spending a lot of time with you guys recently, and she hasn't batted an eye. And if I'm honest, I think that's weird. I mean, I'd be asking questions, but she doesn't."

Avery looked back over the sea and had a very unpleasant idea. All this time, she'd been wondering about how Caspian Faversham could know what they were up to. Someone had to have told him about Anne and their research. *Could it be Alicia?* She knew Gil had told her a heavily censored version of their activities, but maybe she knew more than she was letting on. She exhaled heavily and chastised herself. It was a ridiculous idea.

"Why do you ask?" Reuben said, looking puzzled.

"Oh, no reason. Just curious, I guess," she said offhandedly. The last thing she wanted to do was cause problems with pointless suspicions; maybe she should ask Alex. She decided to change the subject. "Well, I guess we should turn back. At least we know there's nothing else hidden here. The others will think we've got lost."

She stood up and dusted sand off her legs, and then led the way back through the caves to the hidden doorway, both of them dragging a bundle of gorse in an attempt to disguise their footprints, just in case. Once through the exit, they sealed it off behind them, making their way back to the others. Within minutes they heard screams and shouts.

"Crap! What now?" Avery said, hoping it wasn't more demons, as she broke into a run.

20

Avery skidded to a halt at the entrance to the cave, smacking into the back of Reuben, who ran far quicker than her. She pushed him out of the way, wondering what he had stopped for.

The cave was dimly lit with light from the lanterns they'd carried with them. Faversham stood in the centre of the room, a vast creature rearing up next to him, made out of what appeared to be sand and stone. It seemed to have short, stubby legs, but long arms, and it swept them outwards, trying to grab Alex and El, who dodged out of its grasp whilst sending blasts of energy at it. She couldn't see Gil at all.

"What the hell is *that?*" Reuben exclaimed.

Avery didn't answer. She didn't care what it was, but she presumed it was somehow being controlled by Faversham, and he hadn't seen them yet. The sight of him looking smug was enough to infuriate her. *How the hell did he keep finding them so quickly?*

Avery summoned her powers and sent of blast of air towards him at a blistering pace, like a tornado. The noise of the lumbering beast was so loud that Faversham couldn't hear it coming, and he looked around too late. It smashed into him, carrying him into the far wall with a resounding *smack*. He fell to the ground, dazed, and the creature started to lose cohesion as it slowed to a stop.

Avery didn't hesitate. She loosed another wave of air and energy straight at the rock monster, and it staggered, turning towards her with a roar.

Instinctively, she drew on the air again and it lifted her clean off her feet until she floated over the ground. Without having any idea what she was trying to do, she rushed forwards, aiming a blast of pure energy from her hands towards the centre of its mass. The creature came to a stuttering halt.

In the lull from the attack, Avery saw Alex and El release a stream of fire at Faversham, who was trying to rise to his feet. He looked furious, but their attack caught him off guard and he scrambled for cover.

Avery renewed her attack on the beast, enveloping it in another tornado, until, with a deafening roar, it broke apart, sending sand and rock blasting in all directions. A large chunk of stone caught her in the gut and threw her backwards onto the pile of crates, the impact making her dazed and nauseous.

Despite the hit, she couldn't stop. Not now. She staggered to her feet, wobbling on the boxes beneath her.

Avery saw Alex and El standing shoulder to shoulder below her. Faversham was back on his feet, sending a jet of sand and earth at them. They struggled under the onslaught, throwing up a shield in front of them. Avery directed her magic at one of the crates and picked it up with a whoosh of air, hurling it over Alex and El. At the last second Faversham looked up, but it was too late and the crate smacked into him, crushing him beneath its weight.

Once again, Alex and El combined their powers and sent a stream of fire at Faversham's dazed and broken body. Although she couldn't reach them, Avery added her magic to theirs, enhancing their fire with air, until it turned white-hot. Unable to tolerate their combined attack, Faversham disappeared.

Avery collapsed on the crates, vaguely wondering what had happened to Gil and Reuben. And then she heard Reuben's frantic shouts coming from somewhere below her. "Gil, Gil, wake up!"

Avery sat up, and her adrenalin kicked in. Gil must have been injured. She slid towards the sound of Reuben's voice, the crates wobbling and sliding beneath her, and then she saw them. Gil was lying at the rear of the cave, covered in blood, and Reuben was cradling him in his arms. Gil was horribly still.

She half lurched and half ran towards them, until she fell on her knees next to them both, Alex and El arriving at the same time. Reuben was sobbing, almost breathless as he hugged Gil.

Alex leaned in close, feeling for a pulse, but Gil had a huge head injury, she could tell from here, and his head fell at the wrong angle. A wild panic surged through Avery. Gil looked dead. It couldn't be true. She wouldn't believe it.

"I can run back and call an ambulance," she said, feeling her voice breaking, as she desperately tried to remain calm and rational.

El was silent next to her, in complete shock, and Reuben was inconsolable.

Alex looked at Avery. "I don't think we can save him, Ave. I think his neck's broken."

Avery started to shake all over, as tears overtook her, and she sat back, letting grief flow over her. Alex was right.

"El," Alex called softly. "Can you—" he gestured towards Reuben, and El nodded, her face white as she eased her way to Reuben and put her arms around him, while he cradled Gill in his lap.

Alex crawled next to Avery and put his arms around her, pulling her close, and she returned his hug, wrapping her arms around him and burying her face in his chest.

For a few minutes, there was only silence. Avery felt as if she had fallen into a black hole, and the only thing that stopped her from slipping away completely was Alex. His solid warmth was the most comforting thing she could hope for, and she felt his head rest on hers as he pulled her even closer. His body trembled and she looked up at him, smoothing his hair away from his face. His cheeks were wet.

"What happened?"

He shook his head. "I don't know. I have no idea where that bastard came from." He paused for a second, thinking. "We were searching the crates and trying spells, and all of a sudden, Faversham was there, and he blasted us right off our feet. Then that creature appeared. The thing is, I don't think he expected us to be so strong. He demanded that we back off and we refused, and it all went mad after that. Gil was caught by that thing and got thrown against the rock. I didn't even see you arrive. I think he would have killed all of us if you hadn't come."

Reuben spoke then, his voice ragged. "I'm going to kill that bastard. He started a war he will *not* win. And all for a damn book."

Avery pulled free from Alex. "Did you find it?"

Alex shook his head. "No. Not a trace."

"Did Faversham know?" Avery couldn't believe that Gil was dead, and they hadn't even found the book.

"I don't think so. He didn't ask questions."

"We need to get out of here. Faversham could come back at any moment. And we need to call the police. We have to report Gil's death."

"What the hell are we going to say?" El asked, finally speaking.

"We tell them we came searching the caves, and Gil fell from the top of the crates. We keep Faversham's name out of it—no one will believe in witchcraft, and we can't reveal ourselves."

"And what about Newton?" El asked.

"We'll deal with Newton when the time comes. You stay here with Reuben, and we'll come back with help. Reuben," Avery asked gently, "are you okay to stay here with El?"

Reuben nodded. "Whatever. I'm not leaving Gil."

"No, of course not. I'll go with Alex, and El can wait with you." She looked at El, who nodded her agreement.

"And you better find Alicia, too," Reuben added.

Avery felt her heart sink even more. *How would she take it?*

"Of course."

Alex rose to his feet and extending his hand, pulled Avery up next to him. He looked at El and Reuben. "I'm worried about leaving you. Faversham might come back."

El reassured him. "He won't come back. He looked injured to me. I think we broke his arm. And he must have used a lot of energy to control whatever that thing was."

"Come on, let's go," Avery said, and they headed to the passage that would lead them back to the glasshouse.

For a while they walked in silence, Avery wondering how to broach the subject of Alicia, but Alex spoke first.

"Are you all right?"

She tried to hold back tears. "Not really, but we have to get through this first."

He nodded and a guilty look flashed across his face. "I'm wondering if there's some sort of spell we can use for Gil."

She looked at him sharply. "No way. You don't mess with that stuff. People die, Alex."

"I know, but Gil's been murdered! He's gone. He's our friend!" Alex was almost shouting, a pleading look in his eyes.

They came to an awkward stop, their voices resounding in the enclosed space.

"Of course he's our friend, but he's dead, and we *cannot* bring him back." Her voice broke into a sob. "We're not monsters, Alex."

Alex hugged her close again, wrapping his arms around her. Avery cried properly now. Big, long sobs wracked her body as she felt the shock washing through her, and she felt him shaking, too. Alex felt so strong and so warm that she wanted to stay there forever. But now was not the time. She pulled back. "I'm sorry."

"Don't apologise. I shouldn't have asked. It was stupid, and you're right. But I feel guilty. Gil didn't really want to do this. I'm afraid it's my fault he's dead."

Avery shook her head. "We can't do this. Not here. Not now. We underestimated Faversham—we won't again. Come on. We need to get moving."

"But where's the book? It has to be here somewhere. We can't have gone through all this for nothing."

A sudden thought struck Avery, and she smacked her head with her palm. "We've been so stupid! How can we have thought the book would have been in pile of crates used by smugglers as recently as the last two hundred years? They would have found something."

"Shit." Alex closed his eyes for a second. "We need to get smarter about this."

"Come on. We'll think as we walk."

Alex released his hold and the cold air swirled around Avery again as they continued up the passage.

"What do know about Alicia?" Avery asked, deciding she had to bring this up.

"Not much, why?"

"Because someone's betraying us. There's no way Faversham could know where we were today."

"He must be using a finding spell!"

"But he knows too much!"

"And you think it's Alicia? That's a big accusation."

"I know, and I don't say this lightly, but think, Alex! How else could he know what's going on?"

"But how does Alicia know? She doesn't even know Gil's a witch!"

"We don't know that. He could have been deceived by her for years." Avery stopped again and told him about her conversation with Reuben. "All of this started when I received the note from Anne. *Faversham mentioned Anne.* He knew her name! How could he possibly know that?"

Alex rubbed his hands across his face, and the torchlight flickered wildly along the walls. "I suppose that makes sense." He sounded tired and despondent. "So, what do we do? Do we pretend we don't know?"

"I think we play it by ear. It depends what she does now. Gil's dead, and it will be interesting to see how she deals with that." She paused. "Sorry, that sounded really cold, but you know what I mean."

Alex nodded. "I know. Are we going to tell the others?"

"I think we have to. Do you trust the others?"

"Reuben, Briar, and El? Yes! Absolutely."

Avery took a deep breath and exhaled slowly. "Good. Me, too."

"Come on," Alex said. "Time to call the police."

21

Avery woke up at three in the morning in a tangle of sheets in Alex's bed. He was sleeping on the sofa, and she wasn't sure if she was pleased at his gentlemanly behaviour or incredibly disappointed.

She had woken from a deep sleep with a racing mind and lots of questions. And then she thought of Gil, and tears started to well again. Gil was dead. She still couldn't believe it. She rolled over and stretched out, going through the events of the previous day.

It had been a horrible few hours. The police had arrived, and finally Gil's body had been removed from the cave. Reuben and Elspeth had emerged white and shaken, and all of them had been interviewed on site by the police. DI Newton had interrogated them all with barely concealed hostility, and said they were to remain at home and that he would see them all the next day. However, their story had been believed—at least by most people.

Despite trying to call Alicia several times, they couldn't reach her, and had instead passed it on to the police. Avery had felt immensely relieved, but also worried. "Where is she?"

"Gil said she'd gone away on business. She could be busy," Alex reasoned.

Avery just looked at him with raised eyebrows.

Reuben returned to the house with El, and they promised to talk the next day. El said she'd phone Briar with the news. The glasshouse had been sealed off with tape, as had the door to the underground passage, and finally only she and Alex were left.

For a while they sat next to the glasshouse, looking out across the bay to Gull Island. It was late, the sun had set, and a pale moon illuminated their surroundings. Avery wanted to cry again.

"You should stay at my place tonight," Alex said.

"No, I'll be fine," Avery argued, not wanting to put Alex out, even though she really didn't want to be alone.

"All right, I'll put it another way." He reached out to take her hand. He looked tired and sad, and the shadows under his eyes had nothing to do with the darkness. "I want you to stay at my place. I don't want to be alone, and I'll worry about you if you are."

His hand was so warm, and she remembered the comfortable way she had fitted into his hold earlier. She smiled. "In that case, yes please."

So here she was, sleeping in Alex's bed. She replayed everything again and again, and after half an hour of tossing and turning, she fumbled her way to the kitchen in the darkness and poured a glass of water, trying not to disturb Alex.

She heard him stir and he mumbled, "Are you okay?"

"Sorry. I can't sleep."

"Me neither."

"Do you want some water?" She could just see him as her eyes adjusted to the light that trickled in from the street lamps outside.

He sat up, half covered in blankets, his hair loose. "Yes, please."

She finished her water and then carried his glass over, sitting on the edge of the sofa as Alex edged over to make room.

"I'm sorry me and Reuben were gone so long. We could have stopped this," she said. She doubted she would ever forgive herself for yesterday.

Alex finished his drink, put the glass on the coffee table, and then lifted his blanket and threw it over her, pulling her close. His chest was bare and she leaned against him, savouring the warmth and his strong, muscled body. He smelt so good. She immediately felt guilty. How could she even think this when Gil was dead?

"Avery, what happened today is not your fault or mine. If you'd been there, you couldn't have surprised Faversham. We might all have been killed."

"Yes, but—"

"No buts."

He leaned in and kissed her, and she thought she might melt right into him. He was intoxicating. She wriggled under him and pulled him closer until they were wrapped around each other, their kisses long and deep. His hands slid up her back under her t-shirt, and she arched against him. And then he started to peel her clothes off, and she decided that staying at Alex's was the best idea ever.

***

The next time she woke, it was light and they were cocooned in a tangle of blankets. Alex's legs were heavy across her own, his arm wound tightly around her waist. For a few seconds she didn't move, luxuriating in the feeling of him lying next to her.

Her body still tingled from the memory of a few hours ago, and part of her didn't want it to end. She realised that this might have been some grief reaction from him, and if so, she would enjoy it while it lasted. She tried to remember what day it was. Friday. Avery groaned. She should phone Sally. She tried to roll gently away from Alex, but his grip tightened and he nuzzled her ear. "Where are you going?"

"I thought I should phone work."

"Bollocks to work."

"I wish. Sally might have heard about Gil by now. I should let her know I'm okay."

"In a minute," he said, kissing the back of her neck and moving on to her shoulder. Immediately, her stomach flipped and she closed her eyes. Sally could wait. After all, she might not even survive the day.

***

Avery had only been at work for an hour when DI Newton strode purposefully across her shop, the door banging in his wake. She was still upset about Gil, and Sally had burst into tears at the news, which had upset her even more.

Newton's grey eyes bored into hers and he looked grimmer than usual. "Miss Hamilton. We need to talk."

Avery sighed. "Sorry, Sally. I won't be long."

Sally looked between the two of them. "Take as long as you need."

Avery led Newton through the back of the shop and up to her flat. She headed straight to the kitchen and put the kettle on.

"Did you find Alicia?" she asked, her stomach in knots.

"Yes. She'd had her phone turned off."

"Was she upset?"

"What sort of a bloody question is that?" he asked, glaring at her. "Yes. She was upset. She's coming back today. Now, I suggest you tell me what really happened in that cave, because I'm not about to believe the crap you spouted yesterday."

Avery turned her back to him as she prepared the tea and desperately wondered what to say. She had to lie.

"It wasn't crap. Gil had a horrible accident on those old boxes. It's awful, but true."

His voice was scathing. "You're lying. Something terrible is happening in White Haven, and I intend to find out what. I'm on your side, Avery."

"Are you?" she asked, whirling around. "Because it didn't sound like it the other night when we sealed that bloody doorway."

He crossed his arms in front of him and leaned back against the counter, watching her. "All my life I've been hearing about witches, magic, and White Haven, and my place in it. I resisted it then, and I'm resisting it now. Magic should belong in the past."

Avery forgot about the tea. "What are you talking about? What do you know?"

"Not bloody much. What happened, Avery?"

"No! What are you talking about, your place in it?"

"Magic runs deep in White Haven. Our history is soaked in it. Something has woken it up. I think that's you."

Avery felt out of her depth. Things were happening that were out of her control, and now it seemed Newton knew more than he was letting on, too. And she still didn't know what to make of Alicia. Her fear made her angry.

"Nothing has woken up! I have always had magic, as have the others. You just never cared before, and now you do!"

"Oh, I've always cared," he said, stepping closer. "But nothing bad happened before, and now there have been three deaths in one week! And all a result of magic and demons. Something has changed, I know it has, and you are being obstructive."

Newton's anger was palpable, and she retreated, pressing against the sink. "I'm at a disadvantage here, Newton. You know what I am and what I can do. We sealed that doorway the best we could, and I'll be checking it today. My friend, Gil, is dead. And at this moment, I don't really trust you, despite the fact that you're a detective. You tell me about half-whispered myths, but you don't really share them. So, I'm sticking to what I told you yesterday. We were exploring the tunnels and Gil had a terrible accident, one that I will forever mourn. You don't need to fear me, or Alex, Reuben, Elspeth or Briar, in fact."

"Three deaths, Avery. You should be careful." He gave her one last hard stare and then headed to the door. "I'll be in touch."

Avery watched him leave and felt a wave of despair wash through her. What was happening? They had five grimoires to find, and had only discovered two. Why did Faversham want them? If his magic was so powerful, what could the books offer him and his family? Why had they been hidden at all?

There must be something else about the grimoires that was important, something that happened around the time of the Witchfinder. What had Helena and the others done that had earned the enmity of the Favershams? And what had this got to do with Gil's great-uncle Addison?

Avery's thoughts reeled. One thing was certain. Faversham wouldn't stop, and neither would she.

MAGIC

WHITE HAVEN WITCHES (BOOK 2)

UNBOUND
TJ GREEN

1

Avery waited impatiently outside the Witch Museum. It was 2:30 in the morning, and the small town of White Haven was quiet, other than the sound of unearthly grunts and snarls that came from inside the building. The devil's trap had caught something, and the warning she had set up had triggered, waking her from a fitful night's sleep. Any minute now, the other witches would arrive.

It was Sunday night, three nights after Gil's death, and Avery felt gritty-eyed and sleep deprived. If she was honest, she was happy to be woken by the need to do something useful. His death had left her tossing and turning, pondering what-ifs and maybes. She hadn't seen the others since then.

Avery glanced nervously around the car park. If that was a demon in the museum, and it certainly sounded like one, someone had summoned it. If it was Faversham, and she was convinced it must be, was he close by, or doing this from a distance?

As she looked towards the town, she saw shadows edge across the car park. It was the other witches, and she sighed with relief.

Alex blinked back tiredness. "How long?"

"Thirty minutes at most," she said, adjusting her backpack with her grimoire in it.

Briar nodded in acknowledgement. "I can't believe the trap worked. I've got goose bumps." She looked around. "No Reuben?"

Avery shook her head. "No. I didn't think we should disturb him. Have you seen him, El?"

"No. He doesn't want to see anyone right now." El seemed like she was trying to sound cool about it, but Avery detected a tightness in her voice that wasn't normally there.

"Fair enough," Alex nodded. "Let's get on with it. I've brought my new grimoire—there's a spell that I think will work."

"Excellent," Avery said, "because my idea feels shaky. And guys, someone must have summoned that demon. They may still be here." She turned to the back door and with a whispered spell, the door unlocked and they slipped into the museum.

The smell of blood and mustiness was heavy in the air, but stronger than that was the scent of sulphur. The noise in here was louder, too, and her skin pricked at the feral, inhuman sounds that came from inside the main room. A flickering orange light illuminated the doorway.

"What's causing that?" El whispered.

"We'll soon find out," Alex said, leading the way.

A shudder ran down Avery's spine as she saw the dark, multi-limbed, writhing shape, bursting against the constraints of the devil's trap. As the demon saw them enter the room, it howled, revealing a large mouth filled with sharp teeth, and its blood red eyes fixed them with a piercing stare. On the wall behind it was the occult doorway that it had travelled through. The sigils were alight with flames, and acrid smoke poured off them; Avery could see indistinct shapes lurking in the other dimension.

"May the Great Goddess protect us," Briar whispered. She stood, making her personal preparations that Avery was slowly becoming familiar with. She removed her shoes and stood barefoot, grounding herself ready to draw the Earth's strength.

Alex pulled his grimoire free and set it up on a small display case, working quickly and surely, while El pulled a short sword out of her pack and stood poised, ready to strike.

Avery watched them with interest. "What's with the sword, El?"

"After you used the ceremonial sword successfully the other night to help you channel air, I thought I would bind this one with fire—it's smaller and easier to carry, and there's a little something extra in there, too." She grinned at Avery. "Fun times."

"Well, that's one way of putting it."

"Alex, if your banishing spells don't work, what's the back-up plan?" El asked.

"A shit-storm of elemental magic?" Alex looked at them and grinned. "I've got this. Trust me. Just give me one more minute."

Avery took deep, calming breaths and tried to focus. Magic worked best with a clear head and a definite plan. While she waited for Alex, Avery watched the demon. The last time they had encountered them, she had fought them so quickly it had been impossible to study them properly, but now that this one was trapped, she could take her time. Like the other demons, it was made of fire and smoke, its form threatening but seemingly insubstantial. However, this one was bigger, with more limbs. Power radiated from it. It writhed so quickly, it was difficult to make out its complete form, or if it even had one. It seemed to constantly shift, one limb morphing into another, and its eyes moved around within what she assumed was its head. It snapped its huge, gaping mouth, revealing long, sharp teeth, and its growls of frustration were like hearing nails scraped down a blackboard. Fire whips struck against the invisible trap's walls, desperately trying to reach them.

Behind it, the occult doorway was fascinating, fire blazing across its runes and sigils. She wondered if the trapped demon meant the doorway couldn't close.

Alex shouted, "I'm ready! Repeat after me."

They linked hands and Alex started his spell. It was written in archaic English, and at first he stumbled over the words, but then he became more confident and they repeated the words together, each cycle growing in power and conviction.

The demon writhed even more furiously, its shape changing too quickly to register. Avery almost stepped back, its ferocity was so scary, but she held her ground and raised her voice, finding strength in its desperate attempts to escape.

Then, with an almighty crack, the invisible walls of the devil's trap shattered and a rope of flames streaked across the room, whipped around Briar's ankle, and pulled her towards the doorway. It seemed the trap still had some power as the demon stayed within its circle, but more and more flame ropes lashed towards them.

Briar slithered across the floor screaming and trying to break free, hurling energy bolts at the demon, but it was too strong.

El loosed Avery's hand and ran across the room, wielding her sword that now flashed with a white flame.

Avery wavered for a moment, but Alex tightened his grip on her hand, repeating the spell, and she drew on her power once again, binding her strength with his as they repeated the words faster and faster.

Elspeth sliced and hacked at the flame ropes, moving with athletic fury. The ropes shrivelled as she cut them, but she still couldn't get to Briar who was being pulled closer and closer to the demon. She renewed her attack, and Avery tried not to lose concentration. Finally El sliced through the flame rope holding Briar, just as she reached the edge of the trap.

With an insidious whisper, the doorway changed and they all almost faltered. Avery had thought it was open before, but as their spell started to work, the runes faded away, revealing the dimension in all its horror. It was like staring into a gigantic whirlpool of fire that stretched back aeons—it was time that Avery sensed, not space, and it was terrifying.

El grabbed Briar and hauled her across the room, both of them stumbling in their haste.

But the doorway was open for mere seconds. It sucked the demon back within its realms and the doorway shut with a resounding roar, plunging them into darkness.

For a second no one moved, and then Avery spelled a ball of witch light into her hands and threw it up towards the ceiling where it floated, illuminating the space below.

"Everyone okay?" Avery asked. Her heart pounded in her chest, and she felt a little dizzy.

Alex stood immobile, and then he grinned. "Hell yeah! I just banished a demon and closed a dimension—don't thank me all at once!"

"I meant El and Briar," she said with a raised eyebrow. "But well done. It was very impressive."

"Impressive? It was bloody awesome!"

Avery grinned and winked at him. "Only kidding. It's interesting that your grimoire has such spells."

Briar interrupted them. "Don't worry about us—I only almost got sucked into some infernal dimension. El, thank you. You were brilliant." Briar looked pale, and she held her hands over her ankle and calf for a few seconds, murmuring a spell. "That really hurts. It would have been a lot worse without my jeans on."

El smiled and looked at her sword. "This worked better than I thought."

"So what was your special something in the sword?" Avery asked.

"Ice fire."

"Is that even a thing?"

"It is now. Demons don't like it."

"Wow. This night is so weird."

Alex stepped closer to the closed occult doorway, pulling a large potion bottle out of his pocket. "One final thing." He opened the bottle and threw the contents over the doorway with a final incantation, and the runes and marks started to fade until they completely disappeared. "Done. Nothing's coming out of that again."

El looked puzzled. "But who summoned the demon? Where are they?"

Alex shrugged. "Maybe it was done from a distance. Wherever they are, they were trying to disrupt White Haven."

"Maybe it's a distraction," Avery suggested.

"From what?" El asked. "We've protected everything we can."

Briar stood and joined them. "Maybe whoever did this thought the demon would kill one of us. We're too good. I finally feel like we have a win."

"Come on," Alex said. "Let's clean up this place and get out of here."

"Wait," Avery said, moving towards the shattered display next to where the doorway had been. It hadn't been changed since the night they were last here. Underneath the broken glass was a simple ink line drawing depicting Helena, tied to the stake. She was wrapped in a cloak, and her dark hair was flying around her face as if a strong wind was blowing. A man leant forward with a burning branch to light the pyre beneath. Around the pyre, a group of people watched. Avery shuddered. *Poor Helena.* She thought back to their interview with Samuel Kingston. *What if she had been betrayed?* Avery had to find out.

Next to the picture was a display of objects used on an altar. There was an Athame, ancient and worn, its blade dull, the hilt patterned with an old Celtic design. Next to it was an engraved chalice, a ritual bowl made of silver, and two pillar candles that had once been lit. There were two dishes made out of carved wood, the traces of what Avery presumed was salt in one, the other traditionally used for water. The objects were laid out symmetrically on a white cotton cloth, all sealed within a glass-framed display case. Bundles of plants were lined up at the back of the altar, and Avery recognised bay leaves, rowan berries, acorns, oak leaves, and a spiral of hazel branches. She smiled, realising that it really was an altar, placed here many years ago, Helena watching over it.

An old leather book lay to the side, filled with pages of writing. It looked like a ledger, and underneath it was a sign that read: *"Final sales records from Helena Marchmont's business."* Avery flicked through the pages with avid curiosity. *Had this been written by Helena's own hand?* As the witch light glowed from above, a silvery shape began to appear on the open pages in the centre of the book. Avery gasped. It was a message.

No, it was a map.

She reached forward, brushing away shards of glass and reached in for the book.

"What's up, Avery?" Alex asked, coming to stand next to her.

"Look!" She lifted the book and turned it under the light. "It's a map."

He leaned in closer. "A map! Of what?"

She shook her head. "I don't know."

El and Briar joined them, Briar smiling. "This has been here all these years, waiting for you to find it."

"Could it show us where her grimoire is?" Alex asked.

"What else could it be?"

For the first time in days, Avery felt a spark of excitement run through her. After Gil's death, nothing had seemed worth it. Even banishing the demon and closing the doorway, although important, had weighed upon her shoulders. She had questioned what they were doing, and wondered if it was worth the risk. But it had to be. The path to her grimoire was right in front of her.

2

The day of Gil's funeral was overcast and gusty, which was exactly how it should be, Avery thought.

It was Thursday, a whole week since Gil's death, and the days in between had felt long and incredibly sad. Other than needing to banish a demon, nothing out of the ordinary had happened. Avery was grateful for the respite, but it was unnerving. She felt she was on edge, waiting for something to happen while trying to get on with life. She presumed Faversham had summoned the demon, but if he had, he hadn't waited to attack them, and their homes were intact once they returned. Maybe El was right and they had injured him during their battle in the smugglers' tunnels. Well, it wouldn't last long. He would heal quickly, and their brief respite would be over all too soon.

The shock of Gil's death had resonated through the town and it seemed the whole of White Haven was attending the funeral, which was taking place at Old Haven Church, perched on a cliff top overlooking the sea. It had stood there weathering wind, rain, and sun since the 12th century, and the cemetery was snuggled around it, crouched beneath gnarled trees misshapen by the wind. The church was made of huge blocks of stone and had a solid square tower. It was one of several churches in White Haven, and no one was buried there anymore—the plots were full. Only Gil's family status and the fact that they had a mausoleum had allowed for that.

As Avery exited the church after the short service that extolled Gil's virtues without making any mention of his pagan beliefs, she looked around at the grounds, wondering if some of her family might be buried here. They may be witches, but they still ended up in a cemetery like everyone else.

Briar sniffed into a tissue next to her, and Avery put an arm around her shoulder. "Are you all right, Briar?"

"Not really. I think I might start sobbing soon, and then I'd be really embarrassed."

"You and me both, then," Avery said, as she stepped to the side of the path, pulling Briar with her.

Alex and Reuben were two of the pallbearers, along with three of Gil's close friends from the business, and a distant cousin. They exited the church, leading the way down the path to the mausoleum a short distance away under a broad, shady tree. They all looked smart in dark, single-breasted suits, and Avery couldn't help but smile. She'd never imagined she'd see either Alex or Reuben in a suit. Reuben looked a million miles away, his expression grim, and he stared into the distance, seeming to barely register anyone.

Most of the town peeled away after the service, probably heading to the pub where the wake was being held, but El joined Avery and Briar, her eyes red and puffy. She had been sitting at the front with Reuben, and Avery gave her a wan smile as they followed behind Alicia, Gil's widow, who walked with her parents and a few close friends.

Alicia was a petite blonde with sharp blue eyes, and she wore a smart black suit. Avery had met her a few times, but didn't really know her well, and the only thing she had said to her all day was, "I'm so sorry, Alicia. If you need anything..."

Alicia had merely nodded, her eyes red, and Avery couldn't work out if she was furious with her for being part of the events that led to Gil's death, or if she was just in mourning. Or acting. She still suspected her of being a spy for Faversham.

Avery nodded in greeting to a few of the mourners who were joining them at the mausoleum and then slowed down so that they were far enough behind that they couldn't hear. She quietly asked El, "How's Alicia doing?"

El shrugged. "I honestly don't know. She's polite, but that's all. She's barely spoken to me, but I don't see much of her, so why should she?"

Avery nodded and kept her thoughts to herself. She told no one of her fears other than Alex, and they had barely seen each other over the past week, except for the night at the Witch Museum.

"And what about Reuben? How's he doing?"

El dropped her head, silent for a moment, before looking at Avery and Briar. "He can barely look at me, never mind speak to me. I think he blames me."

"You don't know that," Avery said, trying to comfort her. "He's grieving and angry. He'll come round."

"I've never seen him like this before. Whatever we had is gone."

Briar hugged her. "It will be okay. It will just take time."

The mausoleum came into view. It was an ornate stone building with a pitched roof, a double door made from thick wooden planks, and an enormous keyhole. Avery shuddered. It wasn't somewhere she would like to spend eternity. She'd rather be buried beneath a tree or cremated and scattered amongst her plants.

At the entrance the vicar said a few words, most of them lost on the wind, and the pallbearers carried the coffin inside.

The wind seemed to howl in this spot and the leaves above them rustled furiously, some of them flying loose and swirling around them. Avery looked around cautiously. She wouldn't put it past Faversham to be standing by and gloating somewhere in the periphery, but the only person now in sight was DI Newton, stepping between the trees and tombstones to reach them.

Avery nudged El and Briar. "Look who's coming."

Newton nodded to them as he arrived, and then for a moment he watched the vicar speaking to Alicia and her family. Avery had only spoken to him once since they closed the dimensional doorway, and that was briefly over the phone to let him know they could open the museum again. His dark hair was swept back, slightly ruffled in the breeze, and his eyes had dark shadows under them. He turned to Avery. "Thank you for closing the doorway. You should have called me."

"We had no idea if we could do it, and it would've been too dangerous for you to be there. Besides, you couldn't have helped."

"Even so, I'd rather know before than after—should anything like that happen again."

El jumped in, "Let's hope it doesn't. I don't want to have to deal with demons again for a while."

"Nor me," Briar said. "It's taken all week for my leg to heal."

Newton looked concerned. "Why? What happened?"

"Demons have a particularly nasty rope fire." Briar pulled her long black skirt up to reveal a dark red line that spiralled around her ankle and calf.

His face softened for a moment, and then he looked impatient. "You could all have been killed."

"So could you. You haven't got magic to protect you," Avery pointed out. "And you made it pretty clear you hate magic, and what we do. Probably best to leave you out of it."

She found Newton so confusing. He looked concerned, but also disapproving. She kept playing over in her mind what he'd said about his place in the town. He was unfathomable.

He watched her closely, his attention unnerving. "Have you decided to share with me about what's really going on?"

"No, have you?" Avery shot back.

"I'm not concealing anything," he said with searing impatience. He stood over her, his height dwarfing her, and she was forced to look up to meet his eyes.

"Neither are we," she said smoothly.

"So why did you steal from the museum?"

She hesitated for a second. "I haven't stolen anything."

He grimaced. "Really? Because there's a pen and ink drawing of Helena missing, and a book from the display."

"Maybe someone broke in after us." She kept her face straight.

He looked as if he was about to say something else when Alex, Reuben, and the others exited the mausoleum.

"Looks like we're done here," Briar said, glancing nervously between them.

"We are far from done," Newton said, and he stepped forward to join Alicia.

Alex glanced her way and nodded towards Newton, a frown on his face. She shrugged. Alex glared at Newton, and Avery sighed inwardly. More conflict.

She turned and started walking back to the church, the wind stronger now, and her long, red hair whipped around her face. She pushed it back, trying to restrain it, and mulled over the map she had found under the witch light, feeling only slightly guilty over stealing it. It was hers, really, and who knows how long it had lain there, waiting to be found. After studying it for days, she was sure that it was a map. The lines not only seemed to suggest a map, but also appeared to show the grounds of a house or a building of some sort. But she couldn't work out the key that would reveal where to start. A thought struck her suddenly. What if the grimoire was in a vault or a church crypt? It was possible. There were plenty of old churches in the town. She looked at Old Haven Church. It could even be in there.

Maybe it showed where Helena was buried? Unfortunately, that was a real mystery. Being burned at the stake meant burial in non-consecrated ground.

Avery stepped back into the church, the high roof arching above her, and was glad to be out of the wind. It was empty now, and the smell of lilies was overpowering. She sighed and closed her eyes, pondering what to do next, but her reverie was disturbed by the doors of the church opening with a shout. "Avery, we need to go."

It was over. Time to go to the wake.

***

Alex's pub, The Wayward Son, had been closed for the afternoon, open only to mourners. However, seeing as a large amount of people from the town were at the service, the pub looked as full as usual.

Reuben had opened a large bar tab, and the wake was in full swing by the time they arrived. Food was also served, and extra staff had been drafted in to take around trays of sandwiches and canapés.

Avery grabbed a large glass of red wine from the bar and mingled with the guests, managing to find Sally and Dan and some of her other friends who she felt she'd been neglecting lately. Sally hadn't said much about Gil's death, but Avery knew she suspected something other than the official story. She finally worked her way to Reuben's side. He had taken off his jacket and loosened his tie, and he had a very healthy measure of whiskey in hand. He glanced down at her, a wan smile on his face.

"I've been wanting to talk to you all day. How are you?" Avery asked, worried.

"I'm okay." He shrugged, his eyes meeting hers briefly before he glanced around the pub. "It's been a difficult few days."

"Of course. Lovely to see how many people are here, though."

"Yeah." He lowered his voice, turning away from the room slightly. "We need to meet again, I suppose. To discuss, you know…"

"When you're ready."

Reuben nodded and sighed heavily. "I've been left the house, not Alicia. That was a shock."

"Really?" Avery was surprised for a moment that he was bringing it up, and then she shook her head. "You know what—it should be left to you. It's your family home. You live there, too." Which was true. The house was huge, and he lived in a suite of rooms on one of the floors.

"I feel weird about it."

"Don't. Gil's no fool. I presume he left Alicia a good amount of money?"

He nodded. "She's not very happy. It made me think about what we were talking about the other day."

Avery recalled their conversation in the cave on Gull Island, the questions she asked about Alicia, while trying not to voice her doubts about her. Her heart started racing. "Why? Has something happened?"

"She's been weird. More than just mad at not being left the house."

Avery looked around while he was talking and saw Alicia across the room, white wine in hand, glaring at her through the crowd of people. It was as if she could hear their conversation. Avery smiled nervously and turned back to Reuben.

"I wasn't sure you'd want to be involved anymore."

"None of us has a choice," he said enigmatically. "We'll all need to meet. Just give me a few more days."

***

Alex found Avery in the back room of the pub where she'd gone to get some quiet. There was something about this room. It had a feeling of peace and space. She sat at a table on her own, gazing out the window. A fine rain had started to fall, and it blew almost sideways across the courtyard. She was debating at what time it would be polite to leave, when Alex pulled out a chair and sat opposite her.

"The table where we had our first date," he said, grinning, referring to where they'd had dinner only a short time ago.

It felt like a lifetime had passed since then. The thought was immediately followed by the memory of their night together only last week, and she tried to pull herself together. If Avery was honest, she thought about it often, not that she would tell him that.

"You're so funny."

"I know."

She decided to move on. "Have you spelled this room? It's always quiet in here."

"Maybe a little. I like to think some patrons deserve a little peace and quiet. It discourages the rowdy bunch."

Avery nodded. "I like it."

Alex leaned forward, and she could feel his body heat across the small table. "I've been thinking about the Courtney Library. We need to go tomorrow."

That was the last thing Avery had been thinking about, and she looked at him in shock. "Tomorrow?"

"Yes. We've lost a whole week. I don't want anyone else to die, Avery." He looked at her, serious suddenly. "This shit's got real. Gil's dead, there's demons and doorways to other dimensions. It's like White Haven has turned into the Hell mouth. This could just be the start. I don't like being on the back foot."

She closed her eyes and sighed for a second. "You're right. And I need help, anyway." She wondered at what point in the past week she had started trusting and relying on Alex Bonneville. *Life was really weird right now.*

"Why?" His attention was fixed solely on her. It was unnerving, like being caught in a giant floodlight.

"Helena's map. I'm stuck. I have no idea where to look."

"I'm sure we'll work it out. I'll pick you up after my shift here—that okay?'"

"Do we even know where to look?" Avery was flooded with worry, feeling unprepared.

"Trust me. And leave Newton out of this. He seems to be sniffing around a lot."

"He's a detective! That's what they do. And I'm not about to tell him I'm breaking in somewhere. *Again*." She looked at him in disbelief.

He grunted. "Whatever."

"Have you thought any more about Alicia?"

"Not really. I've been too busy here, but it does seem to have gone quiet all of a sudden."

Avery had another thought. "I hear one of the pallbearers is a distant cousin of Gil's. Does he know magic, or about anything to do with their family history?"

Alex rolled his eyes. "I carried a coffin with him—I'm not his best mate!"

Now Avery rolled her eyes. "It was just a thought! I'll ask Reuben. Or better still, I'll ask El. Women are much better at that kind of thing."

Alex smirked. "What, gossip?"

"*Talking.* In fact, I'll do it myself." She gave him a triumphant smile.

"All right then, Miss Marple." He glanced up. "Now's your chance, he's right there."

Avery turned to see an older man with light brown hair streaked with grey in the doorway between the two rooms. He looked lost as he entered the back room, looking around a little sadly. Avery ached to see him looking so alone and she glared at Alex, an unspoken urge for an introduction.

"All right. I'll pick you up at eleven o'clock tomorrow night. Be ready." Alex rose to his feet and called out, "Lindon. There's someone I'd like you to meet."

Avery stood as Lindon approached their table, glancing between the two of them. Alex introduced them and then excused himself, leaving them alone.

"Have a seat," Avery said, smiling as she sat down and sipped her wine. "I just wanted to say how sorry I am. Gil was a really amazing man."

Lindon nodded, gazing into his own drink for a moment before looking up. Avery was struck by how similar his eyes were to Gil's. "Thank you. I haven't seen him in years, not since his wedding. I really didn't think I'd be at his funeral, too."

Avery wanted to ask him about magic, but was unsure how to go about it. "You don't live in White Haven, then?"

"No. Our side of the family decided many years ago that White Haven wasn't for us."

"Why's that?"

He looked at her quizzically. "I think you know."

She swallowed. "Maybe I do."

"My family has always thought our special skills complicated life, and I've kept away from it."

"I don't know how you do that. To me, it's as natural as breathing."

"It's like a lifelong diet—you get used to it."

Avery decided she might as well cut to the chase. "Do you know anything about your old great-uncle Addison?"

"Please don't tell me you think he had something to do with this."

Avery blinked and sat back, perplexed. That wasn't the answer she'd expected. She thought he'd look at her blankly. "Do you know him? Or know of him, and the fact that he disappeared with his family?"

"Don't you mean he was banished?"

"How can you know that when Gil didn't have a clue?"

Lindon gazed out of the window at the swirling wind and rain as it splattered across the pane. It was getting worse, gearing up into a full-on storm. He thought for a few moments and then turned to face her again, weariness as well as grief etched across his features. "He's one of the reasons we left, Avery. Black magic. He sacrificed his family for knowledge. They didn't disappear. He killed them."

Avery almost dropped her drink in shock. "How do you know *that*?"

"My great-grandmother, Felicity, was the youngest sister of Addison— we're not first cousins, just in case you wondered. There was an incident one night, screams, a trail of blood, an altar found in the woods behind the house. The details were not known to my great-grandmother, but steps were taken, and Addison was banished. He was so arrogant, he thought he could get away with it. He was wrong. Magic was a dirty word for years. That story has been told through the generations of our family as a reminder of why not to do magic at all. We don't forget."

"But that's not what magic is!" Avery cried, desperate to defend what she loved. "That was an abomination."

"Is it? Gil's dead."

"There has always been black magic, but there's always been good, too." She sensed she was losing him. "Do you know where Addison went?"

"No, I don't ever want to know." He looked at his watch. "Anyway, I'm going. I have a long drive back."

"You're not staying here tonight?"

"No, I won't stay in White Haven." He stood, easing his chair back. "It was good to meet you, Avery. I'm sorry if I sounded bleak, I know you mean well. Stay safe."

Avery watched him go, and her tears welled up. White Haven was her home, a magical place in many ways, but now, half of her wished she was leaving with him.

3

The next night, Alex arrived at eleven promptly, the engine of his Alfa Romeo Spider Boat Tail idling under her front window.

Avery slipped into his passenger seat dressed all in black—combat trousers, a t-shirt, leather jacket, and boots. "I'm not sure I'm ready for this."

He grinned, his teeth gleaming in the dim light. His hair was knotted up on the top of his head, and stubble grazed his cheeks. "You look ready," he said, easing the car down the street and heading out of the town.

"It's an illusion. I've spent most of the evening sleeping, and then panicking about being arrested. Weren't we going to scope this place out in the light first?"

"No time. We'll be fine, you worry too much."

He concentrated on the road, driving fast but confidently, and Avery leaned back in the seat, glancing between him and the view outside. The lanes of White Haven quickly turned into main roads as Alex headed for the A390 into Truro. At this hour the road was quiet and they made good time.

Sitting this close to Alex was increasingly unnerving. Avery was acutely aware of his build and height and his musky, masculine scent, and found her gaze lingering over his strong forearms and hands as they gripped the wheel. She flushed remembering the feeling of his hands on her body, and she turned away in an attempt to subdue her desire.

He broke the silence that had fallen between them. "So, how are you? The last week's been pretty rough."

"I'm okay, just getting through the day, and trying not to be paranoid about being stalked by Faversham. What about you?"

"I'm trying not to think about killing Faversham, because at the moment, that's all I want to do." He glanced across at her. "Don't you?"

"Yes, but we're not ready yet. I'm not sure I ever will be." Fear swept through her. "You don't mean that, anyway. We're not killers. We'll find another way."

"If he touches you, I *will* kill him."

Avery could barely believe her ears and for a second she struggled to think of something to say. She looked at him as he gazed fiercely ahead, and she decided to make light of it. "Well, I'll make sure he doesn't."

"I mean it."

Avery softened and smiled. "Thank you." She half wondered if she should say something about the other night, and the air in the car seemed to thicken with meaning, but she didn't want to spoil whatever it was that seemed to be there between them. She laughed to break the tension. "I hope he doesn't hurt you, either—I don't think I'm suited to a killing spree. I'm worried enough about raiding a library!"

"You're powerful, more than you know. Look what you did the other night. You were *flying* the night Gil was killed! You actually flew across that room." He glanced at her again, his eyes dark and intense. "Don't tell me you haven't been thinking about that."

"Actually, I haven't." She meant it, too. Gil's death had eclipsed everything. "It all happened in such a rush with this outpouring of fury, and then Gil died, and well…"She shrugged. "I sort of forgot."

"Can you remember what caused it?"

Avery hesitated for a second as she thought back to that moment when she emerged from the passageway behind Reuben. "Pure, blind anger, and the need to stop Faversham and that rock beast from attacking you and El. I literally pulled out everything I could, really focused my power. I needed to act fast, and I knew it." She shuffled in her seat. "What about you and El? You were both channelling some strong power."

"It's ironic, isn't it? Faversham's clearly scared of us finding the books and using them, and yet the fact that he's attacking us is making us draw on reserves of power we never even knew we had."

"He accused us of wasting our power. He's probably right."

"Not anymore, we're not."

"Have you had any more visions?"

"Every night."

Avery looked at him in shock. "Really? What do they show you?"

"Versions of the same thing—black eyes, fires, heat, death. I thought they'd go after Gil died, but they haven't. Are you still reading the cards?"

"Every day. They change, of course, but the threat's still there. There's more than just Faversham, isn't there?"

"I think so," he said sadly.

For a while they made idle chat, until they entered the outskirts of Truro. By now it was after midnight and the roads were mostly empty. Alex cruised through the town, crossed the Truro River, and headed for the Royal Cornwall Museum. It was in the centre of town, and the surrounding streets still had a few people exiting pubs and clubs. Alex stuck to the back streets towards The Leats and turned up a side street to park on a residential road.

"I presume they have a back door?" Avery said, her heart now beating uncomfortably fast.

"Of course. Time to use a little magic."

They had already agreed on the spell they would use, and with a short incantation they were both shrouded in shadows, the spell also ensuring that if anyone saw them, their gaze would slide away.

Avery followed Alex as his tall figure slipped through the streets to the back of the building where an inconspicuous door sat in the wall.

The museum was huge, stretching from River Street where the main entrance was, to The Leats at the back. It was constructed in the 19th century out of large blocks of grey stone, and was solid and imposing.

"Where's the library?" Avery asked, glancing down the street. It was deserted.

"You can only access it from in the museum," Alex whispered.

A security camera was mounted above them. While Alex worked on the lock, Avery used magic to manipulate the angle slightly up and across their heads, pointing away from the door. With a *click*, the door opened, and they slipped inside.

They were in a narrow passage that led into the centre of the building. Immediately to their left was a panel on the wall that housed the security system controls, and the lights blinked, starting to flash red. Alex held his hand over them and within seconds they turned green again. The pair stood still for a few moments, letting their eyes adjust to the dark, but the building was silent. Another security camera sat above them on the wall, and with a whisper Avery disabled it, the red light blinking off.

Alex conjured a witch light and led the way quickly down the passage. They passed offices and storerooms until they reached large wooden double doors, and pushing through them found themselves in the grand central hall. Avery gasped in pleasure. It rose to a high ceiling, the height of the building, and the centre of the hall was filled with glass displays of various objects. Avery took a quick look at the closest one and found that it displayed pots and ceramics that had been found in archaeological digs in Cornwall. In the centre of the room was an old carriage with huge, red wheels.

At the rear of the hall was a sweeping set of stairs that led up to the first floor. Above them, running around the room at the level of the first floor was a mezzanine, edged with a white balustrade, behind which were more display cabinets.

"This place is bigger than I thought," Avery whispered to Alex.

"This is all on their website. The front entrance is through there," he said, pointing to the far side. "I'll grab a guide."

For a few minutes Avery stood alone, hearing Alex's footsteps fading away, and she listened nervously for anything else, but he was quickly back, and he led the way up the stairs and through the galleries on the first floor. Avery paused for a few seconds when they passed the De Pass Gallery, the displays of ancient Egyptian artefacts catching her eye. Alex was quickly at her side, grabbing her hand. "I'll bring you back in the daytime if you want to sightsee," he said impatiently.

They kept going until they reached the far end of the first floor, and within minutes were in front of the double doors of the Courtney Library, its name in brass on the wall above.

The door was locked, but again they enchanted the lock open, and passed through to find a plush-carpeted section with a small reception area, and a few computer terminals behind a desk. The library stretched away ahead of them, the shelves high and densely packed with books. The smell of age-old paper was thick in the air, and Avery breathed deeply, enjoying its comforting and familiar scent.

Alex shut the door behind them and locked it again. "We need to find the archives. You head that way, and I'll try this one," he said, pointing to the right for Avery.

She nodded and passed down the stacks, seeing small rooms leading off the main one with different collections housed within. At the end of the main room was a smaller than usual black door, and she opened it to find a narrow set of stairs leading upward.

She turned and called in a low voice, "Alex!"

He appeared out of the darkness, his skin pale under the strange, luminous white of the witch light. "Found it?"

"Maybe. Did you find anything?"

"Books, books, and more books."

Avery nodded and led the way up the steep and narrow stairs. The decoration was minimal here, and the carpet was thin and worn. They reached a small landing, and after turning saw a warren of rooms with low ceilings stretching ahead of them. These must have been the old servants' quarters or attics—she wasn't sure if it had ever been a private house.

"Bollocks," Alex said. "This is a maze."

Avery's heart sank. "Do you think this is it? Because we're going to waste a lot of time if not."

Alex pointed to a sign on the wall that read, Archives. You must be accompanied by a librarian at all times.

"Great, let's make this quick."

Fortunately, the rooms were clearly signposted, their contents described in decades, subjects, or centuries.

They passed the first few, quickly dismissing them, and then came to a room on their right, labelled *Sixteenth Century Manuscripts*. Metal shelving filled with box files ran down the centre of the space.

They exchanged a quick glance of relief and headed inside, moving to either side of the central stack to search more efficiently. Every now and again Avery pulled a box out to scan its contents, and although she found lots of intriguing papers and treatises on agriculture and the local area, there was nothing about the witch trials. She stood back, frustrated, and looked up and around. A wave of tiredness and despair swept over her. *What was she doing?* She was a respectable witch. She didn't break into buildings and raid other people's property.

"I can hear you huffing from here," Alex called softly from the other side.

"Sorry. I'm having a crisis of faith."

"Don't. I'm not feeling great about this, either. But I think I've found something."

Avery found Alex on his knees rummaging through a box, its contents strewn around him. Avery dropped down next to him, searching through loose sheets of paper and a few bound books.

Alex pointed to another box above them. "I think that one's worth looking at, too."

Avery pulled it free and placed it on the floor, sifting through its contents, both of them working together, side by side. A small bound book sat in the file, and as Avery touched it, she knew. "This is it."

"It is?" Alex said, looking over. "You haven't even opened it!"

"I can tell." She opened the book excitedly, and inside, inscribed in ornate and flowery writing, was the title: *The Trials of the White Haven Witches.*

She looked at Alex in shock, her heart pounding once more. She gently turned the first few pages, and there, in the long list of the accused, she saw the name, Helena Marchmont. The emotion of the moment overcame her, and a few tears sprang to her eyes. She quickly tried to blink them back before Alex saw them. She was such a sentimental fool. But Alex had also fallen silent, and she looked around, wondering why he hadn't commented.

He was holding a very old leather book with the sign of earth on it, an upside-down triangle with a line through the bottom third—another grimoire. He raised his eyes to hers.

"You've got to be kidding me," Avery said, barely able to breathe.

"It's Briar's," he said, his eyes wide.

"Shit. We have to get out of here, and we need to take everything with us. How can *that* be here?"

"Is this a trap?"

"It can't possibly be. If Faversham knew it was here, he'd have taken it by now."

Alex opened the first few pages and swore again. "Look at the pages, Ave!"

She leaned over and saw faint white runes marked on some of the pages, only made visible by the witch light floating above them.

"Have you ever looked at your grimoire under witch light?" Avery asked.

"No. Bollocks! I feel like an idiot. Messages have been hidden under our noses the entire time!"

Alex pulled his backpack out and placed the grimoire carefully inside, then bundled some of the other papers into a cardboard file he'd bought just in case.

"Is there anything about the Favershams in those papers?" Avery asked.

He shook his head, "I'm not sure. Let's take everything."

Avery took another quick look at the book containing the trial transcripts, and saw it contained testimonies from the town members. A quick glance through the file showed a few other articles relevant to the witch trials. She hated doing this, but she copied Alex, loading everything into her own backpack.

A sudden *bang* from below made them fall silent.

"Was that a door?"

"Quickly, put the boxes back," Alex said, setting his own box back on the shelf, now empty.

They heard footsteps downstairs, and two voices calling to each other.

"Did we leave anything open down there?" Avery asked, desperately trying to remember their actions.

Alex shook his head. "No. I locked everything behind us. I doubt they'll even come up here. Maybe they've clocked that the cameras are off."

Despite the fact that her heart was now racing wildly, Avery checked the boxes on either side of the ones they'd already looked at. There was no way they'd be coming back; they had to get everything now. She was glad she checked. There were pages of interviews from witnesses—or at least that's what it looked like at first glance. She stuffed the papers in with the others, trying to be as gentle as possible while working quickly. She pushed the last box in place and ran to Alex's side as he extinguished the witch light, and they stood still, listening together. Heavy footsteps clumped up the stairs, and they heard the door open.

Alex pulled her quickly behind the door, trying not to stumble in the dark, and wedged her in the corner so that she was blocked by his body. Avery knew that if they made a noise, their shadow spell wouldn't stand up to blazing lights.

The main light went on in the narrow hallway, and Avery pressed back against the wall, reassured to feel Alex in front of her. The floorboards creaked as the security officer paced down the hall, stopping every now and again. He must be alone. As he passed their room the flashlight flooded in, sweeping across the open space a couple of times, and then he passed on, and Avery slowly exhaled. They waited for endless minutes as he progressed slowly up and back down the hall, and then the light went off and the door shut.

Avery sagged against Alex. That was too close.

"Do we wait for them to go?" Avery asked.

"They could be here hours," he reasoned. "Let's go now."

They headed back along the corridor, creeping silently through the door and down the narrow staircase until they came to the main library. It was empty and silent, and they risked a pale witch light to guide them across to the main door where they extinguished it again and listened for noise from the galleries beyond.

With a *click* they eased the door open and stepped onto the wooden floor of the museum. It was dark; in the far distance, a flashlight swept around the corridors and two voices carried across the air.

They crept from gallery to gallery, ducking into the entrance of each one, progressing slowly onwards. The men moved down into the main hall, and then disappeared into the other galleries on the ground floor. The lighting in the display cabinets was on, and Alex and Avery glanced nervously at each other and then ran down the stairs. As they set foot in the main hall, they heard another voice approaching from the corridor that led to the rear. Avery froze for a second, and then pulled Alex to the old fashioned carriage that sat in the middle of the floor. Within seconds they were lying flat on its floor, the door shut behind them.

The carriage was small, and while she was able to lie flat between the seats with relative comfort, Alex was squashed in, pressing on top of her.

"Ouch!" Avery whispered, as Alex's weight pinned her down, his knee on her leg.

"Sorry, princess," he hissed, his mouth to her ear.

For endless seconds they heard the security guard walk around, and then they heard him speak. "Hey boss, there's no one here. We've checked upstairs and down. The boys are just finishing the back rooms now." There was silence, and then a grunt. "No. No sign of damage. No forced entry. I reckon the cameras just failed." Another moment of silence, and then, "Yeah, we're out soon."

Avery heard his footsteps fade as he headed to the other rooms.

Alex lifted his head and peered through the window. "He's gone. Let's go. Now!"

He pushed the door open, untangling himself as he pulled Avery out behind him, and then closing the door again softly, they headed down the passage leading to the back door.

Outside, a large security van was on the road, but it was empty. They ran out and onto the street, racing down towards the side street, where they slowed to a stroll as they approached Alex's car.

Avery's heart pounded in her chest, and she expected to hear a shout at any moment. Sweat was beading on her brow and she welcomed the cool night air. She hadn't even realised how hot she was feeling.

With a soft *chirp*, Alex switched off his car alarm and they jumped in. They didn't stop to congratulate themselves until they were on the outskirts of town, both of them glancing over their shoulders nervously.

Avery slumped back in her seat as they hit the A390 and sped up. "That was close."

"But successful. You coming back to mine?"

Avery felt her breath catch, and she looked at him, wide-eyed.

"Surely you want to check the grimoires under witch light?" he said with a grin.

She laughed. "Yes, I do! But I'll need a very strong coffee. Or alcohol. Or maybe both."

4

The witch light floated over the two grimoires, revealing silvery shapes magically marked onto the old paper of the spell books.

"Runes and writing," Alex murmured, gently turning the pages of his own book, as Avery looked through Briar's.

"There are marks on some pages, but not all," Avery noted.

Briar's book was as old as the others, and it contained a mixture of spells, observations on moon cycles, and experiments with herbs and gems. However, the witches who had owned this grimoire had a greater tradition of commenting on the success of the spells, or suggestions for improvements, so that it read as much as a diary as a spell book. The witch light revealed additional notes, some written in English, while some pages were marked with either a single rune or a series of runes.

Avery peered across at Alex's book. "It looks similar to this one in the way the runes are used."

Alex nodded. "There are some marking protection, others denoting months, or what I think are times to best use a particular spell. They seem to provide a hidden level of enhancement for the spells, which is weird. Why would they add a hidden message to an already very private book?"

"Added protection from prying eyes?"

Avery flicked to the unused pages in the back, the grimoire hidden before they could ever be used. Several were indeed blank, but right at the very end the witch light revealed another spell. "Look at this, Alex. This spell has been hidden completely!" She stared at the page, puzzled. "This says: Part Three, The Grounding. Where are the other parts?"

Alex quickly turned to the back pages of his own and swore. "I have Part Five, The Summoning."

They looked at each other as realisation dawned.

"One spell spread across all five grimoires?" Avery wondered, looking back at Briar's book. "I don't know what it's for. Can you tell from yours?"

He shook his head. "No. It's a just a very long spell—no ingredients. It relates to the spirit, like most of the spells in my book, but I don't understand the specifics—yet."

"There are a few ingredients in this one, and then a long chant. It's quite repetitive." Avery's thoughts raced, as she ran through the various possibilities. The spells in Briar's book were themed with the earth element, but not exclusively. "One big spell broken into five parts, each focusing on one of the elements, hidden in the back of each grimoire. The other grimoires must contain the other parts."

"One big spell," Alex repeated. "I have a bad feeling about this. There are a few reasons to split a spell."

"To make all five witches participate?"

"Yes. And to ensure everyone agreed. Or because it was too powerful for one individual alone."

"What type of spell would you want agreement on? A binding spell, or a spell to release something powerful?"

Alex sighed and looked at his watch. "I'm shattered, I can't think straight. It's nearly four in the morning.

"Is it? Wow, no wonder I'm so tired. I think adrenalin is the only thing keeping me going." Avery ran her hands through her hair, trying to release the clips that held it in a loose bun. She looked up to find Alex watching her, his eyes following her hands and her hair, and then her lips.

"Here, let me." Alex said, stepping closer and reaching for her hair clips. He tipped her head so that it rested on his chest, his hands warm on hers as he found the clips and untangled them. He put his hands in her hair, shaking it free, and it tumbled down her back. "You have the most gorgeous hair," he murmured.

Alex's warm, musky scent enveloped Avery, and she inhaled deeply, her hands resting on his chest as she pressed against him. His hands moved from her hair to caress her back, her shoulders, and then her neck, and they were so warm and strong that a sigh escaped her. He bent his head, and she felt his lips upon her neck. A shiver ran through her. This was heaven. His lips moved around her neck, kissing her gently, and then rose slowly to her cheek. As if spellbound, Avery tipped her head back and his lips blazed a trail to hers. She sank into his kiss effortlessly, like slipping into water.

Desire uncoiled within her, a slow stirring in her belly that spread deliciously around her body, her brain incapable of making a rational decision. She wrapped her arms around him, snaking under his t-shirt as he pulled her closer. His hands slid up and down her arms, leaving her tingling and breathless, and then moved to her waist. He lifted her up onto the table and she wrapped her legs around him while their kiss deepened. As her emotions ran wild, a wind once again rose around them, tugging at their hair and caressing her skin, and Alex responded, the candles around them flaring into life. Avery couldn't explain why, but the intensity of their kiss was wilder than before as an urgent lust rose between them. Alex pulled back for a second, his lips grazing hers, his eyes dark with desire as he stared at her. For a moment, it seemed as if time stopped as they both hesitated, and then he picked her up and carried her through to his bedroom.

***

Avery awoke once again tangled in Alex's sheets, his body sprawled next to her. She could get used to this, she thought, as she turned over onto her back, trying not to disturb him.

Daylight filtered through the wooden blinds, casting a pale, barred light across the room. Rain was falling heavily outside. She could hear it pounding on the roof, and it cocooned the flat, drowning out all other noise. Alex felt warm, his arm heavy, and she gently traced the dark shapes of the tattoo that ran across his shoulders and down his arms.

Part of her was annoyed that once again she'd failed to show any willpower at all, but the other half didn't care. She wasn't sure if this was leading anywhere, but it felt good while it lasted. Avery had never felt like this about anyone. It was partly because they were both witches. He knew her, but they also had a connection, a spark that she couldn't explain. No doubt he'd break her heart, but she was resigned to it. As long as she was expecting it, maybe it wouldn't feel so bad when the inevitable happened. She inwardly rolled her eyes. She was such a fool. And then she remembered what he'd said last night about Faversham. *I would kill him he if touched you.* She probably shouldn't read too much into that.

Alex stirred and mumbled into her shoulder. "It feels late."

"It *is* late. It's after twelve."

"Thank the gods I'm not working." He opened his eyes, squinting at her. "I need coffee."

She smiled. "I can get it."

"No, let me. My machine's temperamental. Want one?"

She felt cheeky. "Yes, please. Do I get brunch, too?"

He grinned at her. "Sure. But only if you stick around all day."

She twisted to look at him. "Why do I have to stick around?"

"Well, a—why wouldn't you want to? And b—we have work to do. All that stuff we found last night." He nuzzled her neck again. "I promise I'll make it worth your time."

She thought she might just stop breathing. "You don't have to bribe me with sex."

"It's not bribery. It's a pleasure. Isn't it?" he asked, his eyes questioning as he held her gaze.

"You know it is," Avery said, almost whispering it.

"Good," he agreed softly, before kissing her again. And then he slid out of bed and walked naked across the room and out to the kitchen. She couldn't help but watch him, admiring his long muscled limbs, his flat stomach, and his toned abs. *He was so hot.* She flopped back on the pillow and looked up at the ceiling. *I'm screwed*, she thought, *literally and figuratively.*

Alex cooked an amazing brunch of hash browns, eggs, and bacon, and she gazed at him with new appreciation. He moved competently around the kitchen, and grinned when he saw her watching.

"I didn't know you could cook," she said.

"Must you always underestimate me?" he chided. But she could tell he was pleased.

As soon as they'd eaten, they spread all of the papers they found in the archive on the sofa, the table, and the floor. Avery called Briar with the good news about her grimoire, and the others had agreed to come over later that afternoon.

"I wish I'd thought to bring the picture of Helena's hanging and the ledger," Avery said, making herself comfortable on the sofa. She curled up in the corner, the book containing the trial transcripts and the extra papers about Helena's trial next to her.

"What we find here may make it easier to understand the map, anyway," Alex reasoned. He sat on the rug, the other papers next to him, and the grimoires on the table.

For a while, they worked quietly together. The book containing the trial notes was difficult to read, the language awkward, and the writing faded in places. The first trials were of some old women who had been accused of turning milk sour by a local farmer, as well as ruining crops. Another had been accused of causing a stillbirth. Avery sighed. This was common during the witch trials, and both men and women were the accusers. It was impossible to say now, but more than likely these poor women had had nothing to do with what they were accused of. From the small amount of information available, these women were old widows, living on little money, and struggling to get by.

Initially, the numbers accused were low, and then a fury seemed to ignite the town, and more women's names appeared, along with a few men. Avery's blood chilled. It must have been terrifying. The trials all resulted in a test of witchcraft by drowning. Those who survived were hanged, but most drowned anyway. At this stage there was no mention of burning witches at the stake.

There were a few witness statements at the beginning, defending some of the poor accused, but as time went on, these grew less and less, as those who tried to defend them soon found themselves on the list of accused. And then Helena's name appeared and Avery hesitated for a second, almost scared to read further.

She must have sighed, because Alex called over, "You okay?"

She looked up at him. He had a witch light hovering above his shoulder, illuminating his grimoire and Briar's next to it. "I've just come across Helena's name. This is so horrible. I don't want to read it, but I have to."

"Do you want me to?"

"No. It's fine. I'm being stupid. But I can't help but imagine what if that happened now. What if someone saw a demon, and we were accused in some way?"

"No one would believe it. They'd be locked up in the nearest psychiatric ward. Besides, we could get around that with a spell."

"Could we? Helena couldn't."

"You don't know what happened yet," he reminded her.

"You're right," she said. "I need to focus."

Avery went back to the transcript and had her first shock. Helena was accused as Helena Marchmont, widow of Edward Marchmont, and mother of Ava, aged eight, and Louisa, aged five. *Helena was a widow.* This left her vulnerable. Edward had been a merchant, but Helena had no occupation, and that would fit. She wouldn't need to work as the wife of a merchant. They had money and status—if he'd left her some, which was likely. It was odd, but the address listed was different from the one she had from Anne. Maybe this was a later address. The cottage she'd found on the edge of the town wouldn't have befitted a merchant. Maybe this was Helena's family's home. With any luck, Avery would be able to find the house she shared with her husband. She sighed again and kept reading.

The first charge against Helena was listed on the 9th of October 1589, and they went back several years. A man called Timothy Williams had accused her of killing his wife when she lost her child and then died in childbirth. He said she had done it deliberately, as they were rivals in business. Others had defended her, saying she was a respectable woman who helped her community. Avery recognised the Ashworths' (Briar's family), the Bonnevilles', and the Jacksons' names. They were listed as merchants, too. Again, that made sense, particularly the Jacksons. And then the transcript mentioned another accuser. *The Favershams.* Thaddeus Faversham stated that his wife had almost died in childbirth, but had survived by the grace of God. Their child, however, had died after being cursed by Helena Marchmont, who had attended the birth. He then went on to list failed shipments that had been run aground because of storms. He accused Helena Marchmont of making those storms. Thaddeus cited evidence that Helena's mother had been known as wise woman and witch, and that clearly she had inherited her skills. Joseph Marchmont, Helena's brother-in-law, had defended her, but then it seemed the two girls were threatened. Avery could imagine his fear. Helena stood accused, but he had to protect his nieces.

Then Thaddeus accused the Jacksons, the Bonnevilles, and the Ashworths, too, but none of these seemed to hold weight—at least they weren't formally charged. Maybe they were just too well known and respected. And then someone called Elijah James accused Helena.

Avery felt a rush of anger. Williams, James, and Faversham must have been working together, and maybe had scared others into accusing Helena of witchcraft, too. She did not and would not believe that Helena would be capable of harming others.

Helena had been found guilty. It was impossible to know the details between these lines of accusations—the transcript was dry and devoid of emotion—but whatever the defendants had said hadn't worked, and Avery wasn't sure if they could risk any more for her.

It was interesting that so many of them were merchants in some way or another. Maybe the Favershams had threatened their families, businesses, and livelihoods. One way or another, the accusers had won. A date was set, October 31st, and Helena was burnt at the stake.

And it seemed that Helena was the last name accused, as if her burning had ended the madness. Maybe the town had been appalled at what had happened.

Avery sighed again and looked up to find Alex watching her. "This is horrible."

"Go on, tell me."

She related the story, and as she talked, the events made a little more sense, but she still felt there was something unsaid, something significant. *Why would a witch threaten another in such a public way, just for business?*

Alex tried to reassure her. "Everybody went a bit mad at these witch trials—they whipped people into a frenzy, for a while at least, and then it settled down again. It doesn't excuse their behaviours, though. They were different times, Avery. But, it's interesting that the Favershams led the attack. It could be business motivations, or it could be a cover for something to do with magic. What happened to her children?"

"I don't know. I presume their Uncle Joseph looked after them, or maybe Helena's mother. There's no further mention of her here, so maybe she was in hiding, or had died. I'll have to check my family tree."

He nodded at the pile of old yellow papers next to her. "What's in those?"

"I don't know. I haven't got to them yet." She looked around at the darkened room. The rain was now lashing the windows, the wind surging against the building. She could hear the crash of the surf on the beach. She couldn't see the harbour, but she knew from long experience that the boats would be bobbing furiously, the pavements would be empty, and the pubs would be full. However, it was nice to be curled up on Alex's sofa, even if her reading material was grim. She smiled at him. "How are you getting on?"

"Okay. There are commonalities in the rune markings on certain spells, but I'd like to check the other books first. I still don't know what the spells in the back are about." He shivered. "It's getting cold." He looked at the kindling in the fireplace, and suddenly flames flashed along them and onto the logs laid across them, and then the candles around his flat sparked to life, along with a couple of corner lamps.

Avery groaned. "I am not looking forward to leaving here later. I'm going to get soaked."

"You can stay here," he said.

She shook her head, "I can't. The cats need feeding, and I have work in the morning."

"I'll run you back, it won't take long."

"Thanks," she said, already wishing she didn't have to go, even though she wouldn't be leaving for hours yet.

She turned back to the other loose papers and with a shock, realised they were letters. They were addressed to the magistrate, and they were from Thaddeus Faversham. An even bigger shock was the name of the magistrate. She cried out and looked up at Alex, momentarily too stunned to speak.

"What?" he asked, his eyes narrowing in concern.

"I've found Newton's connection. The magistrate—or Justice of the Peace—was named Peter Newton."

Alex looked stunned. "I presume it would be too big a coincidence not to be related at all to our DI Newton."

Avery's mind raced as she filtered through a few possibilities. "He condemned Helena to death, and many others. Newton said, 'I know my place in the town.' Is he here to protect us, or condemn us?"

"Or protect the town *from* us?" Alex reasoned.

Avery felt vulnerable and looked around the room, as if someone would burst in on them and drag them away.

Alex tried to reassure her. "Avery, it's okay. *We'll* be okay. I won't let anything happen to us—I promise. And neither will you. You're too strong." He nodded at the papers in her lap. "Read the letters, hopefully they'll fill in the gaps."

She nodded and turned back to the letters; there were about five in total. Again, the writing and the language were difficult to decipher, but she persevered, determined to get to the bottom of whatever happened.

After about half an hour, a glass of red wine appeared in front of her. Avery looked up to find Alex grinning. "I thought you'd need fortification. You're miles away. Good news or bad?"

She smiled and took the glass from him, taking a sip before speaking. "Thanks. Well, the news is good and bad. The JP was not running the witch trials, the Witchfinder was. The JP was involved because of his position in the town. He had to be, but it seems he was an unwilling participant. The first letters are from Faversham to Newton, basically complaining about Helena based on the charges he bought against her. It seems they were a polite necessity, basically warning him to support him. There's a letter from Newton telling him to, more or less, consider his actions carefully, and Faversham replied basically telling him to butt out. Then the Witchfinder sent a letter warning Newton that to try to defend Helena would be dangerous, perhaps suggesting his support of witchcraft."

Alex sat next to Avery on the sofa, a bottle of beer in hand, and he took a letter from her, scanning it as she spoke. "So, basically, Peter Newton was damned whatever he did. If he tried to support her, his life and family were endangered."

Avery leaned back against the sofa, looking up to the ceiling. "The bastards. Helena never had a chance."

"But what did she *do*, Avery? And if Faversham was a witch, which he must have been, why didn't he seek revenge using magic? Why use the Witchfinder?"

Avery turned to look at him. "You're right. That's a great question."

He looked smug. "I know. I'm awesome."

She rolled her eyes. "And so modest."

"Anything else in these?" He gestured at the papers.

"Not really, other than really wordy ways of threatening people. Odiousness must run in the Faversham family. The Witchfinder sounds vile, too."

"That doesn't surprise me. But the good thing is, Newton's ancestor wasn't that bad after all."

"He was spineless."

"He was threatened," Alex reminded her. "Maybe that's what our Newton meant by *his place*. Maybe his ancestor was so angry and helpless that since then the entire family line has vowed to protect White Haven and the witches in it."

"He's got a funny way of going about it," Avery mumbled.

"It's a hell of a legacy. Especially if you don't have much choice."

5

It wasn't long before El and Briar arrived, bringing pizza. Avery felt a little self-conscious at already being there with Alex. She felt sure they would know what they'd been up to, and while it really didn't matter, she felt nervous anyway. But neither of them said anything, although Briar did look at Avery with raised eyebrows and the briefest of smirks. Avery attempted her wide-eyed look of innocence, and knew she'd failed immediately when Briar smirked even more. El, however, headed straight to the kitchen with boxes of pizzas, barely glancing at them.

Avery decided to change the unspoken subject. "Where's Reuben?"

El sighed. "He'll be here when he's ready."

The others exchanged worried looks, and Briar shook her head as a warning.

"He's grieving, El. We need to give him time," Alex said.

"I know. I just wish he wasn't angry with me."

"I'm sure he's mad at everyone right now."

"No. Just me." Her tone didn't invite further questions.

This time Briar changed the subject, and grinned broadly. "So, where's my grimoire?"

"Voila, madam," Alex said, pointing towards the coffee table.

Briar gave a barely suppressed squeal that was distinctly un-Briarlike and ran to look at it. "I can't believe it! It's just beautiful."

"I need to show you both something," Alex said. "El, we need your grimoire, too."

El pulled her grimoire from her pack and handed it over. Unfortunately, she didn't look anywhere near as excited as Briar.

"Come over here," Alex said, drawing her to the coffee table, where he placed her book down next to the others. "I just hope this works with yours, too."

El looked mystified as Alex put out the lamps and conjured a witch light above the books. As he'd hoped, El's book also showed hidden runes and writing.

All of a sudden, El's grim mood disappeared and she sat next to Briar. "What? How? It's just like the book we found in the witch museum. I didn't even think! I'm so annoyed with myself..." she trailed off, turning the pages of her book.

"We need to check the back pages, if that's okay?"

El looked puzzled. "Sure, but why?"

Alex didn't answer as he turned to the end, and there, revealed by the witch light was another spell: *Part Two, To Seal with Fire.*

El gasped. "What's that?"

Alex sighed. "In the back of each grimoire is part of a spell. We think they make up one large spell, but we're not sure what it does. Again, yours has no ingredients, like mine, just a spell—a chant. You have part two, I have part five. Briar, you have part three."

El and Briar looked from Alex to Avery and back again.

"I'll sort food," Avery said to Alex. "You explain."

She headed to the kitchen, putting out olives, cheese, and crackers, plus the pizza, hoping that Reuben wouldn't leave them waiting long—if he came at all. She listened as she worked, smiling as the others looked through their grimoires, comparing runes. She was surprised by how comfortable she felt with them all, although really, why shouldn't she? She had spent the last few years keeping her distance from them, and now she wondered why she had. They knew her, understood her, in ways no one else could, even her oldest friends.

And Alex. She paused for a second, watching him. His long hair was loose, falling about his shoulders, his face animated as he talked through the runes he'd found. Whatever preconceptions she'd initially had about him were being slowly eroded away. He was thoughtful, funny, and sexy, and he felt genuine. As if he'd heard her thoughts, he looked up, holding her gaze for a second, before returning to his explanations. *Oh my goddess*, she thought, *be still my beating heart.*

"These runes," he continued, "give protection. It must be a way of categorising the spells. But these," he said, pointing to a few different pages, "add words or extra instructions to the spell. This suggests working with another witch."

"But why wouldn't you put that in the body of the spell?" El asked. "It doesn't make sense."

"This one here," he continued, pointing to another spell in his own grimoire, "suggests an extra ingredient—vervain—and adds a warning: *to lock the heart forever.*"

Briar nodded. "Vervain works better if secrecy is attached to its use. Maybe it was thought to hide it within the spell would add potency."

"Interesting," El murmured. "Like a spell within a spell."

But instead of answering, Alex went still, his face clouding over, his eyes gazing into the unknown.

"Alex!" El shouted. "What's happening?"

Avery dropped the knife she was holding with a clatter. "Don't touch him!" she shouted. "He must be having a vision."

El and Briar both sat back, giving Alex some space. Briar said, "I've never seen this happen before."

"No, nor me," Avery said, watching from the kitchen. "But he said he's getting them regularly."

For a few seconds they watched Alex as he remained immovable. His eyes flickered rapidly and his breathing became shallow, but otherwise he was as still as a statue. Just when Avery was beginning to wonder how long was normal for a vision to last, Alex blinked and looked around, bewildered.

"Are you all right?" Briar asked, narrowing her eyes with concern.

"I am, but Reuben's in trouble."

"*What?*" El leapt to her feet, almost overturning a candle. "Where is he?"

"On the outskirts of White Haven," Alex said, stumbling to his feet. "I'll drive."

"No. I'll drive," El said with white-faced fury. "Keys," she commanded, and her keys flew across the room and into her hand. Without hesitation she raced down the stairs, the others following. Avery helped Alex, who still seemed dazed. He paused briefly to seal the room.

"Maybe you should stay here," she suggested to him as she waited. "Not a chance. I'll be fine in a minute."

Within minutes they were outside, piling into El's battered old Land Rover, and El spun the tyres as she floored the accelerator, racing through the pouring rain.

"Where?" she shouted.

"Old Haven Church," Alex said.

Briar sat next to El, flexing her fingers, muttering softly to herself as she summoned her powers, and Avery joined her, trying to calm her shattered thoughts. *Please let Reuben be okay*, she thought.

"Who was there, Alex?" El called over her shoulder.

"Faversham, and a woman I didn't recognise."

"A woman? Not Alicia, then?" Avery asked.

"Why the hell would it be Alicia?" Briar asked, spinning round to look at them.

"Just a thought I had. I'll explain later," Avery hedged, bracing herself against the seat in front, as El rounded a corner way too quickly.

Briar glared at her. "Don't kill us, El!"

El ignored her, concentrating on the road. Avery turned back to Alex. "Who?"

"I don't know. I couldn't see features, just the sense of a woman. Dark hair maybe?"

"Fuck it!" El yelled, as she got stuck behind a car. As soon as she could, she veered around it, turning onto the lane that led to Old Haven Church.

The rain continued to pour down, and wind whipped the branches of the overhanging trees against the car. The lane was narrow, and if an oncoming car headed their way it would be a disaster. El didn't care. She floored it, and Avery used her magic to help keep the rain away from the car, trying to sense if anything was in front of them.

She turned to Alex. "Did you sense anything else? I mean, was Reuben in the main church?"

He closed his eyes and frowned. "I sensed anger and desperation more than anything. There was a damp smell. I think it was maybe the mausoleum? I don't know." He looked up at her, anguished.

Avery thought of Reuben mourning his brother in silence and then being attacked, and her chest tightened with renewed worry.

Within minutes El was hurtling into the car park at the church. Reuben's car, an old VW Variant, was parked there on its own. They piled out of the door and ran towards the church, drenched before they'd even reached the wide sheltered porch in front of the locked door. It was deserted. El set off again, the others following, running down the path towards the mausoleum, and that's when Avery saw dark smoke spiralling into the air.

The mausoleum door hung at an angle, and a woman with long, dark hair was directing blasts of energy like lightning towards the building. Avery could see a large crack in the wall from here, and the tree that sheltered the mausoleum smouldered. No one else was in sight, and it was clear that she couldn't see the approaching group. El sent a blistering rope of fire at the woman, which snaked around her legs and pulled her to the ground. She turned, her face vicious, even though she was sprawled on the floor. Briar stopped and the rest ran on, but within a few feet, a massive crack erupted down the middle of the path, almost causing Avery to fall. The crack widened under the fallen woman, and although she was struggling to her feet, it knocked her off balance, and she fell into an ever widening, dark hole.

The woman stretched out her arm and flung a blast of energy towards them, causing Avery and El to dive out of the way on either side of the path, but Alex stood firm, holding his hands up and out. Avery wasn't sure quite what he did, but the wave of energy stopped abruptly as the woman screamed and fell to her knees, engulfed now in mud as the earth started to swallow her whole. They were close now, within a few feet, and able to see the woman struggling for control.

Avery squinted through the rain, slicking her hair back from her face, and saw a large, broken branch to the side of the mausoleum, brought down by the wind. She used the wild energy of the wind that raced around her as if it recognised her, and pulling the branch up into a vortex of air, smashed it on to the woman's head. She fell, unconscious, to the ground.

El raced onwards to the mausoleum, and Avery followed, skidding to a halt in the entrance. Reuben was unconscious on the floor, blood streaming from a wound on his temple. El rushed to his side, dropping to her knees and feeling his pulse, while Avery stood panting behind, looking around for any sign of Faversham. But the room was empty, other than for the coffins of Reuben's family; Gil's rested on a shelf, looking far too new.

A wave of sadness and anger, and the weight of centuries pressed down on Avery, and she took a deep breath, trying to steady her breathing. She turned back to the grounds and saw Alex and Briar standing over the woman. They were all completely soaked now, the woman drenched and covered in mud where the earth had pulled her in. Avery shuddered. She had almost been buried alive, and Avery wasn't sure how eager she would have been to save her. She turned back to El. "Is he okay?"

El nodded, looking relieved. "He's unconscious, but alive."

Alex and Briar arrived at the mausoleum, and Alex nodded at the woman. "What the hell are we going to do with her?"

"I want to interrogate her!" El said, looking furious. Avery was shocked; she had never seen El like this.

"I'm all for defending myself, El, but I'm not attacking her now that she's down," Alex said, frowning at her.

"And where's her car?" Briar asked. "How did she get here?"

"The same swirling cloak and dagger way Faversham does, I suppose. I'd love to know how they do that!" Avery said.

Over the sound of the wind and falling rain, Avery thought she heard something else. A car engine. "Someone's here."

Alex ran to El's side. "Let's get Reuben up and we'll drag him to the car. That woman can stay here. I don't care if she gets pneumonia."

But as Avery looked back to the church, she saw two things—the tall, dark-haired form of Newton rounding the corner of the church, and then the unmistakable, blurred shape of Faversham appearing next to the fallen woman.

Faversham hesitated for a second, looking at Avery and back at Newton, who now started sprinting towards them. Faversham knelt down and grabbed the woman's hand, and then with a whirl of wind, he disappeared, taking her with him.

Within seconds, Newton arrived at the mausoleum and sheltered under the porch. He shook water off his jacket, and slicked it out of his hair and off his face. He glanced back at the broken earth, at Reuben's unconscious body, and then at the cracked wall and the smouldering tree, before looking at their bedraggled appearances.

"I think we need to talk."

6

"I think now would be a good time for you to tell me exactly what's going on!" Newton yelled.

He stood in the middle of Alex's living room, soaking wet, trying to towel himself dry with an enormous bath towel. He scrubbed at his clothes and rubbed his hair with fury, until it was standing up on end. He was wearing casual clothes, jeans and a t-shirt, with an old university hoodie, so that despite his anger, he seemed far more approachable now than he had been before. His drenching had removed some of his command.

Alex stood opposite him, also soaking wet, and also trying to dry himself while shouting. "I think it's pretty clear what's going on. Our friend Reuben was attacked and almost killed. Would you like me to file a report?"

"Only if you think you could explain what the hell happened. I'm not sure magic really qualifies for a good statement."

"Well, magic pretty much sums it up," Alex said snarkily.

"Start from the beginning. And tell me everything."

"First, tell me how you knew we were there." Alex demanded, his eyes narrowed with suspicion.

"One of my colleagues had spotted you hurtling up the lane and called it in. I've asked for everyone to watch your cars for suspicious activities."

"Really! You're spying on us?" Alex asked, incredulous.

"For your own good," Newton shot back.

"We're not bloody children!"

"No. You're just unleashing magic onto an unsuspecting community," Newton said dryly.

"Actually, no, we're not! The only people we're unleashing our magic on are other witches who are intent on doing us harm and stealing our grimoires! Witches we didn't know even existed."

Newton stared icily at Alex. "But innocent people have been hurt in the process."

"Not by us."

"Tell me *everything*," Newton repeated.

Alex glanced questioningly at Avery, and she nodded.

Alex sighed and started to explain.

Avery looked from one man to the other, mildly amused, but also slightly amazed at their antagonism towards each other. They were like chalk and cheese, and she decided not to get involved.

She sat in front of the blazing fire, wrapped in a blanket after towelling her hair dry. Reuben was lying on Alex's bed, where Briar was using her healing spells, trying to bring him back to consciousness. El was with her. She presumed they'd call if they needed any help. Avery reckoned Alex must have dished out every towel and blanket he owned.

It was dark outside now, the fury of the storm continuing unabated. They had returned to Alex's flat a little under half an hour ago. They had all helped carry Reuben to the car park, and then split into groups. Briar and Avery brought back Reuben's car, with him on the back seat, while Alex returned with El. Newton had followed behind. Avery had driven, and stopped briefly at Briar's place for her to pick up some herbs and gemstones that she needed for healing. She lived in a tiny cottage tucked on one of the town's back streets, and Avery had waited in the car, and then swung by her own flat to feed her cats. She wasn't sure what time she'd end up getting home later. She was relieved to find that her wards remained sealed.

A huge rumble of thunder cracked overhead and Avery jumped, jolting her out of her reverie.

Newton scowled again, his arms crossed in front of his chest. "You have no idea who the woman is?"

"No," Alex said patiently. "I have never seen her before in my life, but she was trying to bring the mausoleum down on Reuben's head. She meant to kill him. We need a plan."

Alex was right. Faversham had killed Gil, and now they were all at risk; they had to fight back. Before she could think coherently she needed food. The smell of warmed pizza filled the flat, and Avery dragged herself from the fire and over to the kitchen. She pulled out plates and cutting boards and placed the three pizzas out, grabbing a slice for herself.

"Hey, guys, you should eat." She pushed plates towards them, and then carried some through to Briar and El.

The bedroom was only lit by candlelight, and the sweet smell of incense drifted across the room. Briar sat cross-legged on the bed next to Reuben. She had placed healing stones on certain points of his body, a poultice on his head wound, and she held his hand as she quietly whispered a spell.

El looked up as Avery entered, her expression grim.

Avery placed a plate with a couple of slices of hot pizza into El's hand.

El shook her head. "I can't eat."

"I don't care. Try. Force yourself."

El rolled her eyes, and took a bite, chewing unenthusiastically.

"How's he doing?"

"All right. Briar's amazing. She's been sitting like that for the past 20 minutes. His breathing is stable, and his colour's good."

Avery smiled, relief washing through her. "Do we know why he was in the mausoleum?

"To spend time with Gil? I don't know, we haven't talked in days." El's pale blue eyes filled with tears again.

"It'll be okay. Just give him time."

El nodded and turned away.

Avery headed back to the living room and did a double-take. Newton and Alex were leaning on the counter, a slice of pizza in one hand, a bottle of beer in the other. They still looked antagonistic, but clearly hunger had exhausted them.

"Any idea why Reuben was at the church?" Avery asked. "The weather's foul. It just seems odd to me."

"I've no idea. I'm too tired to do this right now," Alex said.

Avery sighed and reached for another slice of pizza. "Me, too. But we need to hide where we are from Faversham. I feel like we have a homing beacon on us. Reuben was a sitting duck on his own. Especially in the middle of a deserted graveyard."

Newton looked at them, frowning. "So, how long has Faversham been involved?"

Avery shrugged. "Since the beginning. We think he's the one responsible for the demons."

"So, he's the one responsible for killing the woman in the car and the cleaner in the museum?'

"Maybe," Alex said. "He did kill Gil. We saw it."

"I think that was a pretty important thing to leave out of your statement," Newton said, clearly annoyed.

"He conjured a bloody great rock monster and slammed Gil against the wall. If it hadn't been for Avery, we'd probably all be dead. How would you like me to phrase *that* in a statement?"

Newton looked as if he would argue, but then he nodded and sighed.

Avery decided she'd had enough of secrets. "Newton, you need to tell us about your part in this. You know magic, you know us. We've levelled with you, now please, be honest."

"You haven't told me everything, Avery."

"We've told you a lot."

"What are the hidden grimoires?" He leaned against the counter, watching her.

It didn't seem worth lying about anything else to him. It was strange, but despite the little they knew of him, she trusted him. "They're our old family grimoires, hidden from the Witchfinder General back in the 16th century. From what we can piece together, Helena—my ancestor—was betrayed, or set up by her accusers—the Favershams—and burnt at the stake. The other families tried to argue for her, but it didn't work, and after she died, they moved and the grimoires were lost, until now. We're still foggy on the details."

Alex added, "We don't have all of the grimoires—only three. Faversham threatened us to get them. He wasn't joking."

Newton groaned and put his last bite of pizza on the counter. He looked at Avery and Alex, his grey eyes tired. "All my life I have been warned about this, warned that it may happen in my generation, but we are always warned, and then the threat passes. But now it seems it's true."

Alex looked nervous. "What's true?"

"That my real job is just starting."

Avery gaped. "What are you talking about?"

"The soul of old Octavia Faversham is bound with a demon's and lies somewhere beneath White Haven. Your ancestors put it there, and it's my job to keep it there."

Alex looked stunned. "Is that a joke?"

"No, unfortunately not." Newton looked as sane as anyone could after uttering such a bizarre sentence.

A horrible trickle of fear ran down Avery's spine. "The spell in the back of the grimoires. Is that what it is? A binding spell?"

"It could be. I have no idea where they put Octavia's soul, or how they did it. I just know it was performed by all the witches to contain Octavia and her pet demon, and as a threat to the rest of the Favershams to back off."

"And you didn't think to tell us?" Alex asked, furious again. "You've known, all this time!"

Newton looked at the floor, and then back at Alex. "I didn't *know*. This information is passed down, generation to generation. How do I know what's relevant or not? I never really believed it, if I'm honest." He appealed to both of them. "I mean seriously, demons?"

He had a point, Avery had to admit. She could scarcely believe it herself, and she was a witch.

"And," Newton continued, "these *activities* have only happened a few times before. Approximately once every century."

Avery sighed. "Addison Jackson."

Newton narrowed his eyes. "Yes. How did you know?"

"Anne's research—Gil's cousin. I've been trying to build a picture as to what happened to Addison. But Lindon said he committed black magic— killed his family for the grimoires."

"No. That was a lie that was fed to his family and descendants. He fled, with his wife and children into hiding to protect them. I believe he did use black magic—blood magic—to conceal them. But he didn't kill them. I'm hoping he had a happy, peaceful life."

"Oh, great," Alex said. "He just left Gil's side of the family to mop up the mess."

"I didn't say he was perfect," Newton said, reaching for another slice of pizza.

Avery's head was reeling, and she was pleased to see Alex looked just as shocked. "The Favershams threatened him back then?"

"So I've been told. And the times before then, too, in other generations. There's a reason witches leave White Haven."

"Yeah, so I keep being told, too," Alex agreed. "Well, it ends here. I refuse to be chased out of my town by some thieving necromancer and his crooked family. And when we find the other grimoires, we'll be more powerful and far harder to manipulate."

"Hold on," Avery said, thinking furiously. "The grimoires have two functions. They detail powerful spells that we've never come across before, and they contain one hidden binding spell that was used to bind Octavia

Faversham and her demon. We have no idea what Faversham wants, but presumably the latter. Does this mean they want to break out Octavia's soul?"

Alex looked baffled. "I guess so."

"But why? What relevance does it have? I mean, what did she do that was so bad that she was bound in the first place, and why is it so important to release her and her pet demon? They have demons coming out of their ears!"

"Didn't your demon-hunting, White Haven-saving ancestors pass that one down, Newton?" Alex asked.

"It seems not," Newton snapped. "I guess your demon-binding, soul-snatching ancestors didn't, either."

Oh great, Avery thought. *Testosterone.* "Guys, we need a plan. You said it, Alex. We're being attacked. Gil's been killed. This is not a game. We need to protect ourselves, and work out a way to attack them first. I hate being on the back foot. And, who are they? We need to know! Faversham and who?"

"Well, I guess that's where I come in," Newton said. "I have access to records you can't get to. I'll check out Faversham's family, his contacts, everyone. Then we'll know who we're up against."

***

They spent the rest of the evening waiting for Reuben to wake, and looking at the grimoires and the documents.

Newton was behaving less like a policeman and more like a friend. Avery had offered to show him what they'd found and he sat on the sofa, looking through the papers and the transcripts of the trial.

"What's your first name?" Avery asked Newton. She was sitting on the floor next to Alex, looking through the three spell books, a witch light hovering between them. "I mean, calling you Newton seems rude."

He looked up, the ghost of a smile on his face. "Mathias, or Matt, but everyone calls me Newton, so you can stick with that."

"Fair enough. What do you think of the papers?"

"Interesting. And chilling. I don't suppose you'd care to tell me where you found them?"

"Not really," Alex said, bristling for an argument again.

Newton raised his eyebrows. "Probably for the best. I've heard about my ancestors and the Witchfinder General, but reading these threatening letters makes it more real. It makes my blood boil, actually."

"At least your ancestor wasn't burnt at the stake," Avery pointed out.

Newton nodded, "True."

Briar came out of the bedroom and stretched. "*Now* I need pizza. Is there some left?"

"Is Reuben okay?" Avery asked.

"He's fine. It was touch and go for a while—his head injury was huge, and his arm was badly bruised." Briar looked shattered, but still very pretty. Her long, dark hair was half tied on top of her head, the rest cascaded down her shoulders. She wore a long, dark red summer dress that set off her hair, and made her skin look even paler. Newton did a double-take, and leapt to his feet.

"Sit down, Briar, let me." He ushered her to the sofa, and then went to get her some food and a glass of wine. Briar seemed oblivious to his attentiveness, but Avery wasn't. Maybe something good would come out of this after all.

Briar sank into her usual corner and within seconds Newton had handed her a glass of wine. "Pizza will be a few more minutes," he said.

"I'm fine," she said, flustered. "Don't rush."

But Newton was already busying himself in the kitchen.

"How's El?" Alex asked.

"Panic-stricken. Things aren't good with those two. Reuben's in a bad space right now."

"Not surprising, but he'll come round, he's a good guy."

"I'm not so sure. He's blaming her for Gil becoming involved in the search for the grimoire."

Avery was stunned. "Why? That doesn't make sense. It was Reuben who pushed Gil to search for it."

"He's looking to blame anyone now. Of course he's blaming Faversham, but El got caught in it, too."

"Why not me? I'm the one who got the box in the first place."

"I think there's a bit of anger in there for all of us," Briar said sadly. "I can't say I blame him."

Newton sat next to her and handed her a plate stacked with pizza, cheeses, and olives. "There you go."

"Thank you," she said, and gave him a beaming smile. "So how are you involved in all this, Newton?"

"Long story."

"I've got time."

Newton started to explain about his family history and Alex nudged Avery, whispering in her ear. "I'm thinking of leaving El and Reuben here tonight. Can I come back to yours?"

"Of course," she stuttered, feeling a rush of pleasure that he'd asked.

"Cool," he said, and leaned a little closer, the warmth of his skin against hers making her tingle. He pointed at the hidden spell in the back of Briar's book. "Briar's book is all about healing, of course, but there are some interesting earth spells, too. This hidden spell, the one we think may be the binding spell, seems to tie the spell to a certain spot."

"Does it? How?" Avery leaned closer, pushing her hair behind her ears.

"This part here." Alex pointed to a line. "The place within the centre of the pentagram, there shall the binding be strongest, rooted to the earth, anchored by the elements, for all of time as the spell desires."

"Within the pentagram? What pentagram?"

"Well, that's the big question, isn't it?" he said, his gaze travelling down to her lips. "Do you think we can get away with leaving now?"

She flushed and grinned. "I don't think so."

"Go on. You know you want to." He smiled mischievously.

"You're a very bad influence," she whispered back, a thrill of anticipation running through her.

"I know. Fun, though." Alex looked up at Briar, interrupting her conversation with Newton. "Do you think Reuben will wake tonight?"

"I hope not. I'm hoping a long, natural sleep will help him heal. Sorry Alex, you've lost your bed for the night."

"In that case, I'm taking Avery back home, and you two can leave when you're ready. I'm going to let El sleep here, too."

Briar's eyes widened in surprise as she looked between Alex and Avery, and then a smile spread across her face. "Fair enough. I'll hang around for another hour or two, just in case there's a problem, and then I'll go home, too."

Newton looked speculatively at Alex and Avery, and then back to Briar. "I'll wait with you, Briar, and then take you home. In fact, from now on, we should all keep an eye on each other."

"Er, okay," Briar agreed, "thank you."

"That reminds me," Alex said, rising to his feet. "Me and Reuben had been thinking about a design of some runes that can hide us from Faversham. The only thing is, it needs to be a tattoo for full protection. Interested?"

Newton frowned. "For me as well?"

"You're part of the team now. You're as much at risk as the rest of us."

"I'll think on it."

"Me, too," Briar said.

"Good." Alex pulled Avery to her feet. "Give me a couple of minutes, and I'm good to go."

7

Alex and Avery were woken the next morning by a loud banging on the front door.

Avery groaned and rolled over to look at the clock. "Crap, it's barely seven! Who's that?"

"I'll go," Alex said, already rolling out of bed and pulling on his jeans and t-shirt.

Avery thought she'd better follow him, although it was unlikely Faversham would just knock at her door. She hurriedly pulled her jeans and t-shirt on, too, ran her hands through her hair, and raced downstairs after Alex.

She heard El's voice before she'd got halfway down. "You have to stop him, Alex! He'll get himself killed, and he won't listen to me!"

El was standing in the middle of Avery's living room, tears streaming down her face. Her face was red and her eyes swollen.

"What's happened?" Avery asked, fear running through her.

Alex was already reaching for his phone that was lying on the kitchen workbench.

"Reuben's gone to confront Faversham."

"He's done what?" Avery said, horrified.

El started crying again. "He woke up half an hour ago and has gone mad. He couldn't remember what had happened for a second, and then when he did he just yelled, and said he was going to kill Faversham." She gasped to get her breath, blinking back tears. "I tried to stop him, but he won't listen. He barely looks at me! We have to stop him."

"He's taken his car, I presume?"

"Yeah. He grabbed the keys and just ran out."

Avery found her own keys, "Alex, let's go."

Alex was on his phone. "It goes to voicemail."

"Keep trying, I'll drive. Try and get Newton, too."

221

They raced to Avery's car, and she pulled out onto the quiet streets. "I'll follow the main road to Harecombe, that would be the quickest way."

She navigated the streets, trying to keep calm, while Alex called Briar. He sat next to her in the front seat, El sitting anxiously in the back. She had fallen quiet now, looking out of the windows, desperate to see a sign of Reuben. The weather was still foul, the wind and rain battering the car.

"Hey, Briar," Alex said into the phone. "Is Newton with you?" He raised his eyebrows at Avery. "Sorry, Briar, no need to yell. Have you got his number? I need to speak to him urgently. Reuben's gone to attack Faversham." He paused and listened. "We're going after him now, on the road to Harecombe. Can you tell Newton? Great, see you later. Don't worry."

"Did you upset her—about Newton?"

Alex looked sheepish. "I think so. She said not to be so bloody presumptuous."

Avery laughed. "I needed that bit of levity right now." She looked at El in her rear view mirror. "Are you okay, El?"

Elspeth continued to look out of the window. "No. I'm worried sick."

"I'm sorry he's mad at you. It's not your fault. If it's anyone's, it's mine."

"No, it's not!" Alex said, annoyed. He turned to face Avery and El behind him. "It's Faversham's. He's the dick here, not us. These are our books. It's not our fault his ancestor, Octavia was such a bitch that she was locked up in some sort of witch's purgatory with her bloody demon."

Now El looked surprised, her attention finally off Reuben. "What the hell are you talking about?"

"Oh! You didn't hear Newton's news yesterday, did you? It's a shocker." He sighed and started to tell her.

Avery half listened, racing down the lanes that led to Harecombe. Once the road opened up, she put her foot down, going as fast as her ancient van allowed. The road hugged the coast, twisting every so often and giving flashes of the sea and coves along the way. There was no way they'd catch him. Then she had another thought. "Hey guys, where am I going in Harecombe? Where does Faversham live?"

"That's a great question," Alex said. "El?"

She looked dumbfounded. "No idea. I'm still trying to process witch purgatory."

"So I'm racing down this road to *where*?" Avery asked, increasingly frustrated.

"There!" El yelled, pointing out the window towards a car park above the beach where Reuben's car was parked.

Avery slammed the brakes on, and turned onto the road to the cove. "What's he doing there?"

"His surfboard's missing." El said, relief creeping into her voice. "Maybe he's changed his mind."

"Maybe he's realised that like us, he has no idea where he's going," Alex said.

"Maybe he's got a death wish," Avery put in. "Surely the weather's too bad to surf. How's he got his wet suit?"

"He always has one in the car," El said.

They pulled up next to his car, right at the edge of the otherwise deserted car park, and looked over to the cove below. The path down to the beach travelled through sand dunes until it hit the beach. The tide was in, smashing against the beach and the rocks either side of the cove. Avery could see Reuben on his board, trying to make his way out.

"Shit. He's really trying to surf now?" Alex was incredulous. "He'll be crushed."

"How the hell do we stop him?" Avery asked, knowing no one could answer.

El jumped out of the car and raced down the path, drenched in seconds. They heard her voice, the words lost on the wind.

"Oh, crap. What now?"

Alex sighed and looked at her. "I suppose we need to go after them."

"And do what? There must be a spell we can use." Neither was dressed for the weather, and Alex looked as rumpled as she felt. "I don't think I'm even really awake yet."

"This was not how I imagined this morning would start."

"Alex, get your mind off sex. Our friends are in crisis."

"A crisis that will not be solved by us getting soaked on the beach. We're going back to bed after this."

"Seriously. Stop it. What is wrong with you?" Avery looked at him in amazement. "Our friend is possibly trying to kill himself!"

"Nothing's wrong with me. For a start, I don't think he's trying to kill himself. I think he's trying to blow off steam, and surfing is Reuben's way of doing that. He surfs. A lot. For hours. He's very good at it. And I woke up in bed with a beautiful woman. Why wouldn't I be thinking of sex?" He grinned suggestively.

Avery was momentarily flummoxed. *Did he just call her beautiful?* "I'm not beautiful."

"Yes, you are." Alex looked away, frowning. "What's he doing?"

Avery followed his gaze, and saw Reuben had paddled out a long way and was standing up on his surfboard, facing out to sea. He seemed to be gesturing towards the waves. Slowly but surely, the waves were starting to rise. El stood on the shore, looking as if she was shouting at him.

"Is he doing that wave thing?" Avery asked, shocked.

The waves rose higher and higher, swelling beneath Reuben, who had dropped to a crouch, looking far too small and vulnerable.

"Oh, shit." Alex said abruptly, getting out of the car and running towards the beach. Avery followed, the wind and the rain shattering her peaceful mood.

Within seconds she was soaked, and she raced down the path, pushing her hair out of her eyes. She could hear Alex shouting. "El, get back, get back!"

But El was already turning and running back towards them.

The giant wave beneath Reuben started to fold and Reuben plunged with it, riding it towards the shore. Avery stopped dead on the wooden path, watching nervously. It looked terrifying.

For a few seconds he disappeared beneath the swell of the collapsing wave, and then he shot out through the end, the spray ferocious.

Alex was up ahead and he had grabbed El's hand, running back with her. The wave hit the shore where El had stood only seconds earlier and raced up the sands. Reuben maintained his balance, crouched, arms outstretched as the wave brought him to the shallows, and as the wave disappeared, he paddled to shore. The waves had crashed just below the sand dunes, and Avery ran to join El and Alex, who stood on the boardwalk just above the water line. Driftwood and seaweed lay strewn across the beach, abandoned by the receding wave.

Alex looked furious and El looked shocked. The wave was lethal, it could have killed Reuben and El. Didn't he see her?

Reuben stood on the shore, looking back at them.

"Wait here," Alex said, and ran to Reuben.

Avery pulled El towards her. "Are you all right?"

El was crying. "What's he doing?"

"He's grieving, El."

"He could have killed me."

"He probably didn't see you." Avery reasoned, trying to reassure herself as well as El.

"I never thought I'd say this, Avery, but I can't look at Reuben right now." El rubbed her eyes and then wrapped her arms around herself. "I want to go."

Avery looked beyond El to where Alex stood in front of Reuben. They were almost nose-to-nose, and Alex looked tense, his fists clenched at his side. He looked over his shoulder, gesturing towards them. Reuben looked across to them and then turned and walked away, back into the sea.

"Come on," Avery said. "Alex will catch up." She turned away and led El up to the car.

8

They dropped El at home. Avery had suggested she came to her flat, but she refused.

"I wouldn't be good company right now, and I've got jewellery to make and a grimoire to study."

Avery looked at Alex after she'd left. "Did Reuben make that wave, knowing El was there?"

Alex still looked annoyed and had been quiet on their way back—all of them had. "I don't know, though I don't think so. But he sure didn't look too worried when I pointed out he could have drowned her."

"It must have been a mistake," Avery said. "Reuben's not like that."

"No, of course not. But it doesn't mean he can't be a jerk occasionally."

"Is he still going after Faversham?"

"No. Even he knows that's dumb right now." He sighed, looking out at the harbour next to El's flat. "My mind really isn't on work right now. If there's enough staff to cover me, do you mind if I come back to yours?"

Avery smiled. "Of course not, although I'm supposed to be working too. I'll ask Sally if she can manage without me today; I really want to go through that stuff again. Do you need anything from your flat?"

"I want to check that it's secure. Not quite sure how Reuben and El left it earlier."

"Sure. I'll let Briar know that Newton can stand down," she said with a grin.

The summer storm showed no sign of stopping, and after picking up some food and a few beers, they parked behind Avery's flat and raced through the rain and into her home.

The cats meowed loudly. "I better feed these guys," Avery said as they snaked around her wet ankles, demanding attention. She bent over, patting their sleek heads.

"And then I think we need a shower," Alex declared, puddles of water forming at his feet. "I might die from pneumonia."

Avery looked him up and down and grinned. His clothes clung to him, revealing every well-placed muscle. "You look pretty good wet."

"I look even better wet and naked. How big is your shower?"

"Not big enough for two," she said, laughing.

"Damn it," he moaned in mock frustration. "Shall I leave it running for you?"

"Yes, please."

He headed up the stairs, and after Avery had fed the cats, she lit a few lamps, brightening the gloom. Her bright Persian rug and colourful cushions glowed in the warm light, and she opened the window an inch, enjoying the smell of the wet earth and the sound of the rain. Alex was singing in the shower. She smiled. She could get used to this.

She unpacked the bags of food, and then headed up to the shower, stripping off her soggy jeans and t-shirt, until she was only in her underwear. Alex was heading out of the bathroom as she went in. A towel was wrapped low on his hips, revealing his tanned, toned abs and arms, and he rubbed his hair dry with another towel. She couldn't help but stare.

He lifted his head, catching her looking, and grinned as he took in her lack of clothes. "Now this is what I was thinking about when I woke up this morning," he said, reaching for her with a wicked grin.

***

After one of Alex's amazing breakfasts, they headed up to the attic, and surrounded themselves with Anne's research and the map they had found at the museum.

The rain sounded even louder in the attic, thundering on the roof and against the windows. Avery put some music on in the background, and then lit a few candles and some incense to aid concentration.

Alex picked up Avery's family tree. "It's hard to believe that Anne spent years doing this research."

"Do you think she knew it would turn out like this?" Avery sat cross-legged on the sofa, the hidden map on her lap.

227

"No idea. Did she know your grandmother?" Alex looked at her curiously. He was sitting on the rug, leaning against a large Moroccan leather pouffe.

"I'm not sure. I'm planning to see her this week—she lives in the nursing home in Mevagissey. I'll ask her then." Avery frowned. "I'm not sure it will be much good. Her memories have gone, she can't even remember who I am half the time."

"Alzheimer's?" Alex asked, looking concerned.

"Unfortunately."

"They say that the memories of their youth can stick around longer than those of the present. She may surprise you."

"Maybe. She would have been a contemporary of Anne and Lottie. They must have known each other."

"Did she tell you much when she was younger and well?"

Avery grimaced as she tried to remember. "I could kick myself. I never asked anything when I should have. Magic was our family secret, of course, and we knew about you and Gil, obviously. I was told we were special and that we mustn't tell anyone, but as I grew older, I didn't ask questions. It was what it was. My grandmother taught me the old ways—the herbs and their properties, the powers of stones, the tarot."

"Not your mother or father?"

"My father left when I was young. There was my mother, my sister, and me. And my gran. So yes, my mom did teach me some stuff, but she was never comfortable with it. And my sister wasn't interested at all."

"Could she use magic, though? I mean, did they have the power, or was it dormant?" Magic could skip generations, or could be suppressed or not used. Like any skill, you could lose it over time.

"A bit of both, I think. They thought it unnatural."

Alex nodded. It was a familiar story, as Gil's cousin proved. Not everyone welcomed magic into their life. "Same for me. My father used it, occasionally. He was prone to strong psychic visions, and he hated them. It all freaked my brother out completely. My uncle pretended it didn't exist, and ran the pub for normality."

Avery leaned forward, her elbow on her knee, and her chin in her hand. "Where's your dad now?"

"A long way from here. Scotland."

"Why Scotland?"

"Because it's a long way from here. He swears it dulls his visions."

228

"What about your mother?"

Alex fell silent for a moment. "Magic didn't run in her family. She found it fascinating, and then she got bored with the weirdness of it."

"So, who taught you?"

"My dad, haphazardly. I didn't respect it enough when I was younger. I took it for granted."

"You were cocky."

He smiled slowly, holding her gaze. "Yes, I was cocky. About lots of things."

Avery was fascinated. "So, when did you start to respect it?"

"When I was about 18 and it finally sank in that no one could do what we could do. I wanted to learn more about it, about me, who I was, and I knew I couldn't learn any more from my dad. I think his powers scared him." He looked at her speculatively. "I couldn't ask you. You kept me at arm's length."

"I did not!"

"Yes, you did. I was cocky. I get it. Your gran would offer me the occasional cup of tea. I should have taken her up on them more often."

"I didn't know that!" Avery felt a rush of guilt. If Alex was lonely and needed guidance, she never knew it. She probably needed some herself.

He carried on, undisturbed. "Gil was a bit older, more serious, and already involved in the family business. El had just arrived, Briar wasn't here then. So I went travelling."

"So I gathered. Where to?"

"India, of course, where everyone goes for spiritual guidance. And maybe weed."

She laughed. "What did you learn about magic there?"

"Not magic so much, but just who I was. I needed to get out of our quaint English seaside town. I travelled around, lived a little, partied a lot, and got dysentery. Then I went to Ireland. I loved it there. I could *feel* magic in the soil. And then I met an old guy on the West Coast of Ireland. He knew when he looked at me."

"Knew what?" Avery asked, confused.

"Knew that I knew magic."

Now Avery was really curious. "Another witch?"

Alex's eyes darkened with memory. "Yes. He must have sensed I was lost. He took me in and taught me how to use my powers, how to spirit walk, how not be scared of my visions, but to trust them."

Avery slowly sat up, seeing Alex in a new light. She'd noticed how different he was over the last few weeks, but talking about this with him was like uncovering another layer.

"That's amazing, Alex. How wonderful for you! Who was he?"

"His name was Johnny, and he lived in an old ramshackle cottage on the edge of the sea on the Ring of Kerry. He never told me his full name, but he knew magic, Avery, really knew it."

"Did he have a family, children?"

"If he did, he never spoke of them. I had the feeling they had gone away a long time before." Alex looked sad as he recalled his memories.

"How long did you stay there?"

"A couple of years, and then I knew it was time to come back. Part of me didn't want to leave—he's old, and I was worried about him. But he knew it was time, too. Said I had to leave, that something called from White Haven that could not be refused. And he was right, so I came."

"So when you arrived here a few months ago, you'd come straight from him?"

Alex nodded.

"Do you hear from him?"

"Occasionally. He only has a land line, and half the time he won't answer it, but I call him anyway." He smiled. "So, that's my story. I haven't told anyone about Johnny before—I'd appreciate it if you keep it quiet."

Avery felt a rush of pleasure that he'd told her such a secret. "Of course, scouts honour," she said seriously. "Was he psychic? Did he know what we'd find?"

"Maybe. He never said what it was." Alex paused for a moment. "What do you know of other witches, outside of White Haven?"

Avery considered his question for a second; she had never been asked that before. "I know nothing of other witches, although I accept the probability."

"There are more of us out there than you realise, Avery. Johnny told me about others."

"How many?"

"I don't know. But like us, they live together in small communities. That's why I reconnected with you and the others when I returned. I wanted all of us to work together. And if there are other witches, I want to know them too."

"But what if they're like the Favershams?"

"What if they're like us?" he challenged, watching her reaction. "If our problems with Faversham get really big, we may need help."

9

Avery's grandmother sat in an armchair in front of a big picture window looking out over the sea. She was petite, white-haired, with bright blue eyes that weren't quite focussed on the view outside.

The residential home sat on a high cliff looking out over the bay beyond. The summer storm had gone, and the sun sparkled off the white-tipped waves. The garden below was filled with roses and summer flowers, and the occasional resident and visitor pottered along the paths.

Avery sat in the chair opposite her grandmother and placed two cups of tea between them.

"Hi Gran, it's me, Avery. How are you?"

The old lady looked at her with flicker of recognition that was quickly gone. She smiled. "I'm all right, my dear. Do I know you?"

"I'm Avery," she repeated, her heart sinking. "Your granddaughter. Diana's child."

Her gran nodded. "I had a daughter called Diana. She was headstrong, that one. Always getting into trouble." She gazed out to sea again. "I miss her."

Avery closed her eyes briefly. This was always so hard. She chatted for a while about what she'd been doing, and asked her gran if she'd been out. Her gran responded, chattering for a while aimlessly, and seemed happy enough.

Avery decided now was a good time to broach what she'd really come to ask. Sometimes calling her by her name worked. "Clea. Do you remember Lottie Jackson?"

She turned to Avery, frowning. "Lottie was a nice girl. We used to meet for tea and talk about magic sometimes."

Avery looked around in alarm, hoping no one was close enough to hear. Fortunately, they were the only ones in the sunroom.

"And what about her uncle, Addison? Do you remember him?"

Her eyes clouded over for a second. "He was always a strange one. We were told to keep away from him."

Avery sat forward. "Why was that, Clea? Can you remember?"

She shuddered and once again turned her gaze to sea. "He disappeared young. Those Faversham boys, causing trouble again."

Avery nearly fell off her seat in shock. "Did you say Faversham?"

Her gran turned in alarm. "Shush! We never say their name. It's bad luck. Almost brought down the whole Council on us once."

Avery's head was whirling. "What Council?"

Her gran frowned. "Do I know you?"

Avery bit back her impatience, and patted her gran's hand. "I'm Avery, your granddaughter."

She smiled. "Of course you are. You look so pretty. Just like Diana."

"You mentioned the Council?"

She looked impatient. "Their water rates are so high! It's scandalous."

Avery blinked. This was useless. What was she thinking? She leaned back in the chair and closed her eyes. She was so tired. After talking to Alex the other afternoon, and reading Anne's papers, she felt she was on the cusp of knowing something, but it was fragile, just beyond her grasp.

She opened her eyes and watched her gran stir sugar into her tea, her hands shaking lightly. She was so old now, so infirm. She wondered if she retained any magic, or if the Alzheimer's had suppressed it. And then she realised her gran's spoon was stirring all on its own. She gasped and pulled it out of the cup. She hoped this didn't happen often.

Some core part of her was still there, buried deep. Avery had to try again. "Why was the Council upset about the Favershams?"

"Oh, they weren't upset with them, they were upset with us."

"With us? Why?"

"Those hidden books caused a lot of trouble. Everybody wanted them." Her gran looked at her earnestly. "We promised not to look for them, and were forbidden to mention them again." She put her finger in front of her lips, her eyes wide. "Silly people. You can't hide magic."

Avery felt a shock run through her. What the hell was going on? "Clea. It's very important. Who are the Council?"

"They're not really a Council," Gran said crossly. "It's all pretend. Some people just like to give themselves airs. We pretended to listen for a while, and then Lottie had a plan. They didn't know that." She broke off, looking perplexed. "I wonder what Anne did with it all? Is there any cake, dear?"

"I'll get you cake in a minute. Who are they, Gran?"

"Nasty people," she said. "There's a reason witches left White Haven."

* * *

Avery arrived at her shop, her head whirling. Despite her best attempts, and lots of bribery with cake, she got no more sense out of her gran.

It was unnerving. The more she found out, the less she felt she knew. Who were 'they?' Why did they call themselves a Council? And most importantly, where were they now?

Sally was standing at the counter, and she looked up as the bell rang on the back of the door as Avery entered. Her blonde hair was taken back into a high ponytail, her reading glasses were perched on the end of her nose, and a pile of new books was stacked on the counter in front of her. "You okay?"

Avery nodded, burying her confusion. "I'm fine. Just stuff on my mind."

She took a deep breath, inhaling the smell of incense and books. Just being here calmed her down. And of course her spell on the place, designed to ease people's moods and help them concentrate. Jazz was playing in the background, Sally's favourite, and a few shoppers perused the aisles.

Sally grinned. "Alex popped in."

"Great. Is he okay?" Avery asked, non-committal. She plonked her bag on the counter and reached for the sweets jar they kept stocked for customers.

"You tell me. You seem to be seeing a lot of him. He had a spring in his step and a twinkle in his eye." She narrowed her eyes. "So do you."

Avery considered her answer, looking at Sally with a raised eyebrow. She didn't want to reveal quite how much she'd fallen for him. "We've reached an understanding. He makes me laugh."

Sally smirked. "I bet he does more than that!"

"Sally!" Avery said, fake scandalised.

"Lucky cow. So, come on, give me the details. Don't think I didn't see his car here the other morning."

"Reuben was at his flat, actually."

Sally snorted. "Yeah, right. So he slept on the sofa?"

"I'm not saying any more."

"I'm teasing," she said, her voice softening. "And pleased for you. Now, get behind here, you slacker, I have stock to check."

"Bring me a coffee?" Avery asked, as she settled in behind the counter.

She nodded and disappeared into the back of the shop.

For the next half an hour, Avery dealt with customers, in between texting El and Briar to see how they were. They all planned to meet up the following evening to swap news, just as Reuben stepped into the shop.

His glanced around the aisles, and then headed to the counter. He looked pale, despite his deep tan. He was wearing a surf t-shirt, shorts, flip-flops and sunglasses. His blond hair was tussled and salt-crusted. He slipped his sunglasses onto his head, and Avery tried not to show her surprise. He looked exhausted.

"How you doin', Reuben?" she asked him, concerned.

He shook his head. "Not great. I came to apologise about the other day. I'm having trouble processing things."

"Not surprisingly," Avery said, her heart heavy. "I'm so sorry, for all of this."

"I didn't mean to put you in danger."

"It was El who was in danger, not me."

He dropped his head. "I know. I've rung her, but she's not answering. She won't answer the door for me, either."

"She'll come around. She was pretty pissed, though." She hesitated a second and then added, "You're both doing a good job of pissing each other off, actually."

Reuben nodded and fell silent, glancing around the room again to check that no one was within earshot. "I want justice for Gil. It seems Faversham is just getting away with murder."

"He won't. We just need to work out what we're going to do. Have you heard about Newton?"

"Yeah, Alex filled me in."

"We're meeting him tomorrow. He's finding out everything he can. We have to do this the witch way, not the legal way."

He nodded, but he still looked down. "Sounds good."

"We'll do this, Reuben," she said softly.

He swallowed and looked her in the eye, his gaze direct and unflinching. "We'd better. Anyway, there's something else I need to talk to you about— two things, actually. Are you free this evening?"

"Sure, why?"

"You need to get a tattoo. I've arranged it all with Nils." Nils was Reuben's friend who owned the local tattoo shop, Viking Ink. "He's staying open late tonight to get us all tattooed."

They'd been talking about this for days. "So you've finished the design, then?"

"Yep, me and Alex. We all get the same tattoo, and it should protect us from prying eyes. And that will help for my second request."

Avery had a flutter of worry. "Which is?"

"I need help. I think I know where my book is."

Avery's glanced around paranoid. "Really?"

"Come to Old Haven Church later. I've texted Alex. I want him there, too."

"Er, sure. What time?"

"Just before midnight."

"Midnight?" Avery wasn't sure she wanted to be wandering about some creepy old church at night.

"It has to be. Trust me." He headed for the door, and then turned back. "Don't bring El." And then he disappeared, striding past the window and down the street, leaving Avery wondering what was really going on.

10

Viking Ink tattoo parlour was located on the floor above an arcade that was packed with kids and teenagers. It was accessible by a narrow staircase, and at the top, the staircase turned and the door opened in a long, airy room.

Big picture windows showed views of the street below, and between the buildings opposite were glimpses of the sea and the harbour. The walls were covered in tattoo designs, the floor was wood, and there were a few partitioned rooms leading off from the main space.

Nils, the owner, was the Viking of his shop name. He was Swedish, and huge. Well over six feet, with enormous shoulders, chest, and well, everything really, Avery concluded. His biceps and forearms were well muscled, and he had a long, red beard and a completely shaven head. And of course he was covered with tattoos. Avery could see the complex designs spiralling down his arms and peaking above his V-neck shirt. He was wearing jeans, so she had no idea if his legs were tattooed, but the likelihood was high.

She'd seen him around White Haven—you couldn't miss him—but she didn't really know him. He was vaguely terrifying, purely because of his size and aggressive look. He had the palest blue eyes, almost icy, and that really didn't help. Avery could imagine him let loose with a massive axe, invading his way across Europe hundreds of years ago.

He looked up as she entered and almost grunted. "We're closed." His words held a trace of his Swedish accent.

She stopped suddenly in the doorway. She was the first to arrive. "Reuben told me to come. I'm his friend, Avery."

"Ah! Avery, come in!" He grinned, showing the whitest teeth, and his scary demeanour vanished. He strode across the room and engulfed her hand in his large one. It was without doubt the strongest handshake she had ever experienced, and she tried not to wince. "So good to meet you. Lucky you! You're the first, come and have a seat."

"Oh, great," she said, trying to sound enthusiastic.

"You are in some club, yes? You're all having matching tattoos."

Avery laughed nervously. "I'm not sure you'd call it a club, but yes, matching tattoos."

He led her to the counter and pulled a sheet of paper towards him. "It's a cool design. Rune work and a pentacle. Very Viking—I approve."

"May I see it?" Avery asked.

"Yeah, sure," he said, his deep voice booming around the room as he handed her the design. "Where we putting this bad boy?"

The design was a complex layering of runes around the outer circle of a pentagram and a protective sigil in the centre, all in black ink. "How big will it be?"

"About the size of your hand."

"Oh." That was bigger than she'd thought, which sounded more painful. "Can I have it on my hip?"

"Sure, right or left?"

"Right, I guess." Avery was so unprepared for this.

A woman came out of a back room as they were talking and nodded at Avery. Avery was momentarily silenced. She was a beautiful, young Japanese woman. Her long, dark hair was tied back, and a section on either side of her head was shaved. She was covered in gorgeous, inky black tattoos, flowers trailing all the way up her arms and at the base of her neck.

Nils started collecting his equipment together. "This is Chihiro," he said. "She's helping me tonight."

Chihiro nodded, but didn't speak. She sat behind the counter and picked up a magazine.

"When are your friends arriving?" Nils asked.

"Soon, I guess."

"Great, I'll start on you. Next one's yours, Chi," he instructed.

He led Avery to a small, partitioned room. "Lie on the table, drop your skirt, and wriggle under the sheet on the bed." He gestured to the long table like a masseuse's bench down the centre of the room. Bright lights were above it, casting a good, even light.

As Avery was getting ready, she heard the door open and Briar shouted out, "Hello?"

"I'm in here, Briar," Avery called, glad of the company.

Briar appeared at the door and looked at Avery with a grin. "Wow, so we're really doing this?"

Nils smiled at her. "Chihiro's doing you. Will be about an hour or so."

"An hour?" Avery exclaimed, her voice muffled as she dropped her head into the space in the table.

Avery was vaguely aware of Briar disappearing, then she heard the *whir* of the needle start, gritted her teeth, and closed her eyes.

When she finally got off the table, her skin burning, Alex and El were also in the main room, debating who was going next. Alex grinned at her. "How's it feel?"

"Painful."

He laughed, "It'll soon go. You bandaged up?"

"Sure she is," Nils said, coming out of the room after her. "Follow the instructions. It looks good. Who's next?" he asked.

"Ladies first," Alex said, nodding to El.

El had already got a couple of tattoos on her upper arm, and appeared to know Nils. "Hey Nils, it's been a while."

"Ah, beautiful Elspeth, come in honey," he said with a wink.

Avery could hear the needle whirring in another room, and presumed Briar was still in there. She sat next to Alex. "That really hurt."

"It won't last long. Sorry I missed the start, the pub was busy." He leaned in and kissed her, his hand cradling the back of her neck as he pulled her close. "I missed you."

"It's only been a day," she said, secretly pleased.

"That's enough. Did Reuben ask you about tonight?"

"Yeah. I'm intrigued, and a little worried."

"I'll feel happier once these tattoos are on. We need to enchant them to activate their power," he explained.

She nodded. "Are we doing that together?"

"May as well."

Avery looked up as the door opened again and Newton walked in. She'd almost forgotten he'd be getting tattooed, too.

Newton looked around the room, taking everything in, and then sat on a worn leather chair next to Alex. He was once again dressed in his work suit and a dark grey shirt. "It's been a while since I've been in one of these places."

"You've got a tattoo?" Avery asked, surprised.

"Yep. A big wolf on my right shoulder."

Alex nodded. "Sounds cool. Where you gonna put this one?"

"Top of my left arm. You?"

Alex looked down at his arms. "No room there. It'll go on my left shoulder."

They were interrupted by Chihiro joining them in the main room, followed by Briar. Newton rose swiftly to his feet. "Briar, are you okay?"

She looked slightly embarrassed as well as pleased, and she held a hand to the base of her neck, securing the dressing in place. "I'm fine. I can cope with ink and my own blood."

Chihiro eyed Alex with pleasure. He stood to greet her, and she reached up and kissed him on the cheek. "Alex, it's been too long." She stood back to appraise him, and Avery felt a trickle of jealousy run up her spine. "You look good," she said, her voice low.

"You too, Chi," he said softly. "You doing my ink? You did the rest!"

"It would be my pleasure," she said, a smile playing across her lips.

I'll bet it would, Avery thought, trying not to snort with derision. She was pretty sure Chihiro had done more than give Alex his tattoos.

As if he'd read her mind, he looked at Avery. "Meet at yours at nine? We can complete everything."

"Yeah, if you know what you're doing?"

He winked. "Trust me."

***

Close to midnight, Avery stood with Alex at the entrance to the Jackson's mausoleum, waiting for Reuben to arrive.

The door was sealed shut, but a huge crack still ran across the stone work from the foundation to the roof.

"I hope the roof doesn't collapse on our heads," Avery said, looking out to the church and the cemetery.

"It's stood here for centuries, battered by the elements. I'm sure it can withstand a little magic," Alex said.

They had met at her flat a few hours earlier as arranged, and together with Briar, El, and Newton, they had recited the spell that activated their protective tattoo. Newton had looked uncomfortable throughout the whole ceremony, but hadn't complained once. His grey eyes watched Briar discretely, and he stood near to her whenever possible.

They drank a potion that Alex had brought with him, and then repeated the spell after him: By day, by night, dispel might, harbour love, harbour life.

By air, by fire, by earth, by water, let us pass unseen, unheard, our spirits hidden.

As soon as they had completed the spell, Avery felt a flare of power on her tattoo, and the sensation of being branded with fire had flashed into her mind before it vanished.

As uncomfortable as it had been, she felt relieved it had been done. Hopefully they'd have no more surprise visits from Faversham. Reuben hadn't joined them; Alex said he'd already completed his spell. El merely nodded, and Avery wondered if anything would be the same between her and Reuben again.

As she was thinking of him, she saw headlights beyond the church, and heard the low growl of an engine and the crunch of gravel.

Within minutes, Reuben was at their side. "You haven't gone in, then?"

"No thanks, mate," Alex said. "It's a bit creepy in there."

"Fair enough," Reuben said. "Have you been tattooed?"

"All done," Avery said. "Nils and Chihiro are interesting characters."

"I'd trust them with my life," Reuben said. "Follow me."

He held his hand over the lock, and muttering a few words softly, they heard the lock release. Reuben turned the large handle and pushed the door open.

"What are we doing here?" Alex said, a hand on Reuben's arm, before he went in.

"I think I've found a hidden entrance. It might be where my grimoire is. After the last time, I thought I'd bring some back-up."

They followed him into the cold, damp building and closed the door behind them. Several doors led off from the main room. Stone sarcophagi were stacked high and deep, and Avery was surprised by the size of it. Her gaze involuntarily fell on Gil's coffin, before she turned to follow Reuben into a small side room.

"This is the oldest part of the mausoleum," he said. "I've been studying old plans, and something looked unusual here."

Avery was incredulous. "You have a blueprint of this place?"

"We have plans of everything. The grounds, the glasshouse, the ice house, the main house, old garden plans, even the old gatehouse. I grabbed all the prints I could find and hid them in part of the attic. But, things have been added to over the years, so I'm not sure how accurate everything is."

"So, this is what you were looking for the other day," Alex concluded, looking around with interest. He flashed his torch around the corners and high ceilings.

"Yes, before I was attacked by that bastard."

"You feeling okay now?" Avery asked.

"Yeah, thanks to you guys and Briar." He turned away, shining his torch down to where a coffin lay on a low shelf, inset into the solid stone wall, a gap of about three feet between it and the floor. "It's here somewhere."

An ornate design of curling plants and flowers had been carved into the stone around a name—*Prentice Jackson, 1388 – 1445.*

Avery gasped. "Is this the oldest grave in here?"

Reuben looked up at her from where he now knelt in front of the stonework, a grim smile on his face. "I think so."

"When was this built?"

"About the early 1400s. Before then, our family was buried in the graveyard. Prentice built this."

"Wow. Most of your ancestors in one place." She wondered where hers were buried, and realised she hadn't even thought about it before—other than about Helena.

Reuben trained his light on one flower, and turned to them, smiling. "Look."

They leaned closer. Within the centre was a simple pentagram, hidden within the design of the plant, the petals curling away from it. You would never see it if you didn't look closely. Reuben pushed it with his finger, and it receded into the stone around it with a click.

For a second, nothing happened, and then the whole stone shelf and the sarcophagus on it started to scrape back into the wall.

Avery's breath caught in her throat and goose bumps rose along her skin. This was seriously creepy. She looked back over her shoulder, but the dark shadows remained unmoving.

Alex asked, "Is that another passageway?"

"We're going to find many more before this is over," Reuben said, watching the space grow bigger and bigger before sticking into position. Stale, damp air wafted up from the dark hole. "Alex, help me push."

Alex got down on his hands and knees next to Reuben and pushed the stone further back; it scraped across the floor painfully and Avery winced. Reuben flashed his torchlight into the space. Shallow steps led downwards.

Reuben grinned, his face shadowed grotesquely. "Shall we?"

Avery's skin prickled. "Seriously?"

"You could stay here if you prefer?" he offered reasonably.

"No, thanks," Avery said, wishing she was still in her warm flat.

"It's okay, Avery. I'll follow you," Alex said. "We'll be fine."

Avery followed Reuben down the steps and grimaced as the cold, damp air hit her skin like a clammy hand. She pulled her coat tighter around herself, and sent up a witch light, in addition to her torch.

The steps were steep, but on the right, the wall opened out and they were soon on the floor of another square stone chamber beneath the mausoleum. Two long stone benches ran along either side of the room. In the centre was a crude fire pit, and at the far end was a carving in the wall—images of the Goddess and the Hunter. Beneath it was an altar, made from rough hewn stone. Brass lanterns hung overhead, spaced across the ceiling at regular intervals.

Alex snapped his fingers and each one lit with a bright orange flame.

"Is this a place of worship?" Avery asked, looking around in shock.

Reuben looked just as surprised. "Looks like it."

"What better way to hide your magical practices than down here," Alex said, pacing around the room.

"But look at the floor," Reuben said. "Devil traps and pentacles."

He was right. Carved into the stone were ornate diagrams and a huge pentagram.

Avery wandered over to the altar. A ritual knife still sat there, next to a goblet and a tarnished silver bowl. "But there's no grimoire."

Alex shook his head. "I don't like this place. I have a bad feeling about it."

"But the image of the Goddess and the Hunter?" Avery said. "Surely these are good symbols?"

"They should be, but I just can't shake this feeling," he said. His dark eyes looked troubled, almost hooded in the light.

Reuben's face had taken on an almost fanatical gleam. "How long do you think our family used this place for?"

"It must have been built at the same time as the mausoleum, so maybe a couple of hundred years until the Witchfinder General scared them off?" Avery ventured.

Reuben traced the carvings with his hands. "Maybe they continued on their own after your families hid their grimoires."

Avery looked at Alex, concerned. "Do you think all of our families met here together at one point?"

He shrugged. "I think so. It's big enough."

As Avery walked around the room, she realised there were narrow channels cut into the floor, leading towards the altar, and lined with a dark stain. Her heart almost missed a beat. "Oh, crap. Is that old blood?"

Alex dropped to his hands and knees to examine it more closely. He sighed. "It looks like it." He looked up at Reuben, who was still examining the altar. "Reuben, let's get out of here."

He turned. "My grimoire is still in here somewhere."

"You don't know that."

"I do," he insisted. "I'm not leaving 'til we find it." He turned away again, his shoulders set.

Alex stood and moved next to Avery. "Let's make this quick," he said softly.

A dark feeling of dread crept up Avery's back. It felt like something was in the room with them. Reuben was whispering spells at the front by the altar as he traced the carvings, desperate to find another mechanism. While he examined the altar, Avery and Alex walked the perimeter of the room, examining the walls for any hint of an opening or a hidden door. The rest of the walls were plain, the thick stones and their fine joins the only marks, other than a couple of small alcoves with old candles in them.

They joined Reuben, who had walked over to the devil's trap positioned in the far corner of the room. Crude runes were cut in the floor in front of it. Despite the bright orange light from the lanterns, Avery felt as if the room was growing darker.

"I think the runes are a summoning spell," Reuben said, dropping to his knees.

"Great, let's not say it, then," Avery said, wishing she was outside in the fresh air.

"Makes you wonder if they summoned a demon regularly though, doesn't it?" he asked, running his hand across the runes. "Maybe it was their own personal demon?"

"For small personal requests?" Alex said, sarcasm dripping from his voice.

"Why else have a devil's trap in the floor?"

Avery turned away towards the altar again, wondering what her ancestors got up to in here. She ran her hand across the engravings on the wall, trying to find comfort in the images of the Goddess and the Hunter and failing. Her gaze dropped to the floor and she saw the channels stained with old blood narrowing to join at the base of the wall, a shallow stone pool just visible before it disappeared under the wall. She felt her breath catch, and the others turned to her.

"What?" Alex asked, at her side immediately.

"Look," she pointed, curious now despite her misgivings. "There's the edge of a shallow bowl—it disappears under the wall. Maybe the wall moves back?"

"Maybe we need blood to move it back," Reuben suggested.

Both Alex and Avery looked at him in alarm, but before they could stop them, he had pulled a small knife out of his pocket and slashed across his palm, just as Alex had done for his spell.

"No, wait!" Alex said, leaping to stop Reuben. "We don't know what it will do."

But it was too late. Reuben crouched down, squeezing his palm, and a bright stream of blood dropped onto the channels and into the shallow bowl.

Avery stepped back, alarmed.

For a few seconds, nothing happened.

"Maybe it needs more blood," Reuben muttered as he repeatedly squeezed his palm to increase the blood flow.

Alex moved closer to Avery, pulling her back into the centre of the room. "Reuben, enough."

There was a loud *click* as the entire wall cracked in half right down the middle, a previously invisible vertical line appearing in the wall between the Goddess and the Hunter. The walls swung back, hinged like doors, and the almost silent *shush* of the mechanism sent chills up Avery's spine.

Beyond the door was a small room, an altar up against the far wall, cast in shadows. They could now see the whole of the stone bowl in the floor. Leading from it, another thicker stone channel led to the second altar.

Avery sent the witch light into the space and gasped when she saw a dimensional doorway carved onto the stone wall at the back, above the second altar. "Not another one!"

"Please tell me your blood isn't running that far," Alex said, his tone abrupt as he addressed Reuben.

"No," Reuben said, throwing an annoyed glance back over his shoulder to Alex. "My palm does not produce rivers of blood!"

"Good. Watch where you drip. We don't want to accidentally open that thing."

But Reuben was already wrapping a portion of his t-shirt around his injured hand. He stepped around the original altar that stood before the wall and went into the smaller room, letting out a short cry of joy. "The grimoire."

Alex and Avery tentatively followed Reuben and saw a small wooden box on the altar, and resting in it was a thick, leather-bound book. Reuben reached forward for it, but Alex shouted, "Stop! Let me."

Reuben stopped mid-reach and frowned at Alex.

"Let's not get your blood on anything else," Alex said, stepping past him and checking the book from all angles before he reached in and lifted it up.

"Sorry, you're right," Reuben muttered. "Is it my grimoire?"

"Sure looks like it," Alex said, turning the first few pages carefully.

Avery saw some objects on the altar and frowned as she tried to identify them. There was what looked like small bone, and maybe a ring, placed together, and next to it a bundle of hair. "Oh, crap!" she said, realising what she was looking at. "That's a finger bone!"

The others turned quickly. "Where?" Alex asked.

"On the altar." She picked the ring up and held it under the light. It was made of gold and it had a large, red stone set into it; the ring was large, undoubtedly made for a man. She dropped it back onto the altar, grimacing.

"Let's get out of here," Reuben said, his bravado from earlier long gone. "We've got what we came for."

As they stepped out of the hidden room, the doors closed softly behind them with a whisper that seemed to come from beyond the grave. Avery desperately hoped they wouldn't need to return here, but had a horrible feeling they would.

11

Alex and Avery followed Reuben down the driveway of Greenlane Manor, the gravel crunching beneath the wheels of Alex's Alfa Romeo. At this hour the grounds were deserted, and the only light came from the window by the huge front door.

"What did you think of the hidden room?" Alex asked her. His face cast mostly in shadow looked grim.

"I hated it. It was oppressive and threatening." She hesitated for a second, wondering if she really wanted to voice what she thought, but this was Alex, and she knew he'd probably feel the same. "It's clear that blood magic, dark magic, was done there, and it worries me that Reuben doesn't seem to care too much."

"It worries me, too. I think his need to avenge Gil may be blinding him to some things."

"And he's inexperienced with magic," Avery added. "I mean, he has power, certainly, but I think he's a bit naive about some magic and its implications. It sounds ridiculous, I know, considering we're what we're all being exposed to, and we're all using stronger magic than we have before, but at least we've been using it a lot longer."

Alex glanced across at her. "Well, he's lost Gil, and isn't really speaking to El, so we're going to have to keep an eye on him."

"And he's here with Alicia," Avery said, feeling her anxiety rise. "We still don't really know what she's up to."

"Reuben's not stupid, though. We need to trust him."

They rolled to a halt in the turning circle in front of the steps to the manor and followed Reuben as he crossed the huge, echoing entrance hall, leading them up the sweeping stairs to his suite of rooms on the top floor. He left the main lights off, and only a couple of lamps casting low light illuminated their way. Avery peeked through open doorways, noting that the furniture looked expensive and antique; it was a very glamorous house. She hadn't been in here for years, and had forgotten how grand it was. It had definitely been refurbished since her childhood.

Reuben's suite of rooms was on the second floor, overlooking the sea. They stepped into a small entrance hall and passed through it into a large sitting room. A small kitchen was located on the back wall, and a door led off to a bedroom, and another to a bathroom. It was nothing like Avery had imagined. She presumed Reuben would live in some sort of disaster of surfboards and shorts, with stuff everywhere, but instead it was all cream linen, dark grey walls, a slick sound system, and an enormous TV.

"You all right?" Reuben asked her, starting to laugh at her expression.

"It's not what I expected!"

He winked, "Not quite the surf dive you imagined?"

"No," she said, feeling embarrassed.

"That's because we have cleaners."

"Lucky you," Alex said, walking over to the window to look at the view. A pale sliver of moon illuminated the sea beyond the bottom of the garden, and Avery could hear the waves crashing against the shore. The glasshouse glinted on the lawn below, and a vision of the hidden passageway and Gil's death filled Avery's thoughts.

Reuben turned on some lamps, and with a flick of a switch, the curtains started to close, dispelling the darkness. He locked the door behind them, and then headed to the rear wall and a section of dark oak panelling. "What I'm about to show you must remain a secret," he said, very serious.

"Of course," Avery said, raising her eyebrow speculatively at Alex.

"Our family is very big on hidden doorways, passageways, and rooms within rooms," Reuben explained, releasing a mechanism which allowed a hidden door within the panel to pop out.

"You've got to be kidding me!" Avery exclaimed.

"We're at the far end of the house, and this passageway leads up to a section of the attic that is separate from the rest. I shared it with Gil, but he accessed it through another door."

They followed him down a long, narrow passage and then up a steep flight of stairs, all hidden in the narrow space between two walls, and then they went through another door and a section of crowded attic space stretched ahead of them.

The centre was dominated by a large table, covered in books. A selection of unmatched chairs were scattered around the place, all upholstered with old fading material. The floor was made of wide wooden planks, and shelves lined the end wall, along either side of a fireplace. There were no windows here at all, and on the far side of the room was another door. Gil's entrance, she presumed.

"How on Earth did you get the furniture in here?" Avery asked, looking around in amazement.

"One of our ancestors brought them in years ago, through that wall." He pointed to the main dividing wall that separated them from the rest of the attic. "And then they bricked it up again. From the other side it's impossible to see that there's anything here, and the attic space is so huge and full of crap, you don't even realise it's shorter than it should be."

"So this spans the width of the house?" Alex asked, walking around.

"Yes, and therefore big enough for our needs. My needs," he said, correcting himself. He placed the newly found grimoire on the table. "It's nice to finally put this where it should be."

He switched on a desk lamp and angled it over the book, and despite her increasing tiredness, Avery looked at the book with excitement.

The cover, like the others, was made of thick old leather, but unlike the others was a dark blue. The arcane symbol for water was embossed on the front, an upside-down triangle, and on the first page was the usual list of all the witches who had used the grimoire before. Reuben ran his hand across it and closed his eyes briefly. He looked incredibly sad. "Gil should be here for this."

"Yes, he should. I'm so sorry he's not," Avery agreed, moving closer to Reuben and resting her hand on his arm. "How *are* you, Reuben?"

"I'm fine. I just want to find Faversham and kill him, that's all."

"There'll be ways to deal with him." She glanced at Alex concerned. "Is Alicia back here?"

Reuben concentrated on the grimoire as he spoke. "No, but she's coming back soon. She texted me to say she'd like to stay here until she's found somewhere else to live."

"And you're okay with that?"

"Of course I am," he said impatiently. "It was her home. I've told her she can take as long as she wants."

Avery glanced up at Alex, and he shook his head. Now was not the time to ambush Reuben by questioning Alicia's loyalties.

Alex changed the subject. "What sorts of spells are in there?"

Reuben sighed as he turned the pages, "I'm not sure—the writing is so hard to read!" He sounded exasperated, and a bit emotional.

"It's been a long night, Reuben," Alex said. "You should rest and read this tomorrow. We'll go and leave you to it, but would you mind if we checked the back first? To see if the hidden spell is in yours, too?"

Reuben shook himself. "Yeah, of course."

They doused the electric lights and produced a witch light that cast a pale, silvery glow over the attic. Reuben turned to the end of the grimoire, and there on the back pages was a spell, the lines of incantation headed: *Part Four, To Suspend in Water.* Avery felt dizzy, and wasn't sure if she was pleased or horrified. Like the others, it was clearly incomplete.

"Just need your grimoire then, Avery," Alex said, "and the spell will be complete."

12

Tuesday passed in a blur of work. Avery found it hard to concentrate, her head swimming with all the new information about the hidden room beneath the Jackson's mausoleum and discovering another part of the spell. She found her mind often drifting back to the map hidden in the old book upstairs, and a couple of times customers had had to repeat questions.

Sally had noticed her distraction, and over mid-afternoon coffee and cake taken in a break between customers, she asked, "Are you okay, Avery?"

Avery took a bite of her slice of coffee and walnut cake, thinking she could eat the entire cake in one sitting. "This cake is fantastic, Sally."

"Cheers, I made it last night, but stop avoiding the question! You're so distracted today."

Avery looked at her guiltily. "I know, sorry, I have a lot on my mind. My life has become very confusing lately."

"Do you want to share?"

Avery took another bite of cake, and wondered if she should. Sally was a good friend, and she valued her opinion, but she also had no idea about the extent of magic in White Haven. It was too dangerous to say much about it. "I'd love to, but it's too complicated. Things are very weird at the moment, and I think it's best if I say nothing for now."

Sally watched her for a second, and then nodded. "Fair enough, if you're sure. But keep safe. I feel whatever you're up to is dangerous."

"Have you still got your hex bag for protection?" Avery asked, with a flash of worry.

Sally reached into her blouse and pulled out the small bag, which she'd placed on a silver chain. "Right here."

"Good. I'll make sure Dan's got his, too."

"Will our other friends be okay, Avery, and my family?" Sometimes Avery was surprised by how perceptive Sally was.

"Yeah, I'm sure they will be. It's you and Dan who are more vulnerable, but don't ask me any more. I can't say." It was improbable that the Favershams would attack them directly; it was much more likely that they'd be caught in the crossfire of whatever magical war was taking place.

Sally nodded, seemingly reassured. "I'll be out back if you need me."

As she was locking up for the night, Avery received a text from Briar inviting her to her house at 6:30 p.m. *Newton's got news*, she'd sent enigmatically. *And don't eat, I'll feed you.*

Avery wound her way through the narrow streets of White Haven, enjoying the early evening sunshine. Locals and tourists alike were strolling the streets, heading to restaurants and bars, and a few shops were open late, enjoying the influx of tourists that the fine weather had brought.

Even in the middle of town, Avery could smell the sea, and the gulls wheeled overhead, their raucous cries echoing around the streets. Lately, Avery viewed the town with fresh eyes. She'd always taken its old buildings and history for granted, but now she felt she was part of its history. She could feel the past stretching its tendrils into the present. She noticed how the buildings from the different centuries all jostled together in a pleasing mix of styles, and she noticed how the town moved from one century to the next in the space of a few feet. It was exhilarating. She loved this place, and there was no way she was leaving, or letting the Favershams dictate what she would do. Despite the fact that she now knew more than she ever had, she still thought there was something else they had yet to find out, something that would reveal the true reason for Octavia's binding and Faversham's attack on Helena.

She turned onto Briar's street, a snaggy lane that stretched up the hill. The pavements were narrow, and the houses had tiny front gardens. She turned up the path and rang the bell, and then heard Briar call, "It's open."

Briar's front door opened straight into the low-ceilinged living room, where a massive old fireplace dominated the room. The space was filled with a comfortable sofa and armchairs, with bookcases on either side of the fireplace. A door at the rear led through to the kitchen, and Briar called again, "Come through, Avery."

The kitchen was small but packed with cupboards and efficiently organised. Briar stood at the counter, chopping salad.

"How did you know it was me?" Avery asked, wondering if Briar had hidden cameras installed somewhere.

Briar grinned. Her hair was wound on her head in a messy ponytail, and she wore a long, loose dress with a belt around it. Her feet were bare and she had painted her nails bright green. "I sensed you—you have a different energy than the others. You're all unique. Haven't you noticed?"

"I haven't, actually." Avery confessed, feeling she was missing something.

"My grimoire talks all about grounding, the earth, and energy signatures," she explained. "It's so much more than just a grimoire!" She grinned and it lit up her face.

"That makes sense. I saw auras when I spirit-walked with Alex, and they're different."

Briar concentrated on mixing the salad together. "I've been practising feeling the energy through the earth. I'm getting better—I feel my customers now before they've even entered the shop. I've started to pick up on moods, too." She stopped for a second and looked at her. "I can feel you and Alex— wow, you two!"

Avery flushed and opened the bottle of wine she'd brought with her, wondering how much to say, and then realised that their relationship really wasn't a secret to anyone. She looked at Briar's expectant face. "Yes, we have a *thing*. It's great so far, but I'm not sure how long it will last."

"You have trust issues. It's quite obvious he adores you."

Avery felt embarrassed and shocked. *Is that what others saw?* "He does not *adore* me! And if he does, he probably won't for long."

Briar rolled her eyes. "Stop it! El's right, the lady's man thing is an act. He's just a flirt—it means nothing."

Avery felt a flood of warmth spreading through her. It didn't matter how often people said it, she still doubted Alex could like her so much that it would last, but it was still good to hear. She swiftly changed the subject to avoid potential embarrassment. "And what about you and Newton?"

Briar turned away to the oven and shrugged. "I don't know. We're just friends."

"Now who's being coy!"

Briar pulled a bubbling, cheesy-topped lasagne out of the oven, and its rich scent flooded the kitchen. "Anyway, El's here."

Within seconds the front door opened and El came in, and they had barely said hello when Alex, Newton, and Reuben followed a few minutes later. Reuben glanced at El, but she looked away. Newton was out of his suit and again in jeans and a casual shirt. He nodded his hellos to everyone, his gaze lingering on Briar.

Alex, however, gave Avery a grin and a wink, and her heart raced. He wore his usual faded jeans and an old Led Zeppelin t-shirt, and his dark hair was loose. He plonked a six-pack of beer down on the bench. "Smells good, Briar. Cheers for cooking."

"My pleasure. I've set the table out back." She nodded towards the small lean-to sunroom at the back of the house. "Have a seat, and I'll bring everything through."

"I'll help," Newton said, immediately finding a tray.

Avery grinned and carried her bottle of wine into the sunroom, smiling at the ordered chaos. The sunroom stretched the length of the house, and a long wooden table ran down the centre, surrounded by old cane chairs heaped with mismatched cushions of stripes, patterns, and flowers. The table was laid with plates and glasses of different designs, but everything worked harmoniously. Plants filled the corners, and a small desk covered in papers was against the far wall. A small, riotous garden was out the back, planted around a tiny paved area, and the double doors to the patio stood wide open, letting in the warm evening air.

Avery sat at the far end of the table at the back, looking out over the garden, and Alex followed her out, sitting on her right, while Reuben sat opposite her. El sat next to Alex, as far from Reuben as she could get in this small place, and ignored him as much as possible.

Anxious to break the awkwardness, Avery said, "I love Briar's house. I've never been in it before."

Reuben nodded absentmindedly, and El answered, "Yeah, it's very Briar. Tiny garden, though—that's why she has an allotment."

"I'll have to visit it one day," Avery said thoughtfully. "I'm sure her new grimoire couldn't make her a better gardener, though."

"Any luck finding yours?" Reuben asked.

"No. It's infuriating. I've examined the map a thousand times, and I still can't work out where it is." She sipped her wine, wishing she wasn't the only one left to find her grimoire. *What if she couldn't ever find it?*

"I'll come round tomorrow evening, and we'll try again," Alex said.

Newton and Briar came out carrying the salad, lasagne, and garlic bread, and Avery inhaled the rich scents greedily. She realised she was starving, and helped herself to a liberal portion.

"Well, I have good news, sort of, to share," Newton began. "I've managed to find out quite a bit about the Favershams."

"And is it good news or bad?" Alex asked.

"Mostly bad." He sighed. "Look, before I start, you need to understand that while I was told about *my role*, I didn't really believe it. It sounded crazy, although my parents were insistent that it was real—are insistent, in fact. And of course now I know they're right."

The others nodded and El said, "It's okay, go on. We get it."

"I'll start with my old family records. The Favershams are definitely on my enemy list, and it started back during the witch trials when my ancestor, Peter Newton, was made to hang Helena because of the Witchfinder General and the Favershams. He felt so powerless that he vowed that it would never happen again. He started keeping tabs on the family, and realised they were rotten and corrupt. He made it his business to know what had happened, and to discover the truth of their witchcraft. Most of the families—your families—left White Haven after Helena's death, but he spoke to Helena's brother-in-law, just before he fled with her children and his own family. He told Peter what had happened with Octavia. He didn't reveal all the details of why, though—he probably didn't know. Peter felt strongly enough, and was worried enough about the implications of it all, that he passed it on.

"So, odd things happened from time to time, but eventually things settled down. Nothing particularly bad happened for decades. The witches left, the Favershams continued to build their empire, and then your families returned and kept a very low profile. And from what I understand, never knew my family knew about them."

"You watched us from a distance," Alex deduced.

"Pretty much. And of course, doubt set in, about everything—although, it was dutifully passed on. There haven't been any specific incidents in recent years—other than with Reuben's great-great-whatever uncle years ago. Addison, more than anyone in years, decided to look for the grimoires. It wasn't enough for him to let sleeping dogs lie. He wanted the grimoires and the power they contained—" he held up a hand to stop any questions. "I don't know why—my family records don't describe those details—we're watchers, remember. But there was enough activity for my great-great grandfather to be aware that *something* was happening. Anyway, Addison started the search, and the Favershams found out. They threatened him and his family. It seems that Addison had found one of the grimoires, and they knew about it. In order to protect his family, he did what we all now know—

he faked their deaths and disappeared, under the cover of black magic and a blood sacrifice. Something designed to scare anyone off searching in future. And knowledge of the grimoire disappeared with him. Your family, Reuben," Newton glanced at him, "continued the lie. Or should have."

Avery groaned as everything dropped into place. "But Lottie shared what she knew with Anne, and Anne was charged with keeping the secret—and the hidden grimoire."

Newton nodded. "Lottie was of a younger generation, but she found out what her uncle had done, and decided it was too big and too important to hide."

"So, they waited until things had calmed down and the story had been forgotten," Avery said, nodding. "How did your family find out, Newton?"

"My great-grandfather was also in the police, and had to investigate the disappearance. He found out what happened, and also played along—but left records of the truth for us." He shrugged. "As I told you the other night, it seemed crazy to me. I barely believed it, and didn't really read the records properly. I've known about you all of course, and your magical history and abilities, but again, I thought it was superstitious nonsense. I didn't even believe the grimoire stuff—I barely knew what it meant. It was only when that woman died on the moors that I really started to believe—it was obvious that wasn't normal. And then you told me about the grimoires the other night, and it all came flooding back—my *other* job became a reality."

"It's like Chinese whispers, isn't it?" Briar said. "Things get forgotten and distorted over time, until we can barely sort the truth from fiction."

"And it started over 400 years ago," Reuben pointed out. "No wonder it sounded crazy."

"But what about that vision you had, in your flat?" Alex asked Avery.

She frowned. "I must have been picking up on the Favershams and Caspian, the blood magic that had been used, and made the wrong association."

"Well," Newton continued after a mouthful of food, "I've checked the family out. Sebastian, as we know is head of the family and the CEO of Kernow Shipping. Caspian is his son and head of finance, and his daughter, Estelle, is head of overseas investments. He has a couple of nephews called," he consulted his notebook, which made him look super official, "Hamish and Rory, and Sebastian's brother, Rupert, is also on the board—he's their father. I have no idea about their magical abilities, of course, but it seems prudent to think they have them."

"So the dark-haired woman who attacked us at the church was Estelle?" Avery asked.

Newton nodded.

Alex narrowed his eyes, "Any suspicion of anything dodgy?"

"No, other than that they're rich and like a say in *everything*. They have their fingers in many, many pies in Harecombe. They're Council members, on the arts committee, benefactors to the art gallery and museum…" Newton rolled his eyes and took a mouthful of lasagne. "You name it, they do it."

"I loathe them even more than I did already," Briar said as she picked at her salad.

Newton paused and looked at Reuben for a second, a flash of concern breaking his police manner. "I've found out that Alicia is related to them, too."

Reuben's head shot up, and he stared at Newton. "*Gil's* Alicia?"

"Yes."

"How?"

"She's another cousin, from Sebastian's younger sister, Honoria."

They all fell silent, and Avery wondered what Reuben was thinking right now. He looked shocked, then surprised, and then finally put his fork down. "Sorry, I'm really confused. Does she work with them? Because I thought she had her own interior design business? And did Gil know?"

"I've no idea what Gil knew, Reuben, but I doubt it. You didn't. And no, she's not part of their business—well, not an obvious one. She's not listed on their company records. It seems she really is an interior designer, and a busy one. She's very popular with some very rich families all across Cornwall, and that includes hotels."

Reuben looked white beneath his deep tan, and he pushed his plate away. "Did she have anything to do with his death?"

Newton looked apologetic and ran his hand through his hair. "I don't know, and I'm not sure I can find out. But you may be able to."

Reuben looked at Avery accusingly. "You were asking me about Alicia, in the caves, just before he died. Did you know something?"

Avery had a sudden jolt of panic and wondered how much she should say, but she felt Alex's leg nudge her own gently, and she realised she had to voice her doubts. "I didn't know anything, no, of course not, I'd have said so. But, I did wonder how Faversham seemed to know so much, and it struck me that maybe Alicia knew more than Gil realised—she did live with him. With both of you."

Reuben looked at her wide-eyed with shock. "But you didn't say a thing!" He sounded incredulous. "I've been living with her ever since Gil died. The grimoire is there *now!*"

He scraped his chair back and stood up, ready to leave, and Avery rose too, as if to stop him. "No, wait! I didn't know! I could have been wrong—*we could still be wrong!*"

"I need to see her. *Now!*" He edged around the table, making for the door into the kitchen.

Newton stood, authority emanating from him. "No. Sit down, Reuben. We need to think this through."

"I don't need to think anything through. Butt out, Newton."

Alex also leapt to his feet and stopped Reuben at the door, his hand on Reuben's arm. "Reuben, as much as I hate to agree with Newton, he's right. We need to have a plan. She could be hiding a heap of magic."

Reuben glared at him and shrugged his hand off. "While I'm standing here arguing with you, my grimoire could be gone and the woman responsible for Gil's death is strolling around my house! Get out of my way. I don't want to hit you, but I will."

"Nice. Resorting to violence again," El said, looking at Reuben with a mixture of sorrow and anger.

Reuben paused for a second, shocked, and then continued relentlessly. "Excuse me for having feelings!"

All of El's anxiety and anger came bursting out after days of simmering resentment. "We all have feelings, Reuben. We don't have to hurt our *friends*, though!"

The magical energy in the room had shot up by then, and as well as feeling wind stirring around her, Avery noticed a flicker of flames in El's hands. *Wow. Things got ugly really quickly.*

Alex was trying hard to keep his cool. "Trust in your magic, Reuben. You have a hidden room, and it's hidden with magic, too—isn't it?"

"Yes," Reuben nodded, "of course."

"Then it should be fine."

"I'm not taking that risk. And I need to know if Alicia betrayed Gil," Reuben said, and he pushed around Alex and into the kitchen, slamming the door behind him.

"We can't let him do this alone, whatever he says," Alex said, turning to follow him. "Newton, come on. We need to stop him before he does something stupid."

"He's right though, Alex, we have to find out about Alicia." Avery reasoned, feeling the need to defend Reuben. "Caspian's already got away with killing him, and for Alicia to get away with betraying Gil as well is too much. I'm coming, too."

Briar looked at El, who remained seated, her face like stone. "I'll stay here with El."

"You don't have to babysit me, Briar."

"Of course I don't, but I'm staying anyway." Briar looked up at the others. "Go on, and stay safe."

13

Newton's sleek BMW sedan raced down the lanes, but despite the fact that they were only minutes behind Reuben, he was already lost to sight. They arrived with a screech of brakes and a splatter of gravel in front of Greenlane Manor and found Reuben's car abandoned and the front door wide open.

They ran up the steps and into the reception hall, and then hesitated. It was dusk and a couple of lights were on, but the rest of the house was in darkness.

"Where the hell are they?" Newton said, trying to contain his anger. All the way to the house they had debated over what to do, but as Newton said, you can't legally accuse someone of black magic and be taken seriously. He darted into the adjoining rooms and shouted, "Reuben!"

Silence surrounded them. They fanned out, checking the ground floor, but every room was eerily empty and extremely tidy.

"Where's her suite of rooms? They must be in there," Avery reasoned, itching to release some of her pent-up energy, while trying to convince herself that Alicia could be completely innocent and just a grieving widow.

"Let's try upstairs, the opposite side from Reuben's rooms," Alex suggested, running up the stairs.

The first floor was in darkness, so they raced up the next flight, coming to a sudden halt as they saw a sliver of light coming from an open doorway, far down the corridor to their left.

They edged closer, Avery trying hard to catch her breath, and heard shouting. It was a woman's voice. "Don't be ridiculous, Reuben. You're scaring me, stop it!"

"Don't play the coy woman with me. You're related to the man who killed Gil, and I want to know what you had to do with it."

"No one killed Gil, it was an accident."

"Bullshit. I was there. He was killed by Caspian Faversham, your cousin. Now, tell me what you know, or I will blast you from the face of the Earth."

They all looked at each other in alarm, and then Newton pushed the door open and stepped in. "Reuben! Calm down."

Alex followed with Avery close behind, both of them stepping on either side of Newton, ready to attack if necessary.

Reuben and Alicia were standing in front of an unlit fireplace, a few feet between them. Alicia stepped back as they entered, fear etched across her face. Reuben towered over her, emphasising how small she was.

Reuben shouted, "Keep out of this—all of you."

Alicia looked as if she might retreat further and then thought better of it. She appealed to Newton. "He's gone mad! He's ranting about witches and magic. You're the detective—I demand you arrest him!"

"The thing is," Newton said, stepping closer, "I know you're related to the Favershams—a magical family—and I know the whole family has a grudge against White Haven. So, you need to prove to me you had nothing to do with Gil's death."

Her face drained of colour. "I may be related, but I have my own life, my own business. I was away when he died!"

"But you're not denying magic anymore, are you?" Newton countered.

Reuben rounded on her again. "He trusted you, Alicia! I trusted you! He hid his magic for years, and you didn't even share that with him! Why?"

"It was a part of my life I've stepped away from." Unexpectedly she stepped forward, appealing to Reuben. "You did, too, I know all about it. You know why that happens."

Avery reeled slightly at her admission. So she *did* have magical abilities. Avery watched her and wondered how true it was that she had abandoned it. Alicia's hands were flexing nervously, and Avery was convinced this was still an act. She'd do anything to stay in the house. Maybe she hadn't found the grimoire yet.

Reuben glared at her. "It would have broken Gil's heart. He loved you, and you lied to him for years!"

"He would have wanted me to practice, and I didn't want that."

Reuben was furious. "Bollocks. You liar. Ever since Avery was gifted that box, you have been betraying us. That bastard Caspian has threatened us, attacked us, and killed Gil. You are the only one who could have told him what we were doing!"

261

"No!" Alicia was pleading now, stepping back again, away from the fireplace. Reuben followed her, keeping only a couple of paces away, and Avery noticed her glancing towards the fireplace.

What was she doing? She seemed to be waiting for something.

And then a horrible thought struck Avery.

Demons.

As soon as she thought it, Reuben stepped right in front of the fireplace, his back to it as he shouted at Alicia, and instantaneously, with a horrendous snarl and smell of sulphur, a demon appeared, flames whirling around it. A long flame lashed at an unsuspecting Reuben.

Avery, however was prepared, her energy already gathered. It was as if she'd had a sixth sense of what would happen. She sent a powerful, targeted blast of air at Reuben, knocking him clean out of the way, and he flew backwards across the room, crashing into a glass-fronted cabinet.

Avery turned her attention to Alicia and sent a second blast right at her, taking her legs out from under her and throwing her into the path of the demon that had now stepped into the room, flames lashing out in all directions. Alicia screamed as she threw up her hands to protect herself.

A second demon appeared behind the first, and Avery glanced at Alex. He sent a powerful flash of energy, which seemed neither flame nor air, straight at the creature that'd just arrived, trying to unbalance it before it could attack. Newton ran to the far side of the room, pulling a dazed Reuben out of the broken glass.

Both demons stepped forward together, advancing on the room. Alicia was back on her feet, shouting something in a language Avery didn't understand, but she appeared to be trying to control the demons.

There was a spell Avery knew that she had never tried before, but it should work perfectly—if she understood the relationship between a witch and their demon correctly. As she uttered it, she felt mean, but it was either Alicia or them. She had tried to kill Reuben, and if she had her way, they'd all be dead. This was no time for sentiment.

It was a spell to bind the tongue.

It was done in seconds. Alicia choked and gagged, and then turned with fury towards Alex and Avery, and then fury turned to fear and then terror as she clutched at her throat, trying to speak the words of command.

Alicia was far closer to the demons than anyone else, but Avery could feel their heat from across the room. Their lashing flames scorched everything they touched. But as Alicia fell silent, the demons stopped their advance and turned on her.

Alicia backed away, but Avery uttered another spell, and Alicia collapsed on the floor. The demons pounced.

They smothered Alicia in their burning grasp. Their voices—if that's what they even were—blood curdling in pitch. Gaping jaws revealed hundreds of tiny teeth, and Alicia disappeared within the dark folds of their nebulous bodies. She couldn't even scream.

Alex stepped forward and started an incantation. Avery recognised the spell they had used in the witch museum, or something similar. He was trying to banish them.

Avery joined him, holding his outstretched hand, adding her strength to his, and Reuben, who had now staggered to his feet, joined in on the other side. Newton, unable to help at all, moved behind them.

They repeated the spell after Alex, their voices growing in power, and the demons retreated, their forms becoming insubstantial. They stepped back into the fireplace, and with a thunderous clap, they disappeared, taking Alicia with them.

Soot poured down the chimney and billowed into the room.

The silence that followed seemed profound. The room was covered in long, black burn marks, parts of the rug smouldered, objects were broken, and the glass cabinet was smashed.

"Is everyone okay?" Alex asked, partially covering his face from the soot.

"I've got a massive burn on my arm and chest, but I think I'll survive," Newton said from behind them.

Avery whirled around and found Newton collapsed on the floor. His shirt was smoking, and parts of it had disintegrated where the flames had caught, burning his chest. She dropped to her knees, examining him. "We'll get you to Briar."

"I'm okay, really." His grey eyes were filled with pain, but he nodded towards Reuben.

Avery turned and found Reuben on his knees, too, crying shamelessly, tears pouring down his face. Alex crouched next to him, his hand on his shoulder. "I'm sorry, Reuben. This just sucks."

Reuben looked past Alex to Avery, and the look in his eyes almost broke her heart. "Thank you for that, Avery. You saved me—I'll never forget it."

She started to well up, too. "I wasn't about to lose you too, Reuben." She looked back at Newton. "What have I done? I've killed Alicia! Will you arrest me?"

He shook his head. "No, you didn't. Her own demons killed her."

Panic flooded through her. "But I made her powerless. I caused it."

"You were a bloody genius," Alex said, looking at her admiringly. "You saved us all."

"Let's just agree it was a group effort. You banished the demons." She wiped away a tear. "How are we going to explain Alicia's death?"

"There's no body," Newton said, wincing with pain.

"But she's gone. Forever."

Newton shook his head, "Leave it with me. I'm here as a friend, not a policeman. I don't have to write any reports. Easiest thing is to say that she's disappeared. But pain is interfering with my reason right now, so if we could go…"

"Of course!" Avery leapt to her feet, and helped pull Newton up. "Are we all going back to Briar's?"

Alex looked at Reuben. "Are we?"

Reuben shook his head, and gestured to the smouldering rug. "No. I'll stay here. I need to make sure the place doesn't burn down and check on my grimoire—and I just want to be alone right now."

"I disagree. I think El should be with you," Alex said, clearly worried about leaving Reuben alone.

Reuben wiped his face with his hand. "I think we both know I've completely messed that up."

Alex looked at Avery and Newton. "I'll stay here for a while. Is there a car I can borrow later, Reuben?"

"Sure. You can use Gil's. It's still in the garage. But, honestly, go now."

Alex stood firm. "No. I'm staying here. I want to make sure those demons don't come back."

Reuben looked relieved, despite his protestations. "Cheers, mate."

Alex had a quiet word with them outside the room. "Speak to El, will you? He needs her."

"Of course," Avery said, and she kissed him on the cheek, thinking how adorable he was sometimes.

14

Briar and El were still in the sunroom when the pair arrived. The table had been cleared, and they sat quietly talking over a glass of wine. Briar leapt up as soon as they entered, Avery supporting Newton. His burns were more severe than she'd initially thought, and although she had used a spell to help reduce the pain, they needed Briar's help.

"By the goddess! What happened?" Briar asked, rushing over and helping Newton into a deep wicker seat filled with cushions.

"Demons," Avery said.

"Where are Alex and Reuben?" El asked, her voice strained.

"They're fine. Alicia is not." She explained quickly what had happened, and Briar gathered her herbs and started to treat Newton, easing his shirt off. A very angry burn stretched across his chest and down his arm, the skin already blistered. Newton lay back, breathing deeply, his face white with pain.

Avery sat next to El, leaving Briar to concentrate. "El, I know you're mad at him, but Reuben's really down. Gil's dead, Alicia betrayed them both, and he's hurting. Really hurting. He needs you. And you know he didn't mean to hurt you."

El's pretty face crumpled and her bravado disappeared as she started to cry. "I love him, Avery, but he really hurt my feelings." She looked at her, desperate and confused. "What am I going to do? I miss him like crazy."

"He misses you, too. He hates himself for what happened at the beach— I know he does. Go to him. Please. You two will work it out."

El nodded and exhaled deeply. "You're right. We're not kids. I'm going now."

"You okay to drive?"

"Fine. I've only had one drink." She stood, and then turned at the door. "Thanks, girls, you're both amazing."

It was another hour before Alex arrived, and Avery and Briar were talking quietly. Newton had gone to bed in the spare room, after having a strong herbal draft to help him sleep.

Alex grabbed a beer from the fridge and sat down, his face drawn. "The grimoire's gone."

"Reuben's?" Avery asked, her stomach churning already.

"No!" Briar cried, simultaneously.

"Yep." He took a long drink. "Reuben is a mess right now. He's veering between anger and grief. He's on a massive emotional roller coaster. Thank the gods El turned up, because I'm crap at that sort of thing."

"Not true," Briar shot back. "You're not a Neanderthal, Alex."

He gave a sad smile. "Well, I think El's comforting arms are far more attractive than my pats on the shoulder."

"Are they okay?" Avery asked.

"They will be. I left them to it. We searched the house first, just in case Alicia had secreted it somewhere to give to Caspian. But it's either really well hidden, or he's already got it."

"She knew where the hidden attic was all along, and was powerful enough to break Reuben's protection. I know this sounds horrible, but I'm glad those demons took her. What a bitch." Avery wondered what she was turning into to think such a thing. "Magic karma is going to hit me where it hurts I think."

"No, it's not," Briar said, soothingly. "You acted to protect others. And I'm sorry I wasn't there to help—I felt I should stay with El."

"You did the right thing," Avery reassured her.

Alex looked thoughtful. "So, Alicia's responsible for the demons then, not Caspian?"

"It looks that way," Avery said. "But who knows, it could be a family trait. I'm sure he had a hand in some of it."

"What are we going to do?" Briar asked, appealing to both of them. "We can't let them get away with it."

Alex stood up abruptly. "I don't know, but we'll think of something. I'm starving, and I can't think on an empty stomach. Any food left? I didn't really eat much earlier—sorry, Briar."

"No problem. It's still warming in the oven. And," she added, raising her voice as he headed into the kitchen, "I have fudge cake in the fridge. Well, some of it. El had rather a large slice."

"Ooh, yes please," Avery said, brightening up. "You are a domestic goddess, Briar. You heal, garden, and cook."

"I'll bring it in," Alex shouted back. He returned with a bowl of lasagne and the cake on a plate with a knife. "Brilliant. So, I think we should do what they least expect and go to the Faversham nest."

"Really? Is that wise?" Briar questioned, alarmed.

Alex swallowed a mouthful of food. "Yep. What are they going to do? We'll be in their public offices. They can't attack us there, or summon demons."

"Well, that's true," Briar agreed.

"I'll either see Caspian or his father, whoever's there. I don't care which. It's time we talked. I want that grimoire back."

"Well, I'm coming, too," Avery declared immediately, through a mouthful of cake.

"What are you going to say?" Briar asked, perplexed.

"I don't know," Alex said, frowning. "But I'll think of something. This has got to stop. We're even now—one down on either side. I think that's enough, don't you?"

"Are you taking Newton?"

"No. This is unofficial—Newton shouldn't get involved."

***

Kernow Shipping was based in an old warehouse across from the harbour at Harecombe, and had been tastefully modernised with large glass windows and solid wooden doors.

Harecombe itself was a larger town than White Haven, with a bigger harbour, more hotels, but far less atmosphere—although Avery conceded that it was still very pretty.

She sat next to Alex in his car; the roof was down and a warm breeze ruffled their hair. They were in a public car park, watching a few people as they pottered around the bay, enjoying the summer sun.

"I presume their big ships dock elsewhere," Avery said speculatively.

"Falmouth," Alex said. "I checked. But they keep their base here. Handily close to us," he added sarcastically.

"So, what now?" She looked at him. "You've been suspiciously quiet on our plan of attack."

"That's because it's really basic." He flashed her a knowing smile. "I'm going to march in, befuddle the receptionist, and introduce ourselves to daddy."

"Is that *too* simple? We are marching into enemy witch central."

"And they employ lots of non-magical people. They'll be limited in what they can do," he reasoned. "I'll do the talking—you're my wingman."

"Cheers! Don't trust me to speak?" Avery was slightly offended, but also quite excited to be Alex's wingman.

"Of course I do, but you're my silent aggressor."

"I thought we were planning on calling a truce—to try for a 'lay our cards on the table' sort of thing."

"Yes, *we are*, I'm just not sure so sure they will want to, though."

They exited the car and sauntered over to the warehouse. Once inside the wide lobby, the outside noise disappeared in the hush of the expensive, double-glazed, carpeted area. Large framed paintings were on the walls, huge potted plants flanked the entrance and the lifts, and two receptionists sat behind a gleaming oak counter.

Both receptionists were in their mid-thirties, and one looked up as Alex leaned on the counter, flashing his most charming smile. Avery stood just behind, scanning the lifts and the entrance. Apart from them, the lobby was empty.

"Hi, I have an appointment to see Mr Sebastian Faversham."

The receptionist looked at the screen for a moment, and then said, "I'm sorry, Mr Faversham doesn't have any appointments booked this morning."

"I think you'll find I'm booked in," Alex said, still smiling.

She looked at the screen again and then looked up, confused, "Oh yes, I don't know how I could have missed that. What did you say your name was? I'll buzz you up."

"No need," Alex said, and Avery felt the fizz of magic as he glamoured her.

The receptionist next to her looked puzzled and went to intervene, and then she smiled vacantly, too. "So sorry for the confusion."

"No problem, ladies. Remind me which floor?"

"The top one, corner office. All the senior partners are on that floor." Her eyes were slightly gazed and Avery knew that once they left, both of them would forget that the conversation ever happened.

"Excellent," Alex said, smiling.

They hurried over to the lifts and waited impatiently for one to arrive.

"I feel I'm in the dragon's lair," Avery said, her senses alert and watchful.

"Fun, isn't it?" Alex said, flashing her a grin.

"You're nuts."

"I know."

As the lift arrived and the doors swished open, Avery saw a figure coming through the main doors. As they stepped inside, he looked up and caught her eye. *Caspian.* As the doors closed on them, she just had time to enjoy the look of shock on his face.

"Oops, we may have company. Caspian's here."

"Good. The more the merrier." Alex muttered a small spell and Avery felt the lift speed up until they arrived at the top with a thump.

"Alex!" Avery said, trying to keep her balance.

"Come on, Ave, time is of the essence. I want to see Caspian burst in on us and try to smooth his father's very ruffled feathers."

"We might be dead before then."

"Oh ye of little faith," Alex said under his breath as he exited the lift.

The first thing they saw was a stunning view of the harbour through a long window, directly opposite the lift. In front of it was a small reception area, with a gleaming white counter and a large vase of flowers. The heady aroma of lilies swirled around them. A couple of chairs and a table were placed in front of it, a waiting area no doubt for visitors to the board members' offices.

On their left, a row of offices led to a large window at the other end, their doors open, but on the right was a small, open plan office area where two secretaries sat, working at computers. They looked up briefly and went back to their work. Avery felt reassured. Witnesses hopefully meant they wouldn't die here.

This time, the lady seated behind the main desk was older. She had silver-grey hair tied back in a neat chignon, and she wore a very lovely pale lilac silk dress. She looked alarmed as they crossed towards her, and rose to her feet. Avery presumed their casual dress was not something she was used to seeing on visitors to the senior partners' floor.

"May I help you?" she asked dismissively, as if that was the last thing she wanted to do.

"We're here to see Seb. I understand he's in the corner office—we won't disturb you."

Avery stifled a giggle. *Seb?* Alex was really pushing his luck.

"I beg your pardon? Do you have an appointment?"

"Of course I do," Alex said as he leaned close to her, and again, Avery recognised a whiff of a glamour spell.

Avery wondered if the receptionist up here had any magical powers, because that might complicate things, but instead, her demeanour softened and she said, "Of course, the end office on the left."

As soon as they were out of sight they ran to the end of the corridor, hoping no one else would emerge from the other rooms, and found themselves in front of two offices, one bearing Sebastian's name, and one that said *Personal Assistant* on it. The door to his PA was ajar, and they could hear the muted murmur of a phone conversation.

Avery felt as if Caspian might arrive at any moment, but before she could say anything, Alex didn't hesitate. He softly closed the PA's door and locked it with a whispered spell, and then threw open Sebastian's door, saying, "Good morning, Faversham! So pleased to finally meet you."

Faversham's corner office was enormous, as was his desk, and the man behind it was imposing. Avery estimated he was in his late fifties or early sixties, but he looked fit. He was slim and handsome, with a full head of silvery hair.

He looked up in shock and then rose to his feet, his eyes narrowing. "Mr Bonneville."

"Mr Faversham."

"And Ms Hamilton."

Avery nodded, but remained silent, standing just behind and to Alex's right, where she could see the corridor behind. She scanned the room, but other than beautiful pieces of antique furnishings, Sebastian was alone.

He regained his composure swiftly. "So, you're here to talk about the terms of your surrender?"

Alex laughed. "No, we're here to talk about the return of the grimoire."

Sebastian also laughed; a dry, unpleasant noise with a smile that didn't reach his eyes. Cold eyes, Avery decided, lacking any warmth at all. "It's good to see you have a sense of humour, Mr Bonneville. Or shall I call you Alex?"

"You can call me whatever you want. I just want the grimoire."

Sebastian stepped around his desk and walked across the carpeted room towards them. He was as stealthy and as self-possessed as a cat.

As he approached, Avery noticed movement from the corner of her eye. Caspian came into view from the corridor outside. He caught her eye and paused for a second, and for a brief moment, Avery was confused by his reaction, and she hesitated, too. He looked worried, not angry. His eyes darted to her and then to the room, and as he stepped through the doorway, Avery called out, "Alex, we have company."

Rather than looking pleased, Sebastian scowled at his son. "Where have you been?"

"Seeking some answers," Caspian replied enigmatically.

Alex stepped aside, and they faced each other in a standoff, all four of them poised and ready to attack.

Sebastian thought for a moment and then gestured to some chairs and a table in the corner of his office. "Let's sit and be civilised, shall we?"

"Let's not," Alex said. "This is not a social call. We are here to try and broker peace."

"Humour me." Sebastian walked over and sat down, looking at them impatiently. Caspian remained standing, too, looking warily between all three of them. He'd lost weight, Avery thought, looking thinner than he had only weeks ago. His cheeks had hollowed out, and dark shadows were under his eyes. He looked ill.

Avery looked at Alex, trying to gauge what he was thinking, but he glanced at her and then at Sebastian, determined to maintain control. He strolled over to the window. "Quite the view you have, Faversham. Don't you think you have enough?"

"There's no such thing as enough." Sebastian leaned back, his legs crossed, his suit elegant, and his eyes watchful.

Alex turned around, and with the light behind him it was difficult to see his expression. "Why do want the grimoires?"

"None of your business," Sebastian shot back.

"Wrong. It *is* our business, because they're ours, gifted to us by our ancestors. And you've stolen one of them. Or should I say Caspian has, your lackey, running around doing your bidding?"

Caspian's eyes hardened, but he still glanced nervously at his father.

Sebastian continued, nonplussed. "Isn't Gil's death enough to convince you that we mean what we say?"

Avery stiffened. They had discussed this on the way over. Alicia had died last night, and it was likely that no one other than them knew what had happened.

"No," Alex said. "If anything, it's strengthened our resolve not to let you have the grimoires. You clearly have no respect for anything or anyone."

Sebastian rose to his feet swiftly and Avery felt the air in the room crackle with energy. It was as if Sebastian had unveiled his power, rather than drew it to him. "How dare you presume to know me!"

Alex stepped forward. "And how dare you presume to know *us*."

The energy in the room magnified as magical power flooded through them. Avery tensed, ready to attack, and she glanced at Caspian, who stood closest to her. He, of all of them, seemed the calmest, but Avery knew how powerful he was, and how quickly he could unleash it.

Alex spoke again. "Why do you want the grimoires?"

Sebastian paused for a moment. "Because they contain something we need."

Alex leaned against Sebastian's desk, arms crossed in front of him. "What if we keep the grimoires, and you tell us what you need, and we'll share that— if we feel it won't harm us. Then we both have what we want."

"Because it is not in our interest to let you keep them."

"It is not in our interest to let you have them, either. Surely," Alex persisted, "we must be able to come to some sort of compromise. Our families have been fighting for generations. Yours engineered Helena's death at the hands of the Witchfinder General, and manipulated others to support you. Haven't you done enough?" Alex was getting angry now, his voice rising with his indignation. "These grimoires are years old. We have no interest in warring with you, or using our new abilities and powers to attack you. We just want to live peacefully alongside you. Two magical communities, co-existing together."

Sebastian laughed, his head thrown back. "You're a fool. You have no idea what those grimoires can do."

"We know there's a hidden spell at the back of them. A spell that bound Octavia. Is that it? Is that what you want? To release her?"

Avery thought she detected a snort from Caspian, but when she glanced at him, he stood impassive, watching his father. He turned to her, aware of her gaze. His eyes swept across her, a look of curiosity and doubt, and Avery had the feeling that they were missing a key piece of information.

Sebastian answered, a carefully schooled response. "Octavia's soul should be released. But we will do that, and we need your grimoires."

"No, you need the spell. Not the grimoires. We'll do it for you, or copy the spell for you. As long as the demon is not released."

Sebastian thought for a moment. "No, that's unacceptable. But a kind offer," he said, sarcastically.

Now Avery *knew* they were missing something. They had just made a perfectly good offer, and it had been rejected for no good reason. It seemed Alex thought so, too.

"You're hiding something, Sebastian. We'll find out what. And then you'll wish you had accepted our offer." Alex looked at Avery and stood, ready to leave, "At least we tried."

Sebastian laughed again. "We have one grimoire, and we *will* get the rest. I believe you have only one left to find?" He glanced at Avery, and she felt the full power in his gaze pierce her core.

They didn't answer, and he laughed some more. "We'll know when you have it, and then we'll take them all. Taking the Jackson's was merely a demonstration of our power. Believe me when I say it will be better to hand them over. Surely, one death is enough?" he said, revealing he had no idea about Alicia.

"Ah, about that," Alex said, stepping closer until he was now only a few paces from Sebastian. "Unfortunately, there was a small incident last night. Alicia, your mole, was killed by her own demons, with a little help from us. So, we're sort of even on the death stakes."

"You're a liar," Sebastian accused, his eyes narrowing. He glanced at Caspian, whose look of doubt rattled Sebastian even more.

"I wouldn't lie about something so serious, Seb. Try and call her. Now. Go on, I can wait."

Sebastian looked as if he was wrestling with obeying Alex's suggestion, but curiosity finally got the better of him and he pulled his phone from his pocket and punched in a number.

They stood waiting silently while Alex moved closer to Avery. When it was clear that no one was answering, he phoned another number. "Put me through to Alicia," he said abruptly. He listened, watching Alex and Avery with hostility. "What do you mean, she's not in?" He paused. "Keep trying, and call me."

He rang off and stared at them for a moment, and then threw his phone at Alex.

Avery was about to laugh, it seemed so unexpectedly juvenile, but in a split second the phone changed into what looked like a dragon, the size of a large bird of prey that screeched as it rushed at Alex, its wings outstretched, cruel talons curving with malice, and flames pouring from its gaping mouth.

Alex rolled and simultaneously threw out a rope of pure energy, lashing at the creature and throwing it back in a high arc across the room and to the window.

At the same time, Avery blocked an attack from Caspian and Sebastian, as they both threw a stream of fire at her. She responded with a jet of super-heated air, knocking Caspian off his feet and into the corridor, where he crashed against the wall. However, Sebastian remained standing, his pupils all black with no hint of white. Avery felt her breath catch. *What was happening?*

He grew taller and broader, and for the first time Avery was aware of how much power he wielded. It was terrifying. He reached out his arm, and although he was halfway across the room, she felt her breath catch as her chest tightened.

Alex, however, had not finished, and as she struggled to repel Sebastian's magic, Alex jumped to his feet. The dragon wheeled and attacked him again, soaring across the room. Alex shattered the huge window at the back of the room and threw the dragon out of it with a well-placed blast of energy.

The sound was deafening. Glass exploded everywhere, and the dragon screeched as it rolled over and over in the air, now outside the building and high above the street.

Sebastian's concentration broke immediately, and Avery was able to breathe again.

For a brief second Avery watched him as he tried to regain control of the dragon, which now out in the open, also seemed to be swelling in size. A dragon was in Harecombe. A real, live dragon.

Alex grabbed her hand and pulled her towards the window. "Jump."

"Are you insane?" The words were barely out of her mouth when he kicked the jagged edges of glass away and dragged her through the window; they dropped like stones.

And then suddenly they weren't falling anymore, but floating, and she had the presence of mind to throw a veil of shadow over them as they streamed down the side of the building and landed at the corner.

It was chaos on the street. Glass was lying on the ground, some people were screaming, cars had screeched to a halt, and horns were blaring at those who were standing in the middle of the road, staring at the creature that now perched on the shattered window, five floors up. No one was looking at them.

They ran across the street to Alex's car, jumped in, and raced away, threading through the chaos with barely a backward glance.

15

Risking being pulled for speeding, Alex kept his foot down until they were well out of Harecombe. He finally stopped at a large country pub, the car park packed with customers, and they grabbed an outside table and a pint.

They both took a long drink of beer while Avery tried to still her jumbled thoughts. Their conversation in the car had been stilted and mostly consisted of, "*Are we being followed?*" "*No, not yet. Keep going.*"

Now sitting in the pub, surrounded by others, she said, "I can't believe you dragged me out of a window. I thought you were trying to kill me."

He laughed. "Idiot. I'm not suicidal."

"I wish you'd have warned me."

"Yes, like I had time for that. While I was battling a *dragon*!"

She stared at him for a second and then burst out laughing, and he laughed, too, until they were both giggling hysterically. Other people turned to stare, and that made Avery worse. "Holy crap," she said, trying to control herself, "It really was, wasn't it? I mean, I wasn't hallucinating. It was a dragon!"

"Bloody Hell, Ave, what have we got ourselves into?" Alex looked like an excited kid who'd just learned he was going to Hogwarts.

"Why are we even laughing? I mean, it's not funny," Avery said, still laughing. "Sebastian's a psychopath, and he conjures dragons. Out of a bloody phone!"

"That was priceless. The look on his face!"

"I think I'm hysterical. This is not a normal reaction to being attacked by a dragon and jumping out of a fifth floor window. Oh, and nearly being crushed by a Darth Vader move."

"Yeah, it was a bit Vader-y." Alex sipped his pint, having finally stopped laughing. "So what's he hiding?"

"I don't know, but I don't think he gives a crap about Octavia's trapped soul. We're missing something. Something big. Something that I think will benefit us, and he's terrified of us getting—and it's not just the grimoires."

Alex fell silent, thinking. "Your grimoire contains the first spell. It *must* tell us more about what it really does. We have to find it." He downed his pint. "Come on, let's go back to yours and get searching."

***

When they arrived back at Happenstance Books, they entered through the main shop and found Sally stocking shelves, while Dan served an old couple struggling beneath a pile of books.

Sally looked across at them and smirked. "You two look like you've been up to no good. You haven't been to Harecombe, have you?"

"Why?" Avery asked nervously.

Alex headed to the rear door and said, "I'll head up and put the kettle on."

"No, no, no," Sally said. "Not until you've seen this."

She nodded to Dan and headed to the back room where she pulled her phone out of her pocket. "It's all over social media and the news. Some guy filmed this." She showed them a short clip of the corner of the harbour in Harecombe where Kernow Shipping stood. The filming was jerky, but they saw cars screeching to a halt, horns blaring, glass on the pavement and road, and people staring and pointing. When the camera swung upwards, you could see a shattered window and a flash of something dark, but nothing else.

Avery glanced at Alex, relieved. *No dragon. How would the Favershams have explained that? How did they get rid of it?* Sebastian must have acted quickly to get it under control.

"There were reports of a strange creature crashing out of the window, but all the company said was that a display from a local carnival had broken a window."

"Well, there you go. What's that got to do with us?" Avery said, wide-eyed.

Sally looked between the two of them, clearly not believing any of it. "So, I suppose you won't be helping in the shop this afternoon?" she asked Avery.

"Not for a couple of hours, but I can relieve you for lunch," she said, checking her watch and finding it was already after one in the afternoon. No wonder her stomach was rumbling. "Sorry, it is lunch."

Sally waved her off, "No, we're fine, carry on. I'll shout if I need you, though."

"Cheers, Sally," Avery said, giving her a hug before following Alex upstairs.

"Bloody hell, I'm starving!" Alex declared, weaving through Avery's messy flat to the kitchen. He looked around, bemused, as he stepped over books and magazines, and paused to fuss over the cats as they wound around his ankles, almost tripping him up. "Have you got any food in the fridge?"

"Of course! It's just cleaning I'm not very good at," she said sheepishly. She switched on the TV and found the local lunchtime news. While Alex foraged through the fridge, she started to tidy, keeping an eye on the newscast. The headline item was the shattered glass window at Harecombe, but other than the short video, all it suggested was that the window had been accidentally broken, and no one was hurt. A representative from the business, who Avery didn't recognise, reassured the news team that it was purely accidental. Avery snorted. Their actions would have only increased tensions between them, but at least they had tried.

Just as the news item finished, her phone rang, and she looked at the caller and groaned. "Hi Newton," she said with a raised voice, attracting Alex's attention. He looked around and mouthed, *Oops.* "What the bloody hell have you been doing?" Newton raged from the phone.

"Whatever do you mean?" she asked, feigning ignorance.

"You know exactly what I bloody mean. Briar *eventually* told me your plans, and we've just watched the news. What the hell have you done?"

"You're still at Briar's?" she asked, avoiding his question.

"Yes I bloody am, covered in demon burns. What have you done?"

She winced. "We went to discuss terms."

"Terms of bloody *what?*"

"Newton. Please stop swearing," she said, knowing it would infuriate him further. "We went to discuss the grimoire, let him know about Alicia, and then he set a dragon on us."

"A bloody *what?*"

"A dragon. A small one, the size of a bird of prey—which is actually quite large, as birds go. But not dragons. I believe they are normally bigger."

"Is this a joke?" he shouted.

"Unfortunately not. Sebastian Faversham is a mean bastard with a lot of power, and didn't like being told Alicia was dead. He made a dragon out of a phone. It was very impressive, if unexpected," she said, pacing across the room with nervous energy. "Alex fended it off and broke the window."

"You could have been bloody killed! Why didn't you ask me to come?"

"Unofficial witch business, you know that. You can't risk being involved, Newton."

He fell silent for a second. "You still should have told me."

"No, better you didn't know at all. Are you feeling okay this morning?"

He grunted. "A bit better. Briar knows her stuff."

"Yes, she does. Are you off sick?"

"Yes, I have no choice."

"Good. Stay there. Hopefully there'll be no repercussions. We kept your name out of things, but keep your head down for a few days. How's Briar?"

"She's fine. Hang on, she wants a word."

Avery heard shuffling as the phone was handed over, and then she heard Briar. "Avery, this is getting worse. Can't we stop this *thing* with the Favershams?"

"We tried, Briar, he didn't want to listen. There's more going on than we realise."

"Were you and Alex hurt?" she asked, sounding worried.

"No. Please don't worry, just keep investigating your grimoire, and protect yourself. Keep Newton there for now, too."

As she hung up, she wondered how El and Reuben were, and while Alex was busy in the kitchen, Avery rang El. She answered quickly. "Hi, Avery."

"Hey, El. How are you two?"

"We're okay, just working through some stuff." She lowered her voice. "Reuben's really down. I've never seen him like this. I can't leave him."

"Have you managed to sort your shop out?"

"Yeah, Zoe's got it covered." Avery presumed Zoe was the immaculate guardian of the shop.

"Well, I've got news for you." She filled El in on their encounter and passed on the same advice she'd given to Briar; keep quiet for a few days and gather strength.

Avery didn't actually say what she really felt, which was that they'd entered a new stage of war with the Favershams. Although she and Alex had laughed about it at the pub, she had a feeling things were about to get a lot worse.

By the time she'd finished on the phone, Alex had finished cooking, and he brought in two plates, each loaded with a thick bacon and egg sandwich on crusty bread, and they headed upstairs to the attic room.

Avery had a large bite and sighed with pleasure. As she chewed, she rearranged some of the research on the wooden table, while Alex stood in front of the map, also chewing and thinking.

He pointed at the map. "What are the pins for?"

"I've marked the original houses of our families at the time of the hanging, but of course there's only Gil's and El's so far." She knew she should say 'Reuben's' now, but still couldn't get out of the habit.

"Now that we have the old records, the other addresses will be in there, won't they?" He turned to the table and rummaged through the trial transcripts.

Avery walked over to the map. "I have an address for Helena, but I think it was her mother's house that she lived in when she was young. She lived in a different one once she was married." She picked up a pin and marked the tiny cottage she had visited the other day.

Alex flicked through the book they had stolen from the Courtney Library. "The Ashworths, Briar's family, are listed as having lived on South Street. I wonder if that still exists?"

"It sounds familiar." Avery said, trying to find it on the map, before pulling her phone out of her pocket to Google it. As soon as the image popped up, she remembered it. "Yeah, it's at the top of the town, heading onto the moors. It's steep, if I remember correctly, and old, so it must be the same one."

"I wonder if the numbers are the same?" Alex mused. "It says number 51."

Avery punched the number in and watched the street view materialise. "Well, it's certainly 16th century. Decent size, too."

"Which is what you'd expect for a merchant." Alex marked it on the map with a red pin. "It's almost directly above El's Hawk House along the coast, and it's opposite to Helena's mother's."

"And diagonally opposite Gil's," Avery noticed.

Alex looked at her, puzzled. "Strangely symmetrical, don't you think?"

"Yes actually, but it must be a coincidence."

"Okay, I'm going to check my family's."

Alex turned his attention back to the book as Avery continued to study the map. She took another bite of her sandwich and then grunted as she remembered something else in Anne's papers. She rummaged through the pile on the table and pulled out an old map of White Haven. She pinned that up and noted the differences between the new and the old. The main shape of the town was the same, and the centre of the town was virtually unchanged, its tight network of streets straggling down to the harbour and along the beach, and inland up into the small valley which narrowed as it followed the curve of the hills down to the coast. The edges of the town were populated with new buildings, houses built in the 19th century.

Avery then picked up Samuel's book and flicked through it, finding a rough map of the town in the 16th century. It was far smaller, but the centre of the town still had the same shape. Layers on layers of history, Avery mused, and its secrets were lost in the foundations and the tide of humanity that had been born, lived, and died here. Until now.

Alex's exclamation disturbed her reverie. "Found it. Parsonage Road. Does that still exist?"

She Googled it quickly, and found it up higher in the centre of the town, close to the Parish Church of St Peters. "Of course, the old church at the top of the town," she said, pointing out the road on the map.

"It's almost dead centre between the Ashworth's place and Helena's," Alex said, marking it with another pin. He grabbed a pencil and drew a faint line between the four on the outside, and then stopped, puzzled. "No, that's not right—what would Parsonage Road link with?"

A thought struck Avery and she groaned, incredulous. "It couldn't be, could it?"

"What?" Alex asked, frowning at her.

She took the pencil from him, and drew a pentacle, linking all five buildings together. "What do you think?"

"Bloody hell. That works. And it aligns to the elements on the compass—each family's strength, each house marking the points. What's in the centre?" he asked, scrutinising the map.

Avery put her head next to his as they scanned the map. "The Church of All Souls. It's been there for centuries."

"The heart of the town, if not the true centre," Alex noted. It was too high to be the exact centre of town.

They both looked at each other, stunned. Avery elaborated. "The spirit of the town, locked within the centre of the pentacle. A place of power. Briar's spell—the grounding."

"A place where you would lock a spirit and a demon?"

"It has to be!" Avery exclaimed. "And where something else may be locked, too."

16

Alex paced the room while Avery again examined the map that appeared on the book they'd stolen from the Witch Museum. She lit a witch light, closed the blinds to block out the sunshine from the bright afternoon, and stared at the fine white markings that must be tantalisingly close.

"Come on, Alex, we need to be logical about possible hiding places for Helena's grimoire. We need an old building, something that's likely to have passages underneath, someplace accessible to her."

"Churches. There are four in White Haven. Old Haven Church where the Jackson's mausoleum is. And where there'll be a crypt. Then there's the Parish Church of St Peter's…"

"And the Church of All Souls in the centre of the pentagram," Avery said, finishing his sentence. "All will have crypts, all are old. The fourth is that Methodist church, but that's far too new."

"True. Then there are a lot of old, 16ᵗʰ century houses, but how likely are they to have tunnels beneath them?'

"And to have been accessible?" Avery added.

Alex continued to list buildings. "The old pubs along the harbour front and the centre of town. They have a big smuggling history, lots of tunnels there, probably."

"What if it's under Helena's family house, the point of Air on the pentagram?"

Alex rolled his eyes as the suggestions grew. "Where's the house she shared with her husband? It might be under there. In fact, the map may not be showing passages at all. It could even be a floor plan of a house, with the grimoire hidden in the walls."

"Or an attic."

"Elspeth's was hidden in the grounds of her house, Reuben's in the mausoleum—again, their property."

"But what about yours and Briar's? Who knows where they were originally hidden."

"There's the aquarium, that's an old building, recently converted, right by the sea wall."

"Or, of course, the Witch Museum."

"Or White Haven Museum?"

"I didn't even think of that." Avery said, annoyed with herself. It was another stone-built house that was on a street sitting along the harbour, with a commanding view over the sea. It had been gifted to the town by the family who owned it, and was now owned by the National Trust.

"But, what link would Helena have to it?" Alex pointed out.

"Excellent, very logical. Let's rule that out."

Alex was already looking for Helena's second address. "Penny Lane, that was Helena's house with her husband," he said, looking up. "That must be the one leading off the high street."

"It is. It's a lovely old street actually," Avery said, remembering its mellow stone and half-timbered buildings.

"Let's try to imagine Helena's thoughts. The five witches—or witch families—have just performed a big spell, one that mustn't be undone, the Witchfinder's coming, and you need to hide your book. Where would you go?"

"I would avoid my house, it would feel too obvious. I'd also probably avoid my mother's house, too," she said, thinking of the tiny cottage she'd stopped in front of the other day. She searched through the papers on the table and consulted her family tree to check dates. "Helena's mother had already died by then anyway, that's why I didn't see her name in the trials—at least she was spared that horror."

Alex frowned. "We're missing something."

Avery smacked her head with her palm. "We're forgetting the Newtons! Is it worth finding where he lived?"

Alex shrugged, "We can, but why would she hide it with the Justice of the Peace?"

"I would have thought it's the perfect place to hide it. Who would think to look there?"

"Fair enough, that does have a certain logic." He consulted the letters that had been sent to Newton by Thaddeus Faversham, scanning them quickly. "Also Penny Lane! Next door to Helena's!" He looked up at her, his pupils large in the muted light. "They were neighbours—he'd have known her well."

"No wonder he felt so annoyed when he couldn't save her. Do you think he knew she really was a witch? But knew she was trustworthy, too?"

"Maybe," he shrugged, unconvinced. "They may have had cellars that could be linked. He would never have known what she had concealed. It's worth checking. Those buildings are shops now, right?"

Avery consulted Google Maps again and then laughed. "Of course they are! I'm so stupid."

"What?"

"Both Helena's house and Newton's are now one building." She looked at him expectantly, as if he should know.

"So? What building? A big shop?"

"It's a restaurant, quite a flash one—Penny Lane Bistro."

Alex grinned. "Public access! Great! What you up to this evening?"

"What I'm up to every evening—looking for this bloody grimoire."

"May I take you out for dinner?"

Avery laughed. "Really? You don't want to sneak in after they're closed?"

"Of course I want to sneak in after they're closed, but we can check it out officially first."

"It's expensive!"

"So?" He frowned, crossed his arms, and leaned back against the table. "You don't want to be seen in public with me?"

Avery huffed at Alex's annoyed expression. *Was he serious?* "I'm seen with you all the time! Are you crazy?"

"As friends. This is a date."

"A date—like a proper, wine-and-dine date?"

"So you'll sleep with me, but not go out to dinner with me?"

Now she knew he had to be winding her up. "I had a pint with you today! Besides, I wasn't sure how serious the whole sleeping together thing was."

His face darkened, and she realised she had made a serious error. "So you're back to thinking I'm just a womaniser? And you're what, the female equivalent? I'm just a quick roll between the sheets for you? You know what? Maybe I should go."

He put the book down, and turned.

"No! Alex, please—I'm sorry!" Panic flooded her at the thought that she'd ruined a perfectly great, if uncertain relationship. "You know what, we're both to blame—we sleep together, and then that's it! I don't know what to think *this* is!" She softened her voice. "You are not *just a quick roll in between the sheets*. You're more than that. And, I know you're not a womaniser. I'm sorry, sometimes I feel a little insecure. You're very..." she hesitated.

He turned back to her and leaned back on the table again, his eyes narrowed. "Unreliable, arrogant, annoying?" He quoted all the things she'd said before.

"Hot. Very, very hot. And clever and quick-witted. And I wonder why you're interested in me," she said in a rush, fearing she'd lose her nerve if she didn't say what she really thought right now. "This past few weeks has been great, but I didn't want to presume too much."

His shoulders dropped and she felt his anger ebb slightly. "Have you noticed how hot *you* are lately? And brave, and funny, and powerful?"

She flushed. "Alex, don't tease. I'm not those things."

He reached forward and brushed her hair from her face, his hands sending a tingle all down her spine. "I think you're very beautiful, Avery, and I can't stop thinking about you. And, as well as being gorgeous, you're a kick-ass witch who I trust implicitly. And trust me when I say that I haven't had as much fun with anyone for a long time as I had with you today. Now, would you like to go to dinner with me tonight?"

She held her hand over his, pressing it against her cheek. "Yes. I would love to."

"Good. I'll meet you here at seven-fifteen." He kissed her softly and then left, a hum of residual energy left in the space.

Holy shit. What had just happened? Her heart was racing, and she paced the room nervously, the cats watching her through their narrowed eyes as they half-dozed on the sofa. *Breathe, Avery, breathe.* He hadn't declared his love, he'd just told her she was beautiful, and gorgeous, and brave, and powerful. And he'd looked at her in a way he hadn't before, even when they were having sex.

What the hell was she going to wear?

***

By the time Alex arrived at 7:15 Avery had wasted hours, unable to concentrate on any of Anne's paperwork, or Helena's map.

She had eventually given up and showered, and then tried on and discarded half a dozen dresses and shoes before sternly reminding herself that she knew Alex, had slept with him, and didn't need to panic. She finally settled on a black, knee-length dress and three-inch tan wedges, which showed off her legs. It seemed with this simple request for a date that everything had changed, had become more serious. Official. But of course, it hadn't. She was imagining things.

When Alex turned up, she couldn't help but gasp. "Wow, you look good."

"So do you," he said, kissing her cheek.

He wore black boots, dark jeans, a black V-neck shirt, and a dark suit jacket. His hair was tied in a man-bun. It was still Alex, not too groomed, but just groomed enough—he still had dark stubble and his usual grin on his face.

He took her hand. "Ready?"

"Ready," she agreed, grabbing her leather bag.

Avery couldn't help but smile as they strolled down the street, but for once they both seemed a little awkward. They ended up both speaking at the same time, and they laughed. "Ladies first," Alex said.

"I've brought the plans with me, just in case."

"You're not planning on having a witch light floating over our table, are you?"

"No! Are we planning on breaking in tonight?"

"I think we should, if it looks likely." He squeezed her hand, "Maybe not in those shoes, though?"

"Oh ye of little faith," she laughed, echoing his line from earlier that day.

Penny Lane, as Avery had remembered, was a narrow, cobbled street lined with 16th century buildings, made of stone and timber. The stone was a warm amber colour, quarried locally, while the wood not only framed the windows but covered some of the upper walls, and were painted in soft whites and muted yellows and pinks.

Most of the buildings were now shops, the lower floors for retail, the upper floors either storerooms or flats. Some buildings were Bed and Breakfasts, and were very popular with tourists. Hanging baskets filled with a profusion of summer bedding plants were hung all down the street, as they were all over the town.

The bistro's entrance was a discreet wooden door, set back under a deep porch. Mullioned windows on either side of the door, with candles glittering on the sills, provided a glimpse into the interior. Once inside, a small counter had been set up by the entrance to receive guests. The inner walls had been knocked out, and it was now a large, open space, broken up only by columns and archways. The ceiling was still timbered, and the whole place was an artful blend of old and new.

Across the room was a long wall of paned glass revealing a courtyard garden, and she heard the clink of glasses and murmured conversation drifting across the room.

Avery breathed deeply with pleasure as she gazed at the white linen tablecloths, soft lighting, glasses, and silverware.

Their table was in the corner, overlooking the courtyard, and as they sat, Avery noticed that many other tables were already filling up. "We were lucky to get a table here."

"Perks of being in the trade—I sort of know the manager."

"Do you think he'd let us in the cellars as a sort of favour?"

"I don't know him that well," he said, looking at the wine menu.

She sighed. "I'm trying to avoid breaking in again. It's becoming a habit."

"Fun, though," he mused, glancing up at her with a smirk.

"I don't think Newton would think so."

"He's got Briar to distract him. And besides, I don't think it will be as bad as attacking Faversham Central."

Avery looked at the menu, finding it difficult to concentrate. Their friends were split into two camps, possibly vulnerable to attack. Briar was on her own, magically speaking, and so was El. Avery wasn't sure how effective Reuben would be right now. The more she thought about this morning, the more rash she felt they'd been. And here they were, having a meal in the gorgeous Penny Lane Bistro. She looked up at Alex, his head bent over the menu, and her heart tightened. *What if he got hurt?*

Alex looked up, startling her out of her thoughts. "Stop worrying and tell me what wine you'd like."

"Sorry. We're all split up tonight. I was just thinking how vulnerable we are."

"All the more reason to find your grimoire, find out what the spell really is, and get more bargaining power."

She nodded. "You're right. A very large Tempranillo, please."

"And this is a date, remember. People will think I'm a crap date if you don't cheer up."

She laughed, "Sorry, this is great, thank you. I haven't been anywhere like this for a long time."

"Me neither." He looked around. "Have you noticed? No cameras in here."

"I should think not. They're hardly conducive to romance and fine dining. I bet there's some out back, though," she said, nodding towards the courtyard.

They were interrupted by the waiter, and once they'd ordered, Avery said, "It's weird, isn't it? This is where Helena once lived. She walked through these rooms, slept here, ate here. Her children were born here. And she'd have been arrested here." She felt a rush of emotion and stopped for a moment, trying to calm her thoughts.

"And now we'll get revenge for her," Alex said. "Somewhere in these walls could be her legacy to you."

She nodded. "There are a couple of doors to restricted staff areas—do you think there's still access to cellars?"

"This is a restaurant now. I bet they use it for storing wine. In fact," Alex said, staring outside, "I can see a large hatch set into the floor. Must be an outside entrance."

Avery followed his gaze and saw a dark rectangle in the courtyard, butting up against the wall of the building. "I see it. Perfect!"

"How agile are you in those shoes?"

"Extremely. Why?"

"Wandering around White Haven in combat gear at night, in the centre of town, will be very suspicious. When we've finished here, we'll head to the pub and then come back after closing. Sound good?"

"Great."

"Excellent, and now we can enjoy our date," he said, teasing her, and making her feel self-conscious all over again.

***

After the meal, Alex and Avery headed to a small pub called The Startled Hare a few doors down from the bistro, and stayed there until closing.

They tried not to talk about the missing grimoires, the Favershams, or magic, and instead talked about anything and everything else. Avery wasn't sure if the meal was a good idea or not, as she now knew that she was pretty much head over heels with Alex. And they had so much fun together. She felt she was like a schoolgirl again, and every now and then she'd find him looking at her speculatively, which made her heart race even faster.

They were nearly the only people left on the street as the bar staff ushered them outside after last orders. They strolled past the bistro, and seeing it was now empty, other than a couple of waiters doing a final clear up, they walked up and away from the town, and then tried to find the alley that ran behind the bistro. The cool night breeze caressed her skin, and Avery pulled her lightweight cardigan close. Alex pulled her into him, wrapping his arms around her as they tried to look as inconspicuous as possible.

Towards the end of Penny Lane they paused outside an alley that disappeared around the back of the buildings.

"This way," Alex said, checking down the street and then pulling Avery after him.

They passed wheelie bins full of rubbish outside the side entrances of the shops on either side, and then turned left heading down towards the bistro. The fences were high at the back of the shops, and most places were quiet as it was long past their closing. They passed the pub and then paused as they saw a gate open and close further down. A waiter emerged from the shadows to put some rubbish into a bin, and then disappeared back behind the fence.

"That must be it," Alex said, and they moved closer, peering through the wooden planks.

"How long until they go?" Avery asked.

"Can't be long now."

They wrapped themselves in a shadow spell, waited another fifteen minutes after the lights went out, and then they eased the gate open with another spell and edged into the courtyard.

Two cameras were high on the wall, one angled towards the glass doors leading into the restaurant, and the other towards the cellar door, and there was a security light. Avery immobilised them all with a whisper, and after checking that the restaurant was in complete darkness, they unlocked the cellar door in the floor and headed down the steps into darkness, pulling the door shut above them.

They stood listening for a few moments, but there was only silence.

Avery conjured a witch light, and its cool, white light showed a paved stone floor, and racks of wine and other stores stretching away into darkness. She pulled the book with the map from her bag and studied it.

The map was long and narrow, much like the cellar space. "This could be it," she whispered, showing Alex.

"Well, there's not much cellar to our left. We're at the edge of the building, but it should go all the way down there," he said, pointing under the main restaurant area.

The cellars, unlike the restaurant above, were still made up of small rooms, all interconnected by archways. The map showed similar-sized blocks, and a tiny pentagram was marked on an interior wall.

"Come on, let's get our bearings," Alex said, leading the way.

They snaked around the free standing shelving housing wine bottles and other supplies, heading into the centre of the cellar. A steep staircase rose to a door set into the wall, but they passed it for now, checking what else was down there. They came to a thick wall, which looked as if it marked where the two buildings would have been divided, and walking through the archway in it, passed another set of stairs which had been bricked up at the top.

The stores ended, and the rest of the rooms were empty, other than a few old boxes, chairs, and endless dust. Avery suppressed the urge to sneeze.

"Which house was which?" Alex asked.

"The one that's now the main dining area was Helena's, the kitchen area is Newton's."

"So we're under Helena's now. Where's that pentagram marked?"

"It's hard to say, I'm not sure which way up the map should be. It looks to be on an inner wall of the first or last room, depending on how it's placed."

"Let's check here then first, just in case."

They headed to the old stone wall and examined it carefully. The stone work was rough and almost a foot thick, but looked intact. Even with the witch light floating above them, nothing was marked or looked suspicious. Then they tried the surrounding walls for good measure, before heading back to the side of the building where they'd entered.

They headed to the far wall, and worked their way back.

"It should be here," Avery said, confused. "If this is the right place. See, the second wall in has the pentagram mark, but there's no wall."

"But there is," Alex said, pointing upwards. Above them was a couple of feet of wall spanning a third of the cellar and forming an archway, separating one section from another. "It's just a very small wall."

Avery pulled a torch from her bag and pointed it at the stones above them. "They're so tightly fitted together, but I think I can see an edge sticking out."

"We need a closer look." He looked around searching for a ladder, but there was nothing in sight. "There's no way I can reach that, it's a least nine feet up."

"But I can, if you boost me." Avery decided there was no way she was leaving without checking this out.

Alex crouched down. "All right. Get on my shoulders. And keep your voice down, just in case."

Avery juggled the torch as she got into position, and Alex rose to his feet slowly.

"Shit," Avery said, as she wobbled and grabbed the wall to steady herself.

When she was in position, she shone her torch onto the spot. Close up there was definitely a seam. "Alex, I'm right," she whispered.

"Well, get on with it," he hissed back, and shone his torch up towards the wall.

For a few seconds Avery worked at the bricks, trying to pull them loose and failing miserably. When Alex shifted position, she wobbled and leaned heavily on one of the surrounding bricks, and with a distinct click, the entire section popped forward. Her heart was now pounding in her chest. She wiggled the bricks free until half a dozen in an uneven rectangle eased into her hands.

"Alex, hold this," she said, passing them down.

For a few seconds they juggled torches and bricks, and then with both hands free, Avery turned her own torch into the hole. It was a small, dry space hollowed out of the wall, and something was in there. She pulled out a thick, heavy object the size of a large book wrapped in oilskin and put her torch in the gap left behind.

"I think we've found it," she whispered. She carefully opened up the oilskin, and beneath it was a leather-bound book.

"Well?" Alex asked, adjusting his position and making Avery wobble again.

Triumph and relief filled her voice. "Yes! It's Helena's book. The sign for air is on the cover."

"Excellent, let's get those bricks back in place and get out of here."

17

Alex deposited Avery at her door with a kiss that left her tingling right down to her toes.

"You're not coming in?"

"I better put in a full day at work tomorrow. And besides, I think you deserve some time to examine the book. I'll see you tomorrow, though?"

"Yes. And thanks for tonight. I really enjoyed it."

"Me, too. Stay safe." And then he disappeared, leaving her with an ache that she wasn't sure the book was going to fill.

After making herself a chamomile and lavender tea, she headed to bed and curled up with the book on her lap, a cat on either side. She could barely believe it. After days of searching, she finally had it. Thank the gods it hadn't been put in one of those crazy rune boxes.

The leather creaked under Avery's fingers as she eased it open and she felt a tingle of magic run through her.

Like the other grimoires, a long list of names filled the front pages of all the witches that had gone before her, and Helena's was the last. She stroked the page, feeling the worn paper, soft beneath her fingers, and suddenly, the awareness of a presence nearby. She looked up, as did the cats, rousing from their slumber as they looked wide-eyed at the door. The room remained empty, but a soft breeze fluttered around her carrying the scent of violets, and she felt a breath on her cheek and the sensation of a kiss, and then it was gone.

Helena.

Avery's hand flew to her cheek and tears filled her eyes as an aching loneliness and sorrow swept through her—and then something else. Relief.

She called out, "Helena, don't go. Talk to me."

But Helena had gone, leaving her blessing, or so it felt to Avery.

She wiped away a tear and turned back to the book. She took her time, turning the pages carefully, trying to decipher the spidery writing. A witch light hovered at her shoulder, and she could see runes and symbols marked on the pages. Unable to contain her curiosity, she headed to the end of the grimoire and found the hidden spell. It began: *The First Part: To Gather the Four Points and Bind them to the Task.*

But then, rather than the spell, there was a note written by Helena.

> *"It is with great trepidation and sorrow that we make this spell. We have lived in White Haven for years, healing, making charms, protecting the poor and rich alike. We seek to do no harm, only good, and we have promised ourselves that we will not bend from our task. And yet, circumstances have made us change our decision.*
>
> *"And it is my fault. So here I make my confession, for it is because of me that this spell has come to pass. Before I met my husband, when I was young and foolish, I lay with Thaddeus Faversham, and before long found that I bore his child. He promised me everything, but in the end, gave me nothing. I could have got rid of the child, it is in my power to do so, but I could not, and so to conceal my shame, I married my husband, cast a spell to delay the birth, and then lied to say it was not full term. And he knew nothing.*
>
> *"My daughter, Ava, is now eight, and is a great joy, and a sweet sister to Louisa. But recently my dear husband Edward died, and Octavia Faversham has decided that Ava must live with them now. She and Thaddeus have finally acknowledged (privately) that she is a Faversham, and is arrogant enough to believe that I do not deserve to raise my own daughter. Ava already shows signs of power well before one would expect it, and I believe it is her power rather than blood that motivates Octavia. And Octavia is powerful enough to steal her, too, and nobody would know or remember.*
>
> *"I will not countenance it. I am furious, and have devised a plan to silence her forever. She will never rest until she has what is mine, and neither will Thaddeus. They think I am alone and vulnerable without my husband, but they are wrong. My power has never been stronger, and the other four families will stand with me. We will banish Octavia forever, locked within the earth with her pet demon she threatens to unleash. Thaddeus will think twice before he threatens me again.*

"But it shall come at a cost. With great spells come real sacrifice, and I am sacrificing my power to keep my daughter. It will weaken all of us, and it may be that the others will live to regret it. But they are also now being threatened by the Favershams, and so they must do this to protect themselves, too. A life without magic—or very little, at least—will be like a life half-lived. It may well be that it takes my daughter's power, too.

"It is my intention to break this spell, when the time is right. I have no idea when that will be, but if not in my lifetime, maybe by the hand and tongue of some ancestor I shall never know. I have therefore written the spell that will bind Octavia, and also the spell to break it, and the exact orders of these incantations are described below. This grimoire is the key to all.

"The spell has been split into five parts, and all five witches must be present to cast it, and all five to break it. It encompasses White Haven itself, bound within the very earth of the town, cast in the heart of it. My part is written here, the other parts are hidden in the other grimoires.

"I have no idea of the repercussions it may cause. It may be that this spell echoes through the years, and I would beg forgiveness of anyone who reads this.

"But a warning to those who choose to break it—the power that is bound within the spell will be unleashed. If you are my descendant, your powers will grow, and your rightful inheritance will be replenished. And I encourage you to do so. You will claim your place within the world, as will all the other witches who stand with you.

"I wish you luck, for once the spell is broken, Octavia will also return. Beware her demon."

Below the note was the spell, complex and layered, with half a dozen ingredients, and then below that, a final word.

"It is done, and I am left weaker than I ever imagined. I fear I have cursed White Haven forever, and our enmity with the Favershams will be sealed down the years. And now I hear the Witchfinder comes, and I must hide the grimoire forever.

Forgive me,

Helena"

Avery felt tears pricking her eyes again. *Poor Helena.* To have had a child with Thaddeus, and for him to abandon her was awful in itself, especially at that time, but to then threaten to take her was even worse. No wonder Helena had chosen to perform the spell. No wonder either that she could not fight back when she had been accused by the Witchfinder—Thaddeus would have known her powers were almost gone. He must have hated her to condemn her to such a death.

And Avery's true powers—hers and Helena's, now one in the same—were bound beneath White Haven, as were Alex's, El's, Reuben's and Briar's. Did this mean that the powers they had now were a fraction of what they could have? Did it still apply? Or had their powers eventually returned over the centuries?

Avery flopped back on the pillow, her head spinning. Helena said the powers would be *unleashed.* What did *that* mean? Would they flood through them like a tidal wave—would it flood the town? Or was all this just a fairy tale? A tale of long ago that had no power over them now, other than with words?

But then she thought of the Favershams. Why would they attack with demons if they didn't think the threat was real? She laughed. No wonder Sebastian had gone along with their conversation the other day. He didn't give a crap about Octavia's soul. He just didn't want them to get their powers back. Why, though? It wasn't as if they would attack the Favershams. They could co-exist as much as they had for years.

So many questions. Avery needed to speak to the others. One thing was certain, however. She knew she wanted to release their powers, regardless of crazy Octavia and her demon. It was their birthright, and she wanted it back. And that meant getting Reuben's grimoire back, as well.

Avery pulled the book to her chest and settled in for the night. She was going to study this book from cover to cover, in case there were more hidden secrets yet to be revealed.

18

Avery entered the shop with gritty eyes and a head full of questions. Sally took one look at her and plonked a coffee down in front of her.

"Here you go. Another late night?"

Avery nodded, sipping the hot drink with relish. "Yes, just catching up on some reading."

Sally smirked. "Really? Because I saw you heading into *The Startled Hare* last night, with Alex."

Avery met her eyes slowly. "We had a meal and went to the pub. And then I went home—*alone*."

"So it's official, then? Rather than this, 'oh, we're just friends doing some research...'" Sally said, adopting a sing-song voice.

"We're seeing how things go," Avery said, itching to spell Sally into silence, but feeling that would be way too mean.

A grin split Sally's face. "Excellent. I've always liked Alex. He's good for you."

Avery spluttered. "Don't be ridiculous. I'm going to open the shop."

Avery took her coffee with her, feeling her cheeks growing hot even as she walked away. She lit a few incense sticks on her way through the shop, and reinforced the spell that helped customers find the book they never knew they wanted.

All day she felt her mind was barely on the job, and she went through the motions as if she was in a trance, pacing out the day until she went to Alex's. He'd texted mid-morning to say he'd invited the others over that evening, and that they'd all accepted. She hoped Newton had some idea of how they were going to get the Jackson grimoire back.

By late afternoon, Avery was tidying the shelves in the far corner of the shop, which housed the esoteric section, when she felt something behind her. She swung around, alarmed, and found Caspian Faversham blocking her from the rest of the shop. His face was white and pinched, and he looked even worse than he had yesterday when they had attacked Kernow Shipping.

"Get out of my shop," she hissed, her hands balling with energy.

"I'm here to talk."

"You cannot possibly have anything to say that I'd want to hear."

"My father suggests a deal."

She was about to push past him, when she stopped and looked at him suspiciously. "What deal?"

"Hand over the grimoires, and no one else dies."

"You can stick your threats up your arse, Caspian. And you can tell your self-righteous wanker of a father to do the same. They're *our* books. Do you think we'd let Gil die in vain? You *murderer*," she spat at him.

She could feel wind whipping up around her, and the chimes hanging in the window alcove started to tinkle. She tried to subdue her annoyance, not wanting to attract attention.

Caspian's dark eyes felt as if they could pin her to the wall. "I didn't mean to kill Gil."

"Liar! I presume you didn't try to kill Reuben, either, at Old Haven Church. Your powers got away from you, did they? And Alicia wasn't trying to kill Reuben when she summoned demons in his own house? And what about the two people killed by the demons here in White Haven? Innocent people. Oh, that's right, you said normal people didn't count," she recounted, remembering their conversation on the beach.

"We started badly, I admit. We suggest a truce," he said, remaining solidly in her way.

She took a step back. "What's going on? Why would you suggest a truce now? Your father set a dragon on us for suggesting this very thing!"

"You shocked him about Alicia. We now believe you, and he wishes to compromise."

Something felt very wrong. She tried to see over his shoulder. *Sally*. She was 'innocent people.' "Where's Sally?"

A slow smile crept up Caspian's face. "She'll be fine. So long as you give us the grimoires."

White-hot anger spread through her, as did ice-cold fear. "Don't you dare hurt her, or I swear, I will kill you."

"You're not the one in the position of power here are you, Avery?"

"Neither are you, without those grimoires. You see, I now know why you want them, and it has nothing to do with poor old Octavia's trapped soul."

Caspian's eyes flashed with a hint of doubt.

She continued, "It's about the increased power we'll have when we unleash the binding spell. And believe me, we'll do it."

Caspian's menace increased as he stepped towards her and she felt his power pressing on her like a wall. "Not without Reuben's grimoire, you won't. And you will *never* find it. Five spells, five witches. You can't possibly do it without that portion. Give it up now, and let Sally come home. She has two children, doesn't she? It would be a shame to see them grow up motherless."

Avery knew he was goading her, and she wanted to let her power fly, to rip off his face and shred his smile to pieces. But then she smelled violets on the air again and felt a presence close to her, filling her with warmth and strength. *Helena.* And then she suddenly knew how they could break the spell.

She took a deep breath and stepped back from Caspian, careful not to give anything away. He must think she was scared and powerless, so she dropped her shoulders and looked defeated. "I need to speak to the others."

"Do it quickly—you're running out of time."

He couldn't possibly know she had found Helena's book. She needed to lie, really well. Witches were good at detecting lies. "But I haven't found Helena's book yet. We can't deliver them."

"But you have a map," he said, slightly annoyed.

"And zero clue as to what it's a map of!"

"Well, you had better work quickly. You have until midnight to deliver them to my father's home."

"It's not long enough—I've been looking for weeks," she said, panic-stricken. "And what do I tell Sally's husband?"

"That's your problem." Caspian's smug smile of superiority returned. "I look forward to seeing you later."

He turned, walked around the corner of the shelving, and disappeared.

Avery raced across the shop, hoping he'd merely been frightening her. "Sally? Sally!"

One of the locals, an elderly man with grey hair, turned and answered. "She headed to the back, love, with a young lady."

Avery now felt sick with fear. They really had taken her. She ran through the door into the back of the shop and found Sally's hex bag on the floor, the contents scattered.

Sally was gone.

***

"They've taken Sally? Your employee?" Newton was seething. "That's kidnapping. I'll arrest every single one of them."

"She's my *friend*. And you know you can't," Avery reasoned, biting back her annoyance. "We have to break the binding spell. That's our only hope. Then we'll have the power to fight the Favershams and rescue Sally. *And* get the grimoire back. And we only have until midnight to do it."

"Midnight! *Tonight?*" Alex exclaimed, his eyes wide.

"Yes. I'm sorry," Avery said, looking at all of them.

She stood in the centre of Alex's flat, dressed for battle. She was wearing her black skinny jeans, a fitted tee, low-heeled ankle boots, and her slim fitting leather jacket.

The lights were low and the mood was grim. Reuben was still distraught about Alicia and Gil's death; his mood had also taken its toll on El. She sat next to Reuben on the sofa, and she looked as bad as he did. The good thing was that they had arrived together and appeared to have settled their differences. Newton was still in pain after his encounter with the demons. He held himself stiffly, and Avery could see bandages around his arm and adding bulk under his t-shirt. They were all weaker than they should be, but they had to act now.

"What have you told her family?" Newton asked.

Avery hesitated, embarrassed. "I told Sam, her husband, that we were doing a late night stock take, and I threw in a little spell to help. It wasn't hard, but it felt horrible."

Avery then told them what she found in her grimoire, and what she and Alex had discovered about the pentagram over White Haven and the centre where the spell had been performed.

"That's where you're confusing me," El cut in. "How can we break the binding spell when we don't have part of the spell—the portion for water?"

"Because we have Helena."

A chorus of "*What?*" echoed around the room.

"She's here with me now. I can feel her. She smells of violets, and she wants us to do this. She made the spell. She *knows* the spell. She doesn't need a grimoire to recite it."

"So that's what I can sense," Alex said thoughtfully. "I thought I was imagining it."

Newton looked spooked. "She's here? *Now?*" He looked around, as if she would materialise next to him.

"I can't see her, Newton," Avery said, trying to reassure him. "It's her presence, her spirit. I *feel* her."

Alex interrupted, "Avery, you know I trust you, I do, and I believe you. But she's a spirit. She has no corporeal body. How can she take part in a spell?"

"Because, Alex, you control the essence of spirit. You have the grimoire. You said yourself it has spells to summon spirits. But she's *already* here. You must know a spell to allow her to enter my body, and then I'll have her knowledge to perform the spell. Reuben can perform the air part of the spell, my part, and I'll do his."

Briar answered first. "That sounds incredibly dangerous, Avery."

"It's Helena, she won't hurt me. Alex?"

For a second he didn't speak, and just stared at her. "Briar's right. It *is* dangerous. And it won't work like that. If she enters your body, your mind will be pushed out of the way—*she'll* control *you!*"

Avery faltered for a second. *That sounded unpleasant, but* … "It will be fine. I trust her."

Alex persisted. "What if you can't get rid of her, what if she sends you mad?"

"It won't. She won't. I feel her. She's gentle and fair—she won't hurt me."

"You don't *know* her, Avery, so you don't know that. And what if the spell goes wrong?"

"So there is one?"

He sighed. "Yes, there is. You would need to surrender your spirit to hers, to allow her in. But I'm scared she would take over, smother you. Then you'd be lost. *Forever.* I don't want that to happen."

It felt as if they were the only two in the room. She felt the others watching them, but she didn't care. "I promise I'll come back."

"You better." He finally broke his gaze and turned to his grimoire on the floor in front of him.

"So it's decided, then." Briar said, her tone even, but her face tense. "I need to prepare my ingredients. My part requires a lot of herbs. What about everyone else's?"

"Mine requires half a dozen," Avery said. "I've already brought them with me. Reuben's, El's and Alex's are incantations only. As my grimoire is the key to the spell, it describes the preparation of the space, too. It seems to be the usual circle of protection. It also describes the order of the incantations to break the spell. It's precise. You need to be familiar with it."

"I presume we're doing this *now*?" El asked.

"We have to," Avery said. She checked her watch. "It's already past six—that only gives us six hours in which to break the spell and get to Faversham's place."

"How?" Reuben asked, looking around at them all. Dark circles were under his eyes, and it looked as if he hadn't slept in days. "You say the centre of the pentagram is where the Church of All Souls is. But *where* in the Church? How do we find it?"

"You're happy to help, then?" El asked him curiously.

"Of course I am. I'm grieving, not useless," he said brusquely.

El flinched, but then he reached out his hand and placed it on hers in apology.

"Right," Avery said, feeling like she needed to get things moving. "Let's check the spells and all the ingredients, and start preparing them here. We'll have to cast the spell that allows Helena in later, at the place where we break the binding. I better go and find it."

"So," Newton said, "what can I do?"

"You can help me find the place."

"Yes, good, I can do that," he agreed, eager to be doing something practical.

"But then what?" Reuben persisted. "Say we're successful, and we break the spell. A demon and a vengeful sprit will then be released. Have we a plan for that?"

"I can handle those, with help," Alex said. "I've been studying the spells in my grimoire like a mad man. And hopefully, if Helena is right, our powers will be released and that will give us some juice."

"She said *unleashed*. That sounds pretty big," Briar said.

"Well, it will be interesting," Alex allowed with a sigh.

"And then we head to Faversham Central and rescue Sally. And your grimoire, Reuben." Avery felt adrenalin rush through her. "And it will give me great pleasure to show daddy Faversham where he can stick his threats."

19

Avery stood next to Newton in front of the Church of All Souls. Its medieval architecture squatted above them, and despite the warmth of the evening, Avery felt a shiver run through her.

The church was typical of its type, with gothic arched windows, a spire, gargoyles and strange, mythical images of the green man on the stonework, and a deep porch with heavy oak doors. It sat just up from an intersection, and it had a small slabbed square in front of it, handy for those attending weddings and funerals to loiter in.

It was still light, and tourists and locals alike were strolling through the town on their way to restaurants and bars. This time last night Avery was one of them, and now she wondered if she ever would be again.

The church doors were still open, allowing late-night worshippers to enter, and Avery and Newton slipped through into the gloom beyond.

All Souls was shadowy and silent, and the temperature plummeted several degrees as they stepped inside the cool confines of the thick walls. Apart from a couple of people who sat near the front in silent contemplation, the church was empty.

Newton looked as serious as she'd ever seen him, and seeing his worried profile, she wondered how he would manage tonight.

"How are you feeling, Newton?"

"Like I'm about to embark on one of the stupidest things I've ever done," he said quietly.

"You don't have to be here. We can manage without you. In fact, you are violating your true role. You're supposed to be stopping us."

He turned and looked at her, his eyes dark and troubled. "That was before I knew the truth of what your families had done and why. I'm also supposed to be protecting you—that's what Peter wanted, too. And besides, the more power you have, the less we have to fear from the Favershams."

"Thank you. We appreciate your support."

"Just promise me you know what you're doing."

She felt doubt surge through her again. "I think we do. But you know we've never done anything like this before."

"You're putting yourself at great risk, Avery."

"My friend Sally's in greater risk than me," she said, hoping that Faversham was true to his word and keeping her safe for now.

He looked around the dark interior of the church. "Well, we'd better find the place, hadn't we? Any thoughts?"

"The crypt," she suggested, thinking about her conversation with Alex. "It's the only place it can be—or at least a place accessed from there."

It was a large church, and they walked down the nave towards the altar, keeping to the aisle on the left, their footsteps echoing around them. They passed the transepts and headed into a small chapel also on the left, out of sight from the visitors.

"Where now?"

Avery pointed to where a narrow, rectangular hole was cut into the floor behind the choir. It was edged with an ornate iron railing to stop people from falling in, and a set of steps led down into darkness.

Looking around cautiously, they made sure no one could see them, and made their way to the entrance.

"Where's the vicar?" Newton whispered.

Avery shrugged. "In his private rooms?"

Avery went to lead the way down, but Newton stopped her. "Let me."

With every step down, the temperature plunged lower and lower until Avery was shivering. At the bottom was a solid oak door, black with age, the arcane face of a gargoyle carved on it. It was locked.

Avery stepped past Newton and laid her hand on the lock, whispering a short spell. The lock released, and she pressed down on the iron handle, swinging the door open.Beyond was only darkness. Avery sent a witch light into the room and then they stepped inside, shutting the door behind them.

They stood on the edge of the long, low roofed room, the walls, floor, and ceiling made of heavy stone blocks. Vaulted archways ran the length of the room, and stone sarcophagi were placed along either side the central aisle. Halfway across the room was another iron railing with a locked gate. Beyond were objects of value—silver chalices and candlesticks.

The crypt was damp and musty, as well as bitingly cold.

At the far end of the room, on the rear wall beyond the railings, was a sign illuminated only by the witch light. It was a large sigil with several lines of runes beneath it.

"Well, at least we know where to look," Newton said. "Isn't it a bit obvious to mark the place?"

Avery shook her head. "The sigil both warns and offers entry, but only to those who are worthy."

"What do you mean?"

"It requires one of us, from the old families, to open it."

Avery walked forward, as if in a trance. With another whispered spell, she opened the locked gate in the middle of the railing and headed to the sigil.

Close up, it exuded power and fear. The mark was complex, but around it, the witch light showed the edges of a door, shimmering with a pale, unearthly light.

"Can you see that?" Avery asked.

Newton nodded. "I can feel it, too. What do the runes say?"

Avery hesitated for a minute as she translated them, glad she'd been researching them recently.

By Air and Fire, Water and Earth, declare your spirit to me.
If I find you worthy, I give entrance to thee.
But if you fail, forever will your soul condemned to misery be.
Are you ready? Declare yourself, and set your powers free.

Avery swallowed. "Well, I think that's pretty clear, don't you?" She turned to Newton. "Stand back. I have no idea quite what will happen."

Newton gave her a long, worried look and then stepped back several paces until he was beyond the railings.

Avery pressed her hands against the sigil.

For a few seconds, nothing happened, but then faint lines like fire began to radiate out from her hands, lighting up every swirling line and mark of the sigil. A tingle spread up Avery's arms and across her chest, radiating down her whole body, just as it was across the sign.

And then it started to burn.

She cried out, and Newton shouted, "What's happening?"

But Avery could barely speak she was so wracked with pain. She was aware of Newton starting to move towards her and she summoned her reserves of strength, shouting, "Stay back!"

The burning intensified until it felt as if her veins and her brain were on fire. Her vision started to dim, and blackness encroached on all sides, until only the sigil remained in front of her, filling her vision.

Her hands were now welded to it, and it seemed to be accessing her mind, pulling out all her secrets. Images flashed across her vision—Alex, her mother, her grandmother, the grimoires, and lastly, Caspian Faversham.

She tried to calm her breathing. This was a test, like it had been for Alex and El. She was pure; she was a descendant of Helena. She deserved to be here. It was her destiny.

And as she thought of Helena, Avery felt her burning-hot flesh flash icy cold for a second, and she became aware of a figure next to her. Avery tore her gaze from the sigil and saw Helena standing next to her.

For a few seconds, Helena's image was translucent, and then it solidified.

Helena was beautiful. Her hair was long and dark, cascading down her back in a thick wave. She was wrapped in a dark cloak, and her face above it was pale. But her eyes shone with fierce desire as she studied Avery.

The smell of violets was strong now, as was the sickening smell of ashes and smoke, and Avery felt herself wretch. She could smell burning flesh, and it was growing stronger by the second, but she held on, willing herself to stay standing and not pass out.

The sigil was now blazing with a fiery light. Avery felt as if her soul was being sucked out of her body. She hung on with every fibre of her being, refusing to give in.

And then it was over. The sigil released her, and she fell to the floor.

With a whisper, the doorway cracked open around the edges and then swung open, and Helena stepped past her into the room without a backward glance.

Within seconds, Newton was at Avery's side.

"Are you okay?"

For a few seconds she couldn't speak, but slowly, the burning subsided and her brain started to function again as her vision cleared. She nodded, taking deep, calming breaths. "Yes, I think so."

Newton's reassuring hands were on her arms, and he helped pull her to her feet.

"Can you see Helena?" Avery asked.

Newton glanced into the room that had been revealed beyond the sigil. "Yes, but barely. She's a ghostly apparition."

Following his gaze, Avery murmured. "Not to me. It's like she's truly flesh and blood."

As if Helena could hear them, she turned and looked at Avery, her eyes burning in her pale face. Her cloak had fallen open, and Avery saw that she wore a long, dark dress with a tight bodice, but then she turned away, dismissing her, and surveyed the room. The feeling of comfort she had given Avery earlier had gone.

Avery felt fear spreading through her. She was about to let this woman into her body.

"I have a very bad feeling about this," Newton hissed.

"Come on. This is no time for doubts," Avery said, trying to subdue her own as she led the way into the room.

Immediately beyond the hidden doorway, a series of shallow steps dropped down to a lower level. As Avery crossed the threshold, light sprang up everywhere, illuminating the magnificent chamber.

Dozens of large-columned candles filled the corners, ran along the walls, lined the aisles, and decorated the altar, revealing the ceiling of vaulted stone, supported by ornate stone columns that formed two rows on either side of the central space.

In the centre of the floor was a giant pentacle—a pentagram, surrounded by a double circle. It was made from different coloured stones—granite, and a red stone that Avery couldn't identify. The signs for the five elements were also marked onto the floor, and in the centre of the pentagram was a devil's trap.

Two large braziers were placed on either side of the altar against the far wall, and they blazed with fire.

Avery could feel the potent magic and power in the room. It resonated with it, caressing her body. It seemed to whisper in her ear like a lover, and she could swear she felt lips on her skin.

She shivered, and it wasn't just from the bone-chilling cold in the room that caused her breath to puff out in white clouds.

Keeping her distance from Helena, who walked with an unearthly grace across the far side of the room, Avery walked around the pentagram to the altar, closely followed by Newton.

"This place is terrifying." Newton said, his face bleak. "It makes my flesh crawl."

"Mine, too," Avery agreed softly, wondering if Helena could hear and understand them.

She turned her attention to the altar, her breath catching as she saw a large jar filled with a swirling black liquid that moved all on its own.

"What's that?" Newton said, eyeing it suspiciously.

"I have a horrible feeling that's Octavia."

"And her demon?"

"Trapped within that, I suspect," she said, pointing to the huge devil's trap in the centre of the pentagram.

Hesitantly, Avery touched the other objects on the altar. They were the usual array of a goblet, bowl, ritual knife, and the powdered remains of what Avery presumed were herbs.

She felt the icy prickle return to her skin, and realised Helena was just to her right, a triumphant smile on her face as she stroked the glass jar. She lifted her head and looked at Avery, sending a shiver to the depths of her soul. And then she turned to Newton, narrowed her eyes, and rushed towards him, causing Newton to stagger back in fear.

But Helena was powerless, and she passed through him, causing Newton to clutch at his chest in shock.

Helena turned back to them, her eyes smouldering with resentment. She was trying to speak, but couldn't, and Avery saw more fury cross her features, transforming her into a witch from the storybooks. And then her anger evaporated, and it was just Helena again.

Avery realised she was holding her breath and she slowly released it, grabbing Newton's arm for comfort.

Newton straightened and breathed easier again, but his face was white.

Avery placed herself in front of him and squared up to Helena. "Things have changed, Helena. Peter Newton never forgave himself for what happened to you. His descendants have helped us through the years!"

Helena cast a resentful glance at Newton, but nodded.

"Will you help us today? Help us break the spell and return our power to us? All five families will be here, but we need your help. The Favershams remain strong, and we cannot fight them without more magic. They already have the Jackson's grimoire. Can you remember the spell for water? Reuben Jackson will swap places, and say the spell for air."

Helena nodded, a malevolent gleam once more springing onto her face. She may not be able to speak, but she understood. She reached out and placed her hand on Avery's arm, and a charge like an electric shock rocketed through Avery. With searing clarity she knew Helena agreed, and she had transmitted one final instruction, as if it was burnt on her brain.

I will lead.

Avery breathed a sigh of relief. She had felt Helena's agreement before, but it was good to have it confirmed. She turned to Newton, a stone in the pit of her stomach. "Go and phone the others. Tell them we're ready."

20

The rest of the group arrived within half an hour, having slipped into the now closed church and down into the crypt.

They were laden with their grimoires and the herbs required to break the binding.

As they stepped into the chamber, their eyes widened, and Alex whistled. "Wow. This is pretty impressive!" He saw Helena standing by the altar and gasped. "I can see Helena."

Helena turned and appraised him, a slow smile spreading across her face, and then she looked at Reuben, El, and Briar standing next to him. Her gaze returned to Reuben, her eyes narrowing speculatively, and then they settled on Alex.

Helena desired Alex, Avery could tell; she looked again at Avery, and a knowing smile crossed her face.

Another chill ran through Avery. She had the feeling that once Helena was in her body, she wasn't going to want to leave it. She subdued the thought. She needed to trust Helena. She was going to save them all.

"Can anyone else see her?" Alex asked.

"A ghost, only barely visible," El said, echoing Newton earlier.

"Same for me," Reuben and Briar agreed.

"I can see her far more clearly," Alex said, looking at Helena warily. "It's not the first time I've seen spirits, but she is far more..." he struggled for words.

"Solid?" Avery suggested.

He nodded, and they both watched Helena pacing up and down, impatient to begin.

"I don't like this *at all*," Briar said, pulling her herbs from her bag. "I don't trust her."

"We haven't got much choice," Avery said. She turned to Alex. "Any tips for expelling a spirit from my body?"

Alex grabbed her hands. "Stay strong. Remember who you are. Hold tight to cherished memories." He pulled her close and kissed her, taking her breath away.

"Guys, get a room!" Reuben said, smirking.

"Sod off, Reuben," Alex said, breaking away and pulling his own grimoire from his pack.

Avery tried to ignore the tingle on her lips. "According to this," she said, reading the instructions in her own grimoire, "we all stand on our respective points of the pentagram. I need to place the glass jar next to the devil's trap. Helena has already indicated to me that she'll lead, so just do what she says. Have you all had a chance to study the spell?"

They nodded, and El clutched the red gemstone necklace that she had been gifted in her wooden box. "I'm as ready as I'll ever be."

"Where should I stand?" Newton asked.

"Just out of this room," Alex suggested. "In the doorway. I suspect that when we start the spell, the demon in that devil's trap will manifest, and it might even get out. Keep well out of the way."

"In fact," Briar said, "maybe you should wait in the church, just in case the vicar comes to call?"

Newton nodded in agreement. "I'll wait in the small side chapel."

"I've brought something for you, just in case," Reuben said, reaching into his sports bag for a large object wrapped in a blanket. He unrolled it to reveal a shotgun and a box of shells.

"Where the hell did you get that?" Newton asked, alarmed.

"Don't worry, we're licensed. We keep it on the estate. The shells are filled with salt."

Alex nodded and laughed. "So that's what you went back for. Good idea."

"Is it?" Newton asked, taking the gun from him and inspecting it.

"Yes. Salt repels spirits, just in case a certain someone needs a reminder of who's in charge." Reuben nodded towards Helena. "Can you use it?"

"I've had firearms training," Newton nodded. "Right then. If you need me, shout."

While they had been preparing, the power in the room seemed to shift and change, as if the energy was rising.

"I can feel the anticipation, can you?" El asked as she took her place on the pentagram.

"Like a charging battery," Reuben agreed, squaring his shoulders. He looked more animated than he had in days.

Apart from Briar, they had all dressed in jeans and boots and jackets, ready for combat. El was wearing her black leather trousers and looked like the angel of death with bright white hair flowing down her back.

Briar, however, still wore her long, flowing clothes, and now she slipped her shoes off, standing barefoot on the cold stones. She saw them watching her. "It grounds me," she explained.

"What do I do about Helena?" Avery asked Alex, once she had moved the glass jar to the right place.

"Stand ready on the Water element sign," he said, bringing a small potion bottle out of his bag and then walking over to join her. "This potion will drug your senses, but only slightly," he added, seeing Avery's alarmed expression. "It will be like when we spirit-walked. There are a few words you need to say, an invocation, to invite her in. Are you sure you want to do this?" Helena was now standing next to Avery, an eager, hungry expression on her face.

Avery summoned her courage. "Yes. We have no choice."

"We do have a choice. We could tackle the Favershams without extra power."

"We'd fail and you know it," she said, casting a wary glance at Helena.

Helena hadn't tried to communicate since they had first arrived, and the sense of calm that she'd first given Avery had now completely gone. Instead, Avery felt Helena resented her, rather than supported her.

Alex took one final worried look at Helena, and then gave Avery a slip of paper he'd written the spell on. It was only a few lines, and she read through them quickly.

"All good," she nodded encouragingly, and Alex returned to his place on Spirit, the point of the pentacle closest to the altar and directly to her left.

She took a long look around the room, taking in the hundreds of candles, the bright braziers, now giving off a smoky heat, and the long shadows from the stone pillars supporting the ceiling, and hoped this would not be the last room she ever knew. Finally, she looked at Helena.

They were strikingly similar, other than the colour of their hair and eyes. They were the same height with small, slim builds, and both had pale skin, but Helena's eyes burned with a fierce desire that Avery wasn't sure she was equal to. Nevertheless, she drank the potion Alex had prepared.

It scorched her throat, and she coughed as the liquid burnt its way down into her stomach. She tasted cinnamon and blackberries, then something peppery and sharp, and then something acrid.

No. That was Helena she could smell.

The scent of burning flesh was back, and smoke now seemed to swirl around Helena as she stood barely an arm's length from Avery, fixing her with a piercing stare. Avery's vision started to swim, and she looked down at the note, quickly saying the words of the spell while she still could.

As soon as they were uttered, she felt her consciousness recede, slipping back into some distant part of her being.

Avery felt Helena ease into her, turning and twisting her way into her body. It was like a cool breeze was running through her veins and tickling her skin. For a few seconds it was pleasant, and then her mind was filled with hundreds of images, some too swift to focus on, others searing in their intensity—particularly one.

The sharp, bitter fear of being dragged to the stake, stumbling on unwilling legs. Anger and the desire for vengeance was so strong that she felt she could almost break free. But the men holding her were too big, their grip like iron around her arms. In a second she was tied to the stake, a huge pyre prepared below her. The firebrands touched the wood and flared beneath her.

Avery tried to scream, but couldn't, her mouth clamped shut by Helena. And then the image was gone, replaced by the memories of her nights with Alex. She could feel Helena examining them minutely, and if Avery could have blushed, she would, but then that disappeared, too.

Avery now started to panic. She felt suffocated; crushed beneath Helena's mind and her considerable will.

If Helena was aware of Avery's panic, she didn't show it, instead focussing on the room and the need to perform the spell.

Avery saw the room through her eyes, the other witches standing ready, looking nervous but determined. She felt Helena's excitement, but also her annoyance and disappointment. She looked down on them and their lack of knowledge, she could feel it simmering in her. Except for Alex. She *wanted* him.

As if Helena suddenly became aware of Avery's presence, she mentally shoved her, and it took all of Avery's concentration to hold on. It was as if she was trying to displace her from her own body.

Alex spoke. Avery could see his lips move, but she couldn't hear him. It seemed as if she was under water.

"I am ready. Are you?" Helena asked. Her words came out of Avery's mouth, making Avery's skin crawl. And it seemed to repel the others, too. They all took one long look at her, glanced at each other, and then nodded.

Helena began.

She spoke the words of the spell cleanly and with authority, her voice growing stronger as she progressed. She never faltered once, and she nodded at each of the others in turn when it was their time to join in.

Power was building in the room, and as the spell was uttered and repeated, each part layered on top of each other, line by line, full of intention and conviction, the devil's trap began to glow with a strange, blue light.

The shape of a demon rose up from the floor, streaming like smoke through a vent, and at the same time, an awful, gut-wrenching growl rumbled around the room.

Helena's excitement began to rise and she pointed her finger—Avery's finger—at the glass jar, which sat a short distance from the devil's trap, and uttered a final command.

The swirling liquid became agitated, speeding up like a whirlpool, until the jar rocked violently and fell over, smashing instantly, the liquid spreading over the stone. A shriek pierced the room, bloodcurdling in its intensity.

And then it seemed as if all hell broke loose.

A wave of sheer power exploded from the centre of the room, throwing all of them off their feet and out of the pentagram.

Avery sailed through the air, and then felt the bone-shaking smack of cold stone at her back, and also Helena's shock. She struggled to breath, wincing at the ache through her entire body, but Helena bounced back to her feet, threw back her head, and called the power to her.

Avery sensed rather than saw it, feeling a rush of power flood through her with such force that her spirit left her body with a jolt, thrown up to the roof above them.

She had a moment of shock as she saw her body below her, now possessed by Helena. The silver cord attaching her to her body curled below her, swaying in the power that had rocketed around the room.

Avery realised she had a birds-eye view of the action below. She could see the aura of magical energy spiralling around the room like a tornado, all different shades of reds, blues, purples, oranges and greens. The different colours were honing in on the different witches, flowing into them. All five witches now stood tall, with their heads thrown back and mouths wide open as the magic poured into them.

In the centre of the pentagram, the demon and Octavia continued to form into their full shapes, as the powerful bonds that had contained them disappeared.

But there was too much energy to be contained in the small room. Avery saw it flood out the door and up through the ceiling, and she followed it, passing through the church and out into the night air.

In the skies above White Haven, a dark purple mass rippled out across the town like a tidal wave, and the giant pentagram that connected the town to this point sparked like fuse wire.

For a few moments, Avery watched, mesmerised, as the magical energy poured into the night, hanging on the air and casting a veil over the town.

Below, people on the street looked around in shock, as if they had heard or seen something, but then with a shrug, they carried on, and Avery realised they subconsciously may have registered something happening, but they had no idea what.

Avery hovered above the church, her cord streaming below her. They had released something fundamental tonight, she could feel it in her spirit body, and with a sense of excitement, but no little worry, she wondered what the consequences would be.

And then Avery experienced a short, sharp tug on her cord and with a feeling of dislocation, she instantly knew Helena was trying to sever her cord.

21

Avery focussed on her physical body and rushed back to the crypt below.

She found a scene of chaos.

The demon had now broken free of the devil's trap and was lashing the room with whips of flame. It was huge, bigger than any they had seen before. Its form was rippling and changing, and it was impossible to predict what it would do next. Alex was desperately trying to subdue it, his lips moving furiously in a chant, his arms outstretched, the other three witches supporting him.

Helena was fully occupied with fighting Octavia, who now appeared unnervingly fully formed. Avery presumed that like Helena, her spirit form had manifested very strongly. Octavia was an imposing woman, with long, white hair streaming over her shoulders and a face full of fury. They were attacking each other with every elemental force they could summon, which was fortunate for Avery because while Helena was engaged with Octavia, she couldn't try to kill her. Because as much as she hated to admit it, that was exactly what Helena was trying to do.

Avery tried not to panic. She focused on being back in her body, but Helena had blocked her in some way; she could see a shield all around her body. How had she done that? Avery could also see a black mark on her life cord. If that severed, she was dead. As the two ancient witches fought, Avery noticed that with every hit Helena took, the shield wavered. That was her chance.

She watched her friends, who were finally getting the demon under control. While Briar and Reuben contained the demon within a magical force field, a doorway started to whirl open in the air behind it, and through it Avery could see the world beyond. Her spirit body could see more than her physical one, and she reeled back in shock. Thousands of tormented and vengeful spirits were pushing at the doorway and some even sneaked out, fleeing the room. They had to close the doorway before more escaped. But before she could think of how to warn them, Octavia blasted Helena with a tornado of air and she flew across the room, collapsing against the wall. The shield wavered and vanished, and Avery streamed back into her body.

Avery could feel Helena's shock and rage—now directed at her *and* Octavia, but as Octavia was still attacking her, Helena could not attack Avery. Avery could also feel the potency of her newfound magic. For a second she found it overwhelming, and then she took advantage and attacked Helena, too, trying to force her out of her body.

For what seemed like minutes, but was probably only seconds, their spirits wrestled as Octavia advanced on them.

Avery was vaguely aware of movement in her peripheral vision, and then Newton appeared, his shotgun raised. He aimed at Octavia and blasted her, sending her flying backwards. He fired again, and then reloaded.

Avery now felt Helena's panic and she yelled, *"Get out of my body!"* She had no idea if she really was shouting, or it was all in her head.

Helena seethed and shouted back, *"No! I died before my time. I will have vengeance!"*

"You have had your time, Helena. You made your sacrifice." Avery was so incensed that Helena was trying to kill her that her anger made her stronger, and with one final, furious push, she ejected Helena.

Relief flooded though her. But Helena stood before her, her face twisted with anger, and she again tried to force her way in. And then a blast sounded to her left, and Helena's spirit wavered and flickered. She turned to see Newton striding towards her, and once again he blasted Helena, shattering her this time into thousands of pieces.

"Get rid of Octavia!" he shouted. "I'll keep Helena under control."

Avery ran on shaky legs over to Octavia, who was now struggling to stand. With a well-timed blast of air, she sent her backwards again. But Octavia regained control quickly and flew at her, hundreds of years of anger fuelling her magic.

In a surprising show of physical force, Octavia dragged Avery to the floor and placed a hand on her chest. Avery felt an icy cold spread through her body. She couldn't breathe, and the more she tried to inhale, the worse the pain got.

Then Avery caught a glimpse of the demon over Octavia's shoulder.

It was being sucked back into the spirit world, the doorway swirling behind it. But it wasn't going alone. With one final lash of his fiery whips, he caught Octavia and dragged her with him. Avery could breathe again.

With a word of command from Alex, the doorway collapsed and disappeared, and the demon and Octavia vanished, with only her echoing scream to remind them she had ever been there.

Newton shouted. "What do you want to do with this one?"

Still gasping for air, Avery rolled over and saw Newton standing over Helena's writhing spirit form, gun pointing down at her.

Alex ran over. "Let me." But before he could act, Helena vanished from sight.

"Where the hell has she gone?" Newton shouted, spinning around.

"No idea," Alex said, "but she won't come back for a while."

"You might have to keep a loaded shotgun in your flat," Newton said to Avery.

"We'll find another way to deal with her," Alex decided. He turned to Avery, his eyes narrowed. "Are you okay?"

"I'm fine, now," she said, sitting up. "Things were a bit scary for awhile there. What about you?"

"Feeling like I could do this all night," Alex said. "That hit of magic was intense!"

Reuben, El, and Briar joined them. All of them looked slightly battered. Their hair was ruffled, dirt was streaked over Reuben where he'd fallen to the floor, and El was cradling her arm where Avery could see a burn.

El grinned, "Alex is right. The power that flooded into us was insane. It feels like it's ebbing slightly, but wow, it was amazing."

Briar agreed, "It's like it's woken up some magical knowledge. Some of the spells from the original grimoire actually make sense to me now."

"It's definitely woken up my magic," Reuben said, rubbing his head. "And yours, Alex. Where the hell did you get the spell from?"

"The doorway spell?" Alex grinned. "Like you say, I was juiced up on magic, and the knowledge just flooded into me."

Newton shook his head. "Well, I couldn't see anything, but I sure could feel something. It was like a wave rippled through the town. If I hadn't known what was going on here, I probably would have dismissed it—like I was imagining something. But clearly, I wasn't."

"Well, there's plenty I can tell you about that," Avery said, "but we have somewhere to be. Are you ready for round two?"

"There's no way that going to Faversham Central can be as bad as this," Reuben said, looking around the crypt.

"I wouldn't bet on it." Avery hedged. "Newton, you'd better come, too. You're pretty handy with that shotgun."

"It's got salt in it, not real shotgun pellets."

Reuben reached into his pocket and pulled out another box. "Proper ones. Just in case."

Newton glared. "I'm a police officer—I'm not going to kill anyone. And neither are you."

"We don't know what we're going to face. Take them."

Newton reluctantly accepted the shells.

"And why are you shooting Helena?" El asked. "I thought she was your friend?"

"That was before she tried to steal my body, but I'll catch you up later. Are we all ready?"

"Yep, let's go." Alex led the way out of the hidden crypt, and as Avery crossed the threshold, the chamber plunged into darkness and sealed itself shut.

22

The group arrived at Sebastian Faversham's mansion, and parked up the lane, well out of view.

He lived in a large Tudor dwelling on the edge of Harecombe, very similar in style to Greenlane Manor, edged with a high brick wall.

They clambered over the wall and landed under the trees on the far side of the garden. The house was visible a short distance away, the windows mainly dark, other than a few on the ground and first floor, and a variety of cars were assembled on the drive in front of the house.

"So, what's the plan?" Reuben asked, checking out the grounds nervously.

"Find Sally first and get her out of here, and then we get the grimoire," Avery said.

"How do we find her?" Reuben asked. "That's a big house."

"I've come prepared. She has a hairbrush at work. I've taken her hair and made a locator spell. I'll release it as soon as we're in the house—we'll just have to follow the light. And then one of us needs to whisk her to safety."

"I can do that," Newton volunteered. "I'll bring her back to the van."

"But how the hell do we find the grimoire?" Alex asked. "There's no locator spell for *that*."

"I'm sure we'll think of something. The important thing is to get Sally out safely."

As Briar finished speaking, a howl set up across the grounds.

"What's that?" Newton said, raising his gun.

"Crap! Dogs," Alex said, pointing to half a dozen animals racing across the grounds towards them.

The dogs spread out in a line, snarling and snapping. They had a feral green glow to them, were twice the size of normal dogs, and as they drew closer, their large canines glinted in the garden lights.

"Oh great, not just any dogs," Avery said, getting ready to defend herself. "I think we've set off a magical alarm system."

"So much for a stealthy approach," Briar said. "Leave the dogs to me. You all head to the house, and I'll catch you later."

Briar was still barefoot, and she planted herself firmly, squaring her shoulders as she uttered a spell. With a juddering shake, the ground cracked open in front of the dogs, and they started to fall in, howling and yelping, but the others didn't stop to watch.

They ran to a ground floor window at the back of the house, well away from the brightly-lit ones.

"There's a spell on the entrances," El said, touching the wood tentatively. "It looks complex."

"Well, we'd better break it soon, because some of those dogs are still loose and they're heading this way," Reuben warned, turning to face them. He directed a blast of energy at the closest dog, and it collapsed on the ground.

"I'll just *fry* the spell," El said, now confident. She placed her hand on the necklace she had inherited with her grimoire. "This seems to store elemental fire, and it's super juiced up at the moment."

She slipped her necklace off and held the stone on the glass. For a brief second it illuminated the web of spells protecting the house, and then flames raced across the window, breaking the spell and shattering the glass all at once.

They knocked the rest of the glass out, piled into the room, and then raced to the door.

Before they opened it, Avery brought Sally's hair out of her pocket. It was stored in a small cotton bag and wrapped with twine. She whispered a spell over it, and it blossomed into a tiny blue light.

For a second the light just bobbed in the air, and then it passed through the door and they hurried to follow it.

Beyond was a passageway, and the light led them down to the main part of the house. They had only gone a few paces when a familiar, dark-haired woman appeared in a whirl of air and magic. It was Estelle, Caspian's sister.

Estelle was statuesque, with long, dark hair and compelling eyes. She was dressed head to foot in black and her arms were outstretched, blocking the passage and ready to attack. Her face was triumphant. "So, you dared to come here with your pathetic powers? You're more foolish than we thought. Did you think you could enter our house and we wouldn't know?"

Avery stepped forward, eager to wipe the smile off her face. "Of course you would know, but we don't scare that easily."

Estelle narrowed her eyes. "Well, you're even more stupid than I thought." And without warning she sent a cloud of black smoke at them. It quickly billowed around them, blinding them all as it grew thicker and more impenetrable. Avery's eyes burned, and for the second time that evening, she struggled to breathe.

But someone reacted equally quickly, and she heard Estelle shout out in pain. In seconds, the black smoke disappeared, and Avery saw El's flaming sword skewered through Estelle's side. Reuben didn't hesitate; he sent a bolt of energy at the ceiling above Estelle, bringing plaster and a large beam of wood down on her head. She fell unconscious on the floor below.

"That was easier than I thought," Reuben said, pulling El's sword free and passing it back to her. "Good aim, El."

"Lucky shot, really," she grimaced.

They stepped over to Estelle's body, and El conjured a fiery rope to wrap around Estelle's prone form. They dragged her into a side room and sealed the door.

The blue light bobbed ahead of them, and they quickly followed it along another side corridor, into the depths of the house. The house was furnished with impeccable taste, and they progressed quietly down the carpeted corridors lined with priceless works of art.

A shout disturbed them, and they turned to find two men they hadn't met before, but had only seen on photos; Caspian's cousins, Hamish and Rory, one blond and the other dark-haired.

As Avery quickly assessed their opposition, she was aware of movement behind her. She turned to find Caspian grinning malevolently. They were trapped.

The next few minutes were a jumble of shouts, wind, fire, and water, and they summoned every bit of power they had. El's sword flashed with fire, balls of energy bounced off the walls, and then the lights went out.

Avery wasn't sure if they were winning or not. The energy balls pummelled her, and several times she fell before getting up again. She realised she had been separated from the others, and suddenly Caspian loomed above her.

Just as Avery was about to throw up a protective shield, the floor cracked and rumbled, and Caspian also lost his balance, falling on top of Avery. She could feel his hot breath on her face, and his weight crushed her.

Briar was here, somewhere.

Massive roots shot up through the floor of the mansion, wrapping around Caspian's ankles and pulling him through the splintered floor and down into the ground.

His face was masked in fury, and he turned and tried to blast the roots free. Some he did manage to break, but the rest were too strong.

Avery was caught up with him, unable to break free, and once Caspian realised it he sneered, grabbed her tight, and pulled her with him.

Avery waited for the horrible, suffocating feeling of earth to cover her, but instead, they fell through space, crashing onto a stone floor below.

The smells of damp and mould were overwhelming. They were in the cellars.

She had fallen on Caspian, which at least provided her with a soft, if bumpy, landing. She fought free of him and the roots that continued to snake around them. Out of the corner of her eye, she saw the blue light bob away to her right.

Sally.

Newton dropped through the hole in the ceiling next to her, winded, but still holding his shotgun. "Are you okay?"

"Sort of," she said, smashing at another tree root. "Better than him."

Caspian was now wrapped in roots that bound him like iron. Avery could see bright blue flashes that encased his body as he tried to free himself, but so far, he was failing.

"Are they okay up there?" She looked up into the darkness of the corridor above. The sizzle of magic snapped like lightning in the dark, and she caught a flash of El's sword scything through the air.

"As far as I could see. Come on, we have to trust they'll be all right." Newton followed the blue light, leaving Avery with no choice but to follow him.

The guiding light led through several interconnected rooms, all in darkness, until eventually they came to another corridor. The air smelt slightly fresher here, and they saw another light ahead.

A room opened up on their left, with a dim light seeping through a small hatch at eye level in a wooden door. The hatch was lined with iron bars, and they edged to it, ready to fight.

Avery peered through the opening and saw Sally lying on a pallet on the floor. There was no one else in sight. She turned to Newton with relief. "It's Sally, and she's alone."

As she reached for the handle, a snarl came out of the darkness, and a dog launched at both of them, mouth wide and dripping with saliva.

Newton pulled the shotgun up and blasted it, twice. It howled and then fell dead at their feet.

"Quick reflexes, Newton," Avery said admiringly. She called out, "Sally, it's us, we're coming in!"

The door was sealed with a very simple spell, and Avery easily unlocked it as Newton reloaded. Fortunately, the Faversham's arrogance was an asset for them.

Sally sat up, looking confused. Her face was streaked with tears and dirt, her hands were blooded and bruised, and she shivered in the cold. "Avery! Where am I? How long have I been here?"

Avery rushed over and hugged her. "Sally, we'll explain everything later. Are you okay?"

"Yes—no, not really," she said and burst into tears.

"Can you walk?"

"Yes, I'm not hurt." She struggled to her feet.

"What did you do to your hands?' Avery asked, concerned.

"I beat the door and made myself hoarse from shouting, but all I could hear was a bloody great dog."

"Can you remember anything?"

"No! The last thing I remember was being in the shop, and then I woke up here."

"Okay, we need to move. We're getting you out of here. Newton, anything else out there?"

"Not yet!" he called.

"Right, follow me, Sally."

Avery pulled Sally out of the room, and then followed Newton along the corridor until they eventually came to a set of steps leading up. At the top of the stairs, they headed through another door to find that the passage led two ways—one back into the main part of the house, and one to a rear entrance.

"Right, leave Sally with me," Newton said. "We'll be waiting in the van."

"Are you sure you can get out of the grounds?"

"I'm pretty sure the family's tied up here. And I can handle dogs." He looked at Sally. "Think you can run?"

Sally's colour had already returned. "Yes, honestly, I'm fine. I'm just glad to be out of that room."

Avery nodded. "All right. I'll see you later. And Newton, if we're not out in an hour, go."

"If you're not out in an hour, I'm coming after you," he said firmly, his eyes glinting fiercely in the dark. And with that he headed out the door with Sally.

Avery turned back toward the interior of the house.

She heard a distant *boom*, and then the house shuddered. Every light went out. *Was that us, or them, doing that?* Avery considered producing a witch light, and then decided against it for now. She edged along the corridor, her eyes slowly adjusting to the darkness. The air changed, and she realised she was entering the large entrance hall, as she saw the broad curve of the stairs next to her. To her right, a long corridor ran away into darkness, and she heard shouts and felt the sizzle of magic. She was about to make her way to it, when a figure ran towards her. She prepared to attack, and then realised it was Alex. He too had his hands raised. He stopped when he saw her and sighed with relief. She ran to the edge of the hall to join him.

"Are you okay?" she whispered.

He nodded. "Rory and Hamish are big thugs and powerful, and then Uncle Rupert waded in. It was touch and go for a while, but we broke free. Briar's coming now, while El and Reuben secure the others."

Over his shoulder she saw Briar's small shape running towards them, grinning as she saw Avery. She was slightly out of breath, but blue flames trickled through her fingers, and she looked raring to go. "Have you found Sally?" she asked, standing next to them.

Avery nodded. "Yeah, and Newton's taken her to the van. Now we just need to find the grimoire."

"Any ideas?"

Avery's shoulders sagged. "Not really."

They fell silent for a few seconds, and then Alex grinned. "What if we used the locator spell with blood? Would it work on Reuben's grimoire?"

"It might do!" Avery said, brightening. "He needed his blood to reveal it; maybe his blood will lead us to it as well."

Alex led them back down the corridor, but they'd only gone a short distance when they met Reuben and El. With their light hair and dark clothes, and El's sword still glowing with fire, they looked like avenging angels. Both of them smelled of singed hair and smoke. Alex pulled them all into an elegant room, lit only by the faint moonlight from outside.

"We need your blood and hair," Alex said to Reuben. "Now?" Reuben asked, clearly confused. "What for?"

"To find your grimoire." Avery looked sheepish. "I just wish I'd thought of it earlier."

"You know the spell?" Briar asked, from where she stood at the doorway to make sure no one appeared unexpectedly.

"Sure, but it will be basic." Avery turned and grabbed an antique silver bowl from a cabinet. "And this will be perfect."

Reuben pulled a few strands of hair out, and then El gave him her sword. He pulled it across the palm of his hand, and a stream of blood trickled in to the bowl. Avery added the hair and then whispered a spell, holding her hand above it. The blood and hair started to bubble together, and as they mixed, it boiled down to nothing, until only smoke remained in the bowl. The smoke then rose out of the bowl, a deep, blood red glow within it, and drifted in the air for a second. Avery said another spell, "Blood to blood, hair and skin, lead us to the spells of the kin."

The smoke drifted to the door where it hung for a few moments before heading right, back to the main entrance, and then up the grand stairs to the next floor.

"Are you sure the others are tied up?" Avery asked El as they followed the smoke.

"Absolutely. Any sign of Caspian?'

"He's downstairs, Briar looked after him."

"So, just Sebastian, then?" Alex checked, hearing them.

Avery nodded. "I hope so."

At the top of the stairs, the smoke headed down a long corridor, passing several doorways. It moved faster and faster, until it streaked down another corridor, and then through a doorway on their right, where they found themselves in an enormous library.

A glimpse of the moon beyond the window cast the room in a silvery light. As Avery's eyes adjusted, she saw that all four walls were lined with shelves, packed with books. Leather armchairs were placed around the room, and in the centre was a large wooden desk. On it was Reuben's grimoire.

Unfortunately next to it, seated at ease, was Sebastian Faversham. He sat very still, his elbows resting on the arms of the chair, his hands together under his chin as if in prayer.

They pulled up short at the doorway, preparing to defend themselves. But Sebastian just stared at them, his face in shadow.

His voice hissed across the room. "What *have* you done?"

"We have defended ourselves," Avery said, thinking he was referring to their fight.

"I don't mean that!" he said, his voice threatening. "You destroy my house, attack my family, but you have done far worse than that."

Reuben was seething. "You have stolen my book, kidnapped an innocent woman, and *killed* my brother! You dare ask what *we* have done?"

Sebastian slowly rose to his feet, seeming huge in the shadows. "I mean the magic you have released from under All Soul's Church."

"Ah, yes," Avery said, shuffling awkwardly. "You noticed that?"

"Noticed?" His voice rose. "The whole magical community will have noticed! The magic even now pools above White Haven, drawing attention and all manner of creatures."

Avery felt her heart thump loudly. She glanced at the others, but they looked as baffled as she felt. "What do you mean, 'creatures?'"

"Anyone or any *thing* remotely connected to magic will have sensed that today. It rocked this house, and beyond. I hope you're pleased with yourselves."

A thousand possibilities raced through Avery's head, but she subdued them. There was plenty of time to worry about his accusations later. *How dare he presume to be so much better than them!*

"We're pleased we've found our old family magic," Avery said, annoyed and stepping into the room. "If it wasn't for Octavia, it wouldn't have been trapped down there, anyway! Maybe, if there was something to worry about, you should have been more honest."

Alex stood next to her. "No, he's just pissed off because we have just as much power as him."

Sebastian threw back his head and laughed, and the sound sent chills down Avery's spine. "Power! It's not just about power!"

"So, we can have the grimoire then?" Reuben asked.

"You think you're so clever, don't you?" Avery could hear the sneer in Sebastian's voice. He lifted his hands, and flames started to crackle in his palms. "You may have released your magic, but I shall destroy your book, and then you'll see what true power is!"

In a split second, he turned and threw flames at the grimoire, but before any of them could respond, the grimoire flew across the room towards them, smacking Reuben in the stomach and sending him staggering back. His hands wrapped around it, holding it tightly. Briar and El stepped forward on either side of him, preparing to attack.

Avery turned back to Sebastian, wondering what had happened, and then saw the bright, burning image of Helena materialise in front of him. The smell of burning flesh was sharp and nauseating, and smoke poured off Helena's body, filling the room.

If it was an apparition, it was a strong one. Avery covered her nose and mouth and squinted through the smoke. Helena had leapt at Sebastian and wrapped him in her burning body. Whatever magic had been released earlier had strengthened Helena, and she now swelled with power.

Not only did Helena appear to have gained physical form, but Sebastian could clearly feel her, too. As she wrapped herself around him, he screamed with rage and pain.

Avery felt Alex's hand on her arm. "Time to go."

"But..." she looked back to Sebastian, horrified. He was burning alive.

"*Now, Avery,*" Alex said, pulling her out the room and down the corridor, running after the others, who raced ahead of them.

The thick, black smoke poured after them, following them like an animal, and they raced down the stairs, out through the front door and across the grass.

Avery risked a look back to the house. She could see the library window from there; it was the only one filled with flames.

23

Newton drove them all back to White Haven as fast as possible without attracting attention. Desperate as they were to get home, he went the long way around, avoiding traffic cameras and anything that might incriminate them in whatever had happened at the manor.

They sat on the floor in the back of the van, propped on old blankets and braced between boxes and the sides, trying not to topple over as Newton steered them to safety.

"Can we please release whatever spells bound the others?" Avery asked, as soon as she could get her breath. "I don't want to think Helena will kill all of them—they don't deserve that."

"I beg to differ," Reuben said, his eyes hard. He still clutched his grimoire.

Briar answered, "Already done. I don't want that either, Avery."

"How the hell did Helena gain physical form?" Reuben asked.

"I'm not sure she really has," Alex explained. "I think it's just a severe and strong manifestation, brought on by the wave of magic we released, and her fury at the Favershams. After all, his ancestor is the reason she was burnt at the stake."

"But the smell," Briar said, covering her face with her hands. "It was awful. I still feel sick."

"Imagine being burnt alive—that would be far worse," El reasoned. "Are you all right, Avery? Things seemed really weird under All Souls when she possessed you."

Avery fell silent for a moment, trying to work through what had happened. "As much as I hate to say it, I don't think she wanted me back in my body. I accidentally spirit walked when the spell broke, so she didn't do that, but she sure didn't want to let me back in, either."

Alex was sitting next to her, and he snaked his arm around her and pulled her close. Avery shivered with pleasure, snuggling into him. He sighed. "I had a horrible feeling that would happen."

"I know you did, but we needed her," Avery said. "And at least we broke the spell, rescued Sally, and got the grimoire."

"But will she come back?" Briar asked. "What if she tries to get back inside you?"

"I let her in last time, remember? I don't think it can happen again."

"I think another tattoo might be in order," Reuben said with a wink.

Avery rolled her eyes. She looked up to the front of the van, where Sally was sitting in the passenger seat next to Newton, silent for now. She called over, "How are you, Sally?"

For a few seconds Sally didn't move, and then she turned around to look at them all, finally resting her gaze on Avery. "I'm not entirely sure, Avery. In fact, I'm not sure of anything at the moment."

Newton called back over his shoulder. "I've been trying to explain a few things to Sally, but—"

She finished the sentence for him. "There's magic, and there's *magic*, and I just need some time for it to soak in. And don't you *dare* think about spelling it out of my head!" She said forcefully.

Avery raised her hands in surrender. "Witches honour—if you'll keep this a secret!"

"Of course I will," Sally snorted as she turned back to look out of the windscreen. "I don't want to be carried off to the local loony bin."

"And how are you, Newton?" Briar asked.

"I'm fine," he said, still concentrating on the road. "Just hoping I can keep us all out of trouble with the police."

"There's no way the Favershams will report it, so I think we'll be fine," El said.

"And what about the magical explosion?" Briar asked. "I think we need to talk about that. We've released something that might have huge consequences."

"Ah, yes," Reuben said. "The *creatures* we will attract to White Haven."

"You know what?" Avery said, "I just want to appreciate having got through tonight. Let's discuss everything else tomorrow night. Meet at mine?"

There were nods of agreement, and then Sally said, "And make me a new hex bag, will you, Avery? Just *way* stronger than the last one."

***

Before Avery went to sleep that night, she sealed her flat tightly with spells of protection—just in case the Favershams decided to retaliate—and then spent some time looking at both of her grimoires.

As she turned the pages, new understanding flooded through her. Spells that she had struggled to really understand and use now made more sense. And with a shock, she found in her new, or rather, *old* grimoire that she would forever call Helena's, the spell that allowed transformation and flight— the mysterious way that Caspian Faversham could appear out of the air. A shiver of excitement and fear ran through her. She would practice that, and then teach the others. She allowed herself a smile at their victory.

Unable to suppress her increasing yawns, she headed to bed, thinking of Alex. Whatever was now happening between them seemed to be more than just physical. He had looked genuinely worried about her earlier, and sitting in the back of the van with his arm wrapped around her had provoked a feeling of peace and security she hadn't felt in a long time.

But the last thought that flitted through her mind as she drifted to sleep was Sebastian's warning about the *creatures* they might attract, and she wondered if that also included the Council—whoever they were.

***

When Avery woke up the next day, she looked out the window, expecting White Haven to look different. But it didn't. The same people wandered down the winding streets, the sun still rose as normal, and her flat looked the same as it always had.

But, she realised, she felt distinctly different. The power they had released yesterday still coursed through her veins, and she felt a subtle awareness of her surroundings and an awareness of her own abilities more than ever. She thought of the other witches, and wondered if they felt the same.

Despite the late night and her lack of sleep, Avery felt full of energy and she headed down to the shop early, planning to ease her way into the day, but Sally was already there and looking surprisingly well, considering her ordeal.

She sat at the small wooden table in the back of the shop with her coffee in front of her, and she looked up as Avery entered.

"Morning, Avery," she smiled. Her blonde hair was in a ponytail, her eyes were bright with curiosity, and Avery realised she was looking at her with new knowledge and awareness that had never existed before.

"Morning, Sally! How are you?" Avery rushed over and pulled her into a hug, making Sally rise awkwardly out of her chair.

"I'm fine." Sally said, a gentle reprimand in her voice. "How are *you*?"

"Good. Very good! But look, I'm so sorry about yesterday, you don't need to be here today. Have the day off—in fact, have the week off," she said in a rush, feeling guilt sweep over her.

"Don't be ridiculous. Sam will wonder what's going on. I don't normally take a week off after a stock take."

Avery grinned sheepishly. "Did he believe it?"

"Completely. I'm not entirely sure I'm comfortable keeping this a secret from him, though."

Avery poured a coffee and sat down opposite Sally. "Do what you need to. I trust your judgement, and I trust Sam."

Sally smiled. "Thanks, Avery. It would make me feel better. Besides, who will I gossip to? *Real* witches in White Haven!"

"But you knew I was a witch!" Avery said, thinking of their conversation the other day.

"Maybe I didn't understand it as well as I do now. And I think it would be a good idea to let Dan in on it, too. Your *magical explosion* last night may be the start of more weird things happening around here."

Avery grinned, pleased to be letting more people into what had been her hidden world. "I agree. Thanks, Sally. I really appreciate that you're not freaking out about this."

"I'm your friend, Avery. And besides, what's life without a little magic?" Sally watched Avery for a second or two, sipping her coffee. "Do you want to tell me what happened last night? All of it?"

"Sure," Avery said with a grin, and she recounted everything in as succinct a way as she could. "Did you feel it? The explosion, I mean?"

Sally shook her head. "I'm afraid not. It must have bypassed us ordinary people. Unless it was because I was locked in a basement."

Avery's shoulders sagged. "Are you sure he didn't hurt you?"

"I am. I was unconscious for most of it."

Avery nodded, and hoped this meant Faversham had some morals. And then she felt a rush of guilt about Sebastian.

"Come on," Sally said, watching her. "Let's open the shop and keep ourselves busy."

The morning passed in the usual way, and as soon as Avery had the chance, she let Dan know what had happened.

They were taking advantage of a quiet moment in the shop, and were both perched behind the counter on stools, nibbling on a pastry. Well, Avery was nibbling on a pastry. Dan had demolished his in two bites.

He looked at her, much as Sally had done, with new knowledge and speculation on his face. "So, does this mean weird old White Haven is going to get weirder?"

"It might," Avery said, shrugging. "Did you feel anything strange last night? It would have been late evening?"

Dan looked thoughtful. "I was in the pub debating life, as normal—"

"You mean football," Avery said, interrupting him.

He adopted a lofty expression and continued, "Debating *life*, sipping on beer, and yes, I might have felt something. Like a ripple of…" He hesitated, puzzled. "I can't quite describe it. It was like a shift of some sort. And then it went."

"A shift?"

He nodded. "Yes, like reality wobbled for a second. But then it went."

Avery looked at him sceptically. "Are you sure you weren't drunk?"

"I may have had a pint or two, but I was not drunk," he said, mock offended.

"Do you think anyone else noticed it?"

"Maybe. For a second some people seemed to look around, and then it just passed."

Avery nodded, thinking about when she had been spirit walking above All Souls and had seen people below on the street. So, some people had felt *something*.

"Thanks, Dan. I hope you still want to work here."

He looked shocked, and then grinned. "Of course I do! This is great!"

24

Reassured after nothing unusual—or more unusual than normal—had happened in the shop or White Haven, Avery locked up at the normal time and went to her flat to prepare for the other witches.

She spent a good hour cleaning and tidying things away, and then organised some food. By the time Alex arrived, the smell of garlic was wafting around her kitchen and living room, and floating out of the open balcony doors, mixing with the smell of incense.

Candles were scattered around the room, and the place looked warm and inviting.

"Hey," Alex said, joining her in the kitchen and plonking a pack of beer down on the counter. His long hair was loose and slightly wild, and his usual day-old stubble was actually looking more like a week's worth.

Avery felt her heart flutter wildly just looking at him. "Hey, you. You're early."

"I know; I wanted to catch you alone before the others arrived."

"Cool," she said smiling. "Any time."

He just watched her for a few seconds, his eyes dark and thoughtful. "You know, you scared the crap out of me last night."

She turned to him, leaning against the counter. "I scared the crap out of myself, too."

"I mean it, Avery. If anything had happened to you, if Helena had killed you or possessed your body, I'm not sure what I'd have done. You mean a lot to me. I just need you to know that." He pulled her towards him, encircling her with his arms, and she looked up at him, willing her heart to behave.

"You mean a lot to me, too."

"The meal the other night, we should do that more."

"I agree. I loved it."

His gaze wandered from her eyes to her lips and back again. "You've always been beautiful. You're one of the reasons I came back to White Haven."

For a second, Avery completely forgot they were standing in her kitchen. "What? No, I'm not."

"Will you stop telling me what I think? I came back for you. All that time I travelled, something was missing, and then I realised what it was. Look at you. You're unfairly sexy."

She unconsciously patted her head and smoothed her hair. "No, I'm not." She struggled to think of something coherent to say, and failed. "What do you mean, you came back for me?"

He smiled and caught her hand in his. "Stop messing with your hair. I missed you. You *know* me. And these last few weeks have just proven that to me."

"But when we were young, you were so … aloof, half the time."

"So were you. We were teenagers."

Avery had to admit that he was sort of right. "But you've been back for months, and have barely given me a second glance."

"I've given you plenty of second glances, you just didn't see them. Or want to see them. You put up very effective barriers."

She gasped. "Liar!"

"You do. To everyone. You just don't want to admit it." He became suddenly serious. "I mean it. I like this. Us. I want it to work. Do you?"

"Yes, I do," she said, breaking into a broad grin.

"Good," he declared, kissing her and leaving her breathless and with desire stirring deep in her belly. And then the bang of the outside door broke them apart, and the others arrived with a clatter of chatter, wine, and beer.

They sat around the table, talking for hours about the events of the previous night.

Avery asked Newton, "Have you heard anything about Sebastian or the Favershams?"

He shook his head. "Nothing. There are no police reports that mention them, which is fortunate."

"Is the house still standing?" Reuben asked. He looked better than he had in days, and Avery presumed he'd finally had a good night's sleep.

"Yes, so they must have been able to limit the damage from Helena's attack."

"Good," Avery said, relieved. "I understand her vindictiveness, I even share it, but I can't condone murder."

"So what now?" El asked, finishing her last mouthful of pasta.

"We learn to master our new powers and spells," Alex said, grinning. "I still feel that magic we released flooding through me, although it has subsided a little."

Briar nodded. "Me, too. I sense a difference in the town, too. You see auras, Alex. Can you see the magic we released?"

"Sort of. It's like there's an extra energy to the place. I see it swirling in certain spots—I wandered up to All Souls earlier, it's certainly there—and there's definitely a cloud of energy over White Haven."

"So, what are the creatures Sebastian referred to?" Newton asked, worried. "Are they dangerous?"

"I've been thinking about that," El said. "I presume he meant more witches, and maybe spirits, too."

"I doubt Sebastian would have called witches 'creatures.' What about more demons?" Newton asked, rubbing his hands through his hair. "I have to think of the town and the surrounding area."

"Maybe," Briar said, glancing at the rest of them. "Maybe other things, like vampires or shape-shifters?"

"*Vampires?*" Avery asked, almost spitting out her wine. "Are you kidding?"

"Just because we've never seen one, doesn't mean they don't exist. After all, we'd never seen demons before. We sure know they exist now."

The table fell silent for a second, and then Avery sighed. "I might start researching, just in case."

"Well, if we've caused this problem," Newton began, and Avery smiled at the 'we,' "then it's our responsibility to manage it, and I expect every single one of you to do that." He looked around the table, meeting their gaze, one by one.

"Of course," Avery said, feeling the enormity of what might happen start to sink in.

"And Caspian, will he seek revenge?" Reuben asked.

"I doubt it," Alex said, sipping his beer thoughtfully. "Not yet, anyway, if at all. We defeated them last night. I think we're status quo now."

"I'd watch out for Helena, though," Briar said to Avery. "I think she'll stick around a while."

A knock interrupted their conversation, and Avery frowned. "I wonder who that is?" She pushed her chair back and headed to her front door, noting that Alex followed her to the top of the stairs.

Half the door was made of opaque glass, and she saw a tall figure on the other side. She opened the door warily, and found a tall woman standing outside. She was dressed in an elegant black dress, and her long, black hair was wound on top of her head in an elaborate chignon. She had been facing away, staring down the alley behind Avery's house, but as the door opened, she turned to face Avery, fixing her with a piercing glare of ice blue eyes. She was very striking, with high, angular cheekbones and dark red lips, full and expressive.

She was a witch.

"Good evening," the woman said, her voice low and compelling. Avery detected an Irish lilt to her accent. "My name is Genevieve Byrne. I am a member of the Witches Council, may I come in?"

For a second, Avery was speechless. Her grandmother had mentioned a Council; she thought it was just incoherent rambling, but apparently not.

Genevieve watched her, amusement mixed with annoyance on her face, and Avery finally found her tongue. "Of course, please come in."

She stepped back as Genevieve entered, bringing in a cloud of perfume.

Avery glanced up at Alex, who was watching with a frown on his face. "Follow me, Genevieve."

By the time they arrived in Avery's living room, everyone was standing, and Genevieve's gaze encompassed the room, as well as them.

Avery gave them all a meaningful glance. "Everyone, please meet Genevieve Byrne of the Witches Council."

"Good evening," Genevieve said in her low, lilting voice to the murmured greetings of the others. "I'm sorry to have interrupted you, but this is urgent."

"Not at all," Avery said, trying to subdue her worry and ignore the shocked faces of the others. "Please, take a seat."

She gestured to her sofa, and they all sat, on the floor or the sofa, watching their visitor.

Genevieve frowned. "I understood there were five witches, not six."

"I'm not a witch," Newton said, watching her as if she might bite. "I'm Detective Inspector Newton."

"Then you have no place here," Genevieve said haughtily.

"Yes, he does," Briar said immediately. "Anything you say to us, you can say to him."

"Really?" Genevieve said, fixing Briar with her inscrutable gaze. "I decide that, not you."

Avery was annoyed, and felt the wind begin to stir around her. "It's my house, and I say he stays. Go ahead, Genevieve."

"I will be brief," she said, looking at them dismissively. "Your actions yesterday were rash and ill-advised. You have angered the Council with your choices."

"What actions were they?" Avery asked, playing dumb.

"You know quite well what. You broke the seal beneath All Souls and allowed the magic contained within to pour forth. You may as well have lit a beacon on the hill by the castle. All manner of creatures will have sensed that power. The Council is greatly annoyed." She glared at each of them in turn.

"Never mind," Alex said, smoothly. "I'm sure you'll all get over it."

Avery suppressed a snigger, and then Briar spoke, an edge of annoyance in her tone. "To be quite honest, Genevieve, we didn't even know a Witches Council existed. Perhaps you should have introduced yourselves a little earlier. How on Earth were we to know this might be an issue? And to be quite honest, this is our families' magic we're talking about, so it really is no business of anyone else's."

Genevieve snapped. "Sebastian Faversham is dead because of you."

Reuben shouted, "You didn't seem to give much of a crap when my brother, Gil was murdered! Not important enough for your attention, you supercilious cow?"

Genevieve leapt to her feet, nose to nose with Reuben, who had stood now too, fists clenched at his side. "How dare you be so rude?"

"How dare you tell us what to do with our heritage?"

The tension shot up, and everyone stood.

Genevieve stepped back, her own hands also clenched, and Avery could feel her power resonating. She looked at them. "Your actions will have repercussions on the witch community. The Council meets in five days. One of you must attend to represent White Haven."

"Or else what?" Alex asked.

She sneered. "I suggest you take the opportunity to attend. Sebastian banned your membership for many years, as have many Favershams before him, but with Sebastian dead and the seal below All Souls gone, you now have an opportunity to sit on the Council and take part in real decisions about our magical community. You would do well to take advantage of it. With increased power comes increased responsibility. Don't miss your chance."

"And who takes Sebastian's place?" Avery asked, fearing she already knew the answer.

"Caspian, of course."

Genevieve headed to the stairs, ready to leave, but looked back at them. "Not many wished to have you on the Council, despite the recent events, but I fought for your place. It is only fitting, after you have been denied for centuries. Don't let me down. I will send word of the venue."

Avery followed her to the top of the steps, watching her as she descended. She vanished before she had even reached the bottom.

Avery turned back to the others, her heart pounding. The room had grown darker as the sun set, and shadows fell across the space, the candles glowing in dark corners and on table tops. Something monumental had occurred; they all knew it, and the relief from their sense of victory earlier in the evening had gone.

"What now?" Newton asked.

"Now we decide who's going to the Council," Avery said softly, her mind made up. "It seems we've been denied many things, for a very long time. I will not miss out again."

MAGIC

WHITE HAVEN WITCHES (BOOK 3)

UNLEASHED

TJ GREEN

1

Avery stood on the cliff top looking out over White Haven harbour and the sea beyond. It was after ten at night and the moon peeked out behind ragged clouds, casting a milky white path over the water.

Alex stood next to her and sighed. "This is crazy. I told you it was a waste of time."

"We have to check. The old guy was insistent he'd seen something. He looked panic-stricken."

"He'd probably had a few too many rums."

"You didn't see him," Avery persisted. "He looked white, and he said he'd only seen something like it once before in his lifetime, and that was just before a couple of young men disappeared and were never seen again." Alex snorted, and Avery punched his arm. "I can't believe you're scoffing after all we've seen recently."

It had been just over a week since the five witches had broken the binding spell beneath the Church of All Souls, marking the end of a fight that had been going for centuries with the Favershams, a family of witches who lived in Harecombe, the town next to White Haven. The binding spell had been cast centuries earlier by Helena Marchmont, Avery's ancestor, and the other four witch families in White Haven. It had trapped a demon and the Faversham's ancestor beneath the church using a huge amount of magic. Breaking the spell had been difficult, but with the help of Helena's ghost they had succeeded, releasing magical energy that increased their own power. They had then defeated Sebastian Faversham, rescued Sally, and regained Reuben's missing grimoire. But Sebastian's final warning had proved correct. Strange things were indeed happening in White Haven.

In the last few days a dozen reports of strange noises and ghostly apparitions had been the centre of town gossip. Lights had appeared up at the ruined castle on the hill in the dead of night, and one fishing boat had reported seeing green lights in the depths of the sea, before they had hurriedly left the area and sailed for home.

On top of all that, Helena had reappeared, if only briefly, in Avery's flat. The scent of violets had manifested first, and then the smell of smoke and charred flesh, and Avery had yelled out, *"Helena! Stop it!"* Fortunately—or not, Avery couldn't work out which she preferred—she couldn't see Helena very often now, but it was unnerving to detect her unique presence in the flat. She hadn't resorted to warding the flat against her, but was seriously considering it.

Although Avery hoped these manifestations would settle down, she suspected they were only the beginning. And then that morning, an old man had appeared in the shop. He looked around nervously, and then approached Sally, who in turn escorted him over to Avery as she sorted some new stock in a quiet corner.

"This is Avery," Sally said cheerfully. "I'm sure she can help you, Caleb." She gave Avery a knowing look and left them to it, Caleb wringing his cap as if it was soaking wet.

"Hi Caleb, nice to meet you. How can I help?" Avery adopted her friendliest smile. Caleb looked as if she would bite. "I've, er, got something to tell you that you might find interestin'."

"Go on," she nodded encouragingly.

"I hear you may have abilities others may not," he said, almost stumbling over his words.

Oh, this was going to be one of those conversations.

She hesitated for a second, wondering what to say. "I may have, yes."

"I was on that fishing boat the other night."

Avery was confused for a second, and then realisation flashed across her brain. "The boat that saw the lights?" She looked at Caleb with renewed interest.

His hair was snowy white, but thick and brushed back from his face, falling to his collar. He had a full white beard, and wore a heavy blue jacket despite the heat, thick cotton trousers, and wellington boots. His face was covered in wrinkles, but his pale blue eyes were alert and watchful. He reminded her of the old sea captain from the fish fingers adverts.

"Yes, the boat that saw the lights. I wasn't going to say anything, but I remember only too well what happened the last time I saw them."

"You've seen them before?" Avery said, surprised. "Are you sure it wasn't just phosphorescence?"

"I know what that looks like, and this was different."

"Different how?" Avery asked, narrowing her eyes and feeling a shiver run through her.

"The lights circled below the boat, even and slow, three of them in all, and then started to weave a pattern below us. The young ones were transfixed. A wave crashed over the side and broke my concentration, but I could hear something." He stopped and looked away.

"What?" Avery insisted.

"Singing."

"Singing?"

"Strange, unearthly, hypnotic. I started the throttle and headed out of there, almost breaking our nets in the process."

Avery knew she should laugh at his outlandish suggestion, but she couldn't. He was so serious, and so absolutely believable. "And then what happened?"

"They disappeared. And I didn't look back."

"And the others?"

"Couldn't remember a thing."

"What happened the last time you saw them?"

"That was a very long time ago—I was only young myself." Caleb looked away again, shuffling uncomfortably, and then lowered his voice. "Young men disappeared. Vanished—*without a trace.*"

"But, how do you know that was related to the lights?" Avery felt bad for asking so many questions, but she half-wondered if he was winding her up.

"They'd been spotted with some young girls, and … Well, things weren't *normal.*"

Avery blinked and sighed. "I know I'm asking a lot of questions, Caleb, but why weren't they normal?"

"They were last seen at the beach, and their clothes were found there, but nothing else. And no, it wasn't suicide." He rushed on, clearly not wanting to be interrupted again. "I think they want something, I don't know why I think that, but I do. I *know* it. And it's only a matter of time before they arrive, so you need to stop them."

"How can I stop something I don't even know exists?" she asked, perplexed.

"I have no idea. I'm just offering you a warning." And with that he left the shop, leaving Avery looking after him, bewildered.

She sighed as she remembered her earlier conversation, and rubbed her head. "It sounds like it's out of a story book. Mysterious lights in the sea, weird singing, loss of memory. Sebastian warned us that creatures would come. What if our magic sent a wave of power out into the sea? I guess it's possible."

Alex nodded, his features hard to see in the darkness on the cliff top. "The old myths talk of Sirens who sing sailors to their doom, but the old guy's story also reminds me a little of the Selkie myths."

"The seals that take human form?"

"Pretty much." He turned to her. "The myths haunt all coastal communities. They were popular in Ireland, particularly where I was on the west coast. And of course here in Cornwall there are Mermaid myths—they come looking for a man to take back to the sea with them to become their husbands and make lots of mer-babies."

"Great, so green lights and mysterious singing under the sea could be a rum-soaked hallucination, or maybe one of three weird myths."

He grinned. "Or a few others we haven't thought of, but I'll keep watch for women shrouded in seaweed or seal coats shed on the beach."

"You're so funny, Alex," she said, thinking the complete opposite.

He turned to her and pulled her into his arms. "I don't care how alluring they're supposed to be, they wouldn't be half as alluring as you."

She put her hands against his chest, feeling the strong beat of his heart and the warmth of his skin through his t-shirt, and looked up into his brown eyes. She could feel her own pulse starting to flutter wildly and wondered if he realised quite what he did to her. "You're very alluring yourself."

"How alluring?" he asked, his lips a feather-light touch on her neck.

"Too alluring." She could feel a tingle of desire running through her from their contact.

"No such thing," he said softly. His hand caressed the back of her neck and pulled her close for a long, deep kiss as his hands tangled in her hair. Pulled so close to him, she felt his desire start to grow, and he stepped away, a wicked gleam in his eyes. "Let's go back to mine. I've got better things in mind than standing on a cliff top."

***

However, when they arrived at Alex's pub, The Wayward Son, Newton was at the bar, sipping a pint of beer.

Mathias Newton was a Detective Inspector with the Cornwall Police, who also knew that they were witches. His history was as complicated as theirs, and although their relationship had started badly, they were now friends. He turned from where he'd been scowling into his pint, half an eye on the football highlights that were on the muted TV screen in the corner, and half an eye on the door. He was in casual clothing, his short dark hair slightly ruffled, and his grey eyes were serious. "Where have you two been?"

"Nice to see you, too," Avery greeted him. She slid onto the seat next to him while Alex leaned on the bar and ordered the drinks.

Alex groaned. "Your timing sucks, Newton. I had better things in mind than a pint."

He just grunted. "Get over it."

"You look as grumpy as hell," Avery said.

"That's because I am. We've had some odd reports at the station."

Avery felt her heart sink. *Not more strange things.* "Like what?"

"Odd disturbances—noises at night, people thinking they're being broken into, electrical shorts, missing items, but no signs of a break-in."

Alex raised an eyebrow and passed Avery a glass of red wine. "People report electrical shorts to you?"

"You'd be surprised what people report to us. But yes. We've had a flood of reports over the last couple of days. I wanted to know if you've seen anything."

"Lots of rumours of weird happenings, but nothing concrete." She related the story the old sailor, Caleb, had told her. "We've been up on the cliff top to see if we could spot anything, but…" She shrugged.

Newton rubbed his hand through his hair, ruffling it even more. "I'd hoped things would go back to normal after the other night, but they're really not. Briar and Elspeth have both had people coming into their shop sharing strange tales, and Elspeth has been selling lots of protection charms."

"Really?" Avery asked. "I must admit, I haven't spoken to them in a couple of days."

"It's my job to, Avery." He finished his pint and ordered another. "Have you heard about the meeting?" Newton was referring to the Witches Council.

She nodded. "Yes. It's tomorrow evening, at eight."

To celebrate defeating the Favershams and breaking the binding spell, they had all met for dinner at Avery's flat, but it had been interrupted by the arrival of Genevieve Byrne, another witch who organised the Witches Council, a group they hadn't even known existed until that night. She had invited them to the next meeting, actually almost insisted that they attend, and after that their celebrations had taken a downward turn as they each debated the merits of whether to go or not. For Avery, it was an easy decision. They'd been invited to something they'd been excluded from for years, and she had no intention of letting the opportunity pass her by.

Reuben had not felt the same. "Screw them all, why the hell should we go to their crappy meeting?"

"Because we'll learn something, Reuben," Avery had answered, exasperated. "Aren't you the slightest bit interested in knowing who they are and what they do?"

"No," he'd answered belligerently.

"Well, I am," Briar said. "But I'm too chicken to go."

"I'm not sure I trust her or any of them," Newton said, "but maybe that's the policeman in me."

Alex had nodded in agreement. "I don't entirely trust them either, but I agree with Avery and Briar. We should go. We need to have a stake in whatever's going on around here."

"Well, unless anyone else really wants to go, I'd love to go first," Avery said. "Someone else can go next time."

Alex rolled his eyes. "Just when I thought things might start to get back to normal around here."

But at least most of them had agreed on attending.

However, now, in the warm comfort of the pub, Avery felt a bit worried about going and the reception she might receive. The other night beneath All Souls now felt like a dream—if it hadn't been for the headlines that proclaimed the death of Sebastian Faversham in an electrical fire at the family home. A fake report. He had actually died after being attacked by Helena's ghost, her spirit made stronger by the extra surge of magical energy that pulsed through her like a bolt of lightning.

"Where?" Newton persisted, drawing her back to the present.

"Some place called Crag's End."

"Where the hell's that?"

"Around Mevagissey, somewhere just off the coast. It seems to be a very large, private residence."

He looked concerned. "I'm not sure you should go alone."

"That's what I said," Alex agreed, gazing at Avery.

Avery twisted to look up at him. "Alex, I'll be fine. They're all witches, I'm sure I'll be quite safe."

"We don't know any of them."

"We were invited. Stop worrying," she said, as much to reassure herself as him.

"Someone should go with you," Newton said.

Avery looked between the two of them. "Something is very wrong with the world when the two of you start agreeing. No. I'm going alone. Trust me. I'm a witch."

2

Avery eyed the house in front of her warily. It looked like a small castle, with three turrets and a stone tower. All it needed was a moat and a portcullis. She hoped boiling oil wasn't about to be poured on her.

It was not the type of house she had expected, and although it looked sturdy and well maintained, the grounds were wildly overgrown and romantic, filled with tumbling roses, honeysuckle, and immense shrubs. Halfway up the drive she wondered if she'd taken a wrong turn, but then the drive opened out and the castle appeared, silent and aggressive in the falling dusk light.

She turned off her van's engine, trying not to panic and get the hell out of there. As she walked up to the front entrance of the castle, she noted only two other cars on the drive. She'd aimed to get there early and find her feet, but now she wondered if she should have arrived late and snuck in quietly.

The castle was slightly inland, set on the edge of the moor. The high walls and hedges protected it from prying eyes, and from the winds that would sweep in off the sea on this elevated position.

She was about to knock on the front door when it swung open in front of her, revealing a large entrance hall softly lit with candlelight. The floor was a chequer board of black and white tiles, and a round table was placed in the centre, on which rested a vase filled with exuberant flowers, the scent filling the room.

As she entered the hall, a deep voice manifested out of the shadows on the stairs, making her jump. "You must be Avery Hamilton. Welcome."

Avery squinted into the darkness and a figure stepped into the light.

The man the voice belonged to was tall and gaunt, and Avery estimated he was in his sixties. His hair was long, slightly unkempt, and streaked with grey, and he wore an old-fashioned velvet jacket and trousers.

He smiled as he came closer and shook her hand, his grip dry, bony and firm. "I'm Oswald Prendergast. Welcome to my home."

Avery looked up at him and smiled back. "Thanks for the invite. I hope I'm not too early."

His sharp eyes appraised her, and Avery hoped she was appearing confident. She wasn't at all sure she knew what she was doing here. "Not at all. A few have already arrived. Come into the drawing room and I'll introduce you."

Drawing Room? Avery felt as if she'd stepped back in time.

He led her up the stairs, the smell of furniture polish surrounding them. "I should warn you that some of our members were unwilling to have you on the Council, but I agreed with Genevieve. In the end we took a vote, and there were more fors than againsts."

"Thank you, we—all of us in White Haven—appreciate it. My grandmother mentioned the Council to me, but I must admit, I thought she was rambling."

"I remember your grandmother. Of course, I didn't really know her, but she's a fine witch. Anyway," he said, gesturing to the door on his left and pushing it open, "we're in here."

Avery entered a room that looked out to the rear of the house. Three large, leaded glass windows filled one wall, revealing the gardens beyond, but it was the interior that really caught her eye. Despite the fact that it was midsummer, a roaring fire filled the large fireplace and the room was stiflingly hot. Someone had thrown open a window to invite a wan breeze in, and in front of it stood three diverse individuals. There was an old man with a huge beaked nose and a shock of white hair and white eyebrows, and he wore a plum silk smoking jacket and black trousers. Next to him was a middle-aged aristocratic woman with auburn hair, a long, straight nose down which she peered at Avery, and she wore a chiffon gown. She reminded Avery of Margot from the sitcom *The Good Life* and she tried to keep a straight face. The next person was the one she least wanted to see—Caspian Faversham. He wore a smart suit and he turned and narrowed his eyes as Avery approached beside Oswald.

Oswald smiled at them warmly. "I'd like to introduce you to Avery, our newest recruit. Avery, I believe you know Caspian, but this is Claudia Everley and Rasmus James."

Avery presumed Oswald must know what had happened with the Favershams, but his tone didn't betray it.

The older two witches looked at Avery with interest, but it was Caspian who spoke first. "Avery. I must admit I hoped never to see you again. I'm sure you're aware that I was against your invitation to this group."

Avery could feel her anger rising already. "I hoped never to see you again either, Caspian, especially after you killed my friend, Gil, and kidnapped Sally, but here we are, having to tolerate each other."

Oswald intervened immediately, his warm, friendly tone disappearing. "Caspian, I warned you. Your family's behaviour in recent days almost meant you lost your place on the Council, so don't push your luck. Your probationary period is not yet over—you haven't got as many supporters as you think you have."

"My father has died too, Oswald…"

"But not by Avery's hand. You know it was Helena's fault."

Caspian shot Avery a look of pure loathing. "You let her in."

As much as Avery didn't want to start a full-blown argument, she was not about to be blamed for everything. "I don't control her, Caspian! She's not a pet."

Oswald laughed bitterly. "You are a victim of your own crimes, Caspian. Stop blaming others."

Rasmus interrupted. "Spirits are wildly unpredictable, you know that, Caspian. I suggest you let it lie." His voice was deep and gravelly, as if it had been dredged from the bottom of the sea. "The Council advised your father against the course of action, and he insisted on doing what he wanted anyway. He brought it on himself."

"Indeed," Claudia said, finally speaking. "I am heartily sick of this vendetta against White Haven."

Avery suppressed the urge to whoop with delight, and instead turned to Claudia and Rasmus, thinking she detected a twinkle of delight in Claudia's eye that was swiftly hidden. "I'm sorry, it was not my intent to argue. It's a pleasure to meet you both."

They both shook Avery's hand, and Claudia pulled her to the drinks cabinet. "Welcome, Avery, let me pour you a drink. Wine, whiskey, brandy, gin and tonic?"

"Gin and tonic please," she said, relieved to be away from Caspian.

"I meant what I said," Claudia continued, dropping her voice. "But others agree with Caspian. You may find you're in for a tricky evening."

"That's okay, I'm a big girl," Avery said, grinning. "But thanks for your support anyway. I'm very curious about tonight, and looking forward to meeting everyone, friendly or not."

Claudia passed her the drink. "This meeting doesn't encompass everyone, just families or coven representatives, much as you are representing your own coven."

"I don't know if we're anything as formal as a coven," Avery said.

"Whether you have declared it or not, you really are. And powerful, too. We all felt that wave of magic you unleashed from beneath the town. It nearly knocked me over. Good thing I was sitting down. I was watching a replay of *Strictly Come Dancing*—I was quite distracted after that."

Avery laughed. "Sorry."

Claudia waved her apology away. "I live close to Perranporth, so I couldn't see the effects, but I hear you lit up the sky—magically, that is."

Avery gasped. Perranporth was on the north coast of Cornwall, so the blast must have been huge—although, no doubt those with magical powers would be far more attuned to it. "I saw it as an aura. It *was* quite impressive. I must admit, we had no idea it would be so large."

"You had no idea your magic was bound?"

"No! We didn't know we had missing grimoires, either. Did everyone know except us?"

"Only Council members knew—no one else. We insisted upon knowing the details if we were to support the Favershams' request to keep you isolated. Many of us thought it extreme, but the Favershams are powerful. Or rather *were*, they have less influence now. But we didn't know *where* your power was bound, or where your grimoires were, either. That has been a mystery to everyone for centuries." She smiled in admiration. "Well done for finding them. Helena's power sits well on you."

"Thank you," she said, flushing slightly. "Before he died, Sebastian suggested we would attract creatures to White Haven, and that we put everyone at risk. What did he mean?"

"That's what we shall discuss at the meeting," Claudia said, her eyes clouding with worry.

Before she could say anything else, another flurry of activity interrupted them. Avery turned to see another few witches arriving, and she took a large gulp of gin and tonic to fortify herself.

Oswald tapped his glass and the sound echoed around the room, magnified by magic. "Welcome, everyone. Please, grab yourselves a drink and let's get this meeting started."

They made their way to the room next door and sat around a long, dark wooden table inlaid with arcane symbols.

Avery sat between Oswald and Claudia. Caspian sat opposite her, and she saw Genevieve Byrne enter and sit at the head of the table. She looked as imposing as she had the other night. The other witches were a mixture of male and female, young and old, mostly white, but there was also a black male witch, and young Indian female. As they all took their places, they glanced at Avery with curiosity, some welcoming, some not.

Silence fell and Genevieve spoke. "Welcome all. Thank you for coming today, I realise it is outside our normal meeting time, but events of the last few days made me act quickly." She glanced around the room, and as her gaze fell on Avery, she smiled briefly. "I'm sure you all felt the wave of power the other night. It was caused by the actions of the White Haven witches."

There was a murmur as heads leaned close together, and Avery was stared at with renewed interest.

She continued, "I'm sure you're all aware of our history. Helena Marchmont and the other witches of White Haven bound Octavia Faversham and her demon over four centuries ago, and then their grimoires were hidden to prevent them from falling into the hands of the Witchfinder General." A collective shudder seemed to run around the room. "These grimoires have now been found and the binding spell broken—hence, the wave of magic we all felt. With the breaking of that spell many things have now changed. I have formally invited the witches of White Haven back to the Council, and they have agreed. Avery Hamilton, the descendent of Helena Marchmont, is our new member, and as such I'm sure you will treat her with respect."

Genevieve looked at each and every one of them in turn, some longer than others, and Avery noticed a skinny, beady-eyed male witch squirm and drop his gaze to the table, as did a young blonde female. *Faversham supporters*, Avery presumed. Caspian glared at her and then stared defiantly at Genevieve.

Genevieve went on, undeterred. "The release of the magic has placed us all in danger. As you all know, many creatures wander our Earth, some friendly, others not, and they are also drawn to magical energy. Our role is to keep our communities safe from them, and fortunately, they mostly keep to themselves. But now…" Her words hung on the air and Avery felt a flush of guilt. She glanced at Claudia, and then kept her eyes firmly fixed on Genevieve.

Caspian leapt into the silence. "So, once again I ask why Ms Hamilton and the other witches should be allowed into our Council. They have caused enough trouble already."

Avery was just about to respond when Genevieve beat her to it. "Because, if they had been part of this Council in the first place, they wouldn't have been in the dark about the threat of releasing this magic. They would have understood their history."

"I agree," another middle-aged witch with grey hair sitting across the table said. "Nothing good comes of secrets, Caspian. And frankly, your family have had their own way for far too long."

There were a few nods of agreement, but the room was otherwise silent. Genevieve frowned at Caspian. "That's the last I want to hear of that, Caspian. The White Haven witches are here to stay. They now provide us with our thirteenth coven, and we have missed that over the years. We all know the significance of that number. Any powerful spells we need to do in the future will now have a far greater chance of success with thirteen covens. Agreed?"

Avery felt a strange realisation settle upon her as she looked around the table at those who nodded their assent. They were now part of a much larger collective, and would probably be required to be involved in decisions and spells previously unknown. That was daunting.

Genevieve hadn't finished. "On to the important question. Has anyone noticed anything untoward in the last few days?"

A young woman of about Avery's age nodded. She had long, dark hair that fell in dreadlocks down her back. They were kept off her face by a bright red scarf, wrapped around her head in a band. "St Ives has had several spirits manifest in the last twenty-four hours, most of them harmless, but a couple have been a little more malevolent. We've managed to banish most of them quickly. One, however, may need a little more time."

Avery wondered who '*we*' was, and presumed at some point in the future she'd find out.

"If you need any help, let us know," Genevieve said. "Anyone else?"

There were a couple more strange reports. The beady-eyed male witch said there had been reports of howls at night on Bodmin. "Something is there. We have no idea what yet, but we're monitoring it."

Almost everyone around the table had noticed increased spirit activity, and Avery felt she should share about the activities in White Haven and the sighting of the strange lights in the sea.

There was a gasp of concern around the room at her news, and Genevieve narrowed her intense gaze at Avery. "When?"

"Probably a couple of nights ago now. Just one report about lights in the sea, but there's some at the castle, too."

Claudia leaned forward. "Lights in the sea are very worrying, Avery. Sea creatures carry their own power that's very different from ours, and the power they exert on humans is significant. You need to start searching now."

Avery was confused, and slightly embarrassed. She felt out of her depth. "But what are we looking for?"

"Unexpected behaviours, such as people acting out of character, strange obsessions, and unexplained absences."

Avery nodded. "We had a few theories, but weren't really sure if we should take it seriously."

Rasmus spoke, his voice unexpected as he'd been silent so long. "Not many of you young ones will have experienced the lure of the Mermaid, but trust me when I say they are evil, dangerous creatures."

"Mermaids?" Avery asked. "Is that what this is? We thought of them, but also considered Selkies."

"Possible, but less likely," he said.

"Mermaids are very powerful, very frightening beings," Claudia said. "We all need to be on guard against them."

"There have been a few Mermaid encounters over the years in Cornwall," Rasmus continued. "Many are romanticised."

"The Mermaid of Zennor," Avery said nodding. "We've all heard of her."

"Yes, she entered the village of Zennor disguised as a beautiful lady, bewitched the men and ensnared young Mathew Trewella. He followed her and was never seen again. Then, many years later, a ship cast anchor off Pendower Cove and a beautiful Mermaid asked the captain to move his anchor, as it was blocking her way back home where her husband, Mathew, and her children were waiting. The captain weighed anchor and got out of there as fast as he could. And then of course there are Mermaids who lure men to their deaths with their singing, much like Sirens of the Greek myths. Also, there was the village of Seaton, which was cursed by a Mermaid because a fisherman insulted her. The sea rose and sand swallowed the whole town."

The table had fallen silent, and all were now watching Rasmus as his dry voice captured their attention.

"Have you ever met one, Rasmus?" a dark-haired witch sitting across from Avery asked.

"Once, as a young man, a teenager. I was poking about in the tidal pools, collecting seaweed and things for my mother's spells, when I heard singing and caught sight of a flash of silvered tail. I squinted, blinked, and then a woman appeared on the beach, literally just appeared out of nowhere, her eyes a shining green. She beckoned to me, singing all the while with her hypnotic voice, and without a second thought I followed her as she walked into the sea. And then my brother shouted, sending a well-timed curse at her, and she disappeared and I never saw her again." He looked up, his vision returning to the present. "Mind you, it was a long time before I went back there again."

"If Mermaids are returning to White Haven, it's likely they'll turn up in other places, too," Claudia said.

"Maybe not," Genevieve argued. "White Haven is the only place which has magic hanging over it."

"Children of Llyr," Oswald said, shaking his head, his eyes haunted. "They're always trouble."

"Llyr?" the young blonde witch asked, the one Avery presumed had sided with Caspian.

"The Celtic God of the Sea. He represents the powers of darkness, and fought the children of Don, the powers of light. Llyr's son is Manawdyan—or in Irish myth, *Manannán mac Lir*—Son of the Sea. They are dark, old gods, best left sleeping. Their children are the mythical creatures of the sea—the Mermaids, Selkies, water spirits, serpents, the Kraken, Leviathan, the Hydra, and others." Oswald turned to Avery. "Let's hope your magic has not stirred the depths of the ocean, or trouble will indeed come."

If Avery hadn't fully understood the threat of the magic they had released before, she did now, and she felt her throat tighten. The spirits that were now rising in the town could be just the beginning.

***

After the formal part of the meeting, most of the witches hung around chatting idly amongst themselves, and Avery had the chance to meet a few of the others.

It seemed the witches represented most of the major towns and some of the villages on the north and south coast of Cornwall. Avery knew that Claudia was from Perranporth, and she found that Rasmus was from New Quay, and due to the distance was stopping at Crag's End overnight, with Oswald. She gleaned he despised witch flight; it made him feel sick. Oswald represented the Mevagissey coven, and the young blonde witch represented the Looe witches, of which there were only two.

Avery met the young woman from St Ives with the dark dreadlocks, who had spoken about the spirits. Her skin was tanned and her smile bright, and she grinned and stuck her hand out. "Hi, my name's Eve. Good to finally meet you, Avery, you've created quite a stir."

Avery knew she'd get on with her straight away. "It seems so. Sorry."

Eve laughed. "Caspian's an ass. Serves him right. And Sebastian was an infuriating, superior nightmare." She lowered her voice. "I should be sorry he's dead, but I'm not."

Avery leaned closer, too. "I do feel bad about it, but then I remember everything he did to stop us, and that helps."

Eve looked at her curiously. "You really had no idea about the Council?"

"No. I feel we've been isolated for years."

"Well, the connections are useful of course, and the wider knowledge about what's happening in Cornwall, but to be honest, the politics are a bit of a drag."

"How many of you are in St Ives?"

"Two of us. Me and Nate." She rummaged in her bag for some paper and scribbled her number down. "Here you go, my phone number in case you need anything."

"Cheers, Eve. What will you do about your wayward spirits?"

"The usual banishment, but there's a lot of activity—it will be hard. But now I'm more worried about Mermaids."

"Yeah, me too. I feel a bit guilty."

Eve shrugged. "It's your magic, you were entitled to it. Don't let Caspian get you down. Or Zane or Mariah."

Avery looked at her blankly. "Who?"

She nodded discretely across the room to where Caspian stood talking to the beady-eyed man from Bodmin, and the blonde witch. "Those two talking to Caspian. Their families had strong links with the Favershams, but without the support of the others, they're no threat to you. Besides, they won't attack you, not like the Favershams did. They just like to suck up to them." She watched them for a few seconds more, and Avery wondered what they were talking about, but then Eve reached out to clink her glass with her own. "Cheers, Avery, welcome to the Council. Prepare to be called upon. Now that you're one of us, you'll be involved in lots of things."

3

Avery had been staring at the words for so long that they'd started to blur. She rubbed her eyes and glanced around, trying to refresh her concentration.

She was in the attic of her flat, and the long shadows of twilight were spreading across the room. The windows under the eaves were open, and the scent of dust, roses, and pollen drifted in, mingling with incense. She sighed, rolled her shoulders, and then looked back at the page, determined not to be defeated by the last few words.

The spell, like many of the others in her newly found, old grimoire, the one she now called Helena's, was written in tiny, spidery writing. The ink was faded in places, but was still just about legible. Avery pulled her own familiar grimoire towards her, picked up her pen, and continued the transcription. Although other witches had added notes to the spells over the years, she was reluctant to write in Helena's grimoire, worried about damaging it. It was far better preserved than it should be, having been protected from dampness and the effects of time by a spell; she could feel the tingle of magic every time she touched the book. In an effort to protect it from further handling, she'd found another spell that worked to cover the book's pages and binding.

Over the past few days, Avery had spent a lot of time examining Helena's grimoire and still couldn't get over the fact that she now possessed this precious item. The worn leather cover felt warm to her touch, and a faint smell of musk and vanilla drifted up from its pages.The first spell she was determined to read and master was the one that allowed flight. She wasn't sure if that was the right word for it, but it was the one she was certain Caspian used to wrap himself up in shadows and air and move from one place to the other. The spell was called the Flight of Spirits, but wasn't anything to do with spirit walking. She carefully transcribed the last few lines and copied the notes made in the margins, then put down the pen. Unlike many spells, there were no ingredients in this one, just repeated lines of incantation that she could only presume got easier with familiarity, as Caspian disappeared with undeniable speed.

She re-read the instructions, and then said the words.

At first, nothing happened, and then the air began to stir around her, gently to start, and then with increasing speed until she felt she stood at the centre of a tornado. Fear gripped her, but she fought through it, strengthened by everything she had experienced in the last few days.

I am a witch, a powerful witch, and I can do this.

She repeated the spell over and over again, her voice strengthening, and she varied the modulations in her tone and words, suddenly realising the meaning of one of the scribbled notes in the margin.

And then it happened. The wind whipped through her and she felt her body pull apart, and then she was standing in her living room and everything went black.

***

Avery stirred, feeling the rug beneath her cheek, and her hip pressing into the floor. *Ouch.* Her head felt like it had been trapped in a vice.

She was aware there was a soft, warm bundle of fur pressing against her arm, and as she moved, the cat stirred, meowing softly. It was Circe. She sounded very different to Medea. Avery patted her, comforted that she wasn't lying there completely alone, and then eased into a sitting position. Nausea washed through her. *How long had she been out for?*

It was darker now, the sky carrying only the tiniest hint of light, but she could make out the clock on the wall glowing with faint luminescence. It was after nine, which meant she'd been unconscious for just over an hour. Wow. But she grinned; she had moved from one room to another—a partial success, at least.

She dragged herself to her feet and headed to the kitchen, pouring a large glass of water that she downed in one go. That was a powerful spell. She hadn't felt that drained even after they'd broken the binding spell. All she wanted to do now was sleep, but she'd arranged to meet the others at Alex's pub, The Wayward Son, and she had lots to share. And besides, she wanted to see Alex again.

She downed another glass of water and decided now was not the time to try that spell again. She'd better walk instead.

***

The other four witches and Newton were already in Alex's flat above the pub when Avery arrived, and they looked at her in alarm when she entered.

El, tall and blonde, with legs up to her armpits, was dressed in her usual black jeans and rock t-shirt. She owned a jewellery shop called The Silver Bough, and silver piercings of her own design sparkled in the lamp light. She leaned against the kitchen counter, holding a bottle of beer, and frowned. "Avery! Are you all right? You look terrible."

"Do I? Why?" she asked, running her hand through her hair.

"You're white."

Alex was in the kitchen, placing some cheese and biscuits on platters, but he walked around the counter, frowning with concern. "What happened? Is it the FaVershams?"

"No, I'm fine. Honestly, everyone relax. I wasn't attacked." She held her hand up as Reuben, Briar, and Newton all turned from where they sat on the sofa or the floor cushions. "I was trying a spell, and it was really hard."

"What spell?" El asked, coming closer to examine her.

"The flight spell, you know—swirly wind and mysterious disappearance and reappearance."

"Bloody Hell, Avery, you shouldn't be trying that on your own," Alex said gruffly. He pulled her in to a hug.

"Why not?" she asked, enjoying his unexpected display in front of the others and still feeling self-conscious about it. "We're all trying different spells on our own. Otherwise, how do we learn?"

"It's a fair point," Briar said. She owned Charming Balms Apothecary and sold lotions, soaps, candles, bath products, creams, and salves. She was dark-haired, petite, and very good at healing and Earth magic. "I've been brewing different potions solidly for the last two days. We can't accompany each other all the time."

"And you, Alex," Avery said pointedly, following him into the kitchen and grabbing a beer, "are always trying out spirit walking."

"Fair enough," he said. "But I don't look as white as a sheet afterwards."

"I admit, I passed out for an hour," she said sheepishly, "but I did move between rooms."

"Wow!" Newton said, looking shocked. "That's impressive!"

"I know!" she said, grinning. "Next time will be better. I'll be awake to enjoy it more."

"Pretty cool," Reuben said, nodding in agreement. Reuben, also tall, blond, and an avid surfer, was trying to master water elemental magic. "You'll have to teach us all when you've mastered it."

Avery joined them in the living room area, Alex and El close behind with snacks. "I will, and you guys will have to share some of your new skills, too."

"So what happened at the meeting, Avery?" Briar asked, leaning forward to grab a cracker and cheese.

"It was interesting. I had no idea that so many other witches were in Cornwall. I feel we've been missing out for a long time—but not anymore!" She related the events of the previous night. "I'd love you all to meet them. I'm sure it's only a matter of time."

Newton frowned. "But you say they're all experiencing some unusual supernatural activity?"

She nodded. "That's a very good way of putting it. Yes, they are. Every single place is having spirit activity at the moment, and it's probably only just beginning. And they gave us a warning about Mermaids. They're deadly. We have to be on our guard."

"Mermaids? Is that a joke? Have I missed something?" Reuben asked, a cracker halfway to his mouth.

"Sorry Reuben, I wasn't sure if Alex had told you. I had a visitor at the shop the other day." She filled them in on Caleb and the lights.

"Great. A few more risks with surfing, then," Reuben said. "I thought Mermaids were hot?"

"No. Not hot, just killers," she said, rolling her eyes.

"Shouldn't we warn people?" Briar said.

"Yeah, sure," Reuben said, nodding. "I'll let the Coastguard know, and we'll put a sign on all the beaches. *'Beware, Mermaid attacks, stick to the orange buoys.'*"

"Oh sod off," Briar said. "That's not quite what I meant."

"Seriously," Reuben said, looking at her incredulously. "What could we do?"

"I don't know," she answered, "but the locals are looking to us for advice. I've had several veiled questions already about whether I offer any other services. I wasn't sure what to say, if I'm honest. I just mumbled and said have a nice day. What are we supposed to do?"

"Well," El said, "the few charms and amulets I sell have sold out. A couple of girls who live in an old cottage said they keep feeling really cold draughts around the place. They're convinced they're being haunted, and I think they're right. I'm making lots of new charms and amulets, because as we all know, this is just the start. Unfortunately, Sebastian was right. We've started something, and we need to protect the town."

"Okay, I have to ask," Newton said, frowning. "Do some people know you're witches? Why did this old guy come to you, Avery? Why ask Briar and El for help?"

Alex shook his head. "No one knows anything. Some of the locals know of Avery's family history, and Avery, El, and Briar's shops trade on herbs, amulets, tarot, and the occult."

Avery added, "Dan and Sally told me that some locals suspect our magic—my magic—may be a bit more *authentic* than others, but it doesn't worry anyone, yet."

"We all know some of the other shop owners that trade on the supernatural, and there's the fake tarot reader at the back of the Angels as Protectors shop—they have had all sorts of enquiries," Alex continued. "It's that sort of town, Newton. Magic, or the pretence of it, is our lifeblood. Bloody Hell, we even have Stan from the Council dressing up as a druid for the pagan celebrations! Not many other towns openly celebrate those. Those rumours are what make White Haven so popular." He looked slightly rueful. "It just so happens that things may get a little more *real* for a while."

"You're right," El acknowledged. "I've always had the odd question about the extent of what I do, because some people really want to *believe*. I always kept it vague, because people love intrigue. Zoe, however—my shop assistant—is always honest about her Wicca activities."

"Well," Alex said, "I've been experimenting with scrying. I've had limited success so far, but I'm going to keep trying."

Newton frowned. "Scrying?"

"The art of divination using water, glass, or mirrors. A useful skill if I can master it. And it allows you a window into someone else's life."

"It sounds a bit stalker-y to me. Be careful," Newton warned.

"I'm not a peeping Tom," Alex said, annoyed. "I was thinking more about keeping an eye on the Favershams."

"Still sounds dodgy."

El interrupted. "Good luck, Alex. I understand it's a hard skill to learn."

Reuben put in, "I've been meaning to ask, how are the tattoos? Healing okay?"

"I forget I've got it," Avery admitted. "It's healing nicely."

"Good. I'll let Nils know. He was worried you'd been put off tattoos forever."

"I must admit, I quite like mine," Briar said, grinning. "I actually might get another."

Avery suddenly thought of something else from the meeting. "One more thing. We also make up the thirteenth coven of Cornwall, too. It means they'll call on us for big spells." She shrugged and grinned. "I think it's pretty exciting."

"Sod them," Reuben said, clearly sticking to his original argument. "They didn't care before, did they? We need to look after ourselves first."

"I'm glad you said that," El said, "because we have a job."

"We do?" Newton asked, looking at her over his beer.

"Maybe not you, but at least a couple of us. The lights up at the castle are getting worse. One of my regular customers told me today that she saw lights again last night and basically said, if you have any other mojo going on, sort out the castle because the town is going to freak out sooner rather than later."

"Have you seen them?" Briar asked her.

"No, anyone else?"

They all shook their heads.

Avery frowned. "I guess we've been too preoccupied. What did you say, El?"

"I merely smiled enigmatically, and told her I'd see what I could do."

"Interesting. And what are you going to do?"

"Rope you lot into a banishing spell, of course," El said. "We've been able to let some of the milder spirit activity play out, but I don't think we can ignore this."

"Spirit banishment seems to be my area of speciality, so of course I'm happy to go," Alex said, reaching forward to get more food.

"Me too," Avery agreed. "I'm trying to increase my knowledge in all sorts of stuff at the moment."

"Sounds like a great idea," Reuben said. "If there's more spirit activity in White Haven, we all need to be able to deal with it. Count me in."

"And me," Briar said.

"I'm coming, too," Newton chimed in. "I want to know exactly what we're up against, And I'll take the shotgun with the salt shells, just in case."

"Excellent. May as well go now, then," El decided, grinning.

4

Avery pulled her van into the castle's car park and frowned. "There's another car here."

Alex frowned. "Who the hell is here at this time of night?"

"Kids, probably," Newton shouted from the back where the others were sitting. "Kids love to spook themselves out with ghost stories."

"Kids who drive?" Alex said sarcastically.

"Well, teenagers then, Mr Pedantic," Newton said, annoyed.

"How're we going to banish spirits with kids around?" Briar asked.

"We're just going to have to glamour them," Alex said, as everyone exited the van and set off across the car park and up the path to the castle.

White Haven Castle sat above them on the hilltop, strategically placed to overlook the sea and the surrounding countryside. It was mostly a ruin now, but large sections of the outer walls still remained standing, and the local conservation group had reconstructed some inner walls creating rooms, although the roof had long since gone. A few trees had sprung up over the intervening years, growing both in and around the grounds. The car park had been built a short distance away so as not to mar the grandeur of the ruin.

Lights were placed at regular points along the wall, and were illuminated at various special times of the year, but tonight they were off. However, torchlight bobbed along at the base of the castle walls, and then disappeared.

"Bollocks," Reuben said, striding ahead with El, "this is going to make things more complicated."

"Are you sure you don't need your grimoire?" Avery asked Alex.

"No. I've been reading these spells and committing them to memory for days now," Alex explained.

Newton was walking alongside them. "What do you mean, 'spells?' Do you need more than one to do the same thing?"

"There are many different types of spells to dispel spirits," Alex said. "In fact, there are many different spells to do all sorts of things. Some work better than others depending on the situation, the witch who's saying the spells, tone, intonation—it goes on. Just as you need lots of ways to catch criminals, we have lots of ways to do things, too."

"Fair enough," Newton said. "What about spells to glamour people?"

Briar answered. "It depends how susceptible they are. It helps if the subject is already attracted to you, too. Men glamour women and vice-versa much more easily. Well, in general, anyway."

"I hope you haven't been glamouring me," Newton said, and Avery smiled to hear the tease in his voice.

"Newton! I would never do that," Briar said, and then she faltered as the implications of his words sank in.

Alex grinned at Avery, and then at Newton. "Nicely played, Newton."

If it wasn't so dark, Avery could have sworn Briar blushed.

"You're both so funny," Briar said, trying to brush it off.

Newton just laughed, and then changed the subject as the castle walls loomed above them. "Well, I know I don't need to say this, but we can't hurt them—whoever they are."

"We'll work it out," Avery said, trying to reassure him.

Reuben and El were waiting for them under the half-collapsed arch that was once the gated castle's entrance.

"There seems to be three of them," El said, pointing to the far side of the courtyard. "We can hear two male voices and one female, and we can see their torches."

"Any sign of spirit activity?" Alex asked, looking up and around.

"Not yet," Reuben said.

Suddenly, as if on cue, a scream pierced the night.

"Crap," Newton said, breaking into a run, the others following.

As Avery ran, she instinctively summoned her power, starting to ball energy into her hands. Torchlight flashed wildly from behind one of the walls, and shouts filled the air.

"It's okay, Cassie!" a male voice yelled.

"No, it's not!" Cassie yelled. "I felt something breathe on me, and it wasn't you or Ben!"

They slowed to a halt as they approached the broken wall. Peering around it, Avery saw three figures in the middle of a large room—although it was barely that anymore. Four partially erect walls encompassed a rectangular space. The floor was made of stone and grass, and broken stones were scattered everywhere.

The three figures carried an assortment of equipment, and they had a couple of lights set up, casting gloomy shadows in the area. First impressions suggested the trio were older than they'd initially thought; Avery estimated only a few years younger than themselves.

Newton stepped out from behind the wall, the witches close behind. "I heard a scream. Are you okay?"

The girl, who must be Cassie, screamed again, and the one of the boys shouted, "Shit! Where the hell did you come from?"

"Sorry, I didn't mean to startle you. My name's Newton, I'm a policeman." He gestured to the others, "These are friends of mine. What are you doing here?"

The man in the centre was holding a camera, and the big white light next to him cast his face into harsh planes and illuminated his dark skin. "Nothing!" he said belligerently.

Newton's voice became hard. "I think we all know that's bullshit. What are you doing with all this equipment?"

The second man answered. He was of average height and a stocky build, and he said proudly, "We're paranormal investigators—it's not a crime. We're not damaging anything!"

Reuben snorted. "Paranormal investigators! Is this a school project or something?"

"Do we look like we're at school? No! We're interested in the paranormal, and thought we'd investigate the lights that have appeared up here lately. It's not a crime," he repeated angrily.

Newton held up a hand to calm him down, which unfortunately drew attention to the shotgun he was holding in his left hand. "It's okay, you're not in trouble."

"Oh my God!" Cassie exclaimed. "Is that a shotgun?" She started backing away.

Avery stood next to Newton, hoping a female might calm things down. "It's okay, no one's going to hurt you. We came up here to investigate the lights, too. The shotgun is just for our protection. The shells are filled with salt."

The first guy, the taller one, said, "Oh, I get it! Very *Supernatural*. Cool. Wish I'd thought of that!"

"Well, unless you have a license, I suggest you forget about it," Newton said impatiently.

"Chill out. I didn't say I'd got one, did I?" He huffed dramatically.

Avery tried not to laugh. This was turning into a very interesting night. She strolled over to look at their equipment and introduced herself. "This stuff looks pretty impressive."

"It should do. It cost loads," the shorter, stocky one said. He reached out a hand. "I'm Ben."

"And I'm Dylan," the taller boy said.

"And you must be Cassie," Avery said, smiling. Cassie was short, with brown hair pulled up into a ponytail, and she looked nervous. "We heard you scream. What happened?"

Cassie glanced nervously over her shoulder. "I felt something breathe on me, over there. It was horrible."

"It's brilliant," Ben said. "That's what we came here for."

"But I didn't *really* expect it!" she answered him, annoyed.

"This is not our first haunting," he said, frowning.

"It's the first time something *breathed* on me," she pointed out.

Avery felt sorry for her. It probably sounded like a bit of a joke before they arrived, but it was very creepy up here. There was very little moon tonight, and the air was cold where the sea wind sliced through the nooks and crannies of the broken walls.

"Have you seen any lights?" Alex asked, glancing around the castle walls.

"No, nothing," Ben said.

"But," Dylan added, "the lights have been reported at hours later than this."

"How do you know?" Alex asked, curious.

"My mate lives on the hill, and he has a clear view from his house to here."

"Well, I suggest you go home now," Newton said in a very policeman-like tone.

"Why? We're not doing anything wrong," Ben said, becoming agitated. "What are *you* going to do?"

The witches and Newton all stared at each other awkwardly, wondering what to say.

"Mm, thought so," Ben said. "Something dodgy."

"Not dodgy at all," Alex said. "Why don't we help each other? We have an interest in ghosts, too. Why don't you show us how your equipment works?"

"Where's your stuff?" Dylan asked, suspiciously.

"I have slightly different methods than you," Alex said with a tight smile.

While the investigators huddled together for a brief second, consulting each other, Alex turned and made a quiet suggestion. "While me and Newton check out their stuff and see if they can help, why don't you check the rest of the place out?"

"Sounds good," El said. "Come on, Reuben."

They turned and headed to the other side of the castle, while Briar and Avery started to explore the room they were in.

"Can you sense anything, Briar?" Avery asked, heading to where Cassie had indicated she had felt something breathing on her.

"Not yet. Maybe an increase in energy in the atmosphere? Nothing concrete. What about you?"

Avery shook her head. "Nothing. It *is* creepy, though. Any idea when this castle was built?"

"Eleventh century, during the reign of William the Conqueror. After he was crowned, he arranged for the construction of many castles. I come here a lot. It's one of my favourite places in White Haven. I love the feeling of the age of the place just seeping around me."

Avery smiled. "I didn't know that! But wow, this is old, then. That's a lot of years, and a lot of ghosts."

"I normally find it such a peaceful place, though," Briar mused as she wandered around the shell of the room, stroking its walls.

"So no previous indication of spirits?"

"No, despite the rumours of a white lady walking the walls. But isn't there always, in these old places?" she laughed.

"I'm starting to think people are just imagining things," Avery said, half-disappointed that absolutely nothing appeared to be happening there.

"But if ghosts do appear, what are we going to do with *them*?" Briar asked. She looked over to where the three newcomers stood with Newton and Alex, showing them their equipment. The sound of static echoed across the space as they demonstrated a small, handheld device.

"They might prove useful," Avery said. "Maybe we should think about working with them. They're clearly open-minded about this kind of thing."

"Even witchcraft?" Briar said, her eyebrows raised. "I'm not sure we should trust our identities with people we don't know. We could end up on YouTube."

"I think we both know we can deal with that," Avery said.

"You know what I mean. I like remaining anonymous," she said, heading through a gap in the wall to explore other parts of the castle.

But then the unmistakable sound of an energy blast disturbed the night's silence.

Avery turned and ran, Briar hard on her heels, heading for the side of the castle where El and Reuben were exploring.

As they sprinted across the grounds, Newton and Alex ran past them, and the three investigators, after a moment's hesitation, followed.

As they rounded a corner, they saw El and Reuben backed up against the wall, as far as possible from an unearthly light in the centre of a large room, and everyone came to a skidding halt, Avery crashing into the back of Alex. Cassie, once again, screamed.

"Holy shit! That's a real, live spirit!" Dylan exclaimed.

"I don't think there's anything *live* about it," Alex said, dryly. He called over to El and Reuben, "Are you okay? Has it attacked you?"

"No, we're fine," Reuben explained. "It just appeared unexpectedly, and kind of gave us a shock."

El looked sheepish. "It appeared right in front of me, and I panicked. But, other than that, nothing. It's just floating there."

The spirit seemed to be just an amorphous blob, with tendrils reaching out around it like grasping fingers.

Briar turned to Ben, Cassie, and Dylan. "I think you three need to get out of here."

"No way!" Ben said, flourishing the monitor in his hand. It was emitting a whining, static noise that was very distracting.

Newton frowned. "I think we all know there's a spirit here, Ben. Turn your damn machine off—it's annoying."

"I can't," he said crossly, "I need to measure this."

Newton scowled, cocked his shotgun, and asked no one in particular, "What now?"

"Can anyone make out what it is?" Cassie asked, finally finding her voice.

As if on cue, the blob started to change, taking on a more human form.

"Looks like a woman to me," Alex said.

He was right. The blue glow made her shape hard to define, but it did appear to be a woman wearing a long dress—a very old-fashioned dress.

Avery snorted. "Crap. So much for us saying there's no such thing as a White Lady here."

The spirit turned in the middle of the space, her arms outspread as she seemed to watch them. Avery felt the hairs stand up on her arms as the woman met her gaze. And then the spirit looked up, over Avery's shoulder, to the top of the wall behind her. A horrible sinking feeling filled Avery's stomach, and she turned to follow her gaze.

There, on the top of the wall, was another blue, glowing ghostly figure. It was a man, and he was aiming an arrow directly at them.

Even though part of Avery's rational mind knew that he couldn't possibly hurt them, she instinctively yelled and ducked. "Move everyone, now!"

A glowing blue arrow sailed over Avery's head, landing at the feet of the ghostly woman with a distinctly solid sounding *thud*. A high-pitched keening sound broke the silence, and then everyone yelled and scrambled for cover.

Arrow after arrow thudded into the ground around them, one narrowly missing Avery's head. She felt it whistle past her ear.

"What the shit?" Reuben yelled, pulling El behind him. An arrow was headed straight for them and he swatted it away with a sweeping motion of his hand. "This feels scarily real, guys!"

Within seconds, at least a dozen ghostly men manifested around them, all wearing what looked like leather breeches, shirts, and cloaks, and all wielding swords or axes. The woman spirit ran from the room, trying to evade their clutches, but she was too late. The arrows finally found their mark as they thudded into her and she fell, facedown.

The men turned their attention to them, and Avery felt a trickle of fear run down her spine.

"Alex?" She looked at him from where they crouched behind a piece of broken wall. "We need to start the spell. We haven't got time to get rid of the ghost-hunters."

Newton was already standing. The men advanced menacingly towards them and he lifted his shotgun and took aim for the closest, releasing both barrels in rapid succession.

Then all hell broke loose as the spirits rushed them.

Avery stood with the others and released wave after wave of energy bolts, but for every spirit they sent whirling backwards, others appeared.

Avery felt cold, clammy hands on her arm and looked up into the white eyes of a scarred man with an evil grin. He lifted her clean off the floor as she gasped in surprise. She should not be able to feel this, and he shouldn't be able to manifest that strongly, but…

Well, in that case, she decided, he could feel *this*. She punched him with a ball of energy straight at his stomach and he dropped her, disappearing only to reappear a few feet away.

Blasts of energy and fireballs ricocheted off the castle walls, and shouts filled the air. The earth trembled beneath her feet as tree roots shot up, grabbing at the legs of the attacking men.

Avery pulled the wind around her and then sent it through the ghosts like a hurricane. Although it scattered them, they didn't stop fighting.

"Cover me—I need time!" Alex shouted above the din.

He retreated as far as he could away from the fight, pulling the three hunters with him, who by now were wide-eyed with either fear, amazement, or both. Newton followed him, still firing, trying to keep the spirits back, while Alex started his incantation, his voice strong as it rose above the noise.

Avery glanced around and saw the scattered witches unleashing their magic in various forms on their attackers, and all managing to hold their own. *But how were the spirits so strong?* It must be the magic they'd released.

She heard a *whirring* noise and she ducked and rolled as an axe whirled past, thudding into the wall behind her. She grinned. *That's mine now.*

Extending her hand and her power, Avery pulled the axe out of the wall into her waiting palm and then turned, wielding her spirit-weapon viciously as she imbued it with extra magical energy. She rolled to the floor and struck out at the closest man's legs, feeling the horrible crunch of muscle and bone as he collapsed on the ground next to her. It was time to try a banishment spell. Her grimoire only had a couple, and she had never tried them before. She uttered the spell, but her incantation didn't seem strong enough, and the spirit just seemed to laugh at her as he dragged himself back to his feet.

Avery started to despair. These spirits were strong, too strong, and she could see the others struggling, too.

But then she felt Alex's power swell around them, and his voice seemed to magnify within the castle walls. As he completed his incantation, a wave of magic passed through the castle like a tsunami, sweeping up the spirits as it passed through, until every single one disappeared and the place fell into an eerie silence.

Now the spirits and their weird blue glow had gone, the place was plunged into darkness, a faint light from the stars overhead their only illumination. Someone sent up a couple of witch lights, and Avery sighed with relief as she saw that everyone was okay. She collapsed to the floor, her heart thudding wildly, and her hands shaking as her adrenaline ebbed away.

It was Dylan who spoke first. "Oh, wow." He stood on slightly shaky legs and gazed around, his mouth open. He grinned, "*Wow, wow, wow!* Guys, that was amazing! What the hell was that? Who are you? You have to teach me that!"

5

Avery gathered some wood from the fallen branches in the grounds and started a fire in the shelter of a reasonably solid corner of the castle, while the three paranormal investigators retrieved their gear. Then they sat and leaned against the castle walls, while Alex lectured. "Guys, we are not teaching you anything. In fact, you need to forget *everything*."

Ben laughed in a slightly maniacal way. "Ha! You're kidding, right? I can't forget that! *Ever*."

Alex glanced at Avery, and she knew what he was thinking. *Should they try and glamour them so they forgot what they'd seen?* But they both knew that there was too much magical evidence to enchant away successfully.

Dylan looked excited, Ben looked shocked, and Cassie looked at them with fear in her eyes. She hadn't said a word.

Briar smiled at her. "It's okay, Cassie, we're not monsters, and we're not going to hurt you. I'm just sorry you were here to see it."

Ben made a strangled sound. "This isn't one of those times when we're made to *disappear*, is it?"

Reuben groaned from where he was lying flat on the ground. "We're not assassins, dude. Calm down. We're just aliens. We have extra-terrestrial powers." El laughed and poked him in the ribs with her toe.

"Not helpful, thanks Reuben," Avery said, laughing despite the horrified expressions on Dylan, Ben, and Cassie's faces. "He's kidding!"

"So what *are* you?" Cassie whispered.

"Can you keep a secret?" Avery asked her.

"And we mean, no blogs, Facebook, Twitter, YouTube chats, leaked camera footage, or *anything* else!" Alex said, looking each of them in the eye sternly.

They all nodded mutely.

"We have the ability to do magic," Avery said, reluctant to say 'witch.'

Ben snorted. "*Magic?*" He started to laugh, but it died on his lips as he saw that no one else was laughing. "Are you serious?"

Newton sighed from the shadows, where he'd sat next to Briar, the shotgun on his lap. "They are very serious. Why, Ben? What did you think that was?"

Ben stuttered. "I-I don't know, I thought maybe they had some sort of weapon. I mean, you have a shotgun!"

"That's because I'm not a witch."

Avery saw the newcomers all flinch at the word.

Reuben rolled over to look at them. "Guys, let them think we're aliens, it's probably more believable."

El sniggered again. "Shut up, Reuben."

He winked at her, grabbed her hand, and kissed it.

"Let me get this right," Alex said. "You're paranormal investigators, you believe in spirits and things that go bump in the night, but you don't believe in magic or witches?"

"Well, I admit to the possibility of them," Ben said defensively. "But we base our findings on rational and scientific investigation."

"Good for you," Alex said. "In that case, you can put this all down to a very active imagination."

Dylan glared at Ben. "Ben, stop being an ass. You wanted to see something tonight! Your EMF meter was off the charts. These guys are the real deal. I mean, look at that weird light thing floating above us."

Ben grabbed his meter from where it lay on the ground next to him, flicked it on, and pointed it at the witch light. He swung the device around and they could hear a low static buzz, steadily rising in volume.

Alex held his hand out and formed a small ball of fire. "Try reading this."

Ben's eyes widened and he leaned forward, pointing his meter at Alex. It started to whine with increasing intensity as Alex made the fire grow, and then decreased as Alex dissolved it again. However, the meter continued to pick up a low buzz from all of the witches.

"Wow. This is really happening, right?" Ben asked, his earlier excitement returning.

"'Fraid so," Avery answered, a trace of a smile on her face. "Are you going to keep our secret?"

All three glanced at each other and then nodded in agreement, and Dylan answered for all of them. "Deal. But you realise you want us to hide the very stuff we're looking for."

"Share what you want about spirits and other paranormal stuff, just not us," Alex said evenly.

Reuben added, "Think of us as your gateway into the unknown."

"I like that idea," Ben said, nodding.

"Good," Newton said, leaning towards them. "Now, tell me what else you know about weird ghosts and sightings lately. And what else do you do, apart from this stuff?"

Ben spoke first. "We all study at Penryn University. I'm doing postgraduate studies in parapsychology, looking at beliefs and experiences, precognition, ESP. I love this stuff—I just remain a healthy sceptic. It's good to have balance."

"Me too, but whereas Ben's background is physics, mine's psychology," Cassie said. "A while ago Ben posted a request on the university messages wall for someone doing psychology to join in his investigations, so I thought, why not? I'm curious. Life's all about experiences. I enjoyed it so much that when I finished my degree, I decided to do postgrad parapsychology, too. We're about to enter our second year. But, this is the first time anything so *obvious* has happened." She still looked wide-eyed and completely out of her depth, but at least she didn't look terrified. "If I'm honest, I thought it would be a load of rubbish and that nothing would happen, ever. How wrong could I be?"

"To be fair," Dylan said, "I don't think any of us expected this. Most of the things we monitor provide goose bumps and a bit of static. This is…unexpected. Anyway, I'm doing postgrad studies in English, focussing on folklore, and myths and legends. I'm an enthusiastic assistant." He grinned again. "This is awesome!"

Avery frowned as she remembered that Dan, who worked in her shop, studied English, too. "Do you know Dan Fellows? He's doing his Masters in something to do with folktales at Penryn."

"Tall guy, glasses, dark hair? I think he's taken a couple of tutorials. Why, do you know him?"

"He works with me in my shop, Happenstance Books."

"Okay," Dylan said, his interest piqued. "And does he know about you guys?"

"Yes, he does. I'll tell him to keep an eye out for you."

"So, how did you know to come here, and what other places have you been told about?" Newton persisted.

"I told you," Dylan said. "My mate lives in White Haven and he saw the lights. The other things have been reported to Ben through his website—it's just a simple one. There's a contact email."

Ben looked thoughtful. "My website's been up for months, but about ten nights or so ago, I picked up a really big EMF surge. It was totally off the charts and completely inexplicable. I was just playing around with the equipment at home, and *wow*! It was just so odd!"

Avery inwardly groaned and glanced at the others who looked as guilty as she felt. It must have been the night they released the binding.

Ben continued, "I thought I'd capitalise on it and put ads in the local papers, and I guess people saw them. I've had loads of reports in the last few days, especially of experiences at castles and other old buildings—you know, churches and stuff. There's no way we can check it all out straight away, but as this seemed to be one of the biggest, here we are. There have been a couple of reports in White Haven, actually."

"Where?" Newton asked.

"Old Haven Church. Apparently, there's a ghostly figure wandering the grounds, in the day as well as at night. Also the Church of All Souls, and the old museum on the hill. I'm going to check them all. Although, I am a bit worried now, after tonight." Ben turned to Alex. "What did you do to make them go? I mean, that was seriously impressive."

"It's my speciality," Alex said, shrugging.

"And harder than it looks," El added. "And you're not witches, so don't even think about trying."

"What worries me," Avery said, "is that these spirits seem to have an almost physical presence. They could grab me, with their horrible cold, clammy hands, and I was able to grab an axe that shouldn't exist in this plane. These are *spirits*. How can this be happening? We were attacked, and that means other people could be, too. And they can't banish them like we can."

Alex groaned. "Damn it. The magic we released has obviously strengthened spirits way beyond their normal means, and this could be only the start. We have to clean up—this is our mess."

Ben looked confused. "What do you mean about releasing magic?"

"Unfortunately, Ben, we're responsible for that EMF surge you picked up the other day. I'm hoping that only spirits that manifest in White Haven have become so corporeal. If you go spirit hunting elsewhere, be very careful."

6

It had been over a week since they'd met the ghost-hunters at White Haven Castle, and Avery had spent the early part of it chasing ghosts. The paranormal investigators had been right about the spirits at the churches, but fortunately they hadn't been as strong as those at the castle, and a few hours' work had banished them. Since then, she had caught up on sleep.

It was nice to settle into the normal rhythms of life again. Avery spent every day in the shop, selling and stocking books, and chatting to her customers. It was also a good way to get a feel for what was happening in White Haven. There were no further reports of weird lights at sea, and events seemed to have returned to normal. She was pretty sure the calm wouldn't last.

When she wasn't at work, she studied her new grimoire, and she knew the other witches were, too. Their individual strengths were growing in unexpected ways, and in every moment of their spare time, they honed their abilities. They all felt they were becoming more attuned to the details of their magic, and could wield it with greater precision.

Avery continued to try new spells, combining new with old, and practising witch flight—with slow but increasing success. She had managed to stop fainting, but it still seemed to take too long, and it was leaving her with headaches.

And of course she spent time with Alex. She could feel herself drifting around with a smile on her face, and had to shake herself out of her dreamy reveries. They had been practising some of their new skills together, and that seemed to be improving their magic, too.

However when Avery arrived in the small room at the rear of the shop on Friday morning, she knew she'd overdone it because Sally, the shop manager and her non-magical friend, looked horrified.

"You look terrible. What have you been doing?"

"Practising witch flight again. It's really hard. I think I'm missing something."

"Avery, I know you're anxious to do this, but you'll harm yourself if you push too hard. Can't you just put that spell aside for a while?"

Avery nodded, and headed to the cupboard under the coffee machine to find some paracetamol. "Yeah, I guess so. It'll be one of those things that will just fall into place—I hope."

Sally frowned, hands on her hips. "I think you should have a few days off from studying that grimoire. It's not going to disappear. You have time."

Avery found the pills and downed them with some water. "I know, but I'm just so excited to have found it—all of them. It's addictive! The spells, the history, the comments in the margins, it's just so…" She broke off, unable to really explain how life changing it had been.

Sally's expression softened. "I get it, I really do, but I'm worried about you. All of you, actually."

Avery smiled, feeling a rush of affection for her friend. "I know, but it's like I've just woken up after a long sleep. It's so cool!"

"It's not cool if you end up killing yourself. I popped into Briar's shop yesterday. She looked so tired. I don't even think she could concentrate. I think she needs some more help in there, she manages pretty much on her own."

"I think we're all trying really hard right now. We're worried about what might happen next, and we want to be prepared." She gave Sally a hug. "I don't know what I'd do without you and Dan. Thank you for being so great."

Sally patted her back. "It's okay. I'm glad to help. Now, come on through to the shop, I've got a few things to show you."

They spent the morning going over new stock and some changes in the store, and Sally ran though some promotions she wanted to implement, and then an unexpected voice interrupted them.

"Hey Avery, long time no see."

Avery looked up to find Ben and Cassie standing in front of the counter, each carrying a couple of books. Both of them looked different in the daylight—older, and less intimidated than the other night.

"Hey guys. Taking a break from ghost-hunting?"

"Are you kidding?" Ben asked. "We're snowed under with sightings. I wanted to let you know, and you're the only one I knew how to contact. And," he gestured to the books in his hands, "I thought I'd add to my collection. This is a great shop, Avery."

"You can thank my manager, Sally, for that," she said, introducing them to her.

"Oh, I don't know, Avery," Sally smirked. "You add a little something I can't."

"We also want to thank you for the other night," Cassie added, looking slightly embarrassed. "I'm not sure we thanked you properly at the time, it was all such a shock. But, you know, without you, things could have been really ugly."

"No problem at all," Avery said, smiling at her. She glanced around the shop and saw a couple of customers listening, and turned to Sally. "Do you mind if I head out the back for a couple of minutes?"

"Sure," Sally said, "just make me a coffee while you're at it."

Once they were safely away from prying ears and she had put the kettle on in the small kitchen, Avery asked, "So, what else have you heard about?"

"More of the same, really," Ben said. "Increased ghost sightings, abnormal noises, disappearing objects, electrical surges, cold spots. And it's happening all over Cornwall. A couple of people have even reported that they've spotted the Beast of Bodmin. You must have seen it on the news."

Avery nodded, remembering the evening news report from the day before. The Beast of Bodmin was a myth that had circulated for years. "I have, although if I remember correctly, there's no footage of it yet." She wondered if Zane, the beady-eyed witch from Bodmin, was having any success finding it.

Cassie continued enthusiastically, "At the moment, we're just trying to document everything, sort of create a database. But we've started to follow up on the more interesting ones."

"Follow up how?" Avery asked, frowning.

"Same as last week, really. We head out with our cameras and EMF meter and see what happens. We went to this old farmhouse a couple of nights ago, on the way to Helston. We picked up really strong signals, and one of the rooms was freezing!"

"Anybody in any danger?"

Ben shook his head. "No, nothing that manifested as strongly as at the castle. Just a really spooked family. They said it started a couple of weeks ago."

"That's good," Avery said, relieved no one could get hurt. "We've been catching up on a few other things." Avery pulled mugs from the cupboard above the kitchen counter. "Do you two want a drink?"

They shook their heads, and Ben said, "No, we've got an appointment at All Souls, actually. We thought you should know."

"All Souls? The Church in the centre of the town?" Avery looked up, coffee forgotten. "What have you got an appointment there for?"

"The vicar said that there's a spirit in the church, and he wanted us to check it out."

Avery felt her heart sink. "Did he give any details?"

"None. He was quite vague actually, other than that he thought there was *something unpleasant*," Cassie said. She looked amused. "He sounded quite progressive. He wanted to know all about the equipment we used and everything."

"Do me a favour and let me know the details. I'll give you my number and I'll grab yours," Avery said, scribbling down her own and Alex's numbers before taking theirs.

Ben raised an eyebrow. "If something needs banishing, do you want me to pass on your number?"

Avery sighed deeply. If anything was happening there it was their fault, and they had to put it right. "I guess so. But keep things vague, okay? I don't need a modern day witch-hunt starting up in town."

"Sure thing," Ben said, grinning.

A thought struck Avery. "Have you heard anything about lights at sea?"

Ben frowned. "Lights? No, but there was a weird accident just out of Mevagissey a couple of nights ago. One of the crew of a fishing boat just disappeared. No shouts, no screams, he just vanished. The crew spent hours looking for him, and the Coastguard was called out, but they never found him. It's been all over the news, but it will be on the net if you missed it. They called off the search this morning."

Avery's heart sank. *Damn it. She'd hoped Caleb had been imagining things.*

Ben obviously caught Avery's expression. "Is there something we should know?"

Avery sighed. "This is going to sound really weird."

Ben laughed and looked at Cassie, incredulous. "Weirder than the other night?"

"Let me update you before you go," Avery said.

Halfway through the afternoon, Avery had another visitor. She was in the Local History section of the shop, seeing what books she had on myths and legends of Cornwall, when someone coughed politely behind her.

"Excuse me, may I have a word?"

Avery jumped, almost dropping the book she was holding. She had been so engrossed, she hadn't heard anyone approach.

She turned to see a man in his late forties, with short brown hair and a hint of grey at his temples. He was of average height and build, and wore smart jeans and a shirt, and a clergyman's dog collar at his neck.

Avery felt her stomach tighten with worry, but she tried not to show it. "Oh, sorry, you startled me. Yes, of course. Are you looking for something?"

"Only you. My name's James, and I'm the vicar of the Church of All Souls."

She forced herself to relax as she smiled, shaking his hand. "Nice to meet you, James. I'm Avery."

He smiled back, but his eyes were wary. "I'm sorry to disturb you, but I met Ben and Cassie this morning. They suggested I speak to you."

"Oh yes, the ghost-hunters. They mentioned they were going to see you." She glanced around and was relieved to find no one was within hearing range. "I gather you're having a few problems."

"If you call a spirit lurking in the church at night a problem, then yes. Is there somewhere more private that we could talk?"

"Of course, come this way."

Once again, Avery headed to the small room at the back of the shop, wondering if this was going to be a really uncomfortable chat. Dan was at the counter, and she saw his eyes widen with surprise when he saw whom she was with. She gesticulated to the back of the shop, and he nodded.

As soon as they were alone, James said, "This is an occult shop. You believe in witchcraft?"

"It's not *just* an occult shop, and I believe in many things, James. The world is a strange place, isn't it? You're here because of a 'lurking spirit,' after all."

He didn't answer straight away. He walked around the room, looking at the boxes of stock along the back wall, many of them new books for the shelves, as well as some second-hand editions, and then he picked up one of the boxes of tarot cards on the table. "Do these sell?"

Avery nodded. "Yes, they're very popular. So are the Angels Cards and the Dream Catchers."

He nodded abruptly. "Yes, people probably put more stock in these things than God now."

"Surely Angel Cards would suggest a belief in God?"

He looked at her sharply. "I guess so. So, what do Tarot cards suggest a belief in? The Devil?"

"Surely if God exists, then so does the Devil. You're the vicar, you tell me. But that's *not* what the Tarot is about, James, and I think you know that. There are many different beliefs in the world. Not everyone believes in the male omniscient being that controls our destiny. The Tarot cards tap into old magic. Or so some believe," she said, tempering her words.

"May I look at them?" he asked.

"Of course." She watched as he thumbed through the cards of the classic Rider-Waite pack, placing them on the table as he looked at their pictures. His gaze hovered over the Devil card before he quickly moved on.

The smell of incense drifted from the main part of the shop, and Avery was sharply aware of how the place would look to someone from the church.

James looked up. "And what do you know about ghosts and spirits?"

"Only that they exist. And you must believe that, too, or you wouldn't be here."

They were silent for a few seconds, assessing each other, and while Avery didn't think he was a witch hunter, he didn't seem as progressive as Cassie had made him sound. And then his shoulders dropped, and he sat abruptly in a chair at the table, worry etched across his face.

"Let me make a coffee," Avery said, moving to the counter, "and I think you need some cake."

James sat mute while she brewed a strong pot of coffee and put the carrot cake that Sally had made in the centre of the table. Half of it had already been eaten, mainly by Dan. It was a miracle he didn't have diabetes.

Avery sat down, pushed a cup of coffee in front of him, and then cut them both a large slice of cake. Before she spoke, she had a couple of bites of her own, hoping to relax herself as well as him. When she woke up that morning, she did not imagine she'd be having tea with the local vicar in her shop.

"So James, this is obviously difficult for you to be here. Why don't you tell me what's happening at All Souls?"

He rubbed his face with his hands, and then reached for his cake, taking a bite and chewing slowly, and all the time he watched her. "Before I tell you, I want to know if you're discreet. I don't want this all over the town."

She nodded. "I'm very discrete. Nobody wants panic in White Haven."

"Why did Ben and Cassie say you could help? They were very vague. There's no point to me telling you anything if you can't help."

"I have a friend who is good at exorcism. Very good, in fact."

James frowned. "Does he belong to the Catholic church? That's the sort of thing they do."

Avery almost choked on her cake. "No, he does not. He has independent affiliations."

James glanced around the room again and Avery felt sorry for him. He was obviously very conflicted.

"James, please tell me. I want to help. What did Ben and Cassie find?"

"Their EMF meter readings were high. They agreed that I was not going mad."

"I'm sure you're not, but I'm going to need more than that."

A small smile crept across James's face and she saw him start to relax. "Sorry. This is all very strange for me."

"I understand. Now, from the beginning."

"It started a couple of weeks ago. The energy in the church changed. It's quite odd, and I can't explain it, but it's like something *else* is there." He frowned as he thought. "Anyway, for a few days there was nothing but this strange feel to the place. I've worked there for years, so I know this is new. And then I was working in the sacristy and I felt as if I was being watched. I turned around and saw nothing, but the air got very cold around me. It was most uncomfortable. And then the next night, the same thing happened, and I saw a ghostly shape in the doorway—just for a second, and then it went. It was shapeless, amorphous, but I sensed intelligence and something malignant. I nearly had a heart attack and I left, right in the middle of writing my sermon."

"Why do you say malignant? What did it do?""

"Nothing, but it just seemed to watch me—study me. I know that sounds strange, it didn't have eyes that I could see. But it was so uncanny. I had to force myself to go in the next day." He sighed, stealing himself to go on. "And then it appeared again, same time, same place, but this time for longer. It was like a dark presence just on the edge of my vision. It didn't hurt me, it was just there. But every night since it has returned, and although it sounds odd, I sense that it's growing stronger. The verger has also seen it, an older man called Harry, and despite his faith, he's very scared. And it's started moving things—the flowers, the Bible, the prayer books. We have to do something before it appears in a service, or at a wedding or a christening, or a funeral. Can you imagine?"

Avery nodded. "I would think you'd lose all of your worshippers."

"And the papers would come, and the archbishop would be involved," he said, his voice rising. "We need to do this quickly. I can't believe I'm even having this conversation."

Avery sat, thinking. They obviously had to help him. All Souls was at the centre of the whole magical release, and it had obviously disturbed a resting spirit. "Do you have any idea of who it may be?"

"I think it's a *what* more than a *who*." He shrugged. "I know that sounds stupid, but you were right earlier. I've come across restless spirits before now. Churches always have them, but this is different. Very different. That's why I called Ben."

"I think we can help, James. Would you like me to contact my friend? We can come tonight, if that helps?"

Relief swept across his face. "Yes, please. The sooner, the better. It appears to be most visible at about nine in the evening. Can you come then?"

"Of course. Probably best if you leave us to it, once you've let us in."

"Oh no," he said, shaking his head. "I need to see this, to know it's done. And I believe Ben and Cassie want to be there, too."

7

Alex leaned across the bar, looking incredulous. "Are you kidding me?"

"No. He's desperate, Alex."

"I get that, but he's a bloody vicar, Avery," he hissed, "at the place where we performed some very big juju."

"I know, Alex. I was there. The big juju is responsible for this," she hissed back. "*We* are responsible for this."

"But we'll be doing magic in front of the vicar."

"Catholic priests used to do this," she pointed out. "They might still, in fact. He asked if you were a Catholic, and of course I said no. But, can we make it look religious?"

"I suppose we'll bloody have to," he said, frowning. "Give me half an hour and I'll be with you."

Avery grinned and grabbed her glass of wine, perching on a bar stool to drink it.

It was 7.00 PM now, and she'd headed to The Wayward Son once she'd closed the shop and straightened up her flat. Having James visit reminded her that she had all sorts of magical things strewn around and she needed to take them up to her attic. If, for some reason, he'd come to her flat, things would have looked really weird.

As Avery sat looking around the crowded pub, she saw the main door swing open and Newton came in with Briar. She grinned and waved, wondering if they were on a date. Briar looked flushed with happiness. *Maybe not*, she thought, as she looked at Newton's face. He was frowning. Again.

"Hi guys," she said, as they each pulled out a barstool. "How are you?"

"Annoyed," Newton said. "Since meeting you, my life has become very complicated."

Briar just grinned. "Hi Avery, lovely to see you. And Newton doesn't mean it. He enjoys it, really. He said so the other night."

"The other night?" Avery questioned, raising her eyebrow. "So you two have been spending some time together? How nice."

"He has asked me to go over the finer points of what we do," she said discretely as Newton turned away to order their drinks. "He feels it will enable him to help us better in the future."

"Of course it will," Avery nodded, trying to keep a straight face. "I presume you did this over wine and a nice meal. Sounds very pleasant. Of course, he does get the added bonus of your fabulous company."

"He's been the perfect gentleman, Avery. I think you're getting the wrong idea."

"Sure I am. Did you cook?"

"No, he did, actually." Briar squirmed slightly. "I went to his house. He said he wanted to repay me for looking after his burns and healing him. He's a very good cook." During their defeat of a demon a few weeks before, Newton had sustained some nasty burns.

"Really? That *is* nice, isn't it?" Avery started to smirk. "Did you enjoy it?"

"We had a lovely evening, thank you, Avery, and then I went home, so you can wipe that smirk off your face," Briar said primly.

"I'm not smirking."

"You so are," she said.

Avery glanced over to Newton, who was still pre-occupied at the bar. "But he likes you, I can tell. You must know, Briar."

"I don't know. I think you're imagining things." Briar looked slightly put out, and maybe regretful.

"He's playing the long game," Avery said, sipping her wine. "Just for the record, I'd like to say that I approve. I like him. He suits you. You'll make a lovely couple."

Briar was just about to say something very rude, Avery could tell from her outraged expression, when Newton slid a glass of white wine in front of her.

"What are you two looking all sneaky about?" he asked.

"Nothing at all," Briar said, breezily. She changed the subject deftly. "You'd better tell her your news."

Avery frowned. "What now?"

Newton leaned on the bar. "Have you heard about the man who disappeared from the fishing boat?"

"Unfortunately, yes."

"Well, it's been logged as an accident, but there's no sign of his body. It was a calm night, and we should have found his body by now, but I guess tides do strange things sometimes. He may turn up yet."

"Any suggestion of lights?"

Newton shook his head. "Nothing. One minute he was there, the next he'd gone. I wonder if there was some sort of Mermaid magic involved—apparently, all the crew looked a little dazed and glassy-eyed. We'll probably never know what truly happened." He gazed into his pint, depressed.

"Are you leading it?"

"No. It's not a murder investigation. I've just been privy to some of the details."

"Well," Avery said, "I have news for you." She filled them in on Ben and Cassie's visit, and then her afternoon call from James.

"I know James," Newton said thoughtfully.

"Do you?" Briar asked. "Is he okay? I mean, will he start pulpit preaching about demons and witches?"

"I hope not. He doesn't strike me as the superstitious type, but I suggest you keep your real nature to yourselves. Not many will like the fact that there are witches in White Haven. Especially the Church."

Avery grinned. "Alex is going to use a Latin spell—it's what they used in medieval times when the priests were involved in necromancy. Hopefully it will throw James off the fact that we're also using magic. I've told James it's an exorcism."

Newton frowned. "Priests were involved in necromancy?"

"Oh yes. In medieval times, the crossover between magic and religion was enormous. I mean, really, what's the difference between a miracle and magic?" Avery shrugged and laughed. "Nothing, except the Church endorsed one and denied the other. The saints replaced the pagan gods. That's how they managed to keep converting pagans to Christianity, by renaming pagan celebrations and incorporating them into the Church calendar. And then they converted everything to Latin—the language of Catholicism. Remember, this was way before Henry VIII and the Church of England."

Newton's mouth dropped open. "Really! I'd never thought about miracles and magic like that before. Sneaky."

"Very."

Briar asked, "Do you need any help?"

"No." Avery shook her head. "One spirit only. Should be manageable. And we want to keep this simple. I don't want to glamour the vicar. It should be pretty straight forward. I hope."

***

The main entrance of All Souls was closed, and Alex and Avery headed around to the side door where they found James waiting nervously. He looked at Alex with interest as Avery introduced them. "I understand you've done this before?" he asked, as he led them inside to the sacristy.

"Several times, and always with success," Alex said, reassuringly.

"Good. I really want this to stop. Harry said he wouldn't return again if I didn't sort it out soon. Like this is something I normally deal with on a daily basis!"

"Are Cassie and Ben here?" Avery asked.

James nodded and called back over his shoulder. "Yes, and their friend, Dylan. They are in the nave at the moment, taking readings."

They entered a small stone and wood-panelled room at the rear of the church. Vestments hung on the walls, and there was a small desk covered in a pile of papers beneath a high window.

"So, this is where you see your ghostly visitor?" Alex asked, looking around.

"Yes. As you can see, my back is to the door when I'm sitting here. The ghost appears in the doorway, and then from there moves to the rest of the church." He shivered. "I can feel it behind me. It's most unnerving."

Understatement of the year.

Avery could feel the magic they had released hanging in the still air of the church. Beyond that, she sensed a different energy signature, which must be the spirit. At the moment, it was faint.

"Let me take you through to the nave," James said, and he turned and led the way out through the chancel, past the entrance to the crypt, toward the pulpit and the nave where the paranormal investigators were setting up some of their equipment.

Cassie turned and waved. "Hi guys. Good to see you again."

"Sooner than I expected," Alex said with a wry smile. He dropped his voice so James couldn't hear. "Not planning on filming us, I hope?"

"Not you." She nodded to where James was chatting to Dylan. "Just the ghost. And James forbade us from mentioning the church on film. Didn't want this getting out on social media or the TV. And of course we honour that. Full confidentiality. But he did give us permission to monitor everything else. I think he's really interested in it all!"

"Good," Alex said, "or else I would have to fry your recording."

Cassie looked at him, wide-eyed. "I suppose you could."

"And would. Never forget that," Alex said, winking. "And it goes without saying that you keep our names out of your reports, too."

"No problem," she answered, almost stuttering.

"Try not to scare Cassie again, Alex," Avery said, patting his arm before looking at their equipment. It was a very impressive, professional set up. "You've got some pretty interesting stuff here, Cassie."

"We get funding through the university."

A shiver ran through Avery as she looked around the church. It looked so peaceful and unassuming. The pews were of polished wood, the flowers were fresh, late evening sunshine streamed thought the stained glass windows casting the interior in a rosy glow, and there wasn't a speck of dust in sight. But, the last time they were here, they had everything to lose—including her life. Somewhere below her feet was the secret space where Octavia and the demon had been bound and Alex had opened up the portal to cast the demon out of their reality, back to its own. And then a horrible thought struck her. When Alex had opened the portal, spirits of some sort had escaped. She had seen them when she spirit walked. *What if one of those was still here in the church, seeking to do harm?*

Avery pulled on Alex's arm and led him away to where they couldn't be overheard. "Do you remember me telling you that I had seen spirits exit through the dimensional doorway you opened?"

He frowned. "I think so. A lot of things happened that night."

"What if we're wrongly assuming it's a regular spirit that the magic has sort of re-energised, and actually it's something else far darker and malevolent? James said it was different from anything he's felt before."

"Like what? I mean, regular spirits can carry a lot of negative energy. It could just be very pissed at being disturbed after centuries of rest."

"I don't know. It can't be a demon, but maybe it's an evil spirit? Something cast in purgatory. Let's face it—we don't know what dimension you opened. Is there more than one? Are there hundreds? That could have been Hell itself!"

Alex's dark brown eyes were suddenly troubled. "As far as I'm aware, the only other dimension is the spirit or elemental world that exists alongside, but separate from, our own. I admit, I don't know the extent of what else is in there. Maybe it is Hell, but Hell is a Christian concept."

For once, Alex wasn't being sarcastic and cocky, and they stared at each other for a few moments, pondering the possibilities of the spirit world.

The scratchy whine of the EMF meter cut through the air and Alex and Avery spun around quickly. Ben held up his hand. "It's okay. We're just taking some basic measurements. We'll be finished soon."

Alex turned back to Avery. "Come on, let's see what they're doing. We can handle whatever it is."

Avery's heart was heavy. While she was pleased that Alex felt so confident, and she did have faith in his abilities, she couldn't shake the feeling that something was *different*—that this wasn't like the spirits they had encountered at the castle the other night.

She shook off her dread and listened to Dylan. "You see, Alex, we have to get base readings first to figure out what's normal and what's not. The great thing about a church is the low levels of electricity." He gestured around. "Sure, there are electric lights and heating, but it's minimal in such a big space. No computers help a lot."

Cassie added, "I'm recording our initial readings, and I've also recorded the temperatures in various parts of the church. Now, if anything happens, we'll have a concrete record of change."

Dylan lowered his voice. "Although, if it's anything like the other night, it'll be pretty freaking obvious."

Alex sighed. "That's very true. But, I think this is going to be a bit different."

"How do you know?" Ben asked, finally putting the EMF monitor down.

"It's my witchy senses."

"Is that a thing?" Dylan sounded doubtful.

"You'd be surprised."

Avery laughed, despite the odd situation. Alex never failed to amuse her. He was so confident and so funny, and yet he never once patronised the others. Alex caught her gaze and smiled, and she felt her stomach somersault.

James joined them. "Have I missed anything? I was just trying to contact Harry."

"No," Alex reassured him. "I was observing these guys. It's pretty fascinating. How is Harry?"

James paused and ran his hands through his hair. "I'm a little worried, actually. I haven't seen him at all today, and he's not answering his phone."

Avery glanced worriedly at Alex and then said to James, "Could he be ill at home?"

"Not as far as I'm aware. He was due in this morning, but maybe he was too spooked to come. However, he hasn't phoned, and he normally would."

Avery felt a dread start to creep though her. "Maybe we should search the church."

"I've been all around it, and he isn't here."

Before they could say anything else, the light dimmed in the church as the sun dropped below the windows, and cold seemed to seep through the nave. Every single one of them glanced nervously around, and James hurried to put on some side lights.

And then Avery felt the energy change. Something else seemed to be with them in the space. Ben obviously felt it too, because he whipped around, pointing his EMF meter around the nave, and the whine of the meter started again. He swung it backwards and forwards, the high-pitched whine intensifying when he pointed it towards the far corner of the church.

"It's over there," he said, advancing cautiously forward.

Alex and Avery joined him, Avery subconsciously summoning a ball of energy into her hands until she remembered that James was still there.

Avery's skin prickled. Keeping her eyes on the corner, she said to Alex, "Can you feel it?"

"Yes. It feels different from what we've experience before. Even Helena."

"It's very different from what we've experienced before, too," Ben agreed as the whine intensified. "This reading is very strong."

The electric lights suddenly exploded above them and glass shattered everywhere, making Avery cover her face for a split second.

In that moment, the EMF meter whined like a wounded animal and then fell silent as the energy signature vanished.

"Where's it gone?" James called out nervously from behind them.

They turned slowly, looking for any sign of the manifestation. Avery pushed out her magical senses, but whatever it was had gone for now.

Alex's shoulders dropped a fraction as he released some tension. "I don't know. Stay together in the centre of the room."

James's voice shook as he looked around. "It feels different again."

"In what way?" Cassie asked, her pen poised over the paper she'd set up to record the events.

"Stronger. More malevolent, somehow. It was…palpable."

The energy had felt malevolent, but more than that, it felt old, like when Avery had sensed the age of the dimensional doorway they had opened in the witch museum. *Very old.*

Moments later, the spirit manifested again, this time on the far side of the church, near the side-chapel where Avery and Newton had hidden before they entered the crypt on the night they broke the binding spell.

"Over there," Avery pointed. "I can feel it again."

Even before she'd finished her sentence the EMF meter exploded into life, and Ben almost dropped it. "Wow. This is vibrating up my arm!"

Before Avery could comment further, Alex stepped forward and started his incantation, his words loud and powerful, echoing around the nave, but he was barely a sentence in when once again the spirit disappeared, and the EMF meter fell silent.

"It's toying with us," Avery said.

Alex nodded. "This thing has time. It's waiting. It has intelligence."

"What do you mean by intelligence?" James asked.

"Most spirits act out repeated events from their previous lives—an experience we had in the castle a week ago. We witnessed old events replayed, caused by a spike in energy in the local area. " He didn't elaborate about the energy, and James didn't ask. "Spirits don't think as such. They exist, lost, drifting around in an existence that isn't their own."

Dylan agreed. "Except for Poltergeists, which are very disturbed spirits."

"But even then, they don't have *intelligence*," Alex said. "This does. I can feel it."

"I agree," Avery said.

Ben headed into the side-chapel, his EMF monitor hissing with low static, and Dylan followed him with the camera.

"Has the basic reading changed?" Cassie asked.

"It's slightly higher than earlier," he said, reading out the levels for Cassie to record.

Avery turned to Alex, lowering her voice. "What are we going to do?"

He shrugged. "Not much we can until it reappears, but I have a feeling it knows exactly what we want to do."

Then, for a third time, the EMF meter roared into life, and this time Avery and Alex turned in unison, looking up high into the vaulted roof of the church. In a split second, the spirit—or whatever it was—charged them, and Avery and Alex fell to the floor, rolling to avoid its attack.

A wave of freezing cold *something* passed through Avery and she struggled to breathe, but Alex had started his incantation again, causing the spirit to disappear as rapidly as it had arrived.

Alex pulled Avery to her feet. "Are you okay?"

She nodded. "I'm fine. You?"

"Pissed off."

"Please tell me you recorded that?" Ben asked Dylan.

"I'm recording, but I don't know what I got," he said. "Not 'til I analyse it later."

"I thought you weren't filming us?" Alex said, annoyed.

"Sorry, dude," Dylan said. "It was instinct. I swear I won't release it. But it could be really useful."

Alex narrowed his eyes as he weighed up his options. "Don't let me down, Dylan."

"I swear, I won't post this anywhere."

James was watching the exchange with interest. "You value your privacy too, Alex?"

"Yep," he said, not elaborating. Alex looked around the church once more and then turned back to James. "I hate to tell you this, but this is no ordinary spirit."

James was pale. "Yes, I'm getting that. I think I need to find Harry."

"Have you checked the crypt?" Avery asked.

James frowned. "No, why? We hardly ever go down there."

"Well, I think we should."

James pulled a bunch of keys out of his pocket and then led the way back to the chancel, down the stairs to the heavy sealed door of the crypt, everyone trailing behind him.

He went to unlock it, and then frowned. "It's already unlocked."

"Let me," Alex said, and he pushed James behind him, entering the crypt first.

The crypt was filled with candlelight and it smelt of blood. In the middle of the floor was the broken body of a man wearing religious clothing.

James released a strangled cry. "Harry!"

8

"What did this?"

Newton stared at the scene in front of him and turned his troubled grey eyes on Avery.

"We don't know," Avery said, feeling more helpless than she'd felt in a long time. In fact, she felt sick at how they had been joking about it earlier, like banishing a spirit was a game. This was a horrible return to reality.

"You don't know?" he said, incredulous. "Your last words to me were, 'one spirit only. Should be manageable.' And now *this*?"

They stood alone in the entrance to the crypt. Everyone else was upstairs in the nave being interviewed by Officer Moore, Newton's red-haired police colleague who worked closely with him, and another uniformed officer.

"I'm sorry, Newton. I feel terrible about this. A man has lost his life because of our actions here only weeks ago. And no, we don't know what caused it, other than some sort of spirit."

Newton was furious. "Shit. Well, you better fix this. The verger is *dead*."

Instinctively, wind began to build around her as she became annoyed. "Of course we're going to fix it," she hissed. "What the hell do you think we were doing here in the first place? We didn't come here to have a chat and a night cap!" Avery turned and started to pace off her anger. "Seriously, Newton. I think you know us better than that!"

"All right, all right," Newton said impatiently. "Get out of the crime scene."

"I'm not in the bloody crime scene! It's over there," she said, pointing to where the body still lay in a broken heap, Harry's head slanted at an unnatural angle.

They had given it a brief examination before calling Newton, desperately hoping Harry was injured and not dead. But his blank eyes had stared up at the roof of the crypt, and they knew it was too late. They were now waiting for the Scene of Crimes Unit.

Newton's face was etched with sorrow. "I'm sorry. I'm just upset and annoyed. It doesn't matter how long you've been doing this, finding a dead body is never easy."

Avery's anger vanished as quickly as it had arrived. "I'm sorry, too. I'm scared, as well. This is different, Newton."

He shook his head. "Not here. We'll talk later. Or tomorrow," he said, looking at his watch. "It's late now."

The thump of footsteps on the stairs heralded the arrival of SOCO; Avery stepped back to give them space, and then joined the others in the nave.

***

"So, what killed him?" Briar asked.

It was the following night and all five witches were in Avery's attic space, surrounded by spell books, herbs, magical paraphernalia, pizza boxes, and beer.

Alex was sitting on the floor, leaning back against the sofa, sipping a beer. "It looks like his neck was broken. And other bones. Like he'd been smashed like a doll. But he was pale, too, and his skin looked dry, as if the life had been drained out of him." He shrugged. "Of course, it could have been the light."

The room fell silent as they thought through the implications, and then Reuben spoke. He sat on the floor, leaning against the wall under the window, his long legs stretched out in front of him. "So, like the other spirits, it has physical capabilities."

"I guess it must," Avery said. "Although, we couldn't feel it when it attacked us. It was like a really strong wind had rushed us."

"But you think it was intelligent," El said from where she sat nestled on the couch. "Maybe it chooses who to be physical with?"

Briar sat next to El, looking thoughtful. "I forgot you'd said you'd seen spirits escape, Avery. I guess I was just so happy to have broken the binding spell that I forgot everything else."

Avery nodded. "I'd almost forgotten as well. Whatever it is—or they are—it's very old."

396

"Which could explain why it feels different," Reuben said thoughtfully. "It's much older than the spirits we've encountered before, and something different from demons—which are fundamentally elemental."

Avery collapsed against the back of the couch, sighing loudly. "Crap. I better hit the books to try and work out what this could be."

"We all should," Briar agreed. "Do you think we should involve the Witches Council?"

"Not yet," Avery said. "Although, I have a feeling they'll involve themselves when this gets out."

"You know this will hit the papers," Reuben said.

"Yep," Alex agreed tersely. "Exactly what we didn't want to happen. James wants to keeps the whole ghost-hunting thing out of this for as long as possible, and so do the police. And of course the police will not believe a spirit did this—except for Newton. They're looking for a real person."

"Which it may prove to be," Briar pointed out.

"Maybe, but highly unlikely in the circumstances," Alex said. "We're saying we were at the Church doing historical research. We'll look less freaky," he said, encompassing Avery in his statement. "Of course, the press has a way of finding stuff out."

"Well, James is more upset than us," Avery said. "Not only has he lost a friend, but he didn't want to alarm the congregation. It's too late for that. The church will be closed for the next few days while SOCO complete their investigation. I have a feeling Newton is going to be busy."

And then Reuben said something that Avery had thought, but hadn't voiced. "What if the spirits that you saw escape, Avery, were the same—all ancient and intelligent. They could be lurking all over White Haven, or anywhere in Cornwall—or even further. What did the Witches Council think about them?"

"I didn't tell them," she said, feeling guilty. "I forgot! The news about the lights in the sea made me forget everything else."

"Great, we'll be outcasts again." Briar sighed and reached for another slice of pizza.

"Good," Reuben said. "We don't need them, anyway."

"I think we will before this is over," Alex said.

"So now we have ancient malevolent spirits of something, and lights in the sea. Just brilliant," El said.

"But we have our grimoires, and we're stronger than we've ever been. Don't forget that," Avery reminded them.

"I think our lives were easier without them though," Briar said sadly.

***

The first person Avery saw in her shop the next morning was Caspian Faversham. The doors had been open for only seconds when he strode in, dressed in his customary dark clothes, setting the wind chimes ringing. Sally saw him and went pale, heading straight to the back of the shop.

"What do you want?" Avery snapped, watching Sally go. "You're not welcome here, and if you touch her, I'll kill you."

"My, my. Aren't we pleasant? We're supposed to be working together now."

Caspian leaned on the counter, looking around her shop in his easy, dismissive manner that made Avery want to smash him right between the eyes. And not with magic, either. She wanted to feel the physical pleasure of actually assaulting him. And it was such a shame, because she'd woken in a great mood after spending the night with Alex. Unfortunately, her warm glow had now gone.

"You made it very clear in the meeting the other day that you didn't want me there. So, why are you here?"

"You haven't seen the morning news, then?" he asked, his eyebrow rising in an infuriatingly superior manner.

"No."

"You don't know about the death in All Souls?"

"Yes, I was there when they found the body." She frowned. *Where was he going with this?* "What's that got to do with you?"

"Humour me. Why were you in All Souls?"

Avery really wanted to tell him to get lost, but she had a feeling there was more to this early morning inquisition than sheer nosiness. She glanced around the shop and, seeing it was still empty, headed to the front door and locked it, reluctant to take Caspian to the back room with Sally there. She turned to find Caspian watching her with narrowed eyes.

She leaned against the door, keeping distance between them. "It's haunted. We were there with a paranormal crew."

He sneered. "Don't you keep interesting company now? Planning to do some ghost-busting?"

"Yes."

"And how did that work out?"

"Caspian, can you please get to the point and then get out of my shop?"

He leaned back against the counter and folded his arms across his chest. "How did the man die?"

"It looked as if he'd been shaken violently. And, his body looked…drained," she said, for want of a better word.

"So you think the spirit did it?"

"It's possible."

He filled his voice with a dangerous tone. "Avery?"

She glared at him. *Why did he have to make her feel like a child?* "Probably. The spirit was strong, malevolent. It was toying with us."

He fell silent and watched her, the seconds stretching between them before he finally spoke. "It seems we have the same problem."

Her annoyance drained out of her, only to be replaced by a sinking feeling. "What do you mean?"

"We have a lurking spirit in St Luke's Church in Harecombe, and it killed the verger last night, too." He watched her, waiting for her reaction.

Avery's heart started racing. "What? How do you know it was the spirit and not a person?"

"Because the body was found in the same manner as the one you found in All Souls. I heard an early report on the radio about both deaths and made a discreet visit to our church. I can feel the spirit there, and it did not like me being there one bit. It's lurking there, like a toad. Unfortunately, I could not linger for too long, there are police everywhere."

"It could be completely unrelated," Avery said defiantly, reluctant to admit that Caspian may be right.

He lowered his voice menacingly. "I think we both know there's no such thing as coincidence, Avery. The news knows that your vicar had paranormal investigators there, too. Speculation is only just starting, and it will get a lot worse. I suggest you tell me what's going on."

She inwardly groaned. *So the historical research ruse hadn't worked.* As reluctant as she was to share anything with Caspian, she knew she had to. It was only a matter of time before the Council was involved. "When we released the binding spell, Alex had to open a doorway to the spirit world to send the demon and Octavia through. Spirits escaped from it. I don't know how many exactly, maybe a half dozen. I think it's these spirits that are causing the problems."

Caspian's face immediately hardened. "Spirits escaped? Then we are in big trouble, Avery."

She swallowed. "Why? Surely we can banish them just like any other spirit?"

"But they're not just any other spirit, are they? They have escaped from one of the dimensions of the Otherworld. And that makes them mean. And strong."

As much as Avery didn't like to agree with Caspian, she knew he was right. And he seemed to believe there were different dimensions. While she was spirit walking, she had seen other spirits trying to get out and failing, which *did* mean these were stronger. "Did you sense intelligence when you were at St Luke's?"

"Yes." He shifted his position slightly as he made himself more comfortable. "Why do you think they're in churches?"

"I don't know. I would think they'd hate churches if they're from some level of a demonic Otherworld."

"Some spirits may feel very comfortable in a church. All those souls to feed on," he speculated. "Something else to think about."

"We'll deal with it," Avery said, sounding more confident than she felt.

"Will you? Sorry if I doubt you," he said, not sounding sorry at all, "but I'll deal with the one in Harecombe. Do you even know what spirits they are? Are they all the same, or did several different types escape?" He stepped closer, closing the space between them. "We need to know, if we're to deal with them properly."

"I'll find out."

"Good. Do it quickly." He smirked. "And I'll inform Genevieve. This matter needs to be brought before the Council."

9

Avery sat at the table in her attic surrounded by her grimoires and books on all things myth, folklore, and magic, quietly fuming. As soon as she could, she had left Sally and Dan minding the shop, and then headed upstairs to her flat to do some research.

She was furious with Caspian, but she was more furious with herself. They had been arrogant when they retrieved their spell books. Arrogant and overconfident. Yes, the grimoires belonged to them, and they had every right to them, but right now, she wished she'd have looked at the possible consequences. Ever since Anne had left them the box, and all of her research that led to their grimoires, there had been death and destruction. And no, not all of it had been their fault, the Favershams were definitely responsible for some of it, but they had to accept some of the blame.

And they had to clean up this mess.

She had many old books that listed varieties of spirits and demons, and something must be in there somewhere. And then a thought struck her. *Maybe Alex could help with his psychic abilities? Maybe they should spirit walk?* But she had a feeling that would be too dangerous when they had no idea what these spirits were.

She thought back to the night when they broke the binding spell and tried to remember what the spirits looked like. The room beneath the church had been chaotic, the witches wielding their magic in huge bursts of action just to stay alive. The demon had been dangerous, and she'd been trying to get back in her own body, which Helena was enjoying being in a little too much. She'd noticed the spirits as an afterthought, really. They were vague and shapeless, with only the barest suggestion of having a human-shaped body; it was the spark of animation and the sense of a soul that marked them as human rather than demon. But whether they were fully human in origin was another matter entirely.

She pushed away from the table and crossed her arms, annoyed. *How could they find out what they were? And if they could manifest at will, how could they trap them long enough to banish them?*

Avery leaned over her grimoires again with determination, summoned a witch light to float above her just in case there were hidden runes and notes, and then uttered a searching spell to look in the books for anything related to identifying spirits. She felt the air shift around her and then the pages started to ruffle in the breeze, as if unseen hands were turning the pages. After a few seconds the pages fell still and she marked the page, but then the pages kept on moving, and Avery marked another page, and then another, until she had almost a dozen spells spread across both books.

Pulling a notepad towards her, she started to make notes on the spells, dismissing some quickly, while deciding to try others, but it was the final spell she looked at that seemed the most promising. She'd left it until last, because it was close to the front of the oldest grimoire—Helena's grimoire—and completely invisible without the use of the witch light. It had been written within another spell, the lines interspersed within the visible spell. The writing was minute and cramped, a scrawl across the page that required time and energy to decipher. Immediately, her pulse began to quicken. This looked interesting. And chilling. There was a line of runes down the side, denoting a warning to only use with protection. It also required objects that Avery didn't have, but she knew Alex did, like a crystal ball for divination. But the thing that interested her most about this spell was that it seemed to offer a way to talk to the spirit in question.

She reached for her phone and called Alex. His warm voice made her smile. "Hi, gorgeous. How are you?"

"I'm fine, how are you?" she asked.

"Busy—it's the lunchtime rush. I shouldn't complain."

Avery could hear the chatter of the pub in the background. "Well, I have a quick question. I've found a spell that should allow us to talk to spirits, but we need a crystal ball. Are you interested?"

He paused for a heartbeat. "Who are we talking to?"

"Our unknown visitor to the church."

"Ah. That sort of thing is dangerous."

"It is?"

"Yes. Opening up a direct line to a spirit can come with a powerful backlash."

She groaned. "Yeah, I sort of got that impression."

"But, I'm always up for a challenge. I'll catch you later—someone's glaring at me for a pint."

"Sure, and thanks," she said as he rang off.

She started to assemble the ingredients for the spell, reaching for a variety of herbs, and wondered if they needed to perform the spell in the church, or would anywhere do. Probably the church would be best. It was where the spirit lived—for now.

She was halfway through the preparation when her phone rang, and she saw Ben's name on the screen. "Hi, Ben? How are you guys after last night?"

"Absolutely psyched," he said excitedly, and then added, "and of course feeling really bad about Harry's death. But we've found something on the camera footage. You need to see it."

"Why? What?" she asked, her own excitement mounting.

"I can't explain it. You just need to see it."

"Can I bring the others?"

"Sure. We'll come to you. What time?"

"Seven?" Avery offered, hoping she'd get everyone by then, and still leave enough time for her and Alex to do the spell.

"Great. Laters," he said, hanging up.

As soon as he rang off, she felt the tingle of magic start to fill the attic. Avery looked around alarmed. *What was happening?* It was like an itch that she couldn't locate, but a strange hyper-awareness started to spread across her skin and beneath her skull. And then Genevieve's voice spoke from somewhere around her, disembodied and surreal.

"Avery. It is Genevieve. We have convened another meeting. Please be at Crag's End tomorrow. 8:00 PM. Do not be late."

Avery groaned. It was like being summoned by your mother. *And why couldn't she just use the phone?* Thank the Goddess it hadn't happened in the shop. That would have been tricky to explain.

It was now late afternoon, the wind had dropped, and it looked hot out. She needed to get out of the attic and get some air in her garden. She could collect some herbs and roots, and do a reading. She grabbed the tarot and her cutting knife, and headed down to the garden.

***

Avery's living room seemed very full by half past seven that evening. All five witches were there, along with Newton and the three paranormal investigators.

The smell of take-out curry filled the room, and foil containers covered the dining room table, alongside naan bread, beer, and wine.

Most of them had come directly from either work or home, but Reuben had been surfing. His hair was still wet, and a fine crust of sand dusted his skin. They had all helped themselves to a selection of different curries, but Reuben's plate was piled especially high.

Avery looked at it, and then at Reuben's lean form. "Where the hell do you put all that, Reuben?"

He grinned. "I surf it off, Avery."

"Wow. Your food bill must be immense."

"It is. Thank the Gods I'm rich, eh?" he said, winking, and then went to sit on the end of the sofa, facing the TV.

Avery grabbed her own food and then sat on a large floor cushion, watching Ben as he finished finding the downloaded file he plugged into her TV.

He turned around, excited. "Guys, I can't wait for you to see this. It's one of the best thermal images we've ever had!"

El grimaced. "Explain. I don't get this stuff."

"Spirits or ghosts work on different levels of existence than us. We usually can't see them or hear them, but we use equipment to try and see what's there. We use EMF meters to read for different electrical signatures, like varying energy levels. But we have to exclude existing phone, radio, and electricity. We've got a Trifield Natural Meter, which we can set to a magnetic setting, and it excludes most electrical interference—but we take baseline readings anyway. Then we have audio equipment, a regular camera, a thermal camera, and a temperature monitor. I've got a motion sensor, but didn't take it, which was stupid, but next time…" He shrugged. "It sounds complicated, but it really isn't. We're just trying to get as much data as possible. And of course, this isn't an exact science."

El looked impressed. "So, you set all of this up at the church the other night?"

Dylan answered while Ben turned back to the TV. "Yep. I got some audio, but it was just static, a sort of hissing that changed in tone, but was inconclusive, and Cassie got some temperature changes. I'm pretty sure we'd have got some motion stuff, because that thing seemed to be moving around the room a lot, but as Ben said, we didn't bring it. But the camera footage was the best."

Everyone nodded, and Avery felt a chill start to run up her spine in anticipation.

"I'll show you the regular camera recording first."

They saw a dim image of the interior of the church fill the screen, the image panning around the entrance, then the nave, the side-chapel, and the choir. The footage recorded Cassie and Ben setting up the other equipment, and the sounds of their low-voiced discussions were only slightly audible. Then the footage stopped, and when it restarted, the camera was pointed to the far corner of the room. Avery could hear her voice and Alex's before the electric lights exploded above them, showering glass everywhere. A faint, white shape seemed to fill the corner before it fled upwards.

Briar gasped. "Is that it, the spirit?"

"Probably, yes," Ben said, nodding. "But it's not clear."

"I switched cameras then," Dylan explained. "The exploding glass was pretty intense, and I thought I might get better results."

Ben then pulled up the thermal imaging footage, and the next thing they saw was a grey image of the church interior and Cassie and Ben looking like photographic negatives. Then they saw James, Alex, and Avery. After some stopping and starting, the footage of the small side-chapel appeared. There was a glimpse of a white image that looked human, but it appeared to have huge shoulders, and it floated off the floor and then disappeared. Then the camera was pointed up at the ceiling, the vaulted roof clearly visible, and there was the most chilling image. A huge, winged creature hovered above them before speeding down in a blur, so fast that it disappeared from view altogether in the jerky footage.

Ben and Dylan looked triumphant, but everyone else looked at each other in stunned silence.

"What the hell is that?" Newton asked, turning to the others in alarm.

Avery felt the blood drain from her face and she struggled to find her voice. "It didn't look like a regular spirit."

"It looks like a bloody great Angel of Death!" Newton shouted. "Why are you all looking at me like that? What is it?"

Alex's usual confidence had gone, replaced by utter confusion. He looked at the others before he finally turned to Newton. "I don't know."

They watched the footage over and over, each of them throwing in suggestions, but unfortunately, no one had a better idea than Newton, which in the light of day, seemed ridiculous.

Reuben turned to Avery. "Is that what you saw flying out of the doorway under All Souls?"

"Absolutely not," she said determinedly. "I would have remembered that. What I saw were formless shapes, small, insubstantial. Although, I was trying to avoid a demon, and struggling to get back into my own body."

Briar leaned back against the sofa looking thoughtful. "But whatever that is had already killed the verger, Harry, at this point. Is that right?"

Avery glanced at Alex and then said, "Yes, I guess so."

Briar looked at the frozen image on the screen and shuddered. "Then maybe the fact that it had fed on Harry—sorry for the choice of word, but you did say he looked drained— had made the spirit, or whatever it is, more powerful?"

Newton leapt off the sofa and started pacing. "Then why hasn't it killed again? And what happens when it does?"

"The Church was sealed by the police," Alex said. "No one is going in or out at the moment. Before we left yesterday, we placed wards of protection around the building—very rudimentary ones, there were too many police around. We hope we've contained it, but honestly, it's unlikely." He looked at Avery. "We should head back and do it properly."

"What about the death at St Luke's in Harecombe?" Reuben asked, finally putting aside his empty plate. "I saw it on the news. Is it the same?"

"First impression says yes, but I'm waiting for the Coroner's report," Newton said, pausing at the window to look out onto the street below before turning back to face them. "However, there's no sign of a break-in."

"Any other suspicious deaths in the last twenty-four hours?" El asked.

"No. But if there are more spirits, and they're linked, then maybe there will be."

Avery mulled over her visit from Caspian, wondering whether to cast more doom on their gathering, but she knew she had to share his visit. "Caspian's already been to see me about that," she said, explaining what he'd said. "And there's another Council meeting tomorrow. I expect to get shouted at."

"Damn it," Alex said, looking concerned. "I'm working, or I'd come with you. I don't like you going alone, especially with vengeful spirits around."

Despite the circumstances, Avery smiled, feeling a now familiar warmth spread though her. "I'll be fine. Besides I have protection—a tattoo and *magic.*"

"Which reminds me," El said, turning to Cassie, Dylan and Ben. "I have amulets for you guys. Wear them always! Strange things are happening, and you are up close and personal with some of it. And don't take any chances."

They all nodded and thanked her profusely, as they took the small silver amulets on chains and examined them carefully.

"Well, guess who's going to come with you tomorrow?" Reuben said, grinning.

Avery felt her stomach drop. "I said I'll be fine. I don't need anyone to come with me. Especially *you*, at the moment. You have a lot of *attitude* going on. I don't think it will help."

"Tough shit. I'm coming anyway. I want to see who these jokers are."

"They're not jokers, Reuben," Avery corrected, sensing conflict already. "Some of them are lovely and welcoming. They're witches. Our friends. We can't afford to alienate them. I don't want to, either. This is our chance to be accepted into the magical community. There's a whole other world of stuff going on out there that we need to know about."

Reuben rolled his eyes. "I know. I'm not an idiot. But two are better than one. I'll tell them I'm nosy."

"You better behave, or we'll fall out," she said, starting to get annoyed.

El snorted. "Good luck with that."

10

Avery drove up the somewhat familiar twists and turns of Crag's End drive, arguing with Reuben. For the entire journey he'd been updating her about his grimoire and his experiments with the spells, and he was teasing and joking constantly, but underneath, she could sense his tension.

"Seriously, Reuben, you need to behave tonight. I will be really pissed off if you deliberately antagonise them."

He dropped his bantering tone. "I'll behave, I promise. Ever since Gil died I've been struggling to deal with this whole magic thing. I thought I'd turned my back on it forever, and now I'm up to my eyeballs in it." He sighed and rested his head against the back of the seat. "Don't get me wrong, I'm glad it's who I am and I've accepted that, although I wish it hadn't taken Gil's death to make me see it."

Avery slowed down and glanced at him, feeling suddenly mean for giving him a hard time. "I know, and I'm sorry, Reuben. You're handling it really well. I wish the circumstances were different. Gil would have been the perfect representative for us, better than me."

Reuben shook his head. "You're doing fine, Avery. I don't doubt you. But, Alex is right. We don't really know these guys, and you being here on your own *is* worrying. If they turned on you, you couldn't fight them all."

She slowed down as she saw a passing bay on the left, pulled to a stop, and then turned to face him, desperate to reassure him. He seemed so fragile sometimes, which frankly was ridiculous, considering the size of him. "This isn't the Wild West, and I'm sure that won't happen. I actually think you'll like them—well, most of them."

He swallowed, and looked out the window, unable to meet her eye. "But, the fact that there are lots of us now—it's really making me question everything. Who I am, who witches are, what other types of things are going on we never knew about. You, Alex and the others, seem to have a handle on it. Even Newton does! I don't think I do. It's too vague—no, too *big*!"

Avery reached out and touched his arm, and he turned to face her, his eyes full of doubt, and she wanted to cry. "It *is* big, you're not alone in thinking that. I feel terrible, Reuben. I started this whole thing off. And look what's happened! With my headstrong insistence that we find those grimoires, I've unleashed something hideous into White Haven…well, the world, actually." The feelings she'd been trying to subdue for weeks suddenly flooded out, triggered by Reuben's heartbreaking honesty. "People are dying, and this time it's not Caspian's fault, or Alicia's. It's mine. I've been so arrogant." She started to well up, a tear trickling down her cheek, and she sniffed, fumbling in her bag for a tissue. "Fuck it. I'm so annoyed with myself."

"We followed you, Avery. You didn't do this on your own."

She wiped a tear away and blew her nose. "You're just being kind. And I'm supposed to be comforting you."

He laughed weakly. "You are. Thanks. Although, making women cry seems to be my speciality lately."

"Have you talked to El about all this?"

He shrugged. "Sort of. I feel I'm being a bit of a crap boyfriend. Have you talked to Alex?"

She smiled wryly. "Sort of. I've been trying to bury all of this guilt, actually. Sex helps."

He laughed, throwing his head back. "Yep, it really does." He pointed to the back of the van. "You're not suggesting anything, right?"

"No, you dick."

He grinned at her, a cheeky glint in his eye. "I'm kidding. Besides, Alex would kill me. And so would El."

Avery pulled the visor down and peered in the mirror. "Wow. I look like crap." She tried to adjust her makeup and took a deep breath. "Well, this is not a good way to enter the Witches Council. Look at us. I'm puffy-eyed, and you look sad."

"By the time we get to the top of this massive drive, we'll look fine. Come on. United front."

She turned and smiled. "United front."

***

The atmosphere in Oswald's meeting room seemed to be frostier than the last, and Avery looked around the table, trying to get a feel for who would be allies.

The room was dark. The clouds were gathering outside and the evening light was dim. A few lamps brightened dark corners, candles were lit down the centre of the table, and incense smoke was unfurling on the air, giving everything a slightly hazy quality.

They had arrived a few minutes late, so everyone was already seated around the long table, engaged in muted small talk. Oswald had greeted Reuben enthusiastically and found an extra chair for him, and Avery and Reuben now sat together towards the end of the table, just inside the door to the room. Oswald was again wearing a velvet jacket, this time with plaid trousers, and Reuben raised a questioning eyebrow at her and glanced towards Oswald's clothes. Avery flashed him a warning with her eyes and hissed, "Behave."

Claudia, the older witch from Perranporth, gave Avery a welcoming smile, as did Eve, the witch from St Ives with the dreadlocks who'd been so friendly at the last meeting, and Avery started to relax. Caspian merely narrowed his eyes at both of them and gave a barely-there nod. If Avery didn't know better, she thought that nod almost denoted grudging respect. But she must be imagining things. Zane, the witch from Bodmin, and Mariah from Looe, were seated either side of him in a show of solidarity, and they barely glanced at her.

Genevieve was once more seated at the head of the table, authority emanating from her in waves. Her long hair was loose tonight, and it cascaded down her back, softening her sharp, refined features. "Right, let's get on with it," she said, the softness of her Irish lilt belying her brusque manner. "There have been three deaths in a very short time, and all of them seem to be the result of spirits or Mermaids." She turned her piercing gaze to Avery, her glance brushing across Reuben. "What happened in All Souls?"

Avery explained about the spirits she had seen escaping from the dimensional doorway, James asking for help and using the ghost-hunters, but held back about the thermal imaging for now. She had every intention of telling them, but wanted to see what the general consensus was first.

Genevieve frowned. "You didn't mention these escaping spirits before. Why not?"

Every single witch around the table was focussed on her, and Avery felt a little embarrassed. "If I'm honest, I forgot about them with everything else that had happened. We were fighting for our lives that night. It was chaotic, crazy—the escaping spirits seemed the least of our worries with that enormous demon in the room. And I was spirit walking at the time. I had to get back into my own body."

"Perhaps," Rasmus said, his rasping voice slightly impatient, "this would be a good time for us to learn what happened that night. We didn't fully talk about it last time. I'd like to know."

"I agree," Eve said, smiling with encouragement. "We all know you had to break the binding, but we have no idea how. What happened?"

"You don't have to discuss this." Genevieve gave a warning glance around the table before looking at Avery and Reuben again. "Our magic and our rituals are private."

"I think we're fine with it," Avery said, looking at Reuben, who nodded in agreement. She saw Caspian shuffle uncomfortably, but ignored him. "I'll try and summarise the lead up. Things got complicated." She relayed the whole story as best as she could, and then described the events that led to them using Helena in her body, and the ritual. She held back from the specifics of the spell—she knew what Genevieve meant. Spells were power, and sharing the details wasn't in their best interests. Witches weren't averse to stealing magic to gain power, Caspian's family was proof of that, but she told them enough to understand the set up. By the time she'd finished relaying the events at Faversham Central, there were more than a few open mouths around the table, and Caspian was seething.

A chorus of exclamations, general swearing, and a huge amount of sympathy and understanding flooded the room. Avery glanced at Reuben in surprise and a smile crept across his face.

Eve's voice broke through the noise. "I had no idea that things were so complicated and dangerous, Avery. I'm sorry you had to deal with that. And Reuben, please accept my sympathies for Gil's death." She shot a look of pure venom at Caspian. "What were you thinking? It's outrageous that you should ever put another witch in such a position. You're a disgrace. I had no idea that things were so bad." Eve then rounded on Genevieve. "Why didn't you explain this before? You gave us a very watered-down explanation of events."

"I didn't know the full details," Genevieve explained, not looking completely surprised at the annoyed faces around the table, but also uncomfortable at the attention.

Avery suspected that was why Genevieve has never asked them for specifics, and didn't give her the opportunity to share the last time. The sympathy she now felt was enormous. She risked a glance at Caspian, and found he was staring at her with grim respect and a challenge flashing in his eyes.

Caspian turned to Eve; he knew he had to make public amends. "You're right, Eve. I and my family must take responsibilities for our actions." Caspian turned back to Reuben and Avery. "We were put in a difficult position by my father. And Reuben, I meant what I said—I did not intend to kill Gil. I'm sorry."

"I'm afraid I really don't believe that, Caspian," Reuben said softly. "Remember, you nearly pulled my family's mausoleum down on my head. Your father cannot accept all the blame. But, I will move on from this, if you can."

Avery tried to hide the shock from her expression. She could not believe Reuben had just said that. She reached her hand under the table, found Reuben's hand and squeezed it, feeling him return the gesture.

Avery had the satisfaction of seeing Caspian's shocked reaction, too. He nodded. "Of course."

For the next five minutes, the table buzzed with questions, either for Avery, Reuben and Caspian, or chatter to each other, and then Genevieve called them to order. "Although this has been very illuminating, I think we should discuss the next death. Caspian, I understand you had a similar experience in St Luke's Church?"

He nodded. "Yes. Another death, another spirit." Caspian relayed the story of the verger's death. "It's almost identical, and that means even more police interest. Your friend, Newton, has already been asking too many questions," Caspian sneered.

Avery tried to bite back a retort. Caspian could not help himself. His sneer was on default. Reuben was not so polite. Their temporary cease-fire was over swiftly.

"He's a detective, that's his job," Reuben shot back. "You should be grateful he understands about this—us—or things would be a lot worse."

"Is that right?" Caspian said, his eyes hard. "So glad he's looking out for *us*. I'd rather he keep his nose out of Harecombe business altogether."

"Enough," Genevieve said, her voice icy. "The police are a necessity. Reuben is right. Better Newton than anyone else. And the death at sea?" she said, turning to Oswald.

"No signs of suspicious activity as far as human intervention goes. The crew are bewildered and understandably upset. Ulysses was able to chat with them. They trust him."

Avery wondered who Ulysses was, but fortunately, Claudia saw her confusion. "Ulysses is the other witch in Mevagissey."

Oswald nodded. "He has strong water elemental magic, and has his own boat. The sailors and fisherman are used to him being around. Of course, they have no idea he's a witch."

"And what does he think of the possibility of Mermaids or Sirens?" Genevieve asked.

"He thinks Mermaids are involved. In fact," Oswald paused and looked around the table. "He is convinced that some are already on land."

Genevieve gripped the table and leaned forward. "What makes him think that?"

"At the moment it's just instinct, but I don't doubt it. He has *very* good instincts," Oswald said.

"Has he any suggestions for what we should do?"

Oswald shook his head. "Not at present, other than to be watchful, and look for unusual activity, especially among men."

Genevieve glanced around the room. "Any other incidents?"

The general feedback seemed to be more wayward spirits, and Genevieve dropped her shoulders and sat back. "So, any suggestions about the spirits in All Souls and St Luke's?"

Avery was about to speak, but Caspian beat her to it. "These spirits broke out of the other dimension, the spirit dimension. That means they are strong, and getting stronger. They seem to be feeding on these bodies."

"I agree," Avery said. "From the brief glance I had at Harry's body, the verger appeared to be drained, and many bones were broken. We wonder if that's why the spirit was so strong when we encountered it in the church."

Eve leaned forward. "What makes you think it's stronger?"

"James, the vicar, said he had only been aware of its presence before. It was watchful, and obviously creepy, but not threatening. Harry's death was a shock for many reasons." Avery shrugged and looked at Reuben. "I must admit, I didn't think spirits could manifest quite so strongly. But we also had an encounter with quite a few ghosts up at the castle grounds, and they were also strong."

"You didn't mention that," Genevieve said, frowning. "When did that happen?"

"Just after the last meeting," Avery said. "The ghosts at White Haven Castle seemed to be re-enacting some kind of event."

Reuben agreed. "It was as if the magical surge we released had jolted them into action again. But they were almost physical...it took a lot for us to banish them. That's where we met the ghost-hunters."

Caspian frowned. "Are you actually trying to advertise the fact that you're witches?"

Avery glared at him. "Stop being a drama queen, Caspian." A few witches smirked and then tried to hide it. "They saw the spirits and would have been hurt if we hadn't intervened. They're trustworthy. In fact, they've also been helpful." She looked around the table, gauging everyone's reaction. "They managed to film the spirit in All Souls with a thermal imaging camera."

Everyone leaned forward now, some frowning, some curious, and the silence around the table seemed to intensify.

"And?" Genevieve asked.

Avery glanced at Reuben, and he nodded almost imperceptibly. "The image appears to be of a large, winged spirit. It rushed down from the vaulted roof to us, and then disappeared."

"Winged?" Rasmus questioned, eyebrows raised. "Like an angel?"

"Or a demon," Claudia said. "They come in many forms."

The black witch that Avery remembered from the first meeting spoke for the first time, his deep voice as rich as treacle. "Or, it could be a Nephilim."

Reuben looked as puzzled as Avery. "What's a Nephilim?"

"They are the children of fallen angels who fled from heaven and mated with human women. They were supposedly giants who dominated other men."

Zane, the weasel-faced witch sitting next to Caspian, looked and sounded annoyed. "That's a Christian myth, Jasper."

Jasper laughed, incredulous, and he spread his hands wide. "Have you learned nothing, Zane? So are angels and demons, but they exist, don't they? As do Mermaids, Sirens, ghosts, Poltergeists, Vampires, shape-shifters, witches, and all manner of other strange, mythical creatures that either exist here or in other dimensions. And there are still other creatures, according to other myths. Many of these spirits or creatures are the same the world over.

It's just that they are named differently according to each culture. We were talking about the Children of Llyr the other day. A Celtic myth, but they exist nonetheless."

Zane looked down at the table, but Avery could tell he was angry at being lectured.

"Jasper, what made you suggest Nephilim?" Avery asked, immediately liking him. She estimated he was in his thirties, his dark hair shorn close to his scalp, clean shaven, and wearing a smart blue shirt, open at the neck.

"I research myths and legends, and the legends suggest that the Nephilim were once winged, which makes sense as the children of angels, but they walked among men without them. As I said, they were tall and powerful. It is suggested by some that God sent the deluge to rid the world of them once and for all. And that is the last time they walked the Earth."

"The deluge?"

"The Flood. There's one in every world myth. The one Noah had to build the ark for."

Avery's head was spinning. Old myths of creation, and monsters that walked among men. But, she reflected, some people considered witches to be monsters.

"Were they giants, or just tall?" Reuben asked.

Jasper shrugged. "It's hard to say. Adults were much shorter centuries ago. Poor diet, harder life, shorter life expectancies. Anything approaching six feet would be seen as giant."

"And why did God want to rid the Earth of them, according to myth?" Avery asked.

"Because they were violent, they dominated men, and more importantly, the Earth was not where they should be. They were the mixed offspring of mortal and immortal. It was considered an abhorrence. But, many things are considered to be abhorrent, and they still exist. *We* know this to be true. But humans do not like to accept the stranger things that walk among us. That's why there are so many fairy tales and myths—to try to explain the inexplicable. We must not be so blind." Jasper allowed himself a wry smile.

Jasper was right. As much as witches kept to their own kind, so did other creatures, but they all knew they existed, even if they didn't mix.

"Avery," Genevieve asked, "would your friends the ghost-hunters be interested in setting up their investigations at St Luke's?"

"No!" Caspian exclaimed. "I forbid them to get involved."

"You are in no place to forbid anything," Genevieve said forcefully, causing Caspian to look furious, again. "We need to know if this is the same type of spirit, and if they're linked to what happened beneath All Souls. I hold you partially responsible, and therefore you will cooperate. Avery?"

"I'm sure they'll be happy to help." *Ben would probably give his right arm to get in that church.*

"Good. Arrange it. And Caspian, be helpful, or you'll find yourself banned from the Council."

11

"In light of what we now think this spirit may be, is it wise you try to speak to it?" Newton asked.

Newton, Briar, Alex, and Avery were sitting around a small table in the back room of The Wayward Son; they had almost finished eating, and Newton was frowning over his pint.

"Yes, it's still important. Nephilim or not, it's still a spirit, and we might be able to find out something," Alex insisted before he almost inhaled his final forkful of rare steak.

Briar sighed. "It is risky, I know what you mean, Newton. But I also agree with Avery and Alex. It would be good to try to get some insight into what's going on."

"But two spirits, two churches, two deaths. It's *very* risky. And since the deaths, they've been locked in by your spells. They might be feeling pretty angry. If they experience any kind of emotion," Newton said, trying to be rational.

Avery smiled and pushed her empty plate away. Newton's protective instincts were strong, and she had a feeling that although some of this was due to his profession, it was also because they were friends now. And on the positive side, Alex and Newton's initial testosterone battles seemed to have settled down.

"We'll protect ourselves well, I promise." Avery said, trying to reassure him.

Alex nodded. "Salt circle, spells, the whole thing. Trust us."

Newton continued to frown. "I don't want any more deaths."

"Neither do I. Especially mine. Or of course Avery's," Alex said with a wink.

"Nice to know, thanks," Avery said.

"Are you going now?" Briar asked, sipping her white wine.

"Half an hour or so," Avery explained. "James will meet us at the entrance and let us in. We wanted to make sure he felt involved in this. But, he stays outside."

"How did you explain that one," Newton asked, curious.

"I said Alex had psychic abilities, as part of his talent for exorcism. He bought it," Avery said with a shrug. "And it is true—I just omitted the witch part."

"Did you see the headlines in the local paper this morning?" Briar asked.

Avery sighed and quoted the headline. "*Unnatural Death at All Souls. Is a violent ghost to blame?* How do they hear about these things?"

Newton answered. "Unfortunately, the press hang around police stations and hospitals, and talk to ambulance staff. They pick up stuff we don't want them to know. If anyone gets in touch with you, deny everything. I've told Ben the same thing."

"I bet it would be good publicity for Ben," Briar said.

"It might well be, but I've ordered him to keep his head down for now."

"Well, he's pretty excited about going to St Luke's in Harecombe," Avery said, recalling their earlier conversation. "Caspian is not."

"I like this Genevieve woman," Alex declared. "She doesn't put up with Caspian's shit."

"Not many do, actually," Avery said, thinking about the previous night's meeting. "It was interesting going to the meeting again. I got more of a feel for the atmosphere and associations. Who likes who, who doesn't. While Caspian has a couple of allies, most people are pretty indifferent, if not annoyed with him. I just get the general impression that everyone's over his grand pretensions. Oswald, Claudia, Genevieve, and Rasmus are too old and too wise to put up with him. I think it was good taking Reuben, too. He's less annoyed now. And of course, we had an opportunity to share what *did* happen recently. They had no idea."

"Well done," Briar said, smiling brightly. "I knew you'd do a great job. And I'm glad Reuben enjoyed it, too."

"He really did," Avery agreed. "It gave him perspective, and me too. I know what our place is in all this now. We really are part of a much bigger thing. Our town, or coven, has been in the dark about so much. No wonder our ancestors left town and abandoned witchcraft. I think it would have been less likely if they'd been part of a bigger community. It explains a lot," she mused.

"Just think," Briar said, "my family may never have left, or El's."

"At least you're back now," Newton said, "and hopefully not planning to leave again."

Avery suppressed a smile as she saw Briar's slightly startled expression. "Absolutely not, Newton. Especially with my shop doing so well."

"Good," he said, swiftly downing his pint. "Must be time for another."

***

James met Avery and Alex at the side door to the church. In the few days since they'd seen him, he looked as if he'd aged by several years.

"Are you all right?" Avery asked, as she watched him fiddle with the keys. Not that they needed them, but they couldn't tell James that.

"Not really. Harry is dead in extremely suspicious circumstances, the church is locked down, and now the Bishop's becoming involved." He looked up, harassed. "Did you see that headline?"

"We did," Alex said sympathetically. "In a few months, this will be old news. Don't worry."

"But where do I see my congregation? Can I come in now, just to see what's going on?"

"No," Alex said firmly. He leaned against the door frame, his arms crossed. "It's too dangerous."

"You can't possibly believe it really was the spirit?" James asked, although doubt filled his eyes.

Avery felt sorry for him. Although they'd all been together when the spirit attacked, James was clearly trying to play the whole thing down. It wasn't unusual. To admit that there was a violent spirit in the church was one step too many for some. Although James had been willing to investigate, the proof now seemed daunting.

"James, let us do what we need to. Who knows, it may have gone?" Avery said, trying to be positive, even though she didn't believe it for a second.

"But if it's not? How long could this take? This Bishop could well insist we re-open."

"We have no idea how long. And if the Bishop does insist, all future deaths will be on his head. Now, can we go in please?" Alex said, pointing at the keys that James still held loosely in his hands.

"What are you going to do?"

"I come from a long line of psychics," Alex explained. "I'm going to try and communicate with it, that's all."

James paused for a second, and then opened the door. Alex and Avery slipped inside, hefting their backpacks with them.

Avery turned to thank him, blocking the doorway. "Thanks. Can you give me a key? We'll lock ourselves in and return the key later."

"I can wait."

"Please don't. Go home, relax. We'll see you soon."

James looked as if he would argue, but then turned and disappeared, his head down and shoulders bowed. He looked defeated, as if every ounce of his energy had been sucked from him. And maybe also his faith. *James would be okay*, she reassured herself. *At least he wasn't a zealot.*

Avery carefully locked the door, leaving the key in the lock, and turned to find Alex had already gone. She looked around and concentrated, feeling with her magic to see if she could detect anything, but the church felt eerily silent. It smelt musty after days of being locked up, and a heavy dampness hung on the air.

She headed down the corridor and found Alex in the nave, already setting up in the space in front of the altar, the noises he made echoing sullenly around the church. "Feel anything?"

"Nope, you?"

"No." Avery paced around, feeling for changes in temperature, or electrical static and pools of energy. She looked at the vaulted roof. "Weird, nothing at all. You'd think we'd feel *something*."

Alex pulled the salt from his bag and poured it out on the floor, making a large circle, big enough for him and Avery to sit in. "We need to encourage it to appear. Come on, jump in."

Avery stepped inside, carrying the bags with her. She pulled out twelve candles, all black for protection, and placed four of them at the compass points, and the rest in between all along the inner edge of the circle of salt, lighting them with a spark from her fingers. Then, while Alex uncovered the heavy crystal ball, she pulled a bundle of incense out, the combination designed to aid with communication and concentration.

She ran the ends of the incense through the flames and watched them spark in an even red glow, and the spicy-sweet smell of incense filled the air; along with the soft light of the candles, Avery felt herself begin to relax and her senses heighten. Her magic started to build as she began to focus in this cavernous space.

She pulled a heavy cotton scarf from her bag, folded it, and then sat cross-legged, watching Alex prepare himself.

Aware he was being watched, he looked up and smiled, his teeth gleaming in the dusky light of the church. The last rays of the sun were setting behind him and falling through the stained glass windows, casting a rosy glow around them. "Glad you're here, Avery."

"I wouldn't miss it," she said, her pulse quickening. She wasn't sure if it was because of the situation or just him. Probably just him. Every time he looked at her she felt his gaze like a caress across her skin.

"We should protect the circle first."

"You lead," she said, as he took her hands in his warm, strong grip. Together they uttered an invocation, reminding her of the first time they had done this together in her attic.

Avery felt a rush of energy and the magic of the spell soared around them, effectively sealing them within its protective embrace. The candles flared, and as the daylight diminished, the church filled with shadows.

And then she felt something stir in the blackness.

A shiver ran across her skin, which was not caused by Alex. "Can you feel it?"

He nodded, scanning the room. "I can't pinpoint where it is."

"No, me neither. It hasn't gathered itself yet."

"It feels old."

Avery reconsidered the spell she'd suggested as a way of communicating, and doubted herself. "Maybe bringing the crystal ball was pointless. If it's here, you won't need it."

"I'll need it," Alex assured her, still searching the room. "It will help me focus."

"What if it's too strong and hurts your mind?"

"You'll have to break the connection."

"How?" she said, worry flooding through her.

"You'll think of something," he said, his calm voice soothing her.

Now that they were sitting there, the candles blazing, with something manifesting in the dark, she realised how ill-conceived their plan was, and how vulnerable they were.

This spirit had killed a man.

Alex seemed to have no such doubts as he confidently reached forward to the crystal ball sitting between them and grasped it with both hands, closed his eyes, and began the spell.

Avery felt his power build and watched the ball at the same time as she sensed movement of the spirit around them. It had drawn closer and she felt a prickle between her shoulder blades. She fought the compulsion to turn around, and continued to watch the crystal ball. For a few seconds nothing much seemed to happen; she could see the distorted images of Alex's crossed legs though the glass, but then it started to darken, and a swirl of smoke filled the centre, until it was completely opaque.

Alex's chanting slowed and he opened his eyes, staring into the depths of the ball. His pupils looked huge, his skin burnished in the light of the candles, and his hair fell around his face, giving him the look of a mystic. "Show yourself to me," he commanded, his voice lowered.

The air seemed to thicken around them, and Avery had never felt so thankful to be within the circle.

Alex continued. "Tell me what you want." The ball within his hands was now impenetrable, and while Avery could see nothing, Alex stared into it, frowning. "Talk to me. You bring fear and death. What do you want?"

Sparks appeared within the smoky interior, and Alex gripped it harder, his knuckles whitening. "That is not possible," he said. "This is not your dimension. Leave! Find peace."

Avery was startled. Alex must be talking to it. She felt the spirit draw closer, circling them slowly, and Avery looked up, trying to see beyond the bright bloom of candlelight into the darkness beyond. For a second she thought she saw something and her heart rate rocketed. The protection spell responded and the flames from the candles flared, shooting several feet into the air to create a wall of fire around them. Immediately the spirit fell back, and it seemed as if there were footfalls in the darkness.

Alex continued to talk in his low monotone, reasoning and coaxing. "Tell me what you are. How many came with you?"

She heard another sound like a sigh, something she couldn't quite identify, and the ball flickered with light again. Alex became more insistent. "Let us help you return, you do not belong here."

Avery watched, mesmerised as the lightshow within intensified, like small lightning strikes hitting the glass. She didn't need Alex to tell her that the spirit was angry, she could feel it. It wanted to escape, but Alex's will was too strong.

Suddenly, the spirit surged, the white light within the ball became blinding, and Avery looked away, but Alex didn't move. He was transfixed, his hands like claws around the glass.

"Alex!" Avery shouted. "Release it, *now!*"

But Alex wouldn't, or couldn't. Was it drawing power from Alex? He wasn't speaking anymore; instead, he seemed locked in his own private battle.

Crap. This was just what they'd feared. If Avery also touched the ball, would she become locked within it, too? Instead, she reached over and held Alex's face within her hands, talking to him urgently but softly.

Nothing happened. The light grew brighter, the spirit grew stronger, and Alex's hands started to shake.

She must destroy the ball.

Avery said the first suitable spell that came to mind, holding her hands above the ball, but not touching it, and sent a powerful shot of energy down through the crystal like a punch. It shattered, chunks of glass flying out in all directions, and Alex fell forward into Avery's lap.

Alex's weight pinned her to the floor. She could see blood trickling down his arms from where he'd been cut. The smell of blood filled the air, and Avery bit back her fear. The circle would protect them. The spirit beyond the flames weakened suddenly, as if a howling wind had suddenly stopped, but she still felt it watching them, and then a second later it vanished, and the church was empty again.

"Alex, wake up," she said, shaking him violently. They needed to get out of there before it came back. "Wake up, now!" She sent a burst of energy across his skin and she felt him stir. He groaned and she sighed in relief. "Alex, are you okay?"

He grunted something she didn't understand.

"Sorry, I didn't get that, but you're alive, so that's good. We need to get out of here." She tried to lift him up, but he was a dead weight. "Alex, please. That thing has gone. We need to go before it comes back."

He rolled his head slightly, his eyes tightly closed, muttering something in a guttural language she didn't understand. *What the hell was going on?*

"Stop being funny. I can't understand you."

Alex sat up suddenly, his eyes opened, and Avery almost shouted with shock. His eyes were white and blinking blindly as he turned his head. His voice rose in panic, and then he fell forward again, the words tumbling out one after another. *Damn.* She had to get him to Briar.

"It's okay, take deep breaths," she said, trying to calm him with her most soothing voice. She stroked his arms, trying to avoid the shattered glass that lay between them, but he tried to throw her off, still muttering, becoming almost hysterical. *Was he possessed?*

She knew a few healing spells, and she tried one then. For a few anxious seconds that felt like hours, she watched him uneasily, hearing the old building settle around them; the squeak and crack of old wood, the eddy of a breeze from ill-fitted windows. And then she felt Alex start to relax, his words slowing.

"Okay. Time to go." She eased away, and started to collect their few belongings, placing them into their packs. She wanted to turn the lights on, but was worried it would damage Alex's eyes even more, so she conjured a witch light before extinguishing the candles. She used a spell to collect the glass from the crystal ball, and the pieces hung in the air before she dropped them into a pocket.

Alex groaned as she hauled him to his feet. "Come on, time to see Briar."

12

Before they headed to Briar's house, Avery needed to return the key to the church. The vicarage was an eighteenth-century house, a few steps from the church. She left Alex sitting in her van, still muttering to himself, and rocking gently backwards and forwards. She didn't want to leave him, but she had to return the key, so she headed up the path to James's front door.

James appeared in seconds, his eyes filled with questions. "What happened? Did you get rid of it?"

Avery shook her head. "We weren't trying to, James. We were trying to find out what it is."

"And did you?"

"I don't know yet. I need to ask Alex." She hesitated. "He's not very well at the moment. I need to take him to a friend."

"Can I see him?" he asked anxiously.

"Not now. Look, I know you're worried, but we need to be careful. Do not go back in that church—whatever the Bishop says."

He looked at the floor for a few seconds, and then looked her in the eye. "Do you believe in the Devil?"

"I believe in many things. The world is not as black and white as some would like it to be. Do you?"

"I believe in God. I believe he cast out his brother angel, and I believe he tries to lure us into evil."

Avery nodded, not sure where James was going with this. "Well, you're a vicar, that figures." *Wow. That sounded lame.*

"Is he in my church, Avery?"

She stared at him for a second. "The Devil?"

"Is he?" he repeated.

"No, I'm pretty sure it's not the Devil, but I don't know what it is yet."

James sighed and passed a hand over his face. Avery could hear the TV in the background, and someone talking. James had a family and a congregation to worry about. Avery felt as if the safety of the whole town rested on her shoulders.

"I have to go. Stay safe, and I'll be in touch."

***

Alex started to become agitated again on the drive, and Avery pulled over and managed to subdue him again, and then made a quick call to Briar to check that she was in. Avery was relieved it was a short trip. By the time they arrived at Briar's small cottage it was after eleven o'clock, but Briar met them at the door, and led them into the small conservatory at the back where they had eaten dinner only weeks before.

The walls of the conservatory were mainly glass in wooden frames, the lower half solid wood. A sagging couch sat under one of the long windows, stacked with cushions, and she led Alex to it.

Rattan blinds covered the windows, but the double doors were ajar, letting in a warm night breeze. Candles filled the space, and incense coiled on the air. Books and papers were stacked on the long wooden table, and it was clear Briar had been working there. An old, battered case that she used for transporting her herbs, gems, and potions was sitting on the table, open in readiness, her grimoires next to it.

"What happened?" Briar asked, once Alex was lying down.

"Well, it worked. Alex could speak to it, I think. I have no idea what it said," Avery explained. "But then something happened. The crystal ball went white and Alex just stared into it. I had to destroy the ball to release him, and now he's talking in some strange language, and his eyes…" She paused as he opened his eyes and started to yell, and Briar cried out in surprise.

"Avery, what the hell?"

Avery could feel herself welling up now that she was with Briar and her adrenaline was wearing off. "I don't know. I managed to subdue him, but the spell doesn't hold for long. Is he possessed?"

"I'm not sure until I examine him. Have you got your phone?"

When Avery nodded, she said, "Start recording, I want to listen to what he's saying properly later."

"That's a brilliant idea," Avery said, pulling her phone from her bag. She sat on the floor and leaned closer to Alex, trying not to get in Briar's way, and then pressed record.

Although they had managed to deposit Alex on the sofa, he was far from settled. He twitched all over, his hands were clenched tight, and he continued to chant and groan, a sheen of sweat visible on his face. Avery watched Briar's deft hands moving over his forehead, and then she did as Avery had done, taking his head within her hands. Every now and again she turned to her case to collect various stones and herbs. She placed a large amethyst on Alex's forehead, held her hand on it, and started a spell, her lips moving quickly.

Avery tried to tune out everything else and just listened to Alex, the way his breath was rushed and shallow, the words falling from his mouth in a torrent. She realised as she sat quietly that he was repeating the same thing, over and over again, but she couldn't work out what it was. Maybe she should call Genevieve or Rasmus, or Oswald. They were older, more experienced. They should know what to do. But as she watched Briar, Avery's thoughts calmed, too. Avery could feel her magic binding around Alex, drawing out whatever it was that was inflaming his brain.

Alex's face turned white and for a brief second he looked terrified, his eyes staring and fixed, and then his eyes closed and he fell into a deep sleep, his head falling to one side as his breathing became deeper and slower.

Avery released a long-held breath she hadn't even realised she was keeping in, and leaned her head on Alex's arm, comforted by his warmth. Exhaustion now washed through her, and felt she could sleep for a week, but there was more to do. She sat up and looked at Briar, taking in her appearance properly since she'd arrived with Alex.

Briar's long hair was tied up loosely on top of her head, and stray strands tumbled down on either side of her face. Her face was stripped of makeup and she looked young and fresh-faced. She was wearing some loose cotton trousers and a t-shirt and it looked like she was ready to go to bed. "Sorry, Briar. I didn't mean to disturb your evening."

Briar pursed her lips. "Don't apologise, you know you can come anytime. And besides, I was doing some reading in here. You didn't wake me up."

"I'm just relieved you're here. You might have still been at the pub, or with Newton."

"He's gone home—he's really busy at work right now. So what happened?"

Avery relayed as succinctly as possible what had happened in the Church. "It was super scary. I could feel it prowling round us." She changed tack. "Is it over? Have you cured him?"

Briar shook her head. "I doubt it. I've just calmed him enough to relax for now. Do you know what language that was?"

"No. His eyes. Is that permanent?" Avery felt her chest tighten with fear. "Is he blind?"

Briar placed a hand on Avery's arm. "I don't know. It's hard to say until we understand what really happened tonight. Sometimes, when the eyes turn white, it denotes the Seer—a vision state. I'm hoping it's that. The crystal ball will intensify such things, and it sounds as if the spirit, or whatever it was, trapped his gaze within the ball. The spell I've used is fairly general, just to calm him for now, but there's another spell I need to check."

Briar rose swiftly to her feet and started searching through her grimoire, while Avery pulled a floor cushion over and made herself comfortable on it, turning her attention back to Alex. She took his warm, strong hand in her own, and stroked it as she watched him breathe. His colour had come back, and he looked healthier in the warm light of the candles. His hair was loose, and stubble grazed his chin and cheeks. She'd always thought of Alex as being unassailable. He was so strong and his magic so powerful, she'd always believed that nothing would get the better of him. And now look at him. She reached out and laid a hand on his cheek. All she wanted him to do was wake up, so she could hold him and tell him how much he meant to her. He would be okay. He had to be.

Avery heard Briar whisper a spell behind her, and heard the pages of the grimoire swiftly turn. A finding spell, similar to one she'd used before.

"There it is," Briar exclaimed triumphantly.

Avery turned. "What?"

"A spell to rid the mind of a forceful vision. It's not perfect, but if I tweak it…"

Her voice faded as she started to assemble the spell's ingredients, and Avery turned back to Alex and thought about the events of the night.

The spirit was old and powerful. It had wings, like an angel or the devil. She paused as she thought of James's question. It wasn't the Devil. Not if there were two or more of them. A shudder ran through her as she thought of the spirit's watchful presence stalking the outside of the circle. *What did it want?*

A cool breeze eddied through the room, and she shivered, looking for a blanket. She rose to her feet, and pulled the door shut. "Do you mind if I close it, Briar?"

Briar shook her head and went back to her spell. Avery locked them in, pulled a blanket over Alex, and then grabbed one to wrap around her shoulders, sitting on the floor cushion again. She noticed her phone on the floor. *The recording. What would it say?*

She played the recording at a low volume so as not to disturb Briar, holding it close to her ear. The words were clear enough, but they meant nothing to her. However, there was a pattern to them. She had been right earlier. It was the same phrase repeated over and over again. *Was there a spell she could use to help her understand it?* She ran through the spells she knew, but none of them would work on this. However, there may well be something in either her own or one of the other grimoires. If—no, *when*—Alex awoke, maybe he would know.

Avery's throat felt like sandpaper. *I need a drink.* Leaving Alex sleeping, and Briar working on her spell, she headed to the kitchen and turned the kettle on. After making chamomile tea, in a vain effort to calm her racing mind, she headed to the living room and idly flicked on the TV, scrolling to the news. She needed a distraction. She collapsed on the couch, filtering through the events in her mind. The Witches Council, the lights in the sea, the threat of Mermaids, the restless ghosts, the church spirits, and the deaths. The magic they had released, their magic, had created so much unforeseen trouble. And then a news bulletin flashed across the screen and she stared in horror.

There had been yet another death, in another church in St Just.

A young woman had been in the church that evening to clean, and the vicar had found her dead. There were no details on how she had died, just the death, but it was clear to Avery that this death was linked to the others.

Could this night get any worse?

"Avery!" Briar's voice broke her reverie, and she ran through to the conservatory.

"What? Is Alex okay?"

"No, but he's talking again."

Alex was still lying down but he was restless beneath his blanket, and half of it was on the floor. A sweat had broken out again on his face, and his eyes were open wide, a wild look to them. His eyes were still completely white.

Avery ran over and held his hand. "It's okay, Alex, you're fine. You're not in danger. Can you hear me?"

Alex's grip was tight on her hand, but there was no hint of recognition in his behaviour.

"I have a potion ready, so it's good that he's awake again," Briar said. "Help him sit up, or even just raise his head," she directed, seeing Avery struggle with him.

Briar knelt next to Avery, holding a small chalice with a thimbleful of liquid in it. With Avery supporting Alex's head, Briar tipped the liquid into his mouth, one dribble at a time, and as he drank, Briar said a spell.

As soon as the spell was completed he fell back, unconscious, and Briar placed a lapis lazuli gemstone on each closed eye. "Good." She smiled at Avery. "That should do it. Now we let him sleep. I'm pretty sure that he's been gripped by a powerful image or vision. His mind is trying to process it, probably replaying it over and over again. This spell will banish it for good—hopefully without him forgetting it completely."

"Thank you, Briar." Avery said, hugging her. "I was so scared. But," she hesitated a moment. "There's been another death. In St Just."

Briar's triumphant expression faded. "There'll be more, Avery. I can feel it. The earth itself is unsettled…it trembles. This is far from over."

13

It was a long night.

Briar had offered Avery a bed, but she didn't want to be so far from Alex, so, like Briar, she slept on one of the sofas in the lounge. Unfortunately, the lounge was small and one sofa was only a two-seater, which Briar insisted on having because she was shorter, but they both hardly slept anyway, woken every hour by an alarm to check on Alex. Not that they really slept in between either.

By the time dawn arrived, Avery felt grubby, her neck ached, and her eyes were gritty. But Alex was better. His breathing was regular and deep, and he had rolled over in the night, pulling the blanket close. The stones had slipped off his head and eyes and Briar collected them up. She smiled at Avery. "I'm pretty sure this is a normal sleep now, Avery. You can go if you want."

"No. Dan will open up. What will you do?"

"My shop can stay closed for a couple of hours," she said, reassuring her. "Let's have some breakfast and coffee."

"Really strong coffee," Avery said, blinking back tiredness.

Briar headed for the fridge. "And really crispy bacon. And eggs. And crusty bread."

Briar had only just brewed the coffee, and the smell of bacon was filling the air, when there was a knock at the door. Briar raised an eyebrow at Avery. "I can feel him from here. Can you?"

"Not like you can, but–" she raised her head and called the air to her, filtering the smells of the morning, "I smell Newton, and determination. I'll go let him in."

When Avery opened the door, Newton looked at her in shock. "What are you doing here?"

"Long story. Come in," she said, turning and heading into the kitchen, Newton on her heels.

"Bacon!" he said, his eyes gleaming. Avery wasn't sure if it was the smell of bacon or the sight of Briar that had given him the bounce in his step. "Morning, Briar. How much you got there?"

She smiled at him over her shoulder. "I've got plenty. Want some?"

"Yes, please. I left the house in a rush, but suddenly I'm hungry."

He reached over to grab the coffee pot, searching in the cupboard above for a mug at the same time, and Avery tried to subdue a smirk as she realised just how familiar Newton was with Briar's kitchen. Despite the early hour, he had dressed with care. His dark grey suit and light grey shirt were pristine, and he smelt of shower gel and was clean-shaven. *Someone was making an effort.* Although, to be fair, he was always impeccably dressed for work.

Avery leaned against the kitchen units. "Well, you're here early and quite jaunty."

"Not jaunty. I'm clinging to normality like a mad man." He leaned back on the opposite counter, watching her. "You look like death. What happened?"

Avery ran her hands self-consciously through her hair, and whispered the tiniest of spells to give herself a little beautification. *Vain? Maybe.* "We had a very unpleasant encounter last night with the spirit. Alex linked with it a little too strongly, so here we are."

Newton stood straighter. "Is he okay?"

"We think so, now. Thanks to Briar." Avery hesitated a second. "We saw the news late last night. There's been another death."

Newton exhaled loudly. "Yes. I was out until two this morning. It looks the same as the others."

"Two!" Briar exclaimed. "And you're up already?"

"It's the job, Briar. So, another broken body, drained, pale, found in the nave of the St Andrew's Church in St Just. It's one of the oldest churches in the town, just like here and Harecombe." He paused for a second, thinking. "And there's no sign of a break-in, no stolen items, and according to the vicar, an uncanny sense of something strange in the church in the last few days."

Briar turned away from the cooker where she'd been preparing eggs and sipping her coffee. Her expression was bleak. "There'll be more. I can feel it in the earth, I told Avery last night. It's like the earth is trembling, from either fear or because power is stirring. I can't quite tell what yet. Maybe both." She looked at Avery. "Take some time if you can today, Avery. See if you feel change in the air."

Before Avery could answer, they heard the door to the sunroom open and suddenly Alex was leaning on the frame. "Do I smell bacon and coffee?"

Avery broke into a broad smile and rushed over, reaching up to hug him. "Alex! You're awake! Are you all right?" She looked at him carefully, relieved to see his eyes had returned to their normal dark chocolate brown. "You scared the shit out of me."

He hugged her, too, releasing her reluctantly. "I scared the shit out of myself, too. My mind was gripped by…something…" he trailed off.

"Coffee and breakfast first," Briar said decisively. "It's ready now, go sit," she commanded, shooing everyone into the sunroom.

Sitting at the wooden table with a strong coffee in her hands, Avery started to feel human again, especially now that Alex was all right. His experience certainly hadn't damaged his hunger; he ate like he hadn't been fed in months.

"Thanks, Briar," Avery said, finally finishing her bacon and egg sandwich. "That was awesome."

"Yeah, thanks Briar. But I have to get to work to investigate a murder, so tell me. What did you see last night?" Newton asked, narrowing his eyes at Alex.

Alex paused for a few seconds, gazing at the table while he gathered his thoughts. When he finally looked up, he sighed. "The spell worked. The crystal ball helped to focus on the spirit and provided a way for us to communicate. It didn't want to at first. It shied away, prowling around on the edge of my consciousness, until its curiosity got the better of it. I think the fact that we were locked within the protective circle annoyed it. So, I found out that it's old, thousands of years old, and it's been trapped beyond our plane for a long, long time. When we opened the door to their dimension, they saw their opportunity and forced their way out, as you saw, Avery. The rest of us were too engaged with the demon to notice."

"And I *was* spirit walking," Avery reminded him. "That allowed me to see things you couldn't."

"True. Anyway, unlike the other spirits there, they were powerful enough to break free. I don't know how many of them crossed. It wouldn't tell me at first. It liked having knowledge I didn't, I could tell."

Briar leaned on the table. "You were talking in some strange language last night we couldn't understand. Avery recorded it. It was as if you were repeating something over and over, like it was locked in your brain. Do you know what you were saying?"

Alex didn't answer straight away, instead picking up his cup and drinking more coffee.

"You found out something bad, didn't you?" Avery asked, her heart sinking into her stomach.

Alex met her eyes and nodded, and then glanced at the others. "I don't know if it's bad or good, but Jasper was right. It *is* one of the Nephilim. Or rather *they* are. No wonder it feels old. It's bloody ancient."

"So, what does this mean? What now?" Newton asked.

"I have no idea. It was curious as to what I was, what we were. It didn't like our power, but it respected us. And so, after this battle of the spirits, for want of a better word, it revealed its name."

"What do they want?" Avery asked. "I could sense you arguing with it."

"They want to return to what they see is their rightful place on Earth— to walk amongst men again."

"That's ridiculous," Newton said, colour draining from him. "They're old, they don't belong here."

"That's not what he thought," Alex explained.

"So why the deaths?" Avery asked, fearing she already knew why.

"They need the energy. They need more to make them corporeal."

"And why stay in the churches?" Briar asked.

"For our particular spirit, it was convenience, since it was where he escaped. But churches carry spiritual energy, which as we thought, is good to feed from. Plus, they're also generally quiet places. The others fled to find their own churches to lurk in."

"So, what were you saying that had been blazed on your brain?" Briar asked.

"We are the Nephilim, we are seven, and we will walk again. Try to stop us and you shall die."

***

When Avery got to work, all she wanted to do was crawl into bed and pretend last night had never happened, pretend one of the Nephilim did not inhabit her local church. At some point she would have to tell James, the vicar, but not now. She couldn't face it. To top it off, Sally had taken a few days of annual leave, as it was now the summer holidays and her kids were off school.

Dan was behind the main counter, his back to the room, leaning his tall frame over the music system when she walked in carrying two steaming lattes and two large, sticky pastries. He was wearing jeans and his university t-shirt, and he turned as she arrived, looked bright-eyed and rested. *Ugh.* That made Avery feel even worse.

Dan took a coffee appreciatively as the sounds of John Lee Hooker filled the room. "Cheers, Ave. You're up early." He looked confused. "You've already been out and it's barely nine. Are you really Avery Hamilton?"

She grinned, despite her crappy night. "Funny. I do get up early sometimes."

"Sure you do. You keep telling yourself that." He grabbed a pastry and took a bite. "So, go on. Why?"

Avery groaned and looked around to make sure the shop was still empty. "We had an eventful night. Alex and I were trying to communicate with a spirit and it gripped Alex in some sort of Seer state. Anyway, thanks to Briar, he's okay now."

"Wow. Your life is anything but boring lately. What spirit?"

She briefly considered not elaborating, but Dan knew what she was and what had happened beneath All Souls, so it seemed only fair to come clean. "I'm not sure how much Sally told you about the death at the church and the spirits I saw escaping when we released our magic—"

"I know it all," Dan said, interrupting her.

"Good. Well, one of the spirits is lurking in All Souls. It turns out that it—*he*—is a Nephilim."

Dan paused, mid-bite, and stared. "Isn't that some biblical something?"

"Yes," Avery said, and explained what it was. "There are seven of them, three deaths in three churches so far, and no doubt more to come. And we have no idea how to stop them. They're very powerful, far more than normal spirits. I need to talk to the Witches Council."

"I hate to tell you this, but there are more than three deaths, Avery. There were another two reported in breaking news only a few minutes ago. I heard it on the radio."

"What?" They must have been reported after she left Newton, or he'd have said so. "Where?"

"Bodmin and Perranporth."

"More old churches?"

"I think so. There weren't many details."

Avery's legs felt weak and she headed around the counter and sat on one of the chairs next to Dan. "This is awful."

Dan cradled his coffee as he watched her. "Yes, it is. Pretty scary, too. There must be a spell you can use, with all your juiced-up magic."

"There are lots of spells…it's just finding the right one."

"Isn't that what the Council is for? You all work together, pool your power. You're not alone, remember that." Dan smiled, trying to reassure her.

"I think I'm feeling very overwhelmed right now." She sipped her coffee again, enjoying the hit of caffeine.

"That's because it's big and it's new, but you'll get your head around it. You always do."

She smiled at him. "Thanks. I'm just tired, I think. Sleep will help."

"Guess who I saw yesterday?"

Avery considered him for a second. "Dylan?"

"Bingo! I saw at him at the Uni library. You've made quite an impression. All of you, actually."

"Have we?"

"Oh, yes," he nodded. "He tells me they're heading to St Luke's tonight."

"Yes. I'm going, too. I'm not leaving them alone with Caspian."

Dan nodded, relieved. "Good, I was hoping you'd say that. Now, go and catch up on some sleep, I'll manage here for a few hours on my own."

"Are you sure? Because that sounds wonderful."

"Yes. Come and relieve me for lunch."

Avery stood gratefully, walking towards the rear of the shop. But before she headed up the stairs to her flat, she strengthened the protective wards on the shop, just in case.

14

"Another night, another church."

Alex leaned on the low wall that edged St Luke's Church. Unlike All Souls, this church was slightly out of the town, and there were no neighbouring shops or houses to witness their activities. "This is becoming quite a habit."

"Not one I'm enjoying," Avery said. She studied Alex's face again, worried that he hadn't yet fully recovered from last night.

He saw her worried expression and laughed. "I'm fine, Avery."

She reached up, cupping his cheek with her hand. "I hope so. I was really worried last night."

He grabbed her hand, pulled it to his lips and kissed her palm. "I know. You're gorgeous, you know that?"

"So you keep telling me." She smiled, warmth spreading through her.

"I mean it." He looked as if he was about to say more when they heard cars arriving, and they looked around to see the three investigators arriving at the same time as Caspian.

Dylan, Cassie, and Ben shouted their hellos, and then started to wrestle equipment from their van, but Caspian grimaced when he saw them. He slammed the door of his sleek Audi, and his sister, Estelle, emerged from the passenger seat.

Avery's only contact with Estelle had been on two instances. The first time was when she had been attacking Reuben at Old Haven Church, and in defence, Briar had half-buried her in soil and Avery had knocked her unconscious with a fallen branch. The second time had been at Faversham Central, their name for Sebastian Faversham's mansion, where Estelle had attacked them in the corridor and Reuben had managed to better her. Today, Avery reflected, was the first time they had seen her and they hadn't been attacking each other. Unfortunately, she looked like she wanted to attack them right now. That was fine. Avery wanted to wipe that dismissive look right off her face.

"Nice to see you, too," Alex said, smirking.

"We don't need you here," Caspian said, turning his back on them as he opened up the church. Estelle stood next to him, glaring at them.

"Well, they do, so get over it," Alex said, joining Caspian at the door. He nodded at Estelle. "Estelle, always a pleasure."

Estelle narrowed her eyes. "Do we need both of you?"

"Safety in numbers. Especially with you two here. Besides, if this is anything like the spirit in our church, it's very mean." He hesitated a moment. "We found out what it is. What *they* are."

"And?" Caspian drawled. "Do you want a drum roll?"

Alex ignored his sarcasm. "They *are* Nephilim."

Estelle released a barking laugh, throwing her head back. "Really?" Her voice dripped with doubt.

"Really. So watch your step, Estelle. It might get all biblical on your ass."

Caspian and Estelle paused on the threshold of the church, staring at each other for a few seconds, and then Caspian looked at Alex, clearly annoyed. "How do you know?"

"I communed with the one in All Souls last night, through a crystal ball." Alex shrugged. "He said there were seven of them. The question is, do we really want to try to record this one, now we know what it is?"

That was a good question, Avery thought, and one they had debated on the way over. They could all be put in more danger than they needed to be. The whole point of allowing the paranormal investigation was to see if the spirits were linked, and it seemed they were.

Ben spoke from behind them. "Yes, we do. The more we film, the more we know."

"And besides," Caspian put in, "you might be wrong."

"I didn't think you wanted them here?" Avery asked sharply, referring to the parapsychologists.

"Let's not upset Genevieve," Caspian said, turning away from her. "Now, let's get this over with."

They followed Caspian into the nave, the dim electric lights throwing shadows everywhere.

Like All Souls, this church was medieval in design, and the high, vaulted ceiling stretched above them. Unlike All Souls, it was much smaller, a country church, similar in size to Old Haven. And it had been smashed to pieces.

Over half of the polished wooden pews had been destroyed, the altar overturned, and candles were scattered on the floor. Set in the walls were small, arched niches that had contained icons, flowers or candles, and all but two of these were now empty, their displays strewn across the floor.

"Bloody Hell," Ben murmured, looking around in shock. "What happened here?"

Avery felt as shocked as he looked. This spirit had actually destroyed objects. Big, heavy objects. Some of the pews were now only splinters of wood.

Caspian rounded on them, eyes blazing. "I presume this hasn't happened at All Souls?"

"No," Alex said, taking in the damage. "Not last night, anyway. It might have by now."

Estelle's cool, clipped tone resonated through the church and she glanced dismissively at Avery and Alex. "Well, so much for it just being a spirit."

"Maybe," Avery began, just as coolly, "the spirit has gained a lot of power from killing its victim. Where was the body found?"

Estelle dropped her eyes and pointed, a glimmer of regret on her face. "Here in the nave, next to the altar. You can just about see where the blood was."

Dylan and Cassie were now behind Ben, and rather than looking dismayed at the damage, they actually looked excited. "Wow. Brilliant," Dylan said. "I wish we'd caught this on camera."

"Be careful what you wish for," Alex said, raising his brows. "Let's get this show on the road."

Cassie, Ben and Dylan worked quickly, falling into well-practised routines, and soon they had their equipment set up, and Cassie had taken her initial temperature readings. Dylan was already prowling the perimeter with his thermal imaging camera, while Ben set up the audio.

While the team organised themselves, Avery and Alex righted the candles and Avery lit them with a word. Estelle and Caspian stood in the centre of the room, and Avery knew they were doing what she and Alex were doing; trying to feel the spirit and locate its presence. So far, Avery sensed nothing, but she knew it must be here.

"You know what?" Alex said, frowning. "I'm going to make a very big protective circle. Guys!" he shouted. "Be prepared to get your ass over here quickly."

Ben, Cassie and Dylan turned and nodded, but Estelle sneered. "Scared, Alex?"

Alex just smiled thinly. "You'll thank me for this later."

Working quickly, he withdrew all the necessary things from his pack, including a large silver dagger, and he used salt to outline the circle, just as they had done before. Avery worked with him, speaking softly. "I think this is a great idea. And it worked well last night."

Alex nodded. "I have a bad feeling about this."

For the next 15 minutes nothing happened, other than their own pacing and waiting.

"It doesn't want to play," Caspian murmured, annoyed.

"Could it have escaped?" Avery asked.

"No. I know how to seal a building, thank you," Caspian said sarcastically. He turned his back to them and watched the ghost-hunters.

The spirit may have been refusing to appear, but the tension in the room increased anyway. Being in such close proximity with Caspian and Estelle was annoying.

Ben and the other parapsychologists ignored them, focussing solely on recording the damage, and Ben even provided some walk-through audio.

Then, without warning, the electric lights that weren't that bright in the first place started to buzz and crackle, the light pulsing.

They all spun around, and Avery threw her senses wide, trying to identify where the spirit was. A large, dark mass started to manifest behind the altar. The EMF meter started to whine, and then one by one, the lights shattered around the room, the candles now their sole source of light.

Alex grabbed Avery's hand and pulled her into the circle. "Everyone, get in here *now!*"

Cassie ran to them straight away, standing close to Avery, but Ben continued to use the meter, and Dylan continued to record. Caspian and Estelle ignored them too, stepping closer to the spirit that had started to manifest.

The dark mass rose taller and taller, its bulk filling out.

Cassie shouted, "Dylan. Ben. Please come here!"

They glanced at them, and then looked back at the spirit, and seemed to decide that retreat was wise. They edged back, step by step, continuing to record all the while.

Caspian and Estelle, however, had poised themselves for attack, their hands raised, balls of energy visible in their palms.

Without warning the spirit grew, becoming more human in shape - except for the wings spread wide behind it. It lunged at Caspian, one large wing sweeping him off his feet and sending him crashing into the wall.

That was enough to make Ben and Dylan run.

Estelle had no such fears, and Avery wasn't sure if she was brave or stupid. She threw ball after ball of energy at the spirit, but instead of retreating it grew in size, its enormous wingspan now reaching halfway along the wall. Avery couldn't work out if she was seeing its shadow from the candles, or the spirit itself. *Would it even have a shadow?*

Alex yelled, "Estelle! Stop! You're giving it power!"

She ignored him, instead conjuring flames and hurling them at the spirit. Caspian, meanwhile, staggered to his feet, and added his power to hers.

Avery looked at Alex bewildered. "Can't they see what they're doing?"

"Blinded by stupidity," Alex muttered. "Caspian! You're not helping. Get back here!"

The spirit continued to change, forming two legs and then arms, but the wings remained. It again lunged at Caspian and Estelle, catching them both with its wings this time, and sending them flying through the air. Caspian landed awkwardly on the top of the broken pews, and Estelle on the stone floor in a crumpled heap.

Avery glanced at Alex and they instinctively had the same thought. They both darted out of the circle, Avery yelling at the ghost-hunters, "Don't move!"

Avery headed for Estelle where she was lying dazed, but still conscious, and summoned air. The gust lifted Estelle up, clean off her feet, enabling Avery to pull her back into the safety of the circle. At the same time, Alex pulled Caspian to his feet, and dragged him away.

The Nephilim, now more creature than spirit, advanced towards them across the nave, but its features were still unformed. A voice filled the air, almost deafening, and Avery recognised the language that Alex had been repeating over and over again the previous night.

Caspian resisted Alex's help, but Alex had clearly had enough and punched him, obviously the last thing Caspian expected, because he collapsed in a heap and Alex dragged him along the floor. Avery helped lift him into the circle, and then uttered the spell that would seal them in.

The flair of magic was palpable and the Nephilim paused, watching them. It then began to circle them, its strange, guttural language still filling the church.

"I did not expect *this*," Ben said. His eyes were wide and his hands shook. The EMF meter buzzed wildly. He asked Dylan, "Are you still recording?"

"Yep. Not sure quite how steady the footage will be."

Estelle rose shakily to her feet and hissed at Alex, "You punched Caspian."

"And I'll punch you, too if you try anything," he said, rounding on her. "Normally I don't like violence towards women, but I'm willing to make an exception for you."

Caspian sat up groaning, clutching a hand to his nose. Blood streamed down his face and he glared at Alex.

"We saved your life," Avery said pointedly, before he could start to argue.

The heavy slap of feet on the floor made them turn back to the Nephilim, but instead of advancing further, it laughed—if that's what it could be called. It was like a howl that sent goose bumps along Avery's skin and lifted the hairs on the back of her neck.

The Nephilim turned away, lifted its wings, and soared towards the closest window. It didn't hesitate, crashing through at speed, sending glass shattering everywhere and splintering the frame. And then it disappeared into the night.

"Great. Just great. So much for sealing the bloody church," Alex shouted. He clenched his fists and with visible difficulty took deep breaths and tried to calm down. He looked at the ghost-hunters. "Are you okay?"

"I think so," Cassie mumbled, while the others nodded.

Avery sank to the floor, depressed and unsure what to do next.

"It was stronger than I anticipated," Caspian admitted. He was still sitting on the floor, and like Avery he seemed deflated, sinking into himself. He whispered a spell and his blood flow stopped, and then he lifted his t-shirt, wiping his face with the hem.

"It will be going after the others," Alex said. "They'll all be out within the hour, and then who knows what will happen."

"Death and destruction. We need to tell Genevieve." Avery looked resolute. "Who knows, with some warning, she may be able to stop the others?"

Caspian shook his head and stood up. "I doubt it, but it's worth trying. Drop the spell, Avery, we don't need to stay in the circle any longer."

Avery nodded and released the spell, watching Caspian as he stood beneath the shattered window. He raised his hands and the broken glass and frame started to reassemble itself, until seconds later the window was fixed.

"Wow," Dylan said admiringly, "that's so cool."

Caspian turned to him, narrowing his eyes. "I trust you will keep our secrets?" His tone didn't invite refusal.

"Absolutely. We value our clients' privacy," Dylan said emphatically, Ben and Cassie nodding vigorously next to him.

"Good." Caspian looked at Alex and Avery. "You better go and check All Souls and repair any damage there, too. We'll stay behind and fix this." He gestured to the destroyed pews. "This is all about damage control now. The less anyone, including the police, knows about this, the better."

15

After the cold and dismal atmosphere at St Luke's Church, Alex's flat was a warm and welcoming haven.

Avery sat with a glass of red wine, curled in the corner of Alex's soft and luxurious sofa, watching the dancing flames of the candles. The blinds were closed, shutting out the night, and Alex was sitting on the floor, turning the pages of his grimoire in a vain attempt to do something useful.

Avery had just taken a call from Genevieve confirming that the others had escaped, too, leaving broken glass and damaged window frames behind. What was worse was that she hadn't blamed her, and Avery felt that if only she had shouted at her, she might be feeling slightly better.

Before Alex and Avery returned to Alex's, they had stopped at All Souls, but that too had a smashed window, fortunately at the rear of the church, away from the road. They had repaired it, and checked the interior to make sure nothing else had happened inside, but unlike St Luke's, the interior was intact.

The ghost-hunters had returned home and Avery reminded them to wear their amulets, just in case. Dylan had pulled his out of his shirt, saying, "Are you kidding? I wear this *everywhere* now!"

That had given Avery some comfort, but she felt more depressed than she had in a long time. She swirled her wine and took a large sip. "I feel helpless."

Alex looked troubled. "Me, too. But the spirits have escaped, so now we have to figure out what to do."

"What was it like the other night, to have that *thing* in your head?"

He shuddered at the memory. "Intense and unpleasant. It was strong, maybe more than it should have been because of the crystal ball, but," he shrugged, "it worked. We know what it is. And it knows what we are, too."

Avery leaned forward. "What do you mean?"

"Well, the whole protective circle meant it recognised magic, but I felt it brushing across my thoughts. I'm sure it knows we're witches, and I'm sure it knows what that means." He smiled softly. "Let's face it—witches have been around a long time, too. Magic is at the root of everything."

"Do you think that frightened it?"

"No. But," Alex looked thoughtful, "I think it respected me. *I think*. Let's hope that works in our favour, eventually. We might even work out what to do with them."

"I don't even know what day it is, never mind how to work out what to do with errant Nephilim."

"You'll be pleased to know it's Saturday, which means a lazy lie-in and Sunday brunch."

"Good, that's something," she said, collapsing back on the couch. "I'm not sure when my Saturdays turned into full-on spirit hunting in collaboration with the Favershams."

"Since *someone* decided to find grimoires, that's when." He caught her foot in his hands, and started kissing her calf, all the time watching her with his dark eyes.

"That's nice," she groaned, feeling like she might melt into the sofa.

"Only nice?" He continued up her inner thigh.

"Very, *very* nice." She watched him, wondering if he was going to stop, and hoping he really wouldn't.

He looked up at her with a wicked grin and took her wine glass out of her hands. "I think we've had enough of grimoires and ghost-hunting don't you?"

✱✱✱

The next morning, there was nothing on the local news about the churches, which was some relief. Their efforts to disguise the spirits and their escape had been successful.

Avery sipped her coffee and watched Alex move competently around the kitchen. "Where do you think they've gone?"

"Good question." Alex pushed a plate of Eggs Benedict under her nose and sat down next to her along the breakfast bar counter. "Somewhere dark and protected."

"A cave?" she asked, through a mouthful of food.

"A deserted building, somewhere inaccessible? But," Alex said, pointing his fork, "so far, no deaths."

"That we've heard of."

"But they're clearly together, and maybe with the other two. Remember the Nephilim I communicated with? He said, 'WE *are seven*.'"

Avery nodded absently, slightly side-tracked by the fantastic brunch Alex had cooked. "Do you think there's a guidebook on Nephilim? Like, how to destroy them and send them back to the Otherworld?"

"Mmm, unlikely, Ave. But maybe you could write one after this? Or, of course, you could cause it to rain for forty days and forty nights. Isn't that what the flood was for?" He smirked infuriatingly at her.

She groaned. "I don't think my weather magic is that good. And neither is your boat building."

Before Alex could tease her any more, his phone rang. "Hey Reuben, how you doing?" He continued to eat as he talked, grunting occasionally, while Avery watched, curious.

She hadn't seen Reuben or El for a few days and she wondered what they'd been up to. She didn't have to wait long.

"Sure," Alex continued. "See you at the harbour in half an hour."

He hung up and Avery looked at him expectantly. "What are you going to do at the harbour?"

"You mean, what are *we* doing?" he corrected, raising his eyebrows.

"We? Can't I go back to bed?" she said, wishing she could summon the energy to feel even vaguely enthusiastic.

"No. A boat's been found out at sea. Empty. Like the Marie Celeste. Reuben heard about it while he was surfing. He's persuaded Nils to take us out to the area."

"Nils, the tattoo guy? He has a boat?" The last time Avery had seen him was when he was putting her protection tattoo on her hip in his shop, Viking Ink.

"He's a Viking. Of course he has a boat."

***

"Morning, guys!" Nils yelled in his slight Swedish lilt from where he stood on the deck of his old fishing boat. He waved and grinned. "Come aboard. I'll give you a tour of my baby!"

It was hardly a baby, Avery reflected as she looked at it. The varnish was peeling, and it had a battered quality to it that suggested it had seen better days. But clearly, Nils loved it. He leaned over the side and extended his hand to Avery, clasping her hand in his very large one. She'd forgotten just how huge he was.

She gingerly walked up the narrow gangplank onto the boat, and looked into Nils's pale blue eyes. He winked. "Great to see you, Avery. Hope my tattoo is looking good. Reuben is inside making tea." He jerked his hand over his shoulder to the cabin, and then looked at Alex, who had followed Avery onto the boat. "Alex! My tattooed friend!" He clasped him in a huge man hug. "We having trouble again, yes? Missing people. It's bad news. I'll go check the engine. As soon as the others are here, we go."

He disappeared to the far end of the boat, leaving Avery bewildered. "Wow. He's a force of nature."

Alex grinned. "He's great though, right?"

Reuben emerged from the cabin at the sound of their voices. His blond hair was slightly damp, and he was dressed in his board shorts and t-shirt. He didn't look anywhere as near as enthusiastic as Nils. "Morning, guys. What a crappy night."

"You too?" Alex said. "You haven't even heard *our* news."

"Does it involve missing fisherman and a drifting boat?"

"No. But there are missing Nephilim."

"Shit," Reuben said, leaning against the side of the boat and cradling his steaming cup. "This keeps getting worse."

"You got any details on the boat?" Alex asked.

Reuben nodded. "Yeah, some. It doesn't sound good. When I had my morning surf, the guys filled me in on the news. One of them had spotted the Coastguard heading out early. You know this place. News spreads. After that, I caught up with Connor, one of the crew." He exhaled with a heavy sigh. "Said it was weird. It was a calm night. There were no distress calls, but the boat was deserted. No missing gear, no signs of damage. The nets were still out. Small family business, too. Dad and two sons. How crap is that?"

"Who was it?" Avery asked, sure she'd know them. Most people in White Haven knew each other by sight, even if they didn't know each other well.

"The Petersons," Reuben said, watching her.

Avery closed her eyes briefly. *Yes, she knew them.* "Damn it."

She turned away, leaving Alex and Reuben talking, and leaned against the side of the boat. Looking out at the harbour and the sea beyond, she reflected on how such a bright morning could exist when there was so much darkness out there. Several women were missing husbands, boyfriends, sons, and fathers. And it sounded as if the Daughters of Llyr were to blame.

The harbour was still mostly empty of boats, many of them still out fishing. Some of the bigger vessels were lined up, ready to take tourists out for a few hours, and queues of people were already getting ready to board.

Beyond the harbour, the town sparkled in the sunshine. Bright splashes of colour marked the plants and hanging baskets outside of shops and pubs, and the smell of salt was strong in the air. It was late July and the tourist season was in full swing; families were everywhere. This was a terrible time to have Mermaids and Nephilim stalking the coast.

Avery heard a shout, and she looked around to see Briar, Newton, and El clambering on board. She waved, unable to summon a smile. "Hey, guys."

They shouted their greetings and crossed the deck to join them.

Nils must have heard them arrive, and he appeared from the engine room, streaked in oil and wiping his hands on a ragged cloth. "Everyone ready?" he asked.

They nodded.

"Great, grab a lifejacket and we'll go."

***

Once they were out of the harbour, a brisk sea breeze ruffled the waves, and they bobbed across the water, heading to the site where the boat had been found. It took them almost an hour to get there, and on the way, they updated everyone about the Nephilim. They stood at the stern of the boat, well away from the wheelhouse so that Nils couldn't hear them.

"Great. Seven Nephilim spirits loose in Cornwall. Just brilliant," Newton said, pacing up and down the deck. "And potentially, they might not even be spirits anymore."

Briar squinted against the sun and lowered her sunglasses. "I can still feel them—not so much on this boat—but I can on the land. They're growing stronger."

"Can you pinpoint where they are?" Newton asked eagerly.

"No, unfortunately not. It's more like I have a subtle awareness of their presence in the atmosphere."

"Well, no further deaths have to be a good thing, right?" El asked.

"I guess so," Avery said. "I really wish we knew what they were up to, though."

"Did Caspian look the slightest bit apologetic for giving the one at St Luke's enough juice to get out of there?" Reuben asked.

"Not really," Alex answered, "but I did enjoy punching him."

"And he didn't retaliate?" Newton asked, shocked.

"There was too much going on there already. A fight would have been dangerous. And besides, I did it to stop him from struggling. God knows what that Nephilim would have done if it had got to us."

"And what about today?" Briar asked. "Other than seeing where the crew disappeared from, what's the plan?"

"I want to see if we can find the Mermaids," Reuben explained. "I have a spell that should work."

"Then what? I mean isn't that dangerous?" Briar asked. "There're five guys on board, and you will all be susceptible to their call. How can *we* stop that?" She gestured toward Avery and El. *It was a great question*, Avery thought. She'd been wondering that herself.

"You're presuming you won't be at risk, then?" Newton asked, confused.

"In theory, no," El explained. "Me and Reu have been doing some homework on Mermaids, and it seems they only target men. We're hoping that means their call won't work on us. Of course, we could be wrong. We can spell you all and tie you to the boat if we have to, but we don't think they'll be around today. This is more of a tracing spell."

Reuben elaborated further. "Oswald was convinced that they were walking the land in Mevagissey. Maybe they're here. I want to see if we can find if they've come ashore."

"Can we detect them on land?" Newton asked. "I mean, will they look different to humans?"

"Folklore suggests they look the same," Reuben said. "That's part of their success, but there should be fundamental differences. If we can detect a signature *something*, we may be able to make a spell to help us find them. I mean, I would imagine there's a strong water elemental nature to them, even if we can't see it."

Avery rubbed her face, frustrated. "So, they won't have bright green eyes or webbed feet or something?"

"Pretty sure not, no," Reuben said, grinning.

"What about Nils?" Newton asked, glancing towards the wheelhouse. "What does he know about us?"

"Not much. He knows I tinker with a bit of witchcraft, but he has no idea of the extent of it. He hasn't asked too many questions about today. He's clever that way."

Avery nodded, knowing what he meant. Like Sally and Dan used to be, he probably knew more than he let on, and sensibly kept out of it. He may not have that luxury for much longer.

As if he'd read her thoughts, Reuben said, "I'd appreciate it if someone distracted him while I'm performing the spell."

"No problem," Newton said.

At that moment, they felt and heard the engine throttle down and their speed drop, and Nils yelled across the boat. "We're coming up to the spot now. It's not one of the common fishing spots—they'd have been on their own here for quite a while."

"Maybe they were lured out here in the first place," El speculated.

Avery peered overboard, wondering where below them the Petersons might be. "Do you think they knew they would die?" she asked.

"They're probably not dead," Alex said, wrapping his arm around her. "Remember the old tales. They could be Mermen by now."

Avery shivered. "Do you think they'd have memories of their life on land? Their loved ones, their friends?"

"Let's hope not," Alex said softly, and kissed her on the forehead. "It would be easier that way."

Newton headed to the wheelhouse to talk to Nils, leaving Reuben free to perform his spell. He pulled a few objects from his backpack, and handed them to El. Avery watched him, curious as to the type of spell he had in mind.

Briar caught on quickly. "You're going to harness elemental water, aren't you?"

Reuben nodded. "Much like you harness the earth and feel its energies, I feel water flow through me. I try not to use it when I surf—it feels like cheating—but I think I'm kidding myself. I probably use it subconsciously, anyway. I can feel it now. And as the earth feels a disturbance, I'm hoping I can feel the Mermaids here."

"You didn't notice anything different when you were surfing?" El asked.

"No. But I'm too busy focussing on surfing and catching that perfect wave," he grinned sheepishly. "It's pretty distracting."

Avery, Alex, and Briar backed away, giving Reuben some space. "So, how are you holding up, Briar?" Avery asked her.

"Not bad. The shop's busy, which is good. When I have spare time, I've been trying to weave some protection into my potions." She looked guilty. "I feel it's the least I can do. I want to protect the town, the people who live here. It's okay for El, she makes protection amulets, but women mostly come to me for creams and potions that have more to do with skin and smells than protection."

"That's a great idea. What about making bundles of herbs for drawers and wardrobes? They could have protection spells woven into them. Or welcome herb bundles for front doors and porches?"

Briar's face brightened. "That's a brilliant idea! I could do that! I've got so many herbs and flowers now in the allotment, it will be perfect. And I could dry them for the winter."

Avery smiled, pleased to have thought of something useful. "I'm happy to help. Why don't you make up a few and I'll sell them in my shop, too? They'd go well with the incense and tarot cards. I'll ask El for some amulets as well, and some gemstones. That way we can try to protect as many people as possible."

Alex frowned. "We have lots of foot traffic coming through the pub. Lots of locals and visitors. I'll ask the bar staff to keep an eye out for suspicious activity, and any strange news or gossip."

Briar looked relieved. "This is great. For the first time in days, I feel like we can make a positive difference."

"The thing is, though," Alex warned, "I think this is our new normal. There'll always be something happening now. If it's not this, it will be something else."

"Cheers, Alex," Avery said, looking at him in disbelief. "Just as we were feeling good."

"But this *is* good," he said. "We're finally awake and aware of the possibilities of the paranormal world. We just need to up our game."

They were distracted by Reuben's shout and he pointed overboard. They turned to see the sea churning behind them, and a strange, silvery trail started to spread from the boat towards the shore. "Nils!" Reuben yelled. "Follow the trail!"

Nils heard his shout and the throttle picked up, and they followed the trail towards the coast.

Reuben and El headed to the prow of the boat, the others right behind them. They followed the trail to the west of White Haven, a small cove out of town. As they neared the coast, Nils slowed down and they entered a deep bay, with high cliffs on either side.

"The Devil's Canyon." Reuben pointed to where the cliff face hollowed out, becoming a cave. "And that's Hades Cave. It gets pretty deep there on a full tide, and it's always dark in daytime."

The boat idled and Nils joined them, his eyes squinting against the light and looking almost icy blue in the full sun. He nodded in agreement. "No one ventures in there, except stupid kids who try to dare each other. They risk drowning. The undertow is massive."

Avery nodded. They'd all heard about this cove and the dangers of the cave. It looked ominous, even in the sunshine. The town council had attached a notice on the side of the rock face, warning of the dangers at high tide. "The perfect place for those who don't care about powerful currents though, isn't it?"

"Can you take us further in?" Reuben asked Nils.

"Entrance only," he said. "The tide's ebbing already. In fact, we really need to get back to the harbour."

"Just a quick look, then."

Nils nodded and headed back to the wheelhouse, and then they eased forward to the cave entrance, nudging just inside. Immediately, the sunshine disappeared and the temperature dropped. The heavy *glug, glug* of the water as it eddied around the cave filled the air. The back of the cave was in darkness.

Reuben reached into his pack and pulled out a huge torch. He flicked it on and trained the powerful beam on the back of the cave. The water looked dark and forbidding, and the walls were slick with moisture. A tiny strip of rock edged the back of the cave, and something on it glistened in the light, but it was unclear what it was, and Avery had the strongest sensation of being watched. She shivered, desperately wishing they could leave. And then she heard something; the lightest splash—something different than the *glug* of the water.

And then another, and another.

Alex must have heard it too, because he said softly but urgently, "Time to go."

Reuben nodded, turning off the light. He turned to Nils and gestured to go, and they eased back, out into the sunshine, heading toward the safety of White Haven.

However, Avery noticed that with the exception of Nils at the wheel, the other three men turned and looked back longingly at the cave.

16

All five witches and Newton were subdued as they sat in the courtyard of The Wayward Son, soaking up the sunshine.

They had barely spoken on the journey back to White Haven, and only Nils seemed unaffected. Avery presumed, and hoped, that in the wheelhouse he'd have been protected from what they had heard and felt. It was only now, with a pint of beer or a glass of wine in front of them, and the promise of food on the way, that they all started to relax.

"I know we've faced some pretty weird shit recently," El said, staring at each of them as if challenging them to disagree, "but that has to be the absolute worst."

"You're right, and I know we didn't see anything, but something *was* there. I could feel it. It gave me goose bumps," Avery said, shivering. "*Something* was watching us."

Briar nodded, looking into her white wine as if the answers to the universe were in there. "It felt different from anything else—demons, ghosts, dark magic, the lot. It felt … Other." She shivered as she finally settled on a word.

Alex, Reuben, and Newton remained silent, and Avery looked at them, concerned. It was Briar who had ordered the drinks, and Avery and El who had sorted seats. The guys had been suspiciously quiet, meekly doing as they were told. "Are you all right? Alex?"

He looked up and finally met her eyes. "I heard something. Something wild and inexplicable, just as we were heading out of the cove. I can't explain it. It was haunting, and—"

"Compelling," Newton finished for him. "I can still hear it." His eyes had a slightly glazed look and he glanced absently around the table. "Maybe we should go back?"

Shocked by his statement, El turned to Reuben, "And what about you?"

"I heard the soft sounds of water, and I had images, sort of, of something beneath the surface, something…" He trailed off, unable to focus.

El acted quickly. She glanced around making sure no one was close enough to witness her actions, and then flashed a short burst of fire to all three men. A jolt of flame flashed across their hands and up their arms, and they shouted in pain.

Newton yelled, "What the hell?"

"Feel better?" El asked, narrowing her eyes.

Reuben shook his head and rubbed his arms. "Wow. Ouch! What the hell was that for? It seems unnecessary."

"Was it?" El asked incredulous. "Because you were all in thrall to something. Not fully, but definitely not your normal selves."

Alex and Newton seemed to focus on their surroundings for the first time since they had arrived.

"I do *not* remember getting here," Alex said, looking around with confusion and concern.

"Me, neither. I just felt really sleepy, actually," Newton said. "Did I doze off? Did someone just burn me?" he asked the table in general.

"Oh, crap," said Avery, incredulous. "In the space of seconds at that cave entrance, you were all enthralled to Mermaids. I mean, seriously. How can that happen? I didn't hear a thing."

Briar agreed. "It's reassuring that we didn't, but worrying that you did. Thank the Gods you didn't dive in."

El frowned, still playing with the flames at the end of her hands. "We need to protect you from their call."

"But how?" Alex asked, bewildered. "I'm not particularly thrilled by it, either. I don't want to become a bloody Merman."

"Does anyone?" Reuben asked, looking around the table. "It's making me think twice about surfing. In fact, I can't believe surfers haven't been attacked yet, but I guess we don't surf in deep water."

"That's a good point," Avery said, frowning. "Maybe deep water is their preferred way of luring men, but then why would they walk on land?"

"There's just too much about them we don't know," El mused. "But so far, both of the boat attacks were at night, so maybe they're put off by daylight. And maybe that's what protects the surfers."

"We must search our grimoires," Reuben said. "There has to be something we can use. And maybe the Council will have some suggestions, too."

Avery looked at him, surprised. "I really didn't expect to hear you say that, Reuben!"

"I know. I've changed my mind about them. You were right. We should learn from them. How else do we grow?"

At this point, the whole table looked at him in shock. He laughed at their expressions and shrugged. "I've been doing some thinking, that's all. And I don't want to end up as a Mermaid mate, no matter how much I love the sea."

From the depths of her bag, Avery's phone started to ring, and she fished around in the bottom quickly, surprised to see Eve's name. "Hey, Eve," she answered quickly, leaving the table so as not to disturb the others. "How are things?"

"So, so," she answered, her voice strained. "I just thought you should know that we've found some dead cattle at Zennor Quoit, the Neolithic burial chamber on the moors just outside of Zennor."

"Dead cattle?" she asked, puzzled. *What on Earth was Eve telling her about cattle for?*

"We're pretty sure the Nephilim have killed them. There were seven of them, all drained of blood, their bodies covered by bracken. The farmer, Carrick, noticed some of his cows were missing, but obviously had no idea to look there. One of the locals was up at the Quoit earlier on a walk, and contacted him."

Avery felt faint and slightly nauseous, and heard her pulse booming in her ears steadily. She pulled a chair out from an empty table and sat down. "Cattle? At least they're not killing humans. Is this a good sign?"

"I don't know, yes and no. That they're not killing people is good, of course, but it means they're gathering power and growing."

Avery thought quickly. St Ives wasn't that far away. It would probably be useful to go take a look. "Would you mind showing us where? I mean, is it worth us looking?"

"Sure, I thought you'd want to. I'm going, too. I know the farmer. He keeps me informed of any unusual things happening, and this *is* pretty unusual. He hasn't called the police yet, but he will. He has to. We have a small window on time, so…"

"I get it. I can come now."

"Great, I'll meet you there," Eve said. It was only when she rang off that Avery realised that Zennor was the place that had been visited by a Mermaid, too.

El's old Land Rover bounced along the lanes and roads to Zennor. It had taken just over an hour to get there, and she pushed the aging motor to move as quickly as possible.

In the end, four of them decided to go. Briar was working on some protection potions for her shop, Charming Balms, and Newton didn't want to interfere with the police investigation, although he really wanted to join them, so Alex, El, Reuben, and Avery made the trip without them.

Avery was lost in thought as she gazed at the moors. They had crossed to the north coast of Cornwall, and after passing through St Ives, had travelled past cultivated fields and meadows for grazing cattle. And then the fields fell away, replaced by wild moorland covered in bracken and heather, an undulating ripple of purple unbroken to the horizon, and the sea to her right.

"What does this mean, then?" Reuben asked, raising his voice so that Avery and Alex could hear him in the back.

"I hope it means they're not going to become cold-blooded murderers," Alex answered.

"Again," Avery tempered. "Five deaths are enough."

"But, it would have been easy for them to kill humans again," Alex argued. "It suggests they have a conscience."

"I suppose so," Avery said reluctantly. "I'm not exactly going to start celebrating, yet."

"Interesting that the cattle were slaughtered at Zennor Quoit though," Alex said, raising his eyebrows. "It's an old burial ground, with a long history of death and spiritual significance to the area."

Avery nodded. "True. Do you think it has significance to them, though?"

"Well, they're old. It may mean something to them to kill at such a place. They are the children of angels, after all, if we're to believe the myths."

"Didn't you ask them about their lineage during your little one-on-one?" Reuben asked Alex, smirking.

"Not really, no," he answered, dryly. "I had other priorities. Plus, I really didn't dictate the conversation."

"Maybe they ritualised the deaths," Avery mused.

"Let's hope this place will tell us something, then," Alex said.

"It's quite a long way to take cattle," El chipped in. "They must have flown them there."

"And I doubt the cattle would have been quiet, either," Reuben added.

They fell silent, and it wasn't long before they passed through the small village of Zennor, and then headed onto a tiny lane that led to the moors. Miles of bracken and heather now surrounded them on either side, and it was only a few minutes later that El pulled to a stop as the track ended at a tiny car park. An old estate car was the only other vehicle on site, and a notice pointed the way across a winding track. Avery could just make out a jumble of stones in the distance.

"It's on foot from here," El said, leaving the car and pulling on her jacket to protect her from the brisk wind that blew from the sea.

The track wasn't long, and in a few minutes they passed large rocks, some of the many that were strewn across the landscape. This land was steeped in history, marked from years of human habitation; the surrounding fields systems were pre-historic and the rocks marked ancient barrows and old settlements for miles around. Eventually, on a slight rise of land, they saw the huge jagged rocks that made up Zennor Quoit, a Neolithic burial chamber. It was quiet and eerie, the landscape all moor and sky, the only sound the wind brushing through the heathers, gorse, and bracken. It was ancient, and Avery felt the weight of the years around her. This land was special.

Two figures had their backs to them, and they turned as they approached. Avery recognised Eve, waving. She could already smell the blood and stench of decay as she led the others over.

"Hey, Avery," Eve greeted her, smiling weakly. "Great to see you. I just wish it wasn't for this." She gestured behind her to the slaughtered remains of cattle visible under the bracken. She nodded to her companion. "This is Nate. He's another witch from St Ives. That makes a grand total of two of us."

Nate muttered a soft "Hey," and shook their hands as everyone introduced themselves. In that brief word Avery thought she heard a northern accent, and estimated he was in his forties. He had short dark hair, streaked with grey. A section above each ear had been shaved, giving him a slight mohawk, and he had a short beard and light brown eyes. He wore old blue jeans tucked in biker boots, a t-shirt, and an old pilot's jacket—brown leather lined with fur. Eve wasn't dressed that differently from him, but a bright blue scarf bound her hair up and off her face, her long dreadlocks visible down her back.

Eve added, "Carrick, the farmer, was here earlier, but he's gone to the farm to get his truck. He won't be long." She looked sad, regretting the deaths for him. "He really didn't believe the cattle were his. Thought he was being told wild stories. He's pretty gutted, actually."

"Where's the person who found them?" Avery asked.

"It was a local walking his dog. He left when we arrived. He didn't want to hang around, understandably," Eve explained. "Anyway, come and look. We haven't disturbed them."

The slaughtered cattle were strewn across an area several metres wide. An attempt had been made to cover them with bracken, but they clearly hadn't meant to hide them properly. All of the cows had their throats slit and their hearts removed. Flies were buzzing around, and Avery felt bitter bile rising in her throat. But, there was very little blood anywhere. She turned into the wind and took several deep breaths before looking back at the carnage.

Alex looked at them thoughtfully. "They've been drained completely. Seven Nephilim, seven cows."

Nate whirled around. "How do you know there are SEVEN Nephilim?" His accent was more obvious now, his deep voice betraying a softened Geordie tone.

"We set up a little psychic one-on-one the other night in the church, and that's what it told me."

"That's a pretty cool trick," Nate said, narrowing his eyes.

"I wouldn't recommend it," Avery said, looking at Alex, exasperated. "He scared the shit out of me. Started talking in a foreign language, probably ancient, and his eyes went white."

"It was *your* idea," Alex pointed out.

El and Reuben had left them talking and were strolling around the site, when El called out from the dolmen. "This stone has been moved. The capstone had fallen years ago, if I remember correctly."

Eve walked over, the others trailing behind. "You're right. The large, flat stone on top of the jagged one is the capstone. They put it back in place."

"Impressive lifting," Reuben said. "They've used it as a sacrificial table. There's blood all over it."

At that moment, a wild wind keened across them, and they all shivered, pulling their jackets closer. Avery eyed the table uncertainly and wrinkled her nose; the tang of blood was sharper here. The press would run wild with this, if they ever found out.

Nate hunched his shoulders and asked Alex, "So, what do they want? Did they share that with you?"

"They want to walk the Earth again. The spirit I spoke to thought they'd been cheated from life."

"So these sacrifices, what will they achieve?" Eve asked.

"We think they want to manifest in physical form, and that's why they killed those people in the church, to give them the power to change."

Avery continued, "And then Caspian and Estelle managed to give the spirit at St Luke's an extra boost the other night, and that's when it escaped."

Nate snorted. "Typical bloody Caspian. Arrogant prick."

El laughed, but without humour. "So, you're a fan, too."

"As much as anyone is on that bloody Council," Nate said, exasperated. "Eve said you made quite an impression."

"I don't know how," Avery said, confused. "I thought we'd annoyed everyone."

"Not everyone," Eve said. "Yes, you've made our life complicated, but it's shaken the Council up, and Sebastian has gone. He was a bully. That's a good thing." She shivered and looked around. "Is there anything else you want to see here? Carrick will be back soon."

Avery shook her head. "I don't think so."

While she was talking Alex leaned forward, touching the capstone and drawing his finger across the dried blood. He immediately cried out and fell to his knees, and then rolled backwards, unresponsive. His eyes were closed, but fluttering wildly.

Reuben ran over. "Shit. What now?"

Avery dropped next to Alex, the springy earth cold through her jeans. She shook his shoulder. "Alex!"

Nate pulled her hands away. "Let it run its course. He's made a connection."

Alex groaned and once again, started speaking in the strange language he had uttered the other night. For what seemed an age, but was probably only seconds, Alex muttered and writhed, a sweat breaking out on his forehead, and then he passed out.

"He needs water," Nate directed. "Anyone?"

"Here," El said, passing her bottle.

Nate lifted Alex's head carefully, and trickled some water around his lips. He then brushed his hand across Alex's brow. Alex immediately stirred and blinked a few times.

"What did you do?" Avery asked Nate.

"My mother had the Sight," he explained. "I've learnt a few tricks over the years."

Alex sat up slowly, breathing deeply. "Wow. That was intense."

"Care to share?" Nate asked, still supporting Alex's back.

"It was a warning to stay away. It knows we're here—that *I'm* here. But also some unwelcome advice. They warn that the Children of Llyr have arrived, and the Nephilim aren't happy about it." He rubbed his head. "Has anyone got any paracetamol?"

Eve crossed her arms in front of her decisively. "Right, you better come back to mine."

17

El followed Eve back along the B3306 towards St Ives, and then on through the town towards Porthmeor Beach and the small nub of land called The Island.

The streets here, like many small Cornish towns, were narrow and edged with a variety of old stone houses built over the centuries, and because of their size, some of the roads were one-way only. St Ives was known for its colony of artists and art galleries, and the streets hummed with pedestrians weaving in and out of shops, restaurants, and pubs. It had been years since Avery had visited, and she looked out of the windows curiously, noting the changes, while keeping half an eye on Alex. He was subdued, lying flat on the back seat, his head in her lap, and Avery stroked his hair and face.

Eve led them through a warren of lanes until they were on the coastal road overlooking Porthmeor Beach, and pulled into a tiny car park at the back of a row of cottages.

Eve lived in an attic studio flat above an art gallery, and while the back view was of the streets and houses, the front looked out over the beach and the wide expanse of the sea, over which was the southern coast of Ireland.

 Avery had not realised Eve was an artist, but it was obvious as soon as she entered her flat. The walls were covered in artwork, either finished or in various stages of completion, and paints, pencils, brushes, pastels, canvases, books, and easels were everywhere. The windows were huge, allowing lots of light in.

Avery looked at some of the paintings, noting they were of brooding landscapes overshadowed by large expanses of sky. Close up, she could see faint images of faces skilfully disguised in the trees and hills.

Avery smiled as she looked around, feeling a kindred spirit. If possible, Eve was even more untidy than she was. The far end of the studio was set up as a living area, and three couches had been arranged around the fireplace on the end wall. It was here that Eve escorted them, settling Alex into a seat, before heading to make some tea. The kitchen was open plan, tucked in the far corner next to the living area, where there was space for a small round table and four chairs. There was a single door in the wall, which Avery presumed led to the bedroom and bathroom.

Avery sat next to Alex who had stretched out on the sofa, while Reuben looked out of the window, and Nate disappeared through the door to the side. El went to find painkillers.

"How are you?" Avery asked softly, her voice low.

Alex squinted, his eyes creased with pain. "I've been better."

"You should stop communing with spirits, then."

"He started it," Alex muttered.

El came over with a glass of water and some paracetamol. "Here you go. Nate's in the back fixing you up something a little more potent."

Alex groaned, sat up, knocked back the pills and some water, and immediately lay down again.

"Is he making a potion?" Avery asked.

El nodded, folding herself gracefully onto the floor, her legs crossed. "I believe so. He has a recipe for something that worked wonders for his mother." She nodded towards the back of the room. "Eve's spell room is back there, beyond her bedroom."

At that point they heard the kettle boil, and Eve came to join them, carrying a huge tray filled with mugs, a teapot, and a coffee pot. She placed everything on a worn wooden coffee table and sat next to El on the colourful rug on the floor.

"I wasn't sure what everyone wanted, so I made everything. And I've got biscuits."

She opened a packet of cookies and offered them around, before sorting out their drinks.

"Awesome," Reuben said, taking a handful of biscuits. "My blood sugar was dangerously low."

"You are a wonder woman," Avery declared, reaching forward to take a mug of coffee. "Thank you. It's great we didn't have to drive straight home."

"No problem. It's good to finally have a chance to talk to you properly." She grinned and looked at the others. "And to meet some more of the famous White Haven witches."

Reuben let out a short, barking laugh and sat on the other sofa, stretching out his long legs. "That's funny. Don't you mean *infamous*?"

"Maybe that would be a better word," Eve said, laughing for a moment before becoming serious again. "We live in strange times, though, so it's good to finally meet you. I'm worried about what your friend said." She nodded at Alex.

"Me, too," he agreed, groaning. "I don't think we're enemy number one anymore."

"Wait until Nate is back with his miracle cure, and then we'll talk more," Eve said. She made herself more comfortable and took a sip of her tea. "Instead, you can tell me about what you all get up to on the south coast."

For the next ten minutes they chatted idly about what they did, and then Eve explained about her work. "I do watercolours mainly, and exhibit in a few places about the town and in various shops. I rent this place long-term. I love it, the light's fantastic."

"And what about Nate?" El asked. "Is he an artist, too?"

"Yes, but he sculpts in metal mainly. He has a place across town."

"So, are you two…?" Reuben asked, meaningfully.

Eve laughed. "No. He has a girlfriend, and I'm between boyfriends right now."

"Are there any other witches in St Ives?" El asked.

Eve shook her head sadly. "No. There were three of us, but Ruth left town years ago. Neither of us are originally from here. Nate's from Newcastle, but moved down here in his early teens with his mother. She married a local after Nate's dad died when he was only a child. His step-father died, too. Nate's mother was a powerful Seer, but she passed away last year after a sudden illness. My family is originally from Glastonbury way, but I moved here on my own. St Ives is the next best place to Glastonbury, in my opinion."

Eve looked a little sad as she said that, but didn't elaborate, and Avery wondered if there was some reason she'd had to leave Glastonbury. Or some reason she wanted to.

They were interrupted then by Nate, who came out of the back room carrying a steaming cup of something fragrant. He knelt next to Alex, who was still lying down, his eyes closed.

"All right, mate. Sit up. I have something for you that'll sort you right out."

Alex squinted at him, and slowly sat up. "I'll believe it when it works."

"It'll work all right," he said, passing him the small, steaming cup.

Alex took a tentative sip and grimaced.

"What is that?" Avery asked, inhaling deeply. "It smells delicious, just like summer."

"I can assure you it does not taste like that," Alex said, wrinkling his face in distaste.

"Interesting you think that," Nate said, addressing Avery and ignoring Alex. "It's called Summer Lightning. It's been fine-tuned for centuries."

"You should share that with Briar. She's our healer—she'd love it."

"Sure. I don't jealously guard my spells like some," Nate said evenly.

"Are you a Seer, like your mother?" El asked him.

He shook his head. "No. That has skipped my generation. Probably a blessing." He looked at Alex. "It's not easy to bear. Especially when your Sight wakes fully."

Alex looked at him. "What do you mean, wakes fully?"

"Yours is just starting, mate. I can tell. The Sight can lie dormant for years, or just turns on and off in fits and starts. But then, for some, something triggers it, and when that happens, it's a battle to stop it."

Avery felt a thread of worry start to run through her, and Alex stopped drinking his potion and looked at her, and then back to Nate. "You mean these things will start to happen more often?"

"Have they been more often lately?"

"I guess so," Alex said thoughtfully.

"I thought so. I can tell. Maybe it's the tail end of my mother's sense. Things might get rough for a while. You'll need to learn to close it off."

"I will?"

"Unless you want to go nuts," Nate said. "Which, I presume, you don't."

"Great. Just great," Alex said, and forced himself to take another sip. "Any tips?"

"I may have a few," he said. "When you feel better, we can talk some more."

Avery liked Nate and Eve. They were friendly and down to earth, and didn't seem to harbour any resentment towards any of them, despite the fact that they had released a cloud of powerful magic and caused some degree of havoc across Cornwall. She felt she knew Eve a little from their brief meetings at the Council, but despite knowing a little bit about Nate from Eve, he still seemed a mystery. He'd shed his leather jacket, revealing an old New Model Army t-shirt full of holes, and up close she could see a slight singeing to his jeans. *Sparks from fire for his sculpting*, she presumed. He wasn't aloof at all, but she couldn't read him as well as Eve.

"And what about you, Nate? What's *your* strength?" Avery asked, looking at him curiously.

He fixed his light brown eyes on her. "Fire, which makes sculpting easier, and telekinesis, of all things. And of course, potions."

There was a brief second of silence in which even Reuben stopped crunching. "Telekinesis?"

Nate nodded. "I barely have to think it, and…" He held his hand out towards the collection of brushes on a nearby table, and in seconds they had lifted into the air, whizzed across the room, and landed in his outstretched hand.

Reuben swallowed loudly. "Wow. It takes a lot of effort for me to do that."

"I have to summon air to do that," Avery said, agreeing with Reuben.

Nate shrugged and looked mildly embarrassed. "What can I say? It's a gift."

"Impressive." El turned to Eve. "And what about you?"

Eve's expression was bright and slightly mischievous. "I'm a weather witch. Of course, I have elemental powers, but they combine to manipulate weather particularly well. However, I don't do that often. It plays havoc everywhere." She gestured to the artwork spread around the room, and Avery suddenly realised why all of her artwork was of stormy landscapes.

Avery had never met a weather witch. It took great control to manipulate huge systems of water, wind, and fire, and weather was a combination of all those things, particularly storms. The chance that they could get out of control was magnified on a huge scale.

"Wanna do swapsies?" Alex asked, still grimacing from a combination of the potion and his lingering headache.

"No, thanks. The Sight does not appeal to me."

Mention of the Sight reminded Avery of something the Nephilim had said. "Alex, the spirit said the Children of Llyr have arrived. They must know Mermaids are here, on land."

He nodded. "I don't know how they know, though."

"It must be like Briar said—the earth trembles because they're here. Maybe they sense that."

"Maybe," Nate said, "the earth trembles because the Nephilim are here."

"True," Avery admitted. "Eve, if needed, is your magic strong enough to drive the Mermaids back to sea? Especially combined with Reuben's ability to manipulate water?"

Eve gazed into her cup and swirled her tea around, releasing steam and scents of cardamom and ginger, before she finally looked up. "I doubt it. While the weather can influence tides and obviously waves during storms, I'm not sure how effective it would be against Mermaids. The water is their strength, their habitat, not ours. It would probably be best to fight them on land. An earth witch would have greater power there."

"Maybe. We just know so little about them. It's infuriating!" Avery exclaimed, feeling hopeless all over again.

Nate frowned. "Are you sure they're on land? How do you know?"

"Well, Oswald said Ulysses could tell in Mevagissey. And then this morning, we found out that three fishermen disappeared overnight, and their empty boat was found drifting this morning. Reuben traced Mermaids to the Devil's Canyon, a small cove outside White Haven. We're pretty sure they're now in the town. We need to find a way to identify them, before any more men disappear."

"You should speak to Ulysses about that," Eve said.

"Really? Why's that? Is he a Mermaid detector?" Reuben asked.

Nate looked at Eve as if weighing whether to tell them something, and then said, "Rumours are that Ulysses has Mermaid blood inside him."

Avery almost dropped her mug in shock. "What? How does that happen?"

"Oswald doesn't talk about it, and neither does Ulysses. But those are the rumours. And if you'd ever met him, you'd know why."

"Has he got scales or something?" Reuben asked, only half joking.

Nate shook his head. "I'm saying nothing. It will be a surprise."

"Okay," Avery said, wearily. "One more thing to add to my list. I presume you aren't worried about Mermaids in St Ives?"

Nate shook his head. "No. But we're not the ones with a big cloud of magic over us. Maybe it's just the south coast of Cornwall that will be affected." He looked at Alex. "Apart from the warning, what else did the Nephilim say? What was the general tone?"

Alex thought for a second. "I can only guess that the blood on the capstone must have triggered it. As soon as I touched it, I felt an intense flood of emotions. I immediately connected to the spirit I linked with last time. I recognised him straightaway, and he knew me." He hesitated and then said, "I think that he had no control over our linking, either. It seemed to me there was a few seconds when he didn't register that I was there at all and his feelings were unguarded. I could see through his eyes, too. He was somewhere dark and damp, and there was a smell around him that I couldn't quite place. I sensed his joy at being released, but also anger and fear. I guess the fear is from us, and the fact that they know we are looking for them, but also there was anger about the Mermaids. Anyway, the connection was short but intense. As soon as it recognised me, I could feel him mentally trying to shake me, and he warned me to stay away. The more I think about it, actually," he mused, "the more I realise how much he was thinking about Mermaids. His thoughts were full of them."

El frowned. "That's pretty scary, Alex, that you could connect so strongly."

"I know. Anyway, the shock was huge for both of us, but after a few seconds he was able to cut it. *After* warning me to back off."

"I think that you should be able to connect again," Nate said. "If you want to."

"I'm not sure I do," Alex said, finally draining his cup. "What do the Nephilim have against the Children of Llyr?"

Avery's grin broadened as a realisation hit her. "The Flood, of course, when the seas rose across the land, wiping the Nephilim from existence. God wanted to eradicate them and used Llyr to do it. I guess that's a pretty big score to settle."

18

When they arrived back in White Haven, Avery left Alex at his flat where he was heading for an early night. Nate's potion seemed to be working, but the psychic link with the Nephilim had left him drained.

As soon as she entered her own flat, she smelled smoke and violets. *Helena.* She looked around, wondering if she'd manifest, but other than her smell, there was no evidence of her. Avery wasn't sure if that was a good thing or not. She'd warded her bedroom against her presence, but otherwise, Helena was free to drift in and out as she pleased. She knew it was odd, especially as Helena had tried to kill her, but she couldn't bring herself to banish her completely. She was connected to her. She was family, after all.

Avery flung open the door and windows, letting the cool evening breeze drift through the rooms in an attempt to get rid of Helena's scent. Circe and Medea were pleased to see her, and rubbed against her ankles affectionately. She rubbed their silky heads and headed to the kitchen to feed them, before curling up on the sofa in the attic with a collection of books on history and myths and legends. She intended to gather every bit of information she could on the Nephilim and the Children of Llyr.

She'd only been reading for an hour or so when her lamps flickered, the music she'd been listening to stopped, and the scent of violets returned, and Helena manifested abruptly in front of her. She was wrapped in her dark cloak, a peek of her long dress beneath, and her dark hair flowed down her back and over her shoulders. She was not as *solid* as she had appeared beneath All Souls, and Avery could see through her to the room behind. Nevertheless, Helena's intense stare was unnerving; the narrowed glare of furious dark eyes that had seen who knows what in the spirit world.

Avery met her gaze, refusing to flinch. "Helena. Nice of you to stop by. Can I help you?"

It was ridiculous to speak to her; Avery knew she couldn't answer, but what else should she do? She couldn't just ignore her.

Helena's gaze was imperious and slightly resentful. It seemed she hadn't forgiven Avery for regaining control of her body, and Avery had no intention of letting her in again. Her eyes fell to Avery's neck and the amulet that El had made her recently, to protect against spirits. She drew her lips back in a snarl.

"Calm down, Helena. This isn't meant for you. What do you want?"

Helena pointed to the table where the grimoires lay. Immediately her grimoire, the original, flipped open and the pages turned rapidly, fluttering like wings before they finally stopped. Helena turned to Avery, hands on her hips.

Intriguing.

"All right. I'll bite," Avery said, unfolding from beneath the papers and heading to the grimoire. Helena hovered behind her left shoulder as Avery conjured a witch light.

The spell in front of her was old, located towards the beginning of the book. This meant it was probably written in the 14th century. The writing was cramped, the language difficult and archaic, and the illustrations obscure. And there, revealed by the witch light, was an image of a Mermaid perched on a rock. She had a beautiful face surrounded by long, flowing hair, and her long fishtail was coiled around her, detailed with tiny scales, but her smile was filled with razor-sharp teeth.

Avery gasped. *A spell about Mermaids.* She turned around to see Helena's predatory smile spread across her face. "Thank you, Helena." But Helena was already vanishing, leaving just a trace of violets behind.

Avery tried to decipher the spell's writing. The title said *Geyppan Merewif.* She turned to the shelf behind her, fingers grazing the reference books until she found the one she wanted, an Old English Dictionary. A few minutes of searching found the meaning. It meant essentially, "To Expose the Water Witch."

Avery grinned. A spell to reveal a Mermaid. If they couldn't banish them, at least they could see them, and that was a start. She pulled the grimoire towards her, grabbed a pen and started to translate the spell.

***

The next morning, despite only a couple of hours' sleep, Avery bounced into Happenstance Books. It had taken hours, but she had finally deciphered the arcane spell, and now she had a way to reveal the Mermaids. She needed to speak to Briar for help with some of the herbs.

She brewed a strong coffee and then walked around her shop, renewing protection spells, and the spell to help visitors find that special book, lit incense, and generally stoked the magic, so that by the time Dan arrived, the place hummed with energy.

Dan loped in through the front door, wearing his university t-shirt and jeans, and a messenger bag slung over his shoulder. He looked around the shop and then at her with narrowed eyes. "You must have had a good Sunday."

"I had an excellent Sunday, thank you. Did you?"

"Pretty good—pub lunch, a walk along the beach, played some football. But enough about me," he said, setting his bag down on the counter by the till. "What have you been up to?"

"I've been researching Mermaids, and have had a little success. I might actually have a way to identify them now." She looked at him speculatively. "I don't suppose you've seen any new women around town, have you?"

He groaned. "Are you kidding? There are loads! It's summer. There are positively gaggles of them, all giggling and surfing and drinking. I got chatted up tons last night. It was great." He grinned, and then his face fell. "Hold on. Are you saying I was being chatted up by *Mermaids*?"

Avery shrugged. "I don't know. But after yesterday, we know they're here, in town somewhere. Didn't you hear about the missing fishermen?"

Dan nodded sadly. "Yeah, I did. It's pretty crap. I didn't know them, but I know friends of them. You think it was Mermaids?"

"It was a calm night, they were in an area not known for the best fishing, and far away from the other boats. We think they were lured there, and then…" She didn't need to finish the sentence.

Dan sat heavily on the stool behind the counter. Fortunately, they had the shop to themselves. "Are they *that* powerful?"

Avery nodded. "We think we found where they've come ashore—the cave in Devil's Canyon Cove. Within seconds they had bewitched Alex, Reuben, and Newton. Not enough to make them jump overboard, but they were distracted, vague—dreamy," she said, searching for a better word. "For some reason Nils was spared, probably because he was at the front of the boat. But," a sudden flash of worry flashed through her mind. "Maybe we should check, just in case."

"And all they want is men? Mates?"

"Yes, we think so. We also think that the magic we released has attracted them here. I suppose like anything that's supernatural, they have their own magic, but are drawn to the magic of others, too. But they're not of the Earth. They are *Other*."

Dan's bright and breezy attitude had disappeared. "For the last few days, there have been about half a dozen long-haired, long-legged young beauties flirting the night away at The Kraken, just off the harbour. They've been attracting men like flies around shit. Including myself. Now that I think about it, it does seem weird. I mean, people flirt in pubs all the time, but these girls exude glamour, confidence. I wonder?" He looked into the middle distance, lost in his thoughts for a second. "I must admit, when you're close by them, it's hard to look away. But, well, they're attractive and funny. It's not that unusual."

Avery fell silent, thinking and watching Dan. "It's a big pub, isn't it? Pretty loud, bands on sometimes?"

"Oh, yeah. It's not the pub I usually go in, actually, it's a bit full-on for me, but my mate, Pete, wanted to go in Saturday night. It has a big party vibe on a weekend, lots of young people out to have fun. One of *those* pubs."

Avery nodded. She knew exactly what he meant. It was the type of pub she usually avoided, too. But maybe she should make an exception. She ran through all the pubs in White Haven. There were quite a few, a mixture of family pubs, upscale bars, chain pubs, those who catered for all sorts, like The Wayward Son, and then there were the party pubs that only wanted singles or couples. Kids were actively discouraged. There were only a few that would fit that description. The Kraken, The Flying Fish, and The Badger's Hat. If she were a predatory female, looking for the biggest selection of young men who'd be drinking, up for fun, flirting, and sex with no strings attached, those would be the pubs that would offer the biggest pool of men to choose from. And she presumed they *were* choosing them. If Avery could perfect the spell, then she could try it out, maybe tomorrow.

Avery looked up at Dan. "Can you spare me for a few hours?"

"I guess so." He looked momentarily confused. "I thought you were worried about Nephilim?"

"Oh, I'm worried about both now."

"Great, just great," he murmured. "Bring me coffee and cake when you come back."

***

As usual, Briar's shop smelled divine. This time it was the scent of basil, rosemary, and...*what?* And then it struck Avery. Tomatoes—fresh, sun-warmed tomatoes. *Delicious.*

Briar looked up and smiled, and then went back to serving her customer, putting the finishing touches on her wrapping.

There were already quite a few customers drifting around the displays, trying out lotions, and sniffing soaps. Another customer, a young woman, carried some creams to the counter, so Avery strolled around the shop, trying out hand creams while she waited.

When Briar was finally free, she joined her at the counter. "What are you doing with tomatoes, Briar?"

"You can smell them? Oh, good. Gardeners' soaps. It's a new range. Delicious, isn't it? And a little something to soothe the joints, too," she said conspiratorially.

"Nice! Well, I know you're busy, but I wondered if you had a couple of dried plants I can have. They're not that common. Well, I haven't got them, anyway."

Briar frowned. "Such as?"

"Agrimony root and Blessed Thistle leaves."

"Follow me." She headed through a door into a room at the back of the shop, and the pungent smell of plants hit Avery like a hammer. The room was filled from floor to ceiling with shelves, and on them were jars and baskets stocked with dried herbs, tinctures, fatty creams, roots, cuttings, and real plants in pots. Everything was meticulously labelled. Above their head were rows of wooden beams, and hanging from them were bunches of drying plants. A long bench ran beneath a window, a little bit like in El's shop, and empty jars sat there, waiting to be filled, as well as ribbons and bags for decoration.

"Wow," Avery said, looking around. "Very impressive."

"I need a lot of stock," Briar explained. She pulled a short step-ladder towards her and used it to reach a small brown jar, and then headed to another shelf and pulled down a bundle of roots. She carefully carried them to the counter, pulled a strand free of the roots, and placed it in a paper bag. Then she measured out a small thimbleful of the dried plant from the brown bottle. "This is strong, so I trust you're using it sparingly. What are you doing with it?"

Avery lowered her voice. "Trying to identify Mermaids."

Briar's eyes widened. "Do you need help?"

Avery thought for a second. "Yes, please. I don't want to take Alex, or any of the men, actually."

Briar nodded. "So what's the plan?"

"I have a spell to unveil Mermaids, but I need to be close by them to use it. I have a few places to try. Which reminds me. Have you got something to aerosolise my potion?"

"Like an old fashioned perfume dispenser?" Briar asked, reaching to the shelf above her and grabbing a beautiful, cut-glass dispenser with gold edging, a fancy purple pump at the top.

"Perfect! You fancy meeting me for a pub crawl after work tomorrow? We'll start at The Flying Fish."

"I'm intrigued. Consider it done. And El?"

"I'll ask her, too. So, another two bottles, please."

***

Before Avery headed back to the shop, she decided to visit James. He had no idea that the spirit had vacated All Souls, and she knew he'd want to use the church again. She hoped he wasn't going to ask her awkward questions.

He opened the door to the vicarage and frowned. "Avery, has something happened?"

"Good news only, you'll be pleased to know."

Relief washed over his face. "Excellent, come in, the kettle's on." He turned and led the way to a large kitchen at the back of the house, overlooking a small square garden filled with children's toys. "Tea?"

"I'm sorry, I can't stay," she said. *Hopefully the less time she spent there, the less awkward questions he might ask.* "I've got to get back to my shop."

"Of course," he nodded, pouring hot water into the teapot. "So, what happened with the spirit?"

"It's gone."

He paused mid-pour. "Gone? How? Where? When?"

474

Should she lie and say Alex had banished it? That might have repercussions later.

"I don't know where." *That was true.* "Sometimes spirits just disappear back to where they came from, or it may have gone somewhere else. But we checked the church yesterday, and it's safe," she said vaguely.

"But, I thought spirits usually remained in one place, somewhere familiar to them."

"Usually, but not always. However, I don't think you need to worry. I'm sure it wasn't responsible for Harry's death after all, and that it was just a horrible coincidence. The police are still investigating."

"Well, how do you know it isn't just hiding again? And how did you get in?" His voice was rising with annoyance.

OH SHIT. "Look James. I can't explain everything to you, but trust me, it's gone. Me and Alex have ways of investigating these things."

James fell silent for a second, studying her. "Why do I get the feeling you're not being honest with me?"

"I'm being as honest as I can. But I can confidently say that you can safely use All Souls again." She smiled tentatively. "Hopefully this will be the last time you'll have a restless spirit in All Souls. We'll keep monitoring the local area, just in case it's gone somewhere else."

He narrowed his eyes. "You know there was a death in Harecombe too?"

"Yes, but no reports of spirits," she said, hoping the vicar there hadn't felt a presence. Surely not, or they'd have heard about it. "Anyway, I better go. I just wanted you to know the church is safe again."

"You know what some of the town believes about you, Avery?"

She felt her heart start to pound, and she took a deep breath. "Yes, I know. Because of the things in my shop and my ancestor, people think I'm a witch. This town runs on rumours of magic. That's how we make our money, you know that."

"Where there's smoke, there's fire," he said, watching her intently.

"Not always," she said evenly. "And you came to me, remember."

"I accept there are many things in this world I don't understand, Avery. I needed help. Maybe desperation was my weakness."

"Not a weakness. You needed help and I gave it, and will do again. You can trust me. If anything else happens let me know."

And before he could ask anything else, she left.

* * *

When Avery dutifully arrived back at Happenstance Books, she carried fresh pastries, Dan's weakness, and lattes. She spent the rest of the day serving customers and reviewing the instructions to the spell in her head, and as soon as the day was done, she headed up to the attic to start. She lit the fire in the small brick fireplace, stoking it until it burned hot and bright. Then she pulled out the cauldron she kept for such work, and set it on her wooden table. Finally, she started to assemble her ingredients.

It was hours later when Avery finally finished, and the potion was now simmering down. Her stomach grumbled, and it was already becoming dark out. The dormer windows were open, and the scent of summer and dust drifted in. Beyond, just visible in the grey twilight, bats swooped for insects. She sighed with pleasure, and once again thought on how much she loved White Haven, and would do anything to keep it safe.

She headed down to the kitchen to feed the cats, now watching her with resentment, and to make some toast, bringing it back up with her to watch the potion like a hawk. One wrong move now and she'd have to start again.

She sat on the rug, eating absently, when her phone rang and she saw Ben's number.

"Hey, Ben. How are you three doing after Saturday night?"

His voice sounded excited, which was a relief. "We're great, thanks, just psyched about the whole night and really pleased with some of our footage. If you're free tomorrow, you should come around to the office we've got set up."

"Sounds intriguing. I think I could do that. Where's your office?"

"We've bagged a room at the university. It's small and poky, but better than nothing."

"Sure—can anyone else come?"

"Whoever's interested," Ben said.

"Cool. Mid-morning okay?" she asked, thinking she could get back and relieve her staff for lunchbreaks afterward.

"Perfect. See you then."

Avery knew most of the others would be working, but Alex might be free in the morning. She called him, looking forward to hearing his voice. It rang half a dozen times before he picked up, and she could hear music from the pub. "Hello, gorgeous," he answered.

"Hello gorgeous, yourself. You busy?"

"Hold on," he shouted, and then the sounds disappeared and she realised he must have moved into the kitchen area behind the bar. "Sorry, had to move. Yes, very. It's a sign tourist season has hit. How about you?"

"The usual. Look, I won't keep you, but do you want to come with me to see our friendly neighbourhood ghost busters tomorrow morning? At the Uni in Penryn?"

"Yeah, why not. Any chance I could come to yours tonight? I can finish in another couple of hours."

She felt the warm pleasure at seeing him flood through her. "That sounds great. Do you need anything? Food, drink?"

"Just you."

She felt her heart skip a beat and she smiled. "Well, I'm all yours."

"Later, then," he said, and rang off, leaving her grinning at the cats like a lovesick fool.

19

Penryn University was a well-designed mixture of old buildings and new, set in green fields close to Falmouth, a town on the south coast of Cornwall.

Alex and Avery arrived close to 10:00 AM, pulling onto the visitors' car park in Alex's Alfa Romeo Spider Boat Tail. The day was overcast but muggy, and they had driven with the roof down and music blaring, both of them singing loudly and laughing all the way.

As Alex parked, Avery called Ben to let him know that they'd arrived, then they checked the map on the visitors' board and strolled across the campus to the entrance of the Pendennis Building where Ben had agreed to meet them. There were very few students around. It was the summer holidays, and the university had opened up for summer school and short courses only.

They approached a dark red stone building, the large windows glinting with reflected sunlight. Ben was leaning on the wall, scrolling through his phone as he waited. He looked rumpled, occasionally running his hand through his short dark hair. His Penryn University t-shirt was creased, his jeans had dropped from his waist and were perched on his hips, and his feet were barely in some old green Adidas trainers. He looked up and grinned when he heard them approach, put his phone away, and shook Alex's hand. "Hi, guys. Glad you could come. You're going to love our stuff," he said, leading them inside.

The interior of the building was modern. The entrance was huge, and bright artwork decorated the expanse of white walls. Granite tiles covered the floors, and a sleek staircase was in the centre, next to the lifts.

"I didn't know you had office space," Avery said, looking around with interest.

Ben headed to the lifts, and pressed the button. "We didn't until about a month ago, when my website really started to take off, and we got lots of referrals. I approached my tutor and stressed that what I was doing was fundamental research, and after all, that is what this building—and this university—is all about. Obviously there's a central research area we all use, but I wanted my own space." He dropped his voice. "He wasn't very happy or very eager to help, but one of the other research projects had just been canned, and the semester had ended, so I argued I should have the spare room. And since it's the holidays, no one's here."

The lift *pinged* as it arrived, and they stepped in, Ben pressing the button for the fourth floor.

"Well, I guess congratulations are in order," Alex said, looking vaguely impressed.

"We've only got it for six months," Ben shrugged, "but it's better than nothing. We'll set up in my flat afterwards if we have to."

When they arrived at the fourth floor, Ben led them through a maze of halls and doors, passing room after room, until they came to the end of the corridor at the back of the building. He flung open the door. "Ta da!"

The room beyond was small, with a tall, narrow window on the far wall looking out over a mixture of buildings and fields. In the distance was a glimpse of the sea and the sprawling town of Falmouth. The room was packed with workbenches, a desk, computers and electronic equipment, huge white boards filled with pictures and scribbled writing, and the hum of electricity buzzed in the air. In the middle of all this were Dylan and Cassie, staring at monitors.

"Welcome," Ben declared. "*Mi casa es su casa!*"

"So, this is where you investigate all the things that go bump in the night?" Alex said, looking around with amusement.

Avery prodded him in the ribs. "This is pretty cool! And exciting."

Dylan slid the earphones he'd been wearing around his neck. "Make us feel legit. I'm going to have business cards printed next."

Cassie laughed. "Your faces are a picture, but he's not kidding. Over the last few days, we've decided we're going to make a go of this."

"Come in," Ben said, shutting the door behind them and ushering them to some spare seats.

"But I thought you were doing post-grad studies, and had—" Avery floundered for the right word, "*other* careers planned."

"When you study parapsychology this *is* the perfect career," Cassie said, leaning back in her swivel chair. "I mean, of course we'll finish our post-grad studies, obviously, but I only had vague plans of what to do with it. Research, of some sort. This is the perfect fit."

"Seriously?" Alex said, looking at her, baffled. "You looked massively spooked at the castle the first time we met."

"It was a shock, I admit that. None of us had ever seen anything on that scale before."

"And potentially won't again," Avery tempered, feeling she needed to add some reason to the conversation. "Ghosts don't normally manifest like that."

"True," Cassie agreed. "But I came back, didn't I?"

Dylan was perched on the end of his chair, his right foot on his knee. The screen next to him appeared to be showing an audio file that he'd paused halfway through. "We know that not every event will be as big as the stuff we've seen recently. Don't worry, we're not getting the wrong idea. But there's way more out there than I realised. And knowing you, and what you are—it's opened our minds to all sorts of things. We're going to be a bit more than just ghost-hunters."

"You are?" Alex asked.

"And we'd like your help," Cassie added.

"You would?" Avery asked, glancing at Alex.

"Nothing that would unveil your identify," Ben tried to reassure them.

"I'm not Batman," Alex said, looking amused.

"No, just a paranoid witch," Dylan said. He held his hands up in mock surrender as Alex glared at him. "I get it, just saying!"

Ben stepped in. "Hold on. We're getting ahead of ourselves. Can we show you some stuff first?"

"Of course you can," Avery said, trying to ignore Alex bristling next to her. "We're all ears."

"First things first. Don't go summoning any of your witchy magic in this room—unless we ask you to. Our stuff's pretty sensitive, and we don't want you shorting it out."

"No problem," Avery said, nodding.

"Great. So, Dylan—want to roll the video?"

Dylan turned to one of the computers behind him. "This video is from the other night at St Luke's. I've edited it a bit…the first part didn't show much. It's in infrared, so the dark blue and green colours indicate cold, and yellows, reds and oranges are heat."

It was odd to see themselves as thermal images. The church was in shades of blue, while their bodies were rendered in a strange, orangey hue, particularly their heads, where they were warmest.

"It's interesting," Cassie said, looking at them, "that all you witches look a brighter range than we do—redder, actually. I think it must be your magic."

"You're right," Alex agreed, nodding. "That is interesting."

"When you use magic, the flare of heat is even greater," Dylan explained. "I think it's the energy you summon, the way you manipulate the elements—or whatever it is you do. I'm going to have to ask you more about that one day."

Great. Now they wanted to study them. Avery had no idea how she felt about that. Surely the magic of magic was its unknowability. She wasn't sure she wanted it reduced to science and graphs. But, on the other hand, the footage *was* fascinating.

For a while, nothing much happened onscreen as they moved around the church, and Alex prepared the circle. They could see the flare of the candle flames and the bright buzz of energy around Avery when she lit the candles using magic, and the glow from the light bulbs.

And then the Nephilim arrived.

"Here," Ben pointed. "You can see a shape behind the altar, a slightly paler blue than the surroundings. Turn the audio up, Dylan."

Again the thermal imaging showed the wide sweep of wings, and they could hear a whining buzz of static as the electric lights started to flash and then overload and blow out, showing as very bright, orangey-red pulses on film. The sound of shouts filled the air, and the zap of magic buzzed again and again. The Nephilim started to get brighter in colour, too, swelling with power, and they saw Caspian sail across the room, caught by the Nephilim's wings. When Estelle started to throw balls of energy at it, it was immediately obvious that it absorbed every single one, becoming brighter and brighter as it grew. When Caspian joined in, they could see its limbs forming out of what was an almost shapeless blob with wings before.

"Wow," Avery said. "That's amazing. I mean, I know, I was there. I saw it happening, but to see it again like this! You can actually see it absorb Estelle and Caspian's magic."

Ben grinned. "I know. This is way better than we expected. Watch this," he said, pointing back to the screen.

Everyone was now back in the circle, except for Alex and Avery, who had left it to get Caspian and Estelle. *They had only just made it,* Avery thought, feeling a chill run through her as the Nephilim advanced on them. They saw the punch that Alex threw at Caspian, the bright burst of blood from Caspian's nose, and then a huge red flare as Avery activated the circle, creating a wall of protective magic around them.

"And that's your magic, Avery," Cassie said admiringly. "That thing can't get close."

The Nephilim stalked around the outside, and then flared brighter again as it headed for the window and smashed through. A wave of yellow flashed across the walls, and then faded.

"That's the spell breaking that sealed the church," Alex noted. He leaned back in his chair, exhaling heavily. "That's actually amazing, to see magic and elemental energy as infrared. And the Nephilim absorbing it."

All three of the paranormal investigators grinned. Dylan said, "I've isolated some of the audio. Listen."

He turned to another computer and played the audio he had displayed on the screen. Over the whine of static they heard a strange, guttural language.

"That's the language Alex was speaking the other night!" Avery said. "Yep. I recognise that," he agreed.

"I can't believe you've captured that."

"That's all we've got," Ben said, "seconds only. Any idea what it says?"

"Not a clue," Alex said, shaking his head.

"Have you noticed how much brighter your energy is, compared to Caspian's and Estelle's?" Cassie pointed out.

"I suppose it is," Avery said, watching the screen closely. "Must be our new influx of magic."

"Anyway," Ben said, "we have some more footage to show you of some other places we've been. Nothing as good as this, but stuff that happened in different houses around Cornwall. We thought you might like to see some of the spirit activity we've captured."

"Sounds good," Alex said. "But first, you said you wanted to ask us something. What did you want?"

Ben glanced at Cassie and Dylan. "We wondered if we set up a paranormal business, could you help us, if we needed a bit of support with any cases? We'd pay you, of course. We're going to charge for this. Or could you recommend someone who could help?" He looked slightly perplexed. "You know, most of the time, it should just be us recording and observing, but we could offer a service, too—to banish unwanted spirits, ghouls, dark magic…" He trailed off, looking hopeful.

Alex glanced at Avery. "I don't mind helping, but I'm pretty busy at the pub, and I'm guessing Avery's pretty busy at the shop, but we could have a think to see if there's someone who could help more often than us."

"Awesome, thanks guys," Ben said, relieved.

"After what we've seen, it would be good to have some support," Cassie added.

"We could probably teach you some simple protection and banishing spells, nothing that needed too much magic," Avery said, already thinking of some basic spells that would work.

"Great! Thank you."

And then Avery had another idea. "You know, I was talking to Briar the other day. She's pretty busy at her shop. She doesn't have help like we do, but I get the feeling she was thinking about looking. Obviously she wants someone trustworthy."

"Me!" Cassie said immediately. "I'd love to help, and it's a great opportunity to learn."

Avery smiled. "Cool. I can't promise anything, but I will talk to her for you."

"Right," Ben said. "Let's show you what else we've been up to."

20

At 7:30 PM that night, Avery was dressed in her heels, skinny jeans, and a slinky top, ready to meet Briar and El for a night out, identifying Mermaids.

After she and Alex had left Penryn in the afternoon, they both headed to work. She had decided to lie to Alex about her plans for the night. She knew he would disapprove and worry.

"I'm just having a quiet night in, catching up with some reading and spell casting."

"Well, I'm working, so have fun."

"If a gaggle of young, nubile women come to your pub, looking improbably glamorous, be on your guard."

"Spoilsport," he said, winking. He dropped her outside of her flat and pulled her close for a lingering kiss. "I'll see you soon."

She spent the remainder of the workday in the shop, and once she was back in her flat, filled the three perfume bottles with the finished potion. She held one up to the light, admiring the pale amber colour. It was always satisfying to successfully complete a spell. *Let's hope it works.* She then fed the cats, grabbed her leather bag, and headed out the door.

Avery strolled through the streets and down to the harbour, enjoying the evening's warmth. Down by the harbour, the smell of brine and seaweed was strong, and she inhaled deeply, feeling invigorated by it. The tide was low, and the boats were half beached. The fish and chip shops were doing a brisk business, and people were perched on the sea wall, eating chips from paper. The scent of the food, and the underlying sharp smell of vinegar, mixed with the salty air of the sea made her smile; she was comforted by the reassuring scents. This was the White Haven she loved.

She was meeting El and Briar at The Flying Fish, the pub perched on the rise of the hill overlooking the harbour, on the road that ran next to the beach. She paused outside it and looked up. It was a large pub, set back slightly from the pavement, allowing a few tables to be set up outside. But it was the large, first floor deck that was the busiest, and the sound of music and the chatter of people filled the air from above. The deck provided shelter for the ground floor seating, and it was edged with pots of greenery and strings of lights. Avery weaved through the already crowded tables, looking for groups of women, but most people on the ground floor were couples or small groups of three or four, both men and women.

Avery headed upstairs, and the noise of music, laughter, and chatter hit her like a wall. This place was *busy*. She leaned on the bar and bought a glass of wine, and then made her way to where El was perched on a bar stool at the far end, sipping on a pint of beer. Her long, blonde hair was loose, cascading down her back, and the light caught her piercings; she was drawing lots of admiring glances.

"Hey El, how are you?"

El nodded and jerked her head back over her shoulder. "This place is nuts."

"I know. I haven't been here in years. I forgot it got so busy."

"I came here once, and that was enough. But, you're right. This is a great place to start looking."

Avery glanced around the room, and caught a glimpse of Briar emerging at the top of the stairs. She waved to attract her attention, and Briar waved back, weaving through the crowd to meet them. "I hate this place already," she said as she joined them. She caught the bartender's eye and ordered a drink.

Avery laughed. "Come on, ladies, it's just a bit of fun. Well, until the Mermaids turn mean."

"So, what's the plan?" El asked.

"I think we just need to keep an eye on the groups, maybe wander around a bit, do some eavesdropping, and spray a little potion," Avery said, reaching into her bag for a perfume bottle for each of them.

"This is your potion?" Briar asked, examining it. "It has a slight amber tinge."

"Yep. It's supposed to. Let's hope I've made it properly, and that it works."

"Do I need to say anything?" El asked.

Avery nodded. "Let's find a quiet spot."

El led the way through the jostling bodies to a corner of the balcony, where the music was quieter, and Avery shared the short incantation. "We just use it like perfume, spray it, but just casually miss yourself, and spray whoever's next to you, say the words, and it should unveil the glamour of their appearance, revealing them properly to us."

"Will they know?" El asked.

Avery frowned. "Not sure. But hopefully not."

"Great," El said, sarcastically. "So reassuring, Avery."

"Sorry," she answered, feeling slightly annoyed. "But it's better than doing nothing."

"Fair point," El agreed. "Why don't we get this party started?" She looked around at the small group of girls behind her, all giggling and chatting together, then spritzed herself and murmured the words to activate the spell. Avery gave the potion a little push with the breeze, allowing the fine spray to reach the group. They didn't even notice. And nothing happened.

"Well, that's one group eliminated," El said, grinning. "Shall we keep going?"

Over the course of the next hour they worked their way through the room, checking out every available group. Every now and again one of them would visit the toilets and try in there, but with no success. Eventually, they stood at the corner of the bar surveying the room, the thumping bass of the music making conversation difficult.

"Should we move on?" Briar asked. "I think we've covered everyone."

"I think so," Avery agreed. "Let's try The Kraken. The Badger's Hat has the club in the basement, so we should leave that to last."

"Do you think a Tuesday is probably a dud night?" Briar asked, looking around doubtfully.

"It's jammed in here," El said incredulously. "And I don't think Mermaids keep work timetables, either."

The Kraken was closer to the harbour and had a large beer garden out the back. Like The Flying Fish, the music was loud, and the atmosphere was raucous. They separated and started to sweep the room, the same as they had done before. It wasn't long before Avery felt a tap on the shoulder, and looked around to see Dan, standing with a tall, blond man.

"Hey, Avery!" Dan nodded towards his companion. "This is my mate, Pete."

"Hi, guys," Avery leaned up and kissed Dan's cheek. "Couldn't keep away, then?"

"He couldn't," Dan said, looking at Pete.

Pete laughed. He was attractive, his blond hair slightly long and falling over his face. His eyes were blue, with laughter lines in the corner, and his attention was on a group of young, pretty girls by the bar. He extended his hand. "Hi, Avery. I've heard all about you. Dan tells me this bar could be bad for my health."

Avery's eyes opened wide at Dan, but he gave a vaguely imperceptible shake of the head that made her think that whatever he'd said, Pete had no idea she was a witch. He laughed and said, "Avery doesn't want you to be fodder for these voracious females."

Avery agreed. "I care about the wellbeing of my friends, that's all." She looked at the girls who were undoubtedly all glowing with youth, vitality, and an undeniable sexiness. Every single one was taller than the average woman, slim, with long hair and fair skin. The more she looked at them, the more she thought they might be Mermaids. "Which one's caught your eye?"

Pete shrugged. "They're all gorgeous and they've been here all week, teasing us mercilessly."

I bet they have. Time to try the potion.

"Let's hope they don't break your heart, Pete."

"I'd recover," he said, smirking. "Come on, Dan. You're my wingman."

Pete turned and headed back to the group, who were already surrounded by men, and Dan hesitated a second. "Do you think…?"

"Maybe. I'll head over soon and test my theory. Are you feeling okay?" she asked, examining his expression carefully for signs of vague dreaminess. "No odd compulsions, or the feeling of being bewitched?"

He looked at her, amused. "No different than usual."

"Well, be careful," she said. "I'll find you later."

Avery saw Briar and El by the entrance to the toilets, and threaded her way through the crowd to join them. It was getting darker now, and the low lights of the pub created shady spaces where couples could gravitate.

El broke her conversation with Briar. "Any luck?"

"Maybe, over by the bar. There are half a dozen women who all look possible." She pointed at them discretely. "They are very good looking, flirting massively, and have a harem of men to choose from."

Briar rose up on her tiptoes to see over the crowd. "Maybe. You tested the potion yet?"

"Just about to. You had any luck?"

They both shook their heads, but El answered. "No. Why don't you go and check those, and then let's move to the last place. I feel my soul being sucked out of me here."

Avery knew what she meant. There was almost a smell of desperation about this place. It should have felt fun, but instead it seemed predatory and sad. She headed to the bar on the pretence of putting down her glass. When she got close enough, she pulled the spray and angled it behind her. She prepared herself to see something unpleasant, and maybe to be recognised.

But absolutely nothing happened.

No one changed or unveiled their appearance; they continued to flirt unashamedly, and didn't seem to notice Avery in the slightest.

Avery worked her way around them all, squirting her potion discretely. And still nothing. She caught Dan's eye and gave him the thumbs up, and he smiled with relief.

She headed back to Briar and El, who had been watching from a distance. "Nothing. Damn it. I felt sure they were them."

El sighed. "So, we have to go to The Badger's Hat?"

"'Fraid so, unless my potion sucks," Avery agreed, as they headed to the final pub for the night.

***

The Badger's Hat was situated in the centre of White Haven, in the middle of a run of shops. Like many buildings, it had stood there for several years and had a certain old world charm. The ground floor of the pub catered to all groups, and it had an extensive menu, but the owners had extended down into the basement, turning it into a club, with a dance floor at the far end.

It was almost 10:00 PM as Avery led the way inside. The restaurant area was on the left, and most of the tables were still occupied, but the kitchen had stopped taking orders and customers were eating desserts and cradling coffees. She didn't linger there; instead, she turned right and heading for the door in the corner with a sign overhead, reading, The Badger's Set. Avery laughed at the name. That was new—but then again, it had been years since she'd been here.

The door opened onto a small landing in a dim stairwell lined with exposed brick walls, lit with shaded sidelights. They went downstairs to the bar and as soon as they stepped inside, Briar said, "Wow. This is cool!"

And it was. The ceilings were low and lined with beams, the walls were of exposed brick, with the occasional smoothly plastered section painted in dark greys or purples. The lights were low, the bar was long and covered in gleaming polished steel, and the seating was funky. It was a great mix of old and new. And it was hot and crowded inside, the murmur of voices a steady undercurrent to the music, which wasn't too loud—yet. Avery could just make out the dance floor on the far side of the room, empty at present.

El headed to the bar, striding confidently through the crowd, and taller than most. "Come on, girls. This round is on me. I think this is the place."

Avery knew exactly what El meant. It did have a feeling of promise in the air. But maybe that was just the mix of alcohol, sweat, perfume, and hormones.

El handed her a glass of red wine, which she sipped with pleasure. None of them had drunk anything except lime and soda water in the second pub, wanting to remain mentally alert and ready for anything.

Briar slipped her shoes off, and pretended to rub aching feet. "Oh yes. I can feel them. I may not be on bare earth, but I can sense a change."

"I guess we are *in* the Earth, in this basement," Avery said. She felt goose bumps run across her skin. *They were here.*

"So, do we split up again?" Briar asked, scanning the crowd.

El shook her head. "No. I think we stick together. There are no easy exits out of here, and I don't want anyone, especially us, feeling cornered, if they work out they've been spotted."

Avery agreed. "Let's start by the entrance and work our way in."

After a half an hour of targeting the bigger groups, and ignoring several terrible chat-up lines, they had still drawn a blank, and they were all feeling frustrated.

"Maybe my potion sucks," Avery said, flopping against the wall and closing her eyes.

"No. They have to be here," El said, remaining determined. "Look at all these side-booths that we haven't tried yet."

She was right. All of the seating was along two sides of the room, and the seats were long, padded benches situated around a table, all partially sectioned off from its neighbouring table to allow for discrete conversations, which left the central area free for standing.

"It's not going to be so easy to spray them though, is it?" Briar observed.

El grinned and pointed to the air conditioner on the wall. "Let's get creative."

She reached up and quickly sprayed the potion several times in front of the vents, and said the spell as the potion was carried across the room. Nobody noticed. They were all too intent on their conversations. "And another couple just to make sure," she said, spraying again. "Now, every couple of minutes I'll keep spraying, and you two will have to go and look."

Avery nodded. "I'll use a little breeze to help."

Halfway down, Avery saw something that made her catch her breath, and she felt Briar stiffen besides her. They both glanced away to avoid staring.

"Do you see them, too?" Avery asked quietly, her heart hammering in her chest.

"Yes. Oh, wow," Briar swallowed, desperately trying to hide her shocked expression. "That's probably what I should have expected them to look like, but still…"

There were four Mermaids seated together in a booth, each next to a man who was gazing deeply into their eyes. With their glamour, they looked like average, attractive women in their late twenties, two with long hair, two with shoulder-length, all with slim builds and nice clothes, but nothing too flashy. With the aid of the potion, they were revealed to be sharp-faced, and their skin was green with a slightly metallic sheen to it. Their hair was long, curling down their backs and coiling on the seats around them, and coloured all shades of blue, green, and purple. But it was their eyes that made them look *Other*—they had a flat, shiny surface, like metal, that reflected the light in an odd way, gleaming with a feral intelligence, and they were completely round—fish eyes. They were flirting with their companions, and every now and again, the Mermaids laughed, revealing tiny sharp teeth, and on the side of their necks were gills, lying flat and unused for now.

Briar and Avery stepped back, trying to watch them discretely through the crowd, and then as Avery turned to look for El, she nearly dropped her drink. At least half of the booths were filled with Mermaids, and she saw another couple at the bar.

She turned her back immediately, trying the hide the panic on her face. "Shit. Briar. We're surrounded."

Briar glanced around and went pale. "What now?"

"Beat a hasty retreat? This was about finding them. And we have."

El joined them, keeping her expression admirably blank. "First, well done. Your potion worked. Now what?"

Avery glanced nervously between them. "I think we need to get out of here, before they realise they've been identified. There are way more of them than I thought there'd be. And then we decide on a plan."

El led the way to the door. They were a long way from the entrance, and trying to get through the press of bodies was slow going. They were doing well, until a Mermaid turned from the bar to get back to her booth, coming face to face with them. Avery couldn't help it. She blinked and averted her gaze, and she knew immediately she'd made a mistake. The Mermaid frowned and turned to look after her, and Avery *knew* she knew.

Within seconds, like ripples in water, head after head turned to watch them, the humans remaining oblivious. Avery felt the atmosphere change, becoming predatory, and the smell of brine bloomed around them. *What was happening?*

They arrived at the door leading to the stairs and freedom, and stepped into the dark entryway, ready to run, when they came to a sudden stop.

A Mermaid stood on the stairs, waiting for them, and one stepped into the narrow stairwell behind them.

The Mermaid on the stairs smiled maliciously, the dim light shimmering on her iridescent scales and glinting off her sharp, white teeth. Her eyes observed them dispassionately. "What are *you* that you can see us?" she asked in a silky smooth voice.

El didn't even bother bluffing. Her hands balled with fire as she said, "We're witches, powerful witches, and we're investigating *you*. What are you doing in White Haven?"

The Mermaid didn't answer El's question. Instead, she narrowed her strange round eyes, stepped forward, and sniffed deeply. "Ah, yes. I see it now. You carry your magic well. It drapes around you like a cloak." Her eyes fell to their bags where they carried the potion bottles, and she smirked. "A clever spell. With all the magic in this pretty place, it was well disguised. And I was a little distracted with all of your lovely men."

"I asked you a question," El said.

"You know what we seek, human," she continued in her lilting voice that carried the soft *shush* of waves. "Searching for mates. And this place is rich with them."

"They are not yours to take!" Avery said, rage flashing through her. "They have families and loved ones here. They do not belong beneath the waves."

The Mermaid smiled seductively and played with her hair, and then turned to catch the light, and Avery realised that she was trying to seduce *her*. "Oh, but they do. Their life will be long and pleasurable with us. They shall want for *nothing*. It is surprising how quickly they forget their human life."

Despite Avery's immunity from the Mermaid's charms, her manner was unnerving, and she had to resist the urge to step back.

"But why White Haven?" Briar asked. Avery noticed her shoes were in her hands, her bare feet planted solidly on the floor.

The Mermaid laughed again. "The magic—*your* magic—falls through the sky." She held out her hands as if to catch something. "It falls even now, like rain, into my hands and into the sea. The currents brought it to us, out in the deep, deep ocean. It called us. It *feeds* us. It falls on your men, even though they don't know it. And now we want them. It is rare to find magic in such rich supply." She looked at them speculatively. "And I think there is nothing you can do about that."

"You need to leave," Avery said, adrenalin making her bold. "You will not take anyone."

"You dare to threaten us?" The Mermaid laughed, and the one behind them joined in. "We are the Daughters of Llyr. We will leave only when we are ready."

The magical energy in the small stairway was strong now, emanating in waves from all of them, and Avery realised with a horrible clarity that the Mermaids had a powerful magic of their own.

El was well aware of it too and she said, "You have your own magic. I can feel it. Why do you need ours?"

"All magic is useful, witch, surely you know that."

The Mermaid stepped closer to El, and then in a lightning strike, pushed El against the wall, her hand against her throat, and Avery noticed her webbed fingers and long nails like talons. Water started to trickle from El's mouth as she struggled to breathe and started to turn blue in front of them, the ball of fire in her hands disappearing.

Avery reacted instinctively, the wind already teasing her hair, and she slammed the Mermaid behind her against the wall as well, lifting her several feet off the ground. "Stop. We can both play that game."

The first Mermaid ignored her, focussing only on El, her face inches away as she watched El struggle. Briar stamped her foot, causing a strong root to snake out of the wooden stairs. It caught the Mermaid around the ankle and pulled her away from El, breaking her concentration. El fell forward onto her knees, spewing up water, and dragging in ragged breaths, but Avery kept the second Mermaid firmly pinned against the wall. She could feel her prodding at her magic, trying to release herself, and hissing with annoyance.

The first Mermaid bent forward and reached for the root, grasping it firmly. Within seconds the wood turned soft and rotten and fell away, and she looked up at them triumphantly.

Avery couldn't believe Briar's spell had been disarmed so easily, but she tried not to show her surprise or any sign of weakness. She stared the first Mermaid down. "This is not a debate. You need to leave White Haven *now*."

Fortunately the stairwell had remained empty, but any minute now, someone could arrive, and Avery wanted to end this quickly. This was not the place for a fight. And she had the feeling they were horribly outgunned.

The Mermaid appraised her with cold eyes. "We are many, little witch, and you are few. We leave when we're ready, and if you continue to threaten us, we will take *all* of your men with us. Now, release my friend."

For a few seconds they locked eyes, and then the door slammed above and voices carried towards them.

Avery dropped the Mermaid to the floor and in seconds, the Mermaids returned to the bar, leaving Avery, El, and Briar to make their way out.

They ran out to the street and down the road, their hearts pounding, and leaned against the wall of the closest chip shop, taking refuge in the handful of people milling around.

"That didn't go so well," El said, her breathing still ragged and uneven as she gingerly felt her neck. Her skin had a horrible pallor to it. "Ugh, I can still feel her webbed hands on me."

"Did she hurt you?" Briar asked, moving El's fingers to examine the area.

"No, I'm fine, honestly. My chest aches a little, and I'll just be a bit bruised." She looked annoyed and shocked. "As is my ego. She was faster and stronger than I expected."

Avery nodded, reflecting on their encounter. "She *was* quick—and she tried to drown you, on dry land! I mean, I knew they had magic, but I guess I really didn't appreciate how much."

Briar rested her hands for a few more moments on El's neck, and Avery felt a pulse of healing magic. "That should help," she said, finally moving away. "Let me know if you need a poultice."

El smiled ruefully. "Thanks, Briar."

Avery glanced at her watch. "If we hurry we can get to The Wayward Son before last call—I'd like to tell Alex what happened."

"I have a feeling Reuben is there, too," El said. "The football's on."

They almost ran to the pub, and got to the bar just as the bell for final orders was ringing. The bar staff were busy serving customers getting their last rounds in, and the hum of noise and familiar surroundings were comforting. Alex was pulling pints with the rest of his staff and he glanced up, noticing Avery's arrival. He shouted, "Be with you in a minute!"

Reuben and Newton were sitting on stools at the end of the bar, watching a repeat of the weekend's Manchester United versus Chelsea match on the television mounted on the wall in the corner, both with a fresh pint in front of them. As the girls joined them, El placed a kiss on Reuben's cheek.

"Ladies," Newton acknowledged, turning around. He looked them up and down and frowned. "What have you three been up to?"

"Investigating," Avery answered nervously. She knew he would not be happy.

"Investigating what?" Newton asked suspiciously.

They were surrounded by people in the pub, and although there was a steady buzz of conversation, it wasn't private. "We've been looking into our latest problem."

"Which one?" Reuben asked.

"The sea-related one," Briar answered enigmatically.

"Oh, so that's why you were so vague earlier," Reuben said to El. "That was very sneaky of you."

El bristled slightly. "For a very good reason!"

"Why is your neck red?" Reuben asked accusingly.

"Er, things got a little ugly."

"What!" he said, eyes wide with worry.

"Please calm down," she said, reaching forward to reassure him. "I'm okay. *We're* okay."

"I think," Briar said decisively, "that we should check out in here—just in case. Glass of wine, please, Avery. El—care to help?"

"My pleasure. Get me a pint of Doom, please," El said, following Briar deeper into the pub.

"No problem," Avery replied, fishing inside her bag for her purse.

Alex finished serving his customer and moved closer until all four of them were leaning together around the bar.

"What have you done?" Newton asked, looking increasingly annoyed. "And what are they doing?" He gestured toward El and Briar, now lost in the crowd.

"I identified a way of finding our *visitors*. And it worked." Avery looked at their astonished faces, trying not to look too pleased with herself. "We have located a healthy number of *visitors* in The Badger's Set. In fact, unhealthy would be a better word. They are already choosing their prey. El and Briar are just making sure there are none here."

"Are you kidding?" Alex said, visibly annoyed. "That was incredibly dangerous. You should have involved us."

Avery looked incredulous. "Really? After you were so quickly seduced the other day? I don't think so."

"It was minor and you know it," he argued.

Reuben looked slightly sheepish. "It wasn't that minor really, Alex. We were enthralled."

Alex grimaced at him. "You're supposed to be on my side!"

"Yeah, shut up, Reuben," Newton added. He adopted his interrogation face and looked at Avery again. "Was the bar in thrall to them? And how many are we talking?"

"I'd estimate at least a dozen, maybe more. And no, the bar wasn't 'in thrall.' Well, not the *entire* bar. They were getting cosy in the booths." They were all glaring at her, and she turned to Alex. "Look, can you at least get me some wine before this interrogation continues?"

He sighed and rubbed his face. "Bloody Hell, Avery. You're exasperating. All right. And then I want to hear every detail!"

By the time El and Briar returned, the bar had quieted down and Avery had informed them about their encounter on the stairs.

Alex asked, "Anything I need to worry about here?"

"Clean bill of health," El said, visibly relieved. "But I think we should do regular checks every night."

"I agree," Briar said, pulling up a stool and sitting down before taking a sip of wine. "There's some potion left."

"And I can make some more," Avery added. "But identifying them is now the least of our worries. They are strong. Or at least the main one we spoke to was. I'm worried our magic is no match for theirs."

"It will be," Alex assured her. "We just need to find their weakness."

"I'll let Genevieve know," Avery said. "I feel we need to keep the Council informed about everything. And perhaps they can help. Someone must know some way to fight them."

Reuben grinned. "I bet Ulysses does."

21

Halfway through the morning the next day, on a break between customers, Avery phoned Oswald. His voice was warm. "Avery, how can I help you?"

"It seems we have a Mermaid infestation, and I was hoping to speak to Ulysses."

Oswald was silent for a moment. "May I ask why?"

Avery faltered for a second, and then thought she should just be honest. "I was told that Ulysses had Mermaid lineage, and thought he might have valuable insight, but if I'm wrong, or we shouldn't know…" she trailed off apologetically.

There were a few more seconds of silence and Avery wondered if she'd just made a horrible mistake, when Oswald finally said, "Let me speak to him and I'll call you back."

Avery then spent an uncomfortable few hours trying to distract herself. She reorganised bookshelves, changed stock, decided to increase the defences on her shop and flat, and drove Dan mad.

After she finally slowed down, Dan said, "Do you want to tell me what's going on? In fact, let me rephrase this. Avery, sit down and tell me what's going on." He gently placed his hands around her upper arms and directed her to the sofa under the window.

Avery felt flustered. She'd been trying to avoid this conversation all day, because she didn't know what to say. But this was Dan, and he'd helped her, and she felt she had to tell him. She just didn't want to terrify him. *But maybe he should be afraid.* "After we left you last night, we moved on to another couple of pubs, and, well, we found *them*. It was all a bit weird."

"By 'them,' you mean…"

"Yes. *Them*."

"Wow. So they're really here. Should we be worried?" he asked, sitting down next to her as if for a long story.

"I don't know. Yes, probably? There are a lot of them." She rubbed her face, as if hoping to rub all of her worries away.

He exhaled forcefully. "Okay. I admit to not taking this as seriously as I should. Now, I'm a little bit freaked."

"I don't wish to alarm you, but join the club. We're a bit freaked, too."

He stared at her. "Not exactly reassuring. Is this in any way linked to the weird deaths in churches?"

"No. Completely unrelated."

"Great. Nephilim and Mermaids, operating independently, both deadly." He raised his eyebrow. "Anything else you want to share?"

"Avoid The Badger's Hat for now. Well, The Badger's Set, to be precise."

"Good tip. Thanks. You didn't mention this earlier, because?"

"I was trying to think of a solution before I freaked you out. Too late!"

"Ha!" he laughed dryly. "You know what? I'm going back to work now, and then I'm going to give up on socialising until all this is over. But I will update my pastry quota. Sugar always helps."

"Pastries on me," Avery said, grateful for a distraction. "I'll go now. Give me five minutes."

She was on her way back from the shop, laden with twice as many pastries as normal, and two mochas for that extra sugary blast, when her phone rang. It was Oswald. She juggled her bags and phone, and tried to keep her tone even as she answered. "Hi, Oswald."

Oswald kept it brief. "Tonight at eight, at mine."

"Can I bring the other witches?"

"I suppose so. But not that Newton man."

And then he rang off.

***

"When I grow up, I want to live in a castle," Alex said, looking up at Crag's End admiringly.

"Idiot. It's not a castle," Avery said, looking at him with affection. He always looked so hot, and tonight was no exception. He'd dragged his hair back into a half man-bun, and all she wanted to do was nuzzle his neck.

"It's pretty bloody close," he answered, unaware of her lustful thoughts.

"It's all right," Reuben said, trying to look underwhelmed. "I prefer my manor house."

"Bragger," El said, narrowing her eyes.

Reuben grinned. "I know. You can stay anytime."

"Only if I get my own wing," she shot back.

"Depends how well you behave."

Briar laughed at all of them, and led the way to Oswald's huge wooden front door. Newton knew about their appointment and was annoyed he couldn't come. Avery still had no idea if Briar and Newton had any type of relationship beyond friendship, and if they had, Briar wasn't telling.

It was a few moments before Oswald answered the door, and when he did, he slipped outside to join them on the covered porch, as if within the house Ulysses would have heard every word. *Talk about paranoid.* His sharp eyes appraised them, and Avery introduced him to Alex, Briar, and El, who he hadn't met before.

He licked his lips nervously. "I would like to point out before I introduce you to Ulysses that he doesn't generally like to talk about his parentage. But, he does acknowledge that many witches are aware of it. It is up to him to introduce the subject, and he often never will. You are lucky this evening. Now, follow me."

He turned and led the way inside, leaving the others to turn and look at each other with stunned expressions, before they hurried after Oswald.

Oswald led the way through a maze of ground floor corridors, panelled with oak, and herringbone wood floors, before finally leading them into a room on the side of the house overlooking an abundant rose garden. It was a sitting room, with elegant, velvet-covered armchairs in rich blues and greens, and a large peacock-blue chesterfield sofa that Avery immediately coveted. The walls were covered in pale blue Chinoiserie wallpaper and decorative lamps were dotted on side tables. It was utterly charming, and very Oswald.

Charmed as she was by the space, Avery's attention was quickly drawn to the man standing in the window with his back to them. It was dusk out, and the room was full of shadows, so that even when he turned at their arrival, it was hard to see his features immediately. One thing was apparent—he was huge. His shoulders were broad, and his arms and thighs were powerful.

"Ulysses," Oswald said. "Thank you again, good friend, for coming. Here are the White Haven witches."

As Oswald introduced them one by one, they all met in the middle of the room, and Avery felt her hand squashed by Ulysses's enormous one. The lamplight threw his face into relief, and she saw the most startling pair of emerald eyes, deep set into a long face, and overcast by a heavy brow and magnificently wild eyebrows. His hair was similarly wild, falling down his back in straggling waves, and his expression was fierce.

Avery smiled nervously, her confidence faltering. *By the Goddess. He looks like Aquaman, but in his fifties. And he's terrifying.*

If Alex or the others had any such fears, they hid them well, but other than muted greetings no one said anything.

Oswald ushered them into seats before bringing over a tray of drinks and glasses. There were cut glass decanters of sherry, whiskey, and port, and Oswald politely filled everyone a glass before pouring himself a sherry and sitting down next to Ulysses, looking like a dwarf in comparison.

Ulysses cradled his whiskey while staring at them suspiciously. As yet, he hadn't said a word.

"Welcome, all," Oswald said. "Before Ulysses tells us about himself, perhaps you could all explain a little about yourselves and your particular problem?"

Oh my God. This is like some hellish chat show or work icebreaker.

"I'll start," Avery said, seeing everyone's slightly baffled expressions, and she told Ulysses about her shop and her family, and about the hidden grimoires, and then Alex carried on, until eventually they had all introduced themselves, downed their drinks, and were still looking at Ulysses's sullen expression. Avery started to wonder if he was mute.

Oswald smiled encouragingly, topped off their drinks, and then said, "Ulysses and I have known each other for many years. He is the only other witch in Mevagissey. His magic is a mix of earth and water—and by that I don't mean the water element itself, of which you young Reuben are a novice, but the magic of the deep oceans, the underwater abyss, and Llyr himself."

Ulysses nodded and finally spoke, all the while looking down into his glass. "Thank you, Oswald. You are very kind, as usual."

Ulysses's voice was not what Avery was expecting. She'd presumed it would be cracked and broken, a barely used rasping thing, but instead it was deep and rich, like hot chocolate, and utterly beguiling. *And actually*, she reflected briefly, *if he were the child of a Mermaid, it would be. Their voices carried the powers of seduction.*

He looked up at them finally, and she tried not to blink and shy away from his bright green eyes. "I don't like to talk about my past, my mother, because it's very painful for me. Even now." His lips cracked a thin smile. "You may feel it's ridiculous, given my age."

"Not at all," Briar said kindly. "The scars of our past can linger a long time."

Ulysses's shoulders dropped a fraction and his smile softened. "What Oswald is not telling you is that he found me, as a child, on the beaches beyond Mevagissey, when he was very young himself. He knew immediately what I was, because of my eyes, and these."

He spread his hands wide, and whatever glamour he was using disappeared, revealing the webbed fingers of the Mermaid, and the slightly green tinge to the skin. Within seconds his glamour returned, and he looked human again.

He continued, "A storm had raged for days, and my father had taken advantage of it. He brought me ashore, desperate that I should avoid the life that he had." He looked around. "You are confused, I can tell. I still haven't got any better at telling this story."

"Perhaps," Oswald said gently, "you should start with your father."

Ulysses nodded. "My father was a witch, and had lived here in Mevagissey with his family, as had generations before him. This was a long time ago. Back in the 1700s. As they do, from time to time, a Mermaid came here searching for a mate, and my father went willingly. He told me he was curious, and of course, my mother was enchanting. But life was not as he expected. The Mermaids' magic will change a man, allowing him to breathe beneath the sea. He grows webbed hands, his legs become a tail, and he develops gills. But even so, the seas are dark and cold. They had many children, and I was their youngest." He paused a second, the memories clearly painful for him. "For some reason, my mother rejected me. I was too *human*. I don't know why—" he spread his hands wide, "some quirk of genetics. My mother tolerated me for a few years, but as I grew older, I became more humanlike and she decided to kill me. My father interceded, bringing me to shore in the storm. My own natural magic allowed my body to change once I reached the shore—my tail disappeared and I could walk the land. But I was otherwise lost."

Oswald jumped in, continuing with his part of the tale. "The day after the storm, I was on the beach—storms always throw up the best things that are useful for magic. When I found him, he was naked, hungry, and covered in seaweed. I knew immediately what he was. There was no sign of his father or mother, and even though I waited with him all day—terrified, I may add—

as you well know, Mermaids are not to be trifled with, no one appeared. In the end, I brought him here. My family has lived here for many years, and it is very private. I have essentially been his father since then."

"It was here that I learned to master my magic," Ulysses explained, his expression haunted and vulnerable. "My father's and my mother's, and learned to live with humans. My father refused to stay, bringing me only to the shore, promising me it was for my own safety, and then he returned to the deep. He was to tell my mother I had died in the storm. As far as I know, he lives there still. Life is long in the depths. I still dream of it."

He fell silent, and Oswald watched him for a second. "So, as you can see, Ulysses is one of a kind. I named him after the great adventurer who battled the seas to finally return home. It seemed fitting."

"And you have never seen another Mermaid since?" Briar asked.

"Never. Until I sensed them the other day in Mevagissey. I confess, I have avoided them. I would see through their magic immediately, and they through mine, even though I cloak myself well. I do not wish to invite conflict." Ulysses's expression was grim. "Because make no mistake, if they knew of me, they would wish me dead, and I would have to fight for my life."

"I have figured out a way to monitor them," Oswald said, "but we are convinced there are only a couple here, and at the moment, they watch and wait."

"Unfortunately, there are far more in White Haven," Avery said. "At least a dozen."

"How do you know?" Ulysses asked.

"I found a very old spell in my grimoire. It has allowed us to unveil their glamour, and we had an *encounter* in a club. They know that we know they're here, but we have no idea what to do next. And they know it." Avery appealed to Oswald and Ulysses. "They're strong, and we're in trouble. It would be awesome if there's anything you can tell us to try to fight them. Of course, we don't expect you to get involved."

Alex placed his glass on the table. "I am curious as to why they want our magic if their own is so powerful. The Mermaid told Avery that all magic was desirable, but I don't buy it."

Ulysses laughed, and it transformed his face. "Of course they desire our magic. Llyr is greedy, and despite his own power, he has always resented the magic of earth and his brother, Don, the Brother of Light. Llyr made his Daughters specifically so that they should need a man of earth to mate with and breed—something to perpetually taunt his brother with. So, when magic is so freely available as it is over White Haven right now—" he shrugged. "It's like Mardi Gras."

El nodded. "She said magic was falling like rain, covering everything and everyone."

"How do we get rid of them?" Reuben asked.

"They are born of water, so that element is like air to them. The air itself does not really trouble them too much, and fire they quench easily. But dry earth—that is a different matter. It is heavy, it suffocates, it saturates water, and could bury them. Of course, powerful blasts of energy will always be effective."

"Well, short of an earthquake, what are we supposed to do?" Briar asked, wide-eyed. "I can rupture the earth, but not on such a scale, and besides, it would be catastrophic for everyone around, not just the Mermaids. We can't just wait for them to take what they want and hope they don't come back. Five fishermen have already gone missing."

"And will never return," Ulysses said seriously, his eyes filled with regret.

"You have a mix of both magic," Alex said. "Does that give you any special abilities?"

Ulysses met his eyes briefly and looked away. "I can swim longer and deeper than any of you could." He dropped his glamour again, lifted his hair, and showed them the gills on either side of his neck. "And I have power over the oceans, but not as much as they have."

Avery looked at the others, and their faces reflected her own disappointment and frustration. She turned back to Ulysses. "Thanks for your time, and for sharing your past. I know it wasn't easy. Based on what we now know, we'll just have to try and figure something out."

"I'm sorry," he said. "I know you wanted more. But one final thing. They have one moon cycle only to live on land, and then they must return to the sea, so they will choose their mates soon—your time is running out."

22

"Genevieve," Avery said, feeling very frustrated. "Surely there's something the Council can do to help us? Men are at risk!"

Genevieve's voice rang out clear and direct over the phone, and Avery held it slightly away from her ear as she paced the room. "No, Avery. I have consulted the covens on this, and although they were happy to admit White Haven to the Council, they feel that this is your problem and that you must deal with it."

"Are you kidding me? Thirteen covens—the magic we could wield together would be huge. I thought that's what witches did? Band together in times of need."

"While some are sympathetic to your plight, many are fearful that becoming involved would invite disaster to their own communities. It seems that only White Haven is subject to this invasion."

"And Mevagissey," she injected.

"Small only, and probably because it is so close to you. No other communities are at risk from Mermaids. And now that the threat of the Nephilim has also gone, many witches wish to keep a low profile."

"The Nephilim are quiet for now. It does not mean they have gone for good."

"May I remind you, Avery, that your magic has caused this. *You* caused this. You insisted on releasing the binding, and now you are paying the consequences."

"But we had no idea what the consequences would be!" Avery shouted. "None! And that is *your* fault for excluding us for so long!"

There was a brief silence, but if Avery expected a change of heart, she was sadly mistaken, because Genevieve ploughed on, regardless. "I'm sorry, Avery, but that is our final decision. If individuals choose to assist you that is different, but there will be no official convening of the covens."

Avery was tempted to scream abuse down the phone, but she resisted. "In that case, we shall manage without you and I won't bother you again."

"Wait," she said, quickly. "We still wish to include you. The celebration of Lughnasadh is approaching, and we are planning to observe that together. It is something we should like you to participate in."

Lughnasadh was one of the big fire festival celebrations, and fell on the first full moon closest to the first of August. It celebrated the start of the harvest, and was a time for giving thanks for plenty, and celebrating the turn of the seasons.

I cannot believe she has the nerve to invite us to this.

This time, Avery decided to celebrate her temper. "Genevieve, go screw yourself." She threw the phone onto the chair in the corner and looked at Alex, who raised an expressive eyebrow.

"Trouble?"

They had returned from Oswald's only an hour or so ago, and Alex was lying in her bed, his hair loose and his chest bare, reading a thriller novel. Medea had curled up on the end of the bed, and Circe was purring contentedly in the crook of Alex's arm.

"That bitch has refused to help us in any way."

"I gathered that," he smirked. "Is this our penance?"

"It seems so. That, that … *Utter cow!*" She continued to pace, desperate to blast something, anything, and when Helena manifested in the doorway, she yelled, "Not now!" and slammed the door in her face with a powerful gust of wind.

"Come and sit down," Alex said calmly, patting the bed beside him.

As fantastic as he looked, the last thing Avery wanted to do was sit down. He had shaved before bed, and now had a very swashbuckling, piratical goatee that added to the wicked glint in his eye.

"I'm too annoyed! Do you know that after refusing to help us, she had the nerve to invite us to Lughnasadh celebrations?"

"Ah! That's what incensed you. And fair enough, too. Clearly, we won't be joining them?"

She had a sudden attack of guilt. "That was terrible of me. What if the others want to go? Do you?"

"No. I'd rather us do our own thing. And I'm sure the others would, too."

"Even Reuben?"

"Even Reuben." He smiled, and she started to calm down.

"You're adorable."

"I know. So are you. Even when you're mad as hell. Now, come and sit down."

She sidled over to the bed, slid beneath the sheets, and slipped under his arm, nestling close to his warm body. "What have we done? What have *I* done?"

"If I tell you I have a plan, will that help?"

She turned abruptly, looking him right in the eye. "Have you? What is it?"

"We have two powerful new arrivals as a consequence of our magic, who fortunately happen to hate each other. Well, the Nephilim hate the Mermaids, the Daughters of Llyr. I have no idea if the Mermaids even know of the existence of the Nephilim. Anyway, it seems the Nephilim merely wish to be left alone, and they seem to pose no risk to us—at least right now. I was thinking, that maybe they wish to avenge themselves. And help us in the process." He smiled enigmatically.

"And just how would they know to do that?"

"I'll contact them again. I have a psychic link."

Avery sat up, sliding from under his arm. "No. it's too dangerous."

"No, it's not."

"Yes, it is. They threatened you last time. You might not survive another link."

"I will. Trust me."

"I trust *you*. I don't trust them."

He smiled, and reached over to brush a lock of hair from her face, sending shivers all over her. "It's nice that you care."

"Of course I care. I don't want anything to happen to you."

"And I don't want anything to happen to you, and yet you rushed off the other night to tackle Mermaids, and didn't say a thing."

"I was protecting you!"

"And who's going to protect *you*? That's my job."

Her heart almost faltered, and she felt locked within his gaze. She didn't think she'd ever felt so—dare she say it—*loved*.

He didn't wait for her to answer, instead pulling her close and kissing her deeply, his tongue exploring her mouth as he pressed his lean, muscled body against hers, pushing her down onto the mattress. She heard the grumpy meow of the dislodged cat, but pulled him closer, one hand exploring his back, the other cradling his head. He smelled and tasted so good.

Alex pulled back, staring at her with his warm brown eyes. "Feeling calmer now?"

Avery teased him. "Not really, but for all different reasons."

"Good," he said, his gaze still serious. "Because we can solve anything together, Avery. Never forget that."

***

The next day at work was busy, especially because Sally was still on leave. A coach of American tourists had arrived at White Haven, part of a tour of Cornwall, and they added to the general busyness of the town.

Avery could tell those that were part of the touring group. She watched them through the window as they clustered together, following the tour guide as he strolled down the street waving a long, red folded umbrella to summon them to see various sights. Avery wondered what they'd think if they knew they'd be seeing witches and Mermaids as part of their tour. Quite a few of them came into her shop, clustering around the books on the locality, and also taking pictures of the occult displays. All she kept hearing was how 'cute' and 'tiny' everything was, and she caught Dan suppressing smirks as he was serving them.

She took a thirty-minute lunch break and headed into the garden to soak up the silence and sunshine, wishing she had all afternoon to potter among the plants. With reluctance, she dragged herself back inside, and then had a horrible shock.

Dan was outside the shop, tending to a young woman who looked as if she had fallen over. He was helping her to her feet, and picking up some of her fallen bags, and he was grinning from ear to ear. Avery could only see the woman's back, but something about her was very familiar. A cold chill started to run down her spine, and she tried to hurry, noting how Dan was focussing only on the woman, oblivious to everything else.

Unfortunately, a customer stepped in front of her and started to ask her about local books she could recommend. Avery tried to deal with her as quickly as possible without being rude, but she was still held up for several minutes. By the time she got to Dan's side, he looked dazed and devoted.

Avery could now see the woman's face, and she felt her own expression stiffen with horror. It was the Mermaid from the other night, glowing with health and beauty. Her long, dark hair had red low-lights running through it, and her skin glowed. She smiled at Avery with triumphant malice, and Avery had to bite down the urge to respond.

"Hey, Avery," Dan said. "This is Nixie. She's visiting White Haven for a while."

So, that's her name.

Nixie held her hand out, waiting for Avery to shake it, and reluctantly Avery reciprocated, feeling Nixie's strong grip. "So nice to meet you," she murmured in her soft, sibilant tones. "I was so silly, I just fell over, and your delightful shop assistant came to help."

"Yes, he's very helpful," Avery said, forcing the words through her clenched jaw. "Dan, can I have a quick word? It's about our earlier conversation. You know, our *visitors*." She sent out a tendril of magic, hoping to break whatever spell it was that Nixie had so quickly and skilfully woven, but she was met with a wall of desire wrapped tight around him.

Dan was oblivious. "I'll catch you later, if that's okay? I'm having lunch with Nixie, down at the Beachside Café."

Avery felt fear rush through her. *What if Dan didn't come back?* But a small queue had started to form inside the shop, and a woman was gesticulating at her, an annoyed expression on her face, as Dan turned away to walk down the street. *She wouldn't take him now. The time wasn't right. This was a threat, surely. A show of power.*

Avery looked at Nixie and her snaky grin. "Sure, Dan, have fun. Look forward to hearing how lunch went."

Nixie answered for him. "Oh, we'll have a great time. See you again, Avery." And then she turned, tucked her arm into Dan's, and led him away.

Avery served the next couple of customers in record time and then called El, relieved when she answered. "El. Thank the Gods. I need your help."

"Hey Avery, what's happened?"

In hushed tones she related Dan's encounter. "Any chance you can have lunch at the same café? I'm completely tied up here, and I know you're close. I'm really worried about him." As she was talking, she noticed Dan's hex bag lying on the shelf under the counter and her blood ran cold. "And he's taken off the bloody protection I made him."

El's voice hardened. "That bitch. Yes, no problem. I'll make sure he's okay."

For the next hour Avery tried to stay focussed, but with every minute Dan was away, she felt her fear rising. Only the regular texts from El kept her from locking the shop and running down the road. El, having found a table in the corner of the café, was watching their every move. She'd said hello to Dan and Nixie, so Nixie knew she was being watched.

When Dan finally arrived back in the shop over two hours later, Avery rushed over and hugged him. "You're back. Great. Are you okay?"

"'Course I'm okay. It was just lunch." He noticed the clock on the wall and the grin on his face slid off. "Sorry. I had no idea I'd been so long."

"Don't worry about the time." She ushered him behind the counter, and turned her back to the shop. "Do you know who that was?"

"Yes, Nixie. Unusual name, isn't it? Pretty, like her." His eyes started to glaze again, and a dreamy smile spread across his face.

"She's a *Mermaid!*" Avery hissed. "Are you mad? Don't you listen to me? And why have taken off your hex bag?"

Dan looked at her with patient amusement. "Oh, Avery. You have such a vivid imagination. She's just a woman. Well, an incredible woman. We talked about everything, from books, to art, to football. I'm meeting her tonight, too. For dinner." He pushed his dark hair back, raking it up into unruly tufts. "And she's invited me to the Lughnasadh celebrations on the beach next weekend. Quite a few of her friends are leaving the area for good—it will be a final farewell, or something of the sort."

Avery blinked, and things started to slide into place. "I'd forgotten about that."

White Haven liked to embrace its witchy roots, and the town Council always put on events to honour the pagan celebrations. The mayor particularly liked to officiate, and Stan Rogers, one of the local Councillors, became their local druid, dressing in robes and chanting around the fire, making libations, and generally kicking off the celebrations. During the summer, the celebrations always took place on Spriggan Beach, on the edge of the town. The beach was edged with sand dunes, and the bonfire was sited close by, on dry sand, above the tide line. The fire was already being built of driftwood and old pallets. During the winter, the celebrations moved to the castle grounds, where it was protected from the strong winds.

These events were always well attended by both locals and visitors, and they attracted people from neighbouring villages. *If the Mermaids had already identified specific men, could they be planning to take them on that night?* Part of her thought that would be crazy. There would be so many people around. But that was also the advantage. Loads of people would be there, drinking and dancing, and although it was a family-friendly event, once the families had gone, the celebrations became wilder, lasting far into the night. If the

Mermaids led the men into the sea, one by one, quietly disappearing, no one would notice a thing until it was too late.

"Dan, I think that would be a really bad idea."

Dan frowned. "Honestly, Avery, she's lovely. I have no idea what you're talking about. In fact, she told me to invite you along. Anyway, I'm going to go and tidy some shelves while you stop being so weird."

She looked after him, flabbergasted. Yesterday, he had been rational and worried, and today, he didn't care. The Mermaids' powers of seduction were impressive. But, what were they waiting for? Why didn't they just take the men they wanted now?

And then suddenly she remembered that Nixie had just invited her, as well. She *wanted* the witches to know when they were leaving. It was a challenge to find out whose magic would be stronger, and clearly Nixie thought it would be theirs.

23

"It's a good thing we weren't planning on celebrating Lughnasadh with the covens," Briar said, looking horrified at the news. "We'll have to be at the beach with the rest of the town."

All five witches and Newton were at Alex's flat after work, sharing pizzas and information, and all of them were worried about Avery's latest announcement.

"We're talking about mass kidnapping," Newton said, looking at them in disbelief.

"Yes, we know." Reuben said, waving his slice of pizza about. "And we're going to do everything possible to stop it."

"But what?" Newton asked, annoyed. "It seems your magic is no match for theirs."

"Wrong," Alex said. "We just have to think creatively. Earth magic is their biggest fear. Well, that's what Ulysses was suggesting, anyway. And I have another idea."

"One that I don't like," Avery added, looking at him with concern.

"Why?" Newton looked between them. "What's wrong with it?"

"It means Alex making another psychic link with the Nephilim."

Newton looked baffled. "And what will that achieve?"

"I'm going to ask for their help."

El almost choked. "You're going to *what*?"

Alex grinned. "You heard me the other day, after I linked with them. They hate the Mermaids—or more generally, the Children of Llyr. They want revenge. If I share the information about Lughnasadh, they may want to help."

"And they may not," El said, ever sceptical.

"So, we'll need a back-up plan," Alex said calmly.

Reuben laughed, a dry un-amused sound. "We haven't even got a main plan!"

"We need to separate them somehow from the men they've chosen. Get them on their own."

"But their Siren call is captivating. They could just use it on the whole beach, then all of you would be affected, too," El pointed out. "The consequences would be catastrophic."

"They are choosing their men with care," Avery said thoughtfully. "They don't just want anyone."

"But if the ones they don't want just drown, they won't care about that."

"Maybe," Avery said, thinking through the possible permutations. "But that would be messy."

"Maybe they want to drown the whole town. Maybe that's why they're waiting for the celebrations," El suggested. "After all, they've done it before."

"The village of Seaton," Briar said quietly. Seaton was once a thriving fishing town, but myths said that after a local man insulted a Mermaid, she cursed the town and it was swallowed by the sands.

"And the Doom Bar," Reuben added, referring to the huge sandbank that was responsible for the floundering of many ships just off the coast of Padstow, again rumoured to have been raised by a Mermaid. "Maybe not the town, just those on the beach. One massive wave would do it."

"Could you counteract that, with our help?" Avery asked.

He shrugged, looking doubtful. "Water is their element, far more than it is mine. I don't know."

"But we know a half-Mermaid, and a weather witch," Avery pointed out, starting to get excited. "Eve can control storms. She could bring a storm in on the night of the celebrations, driving people off the beach. And the great thing about a storm is that it uses all elemental magic. That would be overwhelming to the Mermaids, surely."

"And Ulysses would be able to help counteract their magic with our help." Briar nodded, looking impressed.

El disagreed. "But he wanted to avoid them. He said Mermaids would kill him if discovered."

"But at that point we'd be driving them out of White Haven, back into the sea, and their defeat would be strong enough to put them off ever coming back," Avery said, her voice rising with excitement. *This could work.*

Alex mused, "And if we get the Nephilim on board, the odds are well stacked in our favour."

Newton was not so sure, and he snorted with derision. "And just how are you going to do all this magic stuff with a huge amount of people on the beach?"

"We'll think of something," El said confidently. "The dunes are huge. We can hide ourselves in there easily. And if people start to scatter with the storm, there won't be many around anyway."

Newton looked doubtful. "Why don't you just make a storm and have the event cancelled entirely?"

"Because," Alex pointed out, "they'll just go elsewhere. At least we know—or think we know—where it will happen now. But, I think Avery's right. This *feels* right. They are waiting for the celebrations. There are huge levels of energy that come off crowds of people. They will surely feed off that, especially combined with their own magic and ours already drifting across the town."

Newton still looked doubtful. "I agree with some of that, but I still don't want the Nephilim involved. They killed people. Five people! Don't forget that. They are not our allies."

Avery had to admit that was a sobering thought. She had been so relieved that they hadn't killed again, she was almost feeling positive about them. "No, you're right, of course, Newton."

"What has happened with the police investigation into that?" El asked.

"It's come to a big bloody full-stop," he answered grumpily. "I know what's happened, but I can't say, of course. Everyone would think I'm mad. And there are absolutely no clues at all. No DNA, no fingerprints, no motives. The police chief is going nuts, and there are rumblings about black magic or some religious lunatic, particularly because the deaths were all in churches." He looked at them, and Avery could see the exhaustion etched across his face. "Do you know how bloody complicated my life is right now?"

Briar reached across and touched his arm gently. "We're sorry, Newton. We'll try and resolve this as quickly as possible."

He met her eyes, a flash of longing passing across his face for a brief second before it was quickly veiled again. "But we'll still have five unsolved murders, and the families are still grieving. And of course, there are five missing fishermen, presumed drowned. We know they'll never be seen again. I don't want any more deaths."

"None of us do," Alex said, all humour now gone. "Sorry. We sound flippant right now, but we're not."

"I'm horrified by this," Avery said. "It's eating me up every day. I'm losing sleep over it! And I'm infuriated that the Council won't help. It's not us they're punishing, it's everyone else."

"Right," Alex said, standing up and brushing crumbs onto his rug. "Let's try to reach the Nephilim now. While I prepare, Avery, can you call Eve?"

"Sure." She pulled her phone out, glad to be doing something. "I'll call Oswald tomorrow. I'd rather arrange to see Ulysses in person."

"What should we do?" Reuben asked, as he started to clear pizza boxes and beer.

"Prepare the space. You're all going to help me," Alex said.

***

The only light in Alex's living room was from a few candles, and a low fire burning in the grate. The coffee table had been moved, the rug rolled back, and a huge circle made from salt was in its place. The witches sat holding hands within the circle, and Alex was in the centre, bent over a new crystal ball. Newton had retreated to the kitchen, where he sat watching the events on a stool.

El, Avery, Briar, and Reuben represented the four elements, and they chanted a spell together, summoning their powers to enhance Alex's skills. As the spell intensified, everything outside the circle fell away into darkness, until there was only the five of them and the blackness of the glass orb held within Alex's hands. The room was quiet and hot, and Avery felt sweat trickle down her spine.

For what seemed like several minutes nothing happened, and Alex murmured in frustration. "They are resisting me. I can feel him, the one I spoke to, at the edge of my consciousness, but he's pushing me away." He looked up at them. "Do you trust me?"

"What?" Reuben asked, confused. "Yes, why?"

Avery frowned. "What are you thinking?"

"I have an idea." He shuffled back so he was part of the circle, not removed from it, and linked hands with Avery and Briar, who sat either side of him.

"I'm going to try again, so don't get freaked out. I need your power directly, so you'll feel me draw on you."

They started the spell again and summoned the elements one by one into the circle, magnifying their power, while Alex stared into the crystal ball. Sparks started to dance across its surface, and once again, the outside world fell away until only the crystal ball and its swirling darkness remained. And then, with a sudden snap, Avery felt as if she had plunged headlong into its darkness, falling at a giddy speed she couldn't control.

For a few seconds she was terrified, but then she felt Alex's strong, calming presence, and then Briar, Reuben, and El as their spirits all linked and their thoughts swirled around hers. The darkness cleared slightly, and Avery could make out the indistinct shape of a room. With a shock she heard raised voices, and saw the huge shapes of the Nephilim, still cloaked in shadows.

A deep, resonant voice boomed out, and Avery found she could understand every word. "You intrude again, witch. Have you learnt nothing?"

Alex spoke. "We need your help. I only want to talk."

"You have no right to ask for anything. Leave this place, and leave us in peace."

"I have *every* right. It is thanks to us and the doorway that we opened that you are here. Without *us* you would still be trapped in the spirit world."

A silence fell briefly before their voices rose again, arguing with each other. Eventually, their spokesman asked, "What would you have us do?"

"The Daughters of Llyr are threatening us. We need your help."

Avery felt the anger ripple around the room. "We will not interfere in the affairs of men."

"You have already interfered," Alex insisted. "You are here, killers of innocent humans. You need to make amends."

"We slaughtered cattle."

"And before them, five humans. My memory is not that short. We demand penance."

The figures shifted, moving closer and murmuring together, until another spoke. "You seek to draw us into the light to destroy us."

"No. That is not our plan." Alex's voice was calm and reasonable. "The Daughters of Llyr will kill many. We need help. We are not strong enough to defeat them alone."

"And what will we get in return?"

"What do you want?"

"To live once more among men."

"But you are Nephilim, the sons of angels and human women. Your reputation is one of violence."

"Your stories lie. We were feared for our strength, but we threatened only those who threatened us."

Alex persisted. "But how will you live? Do you even look human? We have seen only your spirit form. The world is not as you left it. Many creatures that are not human have to hide their true nature or risk persecution. Even us."

Again there was silence, and the tension around them was palpable, the shadows deep and impenetrable. Despite her best efforts, Avery could not see the Nephilim. She could feel the other witches, their fear and curiosity, but she could also feel the Nephilim and some of their desperate need to find a way into existence. And then, as if they had come to some unspoken agreement, the shadows lifted and they emerged out of the gloom.

The light revealed seven tall men, all naked, their hair long, faces bearded, and their eyes intense. Swirling tattoos covered their arms and their chests. And they were perfect male specimens. Avery wasn't sure if her spirit form could be seen, but she knew she was staring. She couldn't help it. Their limbs had sculpted muscles, and their abs were well defined, but some were blond, others dark-haired, and their skin colour ranged from brown to white. They looked like warriors.

"Where are your wings?" Alex asked.

One of the Nephilim spoke, his familiar voice indicating he was the one Alex had the psychic link with. His hair and skin were dark, his eyes a bright blue, and his teeth gleamed white in the light. He looked amused as he stared at them, making Avery think he could see them in some way. "Invisible to you now. We can hide them, but they are a part of us and always will be. Are we human enough for you?"

"Very. But you should find some clothes," Alex said, amusement in his voice. "You can speak English now?"

"We are the sons of angels, our language will adapt to anything."

"But how will you *live*?"

All seven Nephilim laughed. "We will find a way. This place," the dark-haired one gestured around him, and Avery realised they were in an old mine shaft, one of dozens spread across Cornwall, "is temporary. A place for us to find our strength. There will be no more killing of humans or cattle."

"Good. In that case, once you have helped us banish the Daughters of Llyr, we will not pursue you, and you will be free to live in peace—as long as you do not kill humans again," Alex warned. "Otherwise, there will be consequences."

The spokesman looked at his companions, and they all nodded. "It is agreed. We will destroy the Children of Llyr. Name the place, witch."

"White Haven. The place you first found when you left the spirit world."

He nodded. "The place that sits beneath the magic."

Avery felt her heart sink. *What the hell were they going to do about that?*

"Yes, that place. On the night of Lughnasadh, under the full moon. Nine nights from now."

"Agreed."

Doubt crept into Alex's voice. "How will we find you?"

The Nephilim smiled, but it didn't quite reach his eyes. "I will contact you again. Our word is law. We *will* be there."

And then they were plunged back into darkness, and Avery felt Alex pull them back into the circle.

***

"Holy crap!" Reuben exclaimed, "That was insane."

Even though the light was low, all of them blinked as they adjusted to returning to their own bodies. *Except they hadn't really left their bodies*, Avery reflected, *not like spirit walking.*

Her heart was pounding and her mouth was dry, and she felt Alex give her hand a squeeze, and she looked at him and smiled. "Well done."

El nodded, stretching like a cat. "Yes. Well done, Alex. That was so odd. I've never done that before."

"Or met a Nephilim, for that matter," Briar said. "Well, seven of them."

Newton stepped in front of them and crouched in front of the fire, just outside of the circle. "Success?"

"You couldn't hear anything?" Alex asked, a frown creasing his face.

"Not a thing. You all fell very silent and still. Like you'd turned to statues."

Reuben grinned. "Like I said. Insane! And yes, success. They will help us, in exchange for letting them live."

Newton looked incredulous. "They have killed five people!"

"And will help save many more," Alex said. He released the power in the circle and broke the ring of salt. "We need them, Newton."

"We shouldn't make deals with murderers."

"The police make deals all the time with lesser offenders in order to catch the big guys," Reuben pointed out.

Briar spoke softly. "So, what's your solution to the Mermaids, then?"

Newton glared at her, and then stood, pacing off his anger. "I haven't got one. Can't you use your magic?"

"We *are* using our magic, but we need them. You know we do," she said, appealing to him.

"Bollocks! I don't like this," he exclaimed.

Avery started to clear the circle, thinking on their options and the days they had left. "Newton, in a few days' time, we could lose many men to these Mermaids. We're running out of time. Our plan is a good one. Sometimes, you have to choose your enemies. I trust the word of the Nephilim. It doesn't mean I like what they've done, but they're trying to survive."

Newton strode to Alex's fridge, grabbed a beer, and took a long drink.

Briar leaned on the counter and watched him. "What will you do about the five deaths?"

"We'll have to blame some nut job who's now disappeared. They will remain unsolved. What else can I do?"

"I'm sorry," Briar said. "But at least you know it won't happen again."

Newton shook his head. "My morals feel very ambiguous right now. I don't like it. It's like I'm living a double life." He stared into the distance for a few seconds, and then downed his beer. "I have to go. I'll be in touch."

Without a backward glance, he strode across the room and out the door, leaving the others staring after him.

24

The next day was Friday, and Avery was relieved it was the end of the week. She was looking forward to Sunday and a day off. She contacted Oswald and arranged to meet Ulysses at lunchtime in a pub in Mevagissey. For some reason, Oswald had insisted on coming too, as if Ulysses needed a minder. Avery didn't care, as long as she could talk to Ulysses again. She had a minder of sorts, too. Alex was joining her.

"I feel two of us will be more persuasive," he argued along the way.

"Alex, you can come with me anywhere," she teased.

Mevagissey was undoubtedly one of the prettiest places Avery had ever visited. It was a small town, little more than a village, nestled on a sloping hill overlooking the sea, and its winding streets ran down to the harbour, the buildings jostling together.

They took Avery's Bedford van, following the main road down to the harbour, where the streets became increasingly narrow. Before they went too far, she found a parking spot on one of the side streets, and then set off on foot to the pub.

Alex pulled her into his side, wrapping his arm around her as they continued to walk. "I hope Ulysses thinks logically. He didn't look too keen to get involved the other day."

"No. But we have a plan now," Avery reasoned.

They rounded a corner and found the harbour spread before them, glittering in the sunlight. Avery could smell fish and chips mixed with the cool scent of briny water. She smiled. *Seaside towns all smelt the same.* It was reassuring.

The Salty Dog Tavern overlooked the harbour, and the sound of voices spilled out of the open door onto the street. They edged through the crowded entrance, where a few smokers hung around, coughing into their cigarettes, and then made their way to the bar. As Alex bought drinks, Avery checked the room out.

It was a small pub with a long bar and a mismatched collection of tables and chairs, and it was filled with sea and sailing paraphernalia—old nets, buoys, shells, and lobster pots. The smell of food filled the air, and most of the tables were occupied.

They found Oswald and Ulysses in a large back room, sitting at a table in the corner beside an empty fireplace. They both looked at them warily.

"Hi guys," Avery said breezily, sitting down next to them and taking a sip of the pint of Guinness that Alex had bought her.

"You don't have to look so worried," Alex told them.

"I think we do," Oswald answered. "You want Ulysses's help. He's said no."

"I get that you're worried, Ulysses, but we have a plan," Avery explained. There was no point in making small talk; Oswald had made that pretty clear.

Ulysses's bulk was still impressive, particularly in a small, crowded pub. He leaned back, staring at them impassively, his green eyes giving away nothing.

She lowered her voice. "We think they will make their move during the Lughnasadh celebrations on the beach in White Haven. I know because Nixie, their leader of sorts, told me herself. She's challenging us to some kind of show of power." Avery could hear her voice rising with frustration. "The Nephilim have agreed to help us. So has Eve. She will bring a storm in on that night, big enough to mask us and what we must do. The storm will dispel the crowds, too, and hopefully allow us to fight the Mermaids unseen."

"The Nephilim?" Ulysses asked, his voice smooth as butter. "And what made them agree to help?"

"The promise of freedom," Alex said.

Oswald's eyebrows shot up. "Freedom? Is that wise?"

"Yes, I think so," Alex said, confidently. "They are now fully physical in appearance, and they want to live among men again. They promise they will not kill again."

Oswald snorted. "So you've made a deal with devils."

Alex leaned forward, his eyes hard and his expression grim. "Your precious Council will not help because everyone's scared, but Genevieve didn't really want to call it that. And of course, it's a punishment of sorts for our transgressions in breaking the binding spell. Except we're not the ones being dragged into the murky depths. We're not the ones who will lose partners, fathers, husbands and sons if the Mermaids succeed! I'm not prepared to just let that happen, Oswald. Are you?"

Oswald swallowed and looked nervously at Ulysses. But Ulysses still watched them, impassive and silent.

Avery spoke, her hand on Alex's arm. "If we do this, the Mermaids will be gone for good. I'm presuming the ones in Mevagissey will join the celebrations in White Haven. They won't be here to threaten you any longer, and they will know that we are too strong for them. They won't come back."

"I knew you would return," Ulysses said, watching them with sadness. "It was inevitable, and it is my fate." He closed his eyes briefly. "I was a fool to fight it."

"I promise we will help you," Avery said.

"You will draw on your reserve of magic above the town?" Ulysses asked.

Avery frowned and blinked. *Of course they could, why hadn't she thought of that? It was theirs to use as they chose.* "Yes. And so will Eve."

Ulysses shifted his massive bulk as he made himself more comfortable. "Let me use it too, and I will help you."

Alex and Avery glanced at each other, surprised. "You'll help?" Avery asked.

"Yes. But I'll need to draw on your magic. The Mermaids will mix with the revellers, they will charm and bewilder, until everyone, man and woman alike, is almost drugged with pleasure. And then they will take their chosen men to the water's edge, and walk them to their doom. The sea will rise to swallow them, and drown those that are left. They have challenged you to a duel. I will need to stop the giant waves, and I must draw on your magic to do so."

"Yes, of course," Avery agreed. "We will lend our strength to yours, and the Nephilim will take on the Mermaids, too. We will attack on several fronts—it's the only way."

"In that case," Oswald said, making a sudden decision that caught them all off guard, "I will be there, too. We will see you on Lughnasadh." And with that declaration he stood, closely followed by Ulysses, and left Avery and Alex gaping at their backs.

***

When she returned to the shop, Dan was there, dreamy and pale, and clearly focussed on other things. Fortunately, Sally had returned to work that morning.

"What's going on with Dan?" she asked, drawing Avery into a quiet corner of the bookshop. "I've never seen him look so distracted."

"Girl trouble," Avery said, watching him surreptitiously.

"Oh, that's nice, isn't it?" Sally asked, falteringly.

"No, not at all. He's in thrall to a Mermaid."

"He's *what*?" Sally exclaimed. "Can't you do something?"

Avery looked at her, annoyed. "I am doing everything I can. Mermaids are very powerful, and their magic is different from ours, rooted in the oceans and the power of Llyr. It's making life difficult."

"But what will happen to him?"

"He'll become a Merman—unless we can break their spell and terrify them with our magic so much that they will not return. We're currently making deals with everyone who can help."

Sally looked horrified. "A Merman! Is that a joke? No, of course it's not, you wouldn't joke about that. Is the Witches Council going to help?"

"No. They're bloody useless. I could strangle that Genevieve woman."

"Oh. So no more Council meetings?"

Avery frowned. "No, I'll keep going to those. We still need to know what's going on. Besides, I'll prove there's more to us, and that we don't *need* them to fight."

"Is there anything I can do? Or," Sally hesitated, "anything I shouldn't do?"

"Do *not* go to the beaches, or The Badger's Hat. And do not go to the Lughnasadh celebrations."

Sally's face fell. "But I love them, and the kids are looking forward to it."

"Not this year, Sally. Trust me. A storm's coming, and you don't want to be caught in it."

***

Over the next week Avery kept herself busy with the shop, and at night she practised spells she thought might come in useful for Lughnasadh. She didn't dare risk returning to The Badger's Hat, but Dan was at work most days, and other than looking utterly lovesick, he remained well.

"So, how's it going with Nixie?" Avery asked him as innocently as she could the following Friday, the day before the celebrations.

He grinned. "Fantastic. She's amazing. We'll be going tomorrow with quite a few of her friends, and my mate, Pete, will be there, too. He's hooked up with one of her mates. We might even have a midnight swim. You should come, too."

Avery's heart sank. She had been trying to convince herself that the Lughnasadh celebrations would be just one big party on the beach, and that perhaps she'd got their plans wrong. She agonised over the fact that she'd persuaded Eve, the Nephilim, and Ulysses to turn up and attack the Mermaids, but that it would all be an elaborate ruse, and they would instead be luring the innocent men to their deaths in some other spot. But Dan's latest update convinced her she was right, and they were looking for confrontation, as if to prove their superiority and unassailability.

"We'll be there," she promised. "We wouldn't miss it. Tell Nixie, thanks."

"Will do." A momentary flicker of confusion passed across his face. "You must have made quite an impression on Nixie. A couple of times she's asked how you are, and if you'll be coming tomorrow. She'll be pleased to know you are."

I'll bet she will be. "Obviously, I don't want to cramp your style, but we'll say hi," Avery said, lying furiously. "Don't you think you should put your hex bag back on?"

"I don't need it anymore," he explained, utterly failing to see its importance. *Too late now, anyway.*

Later that afternoon, Newton came into the shop, looking preoccupied and tired. Avery led him into the back room and put the kettle on for some tea. "You look like crap, Newton. What's going on?"

Newton sat at the table, staring into the distance for a few seconds, before he finally focussed on her. "I'm trying to tie up the investigation into the church murders without creating further complications, but I don't like it. At all."

"I know, and I'm sorry." Avery placed a cup of tea and a plate of biscuits on the table, and then sat down in a chair opposite him. "I wish we could help, but we can't, and you'd never be able to bring anyone to justice."

"I know, but I'd prefer magical justice of some sort at least, and they won't even get that!" He fell silent and sipped his tea.

"But they will make amends," she said, trying to be positive. "They will help save so many people at the beach tomorrow."

He met her eyes with a stony gaze. "Will they? Or will it turn into one big fight with a whole load of casualties caught in the crossfire?"

"You know that's not what we want, and that we'll do anything possible to prevent that."

"I know, but it doesn't mean it will be successful."

"There'll be a police presence there though, won't there?"

"Of course, in case of crowd unrest, but it will be small."

"Will you be there?"

He nodded. "It's not normal for me to be there, but I argued that it's a pagan festival, and that after the church murders anything might happen. So yes, I'll be there in an official capacity."

Avery smiled. "Good. As soon as Eve summons the storm, you must help get people off the beach. We'll isolate the Mermaids."

"And what about the men they've enthralled?"

"We'll separate them as best as we can. I think they'll be confused, anyway. Well, I'm hoping so."

Newton took a biscuit and crunched through it in two bites, and then quickly had another two, as if he hadn't eaten in hours. "We're leaving a lot to chance."

"We're as well prepared as possible," she insisted. "Look, Newton, it's as frustrating for us as it is for you. I'm sorry we can't do more." Avery couldn't help but wonder if Newton's mood was related to Briar, and although she hated to pry, he might want to talk. "Have you caught up with the others since the other night? Reuben? Briar?"

He shook his head. "No, I've been busy at the station, but I might drop into Briar's later."

"Great. Say 'hi' from me."

He lifted his gaze from the table top. "I know what you're thinking, Avery."

"No, you don't," she said, flushing and speaking far too quickly.

"Yes, I do. You're a romantic. I'm single, she's single, and she's attractive. Very attractive, and for a while…" His voice trailed off, and he looked anywhere but at her.

Avery waited, watching his anguished expression.

When he finally looked at her again, his expression was sad. "I know about magic, about your histories. I accept that. I'm your friend, a friend to all of you, and I always will be. And I thought that maybe me and Briar—" he shrugged. "You know. But I think the magic, the blurring of boundaries, is too much. For me, anyway."

"There *is* no blurring of boundaries, Newton. None. We wish no harm—you know that. Especially Briar. She's a healer, a green witch."

"But you're making deals with the Nephilim."

"Just like the police make deals with lesser criminals to get the big guys," she argued. "There's no difference here. You know the Mermaids will kill more."

He shook his head and stood up, brushing crumbs off his shirt absently. "I'd better go."

She stood, too and moved around the table. "No, wait. Don't go yet, I've got time to talk."

"It will solve nothing."

"Things seem complicated right now, but they won't always be. Our lives were peaceful before all of this. They will be again."

He smiled, but it didn't quite reach his eyes. "Will they? I'm not so sure. I'll see you tomorrow."

He left through the back door and Avery watched him, full of regret, without a clue how to make him feel better. And she hoped Briar would be okay, too.

25

Avery stood on the sand dunes overlooking Spriggan Bay, watching the sea and the crowds of people stretched across the sand.

It was the day of the Lughnasadh festival, and in a few hours' time, the bonfire would be lit and the celebrations would begin. For once, it was actually the full moon tonight. On previous years, the full moon had fallen either before or after the celebrations, but the town bonfire was always planned for the Saturday night, regardless. Not that they could see the moon. It was already overcast, grey clouds scudding across the sky, showing only brief glimpses of blue. It wasn't cold, though; instead, it was muggy, a clamminess that kissed your skin. Even the breeze was warm.

A few hundred meters to Avery's right was the harbour wall, and the bonfire was to her left, placed in the fullest curve of the bay, allowing lots of people to be able to spread around it. Even from her height on the dunes, it looked huge, a massive stack of driftwood and pallets, built during the preceding week. Families, couples, and friends of all ages were spread across the sand already. Many had been there all day, but some had arrived recently, laden with chilly bins, rugs, picnic blankets, and baskets of food.

The tide was steadily working its way out, the slow ebb and flow of the waves mesmerising. By nightfall it would be fully out and the Mermaids would have a way to walk to reach the sea.

Avery looked behind her. Below, in the dip of the dunes, the other witches, including Eve and Nate, had set up a base camp. They had picked this spot because it was fairly isolated, sitting a few minutes away from the wooden walkways over the dunes, and out of sight of those on the main beach. They had already placed a spell of protection over the area, causing anyone who did walk that way to turn around and leave.

Behind them were about a hundred metres of dune, all the way back to the road, and above them, on the low hills of the coast, were some houses with commanding views of the sea. The dunes would protect them from their view, too.

Avery took some deep breaths and tried to calm herself down. Her heart was fluttering with anxiety and her mind was racing through all sorts of possibilities. *What if the Nephilim didn't come? What if Eve couldn't summon the storm? What if, after everything they were planning, the Mermaids were too strong and succeeded in taking the men?*

Avery felt movement behind her, and then Alex appeared. He snaked an arm around her waist and pulled her in close, kissing her temple. "Stop worrying," he murmured in her ear.

"I can't help it. This could be a disaster." She turned to look at him, and ran her hand across his cheek. "And I'm worried about you. They could ensnare you, too!"

He smiled, took her hand, and kissed her palm. "That won't happen. You're the only one who can steal my heart, Avery."

"Stop teasing me," she said reproachfully.

"I'm not teasing. I just wanted you to know how I feel, in case anything happens."

What was he saying? I think my heart might explode. I have no idea what to say.

"Avery," he said. "Speak to me. You've gone mute."

"You say the sweetest things. It sort of takes my breath away," she mumbled.

He kissed her hand again. "I'm just being honest. Please be careful tonight. And don't worry about me. I've warded the amulets El gave Reuben and me with extra protection. We'll be immune."

"I'm not convinced. Dan took his protection off, and I still don't know why because he gives me evasive answers when I ask. On the positive side, my protection has held up on the shop. Nixie couldn't get in."

"There you go. They aren't invincible. Anyway, come down to the fire. We're strategising," he said, pulling her by the hand down into the dunes.

The campfire was glowing brightly, the salt in the driftwood burning all shades of blue. The witches sat in a ring, and Eve had a small wooden box next to her, the top open, revealing small glass vials of herbs and potions, all jostling tightly together. A small leather book was open on her lap.

"It's busy, and getting busier," Avery told them as she sat down on the soft, cushiony sand. "There's no wind, it's warm, and the cloud will keep it that way. It's the perfect night for a beach party."

"Not for long," Eve said, rummaging in her box for something. "I'm going to start the spell now. It takes a while to build a good storm. I have to harness energy from all directions, and of course, we want it to look as natural as possible, so slow is better. It's fortunate you have a large pool of energy over White Haven. I'll draw on that."

"Have you ever had to summon a storm quickly?" Briar asked.

"No, never. I summoned rain when we had a massive drought, years ago. The harvest and the cattle were suffering. I also headed off a huge storm a while back, but nothing like I'm planning to do tonight." She smiled. "But don't worry, the principals are the same."

"Do you need us?" Reuben asked.

"No. Nate will help, so that will free you up to get to the beach. What time do they usually light the fire?"

"Not until about eight," Alex explained. He was lying on the sand, chewing a piece of dune grass. "It will be twilight then, sunset is around nine. The cloud cover will of course make it darker."

"Good. I presume the Mermaids won't take the men until it's dark anyway, so I'll aim for the full force of the storm to hit around the same time as nightfall. People should be heading away with their kids then, and the storm will drive off the rest. Then, under cover of the dark, wind, and rain, you can engage with the Mermaids." Eve spread her hands wide. "Of course, weather magic is not always predictable, but it should work out well."

"And what about the Nephilim?" Nate asked. "When do they arrive?"

"In another couple of hours," Alex answered. "I hope."

Nate raised an eyebrow. "I'm curious as to what they're going to look like. And what they're going to do."

"Me, too. I just hope they're dressed," Alex said. "Or things will get really interesting."

Briar smirked. "Part of me hopes they're not. They sure looked good naked."

Eve laughed. "Remind me to ask you more about that later, Briar. In the meantime, while you're all here, lend me your energy to get the ball rolling, and then you can go."

Nate quickly checked that the spell keeping their privacy was still effective, then they linked hands around the fire and Eve began the spell. She tipped her head back and closed her eyes, her voice low as she began the incantation.

She started with an appeal to the four elements, marshalling them to her will. Her long, dark dreads were threaded with beads and framed her strong features, which appeared rigid with concentration. Avery could feel the pull on her magic as it flowed from her and around the circle, mingling with the others'.

Then Eve did something amazing. She opened up and appealed to the four points of the compass, stretching out across the skies above, and with a *snap*, Avery felt the forces start to gather—wind, fire, earth, and water. The magnitude of the distance over which her magic was spread was overwhelming. Eve sat within it all, holding everything together calmly.

She opened her eyes and looked at them. "It has begun."

***

Avery wandered aimlessly across the beach, Briar at her side, taking in everything. The crowds of people, the music that came from all directions, the buzz of conversation, and the hum of energy—no wonder Nixie wanted to return to the ocean here. It was the perfect place.

Historically, men had gone missing alone, or in groups from boats out at sea. This surely had to be a one-off, for so many to be taken at one time. Once again, Avery's thoughts drifted to the power they had released. This was their fault for breaking the binding. But perhaps Nixie and the others had overreached here, and greed would help their downfall.

"A penny for your thoughts," Briar said, and Avery turned to see Briar looking at her, a sad smile on her face.

"Just hoping we're strong enough to do this."

Briar nodded. "It does feel huge. But we have a good plan—well, as much as we can. We don't really know what could happen." She hesitated for a second, and then asked, "Have you seen Newton?"

Avery stopped and turned to face her. "Not since yesterday. He popped into my shop. Have you?"

"Not since then either. He came to see me, too." She sighed heavily. "Magic is freaking him out."

"For now."

"Forever, I think." The smile had disappeared completely from Briar's face, and she turned to face the horizon.

"But he's still our friend. He still cares what happens to us. To you."

"But magic always gets in the way." She shrugged. "I honestly thought that, you know, things might happen."

"You liked him, then? I wasn't sure."

"Yes, I did. He grew on me. Apart from his smoking," she added.

Avery sighed, disappointed for her friend. "Things might happen yet. You're gorgeous, Briar. Trust me, you won't be alone forever."

"How selfish do I sound? Considering what may happen tonight."

"We all want to be loved, and find someone who understands us," Avery said, touching her arm gently. "To find someone who'll put up with our foibles and petty crap. And you will. Not that you have any petty crap I'm sure," she added hurriedly.

"Oh, I'm sure I have," Briar said. "At least you have Alex."

Avery's thoughts flew back to their earlier conversation. "Well, yes, I think so."

Briar laughed dryly. "Avery! Stop it. You doubt yourself, and him. He loves you. It's all over his face. He might not have said so, but it's obvious."

All of Avery's doubts rushed through her. "Seriously? Do you think so?"

"Has he said it?"

"Well, I don't know…he said something earlier."

She huffed with impatience. "I won't ask what. But whatever it was, accept it."

Suitably chastised, Avery nodded. And then she saw Nixie and lots of young and very attractive women on the edge of the crowd, clustered together around a campfire. With them were a number of laughing men, and among them were Dan and Pete.

"There they are," Avery said, turning towards them, but resisting the urge to point.

Briar frowned. "Great, let's go and let them know we're here."

"Is that wise?" Avery asked, catching her arm.

"Yes. It's a game, and we're in play. There are certain moves you have to make, Avery. This is one of them." And then Briar marched off, with Avery running after her.

Before anyone noticed her, Briar strode to the edge of the group. "Evening, ladies. Enjoying yourselves?"

Heads whipped around, and Nixie looked up, a lazy smile on her face. "Avery and a friend. How lovely that you have come to join us."

Dan looked around and smiled, but stayed sitting on the sand next to Nixie. *Like a dog at his master's heel.* He greeted them weakly. "Guys, you came!"

"We're not staying," Avery said, standing firmly beyond their circle. "Just a quick hello."

Most of the group had now fallen silent, and the Mermaids watched them with narrowed eyes and pursed lips, while the men looked contented and oblivious.

"That's a shame," Nixie said, her voice like a caress on the skin. "We're planning on a swim later."

"I'm sure you are," Briar said. "We'll be around, so I'm sure we'll see you later."

"Maybe," Nixie said, her sharp eyes flashing in challenge. "But probably not."

Avery was watching Dan, and she caught a frown pass across his face, but it was quickly gone once Nixie turned her beaming smile on him.

They turned and walked away, aware of being watched. "There are well over a dozen women there," Briar said, worried. "And they looked mean. I'm not sure we're going to manage this."

"We bloody well have to," Avery said, her resolve strengthening. "None of those men had any will left, and I do not mean to lose them. Not one."

On their way back to the others they saw Newton talking to one of the PCs, patrolling as part of the community policing. He waved and strolled over, looking uncharacteristically nervous. "Are we on track?" he asked without preamble.

"Yes," Avery said immediately, hoping to instil a sense of calm. "How about you?"

"Just waiting for the storm." He looked around, perplexed, and Avery noticed he seemed to be avoiding looking at Briar. She had a sudden urge to slap some sense into him. "If I'm honest, it looks unlikely. Are you sure this Eve woman knows what she's doing?"

"Of course she does," Briar said scathingly, and Avery looked at her, surprised. She had never heard Briar sound so abrupt, and neither had Newton by the look on his face. His head jerked back and he focussed on her fully.

He stuttered, "I didn't mean to doubt…"

"Yes, you did. Can't quite make up your mind about magic, can you? But it's fine when it suits you," Briar snapped and walked away, leaving Avery and Newton staring at her back.

A red flush started to creep up Newton's neck, and he couldn't take his eyes off Briar. He looked horrified.

"Sorry, but you did kind of ask for that," Avery said, as gently as possible.

He tore his gaze away from Briar and looked at her. "I didn't mean anything by that! Shit. She hates me."

Avery patted his arm. "No, she doesn't. I better go. Stay safe tonight, and keep well away from—" she pointed across the sand, "*them*. By the campfire, where the crowd is thinning."

She headed back to the dunes, and hadn't gone far when there was an excited yell, and Ben, Dylan, and Cassie materialised out of the crowds. "There you are! We've been looking for you," Ben said.

"I didn't know you were coming," Avery said, shocked. "Are you mad? Things may get rough tonight."

Cassie laughed. "But this is Lughnasadh, and if the Nephilim are coming, we want to see them. It will complete our investigation, sort of."

"I've brought my camera, too," Dylan added, gesturing to his bag. "We don't scare that easily."

Avery eyed them warily. "Well, please be careful. A storm's coming, and we need to stop the Mermaids. We won't necessarily be able to watch out for you, too."

"It's fine," Ben reassured her. "We can look after ourselves." And with that, they headed into the crowds.

＊＊＊

By the time the festivities were about to begin, the skies had darkened, and the clouds were thick with the promise of rain. Not that this development curtailed anyone's excitement.

The councillor, Stan, was dressed in white wizard robes, and he was holding a long, wooden staff. His hair was short and grey, but he had a beard that he had dyed, for some unknown reason, purple. He stood behind the mayor on a small wooden platform in front of the fire that faced the crowds.

The mayor, a woman called Judy Taylor who had bold red hair and short curls, gave a short speech about the importance of honouring pagan traditions and remembering the heritage of White Haven and the witches who once had lived there. Avery and others were standing on top of the dunes, watching the scene below, and they smothered smirks at that. Then, Judy passed the ceremony over to Stan.

With much pomp, Stan raised his staff and offered thanks to the Gods for the beautiful summer, and the promise of a bountiful harvest to come. He gestured to the flowers and fruits that had been placed on the small platform as gifts, making clear they were offerings. He then reminded the onlookers about the church service at the Church of All Souls, which would celebrate Lammas in a more traditional way. The Council were always inclusive. He then turned dramatically and pointed his staff at the bonfire. Two young men stood ready with a flaming torch on either side of the pile of firewood, ready to ignite the fire, but before they could move, a small *bang* emitted from the centre of the pile of wood, and it sparked into life of its own accord. The young men looked momentarily startled, and then lowered the torches to the wood hurriedly, as if it was meant to happen all along, and the crowd clapped and cheered. Stan looked shocked, but he smothered his surprise quickly as he turned and bowed to the crowd, and then proceeded to throw a large glass of beer into the fire as a libation to the Gods.

El was watching with a very large smile on her face.

"Naughty," Reuben said, equally delighted.

"I thought it would be a nice touch," she said with a wink.

Some people stuck around, watching the fire intently, while others drifted back to their groups, their blankets, and their booze.

Now that the fire was lit, the skies seemed even darker. The flames spread quickly and smoke eddied in the air, coinciding with the first stirrings of wind.

Avery stood next to Alex, and she nudged him gently. "How are you? I haven't seen you for hours."

He looked pleased with himself. "I've been contacting the Nephilim."

She frowned, worried. "Are you okay? You managed it alone."

He nodded. "I'm fine. Now that I have a connection, it's easier. And it helps that they're willing to be involved. You'll be pleased to know they're here."

Relief flooded through her. "Thank the Goddess! Where?"

"Beyond the dunes. I'm going to go and fetch them." He kissed the top of her head. "See you soon."

She watched him for a few seconds until he disappeared from view, and then looked at Briar, standing silent, her gaze on the horizon. "Briar, are you all right?"

For a second she didn't answer, and then with visible effort she said, "I'm sorry about earlier."

"You don't need to apologise for anything. I was feeling pretty annoyed with him, too."

Briar finally turned to face Avery. "I'm aiming to work out some of my aggression on those bloody Mermaids."

"Good. Me, too."

Avery looked behind her, down into the dunes, and for a second saw nothing. The veil of magic that protected the space had fallen like a blanket. She whispered the word of unveiling, and it shimmered and disappeared like smoke. Then she saw Eve crouched over their own small fire, and next to her were Nate, Ulysses, and Oswald.

"Come on, Oswald and Ulysses are here."

The small hollow in the dunes was protected from the rising sea breeze, and the fire warmed it beautifully. Even though it wasn't cold, there was something special about sitting around a fire and warming your hands.

Eve's eyes were glazed in concentration; her arms were raised and reaching towards the sky, and she chanted quietly to herself for a few moments. Avery felt the surge of magic around them and its connection to the storm building above, and she shivered with anticipation. When Eve finished, she reached into the small wooden box next to her, chose some herbs, and threw them into the flames. The fire changed colour, sparking with purples and greens, and with it came a huge rumble of thunder in the distance. She smiled at Avery across the fire. "It's shaping up nicely."

"When will it hit?" Ulysses asked.

"In about an hour, as promised. I'll bring the wind before rain. That should start to drive people off the beach."

Reuben laughed. "There's a few down there that will need more than wind to drive them away."

"And that's what the torrential rain will be for," Eve said, grinning. "I have a spell that I'll use to keep me dry here. This, essentially, will be the eye of the storm. I'm afraid the rest of you will get very wet."

Reuben stirred. "Well, I'm going to keep an eye on the Mermaids, in case they decide to bring their plans forward. And I need a hot dog."

"I'll come with you," El said, rising to her feet. She turned to Avery. "We'll stay well hidden in the dunes, and let you know if anything happens."

Ulysses and Oswald had fallen into silence. Oswald, as usual, was wearing his slightly odd, old-fashioned clothing, even on the beach, but he'd replaced his shoes with hiking boots, adding to the incongruity of his appearance. Ulysses was dressed in a t-shirt and jeans, and was barefoot, his hulking build making everyone else look like dwarves.

Avery was restless. "Is there anything I should be doing?"

Nate shook his head. "The action won't start until the crowds have reduced."

"But I feel I should do *something*!"

"This was your plan," Briar pointed out. She was barefoot too, and she dug her toes in the sand, wriggling them playfully.

"I know, but now it feels lame."

"That's how they want you to feel. Overwhelmed and underprepared. You've been *manoeuvred*, actually," Oswald said, suddenly sparking to life.

"What do you mean?" Avery asked.

"As you already know, tonight is a challenge of power. If I'm honest, they have the upper hand. After all, they picked the time and the place. You had no choice but to turn up."

"I know," Avery answered, annoyed. "But what else were we to do? Say, 'no thanks, have a nice night, and help yourself to our innocent men?' That's why we asked for help!"

Ulysses stared into the fire. "Mermaids are wilful, strong, and vindictive. It gives them great pleasure to thwart the Daughters of Don."

"I prefer to think of myself as a daughter of the great Goddess," Briar said archly.

Ulysses carried on regardless, his green eyes reflecting the firelight, which had now returned to a bright orange flame. "To take the men from beneath your very eyes will give them great pleasure."

"We've talked about the possibility of them raising a huge wave to drown the town, or us. Do you still think that's likely?" Avery asked, curious for Ulysses's opinion.

"It's possible," he said nodding. "I thought perhaps they would bring a great wave to wipe the beach, but now I'm not so sure. I think they will want you to survive—to remember their victory."

Nate watched Ulysses thoughtfully. "That makes sense. Our failure will be painful, and horrible."

Ulysses frowned. "It is possible that they will raise a wave over White Haven only."

"But the town is only a few hundred metres away. Could they make a wave so targeted?"

"Absolutely. The tide is coming in, isn't it?"

"It will be soon," Avery answered, wondering where he was going with this.

"And you are bringing in a large storm. This will make it easier to create a monster wave," he mused. "It may not happen, but I think it's a very good guess."

"And what can we do about that?" Briar asked. "We'll have enough trouble saving the men!"

"That's why you have me," Ulysses said, looking up finally. He rose to his feet. "My power over the sea is greater than all of yours. Come, Oswald. We must head to the harbour."

"But we need your help with the Mermaids," Avery said, standing, too.

"You'll have to manage those alone, I'm afraid." And with those ominous words, Ulysses disappeared into the night with Oswald at his side.

Only seconds later, Alex entered their secluded hollow, and behind him stood seven very tall men. The Nephilim had arrived.

26

The Nephilim were dressed in a mixture of army combat trousers, jeans, t-shirts, and boots. They had all shaved, and several had cut their hair, revealing their hard, angular faces, with high cheekbones and square jaws. They looked ex-military and their muscular builds were still apparent, but who knew where their wings were. Every single one of them had an intense stare; the look of those who had seen too much.

There was a second of silence, and then Alex spoke. "Are we interrupting something?"

Avery felt a wave of panic wash through her, and then she took a deep breath and exhaled heavily. *This will be okay.* "Ulysses thinks that the Mermaids may seek to drown White Haven in a massive wave. He and Oswald have gone to the harbour."

Before Alex could respond, Nate leapt to his feet. "So, Alex, are you going to introduce us?"

"Avery, Nate, Eve, and Briar," he said, pointing them out in turn. "We're all witches, and we're here tonight to stop the Mermaids from taking men. There are another two with us who aren't here at the moment."

"Reuben and El are watching the Mermaids," Avery explained.

Alex gestured to the Nephilim. "I'll let you introduce yourselves."

A dark-skinned man detached himself from the group, and Avery recognised him from the cave as the one who had done most of the talking, the one she presumed Alex had the psychic link with. "I'm Gabreel, and this is Eliphaz, Barak, Nahum, Othniel, Amaziah, and Asher."

Each one nodded in turn as he was introduced, but none of them spoke, and Avery knew she'd never remember their names. She wondered if they had any magical abilities, or if brute strength alone was all they needed. If your father was an angel, it must give you some special abilities. *Time will tell.*

There was another ominous rumble of thunder, a gust of wind ran through the dunes, and then there was a flash of lightning far off in the distance.

Eve spoke from where she still sat beside the fire. "I need to concentrate now. I'm going to draw the storm closer—it's going to be big. You better get going."

"I'll stay with you, just in case," Nate said, settling beside her again. "Good luck with the Mermaids."

"Good luck to you, too, and thanks again," Avery said, leaving the warmth of the fire as she led everyone else back to the top of the dunes.

The wind hit them, scouring their skin like sandpaper. Below them the fire still burned bright and hot, and there were a good number of people still on the beach. But it was almost dark now, and Avery could see a stream of people leaving, burdened with blankets and chilly bins.

The wind carried the sound of music from various smaller campfires, the shrieks of children, and the laughter of adults. Silhouettes danced around fires, and there were a few people at the water's edge, barefoot and shouting.

"Good," Alex said. "At least some of them are going. Where are the Mermaids?"

"That way," Briar said, pointing to the left toward an almost deserted area.

They walked down onto the main beach and hadn't gone far when El arrived, out of breath. Her eyes flickered across the Nephilim. "There's some movement in the camp. It looks like they're making a start."

"Right," Avery said, glad to be doing something after hours of waiting. "Alex, how do you want to play this?"

"We've decided that we'll hang back, until the storm fully hits, and then when they're getting close to the sea, the Nephilim will block them."

Gabreel smiled like a shark. "It will be a nice surprise for them."

"What about their Siren call? Will it affect you?"

He shook his head. "No, but they can try."

"Okay," Avery said decisively. "El, take everyone to Reuben, and when they make a move, we'll intervene. Me and Briar will test the waters—sorry, terrible analogy," she said, grinning. "Ready, Briar?"

"I've been ready for hours."

Avery and Briar threaded their way through the remaining partygoers. A flash of lightning illuminated the Mermaids ahead, clustering around the flames of their own small fire.

As they approached, Avery felt the power of their magic, and her skin rose in goose bumps. The wind carried their wild music that emanated from some mysterious unseen place, making her want to run across the sand and fall at the feet of the beautiful women with their pale skin, long hair, and beguiling eyes. She resisted its pull, but quickened her pace, Briar right next to her.

They were only a short distance away when a figure left the fire and walked to meet them. It was Nixie. "Stay away, witches. You won't win."

Avery peered behind her. "Where's Dan?"

She grinned, and her glamour briefly fell away, revealing a row of sharp teeth. "Out of your reach. Do you want to say your goodbyes?"

"You're very confident, aren't you," Avery said. "To invite us here and think we can't stop you? It's not a game. These men will die."

Nixie considered them both for a long moment, her eyes full of hate. "Life beneath the sea is not death. They will have long lives and father many children."

"But," Briar said scathingly, "you're not really giving them a choice, are you? Maybe if they were going willingly we would have less of a problem with this."

"Yes," Avery agreed. "Drop your magic and ask them now. We won't stop those who choose to go freely." Nixie didn't answer, and Avery laughed. "Exactly. No one would go. Blame Llyr for your predicament. The Gods love foolish games, but we won't tolerate it."

Nixie was clearly furious, and she did something so quick that Avery barely registered it before the sand turned into liquid beneath her feet, sucking her in until she was knee deep, and she saw Briar floundering next to her.

At the same time, there was an enormous crack of thunder, and lightning sprang across the sky, slicing it into pieces, and with an unexpected suddenness, rain started to fall in huge, freezing drops, stinging her skin. Within seconds it was pouring down, and then the storm really raged. Crack after crack of thunder and lightning followed.

Excellent. Nobody would notice what she was about to do.

"You'll have to do better than that, Nixie." Avery summoned air, using it to pull her and Briar from the sand, until they were both floating just off the ground. Then she pushed back, hitting Nixie full force in the chest.

Nixie shrieked as she flew over the sand, landing with a *thump* several metres away. She rose to her knees, her face furious, lifted her head, and keened like a banshee.

It seemed this was the signal.

As one, the Mermaids pulled the men close and started to walk towards the sea. They didn't run. Instead, they performed a laughing, teasing dance across the sands. Even from a distance, Avery could see the men's glazed expressions.

Avery saw the Nephilim break free of the dunes, the other three witches next to them, charging towards the mesmerised group.

Briar ran to join them in a pincer movement, but thick strands of seaweed caught around Avery's ankle, dragging her back. Avery whirled around, but Nixie was upon her, tackling her to the ground, her glamour completely gone now. Her nails scratched and pulled and she snapped her sharp teeth at Avery's face. In seconds, Avery felt her lungs start to fill with water and the sand suck her down. Terrified she was either going to drown or suffocate, Avery blasted Nixie away, and spewed water, coughing furiously. She was keenly aware that Nixie would attack her again, so summoning all her energy, she leapt to her feet and then hit back with ball after ball of fire, doing the same to the seaweed still rising out of the sand like tentacles.

Avery harnessed the wild wind that now shrieked around them, muffling all other sound, whisked it into a small tornado, and sent it after Nixie. It pulled her into its whirling circle, and carried her away into the darkness.

Avery didn't bother watching her. Instead she turned and ran after the others. The sand was sodden with water and it splashed around her, slowing her speed, and the torrential rain almost blinded her. They were all now halfway to the sea, the Mermaids still so sure of themselves that they didn't rush, but lazily danced onwards, as oblivious to the weather as the men who followed them, laughing with dazed excitement.

Avery glanced behind her, back to the main fire, and saw it had virtually gone out. The beach, what she could see of it in the darkness and through the sheets of rain, was deserted.

She stood for a second, letting her eyes adjust as she swept her hair back off her face. The witches were darting around the men, desperately trying to break the enchantment, fend off the Mermaids, and blast them out of the way. The men were so beguiled that they were fighting the witches off, too. It was a disaster, and it was clear they were struggling.

And then she saw the Nephilim, black silhouettes beneath the lightning, forming a barrier between the sea and the Mermaids.

Avery ran, finally coming to halt at the edge of the group, which had come to dead stop. The Mermaids faced the Nephilim in a line, the men behind them. Their glamour had disappeared, revealing their silvery, scaly skin and their webbed hands and feet. Their singing rose, but the Nephilim were indifferent to its charms.

Avery ran into the middle of the men, joining the others in trying to break the enchantment. One by one, she jolted the men with a blast of fire, letting it curl up their arms, enough that she hoped to break the spell, as it had done for the witches in the pub. Unfortunately, whatever enchantment they were in now was far more powerful. They shrugged, blinked, and then returned to their dazed state. She found Dan and shook him, but his eyes were vacant.

Frustrated, she caught Briar's eye. She looked frantic, and as impotent as Avery was. There was no sign of Nixie, and Avery wasn't sure if that was good or bad.

Gabreel called out, his voice booming out over the storm. "Return to your ocean, Daughters of Llyr, or you will regret it. These men do not belong with you."

One of them stepped forward, her face contorted with fury. "What men are you that resist our song?"

Gabreel shouted, "We are no men! We are the Nephilim."

The Mermaid's confident manner faltered. "No. It cannot be. You are dead. Fallen in the great flood that destroyed the world."

"And now we are back for vengeance. Flee now, or you shall all die."

Another Mermaid spoke, her voice carrying on the wind like the call of a seagull. "It's a bluff, they're powerless against us."

Gabreel laughed. He flexed his shoulders and two enormous wings spread from his back. He rose into the air and headed straight to the Mermaid. With his strong grip he lifted her high into the storm. Her shrieks made Avery's skin crawl.

The rest of the Mermaids ran at the Nephilim, leaving the men unguarded behind them.

Avery shouted, "We have to act now! We can't break their enchantment, but we can shield them."

"I agree!" Reuben shouted back.

They quickly gathered together, linked hands, and threw out a powerful shield of magic, encircling the men—but they were still transfixed and immovable.

"What now?" Alex yelled.

"Air!" Avery yelled back. "We'll float them back."

Much as she had pulled herself and Briar from the quicksand, she sent a cushion of air beneath the men's feet so they floated inches above the ground, and then with the shield around them, they shepherded them slowly back to the dunes.

Avery looked over at the battle, because that was the only word for it. The Nephilim had taken to the air, plucking the Mermaids up in ones or twos, and they dragged them high over the sea into the heart of the storm. In the searing flashes of light, she saw their broken bodies plummet, and she winced. The ones left on the ground must have decided to salvage what they could, because they turned back to where the men had been, and as soon as they realised they were no longer behind them, they fled into the sea.

The lightning flashed, again and again, illuminating the rising waves as they crashed on the shore. As Avery glanced to her right, back towards White Haven, her breath caught in her throat. An enormous wave was building beyond the harbour. It must be Nixie. She had to trust that Ulysses and Oswald could deal with it alone.

The group arrived at the edge of the dunes, wind-swept and soaked, and she released the spell, floating them back to the ground. Avery sighed with relief as the decked path that led from the beach back to the car park appeared out of the gloom.

A groan grabbed her attention, and she looked around to see Dan rubbing his face. "Where the hell am I? What's going on?"

Beyond him, the other men were stirring, too. Avery shouted, "Not now, Dan. Come on, we need to get off the beach."

With El leading the way, the men followed, all of them awake, but utterly confused.

Before the beach was lost to view, Avery turned and looked back to the edge of the sea, but the darkness and rain obscured everything. Another flash of lightning showed a soaring black shape in the sky, and then it was gone. She hoped the Nephilim would be okay. She turned and trudged after the others, and with every step, Avery felt her worry ebbing away, and exhaustion starting to take hold.

She caught up to Briar, who was drenched and shivering. "Are you all right?"

She grimaced. "Nothing a strong drink and a bath won't cure." And then she allowed herself a smile. "We did good! With help."

"Yes, we did," Avery answered. "But it's not over yet."

A shout up ahead distracted them. For a second, Avery couldn't work out what was happening, and then Newton appeared, running through the men, encouraging them onwards. As soon as he saw them, he grinned.

"You're okay!"

"Of course we are. There was never anything to worry about," Avery said as confidently as she could. But he wasn't really looking at her. Not that Briar seemed to care. She nodded and pushed past him, and Newton turned and followed, leaving Avery to walk alone.

A flash of red and blue lights were visible in the darkness, and as they reached the car park, Avery saw a couple of police cars and an ambulance, and a few people who looked as if they'd come from the houses opposite the beach. The rain was easing to heavy rather than torrential, and a few uniformed officers ran up to the men, ushering them to the shelter in the nearest house. Alex and the others were talking to one of the officers. Newton had stopped following Briar and was standing alone, soaked and smoking a cigarette as he leaned on his car. She headed to his side. "Thanks for organising this."

He nodded to some of the houses behind them. "Someone called it in—which was good, because otherwise I would have had to. I didn't want to risk one of the PCs seeing what was happening and getting involved. They said the lightning showed a group of men on the beach, who looked to be struggling." He gave her a long look, his face clouded and uncertain. "Let's hope there's no video footage. Or it's too unclear to see." He paused for second. "I saw the Nephilim out there battling with the Mermaids."

"We couldn't have done this without them, Newton. Their magic had these men utterly captivated. We might have saved a couple on our own, but that's all."

He nodded as he looked into the distance, and then his gaze drifted to Briar for a brief second, where she stood at the back of the ambulance, wrapped in a towel. A myriad of emotions crossed his face. "All right. Thanks, Avery. I better head to the station and see what comes out of all this." Another couple of police cars turned up and he walked away, as Avery looked for Alex.

She saw him deep in conversation with Dan and she ran over, putting her arm around Alex's waist. "How are you two?"

Alex kissed the top of her head. "We're fine."

"Speak for yourself," Dan said. He looked white and his jaw was clenched, whether from fright or the cold Avery couldn't tell. "I might never go on another date again."

"Can you remember what happened?" Avery asked.

"I remember the beach party, and then things get a bit blurred." He looked behind him to the police. "I better go. I want a lift home. I'll fudge stuff as much as I can with the police. And thanks, guys. I owe you. And you," he said to Avery, "can explain to me exactly what really happened tonight with coffee and a pastry at work."

"Done!" Avery said, smiling.

While the police were distracted with the other men, the witches headed back into the dunes. Briar was visibly shivering, and it made Avery realise how cold she was now that the adrenalin was wearing off.

"There's a big wave heading to White Haven," Avery told the others. "We need to get Eve and Nate to safety, and then head to town."

"Avery," Reuben said, shaking his head. "We don't need to worry about town. Ulysses will deal with it. Come on." And with that he headed across the dunes towards their original campfire.

***

Eve and Nate were still crouched around the fire, in a perfectly warm, dry circle, protected from the raging storm by Eve's magic.

"So glad you two are so cosy here," Reuben declared as they warmed themselves.

"The advantages of being a weather witch. Lesson number one is how to keep dry. Did you save them?" Eve asked.

"Yes, thanks to you," Avery answered. "The men are safe, and the Nephilim were pretty brutal. We left them to it."

"Should we go back and try to help?" El asked. "Although, I would imagine they've finished by now."

Alex shook his head. "Gabreel was pretty clear that we shouldn't interfere. I'll try and contact him later. And they didn't look like they were in trouble."

The three women laughed, and Briar put in, "No. They weren't bothered by the Mermaids at all. I don't think I'll ever forget the sight of them and their huge wings. That was impressive."

El nodded. "Revenge is a dish best served in the heart of a huge storm."

Eve smiled. "Good. Sit with me a few minutes while I ease this bad boy down."

"Much as I hate to leave your toasty fire, I want to see White Haven," Avery said, unable to forget the image of the rising wave. "Anyone want to join me?"

"I'll come," Alex said, rising to his feet.

"Me, too," Reuben volunteered. "It's not every day you see a giant wave."

They reached the top of the dunes and looked towards the town. A rogue wave was rolling in. It was enormous, towering over everything and visible only as an intense blackness against the charcoal grey of the night sky. Avery felt her breath catch, and she heard Alex swear. Viewed through the rain it seemed like a mirage.

"Are we sure Ulysses can handle this?" she asked, alarmed.

But even before she'd finished her question, they saw the wave start to break, well outside of the harbour walls, falling in on itself, and then a wild, keening cry of grief was carried to them on the wind. *Nixie.*

It was over.

"I think we need a nightcap," Reuben said. "Let's head to mine."

27

Reuben's enormous living room was crowded, the fire was roaring, and everyone sat around cradling beer, wine, or whiskey.

Ulysses and Oswald had arrived last with Avery after she went to find them at the harbour, and they both looked very pleased with themselves.

"So, don't keep us in the dark," Eve said, grinning. "What happened?"

Ulysses laughed, his voice as rich as chocolate ganache. "Well, she sure didn't expect to see me."

"Nixie?" Avery asked. She sat on the floor between Alex's legs, who was seated on the sofa behind her. She had managed to dry herself off, and warmth was flooding through her.

Ulysses nodded. "We found her on the harbour wall, calling up the sea. It was her song that led us to her."

Oswald agreed. "She was oblivious and thoroughly enjoying herself. Her face," he mused. "It was vicious. And then she saw Ulysses."

Ulysses laughed again. "It was a good thing you made such a brilliant storm, Eve. No one was around, or I'd have been arrested, because I tackled her straight into the water. She might have been half my size, but she's full Mermaid and it's her element. But I was able to drag her out into the deep. There was more out there than just the wave."

They all looked at him, drinks halfway to lips. "What do you mean by that?" Alex asked.

"There was a pretty big deep ocean creature heading in; a Kraken. Don't worry—it's gone now. And it took Nixie with it. I don't think it was too pleased at being dragged out here."

"A Kraken?" Nate asked, almost choking on his whiskey.

Ulysses nodded. "They're vicious things, but fortunately it took out its annoyance on Nixie, and then I dispelled the wave."

Avery smiled. "Thank you. We owe you."

He shook his head. "No, you don't. And besides, we may need *your* help one day. And it was good for me, cathartic."

Oswald agreed. "I'm sorry the Council didn't help more, but you have proven yourselves tonight."

Nate laughed. "The Council can be a bit precious, especially Genevieve. She definitely wanted you back on the Council, but she always wants things her way. I think she was trying to prove who was boss. I'm not sure it worked."

"She's the lead witch, I have no problem with that," Avery said, "but it was more than us at risk tonight. I'm not sure I understand her stance. Many people could've died tonight—or as good as, to be condemned to a life beneath the ocean."

"You have to remember," Eve said regretfully, "that for many witches, our needs come before the needs of other communities. She didn't want to risk anyone knowing about us, or things becoming more complicated. That's the way it's always been."

With the lights low and the fire crackling, it was hard to believe that just a few hours earlier they had been battling on Spriggan Beach beneath thunder and lightning.

"Well," Briar began, "I'll be glad if life could return to some normality for a while. I have a business to run."

"Agreed," Alex said. He looked across to Eve and Nate. "Our magic that falls over the town. Can you still feel it?"

Eve nodded. "It's certainly fading, and I channelled some of it tonight, which is why my storm was so good. Yes, I still feel it. But you know, you shouldn't worry about that. While some creatures will sense it, not all will want to use it. Some are curious and are attracted to others like them. It can be a scary world out there for those with paranormal abilities. That's why it's best to keep them hidden."

Before anyone could answer, a heavy knock on the door disturbed them, and Reuben went to answer it. When he returned, Gabreel was with him, and his steely gaze swept the room.

Alex leapt to his feet and walked over to shake his hand. "Gabreel, thank you so much for tonight."

"Our pleasure. It felt good to defeat the Daughters of Llyr. They will not come here again. At least not for many years."

"Come and sit," Alex urged him.

He shook his head. "No, I must join my brothers. I wanted you to know we will be on the moors beyond the town. We have found somewhere to stay for now, but we may need your help to become more," he paused thoughtfully, "legitimate."

"We'll do what we can," Alex said, and Avery wondered what Newton would make of that.

He turned and left, saying muted goodbyes, and then Nate rose to his feet, too. "Come on, Eve, we should go. I'm knackered."

Eve drained her glass. "You're right. I'm going to sleep for a week I think. I'll keep in touch, Avery."

Avery stood to hug her. "Yes, please. Safe travels." She turned to hug Nate, too. "And to you. Thank you."

"Time for us to go, too," Oswald said, sounding weary.

After a round of hugs, handshakes, and promises to catch up soon, only the five White Haven witches remained.

"More alcohol, anyone?" Reuben asked. "I've got plenty of beds."

"Yes please, and can we order food?" El asked, stretching like a cat. "I'm starving!"

"It's nearly midnight. No one delivers at this time," Reuben said, reaching for the whisky bottle. "But there's food in the kitchen—if someone wants to cook."

As they were talking, Avery heard the crunch of gravel and a car engine idling up the drive. "Who's that?"

"It's probably Newton," Alex answered. "I thought I'd let him know where we were. I'll go let him in."

Avery glanced at Briar, but she was huddled in front of the fire, staring into the flames.

Newton hesitated at the threshold of the lounge. "Am I welcome?"

"Of course you are, you moron," Reuben said affectionately. "There's a glass here with your name on it."

"I've brought curry to bribe you with, if that helps," he added, and Alex followed him with another couple of bags packed with cartons.

El went to help him. "Brilliant, you must have read my mind." She kissed Newton's cheek as she wrestled a bag from his hands.

Avery smiled. "You don't need to bribe us. You're always welcome."

"Even if you're an ass," Briar added, glancing up at him.

Newton met her eyes and then looked at the rest of them, a rueful smile on his face. "You were all brilliant tonight, and so were the Nephilim. Well done, and sorry if I doubted you."

"You're allowed to," Alex said. "It was risky, but it paid off."

"I'm getting plates," El said, heading out the door. "Newton, sit down, relax, and get drunk with the rest of us."

***

The next day, Alex and Avery left relatively early and headed back to Spriggan Beach, strolling hand in hand across the dunes and onto the flat sands.

The sky was a pale, watery blue, as if the storm had scrubbed the colour from it. The beach was strewn with driftwood and seaweed, and the remains of the blackened wood from the bonfire sat in a soggy pile. The tide was out, and birds settled in the shallows and pulled worms from the wet sand.

"Hard to believe, isn't it, that there was such a massive storm and almost a mass kidnapping last night?" Alex observed, pulling her close as he turned to face her.

"It's surreal! It feels like a dream."

He smoothed her hair from her face. "We've gained some good friends out of this."

"Do you think the Nephilim are friends?"

"I think so. Different, yes, but still friends. And of course, there's Ulysses and Oswald. Oswald's a funny little man, but I like him."

"One of life's eccentrics," Avery agreed. "And I like Eve and Nate, too. Do you think things will be okay with Newton? I'm worried about him. I mean, I know he came round last night, but long term?"

"He'll always wrestle a bit with what we do," he mused. "But he knows we act with White Haven's best interest at heart, and ultimately, he's on our side."

Avery nodded absently. "I hope you're right." She hesitated a second and then said, "I was really worried for a moment last night, in case their magic worked on you."

He winked. "Our spell worked, really well. I could hear their song, but I could control my emotional pull towards it. You won't get rid of me that easily." He wrapped her in his arms, pulled her close, and kissed her until she was breathless. "In the meantime, let's go for breakfast and have an epically lazy day. We deserve it."

* * *

Over the next day or so, the papers and local news were filled with stories of Lughnasadh and the storm.

Unclear footage from camera phones showed strange shapes on the beach, and there was a report about a group of men who became confused and tried to go swimming at the height of the storm. They described how a few locals helped bring them to safety, and that was about all that was said. Quite a few speculated about angels of darkness and aliens on the beach, but most of the speculation died down quickly to muted rumblings.

Sally and Dan were full of questions for Avery on Monday morning, and the tourists who came in the shop couldn't keep the excitement out of the voices about the quaint little town and the beach activities. Every now and again someone mentioned the film *The Wicker Man*, and Avery tried hard not to giggle. And then she thought of what might have happened, and that sobered her up pretty quickly.

Ben appeared in the store halfway through the afternoon, bringing cakes.

Dan smiled in approval. "You know how to make yourself popular around here."

"I always aim to please," he said, helping himself to a cake. "So … Saturday was fairly epic."

"Did you film it?" Avery asked, worried over whether to be worried or not.

"The weather was too bad," he said, shaking his head. "Impressive storm."

"A friend helped," Avery said impassively.

"And the weird, winged creatures over the sea?"

"Our new friends, the Nephilim," she said, quietly.

"Okay," Ben said, nodding in understanding. "Well. The calls keep coming. There are still more spirits in White Haven and other towns. Any suggestions as to who could help us, if needed?"

"I haven't had a chance to ask yet, but I will. I promise. It's just been a bit busy around here." *Underestimation of the year.*

"All good. By the way, Briar called Cassie. She's starting with her next week."

Avery smiled with genuine pleasure. "That's great! I look forward to seeing her there."

"And as for me," Ben said, heading to the door, "I'll be in touch. I have a feeling things aren't going to stay quiet here for long."

"Is that wishful thinking?" Avery called.

"It's good for business," he said, and then waved goodbye.

Dan rummaged in the bag, pulled out a cake, and took a huge bite.

"Glad to see your appetite hasn't suffered after the weekend, Dan," Sally said, smothering a smirk.

"My appetite for cake is fine, not so much for women. But he's right, you know, your friend, Ben."

"Is he?" Avery said, wondering where this was leading.

"Oh yeah. I don't think White Haven will ever be normal again."

Avery groaned. She had the horrible feeling he was right. And then she allowed herself a smile.

What's so great about normal? Absolutely nothing.

End of Book 3 of the White Haven Witches.

Book 4, All Hallows' Magic, is out now.
Read on for an excerpt.

All authors love reviews. They're important because they help drive sales and promotions, so I'd love it if you would leave a review. Scroll down the page to where it says, 'Write a customer review' and click. Thank you—your review is much appreciated.

ALL HALLOWS'

WHITE HAVEN WITCHES (BOOK 4)

MAGIC
TJ GREEN

1

Avery looked out of the window of Happenstance Books and sighed. Winter was on its way.

Rain lashed down and water poured along the gutters, carrying crumpled leaves and debris. The street was populated by only a few hardened individuals who scurried from shop to shop, looking windblown and miserable.

She watched a young man struggle down the road, his arms wrapped around him in an effort to keep his leather jacket sealed. He really wasn't dressed for the weather. He had a beanie pulled low over his head, and she suspected it would be soaked.

He paused in front of her shop and looked up at the sign, hesitated for the briefest of seconds, and then pushed the door open, making the door chimes ring. A swirl of damp air whooshed in before he shut it behind him and shook himself like a dog. He was of average height with a slim build, and his jeans hung off his hips; he pulled off his woollen hat and wiped the rain off his face, revealing light brown hair shorn close to his scalp. He looked up and caught Avery's eye.

Avery smiled. "Welcome. You've picked a great day for shopping."

He smiled weakly in response, but it was clear his mind wasn't on the weather. "I have no choice. I'm looking for someone."

Avery frowned, sensing she already knew what was coming. She'd been feeling unsettled for days, and tried to put it down to the change in the seasons and the coming of Samhain in a couple of weeks. Unfortunately that didn't explain the unusual tarot readings she'd had recently. "Who are you looking for?"

He looked around nervously, noting a few customers tucked into the armchairs she had placed around the displays and in corners. The blues album playing in the background contributed to the mellow feel, and the shop smelt of old paper and incense. Nevertheless, his eyes were filled with fear.

Avery smiled gently again. "Come and talk to me at the counter. No-one will hear you." She moved around behind the till, sat on a stool, and hoped the young man would feel less threatened with something between them.

He followed her, leaning on the counter and dropping his voice. "I'm new to White Haven. I arrived here recently with my family, drawn by the magic here. We've been trying to work out where it comes from; or rather who," he said rushing on, "and you're one of the people I've narrowed it down to."

Up close, Avery could see his pallor under his stubble and his fear was more obvious, but he looked her straight in the eye as if daring her to disagree. She kept her voice low and even. "May I ask how you can detect magic?"

"I may have some ability," he said, vaguely.

Avery hesitated, casting her awareness out. She could sense something unusual about him, but he didn't feel like a witch. He was risking a lot, she could tell, and suddenly it seemed mean to be so circumspect. "Your abilities have served you well. How can I help?"

"My brother is ill. He needs a healer."

"Why don't you take him to a doctor?"

"They would ask too many questions."

"I'm not a healer, not a good one anyway." His face fell. "But I do know someone who is. Can you tell me more?"

"Not here. Later. Can you come to this address?" He reached into his pocket, pulled a piece of paper out and slid it across the counter.

She glanced at it, recognising the street. It ran along the coast on the hillside. There was no way that just she and Briar were going. She didn't sense danger, but she didn't know him or his family. "Okay. But there'll be more than two of us, is that ok? We're all trustworthy."

He swallowed. "That's fine. So are we." And he turned and left, a blast of cold air swirling behind him.

Avery went to the window and watched him run up the street, wondering where he was from, what magic he possessed, and where this visit would lead. It seemed the relative peace of the last few months wouldn't last.

Since Lughnasadh, the night they had successfully fought off the Mermaids with the aid of the Nephilim, life in White Haven had calmed down. She and the other four witches, El, Briar, Alex and Reuben, had been able to get on with their lives without fear of being attacked. Their magic, released from the binding spell, still hung above the town, but it had reduced in size. The unusual level of spirit activity had continued, which meant they were still casting banishing spells regularly, but the three paranormal investigators, Dylan, Ben and Cassie, monitored most of that.

She was disturbed from her thoughts by movement in her peripheral vision, and she turned to see Sally, her friend and shop manager, coming back from lunch.

Sally frowned. "You look deep in thought."

"I've just had a visitor."

"Oh?" Sally raised her eyebrows.

"He's scared and needs our help."

Sally knew all about Avery and other witches' powers. "You don't know him, I presume?"

"No. He's just arrived in White Haven. I need to phone Briar and Alex."

"All good. Have your lunch and take your time. It's not like we're run off our feet."

Avery nodded and headed to the room at the back of the shop where there was a small kitchen and stock room. From here there was a door that led to her flat above the shop and she headed through it and up the stairs.

Her flat was in its usual chaotic state. Books were scattered everywhere, the warm woollen blanket on the sofa was rumpled and half on the floor, and the room needed a good tidy. It would have to wait. It was cool, the central heating turned low, and she adjusted it slightly so it would be warmer for the evening. She pulled her phone from the back pocket of her jeans and called Briar while she put the kettle on and heated some soup.

Out of all of the witches, Briar was the most skilled at Earth magic and healing. She ran Charming Balms Apothecary and lived alone in a cottage off one of the many lanes in White Haven. Fortunately Briar was free that evening and after Avery arranged to collect her at six, she called Alex, hoping he wouldn't be too busy at work.

Alex owned The Wayward Son, a pub close to the harbour, and he was Avery's boyfriend, although she always felt really weird calling him that. It sounded like they were fourteen. But what else could she call him. Her lover? That sounded too French, and somehow seedy. Her partner? Sort of, but they didn't live together. Anyway, whatever she called him, he was all hers and completely hot, and she was smitten. They'd got together in the summer, and things were still going strong.

"Hey kitten," he said when he answered her call. "How are you?"

"Kitten! I like that. I'm good, what about you?"

"Busy. The pub's pretty full for the lunch order. I'm not exactly sure where they're coming from in this weather, but I can't complain."

"It's quiet here," she explained, leaning against the counter and stirring her soup. "But that's okay. Look, I'll get to the point. I've had a visitor, no one we know, but he knows we're witches and needs our help. Are you free tonight?"

She could hear the concern in his voice and the background noise fade away as he moved rooms. "What do you mean? He knows about *us*?"

"Yes, but he wouldn't explain. I sensed some kind of magic, but he's not a witch. He said he needs a healer, so I'm picking up Briar at six. Can you come with us?"

"Yes, absolutely. And I'll stay at yours tonight if that's okay?"

She grinned. "Of course. See you later."

***

It was dark by the time they pulled up outside the white washed house on Beachside Road. It was a double fronted Victorian villa, used for holiday rentals. A portion of the front lawn had been turned into a drive, and an old Volvo hatchback took up most of the space.

"First impressions?" Briar asked, from where she sat next to Avery on the front bench of her Bedford van.

"I can't feel anything magical," Avery said, feeling puzzled but also relieved.

"Me neither," Alex said. He sat at the end, next to the passenger window, looking at the house. "It worries me. Didn't you even get a name?"

"Nope. He didn't stick around long enough," Avery answered. "But I didn't get anything dodgy from him. He was just scared."

"Come on," Briar said, pushing Alex to move. "If someone's hurt we need to get on with it."

The rain still lashed down, and they raced up the path and sheltered beneath the porch as Avery knocked on the door.

A young woman with long purple hair opened the door and scowled. "Who are you?"

"Charming," Alex said, amused. "We were invited."

A voice yelled, "Piper! You bloody well know who it is. Let them in."

Piper glared at them and then turned and stomped off, leaving them to let themselves in.

Briar smirked and shut the door behind them. "She looks fun."

They stood in a large hallway with doors on both sides, and directly ahead stairs led to the upper level. Piper had already disappeared, but the man Avery met earlier bounded down the stairs looking relieved and harassed. "Thanks for coming. I wasn't sure you would. Follow me." He immediately turned to head back up the stairs.

Alex called him back. "Hold on mate. Before we go any further, who are you and what's going on?"

He stood for a second, speechless, and then seemed to gather his wits. "Sorry. I'm not thinking straight. I'm Josh." He shook their hands. "My brother's really ill, and I'm worried he might not survive. That's what's upsetting Piper too. She has a weird way of showing it. Look, I get you're worried, but I'm not a threat. It's easier if I just show you."

It seemed that's all they would get, and he ran up the stairs. Alex glanced at Briar and Avery, and followed him. Avery could already feel their combined magic gathering, but she still didn't sense any magic from elsewhere. She gave a last sweep of the hall and followed the others up the stairs.

On the first floor Avery detected a strange smell. She wrinkled her nose. It was odd, unpleasant, and cloying.

Josh led them into a room at the back of the house, and as soon as they stepped in the smell magnified and Avery tried not to heave.

They were in a large bedroom, and in the double bed in the centre of the room a man lay writhing in a disturbed sleep. A young woman sat next to him, watching with concern, and trying to hold his hand. She looked up when they entered, and a mixture of fear and relief washed over her.

What was going on here?

The man was pale, covered in a sheen of sweat, and his hair stuck to his head. He was bare-chested, but most of his trunk and one of his arms was wrapped in soiled bandages, and it was from these wounds that the smell emanated.

Briar ran forward. "By the Great Goddess! What the hell's happened to him? His wounds are infected!"

The young woman stood, moving out of the way. "Can you help him?"

Briar barely glanced at her. "I'll try. You should have come to me sooner. What's his name?" She placed her box of herbs, balms and potions on the floor, and started to peel the man's bandages away. He immediately cried out, his arms flailing, and Alex leapt forward to help restrain him.

Josh explained. "He's Hunter, my older brother. This is my twin sister, Holly."

Holly nodded briefly at them, and then went back to watching her brother helplessly. Avery could see the similarity between her and Josh. They both had light brown hair, and hazel eyes, although Holly was shorter than her brother, and her hair fell in short wavy bob to her shoulders. The man writhing on the bed had dark, almost black hair, a light tan, and was full of muscle.

Avery asked, "What happened to him?"

Josh met her eyes briefly and then watched Hunter again. "He was attacked several days ago. We've been on the road, and only got here recently; it's taken me a while to track you down."

Avery watched Briar resort to using a sharp pair of scissors to cut the bandages away. Avery recoiled as the smell hit her, and then gasped at the size of the wounds. He had long deep claw marks across his chest, back, and left arm, and they were inflamed and oozing pus. As Briar pulled the sheet away, they saw more bandages around his legs.

Alex looked up. "What the hell did this? And why didn't you go to a doctor?"

"Because they would have involved the police," Josh explained. "We can't afford that to happen."

As they watched Hunter twist and turn, Avery scented magic, and she looked around alarmed. Briar and Alex must have to, because they paused momentarily.

"What's causing that," Avery asked sharply, raising her hands ready to defend herself.

"What?" Josh asked his eyes wide.

"Magic. We can sense it."

"Oh no," he answered. "He's changing again."

"He's what?"

But Avery could barely finish question when Hunter shimmered in a strange way, as if his body was melting, and then his shape changed into a huge wolf, snarling and twisting on the bed.

"Holy crap!" Alex exclaimed, leaping backwards out of the way of his snapping jaws. "He's a *shifter*! Why the hell didn't you warn us?"

"Because we hoped you wouldn't have to know," Holly said tearfully, running forward with Josh to try and calm her brother down. In a split second she changed into a wolf too, leaving her clothes behind as she leapt onto the bed. She yelped and her presence seemed to calm Hunter down. Within seconds he lay back on the bed panting heavily. His wounds looked even worse if that was possible; his fur was matted and blood stained.

Avery dropped her hands and sighed heavily. "You're all shifters?"

"'Fraid so," he said, with a weak smile.

"So, I guess he was attacked by another shifter?"

"You could say that."

Briar leaned back on her heels. "This will probably make things a bit trickier."

"But can you still help?"

"Yes! I'm a good healer, but I have limited experience with shifters."

Like none, Avery thought, just like the rest of them.

Briar continued. "Does he change a lot at the moment?"

Josh nodded. "He doesn't seem to be able to control it. His change won't last long, but we think it's getting in the way of his healing. His wounds keep opening, and we can't get them clean."

She nodded and thought for a second. "I need to give him a sedative. It will calm him down, which will hopefully prevent him shifting."

"You have a spell for that?" Josh asked.

Briar shrugged. "In theory. I'll have to make it stronger than usual. I need your kitchen to make a slight change to one of the potions I have with me."

"I presume you're all witches then?" Josh asked. "I mean I thought that's what I sensed, but I wasn't sure."

"Yes, we are," Avery said. "But we'll talk later. For now, let Briar work her magic."

***

Author's Note

Thank you for reading the first three books in the White Haven Witches series.

I love stories about witches and magic, and I love Cornwall, so I decided to put the two together! White Haven is a fictional town, but reflects the beauty of the beautiful Cornwall fishing villages and the surrounding area. Harecombe, the base of Faversham Central, is also fictional.

The Royal Cornwall Museum and the Courtney Library are real, but the archive is my fictional addition.

Of course, there really was a Witchfinder General who was responsible for many deaths, but he never made it to Cornwall - that's another bit of fiction.

I have lots of people to thank for their help with this book.

Thanks to Fiona Jayde Media for my awesome cover, and thanks to Kyla Stein at Missed Period Editing for ironing out the kinks!

I also must thank Helen Ryan and Terri Cormack for their fantastic feedback on my first draft of book1, which prompted a very important rewrite - you're both awesome!

Thanks also to my launch team, who give valuable feedback on typos and are happy to review on release. It's lovely to hear from them - you know who you are - and their feedback is always so encouraging. I'm lucky to have them on my team! I love hearing from all my readers, so I welcome you to get in touch.

Thanks of course to my partner, Jason, who does most of the cooking while I'm feverishly writing in the study. Without his unfailing support and encouragement, my life would be so much harder - and I'd starve.

I've dedicated this book to my mother, because not only is she one of my biggest fans, but also because I think there's a little bit of witch in all of us, and as the matriarchal head of the family, she's offered plenty of good advice over the years - and plenty of uncanny insight! Thanks mom!

If you'd like to read a bit more background to the stories, please head to my website - www.tjgreen.nz - where I'll be blogging about the books I've read and the research I've done on the series - in fact there's lots of stuff on there about my other series, Tom's Arthurian Legacy, too.

If you'd like to read more of my writing, please join my mailing list by visiting my website - www.tjgreen.nz. You can get a free short story called Jack's Encounter, describing how Jack met Fahey – a longer version of the prologue in Tom's Inheritance – by subscribing to my newsletter. You'll also get a FREE copy of Excalibur Rises, a short story prequel.

You will also receive free character sheets on all of my main characters in White Haven Witches - exclusive to my email list!

By staying on my mailing list you'll receive free excerpts of my new books, as well as short stories and news of giveaways. I'll also be sharing information about other books in this genre you might enjoy.

I look forward to you joining my readers' group.

www.tjgreen.nz

About the Author

I grew up in England and now live in the Hutt Valley, near Wellington, New Zealand, with my partner Jason, and my cats Sacha and Leia. When I'm not writing, you'll find me with my head in a book, gardening, or doing yoga. And maybe getting some retail therapy!

In a previous life I've been a singer in a band, and have done some acting with a theatre company – both of which were lots of fun. On occasions I make short films with a few friends, which begs the question, where are the book trailers? Thinking on it ...

I'm currently working on more books in the White Haven Witches series, musing on a prequel, and planning for a fourth book in Tom's Arthurian Legacy series.

Please follow me on social media to keep up to date with my news, or join my mailing list - I promise I don't spam! Join my mailing list by visiting www.tjgreen.nz.

You can follow me on social media -

Website: http://www.tjgreen.nz
Facebook: https://www.facebook.com/tjgreenauthor/
Twitter: https://twitter.com/tjay_green
Pinterest:
https://nz.pinterest.com/mount0live/my-books-and-writing/
Goodreads:
https://www.goodreads.com/author/show/15099365.T_J_Green
Instagram: https://www.instagram.com/mountolivepublishing/
BookBub: https://www.bookbub.com/authors/tj-green
Amazon:
https://www.amazon.com/TJ-Green/e/B01D7V8LJK/

Printed in Great Britain
by Amazon

52700047R00319